PATHS OF
ALIR

Paths of Alir A Pattern of Shadow & Light Book 3 All Rights Reserved. Copyright © 2014 Melissa McPhail v1.1

Five Strands Publishing Co. http://www.FiveStrandsPublishing.com

Hardcover: 978-0-9906291-0-8

Paperback: 978-0-9906291-1-5

Five Strands Publishing and the "FSP" logo are trademarks belonging to Five Strands Publishing Co.

PRINTED IN THE UNITED STATES OF AMERICA

PATHS OF ALIR

A PATTERN OF SHADOW AND LIGHT

BOOK 3

ALL THINGS ARE FORMED OF PATTERNS...

MELISSA McPHAIL

BOOKS BY
MELISSA McPHAIL

Cephrael's Hand

The Dagger of Adendigaeth

Paths of Alir

ACKNOWLEDGEMENTS

EVERY NOVEL IS a collaborative effort. Even if the bulk of the responsibility for its creation lies with the author, the story would've been quite different—and lessened in that difference—without the input of loyal friends.

This novel is dedicated to those early readers, staunch and enthusiastic supporters all. Many of your inspiring ideas have found their place in this story, and for them, I'm forever grateful.

To Heidi and Shon, for your valuable thoughts and observations, and for the many hours you've both spent working with me through the difficult moments of what seemed at the time to be plot disasters—my gratitude is unending.

To all of my beta readers, and my editor, Melissa, I could not have done it without you. Thank you.

AUTHOR'S NOTE

AS A READER of fantasy, and especially of epic fantasy, I have at times taken issue with authors whose tales have unraveled into so many storylines that the entire length of a book could be expended without ever revisiting some of my favorite characters. I'm left, instead, waiting for yet another lengthy span of years to find out what's become of them. I've complained and I've protested—perhaps even wrongly maligned these authors for their inconsideration, because here I find myself facing a similar branching of paths.

I suppose it's an unavoidable aspect of epic fantasy that the tale—being truly *epic* in scale—necessarily comprises so many characters from disparate kingdoms, so many viewpoints and unique expressions of truth. In many cases, and particularly in the case of *A Pattern of Shadow & Light,* the story couldn't be told properly without revealing to the reader the important roles each of these many characters played.

As my fellow authors likely understood, and which I have recently come to learn, were I to keep these story threads from you, dear reader, I would be cheating you. How could you grasp the vastness of the threat Malorin'athgul posed to the Balance if I never revealed the troubles the Empress was battling in Agasan, or if I merely breezed over Nico van Amstel's attempts to claim the Second Vestal's seat? How could you truly comprehend the Malorin'athgul's purpose if I denied you the viewpoints of Darshan, Shail and Pelas?

Therefore, while I apologize for the continued branching of threads in this third installment of *A Pattern of Shadow & Light*—for introducing yet *more* viewpoint characters for you to keep track of—please know I do so only that I might give you as complete a view as possible into the conflict the First Lord is attempting to overcome, and ultimately, to do *his* story justice in the telling.

For those of you who've been away from Alorin for some time (or a long time), here's a brief summary of where we left off in *The Dagger of Adendigaeth*:

When we last saw Tanis, he'd said goodbye to the Malorin'athgul Pelas and was once again traveling with the zanthyr Phaedor, heading through the high mountains of Agasan towards a place Phaedor called 'home.'

Across the Sea of Agasan, an estranged Trell and Alyneri parted desperate ways beneath the arrows of ambush. Alyneri made a wild flight with an injured Fynnlar to find help at the First Lord's *sa'reyth*, while Trell was delivered to Tal'Shira to be interrogated by Radov's Consul, the wielder Viernan hal'Jaitar.

Also coincidentally in Tal'Shira, King Gydryn learns that Radov has been plotting his overthrow in collusion with the Duke of Morwyk and the Prophet Bethamin. He willingly offers himself in sacrifice as a necessary diversion and launches his own plan to save his kingdom.

The truthreader Kjieran van Stone was also in Tal'Shira, waging his own battle against time, hoping to learn the truth of the plot against his king before Dore Madden's Pattern of Changing binds him eternally to the Prophet Bethamin.

In his final hours, Kjieran saves King Gydryn from assassination at the hands of hal'Jaitar's wielder, Kedar—though the king is mortally wounded in the attempt—and then immolates himself on a pyre before Bethamin can claim his soul.

Gydryn val Lorian is lying beside the pyre of burning tents when he's found by a mysterious man called Prince Farid and taken away.

Finally, at the icebound castle of Tyr'kharta, Ean had just defeated his enemy in Işak'getirmek, only to discover that Işak is actually his eldest brother Sebastian, thought long dead.

And now the story continues in Paths of Alir, Book Three of A Pattern of Shadow & Light.

CONTENTS

Cartographer's Notes: As a result of the last cataclysm, circa 322aV, and the subsequent rising sea levels in the northern reaches of the Sea of Agasan, the Hallovian coastline has shifted in some cases dramatically from the original charts. Since the maps were last charted, abundant reefs have grown. Many of these reefs are not marked on charts predating the last Age. Coastal maps dated prior to 322aV should not be used when sailing the Sea of Agasan off shore of Hallovia.

Sailors have reported unseasonable rough seas on the crossing between Hallovia and Devon in the winter months, especially around 399 N. Captains are advised not to attempt this crossing in the dark months of winter. Sea conditions can be variable and storms severe.

The Empire has received numerous reports of sea snakes infesting the waters surrounding the islands off the coast of Hallovia. As this archipelago include numerous uncharted isles, it has been difficult to confirm sightings.

Captains are advised to set course north of the Jamaian isles or pay ransom to pirates.

Hallovia

Empire
of
Agasan

Rimaldi

Sea of Agasan

Islands of Jamaii

Shoring
Edennar
Calgaron
Aracine
C—ourt Barnes
Dannym
Devon
Stradtford
Towermount
Glas R.
Acacia
Avalon
Jenne
Chalons-en-les-Trois
Valdère
Veneisea
Tregarion
Vienne-Sur-Le Valle
Rogue Valley
Xanthe
Cair Xerxes
Cair Rethyronea
Cair Palea-andeo
Bay of Jewels
Cair Thessalonia
Bemoru
Kroth
Dheanainn

N

On the kingdoms of Myacene, Avatar and Vest and travel between the Middle Kingdoms and the East: The waters of the Fire Sea are navigable along the coastline of the Middle Kingdoms paying regular heed to wind and weather. Storm surges are likely during the deep winter months along the north Salarian coast and all of Daanen and Myacene.

MAP OF ALORIN

...sulfuric geysers and vortices are often reported along with other volcanic disturbances along this unstable coast. Myacene is particularly dangerous at the 45th parallel, where electrical storms spawned by the consistently active volcano of Mt. Veal have been known to generate cyclones several miles wide.

Eastwatch

Wynne

Myacene

Tambarré

Saldaria

Fire Sea

Dhahari Range

M'Nador

Tal'Shira

Nahavand   Taj al'Jabanna

Sand Sea

Raku

Avatar

Abu'Dhan

Kai'ahl

Qar'imali

Sakkalaah

Akkad
Emirates

Duan'Bai

Vest

At the time of this charting, the Slave Trade is active between Avatar, Vest and the Forsaken Lands. Ships suspected of piracy and kidnapping are known to ply the southern waters of the Fire Sea. Captains are warned to run armed and must be ready to fend off attack at all hours of the nation.

The Middle Kingdoms
of Alorin

Charted on behalf of the Empress by the Imperial Cartographer on this date of 517 aV to reflect the missing island of Cair Tiern'aval, which vanished from the Bay of Jewels circa 497 aV.

Additional maps can be found online at MelissaMcPhail.com

THE MIDDLE
KINGDOMS

Shoring Isles

Edenmar

Calgaryn
Aracine
Candred Forest
Dannym
Devon
Stradtford
Tovermount
Acacia
Glixe R.
Highlands
Eastwatch
Wynne

Jeune
Morwyk
Tambarré

Chalons-en-les Trois
Kandori
Saldaria

Valdére
Doane
M'Nado

Veneisea
Nahavand
Taj al'Jahar
Sand Sea
Raku

Tregarion
Vienne-Sur-Le Valle
Rogue Valley
Abi
Qar'imali

Xanthe
Olidine
Sakkalaah
Akkad
Emirates
Duan'Bai

Cair Xeroa
Cair Rethynnea

Cair Palea'andes
Bay of Jewels

Cair Thessalonia

Bemoth

Kroth

N

Dheanainn

disturbances along this unstable coast. A quarter
45th parallel, where electrical storms spawned by
of Mt. Veul have been known to generate cyclone

Wynne

M'NADOR &
SURROUNDING
KINGDOMS

Fire S

ness Range

Tambarré

Saldaria

Dhahari Range

M'Nador

Tal'Shira

Nahavand

Taj al'Jahanna

Sand Sea

Raku

Abu'Dhan

Kai'alil

Kalashak Mts

Haden Gorge

Qar'imali

Sakkalaan

Cry R.

Akkad
Emirates

Duan'Bai

At the time of this charting, t
Avatar, Vesst and the Forsaken
kidnapping are known to ply th
Captains are warned to run ar
attack at all hours of the wate

ssken Lands

THE STRANDS & THEIR ASSOCIATED ADEPTS

⊛ FIRST STRAND ⊛
CREATIVE ENERGY

Healers
Seers

Variant trait:
Foretelling

VESTAL
Alshiba Torinin

⊛ SECOND STRAND ⊛
KINETIC ENERGY

Delvers
Espials
Nodefinders

Variant trait:
Dreamwalking
Twisted Nodes

VESTAL
Dagmar Ranneskjöld

⊛ THIRD STRAND ⊛
ENERGY OF TIME & FORM

Avieths
Fhorgs
Holven
Malchiarri
Nymphs
Shi'ma
Tyriolicci
Warlocks

Variant trait:
Timeweaving
Shapeshifting
Animal Magnetism

VESTAL
Seth "Silverbow" Nach Davvies

⊛ FOURTH STRAND ⊛
ENERGY OF THOUGHT

Truthreaders

Variant trait:
Illusions

VESTAL
Raine D'Lacourte

⊛ FIFTH STRAND ⊛
ELEMENTAL ENERGY

Adepts of the Fifth
Drachwyr
Malorin'athgul
Zanthyrs

Variant trait:
Seeing patterns
Unworking patterns

VESTAL
Björn van Gelderan

THE SORMITÁGE RANKS

(in ascending order)

THE DOCIAN COLLAR: yoked to the honest study of elae. Adepts wear the Docian collar from their earliest years until they pass the Catenaré Invocation Trials, often a span of five to eight years.

THE CATENARÉ CUFF: chained to the dutiful service of elae. Adepts wear the Catenaré cuff until they pass the Maritus Invocation Trials, usually a span of three to four years.

THE MARITUS BRACELET: married to the courageous exploration of elae. Adepts wear the Maritus bracelet until they've completed their Maritus thesis and passed the Devoveré Invocation Trials for their strand, usually a span of five to ten years.

THE DEVOVERÉ RING: devoted to the just and virtuous practice of elae. Adepts are awarded their Devoveré ring upon successful completion of the Devoveré Trials.

A STACKED ADEPT– referencing an Adept who has gained more than one ring in the discipline of a single strand.

A BRACKETED WIELDER – referencing an Adept who has gained a Devoveré ring for each strand of elae and thereby wears a ring on every finger of his or her right hand. A bracketed wielder has ascended from Docian to Devoveré on every strand of elae.

A ROWED WIELDER – having gained a bracket on both hands. A rowed wielder has ascended first from Docian to Devoveré in every strand, then again ascended through the same ranks specializing in the wielder's craft of Patterning, learning to apply the Laws and Esoterics to each strand of elae, as well as building his or her repertoire of associated patterns.

PART ONE

*"Darkness holds eternal sway over he who cannot first find the
light within himself."*

– Isabel van Gelderan, Epiphany's Prophet

PROLOGUE

SHAILABANÁCHTRAN STEPPED OUT of the gloss-black portal into an alley bathed in midnight and the pouring rain. Casting a look at the sky, he solidified a shield of the fifth above his head, lifted his red silk robes out of danger from the muck, and walked with care out of the alley onto a deserted street.

An hour further north and the rain would've been snow—a kinder visitor to be certain, in moderate measure—but the isolation of this Agasi harbor town bordering the great river Vjärna served three purposes: first, it ensured the safety of the king Shail walked to meet; second, it proved the other's troth, his dedication to their mutual aims; and third, it provided witnesses to their collaboration.

Shail believed the king would commit fully to his proposal—no one else could possibly provide what he was offering, and desperate men resorted to desperate means; as case in point, striking a bargain with the likes of him—but he took steps to secure his recourse to blackmail, nonetheless. It had ever proven a prudent and effective practice among these mortal rulers.

Reaching the tavern of his destination, he released his shield and breezed inside to be greeted by the stench of river and sour ale and the tang of unwashed men. He noted three such at a corner table, steely-eyed and beardless, clearly strangers there and most likely guards for the man he'd come to meet. The few other pitiful creatures that passed for men in that town looked up from their mead to watch him cross the room, but he cared only that the man behind the bar paid attention to his arrival.

The fair-haired tavernmaster followed Shail with his eyes, doubtless noting his red silk robes, his long ebony hair bound with black cord, and his earrings. Shail had paid the man for this notice, and he'd dressed so the tavernmaster would readily remember him—should the need arise—in a visual recounting to a truthreader's skill.

The tavernmaster nodded towards a door in the back, his gaze meaningful.

Good.

Shail entered a private room dominated by a long table that supported a goblet and two mugs. One of the latter stood empty save for an uneven line of froth. The fire burning in the river-stone hearth lit the room but cast the hooded man standing before it into shadow. He turned at Shail's entrance.

"By the witchlight of the Disir," he hissed. He pushed his hood roughly back, revealing the face of a man barely twenty and five. Blonde, blue-eyed and bearded … and already bitter to the core. "I've been waiting here an hour for you!"

Shail pressed the door closed behind him and arched a brow. "Your time is so valuably spent? Ruling from a broken throne?"

The young king's expression hardened. His kingdom in the far north of Agasan had long been subject to imperial rule. "Don't patronize me, Lord Abanachtran. I'm not one of your Fhorg chattel to command about."

Shail claimed the goblet of wine from the table and eyed the Dane suggestively over its rim. "No …" A smile hinted in the corner of his mouth, mirthless and sharp. "Merely the Empress's."

The king clenched his jaw. For all the enmity he clearly harbored in his soul, he was not quick to anger. "I'm taking a great risk coming here. The Empress's Red Guard watches me like vultures, her spies as crows reporting on my every move. No doubt they've catalogued every time I take a whore to my bed or a shite in my chamber pot."

Shail's dark gaze flicked over him like the sharp edge of a blade. "A show of courage is an effective means of sealing troth, Ansgar."

The king let out a slow exhale. "Is that what this is meant to be?"

Shail seated himself at the table. "What did you think it was?"

The young king shrugged. "Another test."

"All of life is a test." Shail waved his goblet airily.

The king looked away, and emotions flickered like firelight across his features. "If that's so … then I'm failing it."

Ah … how easy it would be to bind this young king to his will. His brother Darshan used patterns of binding as adroitly and indiscriminately as he worked deyjiin. But Darshan never seemed to grasp the inherent fallibility of compulsion—how it weakened the minds of one's underlings.

Far more effective to bring a man over to one's cause through masterful manipulation—or at worst, subtle influence upon his emotions. But such took time, effort, cunning and above all, an attempt to understand the pitiful races of humankind.

Shail cursed Darshan for a fool. Had he seen fit to convince their brother Pelas to follow their purpose rather than simply compelling him upon it, Shail would not now be dealing with the ramifications of Pelas's embarrassingly obsessive tendencies.

But that was a problem for another day.

"When we're through," Shail told the brooding king, "you will have a new kingdom, one worthy of your ancestors."

Ansgar spun him a heated look. "So you claim, but it will all be for naught if the Empress learns of our activities."

Shail's dark eyes gleamed. "The Empress can see nothing."

"She sees the future!" Ansgar flung his hand in a general southerly direction, ostensibly towards the Empress. "And anything she can't see, the High Lord di L'Arlesé can read on the currents. You bring me ideas thick with promise but thin of credibility."

Shail cracked a bare smile, humorless beneath his black gaze. It was testimony to his patience that his expression revealed none of his immense disdain for this broken king, who but for the fact that he played into Shail's plans would have long ago lost his life.

"You have no idea what I'm capable of," he murmured, lacing each syllable with threat. "I'm telling you, she can see nothing and will know nothing until we're ready to act."

"And I'm just supposed to believe you?" Ansgar threw up his hands and spun away. He set to pacing, a young cougar trapped on a ledge with its prey in plain sight.

Shail arched a cool brow. "That's the price I require for giving you back your kingdom and a throne to rule it from."

"Your price," the king groused, casting him a look. "This is not your only price, and it's high, what you demand."

"The cost of a kingdom."

The comment earned him a glare that time—reproachful, rancorous, and full of resentment at his being so foully used. Since their first interaction, Shail had plucked and played the young king's emotions as a minstrel's harp. Ansgar knew it. Shail knew he knew it. The king was no fool. And the price Shail demanded was high, but Ansgar's youthful idealism yearned to pay it—this they both also knew.

Shail considered Ansgar in silence while he decided how best to stir this soup of animosity into a furious froth. He sat back in his chair and crossed one knee, but his gaze never left the young king stewing in his anger.

After a moment, Shail murmured with a taunting smile, humorless and hinting of malice, "What happened to the great courage of the Danes? Are you all merely shamed dogs, beaten and leashed?" This drew a fierce glare from the king. Shail smiled wider. "Or are you the pinned wolves they fear to bring inside their walls? Warriors they imprison within the deepest dungeon, lest your vengeance be unleashed?"

Ansgar spun around with fists clenched. "My people were the fiercest warriors this land has ever known! Ruthless, courageous raiders who dominated the northern coastlines plundering at will. Our halls were resplendent with the spoils of war. 'From the fury of the Varangians, deliver us, O Lord!'" He cast

Shail a bitter look, chest heaving with an anger closely reined. "T'was a prayer uttered often from the mouths of softer kings."

"So I've been told," Shail murmured.

Ansgar crossed his arms and started pacing again. "Yet here I am," he grumbled, glancing at Shail, "the descendant of those great warrior-kings, ruling from a hall empty of adornment and shadowed as if to hide its absence of glory … to hide its shame."

Shail could feel the young king's deep, simmering anger, and it pleased him.

"Half the noble houses of the Empire were sired by the Danes." Ansgar cast him an astringent glare, his words clipped with resentment. "Yet do they pay homage to our greatness still?" He flung a contemptuous hand towards the distant beyond. "Nay. They suckle like fat babes to a whore's teat while the kingdom of their forefathers withers!"

Shail could feel Ansgar's fury rippling in waves.

The king came and leaned on the table, palms pressed flat, and speared Shail with his accusation for lack of a better target. "The Empress requires us to send any Adept born of Dane blood to Faroqhar for training, but do we ever see these children returned to heal our people, to help with our crops, to call the wind for our ships?" His blue eyes raked over Shail, furious, betrayed. "Nay! Since the last rebellion, I'm forbidden to harbor Adepts in my halls. I'm required to submit to inspection by the Empress's Red Guard, who walk the passages of my fortress as though they ruled instead of me!"

Abruptly he picked up his mug and flung it into the hearth to shatter in a surge of hissing heat. Chest heaving, Ansgar spun a baleful gaze at Shail. "The bitch sent our own people—Adepts from our very halls!—to murder my father when he dared rise against her. Now we're watched like thieves by her Red hounds, who report back to her of every plot and scheme they discover, even the petty bickering among the hedge lords. And she calls this imprisonment mercy."

In a fit of fury, he slammed his boot into the table, sending one end skidding and spilling the ale from the remaining mug. "This is no mercy." Shail couldn't mistake the bitter hatred in the young king's eyes as he looked back to him. "This is castigation."

Shail regarded him with quiet satisfaction. How easily the darker of human emotions could be molded and shaped.

He stood and walked to the king's side. Looking down at him, for he was taller even than the Dane, he placed a steady hand on his shoulder. "With an army such as I will summon for you, think what honor you could recover in battle. Now is your chance to restore the Danes to their former glory. You may never see such a chance again."

All the light had gone from the young king's gaze; only the dark shades of vengeance lingered. He lifted his eyes to meet Shail's. "Adepts are more valuable than diamonds. You give me the Adepts I need to defend my troops, and you'll have your rebellion."

In the dim light of the dying fire, Shailabhanáchtran smiled.

ONE

"I have to go after him, Isabel ... he's my brother."

– Prince Ean val Lorian, at the Castle of Tyr'kharta

E AN STOOD IN Tyr'kharta's shattered hall staring out into the night. A cloudbank had drawn a drape across the moon, casting the river and surrounding mountains into enveloping darkness. The night's icy air burned in his lungs, smoking with every exhale, the remnant coals of his fury. Somewhere in that icebound night, his brother was getting away.

Confusion had resonated through the castle after Sebastian's explosion, and now the sounds of startled and angry men formed a constant backdrop to Ean's own enraged heartbeat. Three of Isabel's men had gone to distract and misdirect, buying them precious moments for discussion.

There was no time to talk, yet time must be made. So Ean had carved it from the spaces between every breath, using the third strand of *elae* to lengthen each moment to its near snapping point while he told Isabel all. The working came to him when necessity demanded it—when Isabel demanded it. Incredible that less than a day had passed since he'd stood in Niyadbakir bristling at his inability to recall what should've been second-nature. Now he'd regained pieces of that skill, but he felt no more whole for having them, knowing that his eldest brother suffered beneath a web of torturous compulsion.

A few steps away, Isabel now conferred with Dorn, the first of four men she'd reclaimed from the clutches of death and dishonor to aid her and Ean instead. The prince barely heard their conversation over the roaring of his blood. He wanted nothing more than to follow his brother, to find him and deliver him from the horrifying evils that wracked his consciousness. Yet his friends—Rhys, Brody, Cayal, men who had served him loyally and bravely—remained in dire peril, hostage to Dore Madden's vengeance.

Ean had never felt so cleaved between duty and desire, nor faced a path so splintered. He'd returned from T'khendar to rescue Rhys and his men but found a lost brother instead. To seek the one now meant abandoning the other, and his honor with it.

Ean gritted his teeth and stared into the night, wondering how fast he would have to run to catch Sebastian, and if he might recall a pattern to speed his way. A hounding sense of wrongness twisted in his gut, urging him to action, yet ... which action?

"Ean." Isabel moved back to him and laid a hand on his arm. "We can delay no longer. You must choose."

He spun her an agonized glare. "You know my mind. I would choose my brother."

"Then your brother we shall follow."

Ean gritted his teeth and turned back to the night. "And abandon my men."

She exhaled a sigh. "Sometimes our only guiding star lies towards the choice we will least regret."

Her words drew knives through his heart. The worst part was that Rhys—with a loyal soldier's simplicity—would likely forgive him for what could only be considered a despicable betrayal. Ean had to hope that he could somehow save both his brother and his men, for he would never forgive himself otherwise.

Isabel's man, Lem, stepped breathlessly between the hall's shattered doors. "My lady—they come."

Isabel shook her head, her lips pressed to a thin line. "The horizon narrows, Ean. Soon there will be but one path, and not the one of your choosing."

Ean clenched his jaw. He knew already that he'd chosen to follow Sebastian, yet still he struggled with the guilt of taking that first step away from Rhys, knowing other steps would follow. Finally, he ground out, "My brother heads north."

Isabel turned her blindfolded eyes to Dorn. "The fastest route to our horses?"

"This way, milady."

She tugged on Ean's arm, and he forced himself to follow.

Through the darkened halls of Tyr'kharta they rushed then. Dorn, Baz, Lem and Poul showed their new color as they fought against men they'd once stood beside in battle. Isabel claimed to have restored their honor when she'd restored the four men to life, and the prince sensed no guile in them, only dedication. Still, he eerily remembered the looks on their bearded faces when he'd first cut them down as he and Isabel had fought their way into the fortress. Now those same men were guiding them out.

The castle sprawled like a crab hugging a hill. Ean barely remembered the path they'd followed coming in, for he'd been singularly focused, drawn towards his brother and that destined moment of recognition and reunion. Then he and Isabel had moved swiftly in silence. Now the corridors resounded with an ear-jarring alarm and the sounds of running men.

Dorn knew the castle well, however, and he had a talent for evasion; they made good time, miraculously avoiding the enemy groups hastening by. Then, just shy of an intersection, Isabel stopped abruptly and reached for his arm, holding him back.

Ean stopped and turned with sudden misgiving, trusting her perceptions over his own. "What is it?"

"Something has changed." She twisted her Merdanti staff between her hands, her brow furrowed. "The paths have shifted. Some have branched, others narrowed." She gave him a significant look.

And a host of armed men came rushing around the corner.

The black-haired man in the lead wore scale armor, dull and dark, that seemed to absorb the light, and his brown eyes held a certain unsavory gleam. As the host of men behind him slowed to match his pace, he looked Ean's party over.

"Who have we here?" When his gaze landed on Ean, his face split in a predatory smile. "No, *no*—it can't be!" he exchanged a grin with a bearded man beside him. "Here I thought we'd be facing a chase and lo but we run right into our quarry! *Ean val Lorian*," he swept one hand before him in a mocking bow, "the pleasure is mine."

"Looks just like his brother," noted the bearded man. His sneering tone set Ean immediately on edge.

A broom formed of the fifth could easily have scattered them, but Ean sensed Isabel's hesitation through their bond, and it confused him as to what he should do. "And you are?" he inquired tightly, buying her time—*but time for what?*

"Raliax." The Saldarian settled the flat of his blade against his shoulder, cupped the hilt in his hands and stood with feet parted. "Fortune works in mysterious ways." He gave Ean an insolent smile. "I handed your brother Trell over to meet his fate just days ago, and it appears you've already had your reunion with dear elder Sebastian."

For these insults alone, Ean might've snapped the man's neck like a twig. He was of a mind to do that very thing when Isabel put a hand on his arm. "Wait," she murmured. "The paths ..." Her fingers tightened around his arm.

Unseen, only sensed, myriad paths converged.

Raliax said, "Dore will be so—"

In the same instant Isabel whispered, "*Dore Madden ...*"

At the exact moment that a white-haired man strode around the corner.

Isabel's blindfolded gaze locked upon him, and she went utterly, completely still. Even her mind became silent. To Ean, it felt as if for a breath of eternity the earth itself stopped turning—all motion in that instant simply ceased while Isabel van Gelderan set her sights on the cadaverous man gaping at her in abject horror.

Then the world started again with a jarring sense of vertigo, and the white-haired man spun and bolted away, leaving a wake of palpable terror.

Isabel sprinted after him.

Ean and all the others stood stunned, still partly caught out of time, but Ean's eyes followed Isabel down the hall, and he watched her morphing ... *shifting* ... as she ran. Color and light blurred, and for an instant she wasn't Isabel but something ... more.

Then Ean's eyes focused again, and Isabel no longer wore her dress but the fighting blacks of the *drachwyr*. She moved like the wind.

Abruptly Ean shook off his stupor and made to rush after her, but Raliax stepped in his path. "Not so fast, Your Highness. You and I have unfinished business."

Any other time, Ean would've happily risen to the Saldarian's challenge—his remarks about Sebastian and Trell certainly warranted vengeance—but in that moment, Ean's beloved was in veritable flight after a man whose face had set off alarms throughout Ean's entire consciousness, and with every second of delay, Sebastian moved a step further towards escape. Thus, Ean knew only an exacting impatience.

He made a fist of the fifth and swept it across the corridor. Armed men flew into the wall and tumbled in a clatter of mail, limbs and exclamations—all but Raliax, who stood there smirking.

"Intriguing stuff, Merdanti." He cast a smug look down at his dull black armor. "They make more than swords out of it, you know. Just absorbs all sorts of magic."

With a growl, Ean lifted his blade and rushed him.

Raliax raised his sword as he leveled Ean a taunting grin in return, certain of his superiority. Just when their blades were about to meet, Ean ducked and spun, twirling inside Raliax's guard. With an upwards sweep, he sliced his blade across the man's armor. It parted like milk. Likewise the flesh of his chest beneath.

Raliax staggered back with a shocked gasp.

Ean stared coldly at him as he collapsed to his knees. "There's Merdanti," the prince murmured, "and then there's *Merdanti*." He spun his Kingdom Blade, reforged by the zanthyr's hand, and sheathed it forcefully. Then he rushed after Isabel.

A pattern of the second aided his speed, and he drew upon the first strand to power his legs as he sprinted down the long corridors following the thread of Isabel's essence, which forever called to him. But his mind was feeling the effects of the long night. No wielder could work *elae* continuously without rest, and he'd been drawing upon the lifeforce since walking into Tyr'kharta.

Ahead, a facade of columns supporting a familiar cornice and bas-relief frieze demarked what could only be a node chamber. Rushing beneath the opening, Ean came to a sudden halt against a wall of energy like a gale force wind—and the *currents!* A torrential vortex swirled around Isabel and Dore.

As Ean watched, Isabel twirled and swung her staff, sculpting the *cortata*; yet not men but patterns were the targets of her spinning fury, the latter being thrown unceasingly by Dore. The domed chamber seemed full of smoke, so soot-blackened had the currents become with the charred vestiges of patterns formed and wielded and blasted away.

Ean gaped at the skill with which Dore conjured and threw patterns, like a dealer spinning out a deck of cards, but viciously, fighting for his life with each pattern slung.

Many patterns Isabel deflected with her staff. Others she torched with a thin beam of the fourth, and still more she let fly to wither into cobwebs as their force drained away. Ean knew she couldn't see the patterns as he saw them, yet she unerringly knew where to move her staff to deflect or destroy them, or how to maneuver her body to ignore them, and not a one caught her unawares.

In contrast to Dore's frantic and desperate conjuring—which often as not sent a pattern off half-finished and already fraying at the edges—Isabel cast her patterns in return with swift and sure perfection, intricately formed in the flick of a thought, almost as if she'd derived them innately—as if she was an Adept of every strand instead of a wielder of all. Ean saw, too, that Isabel's patterns were meant to trap and contain, while Dore's aimed to destroy.

Ean watched Isabel throw a lasso of the fourth. Dore dodged and it passed within a breath of his nose. He flung a fiery bolt of the fifth in desperate return, which Isabel easily deflected with her staff. The bolt blasted a hole in the stone floor, while Isabel's lasso caught on a statue of a lion and ripped it from its base. The marble lion flew through the air—both wielders ducked as it flew past their heads—to shatter against a column across the room in a violent spray of stone and dust that only added to the storm-clouds that the currents had become, black as thunderheads and writhing with power.

Dore's face was a mask of desperate rage. He conjured a series of lightning bolts, a blending of the second and the fifth, and fired them off in rapid succession, trying to drive Isabel back, towards Ean. She spun her staff in the zanthyr's figure-eight form, and the energy either vanished into the staff's Merdanti depths or sizzled out of existence at the breath of its touch. Losing not an inch of ground, Isabel moved closer.

Dore radiated a palpable fear while Isabel's determination charged the air with power. Ean felt it building in the cold void of her mind where she formed and released her patterns; he tasted it on the currents of her every exhale.

Dore and Isabel were so focused on annihilating each other in their own way that neither appeared to notice Ean's arrival. The prince hesitated to interfere, yet he could feel Sebastian getting further away with every beat of his heart. Soon he would be out of reach of Ean's tracing pattern altogether and lost to him—possibly forever.

Ean had many times been warned never to use the fifth in combat, lest he draw Balance against him—never mind that Dore was doing this very thing—yet the prince knew that if he could call upon his own innate gifts, he could end their battle there and then.

Ean called the fifth and stepped into the room.

Isabel felt him and spun in alarm. "Ean!"

But Ean had already gone one step too far.

The pattern had been woven of the thinnest gossamer tracing, yet so broadly as to span the entire rear of the room—he was in it before he ever saw it.

His vision blurred and darkened, and he stumbled. He hardly felt himself fall to his knees, or heard his sword clatter against the stones. His thoughts no longer belonged to him; they belonged to the pattern.

The Labyrinth had him.

Isabel spun her staff and deflected the pattern Dore had just thrown at Ean—the vindictive man would ever take advantage of any weakness in an adversary. Her staff's enchanted stone absorbed the pattern's power and distilled it, dispelled it. She turned her gaze back to Dore radiating immense displeasure.

To her outwardly veiled eyes, the dim, subterranean chamber yet appeared a luminous world of bronze and gold, its walls and foundation reflecting the second and fifth strands in vibrant color. The silver-pale air shimmered endlessly with the iridescent fourth strand, while swirling funnels shone with the first strand's roseate hue.

Björn saw the currents, Ean saw patterns, Isabel saw *elae* itself.

Against this background, Dore Madden stood out as a blight, while his patterns thrown towards her appeared as similar stains, tiny vortices unto themselves, hauling and twisting the lifeforce into unconscionable aberrations. She watched as Dore forced the lifeforce into a new design, his next toxic concoction, stirring the strands together and darkening them with his intent.

Inwardly, she sighed.

Dore Madden was her biggest mistake, her only real regret in all the long centuries of her life. She'd made grueling sacrifices, shed tears for dear friends lost and for the countless innocents claimed on the field of play, but none had bled her as deeply as this one miscalculation. Until she righted the imbalance of their mutual history, she would wear the barbed mantle of this failure as a cilice around her soul.

Dore released his pattern, but in the last moment he threw the second strand behind it to boost its force, pulling upon the kinetic energy of the realm to intensify and speed the impelling. She had to jump to deflect it. Long legs propelled her sideways, and she planted her staff to deflect the bulk of the force just an inch from where Ean lay unconscious.

Even as the killing pattern dissipated around her in a sharp tingle of energy, Isabel cast a net at Dore. He threw himself backwards and spidered away beneath it, but its edges sliced him—she'd made them sharp, so he would feel the sting of her displeasure as he cowered—and thin rivulets of blood sprouted across his face and neck. He seared the net out of the air with the fourth—to her eyes a sizzle of brilliance, but a charred residue traveled away on the currents.

Isabel's tolerance finally reached its end. She'd given Dore his chance, but she didn't possess the drachwyr's patience for toying with prey.

A single thought raised an impenetrable shield around Ean's form. A wave of her staff cleansed the currents of Dore's noxious residue. Then she turned her blindfolded gaze on Dore himself.

He saw this and scrambled back and away, a crab fleeing the incoming tide.

Isabel looked into the space of Dore's mind and saw the scoria of a being feeding on the energies of hate and harm; she saw how *elae* avoided him—he had to summon it forth, for the negative charge of his consciousness repelled the lifeforce now.

Once, she'd hesitated to claim Dore's life.

No longer.

Isabel called the fifth, and the currents swelled towards her. She twirled her staff like a baton overhead—with so much of the fifth coursing through the talisman, the solid stone weapon felt as light as a twig. She opened her mind to frame her intent—

"I wouldn't do that!" Dore's voice introduced discord into *elae's* rushing song, a new and jarring wavelength.

Isabel spun her staff overhead, less a lasso than a building cyclone, and pinned Dore with her invisible gaze. No doubt he'd deduced the purpose of her working from the way the currents swelled to await her will. Already visions of intent stacked within her consciousness, eager for release.

Dore took a tentative step backwards. "I have him, you see. Do you see?" He licked his lips and stared at her with a wild, sharp gaze. "You see much, even blindfolded. But do you see this?" He took another step away from her, one step closer to the node.

She fanned her consciousness around the room. She did see it then. A gossamer thread extended from Dore's Labyrinth—from Ean—back to the wielder. He had hold of the pattern, and what he could do with that simple thread ...

Her staff stilled in her hand. She lowered her arm.

Dore's black eyes gleamed. "He's him, isn't he?" He licked his lips and nodded towards Ean's crumpled form as he took another step in retreat. His gaze hid in the shadows of his brow the way his soul cowered in the desiccated husk of his body, but Isabel felt the glee he now radiated. "Arion. He's Arion Returned—of course he is, you needn't admit it."

Isabel set her staff down in front of her and interwove her fingers around the smooth stone. In her mind, she prepared the knife to sever the thread Dore still held. She'd no doubt he meant to step across the node and pull the thread along with him, no matter what mercy he bargained. It would rip the Labyrinth out of Ean's mind and take his sanity with it.

"Don't try to stop me!" Dore licked his lips, the flicker of a pink tongue across pale flesh. Two steps more and he'd be across the node. "Stay away!" He held up his hand and shook the ethereal thread he held in warning. Then he took that final step.

Isabel cut the thread and simultaneously threw one of her own. She murmured darkly, "Run, Dore Madden."

Dore vanished across the node.

Işak'getirmek stumbled awkwardly through the frostbitten night. His bad leg throbbed a continual reprimand, while his mind had become a ravaged field, thick with the chaff of unraveling patterns. These blew against Dore's compulsive spells and churned into bristly muck. Thinking at all was painful. Işak wanted only to rest, or better yet to lie down and die, but desperation drove him forth—for most of all, he wanted to distance himself from Ean.

Snowflakes floated soundlessly down, disturbed from their rest in the treetops by his rough passing. Deeper snow slowed his progress, and an icy, contemptuous wind stole what breath the steep mountain left to him, but he felt little of these torments, for no worldly chill could approximate the cold radiating out of the raw reaches of his soul.

He knew the truth now.

No more suspicions, suppositions, only certainty: Dore Madden had known his identity from the moment he'd claimed him in N'ghorra—had claimed him *because* of his family name, adding insult to the pernicious injury of imprisonment for the inexcusable wrong of royal birth.

Claiming him as his bright new toy, Dore had twisted and contorted Işak's mind with compulsion, beaten his will to a pulp, and battened any memory of his true identity behind patterns of concealment. Finally, in his most heinous act of degradation, he'd set Işak against his own brother, the final test of his subjugation, a task meant to consume the last vestiges of Işak's honor.

But Işak had failed that test.

And he continued to fail it. This might've been his only consolation as he drove himself through the night fleeing his youngest brother—who had amazingly, *incredibly*, become a wielder possibly more powerful than Dore.

But he couldn't flee the flood of memories swarming his mind.

Dore's iron doors of concealment had been opened, and now Işak struggled to stay afloat amid the deluge of memory—everything he was and much that had been done to break him came flooding back on a tide of understanding. Even before N'ghorra, Viernan hal'Jaitar had begun the process of stripping away his honor, there in the hollow chambers beneath Tal'Shira. Işak shuddered now to remember those days, darker moments even than his penitence in the salt mines.

They'd all tried to break him—Radov, hal'Jaitar, the butchers of N'ghorra, Dore Madden—yet none of them had truly accomplished the deed. But what did honor matter when Dore still imprisoned his mind? All Ean had accomplished was to prolong an inevitable end, for Dore had bound him body and soul.

Işak knew the moment Dore arrived at Tyr'kharta, for the wielder's unwelcome heat suddenly filled his mind, as palpable as opening a curtain to the strong midday sun. Of course Dore would've known his wards around Tyr'kharta had been breached. Of course he would've come. And the moment he arrived, he would've known Işak had failed. Soon he would come in search of him.

Işak ran now as much from Ean as from Dore.

That he ran at all testified to Ean's having accomplished *something* with his unworking. He was climbing awkwardly up a cliff face, using the sparse trees to aid him, when he felt Dore's sudden fury flare through the bond. His muscles spasmed, his bad leg collapsed beneath him, and he lost his hold upon the tree. He fell backwards through the night with wind and darkness an ill support. Then he hit.

Snow erupted around him, and he sank deeply into the drift. Buried rock scraped one leg, bringing new fire, and the compulsion he'd been holding off with naught but the force of his will set back in with a vengeance, making him violently ill.

Even had he the will to move then, Işak couldn't have managed it. His feet were wedged too deeply in, and his leg was soon a throbbing agony. Perhaps he could've worked a pattern to free himself, but to what purpose? Dore was already coming for him.

Işak exhaled a shuddering breath and lay shivering in the damp snow, staring up into the heavens. The stars swirled dizzily above him.

He wasn't sure what was worse: the strange half-life of amnesia that he'd lived in since Dore had plucked him from the salt mines, recalling nothing of himself, only that something important had been lost; or remembering the fullness of his life with vivid clarity and knowing everything they had taken from him.

Amnesia almost seemed a more compassionate path.

He heard Dore approaching long before the wielder arrived, for the man made the noise of an infernal beast and cursed profligately about the inconvenience. Işak admitted there was no easy way to get to where he lay beneath the mountain's rough edge, no node to transport Dore in comfort and warmth. Odd that he hadn't sent Raliax to claim him, but Işak supposed that would've delayed his punishment; Dore felt punishment must be meted immediately after the transgression, as if a man possessed the same incontinent memory as a miscreant dog.

By the time Dore finally reached him, Işak could no longer feel either of his legs, and the queasiness in his stomach had been honed into a sharp ache. Dore stopped above him, and Işak saw in the moonlight that the wielder had undergone some kind of battle, for his clothes were singed and his flesh crossed with lines of blood. He hadn't imagined it possible to make the man look more like the walking dead.

The night had held many surprises so far.

Malice glinted in Dore's black eyes as he stared down at Işak. He licked blood and spittle from his lips. "I see that I must teach you more strenuously to understand the cost of failure."

And he proceeded to do that very thing.

TWO

"Let not your home be a place, unless it is a place
found solely in your mind and heart."

– The Sormitáge Scholar D'Nofrio of Rogue

HOME.
All the days Tanis and the zanthyr were descending from the icy reaches of the mountain pass, the lad tried to process the word. *Home.*

The way the zanthyr had said the word implied mystery and majesty ... even a grave serenity, but *home* brought a different picture to Tanis's mind. To him, *home* meant long days in Her Grace's infirmary, rewards of Mistress Hibbert's plum tarts, and Farshideh's smile, which forgave all transgressions. He was having difficulty reconciling his memories of growing up at Fersthaven with jutting, snow-capped peaks and a lush valley bordering the sea.

Yet for all that Tanis's sense of home didn't quite mesh with the zanthyr's pronouncement, excitement filled him—and anticipation, and even a touch of uncertainty. He couldn't help wondering if somewhere among the deep, tall pines, somewhere near the shore ... would he find a beach covered in pebbles that rumbled with the waves? A small part of him dared hope that his mother might be there.

As they made their way down from the snowbound reaches, Tanis saw again the shapes he'd noticed from their high vantage, only now he could never mistake them for sheep. Though still distant, the herd of silver-white horses milled in graceful silence, their gilded manes streaming like molten sunlight as they pranced and played.

Tanis spun a look to the zanthyr. "My lord ... are those Hallovians?"

"Your mother raised them," Phaedor replied without turning, "but in her absence, the herd has grown wild."

Tanis turned back to the horses. Hallovians commanded a king's ransom in price most anywhere in the realm, and Tanis couldn't count the number of horses that dotted the distant meadow.

Eventually they traded icy trails for rolling hills, then hills for a forest of bare-limbed elms, black oaks and gigantic evergreen hemlocks. The zanthyr led them unerringly through this ancient forest, oftentimes reclining on his horse with eyes closed, letting the animal chose the way. The only sounds were the steady plodding of the horses' hooves, the wind scraping the winter-bare trees, and the occasional foraging animal.

In such moments of enduring silence, Tanis missed Pelas almost desperately. He missed Pelas's passion to experience everything their realm had to offer; he missed his charismatic brilliance of character and his irrepressible curiosity. In contrast, the zanthyr's deep, introspective silence made Phaedor seem ever remote, ever mysterious. Ironically, Tanis understood their innate compositions to be just the opposite: Phaedor was tied to the life of the realm, and Pelas to its demise.

The lad was pondering this grim paradox when he glimpsed a pale structure looming in the distance and noted that Phaedor's horse was heading towards it. Soon they were riding beneath a six-armed archway forming the skeleton of a dome perhaps thirty feet across. Carved patterns covered every inch of the alabaster arches.

Tanis leaned back in his saddle and craned his neck to view the top of the dome where the arches would cross, but too many tree limbs obscured their joining. He estimated the arches hovered at least fifty feet high, however.

He was still staring upwards as they passed beneath the dome's center, whereupon he saw a brief flash amid the fir limbs and felt a static current charge through the air. Tanis got the distinctly uncomfortable impression that the arch had just ... *woken*. He looked down to see the hairs rising on his arms.

"Uh ... my lord ... what is this ... thing?"

Phaedor was reclining on his steed with both hands clasped behind his head and his booted feet propped on his horse's withers. Tanis had no idea how he rode like that without falling off.

"Your father made it," the zanthyr remarked with eyes closed.

"My—my *father* made it?" Excitement thrilled through the lad upon hearing a reference to his mysterious and intriguing father. Then he really *heard* what Phaedor had said. "Wait, my father *made* it?"

Tanis would've pressed Phaedor for more information in that moment except that the energy swirling within the arches was making him feel squashed—never mind the annoying buzzing in his ears—and he noted uncomfortably that the static charge swirling the air was causing the standing hairs on his arms to ripple like wheat in the wind.

Hunching his shoulders with a grimace, the lad pressed, "Um ... why is it *humming?*"

The zanthyr opened one eye to cast him an amused look. "That is the third strand you feel, Truthreader."

"Well and good, but what's it doing?"

Phaedor shut his eyes again. "Its job."

Tanis glared at him. "Which is … ?"

"You might think of the dome as the guardian of this valley." But beyond this, Phaedor would say no more.

The sun was hanging low in the west when Tanis started hearing snatches of a subtle roar that could only be crashing waves. They emerged from the forest atop a grassy hill, where a view spread before them. The lad caught his breath and gave the zanthyr a winsome grin.

The hillside swept down to a line of cliffs crowned by a stately manor and outbuildings, and beyond these, the sea. Built of lustrous limestone and roofed steeply in slate, the manor embellished the cliff with such elegance that the view would surely have been diminished without it.

"The Villa Serafina." The zanthyr's tone held that same wistful timbre from before, a tone Tanis couldn't quite interpret. "Your mother's home—and yours."

Tanis smiled wondrously upon the scene. To think his home could be so beautiful. "So … are you going to tell me now where we are, my lord?"

"On the Caladrian Coast."

"Which is where, exactly?"

Phaedor shook his head. "Have you learned nothing of geography, Truthreader? Caladria lies along the southern coast of Agasan."

"So I *am* Agasi!" The words burst out quite without warning. He'd wondered for so long about his heritage. Finally knowing the truth brought sudden warmth to the otherwise chill day.

Phaedor looked bemused. "Was this not always apparent?"

"Not to me." Tanis stared flatly at him. "But since *you've* clearly known all along, I feel obliged to point out that you might've mentioned it sooner, my lord."

Phaedor cast him a shadowy grin and led away down the hill.

They entered the grounds through a carved stone archway and followed the curving drive past an orchard, a carriage house and then around to the stables. The grounds were well kept, the empty stables stocked with hay and grain, but to Tanis's growing disappointment, no one seemed about. Their only salutation came from the ever–crashing waves.

By the time they'd tended to their horses, the sun was melting into a mercuric sea. Toting his packs and feeling out of place, Tanis followed Phaedor into the silent manor, across marble floors and up a grand, curving staircase.

The zanthyr sent the fourth into the lamps, and the manor blossomed with light, but the lad still felt odd traipsing through such a palatial home with no one to greet him, like a trespasser sneaking in while the family was away.

Two complete turns of the wide staircase brought them to a carpeted landing. The zanthyr led Tanis down a hall and into a corner bedroom paneled in blue silk. A massive canopy bed dominated one wall. The drapes of its rich brocade reflected deeper hues of blue.

"This is your room, lad." The zanthyr walked to the windows as Tanis was staring at the red-lacquered furniture, whose finish crackled with gold. "Tonight we'll forage for ourselves. By morning, your staff will have arrived."

Tanis looked around the room—*his* room—and decided it was all quite surreal, being there in his mother's house—*his* house—surrounded by her things—apparently *his* things—and with the zanthyr as his housemate.

It took a moment for the zanthyr's comment to register, but then the boy frowned. He turned in a slow circle, unable to make sense of what he observed. The manor looked as if it was constantly and carefully tended. Everything shone with polish, from the marble floors to the gold handles on the ornate red furniture.

He turned Phaedor a look over his shoulder. "What do you mean, *my* staff?"

The zanthyr was peering out one of the mullioned glass doors positioned to either side of the bed. "Come, Tanis. I want to show you something."

Phaedor opened the doors and headed out onto a balcony. The wind was picking up, and it tossed Tanis's ash-blonde hair into his eyes as he joined the zanthyr outside. The lad pushed a hand to hold back his hair and blinked at the view.

For the first time, he was able to appreciate the immensity of the spectacular, razor-sharp peaks they'd traveled through, the tops of which were just then being bathed in the roseate sheen of sunset. However *had* they found their way among such a formidable congregation of mountains?

He took a deep breath and tried to wrap his mind around the enormity of this moment, how meaningful it was to be there. This was the place he'd been birthed, and while his fifteenth name day had come and gone unremarked, forgotten amid the thrill of his recent adventures, finding home again was a greater gift than anything he might've asked for.

The lad truthfully didn't know what to make of it. His mind felt stretched by the experience, unable to grasp it all, while his insides fluttered with anticipation like linen snapping in the brisk sea wind.

"Look there," said the zanthyr. He pointed west.

Tanis gazed along the line of Phaedor's leather-clad arm and saw a thin spire of light that erupted from the trees and vanished into the gilded clouds of sunset. He frowned. "What is it?"

Phaedor turned him an elusive smile. "Our card of calling."

Tanis exhaled a long-suffering sigh.

The zanthyr gave him an amused look. "Come, lad. Your stomach is announcing itself loudly and insistently. Let's eat, and I'll tell you what I can of your mother's house."

They ate in the kitchen at a long wooden table that would've easily sat twelve. Tanis's eyes and thoughts kept wondering, wondering if he would happen upon some painting or piece of furniture that sparked a recollection, but so far he'd found no memories of the manor from among his baby thoughts.

It was doubly strange to be sitting with the zanthyr by lamplight after so many nights where their only illumination had been the dancing flames of a campfire. Now Tanis sat with Phaedor in his *mother's* home, and the zanthyr was telling him wondrous things—without even being asked!

"This manor is the Villa Serafina," the zanthyr said as Tanis was reminding himself to close his mouth, for it had several times already fallen slack with surprise. "It and the lands surrounding it have been in your mother's family for generations. The family's main estate, the Palazzo di Adonnai, is located in the adjoining valley, but your mother preferred living here, by the sea."

Tanis *felt* more within this communication than Phaedor's words alone conveyed: intimations of his mother's interests and passions, her pursuits and delights.

"Your mother came here as often as she could. She deeply loved the sea and the forest, and indeed, of all of these lands. It made her sad to return— sometimes after many years—and find that the house had aged."

Phaedor glanced down at his fork, which lay precisely in line with his knife, as though the alignment mimicked the mental organization of his thoughts. His words followed the line of fork and knife, toward Tanis, but the lad knew much lingered unspoken in the narrow spaces between.

The zanthyr rose and walked to a window that looked out upon the kitchen yard and an orchard beyond. Shadows collected around him, and some of them formed into one of his daggers, which simply appeared in his hand. He gazed quietly into the yard as he thumbed the blade. "That he might never see your mother saddened, your father laid a web of patterns upon the villa and its surrounding grounds—protective patterns, patterns of preservation."

"My *father* ..." Again, Tanis's pulse quickened upon thinking of his father, who felt so oddly foreign and yet so important to the lad. It both pleased and excited him to know he'd been a wielder.

Phaedor turned a look over his shoulder, and Tanis sensed a sea of words floating beneath his emerald gaze, vast depths of information about his father. But the zanthyr said only, "The staff from the Adonnai estate come regularly to attend to this villa, but the house needs little attention. It remains exactly as your mother left it."

As grateful as he was to learn these small things, Tanis knew that Phaedor was merely skirting the edges of things ... walking a circle around a vastly beautiful city and describing only its wall. For all the zanthyr had told him more in the last hour than in all the collected minutes of their travels, the *important* information remained frustratingly hidden in that protected city, undisturbed.

"My lord ..." Tanis absently pushed some beans around on his plate with his fork. "Who were they, my parents? I don't even know their names."

The zanthyr arched a raven brow. "Is that so?"

Tanis opened his mouth to again deny such knowledge, but the words wouldn't form. "But I—I mean ..."

No, he really couldn't claim that he didn't know them, yet their names felt so far from his tongue. Tanis set down his fork and fell back in his chair. "My lord, I don't understand why you can't just tell me."

The zanthyr flipped his dagger and caught it by the point. He eyed the boy beneath the spill of his raven hair. "What promise did I make to your mother?"

Tanis frowned at him, for he guessed well enough the zanthyr's meaning. "You promised her you would protect me," he grumbled, "—but I don't see how knowing my parents' names could possibly bring me harm."

Phaedor flipped the hair from his eyes and settled the lad an ominous stare. "Do you not, Truthreader?"

Tanis swallowed, for what he actually heard Phaedor saying was, *One day you will.*

He held Phaedor's gaze as long as he could, but he saw no point in trying to out-stare the zanthyr, and there was no mistaking the warning lacing his tone or the river of portentous meaning rushing beneath it.

Finally the lad cleared his throat and changed the subject to a topic less unsettling. "So ... you said the staff would be coming in the morning?"

Phaedor grinned and flipped his dagger. "*Your* staff, in response to the spire I showed you. It's another of your father's patterns, a beacon high enough to be seen at the Palazzo di Adonnai and far beyond. The spire is raised any time someone crosses within your father's preservation patterns, that is, beneath the dome—which is the only way to reach this villa."

Tanis thought of the luminous spire shooting skyward and marveled at his father's skill. Who were these people, his parents, who led such lives? And where were they now? He wanted so much to push the zanthyr on the topic, but the question simply hid now from his tongue, cowed by the ominous implications of the things Phaedor wouldn't say.

The silence at the table lingered, and the shadows beyond their circle of lamplight felt suddenly heavy. The zanthyr's gaze took in Tanis's drooping eyelids, and a quiet smile graced his features. "To bed with you, lad."

Tanis hadn't realized he was so tired until the zanthyr said the words. Afterwards, he wondered suspiciously if indeed he hadn't *been* tired until the zanthyr decided he should go to sleep. In the privacy of his thoughts, Tanis suspected that the zanthyr's ability actually knew no bounds—that indeed, Phaedor might move mountains if his motives required him to. Putting a boy to bed without argument was certainly not beyond his capabilities.

Yet as Tanis reluctantly trudged up the grand, curving staircase, he wondered how he was ever going to fall asleep. He hadn't even begun to explore his mother's house, and the lure of treasures to be discovered had him fair salivating—either that, or the fact that he'd barely touched his dinner. Most of the day still felt surreal; the enormity of it had barely begun to sink in.

Tanis partly recognized that this new knowledge of his inheritance wasn't just about a house—it was a house and land and titles and possibly peerage in the Empress' court and privilege and his parents' history and their talents and-and-*and!*

But all he really wanted to think about just then was his mother and father and the life they might've led together as a family.

He was quite sure as he stripped out of his traveling clothes and slipped between soft sheets, grateful for the quick warmth of the heavenly mattress and eiderdown duvet, that he would lie awake half the night just thinking about his parents. But no sooner had he closed his eyes with a contented smile than he fell into a deep and powerful sleep.

THREE

"Don't talk to me of Balance. Fortune favors the bold."

– The Adept wielder Arion Tavestra

A BANK OF THUNDERSTORMS squatted along Agasan's Caladrian Coast, blanketing the Sacred City of Faroqhar in fog and rain. The usually bustling harbor lay as empty as the streets, with everyone staying put rather than braving the lashing winds. Most of the city's residents patiently waited out Mother Nature's foul temper indoors, content to sup or share a drink wherever the rains had caught them. Only the occasional pair of Red Guard could be seen passing on horseback, their animals looking as sullen and ill-humored as their crimson-cloaked riders. Storms in the Sacred City were rare, but when they came, they struck with a vengeance.

Atop one of the highest hills, separated from the city by miles of parkland, the inhabitants of the Sormitáge University went about their regular affairs with little interruption. Only the doves that nested among the university's domes seemed bothered by the rains, and they hid their heads beneath sheltering wings, feathers ruffled against the turbulent winds.

Within a gallery overlooking a rain-swept quad, the young Nodefinder Felix di Sarcova della Buonara waited for a gaggle of first-year Sormitáge students—not so affectionately called *frites* by upper-classmen like Felix—to make their way down the passage with an agonizing lack of haste.

Felix's desire for privacy might've been granted sooner had the quad not offered an evening's unexpected entertainment in the form of three *frites* who'd apparently been locked out of their dormitory by some arcane means. Glowing dormitory windows on the far side of the quad illuminated the *frites'* drenched and sullen efforts to regain entry; likewise the host of laughing boys standing safely inside.

Felix might've ordered the gawking *frites* in his own gallery to move on, claiming Devoveré privileges—for he had his first ring at only fifteen, a rare accomplishment that had garnered him many envious new enemies—but then the *frites* might've remembered seeing him.

Felix misliked anyone noticing him while he was about his activities, and especially *frites*. First-years were notorious gossip-mongers. Like fledgling birds, they noisily craved the worms of rumor no matter how many times the disgusting things had been regurgitated.

Like now, for instance. Though they were apparently captivated by their drenched compatriots in the courtyard, the *frites* were running their mouths nonstop about the Imperial Princess Nadia van Gelderan showing up only minutes ago to attend a lecture. Rumor spread in tsunami fashion upon the mouths of *frites*.

Felix waited impatiently in the shadow of a statue, inwardly cursing the fool-headedness of *frites* in general and these in particular, and willing them to find some other place to idle away their evening—he, for one, had somewhere *important* to be. After a nauseating length of time, they finally grew bored of the display and meandered off in a buzz of inane chatter, like a swarm of sluggish flies.

"*Boccalone,*" Felix hissed in his native Calabrian tongue. *Big mouth gossips!*

When the passage fell silent, Felix poked his head around the edge of the statue. He aimed a pair of mismatched eyes—one blue and one green—to the left and right, and then the rest of his body followed his head out into the open passage. Quick as a cat, he darted down the gallery towards the node he meant to travel.

The passages of the Sormitáge were rife with nodes and leis. A Nodefinder had merely to open his inner eye and an onslaught of portals accosted him. Creating a slight hitch in this plethora of potential adventures was the fact that said nodes had long ago been twisted and sealed off. Peering across them revealed only darkness, and traveling them was widely known to be impossible. Indeed, attempting to so much as stick one's head across the threshold of a twisted node was a foolhardy endeavor that even *frites* understood as idiocy beyond contempt. Such a one would go nowhere at best and at worst find himself stuck within the Pattern of the World, trapped until he starved to death or the forces raging within the realm's magnetic grid ripped him apart.

But Felix was no ordinary Nodefinder.

His mother laughingly claimed he'd been bastard-born of a love affair with a handsome avieth named Firenze, which might account for his mismatched eyes and oddly tri-colored auburn hair; but Felix had never seen a handsome avieth and suspected his mother was far too savvy to entertain a Wildling lover right underneath the Lord Sarcova's nose—especially considering how easily Davros Sarcova divested himself of wives who'd displeased him.

Felix didn't really know what divine powers had invested him with the variant talent he secretly possessed, but he knew enough to keep quiet about what he could do. He'd often wondered if his gift enabled him to untwist the nodes as he traveled them, or if it gave him the ability to simply travel their contorted pathways unharmed. Whatever the case, he'd long resigned himself to suffer the mystery, since he certainly couldn't ask any of the maestros about it—they'd only want to know why he wanted to know.

Traveling on the twisted nodes of Faroqhar, however, amounted to illicit use of his talent, and he'd face a tempest of trouble if anyone ever caught him in the act. Raine's truth, the Empress's Red Guard would string him up by his toes, smear him with honey and lower him into a hole of rats. And that would just be the appetizer.

But all the fun of a game lay in its inherent risk.

It's no game tonight though, he thought with the slightest pang of unease.

Tonight he was finally going to find out what had been bothering his roommate, Malin van Drexel, so desperately that the older boy had dropped a whole notch on his belt.

Over the past month, Malin had become increasingly withdrawn and unsociable. He kept odd hours, jumped at shadows, and took his meals alone. Felix had been trying for weeks to get Malin to talk to him. Then, just that afternoon, he'd appeared in their chambers, announced where and when Felix should meet him, and vanished again.

Frowning at these thoughts, Felix stepped across the node and emerged in a hallway leading to the kitchens of one the residential houses. The clatter of pans and dishes underscored the discordant hum floating down the passage from the dining room. This was just the first of several forbidden paths he would travel on his way to meet Malin, each one compounding his chances of being caught.

Lord and the Lady, what are you thinking, Felix?

He'd never attempted anything so utterly reckless, except perhaps the adventure that had landed him in the Princess Nadia van Gelderan's bedchamber—but that had been an accident, inasmuch as he hadn't known the node connected to the Imperial Palace and the private apartments of the Empress's heir.

Still, Evans Hall had better food than his own dining room in Chresten, and his cousin Phoebe lived at Evans, so he had *some* right to help himself to their delectable menu, even if Phoebe had been on holiday for over a fortnight.

See what risks I take for you, Malin? Felix ducked his head and slipped through the shadows towards the dining room, away from the kitchen's glow.

Not much later, Felix stepped off another node into the dim corridor between two rows of high bookshelves. Immediately he collided with a ladder used to access the highest shelves. The spiteful thing tumbled, and Felix just caught it before it crashed to the floor—though not without a considerable amount of cursing that, in retrospect, might've made more of a ruckus than the ladder slamming down.

Regaining his composure, Felix adjusted the diagonal strap of his satchel across his chest and headed to the end of the row to figure out where he was.

In nine hells of misery if they catch you in here, Felix.

Considering that he stood in the restricted section of the Sormitáge's Imperial Archives and had used a forbidden node to get there, it was a conservative estimate.

"Felix?"

Felix turned at the whispered voice that carried easily through the silence and saw Malin approaching out of the gloom.

"Lord and the Lady!" Malin's face broke into a wide grin of relief. "I didn't think you'd actually make it."

Felix scowled at him. "Then why'd you ask me to meet you *here*, of all bloody places?"

"Well, I hoped you would." Malin clapped him on the shoulder. "I'm starving. Did you bring us supper?"

Felix placed a protective hand on the satchel at his hip. "It'll cost you—an explanation for every bite of bread."

That same shadow which had haunted Malin for days returned to his gaze. "I'll tell you everything, Felix. Raine's truth, I'm desperate to tell someone." He tugged on Felix's arm and headed back the way he'd come.

Felix followed, but not without reservation. It was one thing to pop into places unannounced, do your business, and exit again before anyone knew you'd been there. It was quite another to steal into the Imperial Archives for a bloody picnic.

He could just see the faces of the Empress's Red Guard arriving to find him perched on a stack of priceless books munching on a tart. Their imagined expressions were so comical that Felix almost smiled; but the dim light of the vast, vaulted room was too oppressive, the silence too loud in his ears, for any levity to find purchase. The stacks themselves seemed to decry his presence. Felix feared a smile would only further incense them.

"Why here, Malin?" Felix trailed uncertainly behind the older, taller boy. It felt like the shadows were clinging to his body, slowing his pace, leeching the courage from his steps.

"It's the safest place I could think of to talk." Malin shot him a glance over his shoulder. "There's no one about, Felix, don't worry. I've spent many a night here with the Imperial Historian's blessing. Once the sun goes down and the restricted section closes, not even the literatos brave the stacks."

Felix didn't find this point exactly heartening. Literatos were a good deal smarter than them. "Why not?" He spared a glance for the towering shelves, whose ends were each carved with a different effigy. The faces were all glaring at him.

"Superstition, I think," Malin said, but his voice lacked the luster of conviction. "Most of these are books of power—you know, they all have patterns in them—which is why they're catalogued in this section. Even dormant, the patterns collect *elae*. Maestro Greaves cautions all of his interns to be careful when opening any book in the restricted Archives."

"Good to know," Felix muttered. It didn't explain in the least why the literatos stayed out of the stacks after sundown. He could well imagine some monster prowling in the darkness—*Sancto Spirito*, this was the *Sormitáge*. The place was nearly as old as the realm itself. Who knew what lurked in its depths?

Malin led them to an alcove beneath one of the high, stained-glass windows along the west wall. Felix looked up to see rainwater running in rivulets down the panes. For a moment he envied it such escape.

A wielder's lamp illuminated two armchairs and a reading desk piled with notebooks. "So this is where you've been spending all your time?"

Malin gave him a telling look. In the lamp's pale glow, the haunted darkness in his gaze seemed even more brutal. "Let's eat. I'm famished."

"Yeah, so you mentioned."

Felix sat and pulled out several bundles from his satchel. It was everything he could scrounge from Evans' dining room without drawing undue attention. Malin fell to eating with the fervor of the condemned, drawing a true smile from Felix. For a little while he felt like things were almost back to normal between them.

As he was munching on a chicken leg, Malin stared at Felix's Devoveré ring. Felix followed his gaze to the thin gold band, which gleamed like a ray of sunlight twined around his pointer finger. A closer look would reveal the faint etchings of patterns that bound the ring to Felix's life pattern. The ring would never fit another person, and he was the only one who could remove it from his finger.

Malin frowned. "Felix … you've made a *stanza segreta*, haven't you?"

Felix nearly choked on his bread.

Malin lowered his rather gnawed chicken leg to regard him seriously. "I know you must. Traveling twisted nodes? Already Devoveré with your ring at fifteen? Come on—admit it. You've made your coach."

No secret was more taboo among second-stranders than a *stanza segreta*, otherwise known as a coach. Never mind that any Nodefinder worth his salt made one as soon as he could master the necessary skill. Coaches were Nodefinder's lore and better left to myth—if you'd made one, you certainly didn't *confess* to it. Epiphany forbid some *na'turna* bureaucrat actually believe a Nodefinder could pin a leis to his own life pattern and start poking around into what a coach could be used for.

Felix glared at him. "You're a bastard for asking me."

The darkness in Malin's gaze faded slightly, and his lips curved in a smile. "I knew it. You really are a prodigy, aren't you?"

"Bloody Sanctos on a stake." Felix kicked at him. "Tell me what this is all about and get it over with already."

Malin rubbed his Maritus bracelet, absently turning the heavy links in a circle around his wrist. Felix recognized the habit—not so long ago he'd worn the same bracelet. His wrist still felt empty without it.

"Do you ever wonder who you were before?" Malin glanced up at Felix from beneath his brows. "I mean, if you could figure it out—what if you were someone famous, like Arion Tavestra?"

"Tavestra was fifth strand."

"But you know what I mean."

"No, I really don't."

Malin lifted his chicken leg to his mouth, then lowered it again, his expression pensive. "Do you think Adepts ever remember their past lives after they Awaken? If we're always reborn to the same strand ... you'd think something of what we knew would come back eventually."

"So what if it did?"

Malin gave him a long, unreadable look. "Well ... that would explain prodigies like you, wouldn't it?"

"Not really."

"No—think about it, Felix. If we're always reborn to the same strand, it follows that we'd keep the same variant traits."

"No one knows why certain Adepts are born with variant traits. That's why they're called *variant* traits."

"That's not exactly true, Felix." Malin waved an arm towards the stacks looming like mountains in the gloom. "There's centuries of research on variant traits. Back in Cyrenaic times, the Quorum of the Sixth Truth devoted themselves wholly to the study of those with the ability to see patterns. They were all fifth strand Adepts with that particular variant trait." He seemed to finally remember his chicken and pried off a crusty bite, which he then chewed thoughtfully. "You know ... you'd probably have learned much of this yourself if you spent more time in study and less time trying to get noosed traveling forbidden nodes."

"Like the ones I took to get here tonight?" Felix retorted. He leaned back in his chair and eyed Malin irritably. "Is this what you're doing your Devoveré thesis on—variant traits?"

Malin frowned. "Well ... it's where I started. But then ..." He cast Felix a fretful look. "Well, it's just ... then I found this." He pulled a large bundle from beneath the stack of notebooks and laid it on Felix's lap. It was unnaturally heavy.

Casting Malin a wary look, Felix unwrapped the dark cloth to reveal a leather-bound book. It looked old. *Really* old. Like the *Sobra I'ternin* old. Intricate patterns covered the heavy leather binding, while the gilt-edged vellum pages had that particular gleam only acquired after centuries of sitting on a pedestal. Felix noticed that if he looked hard at any one pattern on the cover, his eyes started playing tricks on him, making the patterns seem to twist in painful ways.

Felix's hand slipped inside his shirt, and his fingers absently rubbed the Sanctos amulets he wore, bearing the effigies of his ancestors. Since the day he'd been born, Felix had worn the long-nosed effigy of Sanctos Frangelica, his many-times great aunt who'd died of a broken heart, and whom his mother, in her infinite wisdom, had decided would be the best ancestor to watch over him. He'd also personally chosen the Sanctos of his great-great-great-grandfather Dominico, who'd died fighting pirates. In Felix's estimation, the only thing more awe-inspiring than to die fighting pirates was to live to talk about it.

Still ... he doubted even the sanctified spirits of his ancestors could protect him from the thing resting on his lap. The longer he stared at the patterns, the more they seemed to move.

He lifted a daggered glare back to Malin. "What by the Sanctos *is* this thing and why do you have it?"

Malin had that haunted look again—the one he'd been wearing around for the past fortnight like a death's head brand on his forehead. He visibly swallowed. "It's one of the books of the *Qhorith'quitara*."

"Is that supposed to mean something to me?"

Malin looked immensely culpable. "The *Qhorith'quitara* are the apocryphal books taken from the *Sobra* scriptures."

Felix started in his chair. He felt suddenly like the book was burning a hole in his lap. "The Lost Books of the *Sobra I'ternin*—are you *insane?*" He hastily rewrapped the bundle and shoved it at the older boy. "Put it back wherever it came from!"

Malin took the book and rested it on his knees. "I will, Felix. It's just ..." His brow furrowed as he looked down at the cover. "I found something in it ..."

"Bloody Sanctos on a stake, of course you did!" Felix stood and walked to the edge of the circle of lamplight. He felt like the book was sucking all the air out of his lungs. Pushing a hand through his hair, he turned to stare at his friend. "How'd you even get it, for Epiphany's sake?"

Malin looked tormented. "Maestro Greaves allowed me to look at a section of it for my thesis research. He told me to look at only that section and then replace the volume on its shelf, but I ... hid the book instead and took it with me when I left."

"Malin!"

"I only wanted to look through a little more of it. Maestro Greaves is always talking about the apocryphal books of the *Sobra*. You know ... the ones they're ashamed of ... or afraid of. I never expected to find ... what I found."

Felix's curiosity finally pushed its head out of the sand. "Which was what, exactly?"

Malin's expression rivaled that of an innocent man walking to his own hanging. "You'll never believe it, Felix—Lord and the Lady, *I* don't believe it. I'm *sure* the maestros won't believe it. But I know I'm right, Felix." He dropped his voice to a bare whisper and leaned closer. "There's someone extremely dangerous here at the Sormitáge, a man who's not who he says he is, and I've been so—"

They both heard the footfalls in the same moment. Felix spun even as Malin stood up from his chair. They exchanged a silent look of alarm.

Felix's expression asked a desperate *what do we do?*

Malin set the book down on his chair. "Stay here and keep out of sight." He bravely straightened his shoulders and headed off in the direction of the noise.

Felix lingered, plagued with indecision. On the one hand, Malin being caught in the restricted section of the Archives would get him a slap on the wrist, while Felix's presence would not only likely result in expulsion from the Sormitáge but would also raise a host of unwelcome questions as to how he got there to begin with. Myriad resulting scenarios washed through his mind, each leaving a stain of bloody consequences.

Still …

What if the thing walking nearby wasn't just a literato out for an evening stroll among the horrid stacks? What if it was some kind of gruesome vampire who liked to feast on the flesh of Adepts too stupid to realize that the literatos knew something they didn't? What then? Was he to let Malin face the undead alone and not even get to see him being decapitated and his brains sucked out?

At this thought, the malady which possesses all Nodefinders—that being an innate lack of good judgment and common sense—kicked in, and Felix set off after his friend.

He could just make out Malin's dim form about eight stacks down as the latter turned between the shelves. Soon a man's voice floated out of the darkness. Then came Malin's murmured reply, urgent but low.

Suddenly a feeling of foreboding broke like a wave over Felix.

He sprinted down the corridor, stacks flashing by. Reaching the row where Malin had turned, he grabbed the edge of the massive bookshelf for stability and slung around the edge, only to stagger to a halt.

The row stood empty.

FOUR

"Eat a live toad first thing in the morning and nothing
worse can happen to you for the rest of the day."
— *The Hearthwitch's Handbook*

PERHAPS PHAEDOR HAD cast a spell upon the boy, or perhaps it was merely due to the needs of a growing lad who'd had an incredible day of discovery, but Tanis slept soundly all through the night.

And as the glow of dawn gilded his lids, the dream came …

"Tanis love," his mother said. She touched him gently upon the shoulder.

He opened his eyes to see her standing above him. She wore a blue gown, and her long chestnut hair was caught in a loose plait seeded with tiny pearls. The soft tip of it tickled his skin as she bent over him. Her smile held the grace of divinity in his estimation, and in her colorless eyes he found all of the stars of the sky. She brushed her hand across his forehead and hair. "Welcome home, my darling son."

Tanis wanted to reach out to her, but he felt a great weight pressing him into the bed. Even as she said the words she began to fade, still smiling so lovingly upon him, until he could see the patterns in the silk paneling on the wall behind her. One pattern glowed brightly beneath a long shaft of sunlight.

Then her image faded completely …

And Tanis woke. He opened his eyes to the light of dawn, feeling warmth suffusing him, body and mind. Yawning prodigiously, the lad sat up and rubbed his eyes and looked blearily around. A rose-gold hue tinged the air, hinting at a brilliant day on Agasan's Caladrian Coast. He noticed then that a fire had been lit in his hearth and a morning tea service left upon a round table. The zanthyr had spoken the literal truth: morning had come, and the villa staff with it.

Still tingling from the dream of his mother, Tanis looked back to where she'd been standing in his dream and—

He blinked. Then he blinked a few more times. Funny, but that same pattern looked like it really was glowing. He rubbed his eyes and stared harder, but the vision remained.

Tanis threw off the covers and walked to the wall. He paid particular notice that time to the hundreds of patterns decorating the silk panels of his room. They were formed of delicate silver hand-painted on a field of cerulean blue. Each pattern had its own unique design, though all were about the size of his palm. As he drew nearer to the pattern of interest that morning, Tanis realized it really *was* glowing. His heart started beating faster, and a sudden anticipation hummed through him.

Wondering what it could be, he reached a hand and touched the silk …

"Hello, Tanis love," said his mother.

Tanis spun around.

She stood in the middle of the room.

"No, my darling son, I'm not really here," she said, not quite looking at him. "What you see is but a working of the fourth strand, the illusion of my presence. Breathe now," she advised, smiling gently, "calm your heart. This vision shall not evaporate so quickly as your dream just now."

Tanis stared at her image with his heart thudding in his ears. He thought of sitting down—for his knees felt like noodles and he was suddenly burning up—but nothing stood nearby to collapse upon. So he rubbed uneasily at one eye and watched the apparition in the middle of the room with a nervous feeling in his stomach.

She looked completely real.

From the way her sun-streaked hair shimmered in the morning light like dark honey, to the faint flush upon her cheeks, right on down to the silver charm strung on a delicate chain around her neck. "Come," she said, holding out a hand. "Let us sit together, and I'll explain."

Sure he must still be dreaming, Tanis walked to the bed and took a seat, and she came over to sit beside him. Even up close, she looked utterly corporeal—Tanis almost reached out to touch her.

Illusion …

He knew it was true, for though she sat beside him, she caused no indentation in the mattress. The lad gazed in awe. The fourth strand of *elae* compelled the energy of thought and therefore could be wielded to form illusions, but having seen only the illusions crafted by Master o'Reith, Tanis had no idea they could *feel* so real—that *every sense* could be fooled into believing in that reality.

"Now then," his mother said brightly, "I have attempted to anticipate some of your inevitable questions. I apologize, my love, if I do not answer them all here today. All knowledge must be gained in its proper order and time, lest it be misunderstood, misconstrued or otherwise misevaluated. So I beseech your patience and give you my promise that one day you will gain a fuller understanding of not only the events of your own life, my dearest son, but also of the path that lies ahead." She seemed to be looking directly at him, her starry eyes so brilliantly complex and lovely in their strangeness. "Do I have your agreement then?"

Clearly his mother was waiting for a reply. It made no sense to Tanis how any of this was happening. Surely they couldn't have a conversation ... could they? Still, what else could he do but answer, "Yes, my lady," in a tiny voice full of awe.

She smiled, and the room filled with radiance. "Let us proceed then with some preliminary questions that one need not be a Seer to envision." She seemed to place a hand upon his own. His heart jumped, but then it fell because he hadn't actually felt her touch.

With this, she stood and walked towards the windows. The silk taffeta of her elegant blue gown rustled softly with each step. "First," she began, "I would have you understand that you are *my* son." She turned him a look over her slender shoulder, and her gaze conveyed her deep and unwavering love. "That another woman raised you was necessary for reasons I cannot yet explain, but you remain my son and your father's heir. This is why you were never allowed to take another family's name."

With a throat gone dry, Tanis nodded, though he knew his mother couldn't see him.

"Second, I cannot promise that we will meet again," and she turned away from him at this. "Many days and nights will have passed before you receive this message. But I *believe*, my darling ... and I trust." She stopped beside the east-facing doors and turned to him with the sunlight streaming in behind her. In that moment, Tanis imagined he'd never seen anyone so beautiful as his mother. "Faith is a powerful propellant, Tanis love. Never fail to use it as an agent toward your aims."

Standing sideways by the mullioned doors, she seemed to brush aside the curtains, though they were already open. The long fingers of her left hand played about the charm on her necklace as she gazed out at the sea. "Now then," she said, "we come to the reason for our reunion. You will hopefully have learned much already of our craft, but there are things only I can teach you. This is the purpose of the lessons to follow."

She blessed him with a smile, and then she vanished.

Tanis sucked in his breath in a half-audible gasp. "No!" Suddenly heartsick and desperate to understand what had happened, he spun around looking for her elsewhere in the room. "Where's the rest?" She'd spoken of lessons, but then she'd disappeared.

He jumped off the bed and ran back to the first pattern, but it appeared as ordinary now as any other. Tanis tried pressing on it, slapping at it, alternately tapping it with both hands, beating at it with his fist ... but nothing happened. He wasn't sure what had triggered the first illusion and had no idea how to get it back.

He thought of running down the hall to find Phaedor and asking him about the illusions and how to bring them back, but what if he left and his mother returned? Besides, the idea of facing the zanthyr, with his scrutinizing gaze and inevitable piercing questions, was too disheartening.

Tanis sat for a while on his bed wishing the pattern would come back to life, but eventually he grew cold and decided he'd rather do something than sit there feeling glum. So he half-heartedly threw on a robe and washed his face and drank a cup of tea, which was oddly still steaming though it had clearly been sitting there since before dawn. He felt slightly cheered by the idea that his mother's home might hold other magical things … like teapots that stayed warm all through the day, but it was only a reluctant interest. Finally, Tanis sank down on the edge of his bed again and tried not to feel so dismayed.

That's when he saw the other pattern.

It was glowing softly on the wall near the doors, where his mother had last been standing. No doubt the streaming sunlight had at first obscured it.

Tanis made a streak to the pattern. He studied it closely, and as soon as he placed his hand upon it, his mother reappeared.

"Now, my love," she said, turning from the window as if she'd never left, "let us talk about the Truths …"

By the time Tanis finished his second lesson with his mother, he had the hang of the trick. The next pattern to glow was usually near whatever part of the room she'd just been standing in, and each time, he need only look closely upon the pattern or touch it with his fingers to bring his next lesson to life. By the time midday rolled past, he'd learned more than he had in a year of study with Master o'Reith.

His mother didn't just teach him workings of the fourth strand, but also of the second and third and even some of the first as well. He didn't know why she was instructing him in the Laws and rules governing these other strands, or of the details and patterns of their use—he was no wielder to use the patterns of other strands—but he loved gaining the knowledge and embraced it as much as he embraced the visions of her.

"Now, my darling," said his mother at the end of a lesson where she'd been discussing the second strand's Nine Laws of Travel and the Nodefinders' associated patterns—he'd lost count of all the lessons so far that day, only noting just then that the sun was tilting towards the west and the forest shadows were extending across the hill. "Let us end for today. Feed your body, rest your mind. In sleep, these lessons will take better shape and find their place within your understanding."

She came to where he was sitting at the foot of his bed—where she'd instructed him to sit while they discussed the second strand. She placed ghostly hands upon either side of his head and leaned to kiss his forehead. Tanis saw her face come near and closed his eyes and imagined that he felt her kiss. "Know always that I love you," she murmured.

Then she vanished.

About a heartbeat later, the door to his room opened and Tanis lifted his eyes to find the zanthyr standing in the portal. Phaedor took in his state of undressed dishabille and arched a solitary raven brow.

Tanis grinned sheepishly. "Blame my mother. She's been teaching me."

Phaedor gave him a curious look as he came inside the room. "Your mother. Just now?"

Tanis waved helplessly at the walls wearing a smile that fairly exploded off his face. "At least—her patterns have. They've come alive this morning, and each one harbors a lesson."

"Do they indeed?" Phaedor leaned against the wall and crossed arms before his muscled chest. "Perhaps as you dress you might explain this phenomenon of talking walls to me, truthreader."

Still grinning from ear to ear, Tanis pushed off the bed and went to the red-lacquered armoire, which opened to reveal a full complement of clothing, all of the garments fine enough for the Empress's court—finer even than the jacket Prince Ean had given Tanis and which he'd now quite outgrown, almost as fine as the one Pelas had made for him. "What should I wear, my lord?" the lad asked as he gazed at the array.

"A simple tunic will suffice for the afternoon's practice, Tanis. We won't be heading to Valentina's court for some time yet."

Tanis turned to him swiftly, but the zanthyr merely regarded him with his usual enigmatic gaze. Tanis knew he had to be teasing, yet ... he'd sounded earnest. "Oh, *I* see," the lad returned, affecting a casual tone. "And how will we be traveling to the Sacred City, my lord? Not through the mountains again, I hope."

"Valentina will send a ship."

Tanis gave him a sharp look, for again, Phaedor had sounded sincere. "That's awfully nice of her," the boy replied with sudden misgiving, no longer certain the zanthyr was kidding. "Will she be coming herself then?"

"I suspect she will send her Consort."

At this, Tanis looked to Phaedor in true, for he could tell the zanthyr really wasn't teasing, though the hint of a smile glinted in his emerald gaze. The zanthyr only let Tanis read the truth of his words when it suited his motives.

Tanis turned back to his clothing a little wide-eyed. The idea that an imperial ship might suddenly appear in search of them was both exciting and a little disconcerting.

"About these lessons, Tanis," Phaedor prompted before the lad could dive too far into speculation on *why* Valentina might be sending a ship.

"Oh, right." Tanis selected a green tunic and shoved his arms into it.

"Well … I dreamed of my mother, and when I woke at dawn, a pattern was glowing on the wall."

"Which pattern?"

Tanis pushed his head through the tunic and reached for a pair of dark lambskin leggings. "That one in the middle." He pointed ambiguously towards a patch of wall before attempting to don the pants. "Four up from the wainscoting."

Phaedor walked over to said pattern and laid three fingers upon it, stroking downward. "This pattern, lad?" He turned him a sideways glance, and there was something in his gaze …

Tanis was trying to hold the hem of his tunic with his chin in order to tie his britches. He looked up beneath his brows. "That's it," he muttered.

Did the hint of a smile shadow the zanthyr's lips? Who could say? 'Phaedor' and 'enigmatic' were interchangeable terms. The zanthyr dropped his hand from the wall. "And what happened then?"

"I went over to it and touched it, and my mother appeared."

"How very curious of her."

Tanis was occupied with trying to figure out the way the laces worked on his britches, so he missed the sardonic undertone in the zanthyr's reply.

"Well, not in the flesh, of course," the lad added absently, "I mean, she said she was only an illusion formed of the fourth, but …" He finally managed to tie off the laces and looked up with an expression of supreme excitement, letting his tunic fall around his hips. "But she looked real."

Phaedor's gaze fell softly upon the boy. "No doubt she did, lad."

Tanis grabbed his belt and slung it around slender hips. "When one lesson ended, another pattern would start to glow. As soon as I touched it, she'd be there again, giving me my next lesson."

"Even so?" Phaedor aimed an amused look his way. "And what have you learned this morning, truthreader?"

"About the First Law and the Twentieth Esoteric and the Nodefinder's Nine Laws of Travel." He slid the leather belt through the buckle and knotted it off. "And a bunch of other stuff."

"Do tell me more." The zanthyr motioned Tanis toward the door. "You have my undivided attention."

Tanis finally noticed the multiple undertones in Phaedor's reply. "Wait—is this a test?" He turned him a hard look over his shoulder while the zanthyr was prodding him through the door. "You knew about this already, didn't you? You did come in just as the last lesson finished …"

The zanthyr's emerald gaze glittered.

The manor hummed with activity as Tanis followed Phaedor down the halls, much in contrast to their arrival. While they walked, the boy did his best to

back, saluted with blade held before his nose, and then swung the weapon to the side, readying for the next phase. "Now: the *ta'fieri*."

An already exhausted Tanis felt the words like a knife in his gut and groaned. The *ta'fieri* form of swordplay, known only to the zanthyrs or their beleaguered pupils, was the most difficult of any sword-form to master. The spiraling figure-eight style of fighting seemed to come easily to the creatures who'd invented it, but every muscle in Tanis's body recoiled in horror at the memory of its practice.

Looking the zanthyr in the eye, the boy drew in a breath tight with apprehension and raised his weapon, though he felt despondent about the outcome.

The zanthyr chuckled at his expression. "Now, Tanis, you will never find success if this is your mindset."

"And what exactly constitutes success, my lord?" Tanis countered peevishly, lowering his weapon again. "If success means beating you, I shall never achieve such anyway."

"Yes, but you can get better at losing in the attempt." The zanthyr motioned with his blade. "Come—we'll begin slowly." He pinned his green eyes unerringly upon the boy.

Tanis gave him a harassed look, but he readied his blade again. Two handed, he swung the Merdanti sword back and forth in an exacting figure-eight fashion. The *ta'fieri* was practically useless against any adversary unless you could do it faster than the eye could follow, and Tanis was far from achieving that level of proficiency, so Phaedor sparred with him in apparent slow-motion.

Tanis had barely managed five minutes of the form before his arms were aching and his breath was coming in labored gasps. Sweat soon made his hands slick, and the heat rose from his body to steam in the chill air. Still the zanthyr pressed him, until every muscle in his body had passed through fire and into that overtaxed, wobbly place of barely-controlled motion.

Just when the lad was sure he would drop his sword and was putting all his concentration into just staying on his feet, a man dressed in hunting leathers came jogging across the lawn and halted halfway up the steps to the court. "My Lord Phaedor!" The urgency in his tone interrupted their sparring.

Phaedor stepped back and opened his sword arm to indicate a pause. Tanis doubled over, braced hands on his knees and tried to force some breath back into his lungs. He looked up under his brows at the huntsman, who wore dark leathers and high boots muddied nearly to the knee. Tanis thought him a blessed gift from Epiphany Herself.

The huntsman shifted the longbow and quiver strapped diagonally across his back. "My lord, Dional, the huntmaster, asked if you might come right away." The look upon the man's face made it plain that whatever the huntmaster needed of Phaedor, it was important enough to require his immediate attention.

"Lead on, Kendir." Phaedor swept up the cloth that had protected both weapons and received Tanis's blade from him. They followed the huntsman down the steps. When Tanis thought on it later, he couldn't recall what the zanthyr did with the weapons thereafter, only noting that he never saw them again that day.

They followed Kendir through the forest for the better part of an hour, moving swiftly. Tanis observed the huntsman leave nary a mark of passing and noted with appreciation that he walked almost as silently as the zanthyr. Had anyone been listening from afar, they would've heard but one person approaching—his own fumbling attempt.

Indeed, as he trudged along behind the two men, Tanis reflected that he never had seemed to get on well with forests. Back in the Gandrel, he was always getting tripped up or stubbing his toe on something unseen, and he'd been certain the spiteful roots were always trying to snag his boot or ankle.

This forest treated him little better. The boy tripped twice on their hour-long jog. The first amounted to a spectacular fall to hands and knees, occasioned by a rock that had clearly erupted from the ground just to threaten his steps. The second time, his foot caught within a tangle of fallen branches, and he tripped-skipped-nearly-fell several noisy and harrowing paces across the carpet of leaves and twigs before he'd freed it from its woody captivity.

Phaedor, bless him, never even twitched at these mishaps, but upon Tanis's last dance with the brush, the huntsman had turned an amused eye back in his direction.

The collective mood had become quite sober by the time they reached the waiting Dional, who stood leaning against a black oak as they approached. The estate's huntmaster appeared robust, though he'd clearly seen fifty name days and counting. His shoulder-length hair sported more iron-grey than brown, and his face was as weathered as the elder trees, with deep lines tracing the story of his years.

He straightened as Phaedor arrived. "My lords, thank you for coming. She's this way." He turned and jumped down into the basin of a shallow ravine and headed off.

The zanthyr leapt the distance to the crevice floor with ease, cloak floating behind him, while Kendir slid down the leafy embankment to join the other two. But Tanis stood stricken atop the hill and couldn't bring himself to move.

In the deeps of the pit lay a Hallovian mare.

She seemed to have been dragged quite some distance, for blood, dirt and leaves stained her once-glorious hide, and she lay in an unnatural position, as if pulled unconscious into the ditch. Something had ravaged the poor animal then and left her blanketed in her own entrails. Worse was realizing that she yet lived.

As Tanis gazed upon the mare, a furious sense of loss accosted him. For something to have defiled such a majestic creature … it felt so very *wrong*.

"I found her here," Dional told Phaedor.

The zanthyr knelt next to the mare and placed his hand on her bloodstained neck. She snorted at his touch and tried to lift her head.

Fury, fear and grief all intermingled with the halted breath in Tanis's chest.

"Was it a boar did it, my lord?" Kendir asked.

"Not likely." Dional looked grim.

"You know what did this deed, Huntmaster," the zanthyr murmured without removing his eyes from the mare's. He stroked her neck, and Tanis somehow knew the Healer in him searched her wounds for answers.

"Then it's as I feared: a *drogue* wolf." Dional spat in the dirt and ground his boot over the mark.

"The mountain wolves have never ventured into this valley before." Kendir's voice sounded strained.

"The dome sings too loudly," Phaedor said by way of agreement. "Only a crazed thing, half out of its mind already, would stay within the arc."

Dional cast the zanthyr a tense look. His thoughts were loud, and Tanis imagined the words must be ready to come, but something stayed his tongue so that only his thoughts shouted, *A rabid drogue wolf on the prowl. Lady of the Rivers help us all.*

Seeming equally disturbed by the same unspoken conclusion, Kendir cast a predatory eye around the forest and fidgeted with the longbow slung across his chest, clearly itching to use it.

"Come, Tanis." Phaedor waved him over while still holding the dying mare's lambent gaze.

Tanis slid awkwardly down the embankment and knelt at his side, whereupon the zanthyr murmured, "Place your hand on my shoulder and follow my thoughts. See how we trace this deed to its source."

The zanthyr had never before offered to share his mind with Tanis. Made somewhat nervous by the prospect, the lad placed his hand as Phaedor instructed and closed his eyes.

Instantly he felt swept away.

The zanthyr was immersed in the currents—a wild, rushing river of colorful light—and his agile mind swam upstream at incredible speeds. Tanis latched onto him as a minnow to the salmon, feeling the force of the current pushing him backwards while Phaedor's powerful intention pulled him inexorably forward.

Soon the zanthyr had isolated a single current and was following it off onto a tributary river that seemed vaguely greenish in hue. Tanis knew—because Phaedor knew—that they were now tracing the third strand solely, and within that, one particular life-thread. In nearly the same moment, the lad felt a wash of warmth that he soon identified as the first strand, which the zanthyr was using somehow to cross-index the third strand thread he was following with the horse's own terrible experience.

All of this occurred in less than a teaspoon of sand's passing through the hourglass—mere moments—and Phaedor had found the answer he sought.

He moved his hand from the horse's flank to her brow, and because Tanis still had his hand upon the zanthyr's shoulder, he understood the foreign words when Phaedor whispered in Old Alaeic, "*Go Lilionath. Go into the Doors of Morning. Take with you the gilded memories of your life; let your children carry forward the blood of your ancestors while you find your path anew.*"

Phaedor paused there, letting the rush of *elae's* currents wash over them, letting *elae* swirl and press, but the zanthyr was now the rock, solid and unyielding, and the flow merely altered its course around him.

Feeling buffeted by the unyielding energy as if standing in the pounding surf, Tanis wondered what they were waiting for ... and then, finally, a breath of warmth flowed past them on the currents, and Tanis knew—because the zanthyr knew—that the mare's spirit was departing on *elae's* tides.

Phaedor withdrew from rapport.

Tanis opened his eyes and let his hand fall to his side. The horse exhaled a long sighing breath, and all of the tension that bound her to life eased gently into the night. Silence embraced the darkening forest, a fitting homage to the lovely creature whose spirit galloped away on the crest of twilight.

The zanthyr stood and looked down on the horse. In his stillness, the shadows of the evening collected around him. "Burn her."

Dional shifted from foot to foot, looking uneasy. "What of the beast that did this, my lord?" Tanis sensed the tension in his tone and felt his thoughts lying heavy and troubled.

Phaedor turned his gaze into the darkening forest. After a moment, Tanis saw the faintest tightening around his eyes and knew he'd gained knowledge of the beast. "He lingers within the arc."

Dional grunted. "I'll call a party to the hunt."

"Set traps," Kendir added.

"No traps." Phaedor turned him a swift and penetrating look.

The man started at the intensity of his gaze. "My lord? I only—"

"A *drogue* wolf is a *thinking* beast." Dional's critical tone held rough censure of his subordinate. "Even a rabid one has the wits to lure its prey into any trap we set for it." The huntmaster looked back to Phaedor. "No traps, my lord. We'll track it from here. Lady of the Rivers willing, we'll find him tonight."

Phaedor gave him a long look. "Perhaps the goddess will grace you this eve, Huntmaster ... but don't count on it." With that, he spun away and in two quick leaps had cleared the ravine.

Tanis gazed after him wondering if he would ever come to understand how much of the future lay at the zanthyr's easy disposal.

"Come, Tanis." Phaedor's voice floated down from the darkness above.

With one last glance at the hunters—who seemed less than enthusiastic about their ill-fated task now that the zanthyr had doomed it from the outset—the lad followed, scrambling up the leaf-strewn hill to rejoin the regal shadow that was bound to him body and soul.

FIVE

"He conceals his honor beneath a cloak of shame."

– Isabel van Gelderan, on the Espial Franco Rohre

F RANCO ROHRE PRESSED fingertips to his brow just above his left eye, where a vein throbbed painfully. He'd been having recurring headaches ever since beginning work on the Sylus node. Dagmar had assured him the headaches would fade now that Franco had completed this task, but the Great Master had also been frustratingly vague as to how long such recovery would take.

That's what happens when you stand in place of a node, you idiot. This wasn't the first and it won't be the last time you nearly kill yourself trying to appease the First Lord's demands.

Franco grimaced. It seemed he was increasingly having full conversations with his conscience. He might've worried about his sanity if he hadn't already been sure that he'd lost it.

Ha! That's a certain text! No man in his right mind would swear an oath to Björn van Gelderan.

Franco gritted his teeth and tried to focus on something besides his own insanity. He let his gaze stray across Björn's elegant gallery, noting the rain-spattered windows, the armchairs of misty velvet, and the colorful paintings on the dove-grey walls with equal disinterest. Who knew headaches could be so all-consuming? He wanted nothing more than to drown his brain in wine and pass out on the bed.

The high-minded dreams of the inebriate.

His gaze fell upon the Nodefinder Carian vran Lea, who stood across the long gallery talking to the Great Master. Franco still hadn't decided what he thought of Carian. The pirate certainly seemed capable in their mutual craft—brilliantly so, considering he'd had no formal training—but could he be trusted beyond his own self-interests?

Can anyone? Can you?

Franco pinched his brow with thumb and forefinger.

At that point, his only interest was self-preservation, for it seemed the only goal left to him. If Björn hadn't demanded he work the Pattern of Life centuries ago on Tiern'aval, he'd have taken his chances in the Returning by now.

And where would you be then? Just one more Adept that never Awakened?

Franco banged his fist against the arm of his chair and pushed to his feet. Better to intrude on the conversation of others than to continue this one inside his own skull. He walked to where Dagmar and Carian stood talking.

The Vestal turned at Franco's approach, and his features lifted with a smile. "I apologize for pulling you from your own affairs so soon, Franco, but thank you again for joining us here. I don't think we'll need wait much longer for the others to arrive."

"I'm happy to be of service in any way required, my lord."

Liar.

Dagmar clapped him amiably on the shoulder by way of acknowledgement. Then he nodded to the pirate. "Carian and I were just discussing the theory behind laddering nodes, but perhaps you'd like to share with him your recent work on the Sylus node instead?"

Yes, go on. Tell him how for that endless moment you became one with the Pattern of the World—oh wait. Two worlds.

Franco pushed his fingers to pinch his brow, wishing he might purge the headache and the inane chatter of his conscience along with it.

"You look knackered, mate," Carian observed. "Perhaps you should sit down again."

Dagmar gave Franco a compassionate smile as he explained to the pirate, "Franco is feeling the aftereffects of plus-crossing nodes."

Carian's eyes nearly popped out of his head. "Plus-crossing—you mean *two* doublebacks?" He spun a look from Dagmar to Franco and then threw up his hands and exclaimed, "*Ho-ho*—I am your most humble servant! Let me get you some wine, Admiral!" He made a bow of shameless reverence before skipping off to fetch Franco a drink.

Franco cast a pained look after the retreating pirate. "I suppose you had to tell him about that."

"Carian will be a needed ally, Franco." Dagmar's lips twitched with a smile as he watched the lanky pirate literally waltzing back to them with a bottle and goblet as his partner.

Carian came to a halt and poured the wine with a flourish. He shoved the goblet at Franco. "Drink up, my handsome. Björn's wine is the best around."

Franco eyed him uncertainly, but he took the wine.

"Ah, good, you're all here," came a voice from behind them.

Franco turned to find the Fifth Vestal entering from the gallery's far end. In his wake followed Dämen, Lord of Shades, and the Fourth Vestal Raine D'Lacourte.

Franco stifled a grimace. He couldn't look at Raine and not also see the face of his own many betrayals while in service as the Fourth Vestal's Espial, or the hundreds who fought and died at the Temple of the Vestals ... or the look on the Malorin'athgul Rinokh's face as Creighton's Shade pulled him across the node Franco was holding open while Ean hung onto his life pattern, unmaking the man in the crossing ...

"Franco, I hear you completed the Sylus node." Björn looked his usual immaculate self as he joined their group. Franco couldn't remember ever seeing him discomposed—at least not since that fateful night on Tiern'aval. The First Lord gave him a pleased smile and gripped his arm. "Admirable work, from everything Dagmar has told me."

"Thank you, my lord. I'm grateful for your confidence in my ability."

"Are you?" Björn arched a sardonic brow, reminding Franco with a jolt that colorless eyes did not solely the truthreader make. No man in history had accumulated more Sormitáge rings than Björn van Gelderan. They didn't make enough rings to account for what he knew.

And with that skill, Björn seemed to have easily plucked from Franco's thoughts the truth of his devastated state and the many fears that plagued him. No doubt the man knew his mind better than Franco himself did.

Franco cleared his throat and dropped his eyes to the goblet in his hand. "Well ... my lord, I suspect you know what I mean."

"Indeed, Franco Rohre. Would that I had less personal experience myself with the feelings that plague you. But it's my hope this will bring you some cheer at least." He turned to Dagmar. "Have you the letter?"

Flashing a sudden knowing smile, the Vestal withdrew an envelope of black leather from inside his coat and extended it to Franco.

Franco noted the sigil embossed in the leather with rising unease. He hadn't seen the Citadel's seal since Tiern'aval, when a marble version of it had come shattering down from a crumbling dome.

Franco drained his wine. While the liquid was still flaming his throat, he somewhat gasped, "... What's this, my lord?"

Dagmar pushed it towards him insistently. "Isabel bade me deliver this to you once you finished the Sylus node."

Franco darted a glance at Björn as he handed Carian his goblet and reluctantly took the envelope from Dagmar. Then he opened it and drew out the small velvet pouch it contained. But when he emptied the pouch's contents onto his hand, his eyes flew back to Dagmar. "*Great Master* ..." The words barely scraped out through vocal cords frozen in shock. He looked from Dagmar to Björn, seeking explanation. "But ... First Lord, you stripped me of my rings on Tiern'aval."

"And now the High Mage of the Citadel returns them to you." Dagmar grinned broadly at him.

"You've earned them, Franco." Björn graced him with a smile of equal measure.

Franco stared at the three thin gold rings lying in his palm while his eyes grew hot and a painful clenching constricted in his chest. Prior to the wars, his two Sormitáge rings—so long sought and hard-earned—had formed the core of his entire identity. When Björn had stripped him of the right to wear them, Franco felt like his soul had been flayed.

He managed a dry swallow and pointed out weakly, "Um … there are *three* rings here, my lord."

The First Lord nodded to the envelope in Franco's other hand. "I believe Isabel included a message to explain the presence of the third ring."

Indeed, Franco saw a sheet of parchment inside the envelope. The letter detailed his many accomplishments—a surprisingly long list, even to his own eyes, and most of them since his Calling—but all he really saw was the last line of investiture, and beneath this, Isabel's signature between the official seals of the Citadel.

Franco lifted his gaze back to the Vestals. His hands shook.

Dagmar grinned and clapped him on the shoulder. "Welcome to the Third Echelon of the Guild of Espials, my friend."

Carian let out a whoop and grabbed Franco's hand, shaking it vigorously, and then a sudden storm of congratulations descended on him. Smiling faces swirled around him, hands and arms embraced him, but all his blurry eyes really saw were three gold Sormitáge rings.

Once congratulations had been adequately bestowed, Björn lifted his gaze to include everyone in the group and his expression sobered. "On to our next matter. Based on the strength of your work, Franco, and yours, Carian, Dagmar recommended that I call you both to attend this council today." He motioned them towards a grouping of five chairs, and each of them took a seat. Björn said as he settled, "Dämen will explain."

The Shade came to stand between Björn and Raine. His chrome features reflected the storm beyond the long windows, shifting in sequence with the clouds. "The First Lord's contact in Illume Belliel informed us that Alshiba has granted a vote to Niko van Amstel to be elected as the new Second Vestal."

"Balls of Belloth!" Carian leapt to his feet. "Great Master! We have to stop—"

"It's done," Björn said quietly. "They voted."

Carian spun hotly to the First Lord. "Who voted? *I* didn't!"

Dagmar said, "Niko only needed a majority of Guild members." He frowned at Carian and waggled his fingers for the pirate to sit down again.

Carian shoved his wild wavy hair behind his shoulders and complied, but he looked disgruntled about it.

"It came to our attention some time ago how Niko intended to gain this majority," Dagmar informed them then. "Working with the Guild Master of Rethynnea, a man named D'varre, Niko succeeded in redefining the status required to sit as a voting member of the Espial's Guild."

Carian shifted disagreeably in his chair. "Which is?"

"Rings."

Franco felt a sudden hollow pit open in his stomach.

"*Sormitáge* rings?"

Franco's head throbbed in accompaniment with his sinking hopes. He leaned an elbow on the arm of his chair and braced his temples with thumb and middle finger. "That would limit the number of voting Guild members to less than what?" He looked up at Dagmar beneath his hand. "Five hundred?"

The Second Vestal nodded. "So we think. Of those brothers of the strand who Return, fewer each year seek formal instruction."

Björn gazed severely upon them. "Once the Guild included thousands of voting members. Now five hundred is a fair estimate."

Franco exhaled a slow breath. "Niko could easily have mustered the manpower to contact a majority of voting members and invite them to sell their souls."

Carian launched out of his chair again, all flailing arms and indignation. "Niko can lick my hairy arse—he's not the Second Vestal! That great man sits there!" And he slung an emphatic finger at Dagmar.

"While Dagmar no doubt appreciates your loyalty, Carian," Björn noted, "we've assembled not to argue the legitimacy of Niko's claim but to determine what we must do to intercede between his ambition and the sanctity of our realm."

Caught mid-flail, Carian sort of stared at him. "Oh ..." He sat back down.

Franco remembered seeing the Alorin Seat Alshiba Torinin in Mark Laven's home, remembered her calm rationality in the face of the avieth Seth Silverbow's belligerence, remembered the dual sense of duty and devotion she'd emanated. It made no sense. "How could she do this?" he muttered.

Raine seemed keen to his thoughts. "Alshiba never would've ratified Niko's claim if she'd known of his crimes on Tiern'aval. This is an act of desperation."

"Desperate times, desperate measures?" Franco inquired tightly.

"Desperate mistakes," Björn murmured. He gave Raine a pensive look. "But you're right ... perhaps it is time for the world to have the truth of the Citadel's fall."

"Which is what exactly?" Carian asked.

Björn looked to Franco. "Perhaps you would prefer to tell him?"

Upon this inquiry, Franco felt something release in his mind—like the sudden snap of a lace too tightly bound—and a flood of words fell upon his tongue. His eyes widened while his mind rejected comprehension.

Had Björn really just released the truthbinding of his treason on Tiern'aval?

"Well?" Carian flicked at his chair arm impatiently.

Franco's heart beat a rapid rhythm of disbelief. He stared at his knees while his tongue attempted to work some moisture back into his mouth. After all this time—*centuries* of bearing the burden of this secret—could it really just end with naught but an ignominious *snap*?

"They'd planned an overthrow, Carian." Dagmar offered explanation when it became clear that Franco couldn't speak. "The Fifty Companions—most of them either duped or woefully misguided—believed the Hundred Mages had been infiltrated by a wielder who walked the dark path of *elae*, called *mor'alir*. They claimed the High Mage had succumbed to this wielder's influence and had been using forbidden patterns—dark patterns known as *inverteré*—to bind others to her will. Many of the Mages were in collusion on this overthrow. They attempted to slay the High Mage and any who stood to protect her."

Carian blinked. Then he frowned, perhaps recalling that the Citadel's High Mage was Isabel van Gelderan. Then he spun a glare at Franco. "Were you really so *insanely* stupid?"

Franco pushed a hand over his eyes. He honestly wondered if his head might feel better with a dagger shoved into each temple.

"Well, what's the rest of it?" The pirate looked appropriately disgusted.

"Things somewhat disintegrated from there," Franco muttered.

Björn exhaled a measured breath. "Tiern'aval was the site of a massacre long before we unwittingly ripped it from the realm."

Dagmar said tightly, "Many innocent Mages fell to Dore's revolt."

Franco thought of the rest of that night and felt ill all over again.

"I don't get it," Carian grumbled. "Alshiba—along with most of the bloody realm—thinks *you* slaughtered the Hundred Mages, First Lord. Can't we tell the Alorin Seat the truth? If Niko had a hand in such treason, she should know. Surely then—"

"It would make no difference now, Carian." Raine looked grim. "Alshiba would only think we're trying to defer blame to Niko in order to suit our own aims. She'd never believe such a truth now."

Carian threw up his hands. "So what do we do? I suppose you're about to tell me I can't just kill him—because you know I *want* to—"

"I think we all agree the realm would be better off without Niko van Amstel's stain upon its mantle," Raine cut in with uncharacteristic enmity, "but there's more at stake here than mere vengeance."

Dagmar nodded his agreement. "The chain reaction of Niko's appointment is already casting tremors through the firmament. We have to make haste to counteract events he's set in motion."

"I don't understand." Carian flicked discontentedly at his chair arm like a child called to heel. "If you went back to Alorin, Great Master, they would have to stop this. Aren't there regulations—*by the thirteen hells*, can't we appeal to Illume Belliel?"

"There are statutes, Carian," Björn said. "Alshiba has disregarded them." He stood, pushed hands into his pockets and began walking around the circle of chairs. His expression fell into a pensive frown. "Niko couldn't have accomplished this alone. He's only ever been the figurehead for smarter men's ambitions."

Dagmar grunted. "We must learn who's backing Niko and what their ultimate plans are."

"As if purloining the Vestal appointment isn't enough?" Carian complained.

"Perhaps for Niko," Björn answered, turning cobalt eyes upon the pirate. "Not for those who're surely manipulating him. We need to understand their end game."

"I still don't see why I can't just kill him—end of problem."

Raine muttered, "This serpent will just grow another head, Carian."

"Niko is our best chance of learning of the larger prize in their sights." Björn came to a halt behind Dagmar's chair. He eyed each of the others in turn. "This is a trail laid of water on rock. Without Niko, it evaporates."

Franco gritted his teeth. He already suspected what they needed from him. "What would you have me do, my lords?"

Dagmar's gaze fell apologetically upon him. "No doubt you've guessed that we need you to once again be Niko's ally, Franco—as odious as that task will no doubt prove for you. Take Carian and attend his celebration. Do whatever you can to learn of his plans and activities—and most of all, do your best to learn anything of those backing him."

"*Then* can I gut him?" Carian asked hopefully.

"This task holds an added danger," Raine advised, ignoring the pirate.

Franco lifted his gaze to meet the Vestal's.

Raine's expression conveyed both concern and apology. "By now, the entire realm will have heard of the destruction of Rethynnea's Temple of the Vestals." He exhaled as he added, "And if I know Seth, your names will be unquestionably and contemptuously linked to its fall, and …"

"And to your notable absence, my lord?" Franco finished.

Raine nodded.

Standing behind Dagmar, Björn settled his cobalt gaze unerringly on Carian and Franco. "Information. We need it, you two must collect it."

Carian left his meeting with the Vestals with lightning strikes of disagreement twitching in his lanky frame. He wasn't used to having to report to so many captains, all of whom thought they ran the ship—*his* ship. Yet it never occurred to him to set a course that varied from the heading the Great Master had chosen. If Dagmar was allied with Björn van Gelderan, then Carian was too, even if that meant merging his vessel into the armada of an unknown admiral.

But he didn't have to be cheery about it.

Thinking of irascible dispositions, however, reminded him of Gwynnleth, who he hadn't bothered in a few days, so he went in search of her. Gloating in front of the avieth always improved his mood.

After looking in all the usual places, he finally spotted her sitting on the roof of one of the palace towers beneath a clearing sky. He made his way to the balcony that circled the tower roof and leaned back to stare up at the near vertical pitch of the slippery slate. He spent a while trying to decide if the joy inherent in bothering Gwynnleth was actually worth the effort of reaching her. As part of this analysis, he peered down over the edge of the balcony, automatically discerning his potential angle of fall. His prospects weren't that promising; one misstep and he'd plummet a thousand paces to the palace's craggy foundation.

Death by pancake. Joy.

Sucking on a tooth, Carian turned and assessed the roof again. He'd grown up clambering along rain-slicked masts, weaving in between rigging and lines while all around a storm raged and the ship pitched and hawed from one near-horizontal angle to the next. But this? This was insane.

Yet there sat the avieth, her slender form perched effortlessly on the sheer tiles, no safer from a fall than he would be.

If I don't go up, and that bloody bird finds out that I stood here like this, she'll make me the butt of her mockery for a century.

Still … it was a really long way down.

Finally Carian growled an oath, shrugged out of his boots, jumped to grab the gutter and swung a leg up over the edge. Gaining the tiles on all fours, he paused, feeling the pull of a thousand foot drop in the rapid beating of his heart. He cast an irritable glare up at the avieth, much the wolf eying an offensive owl on its perch of safety—and with a similar lack of notice in return. The wind lifted and twisted his wavy hair into wild designs as he climbed then, macaque-like, hand over foot to the very peak of the tower.

"*Winds*, birdie, I've been hunting for you everywhere." Carian settled in beside her on the damp tiles, hugged his knees, and noted that his hairy toes were all that stood between his body and a thousand foot tumble. The stubby appendages seemed unnervingly overmatched.

Gwynnleth angled him a narrow eye, at last deigning to notice his arrival. "Indeed, Islander? Where were you looking?"

"Let's see …" Carian scratched at the scruff shadowing his jaw. "I checked in the kitchens—you know, in case you'd gotten hungry." He disentangled his whirling hair from its attempts to strangle him and shook out his head so it flew behind him like a tattered veil instead. Then he grinned as he added, "Plus, there's this poppet in the bakery who fancies me."

Gwynnleth arched a brow to express her infinite disinterest.

"I also checked the First Lord's game room, but the blokes gaming today only wanted to play Shari. I can't fathom their interest in that bloody game.

What's the point of moving a bunch of glass stones from place to place? Trumps is the only game worth wagering on."

"I despise your reckless games of chance."

"Yeah," he snorted, looking down again. "You'd rather recklessly gamble with your life."

This drew a twitch of a smile.

The wind caught their hair in a sudden upwards draft, such that both Carian and Gwynnleth's locks formed undulating black and auburn flames. With much cursing and complaining, Carian gathered his mass of wild waves into a knot behind his head so that only Gwynnleth's hair remained free to spit and sting him in the face.

He shoved another snapping end of it away from his mouth, spat and waggled his tongue to free the last of it. "After that, I looked in Mithaiya's chambers."

She eyed him askance. "You looked for *me* in *Mithaiya's* rooms."

"You know, just in case her lizardness was in the mood," and he shrugged his eyebrows saucily. "Sadly, my dragon-love wasn't there."

Gwynnleth arched a dubious brow. "I fail to see where in any part of this you were actually searching for me."

"The part where I came out here and looked up."

She turned away again wearing an expression of supreme indifference. "So now you've found me—miracle of miracles. What do you want?"

"I just thought you'd want to know that we're heading back to Alorin."

The avieth—damn her—didn't even twitch a brow at this enticing news. "Who is we?"

"That Rohre character and me. We're heading to a party—thought you'd want to join."

"Whyever would you think I'd want to participate in such repulsive activity?"

He glared at her. "Oh, let me see ... because it's in *Alorin*, maybe? Last I knew you were creaming your linens to get home."

She gave him an arch look. "The only thing likely to bring me that sort of pleasure is the sight of my blade across a certain pirate's throat."

Carian grinned lustily. "You can hold your knife to my neck all you like, birdie, so long as you're riding my cock at the time."

Gwynnleth gave him a withering glance—whereupon his bare feet caught her eye, and she frowned. "You have the toes of a yeti."

Carian waggled the hairy appendages for her pleasure. "You wouldn't criticize them if you knew their many talents."

"Perish the thought."

He shook pieces of flying hair from his eyes. "What's got your feathers all tizzied up, chickadee? You're even more snarky than usual."

She cast him a critical eye. "A defining aspect of choosing an isolated tower so as to be alone is that one is actually left *alone*."

"I might've left you alone in limbo between the worlds." Carian shoved her hair out of his eyes again and glared at her. "That's gratitude for you."

Gwynnleth pressed her lips into a line and considered him, her tawny-gold eyes unreadable. Finally she made the slightest of shrugs with her shoulders and turned her gaze back to the immense valley spreading before them. Carian admitted it was quite the view. The world appeared larger from atop their tower, a thin spire linking charcoal clouds to the lush, fertile plains as if a single needle stitch in the vast tapestry that held T'khendar together.

"The Fourth Vestal told me earlier this morning that you'd be returning to Alorin," the avieth finally admitted. "He suggested I might accompany you if I so desired."

"And?"

Gwynnleth pried at her thumbnail with her teeth. "I said no."

"Shadow take me, *why?*"

She peered at him for a long moment with a furrow between her pale ginger brows. "When the Second Vestal took us to T'khendar's edge, to the valley of unmaking where that creature Rinokh lurks ... what did you think?"

"It was a bloody shock." When Gwynnleth just watched him, expecting something more profound, perhaps, Carian grumbled, "If you mean what did I think about all of this—" and he held out one hand to the world at large, "let's just say, I got the picture."

The avieth turned and frowned out at the view. "The Fifth Vestal has gone to great lengths to ensure Alorin's safety, even enduring ages of vilification innocently and unnecessarily. I wouldn't have believed it without coming here." She dropped her hands to press against the roof and lifted her gaze to the sky as if searching for something in the clouds. "Seth never will."

"So?"

She spun him a severe look. "We know things for having been here, Islander. Things that as yet must remain unknown to others, and especially to Seth Silverbow, who would take every truth we've learned and twist it into a new form of blame. In Seth's mind, Björn van Gelderan deserves no mercy, no matter how justified his actions might've been. If I return ..." She shook her head resolutely. "The moment I take the form, Seth will know my mind. I won't be able to hide this knowledge from him. He'll use it to harm the Fifth Vestal and anyone who serves him."

"So don't take the form."

She grunted. "Another impossibility."

"Just because your feathered head can't conceive of it, chickadee, doesn't make it impossible. It just makes it difficult. Welcome to the Guild of Hard Knocks—on Jamaii, we call it the Account."

Her tawny gaze narrowed. "You're comparing my natural state of existence to *piracy*?"

He shrugged. "You're an avieth by birth, I'm a pirate by birth ... where's the difference?"

Gwynnleth glared icily at him.

Carian was just opening his mouth to begin upon a lecture in support of his point when a raucous cry split the near air. He shoved hands over his ears and glared upwards just as a *drachwyr* erupted out of the cloud bank and surged past them in a powerful rush of wind. "Bloody screeching!" He leaned to shout after the dragon, "Screw knives into my ears, why don't you, woman!"

Gwynnleth watched the soaring dragon with the ache of longing in her gaze.

The *drachwyr* banked in a spread of gilded wings and turned towards the crenellated roof of the next tower over. Letting out another cry, which sounded to Carian like a bleating goat mating with a lion—or a hundred such pairings, all crying out at once—the *drachwyr* thrust back her wings and extended talons to the flat roof. Her wings began shimmering as she alighted, and a blinding sparkle of brilliance followed. This waterfall of light eventually evaporated into the form of a woman in a blue gown.

"I cannot imagine what she sees in you," Gwynnleth remarked, eyeing Mithaiya across the way.

"It'd be my pleasure to give you experiential knowledge, birdie. You need only beg on hands and knees, preferably with your hands tied behind—"

"Careful you don't overextend yourself offering your loins to so many women." Gwynnleth's tone was flat.

Carian grinned. "Not likely."

"Or exaggerate your apparent plethora of skills."

He gave her a bigger grin. "Even less likely."

Across the way, Mithaiya blew upon her hand, and a fiery streak spread towards them, leaving a wake of luminance. The *drachwyr* stepped between the crenels of her tower and began walking across the glowing path.

Gwynnleth grunted. "Subtle isn't she?"

Carian cast Mithaiya an appreciative grin. "She likes to make a dramatic entrance."

"How well suited you are for each other."

"Now, birdie, you needn't be so petulant. You can join us any time. That would make for a good tale, wouldn't it? The pirate, the hawk and the dragon ..."

"Wherein the dragon eats the pirate and the hawk flies away."

Mithaiya reached their tower, lifted the silk skirt of her cerulean gown and stepped barefoot onto the roof.

Gwynnleth turned Carian an accusatory glare at the continuing egregious infraction on her solitude.

"Carian vran Lea, Gwynnleth of Elvior." Mithaiya gave them both a nod of greeting. "You choose unique places from which to appreciate the First Lord's wondrous realm."

"The sight is so glorious," Carian replied with eyes only for the exotically beautiful Mithaiya, "it must be viewed from all available angles."

She arched a delicate raven eyebrow, and a suggestive smile hinted on her lips. "I did not think there were any angles as yet unexplored."

"My lady, you underestimate yourself."

Gwynnleth cleared her throat purposefully.

Mithaiya gave her a curious look.

"Don't mind birdie," Carian remarked. "She's just ruffled because she can't return to Alorin and take the form without Seth knowing all about our plans."

Mithaiya's brow furrowed in a little frown. She moved to kneel between Carian and Gwynnleth and placed a gentle hand on the avieth's arm. "We *drachwyr* share the intimacy of this sacrifice, Wildling child. It is sometimes necessary, but it never comes easily."

Gwynnleth cast her an unfriendly stare.

Carian tugged on Mithaiya's skirt. "How was your day, your lizardness? Find any holes to patch in this fair world?"

She frowned at him. "Ever so cavalier, Carian vran Lea, but if T'khendar falls, so soon will fall all of the Realms of Light."

Gwynnleth cast her a sideways look, tawny eyes narrowed speculatively. "What do you mean?"

"T'khendar is a buffer, Gwynnleth, my fair sister of the skies." Mithaiya turned her blue-eyed gaze out across the land as if seeing far beyond the mountainous horizon. "The Malorin'athgul were never meant to know about Alorin or any of the Realms of Light. *These* realms the Maker fashioned with permanence intended. Yet somehow the dark creatures of Chaos found Alorin, and in that knowledge they grew lust for our fair realm. Yet they know joy only in unmaking. Having found Alorin, they would have set their teeth into its tender flesh had they not been immediately brought within her bosom."

"I'm confused. *We* brought them here?"

Mithaiya shrugged a delicate eyebrow. "How they arrived is of lesser importance. The Mage and his Council made T'khendar to ensure the Malorin'athgul couldn't reach Alorin from the plane of Chaos, where their power is greatest—T'khendar now stands in their way."

She smoothed a strand of dark hair from her eyes. "We *drachwyr* now patrol empty skies seeking those aetheric places where the walls between Chaos and T'khendar grow thin, that the Second Vestal might shore them up so our fortress remains strong. Do you see? T'khendar is a fortress—Alorin's fortress—the last bastion between the chaotic fringes of the cosmos and our precious realm."

Carian sucked on a tooth as he considered her. "What I don't get is if the damned creatures are already in Alorin, aren't they unmaking it as we speak? Isn't that the bloody problem?"

"At this point, with the knowledge they have, it would be much worse for us if they were outside the realm."

Gwynnleth grunted. "I cannot fathom how."

Mithaiya arched a brow. "Floating among the stars of Chaos, they're capable of unmaking worlds, but inside the realm they can claim only a fraction of their power, for *elae* is strong here and forms a natural counterpoint to *deyjiin*. The realm cannot be unmade from within, sweet sister-kin."

Mithaiya smoothed her flying hair back from her eyes again and looked Gwynnleth over with them. "You still do not see, do you? *Inside* Alorin the Malorin'athgul are deadly; their presence is corruptive and disrupts the Balance, their intentions are ever aimed towards engendering chaos, and their power remains formidable. But outside … *outside* the realm, where they could draw upon the endless power of Chaos to unravel Alorin's aether? Outside, dear one, they would be catastrophic."

"So you're saying it's a boon to us that they're in our realm?"

Mithaiya exhaled a discontented sigh. "Better within than without is all I'm saying." The *drachwyr* turned to Carian then. "But I would we spoke of more cheerful things. I have some news."

Carian gave her a lusty grin. "I will pay handsomely for it."

Her eyes sparkled darkly. "Indeed you will."

"What news?" Gwynnleth prodded with a glare at Carian.

"Your friend Fynnlar val Lorian will live, despite the grievous wounds he sustained at the ambush in the Kutsamak when his cousin Trell and all of his men were also taken." Mithaiya frowned slightly as she added, "The zanthyr Vaile risked upsetting the Balance to Heal him. Fynnlar will stay at the First Lord's *sa'reyth* while he recovers. In the meantime, the First Lord's allies search for Trell of the Tides."

Carian's felt his mood sobering like a sudden dead calm. "Still no word where they're holding Trell?"

Mithaiya shook her head. "We know only that the prince was taken to Radov. Unfortunately, the Ruling Prince of M'Nador has many fortresses, many prisons in which to bury his enemies alive. But the First Lord has eyes and ears throughout the realm, and all are watching and listening for news of the prince's whereabouts."

"Well, that's something at least." Carian had grown fond of Trell of the Tides, and he bristled at the idea of the prince falling into the hands of that lunatic, Radov, or worse, his psychopathic wielder, Viernan hal'Jaitar.

Carian caught a floating lock of Mithaiya's dark hair and spun it between his fingers. "My lady … we should retire if I'm to pay you for this information today. Soon I must be off."

She met his gaze with her very blue eyes. "Off? To where?"

"Rohre and I are attending a feast thrown by Niko van Amstel, High King of Treason, Treachery and All Things Ignoble. The Great Master, unfortunately, has forbidden me to gut and castrate him—not necessarily in that order should I not exactly disobey his command."

"Niko van Amstel." Mithaiya's eyes narrowed like a cat's. "He lays his bed with Dore Madden, and the two ever were about seditious lovemaking."

Gwynnleth frowned at them. "I know these names."

Mithaiya turned to her. "No doubt you do. They are two of the so-called Fifty Companions, of whose number the Espial Franco Rohre also belongs."

"But Franco serves the First Lord," Carian pointed out.

"As do many more, though few know each other in this troth as yet."

Carian flicked Mithaiya's blowing hair from his eyes. "What—you mean other Companions are sworn to the Vestal also? Who?"

"You will come to know them, I believe, by their alliances." She stood and pulled him to his feet—close, so that their bodies pressed together. "You have a debt, Carian vran Lea. I would see it repaid."

The pirate eyed her hungrily. "Let thy bosom release its godly nectar my way."

Mithaiya flashed a fang-sharp smile and slid past him towards the roof's edge and the waiting balcony.

Carian swept the hair from his eyes and looked to Gwynnleth to find her glaring at him. "What? Amithaiya'geshwen means the Bosom of God's Nectar—"

"Get off my rooftop."

He grinned. "Take care of yourself, birdie." Then he jumped down to the balcony and his waiting lady love.

SIX

"No man can achieve a praiseworthy life unless he listens
to the whisper which is heard by him alone."

Emir Zafir bin Safwan al Abdul-Basir,
Unifier of the Seventeen Tribes of the Akkad

THE SACRED CITY of Faroqhar, seat of the Empress of Agasan, languished beneath the fourth day of a lashing late-winter storm. Sitting atop the highest hill opposite the Sormitáge campus, the domes and towers of the sprawling Imperial Palace made brief appearances among the overcast, while the occasional golden glow peeked through from many a lighted window.

"It's really raging out there," Empress Valentina van Gelderan noted to her lover as they lay upon her ornate marble bed entwined in the aftermath of lovemaking. Rain dashed itself against a wall of glass-paned doors, while lightning flared in brief displays of brilliance and shadow, a turbulent dance set to thunder's forbidding rhythm.

The Adept wielder Marius di L'Arlesé twirled a lock of Valentina's raven hair around one gold-ringed finger. "I remember when you wore it like this," he murmured with only a hint of the weariness that plagued him these days, "long and flowing … free. Ah, to be so young again."

Valentina turned her head to better smile upon her Consort. "I was a girl then and already smitten with you, the most promising wielder to walk the halls of the Sormitáge since Arion Tavestra."

Marius held up his hands and observed the thin gold bands that graced all ten of his fingers. Every ring had been hard-earned in trials that had often lasted not hours but days. He'd gained the last of his rings in the aftermath of the Adept Wars, when some knowledge yet remained. Now, three centuries after the slaughter of the Hundred Mages, it was a rarity to find wielders who could claim even a handful of rings.

"Marius … ?"

He lifted his eyes back to her and realized she was still waiting for his response. "A man in full, yes." He gave her a soft look. "Yet when it came to matters of love, I was but a boy who fashioned himself a man, and you …" His expression turned chastising. "You were a tigress, relentlessly pursuing me across the years until you made me your own."

Valentina regarded him lovingly. "You'd already stolen my heart; what choice was left to me?"

"Ahh …" Marius exhaled a sigh and lay back on his pillow. "If only I'd known the burden its possession would prove."

Valentina arched an ebony brow. "You're not so aged as your tone implies, *mio caro*—surely no less virile in this moment than the day you first worked the Pattern of Life." She ran a finger along his sideburn and added with a slight smile, "No matter the silver you let come into your hair."

Marius sighed. "We can trick the body but never the mind, Valentina." He turned his head to gaze into her colorless eyes. "My soul feels the ever-lengthening ages."

"My, but you're maudlin tonight."

He grunted. "Centuries have passed since I first worked the Pattern, and though my love for you remains undiminished, I confess no similar sentiments towards life in these times."

Valentina frowned. She slipped from within the curve of his body and stood to retrieve her robe. Marius followed her with his eyes, noting as ever that her form was more exquisite naked than garnished with the diamonds of her imperial gown. Incredible that this vision had produced eleven offspring; such was the power of the Pattern of Life to restore youth and vigor to the body, even if not to the enduring spirit inhabiting it.

"What troubles you, Marius?" Valentina's voice carried a husky, melodious resonance that always stirred his blood. "These wistful musings are hardly like you." She tied the waist of her silk robe and walked across opulent carpets towards the wall of glass doors and the storm.

Marius sat up and spun his feet over the side of the bed in one smooth motion. He pushed a hand through his dark hair, barely touched with grey at the temples, and looked up at her under his brow.

Scarcely a day had passed of late without a particular argument sprouting between them, and though he loathed bringing it up again, he couldn't keep it from his thoughts—the matter pressed upon his conscience like an arrowhead beneath his armor, with every motion grinding its way further into his flesh. "You know my mind, Valentina."

Even as he said it, he wished he could've withdrawn the words.

"And you know mine." She turned him a level look over her shoulder.

Marius shook his head. "Valentina, Ansgar *is* conspiring against you."

"No doubt he is." She cast him a rueful smile. "But I will not bring war against the Danes without provocation—without proof." Her gaze was steady, her tone uncompromising. "Why must you plague me with this matter? I publicly granted Ansgar clemency to rebuild his father's domain, and I cannot be seen to renege on that promise, especially not so soon."

"It's been seven years, Valentina. Time enough for a young king to become embittered by the sanctions leveled in punishment for another man's crimes."

Her gaze remained uncompromising. "Denying one covenant calls all into question—overnight I'd have a dozen would-be dictators biting at my heels. Would you risk the stability of the Empire on the whispers of spies?"

Marius leaned to brace elbows across his bare knees. "You've acted on whispers from the Order of the Glass Sword before, Valentina, and with less provocation."

"Spies trade in whispers. Offer me proof of his treason, Marius. *Then* I will act."

Marius felt frustration rising inside him. Was the Empress losing her taste for war? The thought increasingly troubled him of late, especially with the inexplicable darkness he perceived on the currents. Then again, he remembered too well the way she'd looked upon the young Dane as he'd stood humbled before her throne. "Mayhap your own emotions on the matter confuse you, Valentina."

She spun him an icy look over her shoulder. "Marius, you forget your place."

Marius bit his tongue rather than provoke her further. In all their years together, they'd never faced such discord between them. It only heightened his sense of unease.

"The currents show nothing to substantiate the Order's claims of high treason from the Danes," Valentina pointed out stiffly. "You said as much yourself."

"I said I didn't know *what* they showed." He remained frustrated by his inability to understand the strange influences he'd been seeing on the tides of *elae.* Something odd was happening in the far north, near the Dane's city of Kjvngherad—this much Marius had ascertained—but he couldn't explain the darkness he saw.

The burden in their discord lay upon his shoulders. Had he been able to bring her any shred of proof—blood on stone, ink on paper, treason upon the currents—anything she might hold before the Patrician Senate, there would be nothing to discuss.

Marius frowned and lifted hazel eyes to view his Empress across the room. She stood regarding him regally from her position at the windows, a slim figure in white silk, with raven hair and eyes like the diamonds of her famous throne. There were times when Valentina seemed simply Valentina and not the poised figure of the Empress of Agasan, but such glimpses of the mere woman—of the girl who'd claimed Marius's heart so many decades ago—were few and far between.

"If not the currents, Valentina," he reasoned, holding her gaze, "surely your Sight has shown you something."

He saw the tightening around her eyes, but she smothered this response with a cool brushing away of her hair and turned to look outside again. "My Sight …" she repeated after a long silence, her tone unexpectedly astringent. "My Sight, Marius, is … blurred."

It pained her to admit it—Marius saw this at once, even as a number of ill-fitting pieces fell into place for him. This then was the crux of the matter, the reason for their quarreling. Never before had the Empress's Sight defied her, and long had Valentina relied upon it to govern her decisions. Without it, she was blinded.

As was he, without the currents to guide him.

Marius stared at her upon this thought. "This *cannot* be a coincidence … that your Sight eludes you while the currents also defy my reading? What are the chances of us both being so blind, Valentina?"

She turned him a look over her shoulder.

"It's Kjvngherad. It must be."

She barked a laugh. "Ansgar? You think *him* capable of obfuscating my Sight? A mere *na'turna?*" Valentina shook her head, and he read much from her grim expression. "This treachery has but one obvious source: the realm is out of Balance, and *elae* is dying."

Marius eyed her sharply. "Dying our race might be, Valentina, but it's been waning for centuries. *This* is new. This is different. And I daresay it's manmade."

"I would like it to be so, *mio caro*, but we cannot deceive ourselves—"

"Are we?" he challenged, straightening. "We have no more proof that this obscuring is a product of Balance than one of direct malfeasance aimed against us."

Valentina frowned as she considered him. "I've no knowledge of anyone being able to confound the Sight."

Marius stood and walked to her. "Nor have I." He brushed a strand of long hair off her shoulder and settled hands around her slender arms. "But I'd never heard of a wielder creating a realm whole-cloth out of the aether before Malachai … did …"

When he failed to finish the thought, Valentina looked at him curiously. "What is it?"

Before Marius could put words to explain his idea, a knock came twice upon the outermost doors to their chambers. "Aurelia!" The guard used the Empress's formal title. "High Lord? Pardon my interruption, Your Grace—a missive has arrived for you."

Releasing Valentina with a look that said their discussion wasn't finished,

Marius donned his robe and crossed the distance between bedchamber and sitting room with long strides. He sent a flow of *elae* into the doors to unbolt the latch, and they swung open just as he reached them.

A Praetorian stood in the portal, resplendent in his red-violet cape and elaborately etched silver cuirass, yet for all his weaponry, he was no more impressive in breastplate and greaves than Marius di L'Arlesé in the simplest of garments.

"High Lord." The Praetorian gave a respectful bow. "This just came for you." He held out a red leather case inscribed with a well-known seal.

At last, Marius thought. *The report from the Order.* He took the case and thanked the guard, then walked slowly back to the bedchamber while working the trace-seal that bound the leather. Unfolding the parchment inside, he began to read ...

After a moment of silence, Valentina turned to him and found him standing still in the middle of her sitting room. "What is it, Marius?"

Marius frowned as he read. "The Order reports visitors in the night to Kjvngherad, and two Red Guard were found dead upon the rocks at the fortress's base."

"Treason?"

"The Danes said a storm must've claimed them, but the Order is investigating further." Marius scanned the rest of the report, which detailed shipments into and out of Kjvngherad and the odd comings and goings of the Danes' young king—suspicious, but not enough to prove ill-doing.

Marius flipped to the next page and continued reading, whereupon he lifted his gaze to Valentina. "Three more Adepts of the Fifty Companions have been found murdered."

Valentina arched an ebony brow. "This is becoming an epidemic. Who have we lost this time?"

"The Order's operative included descriptions of what was left of the bodies he found. Here." He held out the report to her. "Read for yourself."

Valentina crossed the distance and took the parchment from him. While the Empress looked it over, Marius returned to the bedside to retrieve his clothes.

Valentina's gaze became ever more troubled as she read. Lowering the report, she looked to him and shook her head. "I fear we are facing the beginning of the end of days."

"It wasn't divine vengeance that shredded those Companions, Valentina," Marius remarked with some asperity. He had donned his white shirt and was now attending to his pants. "Not unless Cephrael takes the form of a Whisper Lord."

Valentina sank onto the edge of her desk. "The Alorin Seat is convinced my great-uncle is behind these deaths."

Marius gave her a telling look by way of agreement.

"I'm not certain the truth is so simple," she remarked with a little frown, the barest narrowing of her brows. "The absent witness is conveniently blamed."

Marius knew better than to voice his opinion on this topic; experience had proven that any discussion involving Björn van Gelderan would open an argument he could never win.

Valentina shook her head and then gazed at him for a long moment of silence. "I fear illusions of hope, Marius. The realm is dying, and our race dies with it."

Exhaling forcefully, Marius pushed off the bed and took up his long crimson coat as he walked to her. Fully dressed, he posed a striking form. He placed hands upon her silk-clad shoulders and gazed into his Empress's eyes. "Whoever is behind these deaths and disappearances, the Order shall uncover them, as well as their motives. I head now to the Sormitáge."

She ran fingers across his cheek and then through his dark hair. "You go to study the currents?"

"I go to the Archives. Perhaps our ancestors can teach us something of this threat."

She eyed him speculatively. "And there is the other matter hanging upon your conscience."

He grimaced—for she knew his mind too well. "Admittedly, I would also know what the Endoge has discovered about the Adepts gone missing from the Sormitáge. The Order has found no trace of Malin van Drexel or any of the others."

"Which may indicate there is nothing to find. The Sormitáge produces more dropouts than graduates, long an effective means of winnowing the gold from the dross."

Marius regarded her with a frown. His gut told him the three missing Adepts played some role in a larger conflict, but these days his Empress required proof before action was taken, and he had none to give her. "Valentina—"

She leaned in with a kiss, capturing him as ever with the simplest of means. Pulling away, she looked up into his eyes. "Go then, and bring back the truth of things."

Marius bowed in gratitude for her parting kiss, which was all the apology either of them ever needed.

The High Lord exited the imperial apartments beneath a marble archway sculpted in a rendering of the Lady of the Rivers reaching to embrace the Lord of the Forest, one of the oldest and most enduring legends of the Agasi culture. The four Praetorians on guard slammed vambraces across their breastplates in salute as he passed.

Beyond the impressive threshold, Marius's own men waited in an antechamber, lounging among a collection of low couches. Seeing him, they dropped their cards on a table and leapt to their feet.

"*Buona sera, Signore* di L'Arlesé!" greeted the shorter of the pair, a truthreader named Giancarlo. He flashed a toothy grin, bright against his olive complexion.

"Giancarlo, Vincenzé," Marius returned. "Walk with me."

They jumped into step with him as he headed swiftly down the corridor. "*Dove*, High Lord?" asked Vincenzé, Giancarlo's taller, leaner Adept cousin. His blue eyes gleamed with curiosity as he waited for the High Lord's reply.

Marius eyed the both of them askance. "To the Sormitáge."

Giancarlo whacked his cousin on the arm and then presented his palm, waggling his fingers expectantly. "Pay the piper, *mio fratello con il cervello di topo.*" My brother with the brain of a mouse. Giancarlo's Calabrian accent fell heavier than his cousin's, though both had been raised within an hour's ride of each other's homes.

Vincenzé dug two silver coins out of his pocket and slammed them into his cousin's open palm. Marius was used to their constant wagering—the two of them bet on anything and everything conceivable to man—but they were unquestionably loyal and deviously inventive, and Marius depended on them for all manner of assignments.

"*Che cosa avete sentito?*" What have you heard? the High Lord asked. Though he read all of the reports from Agasan's unparalleled spy network, the Order of the Glass Sword, he trusted first what he saw with his own eyes, either in the flesh or upon the currents. Next, he trusted Vincenzé and Giancarlo.

Come to think of it ... he might list quite a few additional others that he trusted before he trusted the Order. This didn't mean their information was incorrect, but spies ever had their own agendas, and Giuseppe di Creppo, the Order's Grand Master, stood as no exception.

"Loudest upon the tides of rumor, High Lord," Vincenzé replied, keeping his voice low even though they spoke in their private dialect, "is talk of the boy Malin van Drexel, the latest Adept vanished from the Sormitáge."

Yes, he is heavy in my thoughts as well.

It wasn't unheard-of for an older boy to abandon his studies and flee the university—often with a girl in tow—or to expatriate to Jamaii or the Akkad to seek wilder fortunes, but three boys in fewer moons was too many for coincidence.

The High Lord shook his head at their own failure to uncover the perpetrator thus far. "Suppositions?"

"Oh, most everything is floating around." Vincenzé rested a hand on his sword hilt as they walked. "The students claim malfeasance on the part of various docents—clearly ill attempts to exact some personal vendetta— while talk among the literatos and maestros is that the boy ran away. The administrative staff whisper a dozen different theories, each more wildly variant and unlikely than the last."

"And the family?"

Vincenzé exchanged a look with his cousin, who replied, "The family is rattling sabers at the Fifth Vestal, High Lord, demanding he return their son unharmed or else appear before them and declare his innocence."

"*Che mi tocca sentire,*" Vincenzé touched a hand to his temple and then threw it into the air incredulously. "As if the Vestal need speak nothing to the *Empress* of the *wars*, yet they expect he will appear before *them* to address allegations of kidnapping?"

"The vain hope of a grieving family," Marius murmured by way of agreement. There was nothing else to be gleaned from such hearsay, so he moved on. "What other news?"

"Giancarlo lost his shirt dicing with a pair of gypsies," snorted Vincenzé. His blue eyes sparkled with mirth.

"Hey *stronzo*," Giancarlo smiled daggers back at him, "my balls have a little itch." He pointed to his crotch. "Come do your duty. I know you enjoy it."

"What's the latest among the Guard?" Marius prodded.

"Complaints about the weather," Giancarlo offered. He grabbed his crotch and made kissing sounds towards his cousin.

"And the food." Vincenzé clapped his hand on his forearm and waggled his hand, an oblique reference to the length of his shaft and Giancarlo's taking it in the arse.

"And the officers," Giancarlo added in answer to the High Lord while simultaneously thumbing his teeth at his cousin.

"And the ale." Vincenzé shot Giancarlo a predatory grin.

Giancarlo's look was withering. "And the lack of suitably amenable women."

"Don't you mean malleable?" smirked Vincenzé.

"That too. Then there's the usual mutterings about duty assignments."

"And respectable pay."

"Or rather, the lack thereof," Giancarlo corrected.

"Lots of talk about the Danes and whether they mean to revolt again," Vincenzé said.

Marius had expected this. The Red Guard always worried about the Danes.

"And recently there's been some chatter about a disaster in the east, some kind of temple destroyed in Rethynnea."

"I heard it was Thessalonia," Giancarlo said.

"No, it was Rethynnea."

"The Temple of the Vestals," Marius meanwhile supplied in answer, having learned of its destruction from the Order many weeks ago.

"*Esattamente.*" Vincenzé shot his cousin a triumphant look. "In Rethynnea."

"Nothing else, then?" Marius asked.

"No, High Lord. It's been remarkably quiet."

If it's quiet, it's a dangerous kind of silence.

All of Marius's senses shouted that the realm was tipping towards disaster. The unexplained taint upon the currents indicated *some* impending ill, but no matter how clearly he recognized the danger, he had no understanding of what he saw and no way of acting upon it. He felt a stallion thrice bound to its stall, unable to move in any direction save backwards into the wall.

"You will tell me if anything else comes to your ears," the High Lord murmured.

"*Naturalmente,*" Vincenzé said with a flourish of his hand that was almost a salute.

The Sacred City of Faroqhar hosted two kinds of nodes: the kind that were twisted, and the kind that were bound into *soglia-varcarés,* often shortened to *soglia'res*—gateways that anyone could use.

One such *soglia're* dominated the center of the Imperial Palace's *Piazza di Sacro Cuore della Verità,* so named because legend claimed it was the spot upon which the blessed *angiel* Epiphany had been birthed into the realm.

Reaching the piazza, Marius called the fifth to fend off the lashing rain and headed to the marble rotunda dominating the plaza's center.

He and his Calabrians had made the *soglia're* crossing so many times that they no longer noticed the blur of disorientation as they trod upon the very Pattern of the World to move from the palace to the Sormitáge campus, several miles distant. Certainly as they emerged at the other end, the winds thrashed the Sormitáge's limestone forecourt just as fiercely as they'd been striking the palace's.

Still draped in the fifth, the High Lord di L'Arlesé approached the Sormitáge's grand edifice with Giancarlo and Vincenzé close on his heels. Several groups of students hung about beneath the mammoth portico that formed the building's façade, some gazing dispiritedly into the rain, others chatting or smoking the pungent leaf that the students seemed to favor.

Two adolescent truthreaders were practicing their craft on one another as Marius began his ascent of the fifty long stairs leading up to the entrance. When they saw him, however, they quickly turned shoulder to shoulder and bowed. Surprise rippled through the rest of the students then, such that whispers of the High Lord's arrival preceded him into the building.

By the time Marius and his men entered the main hall, an administrative line was gathering in a hasty display of rustling robes, with the willowy, violet-doused Endoge at its crowning head. "High Lord di L'Arlesé." The Endoge greeted him with a stately bow. "You honor us. I'm ashamed to say I knew not of your intended visit, but be assured—"

"I mean only to study in the Archives, Liam."

"Of course." The ever-composed Endoge held a hand toward the Sormitáge's Grande Passáge while his colorless truthreader's eyes watched Marius with a shrewd intelligence. "Allow me to escort you, High Lord?"

"Your guidance is welcome."

The Endoge made a formal and elegant nod of acquiescence and led away with his hands clasped before him.

Marius looked to Vincenzé and murmured, "See what you can learn."

The two Calabrians bowed and slipped away to their own investigations.

The Sormitáge's Grand Passáge arched six stories and boasted some of the realm's most spectacular sculpture and art. The paintings on the walls and immense ceiling told the story of Alorin's genesis as recounted in the *Sobra I'ternin*, as well as gave a history of five millennia of kings and emperors. At a quarter of a mile in length, and painted by the hands of master artists over many decades, it stood as the greatest work of artistic endeavor the realm had ever witnessed.

Domes crowned each junction where new passages branched to other parts of the university's vast main building, and each dome's frescoes depicted a different legend. Some claimed the entire mythology of Alorin might be understood from a detailed study of the domes of the Grand Passáge.

As the High Lord and the Endoge made their way down the corridor, literatos and other faculty stepped aside with low bows, while docents held back whispering students to leave a wide path free for the High Lord's procession.

They were walking beneath vivid scenes from the Creation when Marius said to the Endoge, "Since I'm here, Liam, what student progress is worthy of note?"

"All are in keeping with expectations, Your Grace, but we've seen some impressive achievements from among the Catenaré ranks this term."

"How many are expected to finish?"

"One hundred and forty-two have been invited to Invocation Trials, which begin in a few days."

"And how many among the recent Devoverés have demonstrated an aptitude for Patterning?" As a wielder himself, Marius strongly supported screening all Adepts for an aptitude in the craft, though it pained him how rare it was to find any with both aptitude and interest. Rarer still were those who could learn to work patterns of the fifth with any regularity. In fifty years, he could count them all on his own hands.

"Over thirty Devoveré have submitted requests to advance their study across the strands. One I might call to your attention, High Lord, is the eldest of the Mavellias boys, a Nodefinder."

Marius pepped up. "Has he shown an interest in pursuing the art?"

"He's shown great interest in pursuing the Healer Penelope van der Meer," the Endoge offered sourly. "And before her, I believe it was the truthreader Mariana d'Ancarré, eldest daughter of the Veneisean ambassador."

"I see."

"Maestro van Reinlein, the young man's sponsor, is speaking to him about his shameful dilettantism."

"Let's hope the maestro's lecture takes root. By Epiphany's light, if Malachai's scourge had beset us in this age instead of three centuries ago, he'd have wiped us from the realm."

The Endoge arched a rueful brow by way of acknowledgment of this truth. "I share your concerns, High Lord. Despite all efforts, our numbers decline every year."

Passing beneath a dome whose frescoes told the story of the birth of the Lady of the Rivers, they turned off the Grand Passáge and headed down a staircase and outside beneath a cloister being bombarded by rain. Their clothes were damp when the Endoge led them back inside and up another staircase.

Marius noted the Endoge's pale hand as it traced the line of the marble balustrade. The truthreader wore three Sormitáge rings on his fourth finger, and the pale gold gleamed brightly in the dim stairwell. A stack of three was a remarkable accomplishment for an Adept of any strand, yet not an unexpected standard for the Sormitáge's chief administrator.

Marius exhaled a slow sigh. How few they were, those who'd survived the Adept Wars, and how dire their race's future appeared to him. That someone— or several someones—seemed intent on finishing Malachai's work and exterminating the last of them only rubbed salt in the wound.

Marius pushed a hand through his hair and sent a sideways look at the Endoge. "Any progress on locating your most recent missing Adept, Liam?"

The Endoge cast him a reticent eye. "Regrettably no, Your Grace. The boy seems to have completely vanished—I believe your own Order found no more than the regiment captain did."

"I heard as much, yes."

"I daresay, the lack of evidence implies some form of arcane malfeasance, yet if *elae* was somehow involved in the act, the currents showed none of it." Liam glanced uncertainly at him. "Malin van Drexel had his Maritus bracelet. He could not have left the grounds without being traced by the wards. It is most perplexing—we should've found *some* sign of him."

Marius thought of the taint he'd been seeing on the currents and wondered with a surge of unease if those scars might conceal such dark deeds as forcefully removing a student through the wards.

The Endoge continued meanwhile, "I confess, the idea of *elae* being put to despicable use within our pristine halls … I cannot sleep at night for the horror of it."

Marius cast the Endoge a look of agreement.

At last they reached a pair of towering double doors framed within five recessive marble arches, and the Endoge came to a halt. "On my desk I have the regiment captain's complete written report on Malin van Drexel, which I would be most obliged to share with Your Grace once your study in the Archives is concluded."

"Thank you, Liam. I'm interested in seeing what avenues were followed in the captain's investigation."

"I await your calling." The Endoge bowed and departed.

For a moment, Marius watched him making his way back down the hall. Then the High Lord di L'Arlesé sent the fifth into the doors and entered the Imperial Archives to see what history could teach him.

SEVEN

"The darkness at the end is that of the beginning;

thus are life and death of equal value."

– The Book of Bethamin

DARSHANVENKHÁTRAMAN STOOD ON the tower's crenellated roof gazing north as the wind whipped and swirled around him. The air tasted of earth, and heat, and carried upon it the peculiar tang of static that felt such a balm to his troubled mind. A storm was coming. In the east, turbulent clouds clashed in variegated mounds, lightning flashing in their depths, while a broad swath of rainstorm shadowed the lower horizon.

Saldaria. Tambarré. That liminal place between desert and northern forest birthed fierce storms. Lightning commonly struck the land while its mother storm swept above, marking her path of passing with sand melted into curling spires of glass. And when the tempestuous wind drove the desert into the sky, mud rained down upon the Prophet's temple.

Storms called to Darshan, though it was his brother Shailabanáchtran whose name meant Maker of Storms. He and his brothers had been birthed among a contentious clashing of elements that charged space with power; their nascent forms had been swaddled in voluminous clouds of electrified dust that refracted starlight into colors inconceivable by mortal eyes. Though the worst storms of this realm were calm by comparison, they yet harbored some quieter harmonic of the Chaos out of which the Malorin'athgul were birthed, and to which Darshan would return when their work was done, when all that was left of Alorin was a similar elemental storm.

"Missing home, brother?"

Darshan turned to find Shail rounding the last stair leading up from inside the tower. The wind grabbed Shail's long hair and tore at the crimson silk of his robes. Darshan wore nothing, preferring the feel of the storm's electricity flowing across his muscled flesh. *Elae's* fifth strand was powerful during storms, resembling in its ferocity their own consumptive power. Darshan looked back to the view. "Sometimes I envy Rinokh his vanquishment."

Shail reached his side and joined him in gazing at the northern line of mountains, whose jagged peaks were tearing into the band of clouds that formed the storm's vanguard. "Feel free to join him any time."

Darshan cast him a sidelong eye. "Yes ... you would happily be rid of me, too. Don't think I don't know it."

Shail wore a feral sort of grin. "This world is too small for all of us."

"You would make of it your private sandbox," Darshan murmured critically, "to wage wars and build cities and tear it all down in a swipe of one hand."

"And why shouldn't I? We're gods to these creatures."

Darshan radiated disappointment. "You adopt a naïve view, Shailabanáchtran. The Chaos Father made us for a purpose, and we should be focused upon that purpose—not engaged in infantile games, pushing our toys hither and yon."

Shail arched a dubious brow but held his tongue.

Darshan turned to him. "You mock me even in silence. Why did you come here if not to listen?"

"Why did you summon me if not to speak?"

"I suppose for another lesson in futility." Darshan's gaze flicked irritably across his youngest brother. "How goes your obsessive hunt for your northern prince?"

"*My* hunt?" Shail arched a patronizing brow. "I understood you also wanted him called to heel—something to do with breaking the bond with one of your Marquiin pets?"

Darshan looked dismissively away. "You and Dore spend too much time together. It's absurd to think one man could pose a threat to us."

"One man can raise the hopes of millions."

Darshan grunted. "Deluded millions."

"Perhaps, but those delusions provide them surprising buoyancy in weathering the storm. Take care, brother." He looked Darshan over as the wind whipped his long black hair into violent designs. "If you don't soon remove your head from the clouds, when you do, you may discover you've no ground left to stand on."

"Ground you haven't claimed for yourself, you mean."

Shail's dark eyes gleamed dangerously. "In any case, Dore reports that the val Lorian boy escaped his pet wielder—a pity, although I'd warned him not to underestimate the prince. Ean val Lorian continues to prove himself a threat worthy of our notice."

Darshan grunted at this.

Shail drew his silk vestments tighter around him. "You would be wise to take heed of this man, Darshan. He brought a woman with him to Tyr'kharta. Whoever she was, she has Dore in a frenzy."

"Dore is easily excitable." The man had far too many idle pursuits that did not immediately benefit their aims. It vexed Darshan somewhat that Dore thought to report to his brother before himself. Never mind that he'd made it abundantly clear to Dore that the matter of the val Lorian prince fell beneath his notice.

Shail wandered along the wall. "Dore thinks the prince may try to rescue his brother. He sent the val Lorian men to Ivarnen while he holds the brother in Tal'Afaq. No matter which fortress the prince chooses, we'll have him."

Darshan appeared unimpressed. "Would that Dore might be diverted from this obsession with Ean val Lorian, but he will not." He looked his brother up and down. "Much like yourself."

Shail arched a sardonic brow. "I'm averting a future your current view is too narrow to foresee, brother. One day you may thank me for it."

"More likely I'll curse you, but I see nothing new in that denouement." Darshan exhaled an annoyed sigh. "Tal'Afaq, Ivarnen … these are poor choices for ambush. Dore risks the *eidola*, who are vulnerable while still in conversion."

"Ivarnen is the most fortified of your outposts. The prince will be unable to gain entry save through the channel Dore creates for him. And four *eidola* lord over Tal'Afaq. It is impenetrable."

Darshan heard this statement and thought Shail was proving his own naivety, but it would serve no purpose to argue the point. "What of the *eidola* you've been experimenting with using the *inverteré* patterns? How fares their conversion?"

"As well as your own."

Darshan eyed Shail circumspectly. Something in Shail's coldly smiling gaze hinted that he thought his creatures better formed and far superior. Darshan suspected his youngest brother would think thusly of any working held in competition against his own.

Shail swept a strand of blowing hair from his face. "Soon we will raise armies unlike anything this realm has ever known."

Giving Shail a long look, Darshan walked to the tower's edge where part of the crenellated wall had crumbled and fallen away. There, he braced his feet, lifted his arms, and with his mind pulled the storm closer, calling its power for his own.

White-hot kinetic energy scraped along his skin. It roused the dark hair on his arms and chased and sparked from band to band among the hundreds of braids hanging down his back. It sang through his flesh and stirred his loins, savagely arousing him with a rapturous pain. For a moment, he seemed unearthly, a being encased in light. Then the raw power exploded upwards, splitting the sky, throwing the world into blinding negative.

Somewhere far above, thunder sounded.

Darshan slowly lowered his arms. Steam rose from his flesh, and his chest lifted and fell with his rapid breath. The lightning had left jagged ebony streaks across his skin, vicious brands that even then began to fade. He turned his head to look upon his brother, and his eyes were wholly black.

I would see this realm returned to Chaos, he said mind to mind, his thoughts as dark and violent as exploding stars.

Shail eyed him inquisitively. One could almost see the picture spinning into shape in his calculating gaze. "I had only to follow the path of the dead to find you tonight—truthreaders like a trail of breadcrumbs from temple to tower." The wind funneled into the wide sleeves of his robe, and the silk billowed about him. "It seems excessive, even for you. Your appetite for the flesh of young men must've grown tremendously."

Darshan gave him a withering look.

"Or ..." Shail pressed a finger across his lips. "Is it that your favorite flavor is gone and none of the others taste as sweet?"

Darshan looked back to the storm. Kjieran's loss was a wound that wouldn't heal, his death a mystery with no answers, only agonizing questions shaped of jagged blades. Yes, none of his other truthreaders even remotely filled the void Kjieran's death had opened, no matter how many he consumed in one meal. But it was no business of Shail's.

Darshan arched a brow. "You should know better than to believe the things Dore whispers across your pillow."

He called the wind this time, drowning out Shail's affronted retort. The wind funneled down from the charcoal skies, dragging a cyclone of clouds. It buffeted and enveloped him where he stood. Stinging ice whipped his body, sharp as the knife of betrayal Kjieran had plunged into his heart, and the rough wind scoured his naked flesh. He willed that it would take these strange and inexplicable feelings with its passing, leaving him cleansed of their constant ache.

The wind tore away from him and fled past Shail, ripping through his silken robes as it left. He stood glowering with his fists clenched.

Darshan sighed. The gust of wind was gone, but the ache irritatingly remained. He looked to Shail. "Have you done something to Pelas?"

His brother's gaze tightened. "Why?"

"This will be the third summons gone unanswered in as many moons."

Shail gave an indifferent shrug. "The last I saw our brother, he'd taken a truthreader for his sodomite."

"And?"

"You know how he is. Perhaps the boy is more intriguing than you or I."

"What do your spies say of his activities?"

"They've proven annoyingly silent."

Darshan grunted. "I believe Pelas has killed all of my spies. He seems quite adept at ferreting them out."

"Or else they're inept at keeping their mouths shut." Shail strolled to the edge of the tower and looked down. The stones at its base joined with the sheer mountainside, which fell away into a boulder field hundreds of paces below. He bared his teeth in a sharp smile and murmured, close and low at Darshan's ear, "Then again, maybe he learned what you did to him and chose another side."

Darshan's eyes flashed. He spun nose to nose with his brother and murmured darkly, "Pray you are incorrect."

Lightning split the sky in a blistering line and thunder shattered the world. The storm's tumultuous blanket now claimed the entire eastern horizon, while rain washed across the plains. In moments, it would be upon them.

"Pelas is of far less concern than Ean val Lorian," Shail remarked then, turning away. "Pelas *believes* all the drivel you've planted in his head. You waste all your efforts worrying about our brother's inane dalliances a continent away while a real danger cavorts upon your doorstep."

"I'm relieved to know where I stand in the order of priority." Pelas noted from behind.

Darshan whirled to find him sitting on a merlon on the tower's south side, one elbow resting on bent knee. There was no telling how long he'd been there listening—*damn him.* Pelas had tricks that eluded even Darshan's understanding. This is what Shail failed to recognize about their intrepid middle brother.

Darshan frowned. "Make yourself at home, Pelas."

"Thank you, I *am* quite comfortable." His copper eyes swept Darshan's naked form. "Laundry day?"

"How droll," Shail sneered.

Darshan eyed Pelas darkly. It troubled him not knowing how much Pelas understood of their activities, how much he'd overheard in this or any other conversation where he'd deigned to listen in similarly unannounced. "I suppose it would be too much to expect you've accomplished something since last we met."

Pelas flicked at a speck on his boot. He'd bound his long hair at the nape of his neck, but the wind still whipped stray strands across his face and around his shoulders. "The last time we met ended in a rather spectacular fight."

"So I recall," Darshan said, eyes cold and very, very bleak.

"I believe at the time you swore to end me if I defied you again, and I … think I answered that by throwing you through a wall."

"That is my recollection as well."

Pelas leaned back on one elbow. "Well, if you mean since that last meeting? Then, no."

"It's always such a pleasure catching up with you, brother," Shail remarked as his gaze took in the approaching storm. "One day you *must* tell me all about your dabbling with colored mud and *oh*, the latest *carvings* you've made of the realm's Healers. No doubt they're all true works of art." He cast a look at

Darshan by way of departure and then descended the steps into the tower amid a billow of crimson silk.

Thunder cracked overhead, splitting the sky, and rain poured out of the fissure.

Darshan lifted his face to the heavens and closed his eyes to the wind and the icy, stinging rain. He could sense the rain's deconstructing of the clouds, molecule by molecule. The chill downpour washing over him was not unlike the rush of unmaking. Would that he could return now to those chaotic fringes of the cosmos. No doubt there he would not feel so empty.

As the rain roared down around him, pelting earth and stone with equal fervor, Darshan exhaled a slow breath and opened his eyes. Droplets clung to his lashes, tiny globules, worlds unto themselves. He blinked them away like tears and turned to look at his brother.

Unlike Shail, who'd shamefully fled the storm, Pelas stood now atop the merlon balancing on its edge, even leaning somewhat into the wind, foolishly trusting to its support. His coattails flapped behind and beneath his outstretched arms, while his dark hair lay in drenched waves down his back.

It troubled Darshan how alike they were, he and Pelas. Diametrically opposed philosophically, yet entirely too akin on an instinctive level. It was one reason he considered Pelas so dangerous. One of many.

"Why have you come, Pelas?"

"You summoned me, Darshan."

"Were I to collect a drop of rain for every time I've summoned you without a response, the resulting sea would fill all of Saldaria."

Pelas turned him a look over his shoulder. "Is that all I need do to claim your trust? Attend you even as Shail does, like a dutiful lap dog attentive to your call?"

"It would be a beginning."

Pelas's eyes tightened. "A beginning with no end. You would make me your lackey, just another fawning sycophant vying for the favor of Bethamin's *divine* grace."

Darshan exhaled a frustrated breath. "I tire of this argument, Pelas. It serves neither of us."

Pelas stepped down off the merlon, landing with a splash of boots in the puddles rapidly filling the roof. When he looked up, his eyes shone like glowing amber. "Why have I come?" He gave Darshan a humorless smile. "*Why* have I come? I've come so you can *remove the compulsion you placed on me!*"

His words thundered, and an expanding bubble of sound ripped through the storm, blasting the water from Darshan's flesh. The puddle beneath his feet vanished, seared away by sound, and then reformed seconds later as the rain returned.

Pelas faced him now, arms poised aggressively at his sides, his eyes fiery and his body thrumming with power.

Darshan pressed his lips in a tight line. "What have you done since coming to this world? What have you accomplished towards our aims?"

Pelas stared at him. "Shail means to destroy you, even as he destroyed Rinokh. Yet you stick your bloody claws into *my* mind—"

"Shail is at least pursuing our purpose!" Darshan gave his brother a piqued glare—*by Chaos born*, Pelas was the most obstinate being ever created! "Whether or not Shail thinks he can somehow eliminate us, his brothers—to whatever end that might prove—our purpose is still being accomplished. But you, Pelas … you don't just fraternize with these human toys. You're *in love* with them!"

"As are you."

Darshan sucked in his breath with a hiss. The words were accusation and victorious coup in one.

"What happened with Kjieran? Why did he betray you?" Pelas made a slow approach behind the lance of his words. "What did you do to the poor man to make him *hate* you so desperately that he would rather burn to death than endure one more breath bound to you?"

Darshan gaped at his brother. How could he have learned these hateful truths? If there was anything in the cosmos Darshan feared, it was the mistake of underestimating Pelas.

Darshan lashed out with a mental bite of jagged power that tore through Pelas's mind. His brother stumbled, shook his head, but then he straightened, and when he looked up again, his face was set with a grim smile.

Darshan grew wary and his gaze narrowed. Pelas shouldn't have been able to throw off his assault so easily. His brother had changed since their last confrontation, grown stronger somehow.

"The laughable irony in all of this is you imagine I have some choice," Pelas observed bitterly. "If I indeed love these beings, or even if I love killing them, is it not what I'm made to do, brother?" His gaze darkened. "I know it's what you've *compelled* me to do."

"I've compelled you to follow our purpose!" Darshan cast his brother a heated look. Why must Pelas ever rouse such feelings of revolt and reprimand within him? He might watch a hundred Adepts dying in the thrall of *deyjiin's* dark grace without a single twinge of feeling, yet a wrong word from Pelas could set his blood to boiling. "Choice, choice—of course you have a *choice.*" He flung his hand at this absurdity. "Do you imagine that the rules that define *their* existence somehow equally define ours? We're gods to these creatures!"

Pelas shook his head, his face a mask of disgust. "Can you not see your hypocrisy?" As if in equal accusation, the skies flashed and thunder sounded. Pelas swept his dark hair back from his face and flung a hand at Darshan. "By *Chaos born*—is there even a *thimbleful* of truth amid your mountain of lies?"

Lightning split the sky again, and a resounding crack followed on its heels, reverberating through the valley. The tower gave a little shudder.

Darshan lifted one hand in entreaty. "I don't want to battle with you, Pelas. I never have. We are too alike—"

"We are *nothing* alike!" Pelas's lip curled in contempt. "Remove the compulsion you put upon me, Darshan."

Darshan's gaze smoldered. "That compulsion is the only reason I suffer you to remain here."

They locked gazes upon each other and started pacing a slow circle with their bodies as magnets, both repelling and compelling. "You have no right to attempt to control me."

"I have the skill," Darshan replied blackly, resolutely. "I have the power. That gives me every right."

"Might defines right?" Pelas's tone was crystalline in its iciness.

"Only the feeble complain of injustice, Pelas. The concept is a fabrication invented by the weak to justify their failures." He regarded Pelas with grave censure, his dark gaze raking across him. "I fear you have become feeble … weak, like these creatures whose insignificant lives you covet."

"Or perhaps I am become bold," Pelas returned with a sudden defiant smile that unnerved Darshan no end. "Perhaps I will choose my own purpose instead of the one you've chosen for me."

The very suggestion roused Darshan's rage beyond measure. "I will destroy you if you defy me, Pelas." He filled himself with power, feeling it electrifying his skin. "I won't allow you to impede us in accomplishing our purpose."

"As if I *could* with your COMPULSION IN MY HEAD!"

Abruptly Pelas became a streak of darkness that slammed into Darshan. He grabbed his brother as they both flew backwards into the tower wall. The stone exploded behind them, broken bits pelting down as they struggled, each encased in *deyjiin,* arms and legs scrabbling for leverage over the other.

Pelas's fist connected with Darshan's nose, and blackness and blood darkened his vision. He fought back, feeling his knuckles slamming into the side of Pelas's head. They spun, entangled, tumbling through puddles and across broken shards of stone that dented their flesh, until Darshan finally flipped Pelas off him with a forceful thrust.

His brother went sprawling backwards into a merlon. His temple struck against the stone's edge, and he pitched sideways to land in the crenel between. Darshan rolled to his feet and threw *deyjiin* at Pelas, but his brother dove to avoid the violet-silver streak, which exploded in a shattering of stone.

Pelas launched at him again, and his head caught Darshan just below the ribcage, painfully forcing the breath from his lungs. They tumbled head over heels and stopped in a tangle of limbs.

Faster to regain his bearings, Darshan again kicked his brother away. This time he simultaneously threw a stunning pattern, which caught Pelas at the hip while still in the air. He crashed down, skidded in a spray of water, and stopped just short of the stairway leading down into the tower.

Darshan slowly got to his feet. His body thrummed with power, but rage still had him shaking. He walked to stand over his brother and watched him as he struggled to recover. Then, decided upon his course, he straddled Pelas's body and clamped iron hands around his neck.

Pelas's eyes flew wide and he struggled, but his blows landed weakly, and with one leg useless and the other pinned beneath Darshan, he had no means of escape.

Darshan watched dispassionately, his fingers a vise around Pelas's throat, as his brother's handsome face reddened and his eyes bulged, as veins stood out in his temples and his lips began paling.

Their gazes locked; Pelas's in merciless accusation, Darshan's resolute.

And then the unthinkable happened. Pelas twisted violently in his grasp—somehow, so unexpected—and Darshan felt fire sear across his chest. He fell sideways with disbelief. Looking down, he saw a long gash striping from shoulder to abdomen, the gouge deep enough to reveal his rib bones.

Pelas rolled to his feet and climbed one-legged onto the nearest crenel. He turned to face Darshan, chest heaving. In his hand, he held a Merdanti dagger—a zanthyr's blade, from the look of it.

Pelas's gaze burned into Darshan with remorseless condemnation. "Thank you, brother," he murmured just as thunder shook the world again, its anger equally relentless, "it's a relief to see my enemies more clearly." He turned and dove off the tower.

Darshan jumped up after him. His hands caught against the crenel in time to see Pelas somersaulting through a jagged black scar that sliced the air.

Then the portal winked shut, and Darshan stood alone.

EIGHT

"A fool sees with his eyes, a wise man with his heart."

– Aristotle of Cyrene

"TIMEWEAVING," SAID TANIS'S mother as the lad was breakfasting one sunny morning. She stood at the east-facing windows, a position she often occupied when instructing. "It's possible you may have learned something of this skill during your travels, but I must assume that you haven't."

"What's timeweaving?" Tanis asked through a mouthful of biscuit crammed with salted pork—he had three left of the dozen that the cook, Madaé Giselle, had included among that morning's fare.

He knew his mother's illusion couldn't hear him, but he'd noticed that she often anticipated his next question so perfectly that it seemed she was reading his mind from the distant beyond; so he'd started asking the questions aloud, because doing so lent a sense of normalcy to a situation that was otherwise too entirely unnatural.

"I've mentioned before the variant aspects of the strands." His mother gazed out the window with her silver amulet caught between her fingers, its delicate chain but a faint sparkle around her neck. No matter her other accoutrements, this amulet she wore always, though sometimes Tanis caught merely a glimpse of the chain within the neckline of her gown. "All five strands have peculiarities associated with them. We call these peculiarities 'variant traits.' Healers, for instance, are sometimes born with the latent attribute of the Sight. Nodefinders may also walk the world of dreams. Many truthreaders are blessed with a talent for crafting broad illusions."

She turned to smile at him. Tanis thought even the sun stood diminished next to his mother's radiance. "I should remind you, Tanis love, that the power of the fourth may be harnessed—*harvested*, if you will, the energy of thought skimmed like cream from the minds of men—in such a way as to impact the elements themselves. Many conceive such workings as being of the fifth, for the harvested power of the fourth can exert similar force over matter, energy and space, but the patterns used are not the same."

She left the window to stroll the boundaries of the room as she continued his lesson. "But I digress. In natives of the third strand—which strand many have aptly named the Wild magic—variant traits range broadly. Geishaiwyn, for instance, have a double gift. They can shift their features in small ways—nothing like the avieths, who change forms as completely as those creatures of the fifth strand. Geishaiwyn can also travel the leis. But the dual gift of shapeshifting *and* nodefinding limits them—for they cannot fully change themselves, and traveling the nodes and welds is quite beyond their ability.

"In avieths we find yet another example of a variant aspect of the third strand. Alone of the third strand races, avieths can wholly shift forms. When avieths are in their human form, they are as human as any other Adept. While unusual, it is not unheard-of for avieths to cross-breed with Adepts of different strands."

His mother brushed a long lock of hair back off her shoulder and smiled.

Tanis washed down the last vestiges of the crumbly biscuit with two large gulps of tea. "And timeweaving?"

"Timeweaving," she seemed to answer as she paused to examine a long wooden box upon one of the lacquered chests, laying her hand almost reverently upon its golden wood. Tanis had often seen her pause as she passed it. "Timeweaving is predominant among the Tyriolicci—a race better known as Whisper Lords—but only latent among the avieth clans. No other races are known to inherit timeweaving as a variant trait, though wielders in their graduate years may learn the patterns of its execution if they dare."

She'd reached the bed by then and leaned to straighten the covers, though the silk duvet remained rumpled as she moved on. "Not to digress too far," she added, thoughtfully tapping a finger upon her lips, "but it is pertinent to note that many other variant aspects of the strands exist—too many to impart in this lesson. Likely you have heard of someone with the ability to unwork patterns. This is a particularly rare variant trait found only in Adepts of the fifth strand; and Nodefinders exist—equally rare—who have been known to travel deftly across twisted nodes that none should be able to follow. Men who are born as Healers, and female truthreaders, are also bequeathed their talent due to a variant trait. So there are talents even among the talented, obscure attributes inherited or graced.

"While not one of these exactly," she continued then, coming around at last towards where Tanis sat at the table, chin in hand, utterly entranced, "timeweaving is neither common nor easily mastered, even by those graced with the inherent understanding of its patterns. Perhaps this is well, for the manipulation of time itself is dangerous. While the Tyriolicci take but the slightest skips through time, were they to apply this talent on a larger scale, they might take themselves far into the future."

She slowly lowered herself into an armchair close to Tanis's table and settled hands demurely in her lap.

Tanis thought there was something deeply magical about his mother—never mind that her entire lesson was an illusion so well-crafted that she seemed utterly corporeal. Even more than her skill with the fourth, his mother exuded a mystical aura that made Tanis think of her as nearly otherworldly.

"Were they to embark upon such a tremendous journey into the future," his mother went on, still talking about the Tyriolicci, "it would be for eternity." The tiniest furrow between her brows emphasized the enormity of this truth. "This is something you must understand, Tanis my love. For Adepts anchored to the tapestry, the future has endless paths; the past has but one. The past cannot be unmade, nor reached again once the moment has departed. Perhaps the Maker willed it so, that consequences might have meaning." She ended this sentence with a long, thoughtful look that didn't quite meet his eyes—for of course she wasn't actually there.

Then she gave him a gentle smile, pressed fingers to her lips in a kiss, and faded.

The lesson had ended, but Tanis understood that even this ending was an emphasis.

That consequences might have meaning.

He'd surely never thought of such concepts before, but now that he did think on them, the rationale appeared obvious. If the past could be blithely undone, even by a select few ... if the world might be remade over and over again, what lessons might never be learned? Without consequence, how could anyone gauge the justice or injustice of an action? And in the long term, what would happen to the culture? For no actions would truly *mean* anything.

Shoving his last biscuit into his mouth, the lad chewed thoughtfully and looked around for the next pattern. Then he paused in his chewing and looked again more closely. Finally he frowned. Nothing was glowing.

Odd.

Always before there'd been another pattern waiting for his attention, another lesson to be taught, at least until the sun cast short shadows on his balcony. But it seemed he was meant to ruminate—or at least to reflect—on his mother's single lesson of the day.

Pushing away his empty plate, Tanis reckoned he could reflect just as easily outside as in, and the day had dawned clear.

The cook, Madaé Giselle, called the weather along the Caladrian Coast 'fickle and tempestuous as a Hallovian tart,' and Tanis knew she didn't mean the kind of tart made with fruit. Since it could be sunny one hour and raining the next, Tanis dressed quickly and headed out.

He gave cheerful hellos to his household staff—so strange to think of them as *his*, though the zanthyr had insisted that he must—and exchanged pleasantries with his seneschal, Madaé Lisbeth, an older woman who was diminutive and soft-spoken yet often eyed him in a way that made him slightly nervous. Actually, most of the staff made him a bit nervous, for they either looked at him with embarrassed awe, like the rosy-cheeked chambermaids, or with all-knowing gazes, like Madaé Lisbeth.

His use of the Agasi tongue had become natural, and while he felt his vocabulary somewhat lacking for adjectives—or expletives, especially while sparring with the zanthyr—Tanis decided he was getting on all right. Much of his progress with the language was aided by the fact that his mother lectured in that same dialect, and what words she spoke Tanis couldn't help but immediately recall then and thereafter.

Before heading outside, Tanis looked for the zanthyr. When he didn't find Phaedor in any of his usual places, the lad sought out the one person who would certainly know his whereabouts: the tall, wiry cook, Madaé Giselle.

Neither tiff nor tryst went into the soup of everyday life at the Villa Serafina that Madaé Giselle didn't inspect. Her fingers touched every conversational pie constructed or consumed within the villa grounds, and she swept up crumbs of gossip just by passing through a room.

Besides which, his stomach was already growling again.

He found the villa's inimitable cook in the kitchen, furiously pounding chicken cutlets into pancake-like abominations on a long, marble-topped table. Suddenly unsure of his own position near the violence of her enthusiasm, the lad remained stationary until Madaé Giselle took a break to wipe her brow with her sleeve and saw him standing there.

"Why Tanis, lordling, what are you doing a-standing and a-watching?" Madaé Giselle wore her long, ash-grey hair in a sort of turban formed of a great swath of blue cloth, which was dusted that morning by floured handprints. She set down her mallet and pushed an errant wisp of grey hair from her eyes. "Didn't Birger a-bring your breakfast?"

"He did, Madaé. I was looking for Phaedor, and—" The sudden growl in his stomach announced his alternative reason for venturing down to the kitchens.

"My, you are a-growing yet," Madaé Giselle noted with a crinkling of wizened eyes, "and the Lady of the Rivers knows I've been a-pounding chickens since dawn. Come then." She waved him over. "We'll see what Nathalia has in the warming oven, and you can keep me company while I take my pipe."

She called one of her assistants to resume the beating of the chicken flesh and the woman Nathalia to fetch Tanis a second breakfast, and they sat outside at a wrought-iron table near one of the wide brick ovens that the baker's boys kept stoked all day.

Between the heat coming off the open-mouthed oven and the hot pear and turkey pie that Nathalia brought Tanis, all balanced by the brisk chill of the sunny late-winter morning, the lad soon attained a perfect state of bliss.

Madaé Giselle packed her long-stemmed briar pipe and fired it up, letting off a haze of smoke that smelled faintly of apple. "As to the Lord Phaedor, now my dearest," she said then, "he was a-called away before dawn to see about another horse claimed by that *drogue* beast." She shook her head and propped a scrawny ankle swathed in heavy woolen socks over the opposite knee. Tanis thought she must be at least sixty and twelve again, but she was a spry old woman for all of that, as knotted and strong as one of the Gandrel's ancient white oaks.

"I hope they catch the beast this time," Giselle grumbled with teeth clenched around her pipe. "Dional's been at naught but stalking of the thing since you and the Lord Phaedor were called that first day, and our ovens are a-feeling the Huntmaster's absence." She shook her head. "Naught but turkey and chicken is poor fare for the Lord Phaedor and our lady's treasured son."

Tanis was much more concerned about his mother's horses being killed than he was about what went into the pot for dinner. There was something inherently evil about destroying a Hallovian as that wolf had done. The image of Lilionath still sat with him, especially when he closed his eyes at night. "I don't know why Phaedor doesn't just help them find it," Tanis muttered, more to himself than Madaé Giselle.

"Well, it's not his job," Madaé Giselle commented, puffing twice on her pipe, "and the Lady of the Rivers knows he cannae be a-going round and righting all the wrongs in the world, now can he? What would become of the rest of us?"

Tanis gave her a long look upon this comment, for his truthreader's sense told him that she truly believed the zanthyr *could* make right everything that went on in the world.

Faintly unsettled by the prospect, he asked, "How long have you known Phaedor, Madaé?"

She eyed him askance. "Oh, as the years a-go, a long time, Tanis lordling. I've been a-cooking for the estate and your mother's many guests who come and go for longer than I care to admit. The Lord Phaedor appears but like the great southern storms—once or twice in a decade's time. Can't say as I know him well," and here she turned to look Tanis full in the eye, pulled her pipe from her teeth and gestured with it, "but I know well his reputation."

"But you knew my mother?"

Madaé Giselle gave him a long, considering look, one eye spying him slightly narrower than the other. She shoved the pipe between her teeth again and took a long draw. "There are things you haven't asked him as yet, I take it."

Tanis popped the last of his tart into his mouth and mumbled, "Phaedor tells me only what he thinks I need to know, and that's little enough." He brushed the crumbs from his lips with his fingers, sat back in his chair and crossed his arms before his chest, turning a look towards the apple orchard and the glimpse of blue sea beyond. "It's no use asking, really. I know that he only withholds what he feels is important to my welfare, and foremost, he would never do anything that would bring me to harm, even if that means not telling me some important truth."

"My, yes." Madaé Giselle's brow creased compassionately. Then she flashed a smile, and Tanis saw the shadow of a much younger woman in her features. "But I never thought I'd see this day," she said with a sigh, "the day you returned. What a joy this is to all of us—and what a handsome lordling you turned out to be! And so tall already, just like your father."

Tanis reddened under her admiring gaze. "Thank you, Madaé."

She gave him a tolerant nod.

"Do you get many visitors here?" It seemed an odd sort of existence, appearing overnight to cook for perfect strangers.

"Oh, your mother has many friends, but it's a rare few as know the secret path through the formidable peaks of the Navárrel to find this valley. We've a-plenty to keep us busy at the main estate in any event." She puffed a halo of apple-scented smoke around her head. "I vow it's a nice change when we do get company at the Villa Serafina, for 'tis only your mother's friends as a-stay here," and she added, winking, "and they're an interesting bunch."

Tanis was sort of regarding her in awe when Madaé Giselle pushed out of her chair and stretched with hands supporting her lower back. She was very tall for a woman, taller even than Tanis—though he had to admit that a year ago he'd have been looking well up at her. The years didn't seem to have diminished her spirit or her height. "Off with you now," and she gave him a smile that made deep wrinkles around her eyes. "I've got work to do or there'll not even be chicken for your dinner."

As Tanis was rising, Madaé Giselle tapped out the remains of her pipe over the oven grate. "His lordship mentioned you might want to work your forms in his absence."

"Of course he did," Tanis muttered. He wasn't exactly looking forward to another grueling day of swinging that Merdanti blade, although it *was* getting easier.

When they'd been traveling the Navárrel together, Phaedor had woken him before sunrise every morning to spar with him. Among those icy reaches, the zanthyr had taught Tanis hand-to-hand combat, starting with maneuvers that Tanis would use in specific situations—someone attacking him, coming at him with a knife, grabbing him from behind. They'd practiced these maneuvers together until they became second nature to Tanis, and he'd grown adept at them.

Gradually the zanthyr had broadened Tanis's repertoire, adding new maneuvers and connecting each move with others so Tanis would eventually be able to think with all of them and adapt what he knew to varying situations. At the time, Tanis had found this training remarkably grueling—getting repeatedly flipped upside down and slammed onto your back by the zanthyr was not an experience he'd wish upon anyone.

Yet in comparison to training *swords* with Phaedor, being shoved, spun, tumbled, flipped and otherwise tangled into painfully unmanageable positions was far preferable.

Contemplating the day's suddenly lackluster prospects, Tanis headed off, but just as he reached the kitchen gate, Madaé Giselle called after him from the door, "Oh, I nearly forgot, Tanis lordling. You've a guest came in late last eve. A friend of your mother's, don't you know," and she chuckled at her own joke. "Don't be squeamish if you see him about. He's a wretched face but a kind soul."

A friend of my mother's is here? Suddenly quite excited for the day again, the lad waved in acknowledgement and headed off.

A friend of my mother's!

A part of him wanted to immediately rush to this man with 'a wretched face but a kind soul' and ask all of the questions that Phaedor had refused to answer. Yet this very potent desire put Tanis in a quandary. He'd just admitted that if the zanthyr hadn't told him something, it was likely for his own good. What terrible consequence might claim him if he demanded answers of another ... answers that Phaedor was determined not to give? Would Tanis be testing the Balance? Or was it only a natural course of events if someone *else* told him?

How was he to gauge the right time to learn some vital secret?

Walking beneath the high morning sun, feeling its heat upon his head even as a gust of wind chilled his face, Tanis exhaled a sigh. Even his own conscience stood defiantly against him.

He'd just reached the centaurs' courtyard where his sword awaited when a sudden echo of surging waves and a brisk wind off the beach brought the smell of salt and sea and an unexpected sense of calling; Tanis felt the ocean's pull as clearly as if its waves shouted his name.

He'd barely had any time to explore the shore—certainly not time enough to find that beach whose song of rushing pebbles he so dearly remembered. But he could practice just as easily by the sea as he could in the courtyard, couldn't he? So he retrieved the bundle of weapons from the chest where Phaedor kept them and followed the ocean's call.

The apple orchard gave way to long scrub grass and twisted, knotty trees. With every step, the ocean's roar grew apace with Tanis's excitement, and soon he was fairly running.

That moment when he cleared the trees was as exhilarating as his first gallop upon a worthy stallion. Tanis stood and basked in the view of rugged coastline and cliffs, his cheeks flushed from the chill morning air as much as from the brief exertion, and then he descended the path to the beach.

A swath of sand spread between two jutting cliffs. Eddies in the dark water marked each end, rip currents vicious and cold, and between, the deep ocean pounded into froth against the shore. This was not a gentle beach—more akin to Dannym's rough shores than the tourmaline waves that lapped languidly in the Bay of Jewels. Tanis found it exotic and thrilling.

As he headed out across the sand, motion at the base of the far cliff caught his eye, and for the first time he noticed a man standing there. The stranger turned his head to look at Tanis, and then—in what seemed the very next instant!—he was standing just five paces in front of the lad.

Tanis might've made more than a half-uttered gasp had his attention not been claimed in the same moment by the flash of a pattern imprinting itself upon his consciousness like the painful afterimage of the sun.

The man's skin shone as black as pitch, while his long nose hooked over a mouth that seemed frozen in a perpetual scowl. Dressed all in black, his boots and britches were bound at ankle, knee and thigh, while his belted jacket belled loose through the sleeves. Tanis appreciated Madaé Giselle's warning, for who else could this be but his mother's wretched-faced friend?

The stranger offered unexpectedly in the Common Tongue, "Storm-surge." He flicked one leathery hand towards the waves. "Swell came in this morning." His face seemed frozen in a fierce scowl, but he'd the soft-spoken voice of a poet. "Any time one of the volcanoes on the island of Palma Lai erupts, there are stormy seas on the Caladrian Coast."

Tanis asked by way of nervous greeting. "So it's not always this raging?"

The man grinned, shrugged. "Well … Palma Lai erupts a lot."

Tanis noted that the grin did little to lessen the ill-aspect of the man's features, but his gold-flecked eyes were wonderfully warm.

Still feeling a little rattled by the man's sudden appearance so close to him, Tanis shifted his bundle of weapons to his other arm and extended his hand. "I'm Tanis." He willed himself to relax in the company of the Wildling, whom he'd immediately and correctly recognized as a Whisper Lord.

"Loghain," replied the Tyriolicci. He clasped wrists with Tanis in the western fashion. "But of course you could only be 'the babe Tanis,'" Loghain noted as he held Tanis's wrist in a firm grip, winking at the moniker, "though clearly a babe no more. To hear Madaé Lisbeth speak of you all these years, you'd think she expected you to be in swaddling still."

Tanis gazed at him in surprise. "Madaé Lisbeth spoke of me?"

Loghain gave him an amused look—or at least his eyes appeared so. "Ah, but you're legend, lad. Since the zanthyr left with you, the story of 'the babe Tanis' has gained near religious status to these folk, and you their long-awaited messiah."

Tanis barely heard the end of this, for his ears had hung like a fish on the line from the very start. "Since Phaedor left with me?"

Loghain gave him an odd look. "Well, yes, lad. On your mother's instruction, t'was the zanthyr took you across the sea." Missing Tanis's astonished expression, the Whisper Lord continued quietly, his voice floating upon the breeze just loud enough to be heard above the crashing waves, "I suppose Madaé Lisbeth has her right, if anyone does. T'was her cared for you in your cradle."

Tanis had never even thought to wonder if any of 'his staff' had known him as a baby. Now, not only did he find out that they had, but also he knew how he'd come to live with Melisande d'Giverny. This was more information than he might've gotten from the zanthyr in all of a week with Fortune on his side!

Fair beaming at the Whisper Lord, Tanis asked, "How did you do that just now? Cross the distance so fast?"

"I but walked, lad."

While Tanis could hear the amusement in Loghain's tone, he also knew that the man spoke the truth. That's when he understood.

Convenient that his mother had just been teaching him of timeweaving, how it was a talent of Whisper Lords, and now here he stood meeting one. Entirely *too* convenient. But what else could it be but coincidence?

Tanis realized he'd sort of been staring at Loghain while these thoughts found their place in his understanding, and he dropped his eyes again with a smile. "Sorry, sir. I … it's—I was just learning about timeweaving this morning." He looked back to the man. "That *is* what you did, isn't it?"

"Just so, lad. We call it *foléim beag*, the little skip."

Tanis hitched up the weapons under his arm—they were really growing heavy. "I saw a pattern a moment ago. I mean, not actually," he corrected, trying to understand the experience himself. "It was more like the afterimage of a pattern … a reflection, maybe?"

Loghain arched the ridges that passed for eyebrows on his leathery face. "Did you now?"

Tanis frowned. "I don't normally see patterns—not like Prince Ean does. Not like the zanthyr. I only see the ones on my walls when they glow."

Loghain gave Tanis a curious look and then glanced over towards the cliff he'd just left. "Have you ever seen a fire-starfish, Tanis?"

The lad shook his head.

"Well, you should, and you have some spectacular ones along this beach. Come, I'll show you."

Tanis hiked up the bundle beneath his arm and followed the Whisper Lord. "My mother told me most people who can timeweave just take little skips through time, like you did, but she also said it's possible to move further forward through time, though only forward, not backwards."

Loghain gave him a curious look. "When did she tell you this?"

"This morning." But at Loghain's astonished stare, Tanis hastened to add, "It *was* her, but it wasn't. It's … complicated."

"Apparently." The Wildling's golden eyes glittered as they gazed upon him, reminding Tanis for some reason of the zanthyr. "Well," Loghain turned forward again, "it is possible to move ahead in time, but it's perilous. There's no certainty of the span one skips when moving through wide swaths of time; gauging the moments rests solely upon the wielder's skill. For most who attempt it, there's no going backwards again to find the years that were lost. A grave undertaking."

Tanis looked to him, for he spoke with feeling. "You said for *most* who attempt it. Are there people who can travel back in time?"

Loghain studied him for a long while, his eyes now frowning in union with his other features. Then he looked away and said in a low voice, "*Theoretically,* under certain extremely rare conditions, such *might* be accomplished, but I know of no Adept who's ever succeeded." Looking slightly uncomfortable with the topic, the Whisper Lord motioned to the bundle Tanis kept switching from arm to arm as they walked—a long way through the sand, which Loghain had crossed the first time faster than a breath of wind. "But what have you there?"

"Oh, this." Tanis's face fell as he turned his attention to the swords and his purpose for carrying them. "Phaedor's gone with Huntmaster Dional, so I thought I'd come here to work my forms."

Loghain brightened upon these words—if such could be said of the way his brows seemed to lift and soften slightly. Tanis realized the man's ill-disposed features were quite expressive if one knew how to read them. "I'll be your sparring partner, lad," the Whisper Lord offered. "That is, if you'll have me."

Tanis gave him a grateful look yet tinged with uncertainty. He recalled too well what had happened to Prince Ean and Lord Fynnlar when they met a Whisper Lord on the streets of Chalons-en-Les Trois.

"That would be ... um, great."

Loghain chuckled and clapped him on the shoulder. "I vow I'll be a kinder pairing for you than the First Lord's zanthyr." He laughed again at this near absurdity and then spared a look around. "This seems as good a spot as any, wouldn't you say?"

Tanis set down the bundled weapons in the sand and asked as he unwrapped them, "Who is the First Lord, sir?"

"The man Phaedor serves, lad." Tanis heard more in Loghain's words than the Wildling had likely intended, but Loghain's thoughts were strong and full of reverence and obligation both. The Wildling added as Tanis was watching him, "The man I'm sworn to as well."

Tanis held the Whisper Lord's gaze, feeling suddenly apprehensive. "Raine D'Lacourte believed that Phaedor served the Fifth Vestal."

Loghain cracked the knuckles on both hands and then shook out his arms in preparation for their sparring. "And what did the zanthyr say to that?"

Tanis grunted. "He says his motives are his own."

Loghain seemed to suppress a smile. Then his gaze softened, perhaps in understanding of Tanis's apparent dilemma. "And which do you think is true, lad?"

Tanis sighed. "Both." He threw off the last of the canvas and revealed the blades within.

Loghain barked a laugh. "Merdanti!" He shoved hands onto hips and grinned broadly, his leathery black face looking ever the mummer's mask. "He teaches you swordplay with *Merdanti* blades. By Cephrael's Great Book, the creature has balls bigger than Belloth!"

"The blades are dormant," Tanis offered, albeit a mite resentfully. He held one to Loghain.

The Whisper Lord pushed both hands before him in amiable rejection. "Oh, I'd rather not put my skill to such a test as that would prove, young Tanis, dormant blade or no." He patted the chest of his jacket. "If you will permit me instead …"

Tanis nodded while his apprehension waxed and his courage frustratingly waned.

From inside his jacket, the Whisper Lord pulled two rolled leather bundles and carefully unfolded his daggered gloves. The razor-edged blades were nearly as long as Tanis's forearm. They were frightful to look upon and extended out of the glove's fingers like a dragon's claws. The lad couldn't help but think of Lord Fynnlar's wounds, the scars of which he'd been all too eager to share with Tanis, along with a morbidly detailed and dramatic retelling that necessarily emphasized his bravery.

Loghain smiled at Tanis's faintly horrified expression. "Would you like a closer look, lad?"

Somewhat in awe, Tanis accepted the proffered glove. At a look of prodding from Loghain, he slipped his right hand inside. Soft fleece lined the thick leather, while each finger fit inside a metal sheath—a fitted tube, even—that formed the hilt of its accompanying dagger. Tanis couldn't bend his fingers once inside the metal casing. The daggers were scary even wearing them on his own fingers. Tanis took care to point them away from his face.

He slipped off the glove and returned it cautiously to its owner. "A friend of mine was nearly killed by such as this."

"Oh, indeed, they're deadly things." Loghain pushed his hands into his gloves. Then he clicked his daggers together and added with a wink, "Though no more so than a Merdanti blade." He motioned Tanis up and into position.

Calling his courage sharply to heel, the lad took up his blade and faced off against the Whisper Lord.

With grave solemnity, Loghain pressed palms together before his chest, bowed slightly, and then let his blades slide off each other with a deadly scraping hiss as his arms flew wide.

Tanis took a reflexive step backwards.

"Intimidation is half the battle, lad." Loghain watched him in a quietly intense way. He drew one arm back at the shoulder, lethal daggers fanned forward, and held his other hand low and partly hooked, ready to eviscerate.

Tanis eyed him uncertainly.

"Come now." Loghain encouraged with gentle guidance. "Let's see what the zanthyr has taught you. We'll take the forms at half-speed." His golden eyes met Tanis's and held them firmly. "Begin."

Tanis's throat felt suddenly dry and his heart started pounding even before he took that first step forward, but to his great relief, he actually *did* take that step.

The first form was a simple combination, Cardinal Skims the Water, which involved cutting down right, crouching and then sweeping from low to high. Cardinal Skims the Water naturally flowed through Searching the Sea and Crouching Leopard into Holding the Moon.

Loghain didn't press him into Black Dragon Whips His Tail or Green Dragon Emerging from the Water, yet Tanis came easily to understand why Lord Fynnlar had nearly been killed by the Wildling in Chalons-en-Les Trois: no matter the form Tanis used, a single sword was just ineffectual against the Whisper Lord's daggered gloves! Every time Tanis thought he'd blocked an attack, Loghain would pause their practice to point out his other hand—the one Tanis didn't have blocked with his sword—which was invariably aimed at some part of his body that he very much wanted to keep.

Thus did their practice continue, with Loghain working him carefully through the first nine forms while also pointing out what *not* to do if Tanis was ever unfortunate enough to actually battle one of Loghain's Tyriolicci brethren.

Sparring with the Wilding was a vastly different experience from sword practice with the zanthyr. For one, the Whisper Lord took great care not to harm Tanis, and he would frequently stop their interplay to discuss a maneuver or to show Tanis how he was putting himself in danger. Once Loghain had assured himself that Tanis knew how to use his blade, he pushed the lad faster, with Tanis working hard to fend off quickly thrusting attacks.

Yet even this felt like practice; it had none of the vital desperation present in the zanthyr's teaching, for even in instruction, Phaedor fought with such fury and carefully measured force that Tanis's every decision truly felt critical to his continued survival.

The sun was climbing toward midday and Tanis had worked up a healthy sweat when Loghain gave them a moment to rest. Their respite was necessarily short-lived, for the brisk wind whipped the ever-present crashing sea into spray, and Tanis quickly grew chilled when standing still.

As they faced off again in their circle of trampled sand, Loghain pressed gloved hands together, bowed, and sliced his blades apart, assuming his position once more.

"You're far more advanced in your training than I imagined," he complimented with arms held ready, spiny blades aimed at Tanis's head and gut. "Let's move then to more difficult terrain. No doubt he's been instructing you in the *ta'fieri*."

Tanis grimaced. "Yes, sir."

Loghain smiled at his reluctance. "Come then. The *ta'fieri* is the only form effective against Tyriolicci blades."

If only not to appear ungrateful for Loghain's instruction, Tanis reluctantly reawakened muscles already taxed and began sweeping his sword back and forth in the zanthyr's torturous figure-eight style.

The *ta'fieri* of course involved more than merely making that sign in the air with one's sword. It was an incredibly complicated form to master, and Tanis faced only the beginning of its instruction. The moment he clashed blades with Loghain, however, he saw for the first time how truly effective the *ta'fieri* could be. Though they practiced in much slower motion than any reasonable battle would prove, Tanis could yet see that were he to build up the strength to perform the *ta'fieri* in true, he might yet hold his own against such a Wildling—if not, perhaps, against Loghain.

He couldn't keep up the *ta'fieri* for long, however, so he felt immensely relieved when he saw a man carrying a wicker basket descending the cliff and recognized him as his valet, Birger.

Loghain saw him, too, and he disengaged with a long step backwards and away from Tanis, followed by a brisk bow. "So … it would appear reinforcements have arrived." He cast the lad a wry smile. "I'll get a fire going."

Deft with flint and steel despite the blustery wind, Loghain had raised a nice blaze by the time Birger reached them, the valet having trudged unwaveringly yet slowly across the deep sand.

"Madaé Giselle sends luncheon, milords," Birger announced. He set down the wide basket and began distributing the meal while Tanis basked in the heat of Loghain's fire.

Birger dished out herbed chicken stuffed within round loaves of bread and smothered in wine gravy just off the stove. A flagon of mulled wine steamed when the valet pulled the cork, and Tanis and Loghain drank the spiced wine from deep copper mugs lined in tin, the cup's warmth a balm to Tanis's icy fingers. The lad wondered yet again what patterns Madaé Giselle had learned to keep the meals—like his morning tea—hot despite the elements, and who had taught them to her.

Then he realized he knew after all: it had to have been his father.

"Do you visit often, sir?" Tanis asked Loghain as they sat side by side with backs resting against a bleached driftwood log.

"It's been more than twelve years since I last partook of your mother's hospitality." Loghain's golden eyes flicked to Birger who stood a discreet distance away and back to Tanis. "It's a privilege beyond measure to be welcomed here."

Tanis was finally feeling his fingers again; food and wine warmed his belly, and his spirits were climbing. "What brings you this time?"

Loghain gave him a grave look. "Alas, I'm upon a regretful task, young Tanis. Would that it were happier circumstances that drew me to Agasan and your mother's home." He shook his head. "A grim task," he added then, "and one I don't relish. I needed some respite from this work … if not from my unrelenting conscience," he added under his breath, "and the Villa Serafina has ever offered both."

Tanis's eyes alighted on the daggered gauntlets lying in the sand at Loghain's side and he thought he could imagine what grim task the man was upon. "Why do you do something if your conscience is at odds with it, sir?"

Loghain gave him a rueful smile. "There is much in the First Lord's game that engenders regret, Tanis. There are enemies and traitors aplenty who would seek to undo everything the First Lord has sacrificed so much to achieve. I feel no compunction about stopping them from committing such acts, but …" and here he sighed, "a life is a life. One must never claim a man's life cursorily, nor be indifferent to its passing, no matter the doomed man's crimes."

Tanis wondered why learning that Loghain was upon an assassin's path troubled him so little, but he supposed it was because his instincts told him that the Whisper Lord was an honorable and kind-hearted soul. *And my mother's friend.* Even had his own instincts tended otherwise, Tanis knew he would have trusted Loghain merely for claiming an association with his mother—for Tanis had come to know *her* well enough through their lessons to know he could trust any man who rightfully claimed her friendship.

As the lad finished off his second sandwich and retrieved his copper mug from between his legs, Birger appeared at his side to refill it with more piping hot wine. Tanis thanked him and then looked back to the Whisper Lord.

Loghain's amiable nature and willingness to speak on things emboldened the lad toward questions he wouldn't have dared ask the zanthyr. "Sir," he posed as he sipped his wine, "how did you meet my mother?"

The Whisper Lord's face split in a grin. "Your mother," he murmured, eyes sparkling. Tanis caught flashes of his strongest thoughts, images of his mother on horseback on a deserted road … of her crystalline eyes gazing over a goblet, captured in darkness and firelight …

"We traveled together in my youth." Loghain shrugged bony brows. "I'm not sure why she chose me to accompany her. I thought at the time I was meant to be her protector." He laughed heartily at this idea and leaned toward Tanis as he confessed, "The ego of my youth stood taller than Mt. Pisah and even more firmly rooted! Not that I alone suffered this folly. I'd wager you could float a barge across the South Agasi Sea on naught but the inflated egos of adolescent Tyriolicci warriors. Truth was," he added, winking, "more often than not, she was the one protecting me."

Tanis heard a deeper truth in these words, but he didn't understand its meaning.

"Oh, to be sure I handled many a company of outlaws who got above themselves and thought to disrupt our caravan, but these were base ruffians, their attempts easily thwarted. And your mother is no fool."

"Did you travel together for long?"

"Two years." He cracked another smile. "I'm still not sure what task she was upon. We traveled at her bidding, sometimes staying but a night in a town and betimes a score of weeks. Your mother is unvaryingly fond of Kandori, and she spent some months there collecting stories and myths from the oldest villages and recording them in her journals." Loghain smiled with the memory, whereupon his golden eyes flicked back to Tanis. "Women are ever indecipherable, are they not, lad?"

Tanis thought of Her Grace and had to agree. "Utterly, sir."

Birger appeared at their sides again, this time offering lighter fare, and they finished off their meal with frothy meringues filled with apricots and tart cherries.

As he was masticating a particularly chewy morsel, Tanis felt suddenly compelled to ask, "Sir ... does my mother serve your First Lord, too?"

The Whisper Lord watched Tanis in silence at this, his golden eyes pensive while visions danced within his thoughts. "I think that's a question I'd best leave her to answer." He stood and looked to the near cliff, whereupon he frowned slightly. "Tide's coming in. It's now or never if you wish to see those starfish I told you about."

Feeling well stated with food and wine, Tanis willingly followed the Whisper Lord to the tide pools near the blustery cliff. As he clambered over slippery, wave-washed rocks behind the long-legged Wildling, Tanis felt a little like a sea creature himself.

They reached a crevice in the lengthy outcropping of volcanic stone like a blackened finger of blistered land, and peered down into a narrow corridor as the waves rushed in and out. Mollusks clung anywhere anemones didn't, and amid the display of tri-colored sea life, huge orange-red starfish staked their own claims.

As Loghain reached down to collect one for better inspection, Tanis crouched on his heels beside him. Looking up, he noted with a frown that Birger was heading back to the cliff, carrying his wicker basket with him. "Did you know my father also?"

Loghain glanced up beneath leathery brows. "By reputation alone. *Aha!*" Looking triumphant, the Wildling brought up a starfish and showed Tanis its myriad tube feet.

But the lad wasn't interested so much in starfish anymore. He rested elbows on knees and watched the Whisper Lord pensively. Both of his parents seemed whisper-thin outlines of once great individuals, and the lad fervently wished he might gather more details with which to fill in the bare sketch in his mind. "Will you tell me of him, sir? That is, what you know of him?"

The Whisper Lord returned the starfish to the tide pool and sat back on his heels to consider Tanis. "If I know anything of your mother, lad, it's that she's some plan for you in all of this. Trust her to tell you when the time is right."

Tanis dropped his gaze to hide his disappointment. "You'll say nothing then?"

"I dare not." He clapped a strong hand on the lad's shoulder. "Come. The day grows short, and I'd like to think myself less a fool than to rouse Phaedor's ire by idle chatting when there's daylight left for sparring."

As Tanis was reluctantly getting back to his feet, Loghain motioned to the empty scabbard at his belt. "I noticed that you wear a sheath but no blade. Where's the dagger that belongs there?"

Tanis looked down and fingered the leather sheath he still wore every day for reasons he couldn't quite explain. He remembered too well the morning he'd purchased it and all that had followed. It was almost as if the sheath had indeed fulfilled Her Grace's prophecy when she'd claimed that sporting a Merdanti blade was only inviting trouble. Sometimes he really missed Her Grace.

Looking back to Loghain, Tanis exhaled a long sigh. "It was Merdanti." He felt a pang of heartache, for the dagger represented so much now. "I gave it to a Malorin'athgul."

Loghain drew up short. "Surely you jest!"

Tanis grimaced. "It seemed like a good idea at the time."

The Whisper Lord let out a low whistle and observed cryptically, "My ... you *are* your mother's son." Then, casting Tanis one last wondering look, he jumped into the shallow surf and headed back up the beach toward their fire and his blades.

Tanis looked down just in time to see the starfish tumbling away on the retreating waves. He felt strangely connected to the little creature, as if they both pitched within a tumultuous sea, each of their futures full as much of mystery as promise.

"Coming, Tanis?" Loghain's voice echoed on the breeze.

And the lad hurried to join him.

NINE

"The difficult is done at once. The impossible takes a little longer."

– The Fifth Vestal Björn van Gelderan

E AN STOOD IN a maze formed of towering black walls beneath a bleak
sky. Rising from his knees, he put a hand on the stone wall nearest him.
It felt smooth, cool, and thoroughly solid. A part of him recognized
the Labyrinth, even remembered having escaped this trap many times …
innumerable times. Oddly, he couldn't think of the means by which he'd
accomplished any of those escapes now.

The Labyrinth's ingenious construction traps an individual's attention—
one experiences the feeling of being wholly caught within it. Yet in truth, a
single pattern could never hope to encompass an entire mind, for a man's mind
forms a universe unto itself.

The key to the Labyrinth's power is its effect on units of attention. These
nerve channels of reason connect experience with understanding; the lightning-
swift translation of memory into consequence. When attention becomes
trapped—when a mind is compelled to focus only on the Labyrinth—the
Adept experiences an inability to think other thoughts. His attention is trapped
inside the pattern and he's cut off from his own mind.

Ean couldn't reach the experience from which to derive the solution to his
escape; he couldn't extend his thoughts beyond the maze. Every time he tried to
reason through the problem, he felt his attention drifting off. He recalled only
that he shouldn't fight it—that fighting the Labyrinth meant giving it more
power.

Most patterns expended their energy creating some effect—a blast of heat,
the shifting of elements, movement through time and space—but the Labyrinth
was the pattern. Formed of the fourth strand, it devoured any energy put into

it, making its hold upon the Adept's mind that much stronger. To fight it was to surrender to it.

Ean exhaled a frustrated sigh and turned a look around. He stood at a crossroads of spiraling corridors. A glance upwards showed the stars seeming to form a similar dizzying spiral. Standing still, resisting the maze's call, felt like fighting it. So Ean picked a passage and started down its path.

The mind forms a universe that is shaped by an individual's thoughts and bound by laws of his own construction; thus, every Adept experiences the Labyrinth differently, and each one must devise their own means of escaping it.

For Ean, who had once been called Arion, walking was the key. Walking the maze somehow freed his attention ... as if in complying with the pattern's intent, it slowly released its hold on him. Bit by bit, pieces of Ean's attention slipped from the Labyrinth's hold as he walked. These pieces collected outside of the pattern's binding and began traveling the nerve channels of memory again.

Ean walked, and he remembered ...

Oddly, the first memories that returned to him were of Dore. Perhaps because the wielder's own pattern held the prince's consciousness bound, or perhaps due to Ean having seen and recognized the man on a fundamentally aversive level, but Dore's face had been seared into Ean/Arion's mind in association with a slew of vehement curses.

Each curse seemed to have a specific associated memory. Ean got the idea that Arion had attempted to pin Dore's crimes in mind for all eternity, permanently searing them into his own mental consciousness with a sort of marker, so that Arion—no matter who he became in a future life—would see Dore's face and remember the man's crimes, and thereafter exact his promised vengeance.

The first scene presented itself to Ean with startling clarity, all wrapped up in a complete package of recollection as if bundled and sealed, to be opened later upon utterance of the appropriate curse ...

Ean saw himself as Arion for the first time. He stood looking in a mirror—a tall man, fit, with dark blonde hair and aqua eyes. Ean saw intelligence in Arion's gaze, and perhaps a hint of humor, but mostly the gaze struck him with a certain compelling intensity. Something in the shape of Arion's eyes and straight nose stirred a different memory ... but no, that memory wouldn't come. Only this memory had returned, complete and whole unto itself.

Arion rubbed a hand along his jaw and frowned as he stared at himself. His manner was that of a man in his prime, confident, secure in the love of an incomparable woman.

He saw her behind him in the mirror in that moment and turned quickly to her. Sudden feelings of dismay and fury flooded him. "Isabel, what in Cephrael's name—?" She came and pressed fingers to his lips. As ever, her touch sent an electric current through him, but just then his fierce protectiveness overshadowed any other sensation. He took her hand. "The charges against you—"

"Any Questioner will see the truth." Her smile soothed, but her eyes held a deep sadness. "This is meant to be a warning."

"From whom?" He took her by the shoulders and captured her gaze. "Who would dare threaten you?"

She frowned and did not answer him.

The scene shifted, as if in a dream, and connected to a later memory that Ean somehow understood was part of the same recollection, though separated by a span of weeks.

Arion stalked down the central atrium of a massive library. Four floors of shelves towered above him, while the moon shed its light in gentle beams through the glass oculus of a dome high above. Circles of lamplight illuminated each table, but all stood empty save for one in the far back, near the doors to the restricted section.

At this table sat a slender man with longish hair that gleamed pale in the lamp's muted light. He was absorbed in reading a book. His hair brushed his shoulders as it fell towards the table, obscuring his features from view, but Arion knew him—there was no mistaking Dore Madden from any angle.

Arion slammed his hands on the table, and Dore recoiled in his chair. "I know it was you!" Arion captured Dore's hooded eyes with his own and bound the fifth around him, pinning the startled man to the mercy of his inspection.

The face that confronted him appeared much younger than the one that had cast the Labyrinth over Ean, but his gaze hadn't changed. Something foul ever seemed to lurk behind Dore Madden's eyes. You could catch a glimmer of it, if you could stand staring into them long enough.

Pinned against the back of his chair, Dore licked his lips. "If she did it, she should be convicted."

"But she didn't do it!" Arion felt his fury bleeding into the currents and quickly curtailed his emotion. A great many people would be vexed with him if he carelessly disintegrated Dore Madden and the Sormitáge Archives along with him—though he couldn't imagine any of them thinking Dore alone would be any great loss.

Dore smiled thinly. "The evidence is compelling."

"That evidence was planted."

Dore arched the faint wisp of hair over bone that passed for his eyebrow. "Be wary, Arion—the evidence was found in her own chambers, I'm told." He gave a fitful, fleeting smile full of cowardly threat. "Careful they don't call you in for Questioning, too."

Arion pressed his hands hard against the table lest they claw for Dore's throat. He said through gritted teeth, "I would die a thousand deaths before I see harm come to Isabel."

"You may get that chance," Dore smirked. "I hear Questioning in Illume Belliel can last for decades."

Abruptly Arion growled an oath and spun away. "In what universe could it possibly be imagined that the High Mage of the Citadel would work forbidden patterns?"

The question was rhetorical, but Dore replied in his abrasive tenor, a voice like the churning of grit left in a prospector's pan, "People cannot be trusted with power, Arion. Not even the greatest of them can drink it without falling prey to its corruptive allure. Isabel van Gelderan has drunk from that well for a very long time, and it has clearly tarnished her, even as it erodes the Fifth Vest—"

Arion spun and slammed his hands on the table again. "*Dare* you?"

The fifth snarled with his anger; an elemental wind snuffed the lamp, tore through the pages of the open book and spit Dore's hair upwards. Pinned as he was, Dore could do no more than return a wild stare at Arion. His breath came faster, however, pushing against the ribs of his bony chest.

"I could snuff you like a candle." Arion's voice was coolly controlled, but the fifth thrummed with warning.

Dore licked his lips again. It was the furtive advance of what loosely passed for courage in the man. "But you won't," he murmured, his eyes burning with a dark light, "because you're the magnificent Arion Tavestra, so incorruptible and bright, like a newly minted coin with the Fifth Vestal's head gleaming upon it."

Arion bared his teeth. "I could make it look like an accident."

Dore cast him a hollow smile. "How would it appear for the High Mage's lover to become aggressive towards a witness who may be called to testify against her?"

Arion straightened. He'd never wished to harm another being as desperately as he wanted to harm Dore Madden. Choking the ill-born life slowly and torturously out of the man would've been the fiercest of joys. It took all of his considerable will to simply stand there.

"You may have the rest of them fooled," he said quietly, "but you won't escape my vengeance, Dore. I will pursue you across lifetimes if I must—until I've made you pay dearly for what you've done."

It sounded a bold threat, but Dore's face went slack. "You have no proof," he whispered.

Arion tapped one finger to his temple. "In here is all the proof I require ..."

Time whirled. Suns rose and set and rose again, and images spun in a dizzying kaleidoscope of memory until the next one bubbled to the surface …

Arion ran.

In one hand he held a Merdanti sword while the other hand supported a shield of the fifth against an onslaught of fire and flame. Cannon blasts of power rocked the firmament and shattered the stone beneath his feet, or reflected off his shield to shatter the walls instead. He leapt fallen statues and dodged crumbling columns and missed not a step in pursuit.

Smoke and flame filled the wide corridor, but occasional breaks revealed the huddle of traitors fleeing ahead of him. They threw patterns in an unending stream, their conjuring growing ever more desperate.

Arion ripped these patterns out of the air and cast just as many of his own. Where his landed, men fell to the stones to be trampled first by their friends and then by Arion's fury. He left a continuous trail of bodies in his wake.

He couldn't see Dore among the mass of traitors, but he knew the wielder ran at the head of that bunch. Many of the patterns he ripped out of the air reeked of Dore's particular poisonous tang.

A thunderous roar shook the air and the walls and floor trembled beneath him, but this eruption was the product of another battle happening elsewhere in the massive Citadel: Illume Belliel's Paladin Knights battled Malachai's Shades and Björn's Council of Nine, with the fate of T'khendar and all the Realms of Light teetering in the balance.

No mercy would be found in any corner of Tiern'aval that night.

Reaching the dome still some distance ahead of him, the traitors sought to bar Arion from entering. They threw a net of patterns layered scores deep across the archway. Meanwhile they attacked the doors inside the dome that led to the node chamber—doors he'd bound with the fifth. Eruptions of power buffeted Arion as he chased.

The patterns barring the corridor were too many and too complex to unwork quickly. Instead he called the fifth. The elemental force of the world coursed through him, electrifying his blood, sparking in his eyes; for an instant he became a being charged of energies violent and reactive. Then, still running, he released his intent.

The floor beneath the archway mushroomed. Stone turned aqueous and rippling, and as it rose up, it pushed the net of patterns above it. With a thought, Arion reordered the molecules of the morphing stone, and crystal formed before his eyes. He cast the fourth into the glassy wall, while his running feet pounded in time with his raging heart, and he flung the fourth along his blade.

The wall shattered like a great chiming bell. Running through the eruption of crystal shards, Arion entered the dome.

They were waiting for him—Mages all. And Dore. The other cowards who'd waged this coup had already fled somewhere—elsewhere. The traitor Mages formed a line before the towering doors, a score and ten left from the sixty who'd first stood against him, and they raised their hands as one.

A storm of patterns pummeled Arion, forcing him to one knee. He might've used the fifth to push the patterns back, but he saw the Labyrinth concealed in every one. He pressed his fist into the floor to support himself while his other arm braced the shield that held the patterns off, his thoughts holding tight to that tiny globule of safety protecting him from a rain of destruction.

On and on the onslaught came. No man should've been able to withstand that bombardment. Certainly the Mages thought as much. Their faces contorted with effort and rage, eyes fomenting with violent power. They meant to annihilate him.

Well … he intended the same.

The currents told him enemy reinforcements were coming—Illume Belliel's Paladin Knights in force, coming to help the traitors they thought were true.

This would've been a very different battle without their interference.

Arion couldn't splice his thoughts into any more pieces—already his mind felt fractured, flayed. When he paid attention to his body, his breath came raggedly and every muscle ached. But he rarely paid attention to his body.

He would've liked to have stretched time to give himself the edge, but he couldn't summon the attention or the energy. Instead, he reached out to the currents. He let part of his mind flow with them across the room, and—

Ripped the fourth from the Mages' minds, purloining it for his own use. While they shrieked in fury, he spun his stolen power into a combustible ball and ducked as the explosion erupted in every direction at once with volcanic force.

The Mages flew through the air like tumbling dolls. The dome's glass ceiling exploded into a rain of deadly shards. Arion put kinetic propulsion behind the deadly glass. More Mages fell.

Now a net of compulsion bombarded his shield. It felt like barbed wire against his mind, a last-ditch attempt to hold him off. He jumped to his feet in alarm—yes, as he'd feared, they'd gotten the doors open and were slipping through the parting like rats fleeing a sinking ship.

A storm of running feet now pulled his gaze back to the corridor. The Knights were nearly upon him. And the Mages … he spun back to find them vanished through the doors.

All but Dore. He stood in the parting with a hand on the edge.

Their eyes met. Victory, challenge, fury, threat … all were conveyed in this single locking of gazes. Then the Paladin Knights came pouring into the chamber intent upon him—they thought *him* the traitor.

Arion breathed in determination and exhaled duty. The two were eternally interwoven in him, threaded into his very life pattern.

Dore and the Mages would have to wait.

He lifted his blade and turned to face the Knights ...

On and on came the visions as Ean walked through the Labyrinth. Every step worked the pedals of the wheel, spinning memory into threads of another man's life. Many of the scenes seemed to have no relation to the Labyrinth but only to Arion, perhaps connected to those years in which he was exploring the Labyrinth himself and structuring his methods of escape.

After a time, Ean grew tired of the steady influx of memories, many of them confusing and lacking in context. He had no idea how long he'd been walking either, for the Labyrinth contains no time—a memory can be just as vivid in recollection whether it happened seven decades or seven minutes in the past—but Ean had the sense that his physical body was growing weary, and this translated into a similar weariness of thought.

Reaching another crossroads, Ean sat down and exhaled a long sigh. Then he stretched out on his back, clasped hands behind his head and gazed up at the heavens. Once again, the stars seemed to mirror the crossroads where he lay. Wait—

The stars mirrored the crossroads.

Ean sat up swiftly, and a tremor of excitement thrilled through him, for he remembered an important truth: the stars weren't *part* of the pattern, they were its mirror! They could show him the way out!

But no ... that didn't seem right.

After a moment of frowning over this, he exhaled explosively and fell onto his back again. He'd obviously played the Labyrinth game countless times. Surely he would've left himself keys, hints to help himself remember the way out ...

Walking the maze had been the first clue. The order of the stars was another, but what was their message?

As Ean pondered this, his attention began to wander again. Some of his attention meandered back along the route he'd followed through the maze and the stories of Arion's life he'd encountered along the way. Other pieces spanned tentatively ahead. Most of his attention stayed on the stars, watching, exploring the relationships of their placement, seeking a pattern in their arrangement. After a while he imagined himself among them, staring down at the maze.

He could see it spreading out beneath him almost at once, a vast circular pattern of intersections, canals and dead-ends. It seemed to have no beginning and no end, no clear way in or out. Ean inspected the wall along its outer rim, finding not a single opening.

Then it occurred to him with a shock of awareness.

He was actually *in* the stars looking down at the maze.

In that moment, he understood.

He didn't need to *solve* the maze at all. The end was as unimportant as the beginning. All he needed to do was continue to free his attention until *he* was free.

It came back to him in a sudden flood—all the tricks he'd discovered in beating this pattern. This was *his* mind, after all. He could be anywhere within it. Be the sky, be over the pattern. See its structure. See its end. Be *at* its end with a simple thought.

He remembered now making the heavens, constructing them to mirror the pattern as a message to himself. He understood the meaning of that message now.

With a thought, Ean returned to the Labyrinth. He wanted to leave himself a better message—one that would help him escape faster the next time. The conundrum lay in where to leave this note for his future self, because every wall looked the same, and he couldn't know which crossroads he might next arrive in, if ever trapped again.

Arion had left a message in the heavens.

Ean decided to leave it on the walls—but upon *every* wall. He extended a finger and wrote in light, *Walk the path, but be in the stars.* He pushed this message into the stone and made it glow. Then he multiplied it, so that as he turned around in that circle of intersecting routes, the message glowed on every wall, endlessly repeated.

Satisfied, Ean returned his awareness towards the distant stars and took a mental leap. Pinpoints of light became gilded streams, a tunnel of brilliance. Soon he felt himself falling, but he sensed it was only towards the unconsciousness of sleep and restful recuperation.

He'd already left the Labyrinth far behind.

TEN

"You see things that are and ask, why?
I imagine things that never were and say, why not?"

— The artist Immanuel di Nostri

PELASOMMÁYUREK PERCHED ATOP a rock formation overlooking an arid valley and the Saldarian fortress of Tal'Afaq. The natural sandstone tower fell away steeply to either side of where he sat hugging his knees. He didn't fear the edge, yet he remained acutely aware of its danger. He'd gone to Tal'Afaq in part because Darshan had spoken of making *eidola* there, and Pelas wanted to see if his brother had truly done what he'd claimed. But he'd also gone there to brood, for the lonely sandstone towers of Tal'Afaq were unmatched in their isolation.

Pelas felt a crushing sense of betrayal at what his brothers had done. Learning that they were equally complicit in forcing him along a path of their choosing had him in turmoil. He'd often fought with his brothers—especially with Darshan, though he *liked* Darshan and rather despised Shail—yet he'd always believed they held each other in mutual esteem. Now he knew better.

Learning that Darshan had compelled him upon their purpose had infuriated him, even if it hadn't surprised him; yet he would've forgiven Darshan if his brother had agreed to free him. Odd that an act so egregious could be so easily put aside, but something so small as learning how little his brothers actually thought of him … this betrayal could never be forgotten.

Pelas exhaled a long sigh, wishing his breath might release the tension binding body and thought, might dispel the raging currents that clung to his anger. He didn't want retribution—though watching Darshan endure a few centuries of agonizing punishment held a certain appeal. Yes, Darshan had threatened him, incensed him, even broken his heart, but Darshan's argument had merit: they *had* been created for a single purpose.

Yet ... Darshan had emphatically declared that *they* had choice where the races of Alorin did not. To Pelas, this meant that they should've been able to choose their own purpose. The problem, he suspected, lay in Darshan's limited view—he couldn't see any other path for them than what they'd been created to do.

When Pelas thought upon it, it all traced back to his little spy.

Odd that a mortal boy could have such a profound effect on him, but until he met Tanis, he hadn't realized how dark his days had become. Darshan had compelled him to walk a path of burning stones, and the longer he'd stayed upon it, the rawer his soul had become. Tanis had braved walking the smoking stones of his mind with him, and in so doing, he'd shown Pelas there *could* be another path, even though he hadn't believed it at the time.

Pelas ran his thumb across his fingernails and eyed the fortress of Tal'Afaq in the distance. The concept of *eidola* intrigued him, but the idea of potential new paths intrigued him more.

Before Darshan took it upon himself to compel him onto a path of *his* choosing, Pelas had spent decades at Agasan's Sormitáge. Though he'd been upon a work of artistic exploration instead of adventuring with *elae*, he'd listened, he'd learned, and he'd made many friends. Centuries had passed since he'd lived and worked there ... dark years, with darker tragedy in between. Many faces had been lost to the turning of the Fourth Age, but he knew one would remain, one he could trust—a near miracle, that, for trust came to him as rare as diamonds in the sea.

He would take a risk going to the Sormitáge now, of course, what with his brother's compulsion in his head and the campus so rife with Healers. Living as Pelas did in the isolation of Hallovia's storm-washed coast, those dark passions implanted in him often slumbered, but they would come to vivid wakefulness again if disturbed by the resonance of the first strand.

If there was any grace in what his brother had done to him, though, it was that only the strongest Healers compelled that darkness from its slumber. Even then, with enough distance between them, he could often resist its demanding call.

But Healers weren't the only danger. His brothers had spies like spiders among the university's halls, and he had been well known there once, albeit as his other identity: the artist Immanuel di Nostri.

Still ... all experience was worth having.

Pelas stood and stepped to the crumbling edge, barely a foot before him. The ravine lay in shadow, but Pelas was of the fifth—he could sense the density of the earth or the exact molecular composition of the air with the same refined clarity as a master chef's expert tasting of a sauce, differentiating elements as the chef discerns flavors. Pelas knew intrinsically the distance of the stone tower to the earth below, the gravitational forces acting upon it, the humidity of the air, and the elemental construction of the rock. These perceptions were as natural as drawing breath.

A breeze rose as Pelas lifted his arms. Then he dove. Wind rushed in his ears and buffeted his eyes, making them squint and tear as he fell. Few sensations in Alorin approximated the feeling of unmaking, but falling at terminal velocity came close.

Too quickly, the ground rose up to greet him. Pelas summoned a portal and somersaulted into Shadow just inches before they met.

Socotra Isio leaned against the marble balustrade, feeling the press of conscience like the tide-pull of the years behind her. Her aging brown eyes gazed out across a valley of forested hills in a patchwork of bare hardwoods and evergreen pines—hunting grounds of the imperial family of Agasan—and beyond these, peeking among the highest firs, the spire tips of minarets belonging to the Empress's palace.

The Palmer's white habit and wimple covering Socotra's head and face kept her from smelling the forest's scent, but she imagined that she could. Indeed, she imagined herself back in her native Malchiarr, where the hills were steep, the trees immense, and mist clung jealously to the valleys even when the sun won its battle with the clouds. Increasingly she imagined herself there.

Odd how entering one's twilight years cast the mind back to one's earliest days to dwell. A century or more might've passed without thinking of herself in those forests—a barefooted child with a Nodefinder's adventurous spirit and a Geshaiwyn's nose for trouble—yet now such moments were the only parts of her life she wished to recall. She'd taken the Palmer's religious vows at a time when hiding her face appealed to her vanity. Now this same anonymity appealed to her conscience.

"Socotra Isio."

She turned at the address. Had she recognized the voice brought to her by her sluggish ears? Certainly her eyes made no mistake of the man standing before her.

A flood of warmth carried a smile to her features, though her wimple hid it from his view. "Immanuel di Nostri." She nearly laughed to say his name, it had been so long. *So* long, yet the man looked not a day older—still as strikingly handsome as the day he'd kissed her hand and lifted those devastating copper eyes to capture her heart. And then proceeded to break it. But she'd understood from the first that no woman could command Immanuel di Nostri; he was the kind to live free or not at all.

"I thought I might find you here." Immanuel's eyes danced as he looked upon her in her Palmer's habit. There wasn't much to see: an old woman in swaths of white silk. But then she remembered that Immanuel had a knack for seeing what wasn't there as much as what was—sometimes in spite of what was—a talent all great artists seemed to possess.

She held a hand out to him, and he came and took it. Her brown eyes smiled into his. "Startling that you remember my habits after all these years," she said, grateful for the silk that hid her flushing cheeks—*so* unseemly for a woman her age! "... but even more so to realize I've had the same habits for so long."

He kissed the back of her hand. "Our habits define us in profound ways."

"Spoken like a painter who sees the world only in color and light."

"No, Socotra." He held her wrinkled hand to his cheek endearingly. "An artist must see the entire spectrum to paint its many shades."

"Gah!" She tugged her hand good-naturedly from his grasp. "I'm too old for these flirtations."

He wouldn't release her from his gaze. "Do you miss them?"

"If by that you're asking if I miss our interludes, well ..." she shrugged. "My heart has mended."

He smiled and shook his head. "Women are marvelous creatures."

She eyed him askance at this. He wore his dark hair flowing and free that day, the way she liked it. She wondered if he'd done it especially for her and decided that of course he had. "And men are mules who need a good switching to learn their heads from their arses," she replied, "but you didn't come to me after all this time to listen to lectures on the nature of mules." Her wizened eyes looked him over. "Why have you come, Immanuel?"

"For your wisdom, my lady." He took her hand again and ran his fingers gently across her palm, as he'd done when they used to lie abed together, back when her belly was flat and her breasts full. "But what if I said I'd come merely to assure myself of your welfare?"

"Then you'd be a liar." She gave him a look of speculation. "And whatever else Immanuel di Nostri is, a liar he is not."

His chuckle reminded her of a zanthyr's rumbling purr. "Will you never give this up? I'm a man like any other."

"And I'm the Empress's heir!" She laughed then, and grasped his hand and tugged upon it. "Come, walk with me. Standing too long in one place now makes my bones weary."

Immanuel bowed and extended his arm to her. Socotra smiled as she accepted it, and they headed down a path together through the Sormitáge's Morning Gardens.

After a time, he said to her, "I sense deep turmoil within you, Socotra."

She grunted and flashed a look his way. "You always were too perceptive to be human."

"Tell me." He placed his smooth, caramel-skinned hand over her aging fingers. "What's troubling you?"

"Ah ..." A regretful sigh escaped her. "You've merely caught this pig wallowing in mud flats of her own making." She cast him a sideways look. "I don't want to bore you."

He smiled into her eyes and shook his head.

"Ah well …" A grimace as of pain pinched her expression. Thankfully her wimple hid all but the shadows in her eyes. "You may've heard rumors but now it's fact: Niko van Amstel is going to be the new Second Vestal. I've just received an invitation to his fête."

To his credit—for he'd famously eschewed Adept politics while keeping remarkably abreast of them—Immanuel at least had the decency to look surprised by this news. "I've spent many moons at Niko van Amstel's estate …" he frowned, cast her a curious look. "I wouldn't have thought him the best candidate to lead the strand."

She harrumphed an emphatic agreement. "Franco Rohre would've been a far better choice—not a one of us doesn't know it. The Alorin Seat knows it. Even Niko knows it."

"Then why not select him?"

She snorted. "He'd never accept! Franco is …" Socotra exhaled a sigh and shook her head. "I suspect Franco would know better why this whole idea reeks of wrongness."

His eyes crinkled with a sudden smile. "He was another of your lovers, this Franco?"

She stiffened at his impropriety. "*Former* lovers have no claim to make such inquiries."

Immanuel chuckled. He took her hand from his arm and brushed his lips across her fingers instead. "And what rights are invested to current lovers?"

"You're shameless to flirt so with an old woman." Her tone hinted of peppery affront, but her laughing eyes quite ruined its burn. The doors of a woman's heart never grew so hardened as to deny quarter to a handsome man. "Franco is … *friend* is perhaps too generous a word, but we've always understood one another. Of any of us, he had the firmest hold upon his honor."

"What do you mean, 'of any of us?'"

"We survivors … they call us the Fifty Companions, but *companions* we've never been."

Socotra sighed. If ever there was a time to speak the truth of Tiern'aval, these times called for it, yet the oath she'd sworn still bound her tongue to silence. More than frustrating, for her conscience knew no relief from its burden.

"Ah … of course."

Socotra eyed him quietly. She'd long wondered how much Immanuel di Nostri understood of the Adept arts, how knowledgeable he was of their history and trials. He'd lived through the Adept Wars yet remained indifferent to the tragedy—no matter the words he'd tried to use to paint some other picture in her mind. He claimed himself *na'turna*, only learning and working the Pattern of Life as gifted artists were sometimes wont to do, but she didn't believe a word of this nonsense. In her private speculation, she thought him a zanthyr's Wildling offspring, for she'd wager her last tooth he had something of the fifth in him.

"So Niko van Amstel will become the Second Vestal," Immanuel remarked, sounding thoughtful. They were approaching Tilden Hall and her chambers. "What in this most disturbs you?"

Socotra turned her gaze away. *A truth I may never share.*

Once, her secret troth with Björn van Gelderan had buoyed her, firmed her resolve, but now the same oath of secrecy served Niko's ambitions and drowned the rest of them in guilt. "Niko ... has not a clean soul."

Immanuel smiled crookedly. "Has anyone?"

She shook her head. "I fear the colors of Alorin's tapestry if Niko van Amstel takes power."

Immanuel considered her quietly. Then he nodded. "This is a fear I understand."

She served him tea in her drawing room while he stoked her fire.

Stoked indeed ... never more apt a metaphor had she found to describe Immanuel di Nostri's effect on anyone. Man or woman, he caught and held them captive with the simplest of glances. His every motion held a calculated grace, using never more nor less effort than efficiency required, and his gaze conveyed intelligence and a wry sense of humor. But Immanuel's vivid passion for experience is what truly enflamed Socotra—none could long remain around the artist without feeling that vibrant pulse of life filling them as well.

Immanuel replaced the poker on its hook and straightened to face her as she was setting the tea service down on a table between two armchairs. He stood waiting then, watching, expecting her to reveal her features or else the miracle of consuming tea without touching porcelain to her mouth.

Sitting down, Socotra unfastened the lower flap of her wimple. But this was not all she did.

The cloth came away to reveal a woman of perhaps thirty and five, exotically beautiful, with slanted eyes and the nut-brown skin of the Geshaiwyn people. She next removed her head-covering and drew forth a curtain of shining black hair.

His eyes softened. He came and bent one knee beside her and placed fingertips to her cheek. "Socotra," he whispered, "show me what is real."

She pressed her lips together and regarded him in silence. *Would that I adored you less.* A deep breath and slow exhale, and her face resumed its natural shape—eyelids drooped, flesh sagged, reforming before his eyes.

She knew what he saw then: hair still lush and long though it had shed all of its darkness, and the lines that deepened the folds of her slanted eyes and creased her cheeks like dry riverbeds.

Yet his smile showed none of his surprise at how deeply she'd aged—if he was surprised at all—and his fingers tracing her cheek still brought a flutter to her heart. As he rose, he leaned and kissed her, instantly reminding her of their heated nights and a shared intimacy that had defied words. He'd been an incomparable lover.

"You still flush at my kiss," he remarked with a hint of pride as he took his chair.

Socotra grunted. "I'd like to meet a woman who doesn't." She poured him tea and handed him the cup and saucer. Sitting back again, she observed, "I would ask where you've been these long years, but I'd rather know what knowledge you think *I* possess to bring you back."

His copper eyes danced as he looked her over. "One of the Sormitáge's leading *Sobra* scholars need not be so humble."

"But the youngest child of Gilden Isio had best be." She stirred honey into her tea. "What's your question, Immanuel?"

He settled back in his chair and crossed his knees with aristocratic elegance. "I've recently become interested in the philosophy of paths."

Socotra arched brows. "Just when I thought you couldn't become more intriguing." She considered him while he chuckled. "This interest is general? Personal?" When he didn't answer, merely smiled at her, as was his way, she said, "We Palmers believe all natural men have a path. Some walk the Greater Path, weaving a broad thread in the tapestry of all; some walk the Lesser Paths, so their choices have no impact on the larger pattern of the tapestry. Finding and knowing one's path is at the core of our faith. But this, I believe, you already knew."

He nodded.

"So ... ?"

"Do you choose your path, or does it choose you?"

"As in, are we destined to one path only?" She sipped her tea and eyed him over the rim. "Some think Cephrael moves us, that whatever path we walk, whatever choices we make, His hand is guiding us. Whether this amounts to one path or many, they believe each step is framed by His intent.

"Others believe every man's path is of his own choosing; that no matter where his choices take him, he is still upon *his* path. Epiphany's Prophet wrote lengthily on both ideas."

She set her tea in her lap. "Then there are those, such as in the Sorceresy of Vest, who believe only Adepts have paths, but that each Adept must choose between the two Paths of Alir—the heart-light. Every Adept is called to one path or the other, based on the song in his or her heart."

"These paths are?"

"*Hal'alir*, the light path, and *mor'alir*, the dark path. They're echoes of each other—harmonics—and in treading one path an Adept is ever above or beneath the other, its lighter or darker reflection. Every step, every act, reflects that harmonic connection. Since it is through each act of power that the paths are walked, an Adept is only ever one step away from either path."

"Is there a 'right' path?"

"The Sorceresy claims both paths are valid journeys, though I cringe to imagine the corruption the dark path works into an Adept's soul." She picked her tea back up. "But I could advise you better if I knew what you were hoping to understand. The subject is as broad as that of Balance."

"My interest is merely scholarly, Socotra." He smiled innocently. "You know how I am."

She grunted dubiously.

He chuckled at her. "So which of these multiple divergent ideas is correct?"

"That inevitably depends on who you ask."

"And what do you believe, Socotra Isio?" His gaze captured and held her. "Can a man choose his own path, or even change his path once he finds himself upon one he regrets?"

The question launched her back through time, through her hundreds of choices, for good or ill, through a Citadel dissolving in flames and a tortured oath of contrition beneath the Fifth Vestal's cobalt gaze ...

"Epiphany's Prophet says we choose. We *choose* what to do with our lives, what to make of them, or not, who to harm and who to love, who to protect and who we allow to harm us. She says the choices we make every moment of every day cast the path anew before us. Our paths can be straight or winding depending on how closely we listen to our hearts."

"What does this mean, to listen to your heart?"

"Epiphany speaks through our hearts. She speaks the Maker's will for us."

"If your Maker has a will for each of you, is this not the same as destiny?"

"Destiny implies you have no choice," she corrected, "but every man chooses first to listen and next to act, or not, upon what he has heard—or what he *thinks* he's heard."

His gaze narrowed slightly at this concept, so she clarified, "If two warring dukes both listen to their hearts, and both of their hearts tell them to go to war ... can they both really be acting on the Maker's will?"

He shook his head. "Can they?"

"Epiphany's Prophet tells us the answer lies not in the deed but in the conviction behind it."

Immanuel barked a laugh. "I see now why it takes so many of you to understand this subject. It lacks logic in every sense."

She smiled sadly upon him. "Faith often does."

He bowed his head to her in acknowledgement of this truth. Then his eyes strayed, and for a time he sat with his wrist draped across the chair arm, tea cup captured beneath his hand, one finger idly tracing along its rim. She could always tell when Immanuel's thoughts had taken him elsewhere, even if she couldn't tell where those thoughts traveled.

"What did you mean when you said natural men have a path?" he asked after a time, looking back to her. "You imply some don't?"

She searched his eyes, again seeking any clue to why he fixed on this topic now, when he'd shown so little interest in it before. Finally, finding nothing in his gaze, she said, "My Order believes that fifth strand creatures have no path."

He arched brows at this and shifted in his chair, settling chin in hand. "Whyever not?"

"Because they lead immortal lives." She held his gaze with a tilt of her head to see that he understood. "Unlike Adepts of the fifth, who must work the Pattern of Life to live immortal through the ages, the lifelines of fifth strand creatures are tied to the life of the realm. But the paths of the tapestry are woven of individual lifetimes. Thus fifth strand creatures have no place in the tapestry, nor a path through time."

"So *no* fifth strand creatures have a path?"

Was that a hint of disappointment in his tone? It was so hard to tell with him—he kept his emotions so close. She shrugged with a look of apology. "It is but one theory to explain their natures." She shifted uneasily in her chair then. "But when we speak of fifth strand creatures—zanthyrs, *drachwyr*—we necessarily speak also of Balance, Immanuel, for the two are inseparable. We Palmers believe such creatures have no path within the *tapestry*, but any study of Balance will show you that it all but *clings* to them like their own shadows, that their every action influences it."

Immanuel finished his tea and set his cup down on the table. "Intriguing, Socotra … as ever." His eyes that time looked her over appreciatively, making her flush, but she didn't chastise him again, for the places his gaze warmed in her hadn't known the heat of desire in many years. Holding her still with his gaze, he rose slowly, took her hands and drew her to her feet.

"I'm old, Immanuel," she whispered breathlessly.

One corner of his mouth curled upwards. "So am I, Socotra."

But when he fastened his mouth on hers and lifted her effortlessly into his arms, she suddenly felt very young indeed.

Pelas rose from Socotra's bed and dressed in silence. It had been a long time since he'd sought carnal pleasure from a mortal woman, a long time since a mortal had aroused him. But Socotra had always stirred his passions. She understood him in ways no other woman ever had.

As he was donning his pants, he felt admiring eyes on him and turned her a smile. His lean physique was not so imposing as his brother Shail's, rather the jaguar to Shail's tiger, nor had his bones climbed so tall as Darshan's, but human women had always found him attractive, which suited him fine.

"There is another group who affects the tapestry that I failed to mention." Socotra bent an elbow and rested her head in her hand as she watched him dress. He still found her beautiful; it had surprised him that she didn't agree.

"Who?"

"My Order describes them as vortices."

He cast her a look at this, for he knew vortices of an elemental nature; at the fringes of space, they became pools of chaotic power.

"These Adepts attract the paths of others and align them along their own, forming a broad swath in the tapestry, rivers into which numerous tributaries flow. No matter their intent, vortices bend the paths of others to suit their aims, even calling into their path those they'll need to accomplish their objectives—whether or not they even know they'll need them. Björn van Gelderan was such a one. He drew many men—*great* men—to his path."

"Björn van Gelderan ..." Pelas frowned slightly as he fastened the tiny hooks lining the placket of his silk shirt. He cast her a look. "He was fifth strand."

She lifted one shoulder in a shrug. "Vortices usually are."

Pelas fastened his belt and sank down on the bed at her side. He smoothed a strand of hair from her shoulder. "Thank you for today."

She rolled her eyes. "If you want to thank me, paint me as I was when we were lovers, not as I am now."

He planted a kiss on her forehead and murmured, "When I paint you, Socotra, it will be as *I* see you."

"Immanuel—" She took his hand as he made to withdraw. "What *are* you?"

Pelas gazed at her for a long time. Then he sighed. "If I told you my nature, Socotra ... you wouldn't like it."

"But I would believe it." Her eyes searched his. "Truth may be a stinging balm, but it's the only one that heals in the end."

He took her hand and kissed her palm. "I'm grateful for your wisdom."

Then he grabbed his coat and departed. She didn't ask him if he would return. In all their years together, she never had.

Night had fallen by the time Pelas emerged from Socotra's apartments. He paused at the top of the steps leading down from her building and surveyed the campus. In daylight's stead, the lamps lining the manicured paths had come to illuminated life; miniature suns, captured stars, they formed an earthbound constellation across the wide expanse of lawn. Dark forms passed here and there along the shadowed channels between—Adepts and faculty heading to and from their evening classes.

But Pelas observed the night in search of his brothers' spies.

Some he knew by sight, most by the feel of their minds, which ever remained darkened after a brush with Darshan or Shail's. He might've called a portal while still inside Socotra's chambers and avoided any confrontation, but he'd lingered for two reasons: first, he wanted the men who trailed him to know he'd left Socotra's home, that they might find no reason to molest her. Second ... he had a message for them to pass along to his brother.

He thought he felt their watchful presence as he descended the steps. They wouldn't attack him openly, not in that venue thick with wielders and *raedans*, not where the world could so easily learn of their activities. But he wanted to hasten their approach, so he headed across the lawn and into the woods, back towards the Morning Garden where he'd met Socotra and where groves of towering elms would hide their interaction.

Reaching an open grove he found satisfactory, he removed jacket and shirt and draped both neatly across a sapling. Then he turned a circle, gaze uplifted, searching for the right vantage. He found it in an arching limb thirty feet above. Thick as four men, the limb spanned the range of the clearing to mingle its branches with those of the facing giant.

One leap and his hands found purchase around the broad limb. The jaguar might not be as imposingly framed as the tiger, but it often showed itself faster and lither; it made up in speed and ingenuity what it lacked in strength.

One day his brothers would realize this about him.

In moments, Pelas crouched on the tree and cloaked himself in night. He marveled that neither of his brothers had yet learned the trick—a simple working of *deyjiin*—but it had helped him listen in on numerous of their conversations unnoticed.

He felt the spies before they reached him, for they pushed the currents in front of them in a steady, warbling wave, a reaction he hadn't observed in the currents before. Presently the spies appeared out of the gloom, and Pelas understood why they made such an unusual impression on *elae's* tides: they wore only their skin—night-black skin with even blacker eyes—and they reeked of *deyjiin*, heavy as a drunkard's stench. These then must be two of the *eidola* his brothers had been talking about.

Pelas remained quiet on his high branch, listening, frowning at the wood-slat clatter that passed for language between the two of them. He knew many languages of this realm and should've known the one they spoke ...

Then he had it. These *eidola* had once been Fhorgs—that told him immediately which brother had created them—but their stilted vocal chords made the language of Myacene—already guttural and chopped—into a clattering farce.

He watched them pick up his jacket, sniff it and look around. Then he scowled as they dropped it onto the grass. Apparently being bound to his brother didn't make them any more intelligent.

Or perhaps these two weren't bound at all. Shail and Darshan had intimated using different methods to make their *eidola*. Tainted by Dore Madden's influence and already too fond of compulsion, Darshan would've used the darkest patterns to sculpt his creatures, but Shail would've chosen only the most effective. Pelas couldn't be sure how these *eidola* had been crafted without inspecting them closer.

How simple to make the ground as mud beneath their feet. They sank like stones—he had to harden it quickly lest it swallow too much of them. The two creatures hissed and spat and pulled impotently at their thighs, but unless they could work the fifth—which he severely doubted—they'd remain there at his pleasure.

Pelas released his nightcloak and jumped down from the limb. The ground leapt to meet him in a sweep of wind. He landed in a crouch near the two *eidola*, who snarled what had to be curses; he thought he recognized a few words out of the flotsam their voices made of their native tongue.

Baring black bone for teeth, one pulled its blade—Merdanti, of course—and swung it at him, which Pelas easily avoided. The other's blade had been caught in the earth along with its legs. It growled a black-gummed snarl instead.

Just to appease his curiosity, Pelas tried a number of ways to harm them, but the fifth strand slid off their skin like water over tarred wood.

Interesting.

First taking a moment to refold his jacket, he moved to the *eidola* closest to him, the one still swinging its blade, and thought: *free.*

The earth practically spit the creature out.

It streaked towards him—a flash of dark lightning, faster than Pelas had expected, which impressed him. Fast, but not faster than him. He slipped into its guard, grabbed its arm and spun it over his back. It slammed into the earth with a thud, and its blade went whipping end over end into the grass.

It was stronger than he'd expected, though, for it yanked free of his hold and rolled-jumped-flipped towards him. It caught itself on one arm and slammed its feet into Pelas's chest. He flew backwards, somersaulted, and came up in a crouch just as the *eidola* sprang for him again. Pelas launched up underneath it and caught his arms around its waist. They hit the earth in an explosion of grass and dirt and tumbled again.

Pelas came up on top. He straddled the creature quickly, grabbed its head and twisted with a grunt of effort to the reward of a resounding crack. The creature jerked and then stilled beneath him. Just to be certain it was dead, Pelas put a hand on its stony chest and ripped *deyjiin* out of it. The body crystallized and then crumbled into black ash between his legs.

He looked to the other *eidola.*

It had gone quiet and was watching him with those dark eyes, perhaps contemplating its own hitherto unanticipated mortality. Pinning it with his gaze, Pelas stood and approached.

Bury, he thought, and the earth complied. He hardened the earth again just beneath the *eidola's* chin. It spat a clattering curse at him.

Pelas crouched in front of its head. "Would you prefer I bury you up to your nose?"

In reply, the creature glared malevolently.

Pelas held its obsidian gaze. He noticed the hint of *deyjiin's* violet-silver gleam in the depths of its eyes. "If you would live, tell my brother this: if he wants me to stay out of his business, he'd best stay out of mine."

He walked to retrieve his clothes.

"You're just going to leave me here?" The creature's crackling voice sounded like a spray of falling pebbles. So it *could* speak something other than wood-slat. "Like *this?*"

Pelas pushed his arms into his sleeves. "You object to being left alive?"

The creature glared sullenly.

"No doubt my brother will send someone along after a while. I suppose you've some way of calling him."

"He'll gut you for this."

"All families have their disagreements." Pelas slipped his arms into his jacket, gave the glaring *eidola* a cool smile of farewell, and called a portal for home.

ELEVEN

"He whoe suffers shipwreck twice complains wrongfully to the sea."

– a Caladrian proverb

TWO RAPS CAME upon the heavy doors of the High Lord Marius di L'Arlesé's office. He looked up from his desk as a pair of Praetorians opened the doors and clapped vambraces against their etched silver breastplates in a military salute. Through the parting breezed Giancarlo.

"High Lord," he said as he swept inside, "Vincenzé comes from the Sormitáge with the Imperial Historian in tow. You'll want to hear what the maestro has to say."

"Monseraut Greaves? Regarding?"

"T'were better the man confess to you directly, High Lord."

Marius considered Giancarlo curiously. "Very well. Have Vincenzé bring him to my salon."

Giancarlo nodded and withdrew, and the Praetorians closed the doors behind him.

The High Lord slowly closed the cover on the book he'd been reading. He'd hoped that reviewing accounts from the Adept Wars would shed some light on the strangeness he kept seeing on the currents—which ranged at times from a single thread of inky darkness to an entire tide of it—but he'd spent hours reviewing descriptions of *deyjiin's* effects, and none of those sightings matched his own present observations. He could do no less than count them as hours wasted.

Instinct told him this taint was manmade, but the Empress's repeated bleak conjecturing about the end of days had him mired in doubt. For all he argued against her on the matter, Marius couldn't entirely discount the possibility. What if the taint *was* a precursor to something far more dire? Was *elae* itself failing?

Marius leaned back in his chair and exhaled a heavy sigh. To think he'd lived to see such times. He resented how often he felt the temptation to take the palace's weld elsewhere—anywhere, just to some realm where *elae* didn't reek of death.

The High Lord thrummed his fingers on the worn leather cover and then he pushed out of his chair. He would hear what Monseraut Greaves had to say.

He entered his salon to find Giancarlo and Vincenzé standing to either side of the portly historian, who was wringing his hands anxiously. Marius frowned. "Monseraut, welcome. May I offer you a glass of wine?"

The historian looked up with immense gratitude. "Wine would be most appreciated, Your Grace."

Giancarlo went and poured the man a goblet while Marius took a seat.

"Well then," said the High Lord as he settled in an armchair. He considered each of the men in turn. "What have we?"

"Monseraut Greaves has been withholding information concerning the disappearance of Malin van Drexel." Vincenzé gave the historian a piercing look of censure.

Likewise offering a disapproving stare, Giancarlo begrudgingly handed Monseraut his wine. The historian drank half of it in one gulp and then lifted his baggy eyes to the High Lord.

Marius arched a brow. "Well? What say you to this accusation, Monseraut?"

"I know nothing of Malin's disappearance, Your Grace, would that I did!" He cast a despairing look of entreaty at the two Caladrians. "I—I had intended to find and confront Malin on the very evening he disappeared."

Marius folded hands in his lap. "And?"

The historian wetted his lips. "I went to the Archives the night Malin disappeared. I didn't find the lad, but I did see evidence that he'd been eating at his desk not long before I arrived."

"This is all documented, Monseraut."

Vincenzé flicked the man's arm with the back of his hand. "Dare not waste the High Lord's time, Maestro."

First shooting a fearful glance towards each of the looming Caladrians, the historian pulled a kerchief from inside his vest and wiped his brow. "Malin was working on his Devoveré thesis under my tutelage, Your Grace," he said then. "He'd been researching variant traits and their influence in history—it's quite an interesting topic, actually, it—"

"My patience wanes, Monseraut." Marius pinned the historian with a penetrating gaze. "Speak quickly and forthrightly."

Vincenzé seized his arm. "Tell the High Lord *why* you were looking for Malin."

The historian looked around at the host of inhospitable gazes leveled upon him and paled measurably. "I fear Malin has taken an … important work from the Archives."

"Taken." The High Lord drew back in his seat. His voice deepened with his alarm. "Which important work?"

The historian turned even sicklier in hue. "The first volume of the *Qhorith'quitara.*"

Vincenzé released the man's arm with a shove of contempt.

Marius stared at Monseraut. He feared his ears had tricked him, for surely the man had not just said what he thought he'd heard. "Are you telling me that Malin van Drexel vanished with one of the apocryphal books of the *Sobra I'ternin—in his possession?*"

Monseraut whimpered, "The Lady preserve me, it were not so! I don't see how it's possible. No, not possible. *Not* possible!" He squeezed the goblet in his hands and kept muttering fervent denials.

Marius looked to Vincenzé. "Get the Order onto this." He fastened an incendiary gaze back on the historian as Vincenzé speeded off. "Who have you told, Monseraut?"

"No one, Your Grace!" The goblet in the historian's hand trembled. "I dared not." He patted his brow with his kerchief again and said by way of seeking the High Lord's mercy, "It was a—a copy only. The originals are held in the Empress's vault, as you well know."

Marius cast him a critical eye. "Even a copy of one of the books of the *Qhorith'quitara* is still a book of power."

Monseraut swallowed and dropped his gaze. "Yes, Your Grace. Quite so."

Marius rubbed his jaw and considered the ill news. The apocryphal volumes known collectively as the *Qhorith'quitara* comprised writings and patterns from the *Sobra I'ternin* which were deemed too dangerous for broad study—even among a public of highly vetted and trusted scholars. In some cases, the patterns were considered so treacherous that any propagated knowledge of them had been deemed potentially hazardous to the realm. The works were also known to contain legends of near-mythical creatures—powerfully dark beings—whose names and abilities were better kept secret.

The High Lord cast Monseraut a fierce stare. "How by the Lady did Malin van Drexel get his hands on *any* volume of the *Qhorith'quitara?*"

Monseraut wiped his brow again. "Malin was assisting me in the archival chambers, and … I let him read a page out of the first volume." The confession came out as a squeak. "Under my supervision, of course! The passage applied to his research. We—we've let older students view isolated passages as they applied to their studies, Your Grace. There is precedent for it. My grave mistake came when I handed the book to Malin to replace upon its shelf, trusting too deeply and foolishly of his character." He gave the High Lord a look of heartfelt contrition. "I should have known the book would speak to him."

"*Speak* to him?" Marius shifted in his chair. "What do you mean?"

The folds of Monseraut's flabby face contorted with equal parts chagrin and shame. "As you noted, High Lord, even a copy of the work remains a book of power. I've handled the volumes enough to have become inured to their magnetic lure. I'd forgotten how intrinsically the patterns within them call to an Adept—it's almost as if the books exert some inherent compulsion that requires a man to read them, the deadly oleander calling the unwary to partake of its nectar."

Marius thrummed his fingers on the arm of his chair. "What information does the volume contain?"

Monseraut pulled at the collar of his robes to get at his neck with the handkerchief. "The history and nature of the *angiel* and the ancient races, a treatise on existential equalization—"

"By this you refer to Balance," the High Lord muttered.

"Yes, Your Grace. It covers some of the more esoteric concepts regarding the qualities and interrelationships of the strands ..." He cast a vague look from his empty goblet towards the distant decanter of wine. "Other things ..."

"I would like a complete listing of the subject matter covered."

"Yes, Your Grace. But if I may ..."

The High Lord gave him a mildly irritated look but nodded for him continue.

Monseraut wrung the goblet between his hands. "I mean only to bring to your attention that the volume doesn't appear to have left the Archives, though ... well, we cannot find it. As Your Grace may recall, all of the restricted level materials are branded with a trace pattern. They cannot be physically removed from the Archives without setting off a series of alarms, including fourth strand containment fields that activate around the entire building."

"Yet you cannot find the book using its trace pattern."

The historian shook his head.

"Vanished," Giancarlo observed, "just like the boy."

Marius found the news increasingly disquieting. He cast a troubled look at Giancarlo. He trusted the truthreader to tell him if the historian spoke an untruth, yet the entire affair remained so bewildering that it seemed some lie must yet be hidden within the chain of inquiry, befuddling and obscuring all that followed. "When did you notice the book missing, Monseraut?"

"The day before poor Malin vanished, Your Grace."

Marius exhaled forcefully. "Did you not think the boy's disappearance might be *due* to his having the book? That the investigating captain and especially the Order might need this information?"

Monseraut's shoulders slumped. "Your Grace ... it's the *Qhorith'quitara*—free of the vault, free for the taking." His eyes searched the High Lord's gaze imploringly. "To those who know its name ... would they not go to any lengths to claim such a work? There are Arcane Scholars who would kill to possess *any* verified copy of its volumes. Even among the Order, can all be trusted?"

"Someone may have claimed it already, Monseraut," the High Lord groused, but he conceded the historian's point.

Marius's gaze narrowed as he thought through the matter. "I must know everything about Malin van Drexel: his work with you, Monseraut; his thesis, his friends and acquaintances—*everything*. You will include what steps have been taken to recover the book thus far." He looked to Giancarlo then. "Tell Vincenzé I want a web of patterns crisscrossing the Sormitáge campus. If the book stirs even a breath of air outside the Archives, I would have alarms sounding across the Imperial ity, so even I may know of its appearance."

Marius leveled the historian an acute stare then. "Giancarlo will go with you to ensure your immediate compliance to these orders, Monseraut."

The historian's gaze flickered fearfully to the stone-faced truthreader and back to Marius. "Your will, High Lord."

TWELVE

"Few vices are more blinding than ambition."

– Errodan, Queen of Dannym and the Shoring Isles

THE ACOLYTE ORKAN Banh followed Dore Madden into the Prophet's chambers with the specter of death looming close behind. He felt its ominous presence hovering in delight, as if waiting for him to make some calamitous error and offend the Prophet.

Most who entered Bethamin's private chambers never reemerged standing but were carried out on stretchers, or wheeled out in a tangle of grey-limbed bodies by the two silent brothers walking behind Orkan. He only hoped they weren't following him just to watch him die.

Orkan's greatest desire was to Ascend, to receive the Prophet's blessing and go out into the world to spread Bethamin's doctrine with a Marquiin at his beck and call—at least, that was his expectancy, gleaned from his limited view of Ascendants and their Marquiin—but none Ascended who did not first please Dore Madden. Thus any time the Prophet's Advisor called upon him, Orkan jumped to attend.

He could just make out the Advisor across the dim hall. Orkan felt uncomfortable in the Prophet's chambers. The towering marble columns seemed placed there merely to emphasize the dark spaces in between ... vast spaces, as empty and cold as the Prophet's distant gaze.

A slimy tongue of fear licked along Orkan's spine at the thought of meeting the Prophet's eye. He suppressed a shudder and forced his legs to move faster.

The men following Orkan matched his increasing pace with shuffling steps. He cast an uncertain look over his shoulder at them, noting a pair of round, dull faces typical of the Saldarian peasantry—the kind of inbred hill folk that mingled their blood with M'Nador's Bedouin tribes. This pair looked too stupid to have the Sight, so Orkan decided they must be accompanying him for some other reason than his imminent demise.

Then he wondered: could it be that he'd pleased the Advisor already? Mayhap the Prophet intended to grant his Ascendancy even then! Surely he'd shown his dedication, proven his devotion in his unflinching service.

Orkan felt the specter of death receding. He straightened his shoulders, cast a haughty look at the two stupid-faced men behind him, and marched taller to the cadence of the Advisor's quick steps.

Eventually they emerged in a long, open-air gallery. A rain-drenched wind whipped in through an arcade of arches open to the storm. Every night that week Tambarré had seen another storm, as like the elements shared the Prophet's ill mood of late.

On a balmy night, the sunset would've illuminated the chamber with golden light and set flame to the many low couches, divans and ornate curule seats arranged throughout the room. But with the tumultuous sky and lashing rain pelting the balcony beyond the arches, the space seemed to stand on the verge of the world as if to bear witness to its imminent end.

The naked bodies lying face-down on the floor somewhat intensified this unsteady sensation.

Orkan thought it odd they were both prone with their naked cheeks mooning him. Though Death's grey flag had staked its territory upon their flesh, their buttocks still showed bluish bruises in the shape of fingertips—and not just buttocks but backs and arms and any number of other places where Bethamin had clenched them.

Verily, the Prophet had worked these men hard, claiming their bodies for his indifferent pleasure before apparently sating his hunger on their doomed souls. Orkan wondered grimly if those brands of the Prophet's attentions would cling to the dead men all the way into the Returning.

The Advisor stopped before the bodies and looked Orkan over with eyes like dark pools. "Are you ready to prove your worth to the Prophet, Orkan Banh?"

Orkan crossed arms before his chest and bowed reverently. "I live to serve the Prophet, Advisor."

Dore's black gaze licked over him again. "We'll see." He reached inside his robes and withdrew a bulbous rubber syringe, crudely forged, with a long, hollow snout. This, he extended to Orkan.

As Orkan took it from him, he noted the two stupid-faced men shuffling up behind him. He looked blankly from the syringe in his hand back to Dore. "What am I meant to do with this, Advisor?"

Dore's gaze swept the naked dead. The tip of a pink tongue feathered across his lips as if tasting sweetness , and his breath came faster. "The Prophet has expended his seed in these men. You must retrieve it."

As if on cue, the silent brothers withdrew their hands from their robes, each one holding a glass tube with a cork at its open end.

Orkan felt blood rushing to his face. He didn't want to understand what was being asked of him. "I'm not sure I …" He looked back to the dead men, and his face twisted with revulsion.

Dore placed a hand on Orkan's shoulder and leaned close. His spindly fingers undulated as they squeezed the joint, like the massaging tentacles of an octopod. "The Prophet's seed is valued beyond measure, Orkan Banh." He brought his mouth close and whispered, "Only the most revered might be entrusted with reclaiming it."

Orkan's stomach turned, but whether this response came from contemplation of his task or from Dore's probing touch remained unclear.

"Every orifice must be *meticulously* probed," Dore whispered. Abruptly his hand dropped and clenched Orkan's genitals.

Orkan drew in his breath sharply.

Dore squeezed. "Leave not one precious drop of the Prophet's seed unclaimed." His tentacle fingers undulated at Orkan's loins before releasing him. Then he departed without another word.

Orkan dropped his chin to his chest. His breath came painfully, clenched by disgrace. The specter of death may have receded, but only so humiliation could step into its place.

The peasants behind him began snickering, and Orkan's face reddened. He knew they'd be watching with impunity as he performed yet one more detestable, ignominious act in the Prophet's name.

Darshan was standing beneath a rain-swept portico that adjoined his private chambers when the sensation of Dore Madden's nearing presence interrupted his thoughts.

Ever the man reeked with the smoke of unwholesome desires. Wanton lust clung to his breath, making every exhalation a noxious fume of the darkest enticements, while the aftertaste of palpable need laced his thoughts. The Prophet compelled devotion from his followers—all that is, except Dore Madden, for Dore already thrust it forth like seed spilled from his withered loins.

Darshan traced the edge of his chin with one long finger while casting a penetrating gaze into the storm. Dore undoubtedly thought he concealed his deepest desires behind screens of the fourth, but no mortal could hide their thoughts from Darshanvenkhátraman, Destroyer of Hope.

He knew Dore lusted not for his affections but for his submission. The man dreamed of dominating the Prophet as the Prophet dominated his lovers. Often these boiling urges came to Dore while in the Prophet's company, and they gave vent to unbridled imaginings that Darshan found faintly repulsive.

A gust of wind brought the damp breath of rain sweeping beneath the portico and across Darshan's bare arms and chest. It was the season for storms, but Darshan's thoughts lingered on a different sort of storm.

"My lord, you summoned?" Dore's lust preceded his person as the man joined the Prophet under the vaulted limestone canopy. Even the wind and lashing rain couldn't cleanse Dore's reek from the air.

Darshan clasped hands behind his back. The wind whipped through his fine linen pants, reforming their shape around his muscular legs, but it barely stirred his heavy mane of hundreds of long braids.

"I'm concerned what my brother Pelas knows of my activities." Darshan aimed a look at Dore. "He cannot be allowed to interfere."

Dore's pale pink tongue flickered across even paler flesh. "Would you do another binding, my lord?" His eyes gleamed with the prospect. Compulsion patterns were Dore's favorite.

Darshan's gaze tightened, the only conveyance of his displeasure. "No. The existing binding you suggested has already fomented too much contention between us."

Dore took a step forward, and a dark light came into his eyes. "No doubt you're right to suspect him, my lord. My informants tell me the Lord Pelas has been seen often at Niko van Amstel's manor, posing once more as that painter, Immanuel di Nostri."

"I don't need my own perceptions validated by you, Dore Madden." The Prophet's words lashed like a whip.

Dore ducked his head and backed off, whispering, "Yes, my lord," but his thoughts quivered with pleasure.

Darshan turned away with a scowl. "What can be done besides binding Pelas? How else might I stop his inevitable intervention?"

"Perhaps ..." Dore sought the Prophet's favor with an unctuous smile, both ingratiating and corpselike. "This is only an idea, my lord ... but ... might you take away his power?"

The Prophet's eyes flashed. "Our power is not extended and denied as a woman's affections, Dore Madden. We are immortal; likewise our ability. Yet ..." Darshan exhaled a slow, contemplative breath, and his gaze narrowed as the idea took on a dangerous attraction. "I confess ... a helpless Pelas appeals to me mightily. I mislike his intimations of late. He means to betray me."

The wind gusted beneath the portico, bringing a sting of rain. It pushed Dore Madden's pale hair into his eyes. He licked his lips once more. "There *is* a way it could be done, my lord."

The Prophet looked to him sharply. "Tell me how."

Dore brightened. "Trickery. Deception. The same principles that worked the first time in claiming Lord Pelas's mind will aid you again. We must act quickly and call upon the Lord Abanachtran to be certain the trap is effectively laid."

As Dore continued explaining the details of his idea, Darshan felt a lingering dissonance smoothing inside him. His recent interchanges with Pelas had formed a discordant harmony, but this ... surely this solution would resolve Pelas's fractious belligerence into melodious obedience.

Yes ... Darshan saw at last the two of them working side by side to claim this world and exact their purpose upon it. The idea pleased him mightily. Darshan stroked his chin with thumb and forefinger and idly contemplated what he and his brother might accomplish once they were reunited in purpose.

"Pelas must be contained and brought to me," he ordered, seeing already a new future expanding to the horizon. "This should not prove difficult, for he maintains a foolishly innocent trust of others—" and he added with a glance at Dore, "even of me. Even now."

Dore's eyes burned with dark delight. He bowed, murmured, "Your will be done, my lord," and departed to become the mortal hand of his master's divine intent.

THIRTEEN

"Time makes heroes of traitors and fools of the wise."

– The Immortal Bard Drake di Matteo

F RANCO PAUSED AT the jungle's edge overlooking the impressive length of lawn. It spread like a luminous, silver-dark skirt around Niko van Amstel's candlelit mansion. As he stood there battling with indecision, a sudden flare pulsed along the second strand and sent a current of additional pain through his still-pounding head. A moment later, the pirate stepped across the node behind him.

The stone archway at his back was one of many that newly graced Niko's estate. Franco could see three similar portals from his high vantage, each demarking a node rerouted from elsewhere in the realm directly to Niko's door.

Just like Illume Belliel ...

Franco watched a group of men arrive through an archway nearer the house and join the end of a long line snaking out from Niko's front door. He doubted even a fraction of Niko's guests knew how the arrangement of archways mimicked the nodecourts on Illume Belliel. With typical outrageous presumption, Niko was setting up his home as Alorin's unique version of the cityworld—*Shadow take the arrogant bastard.*

"You never mentioned he was so popular," Carian observed as he moved to Franco's side.

Franco turned the pirate a rueful eye. The islander looked uncharacteristically venerable in a formal velvet jacket and matching waistcoat of muted grey. With his wild hair neatly plaited into a club and his usual five-day beard shaved clean, he could nearly be mistaken for a nobleman—except for the ear and nose-rings, which somewhat sullied the effect.

"Niko cultivates popularity like cooks grow tomatoes," Franco muttered. He looked back to the mansion wearing a sour expression.

"Sounds like a real charmer."

"Unfortunately."

Carian sucked on a tooth and eyed the distant manor. Guests crowded against the illuminated windows and spilled out onto terraces bordering the lawn. "So ... what's our plan, Admiral?"

Franco cast him a strained look. The pirate insisted on calling him admiral despite his protests. "What makes you think I have a plan?"

"Don't you?"

"Trying to outthink Niko's megalomania results in unpredictable outcomes, Carian. I've found it best to play things by ear."

"So we're sailing it close to the wind, eh?" Carian grinned and elbowed him in the arm. "No worries, Admiral. I've got the helm." He sauntered off down the hill with his usual long-legged gait.

Franco followed, cursing silently to himself.

They made their way inside via one of the terraces and began the tedious process of maneuvering through the throng. Already feeling like one of a thousand carp in an overstuffed vat of brine, Franco chose a goblet of wine from an offering steward and nodded to Carian to follow him towards a drawing room. He stopped just without the archway and scanned the guests inside with an eye for faces known to him. Guests milled like trees shifting in the wind, and through a break, Franco saw a gathering of Companions.

Coldly beautiful, a tall woman stood talking to another, portly and shorter, who stood with her back turned but whose round form was unmistakable. "The blonde woman is the Healer Laira di Giancora," Franco murmured to Carian as he took a sip of wine, "and her companion is the Healer Mian Gartelt. They're two peas in a poisonous pod."

Just beyond the women, the darkly bearded truthreader Gannon Bair was casting his colorless gaze across the top of his goblet as he drank amid a circle of well-dressed men. Loudest among them was the ever-rakish Demetrio Consuevé, whose very presence made Franco's wine sour on his tongue.

If ever Dore Madden had a protégé, Consuevé was it. He'd been the type of twisted boy to put a hungry rat in a box of mice and watch the creature feast, the type to pull the feathers from a bird's wings and then drop it from a roof to see if it could fly. Consuevé's dark sense of humor had appealed to Dore, and Franco had often seen them together in the Sormitáge halls, with the elder Dore whispering gleefully into the younger boy's impressionable ear.

During the wars, Consuevé had been too young to fight for the Adept resistance and too unreliable even for Dore to have involved him in their failed coup. He'd stayed at university while his compatriots died. Franco loathed him.

"Recognize anyone else?" Carian asked low into his ear.

"The truthreader in the kilt is Gannon Bair. He hails from Hallovia, but he serves in Queen Indora's court in Veneisea alongside the man on his left, Elien ap'Gentrys, who is one of Indora's wielders."

"What about the dark drink in the middle there? Is he their leader?"

"That's Demetrio Consuevé," Franco growled, not caring to keep the disgust from his tone. "He's an Espial for the Arch Duke of Rimaldi and in our day was Dore Madden's favorite disciple." Franco took a long draw on his wine, but he couldn't wash away the aversion that flavored it now. "We should go."

Carian peered curiously at him. "If we're supposed to be gathering intelligence, we'll have to start somewhere."

"Not here." Franco nudged the pirate away, taking care to avoid the Companions' notice.

The press of guests moving through the mansion pulled Franco and Carian along, and they followed the flow of others ogling Niko's vast art collection. The current of bodies took them into a long gallery split down the middle by marble sculptures set on identical bases of black onyx. Along the ceiling and walls, colorful oil paintings depicted august men and scantily clad women frolicking within their gilded moldings.

"Franco Rohre."

Franco turned at the familiar voice—one of few he actually welcomed—to see Devangshu Vita approaching through the crowd. The Bemothi Nodefinder wore a knee-length emerald coat covered in gold embroidery. Dark-haired, caramel-skinned and brown-eyed, Devangshu walked with challenge at one hand and cunning at the other, imparting him with a roguish demeanor that his aristocratic blood only partially dampened.

He eyed Carian speculatively as he took Franco's arm and said low into his ear, "I thought I saw you head this way. Half the hall is on the lookout for you."

Franco clasped wrists with the Nodefinder and then held a hand towards Carian. "Devangshu Vita, may I present the Nodefinder Carian vran Lea."

Devangshu did a double-take on the pirate. Then he turned a fierce look back to Franco. Abruptly he snared both Franco and Carian by their elbows and moved them rapidly into an isolated alcove, half-obscured by a curtain. He whispered, quick and low, "I've heard your two names mentioned often of late, and among company that I daresay you'd not want speaking of you at all."

Carian smirked. "Is that so?"

Devangshu eyed him critically. "Coincidence, perhaps, that your names are both spoken of in association with the destruction of Rethynnea's Temple of the Vestals, and now here you appear together?" When neither Carian nor Franco said a word to deny this, Devangshu hissed, "By Cephrael's Great Book, if there's any truth to these rumors you can't be seen together here. You're the talk of three continents. Franco, Seth is loudly declaiming you've allied with the Fifth Vestal and curses your name to anyone who will listen—which is quite a few among this bunch." He turned his dark Bemothi eyes to look over the pirate. "And you, Carian vran Lea, he won't say what role you played, but he's got the entire Guild on the lookout for you." Devangshu grunted incredulously and shook his head. "Alshiba *herself* is here, Franco, and rumor has it she hasn't come for Niko but in search of you."

Franco could barely think for the pounding in his head. He desperately wanted to crawl into a dark corner and drown himself in wine.

Yes, dissipation is ever the coward's retreat. Go on then. Hide your head in the sand—as though the crimes etched into your flesh won't be visible if only you close your eyes.

Franco pinched his brow. He felt woefully ill-suited to a spy's artful and devious craft. Espionage didn't suit him.

No, craven despair fits you so much better.

Carian meanwhile saluted Devangshu with his goblet. "Rethynnea is the least of my accomplishments, mate. But I've heard of you, as well. My pal Kardashian had plenty to say of your work for the Grand Duchess of Kroth. Said he had quite a time getting to her jewels, thanks to you," and he winked at this last.

Devangshu's eyes widened. "*Kardashian.*" He bent his head and asked low in Carian's ear, "You know the thief well, do you?"

Carian drew back to cast the man a guarded look. "Possibly."

Devangshu dropped his voice even lower. "I've heard word Kardashian is here tonight. You would recognize him? Even ... put me in touch with him?"

"Well, that depends."

Devangshu eyed him critically. "On?"

Carian flashed a toothy grin. "On how much you're offering for my introduction." He clapped the Bemothi on the shoulder and aimed a look at Franco as he guided Devangshu away, saying, "Let's you and I have another drink and discuss the terms of our accord."

As Franco watched them go, he silently cursed the Vestals, the Malorin'athgul Rinokh, and every Companion he could think of. Yet in truth, he knew if it hadn't been for his own stupidity three centuries ago, he'd have been several lifetimes distant from Björn van Gelderan's infernal game by now.

Once the pirate's tall head finally vanished into the crowd, Franco turned and headed in the opposite direction.

Shade and darkness. Alshiba is here?

Dread filled the air so thickly that he nearly choked on it. He'd understood and accepted some risk in coming to Niko's fête, but he'd never imagined having to face off against the Alorin Seat herself. At the slightest provocation, Alshiba Torinin would drag him to Illume Belliel for interrogation—and it was now his word against the Third Vestal Seth Silverbow's. He felt ill just contemplating the mush his brain would become when set as the battleground for a duel between Illume Belliel's Questioners and the truthbindings set in place by the Fourth and Fifth Vestals.

"Franco? *Franco*, it *is* you!"

Franco halted and closed his eyes with a grimace. Fate was pulling no punches that night. In fact, Franco was coming to fear Fate quite had it in for him.

The courtier's role he'd played for so long came to his aid, fitting him like an old cloak worn thin but still conformed to his shape. Summoning a smile, he turned to greet the Healer Mian Gartelt, took her hand and made a little bow as he kissed it. "Mian, always a pleasure."

Mian's cherubic face beamed. "We've been on the lookout for you all night." She looped her arm through Franco's and drew him towards the room of Companions he'd been so eager to avoid. "I must say, countless people are asking to meet you. You must tell us what happened at the Temple of the Vestals. Have you seen Raine D'Lacourte since the devastation? Does he live?" Mian ever thrived on bloody gossip, and her eyes were bright with the expectation of juicing Franco for all he was worth. She gave a little giggle. "Oh, it's quite the topic of speculation!"

"I really don't know what I could add, Mian."

"But you were there! Everyone says so."

"I suppose everyone would know."

She gave him a chiding look and a little pout, which on a lovelier lady might've been provocative but on her chubby face merely appeared sullen. "You're not going to be uninteresting and declare yourself truthbound, are you, Franco? You were so dreadfully honorable before the wars, but I thought you'd changed."

He arched a brow. "I can't say honor has been foremost among my surviving attributes, Mian."

"That's a relief." She pushed a lock of hair from her blue eyes with absent annoyance. "Honorable men are ever so tedious."

Mian drew him further down the gallery, prattling gleefully about those of their Companions who'd recently been found a bloody ruin, fodder for a Tyriolicci's blades. Franco barely kept his loathing in check, yet none of this showed in his face; how easily dissembling came to him now.

The Fifth Vestal was right to condemn you on Tiern'aval. You deserve this fate.

"Are you listening, Franco?" Mian tugged on his arm. "I said *Niko* is waving us over—look!" She made a beeline for the realm's newest Vestal.

Feeling like he tumbled ever deeper into an abyss, Franco steeled himself to meet their host.

Niko's handsome face lifted with a smile as they approached. "Ah, Franco—Franco!" Niko embraced him and then drew back to take him by both shoulders. "How honored I am by your presence here on this special night, my old friend."

Franco forced a smile. "Where else would I be?"

Niko looked to Mian. "Thank you for unearthing this treasure, Mian, but will you excuse us a moment, my dear?"

"Of course, *Your Excellency*." Mian bobbed a curtsy and fastened Niko with a look of vapid adoration as she moved off.

Niko took Franco by the arm—Franco was beginning to feel everyone's favorite ragdoll, dragged by the arm hither and yon—and remarked in a low voice, "I detect your usual dry humor, my friend, but there are some—albeit a very few—who did refuse to attend my fête tonight. In their vanity, no doubt, they felt themselves more worthy of the Vestal ring and now use my elevation as a reason to bemoan and sulk like petulant children—oh, thank you." He chose two goblets from a steward, offered one to Franco in exchange for the empty one in his hand, and sipped his own as he continued, "Such misbehavior cannot go unpunished, you will certainly agree."

A cold unease coiled in Franco's stomach. *And just how are you planning to effect such punishment?*

Niko started them walking down the gallery again, giving Franco the repulsive sensation of being on parade. He said low into Franco's ear, "As I promised when you came to me so many moons ago, you will see changes now that I'm in power." He smiled and nodded at someone in the crowd, but he kept Franco clutched firmly in his hold as he continued, "The realm has long withered from lack of strong leadership—and especially our strand. It's a burden to be certain, bearing sole responsibility for restoring Balance in the land."

Franco managed a thin smile of encouragement while his stomach churned in violent somersaults of outrage.

Niko sighed and affected a look of significant forbearance. "Tis a grave weight I've taken upon my humble shoulders."

"How noble of you to accept the Vestalship when it has so clearly been thrust upon you." Really the man could not have been more vile.

Incredible. You actually made that sound sincere.

"I knew you would understand, Franco." Niko wrapped his arm around Franco's shoulder, still guiding them down the gallery. Everyone stared as they passed—some with curiosity, most with envy. "Since we were roommates together, you have ever understood me."

Better than you can imagine.

"But I've been hearing distressing tales of you, my old friend. Of course I never believe such gossip." He gave Franco a smile saturated with insincerity while his eyes speared Franco, probing for explanation. "As the Second Vestal, of course I must investigate such remarkable rumors, even when they involve old friends." When Franco said nothing, Niko added, "Alshiba herself has come in the hopes of speaking with you, but perhaps things would go better for you if I might stand in support of your name. Of course, I would need to know the truth of things."

Franco eyed him remotely. "A magnanimous offer, Niko, but I couldn't bear the thought." *Really, I couldn't bear it.*

Niko took the comment as Franco expected he would. "How honorable you are, Franco. You never were one to foist responsibility on another's shoulders. But don't be so hasty to disregard my help. These are serious accusations leveled against you—sedition, betrayal, alliance with the Fallen One ..."

Franco snorted his feigned disbelief. "You think I would ally with Björn van Gelderan?"

Niko's tense expression softened somewhat. "No. No, of course I don't. But Seth Silverbow ..." He shook his head resolutely. "His fervor can be quite convincing. Perhaps if I had some sense of the story myself—"

A hush spread through the gallery suddenly, and Franco followed the gazes of the other guests to see that Alshiba Torinin now stood in the distant archway surrounded by a host of white-cloaked soldiers. *Paladin Knights from Illume Belliel.* Franco swallowed in spite of himself.

Niko gripped his arm tightly and dragged him beneath an archway leading to another gallery, pulling him out of the rush of guests now mobbing the Alorin Seat—and out of sight of Alshiba.

"I must know, Franco," Niko whispered, urgent and low. "Are you still with us?"

Franco held his searching gaze. He thought of the oath binding him and murmured, "My loyalties have not changed in three hundred years, Niko."

Niko pressed his lips together and nodded. He motioned them on into the adjacent gallery and stopped in the shadow of a massive statue depicting the Hallovian god Laocht wrestling with a serpent. "I fear my responsibilities tonight must prevent me from hearing your side of the story now, Franco, but I'll find you later to resume our talk. I want nothing more than to swap tales of our adventures in privacy and peace." He paused, smiled. His expression seemed amazingly genuine. "I recall so fondly our evenings spent fireside while all the Sormitáge went about its business. It's been too long since we shared confidences." At this last, Niko gave him a meaningful smile. Franco stifled a shudder.

Carian's arrival spared him further of Niko's particular intimacies. "*There* you are!" The islander ambled cheerfully up and turned his brown eyes between Franco and Niko expectantly.

Franco was just about to make a reluctant introduction when Niko bowed his head in gracious acceptance of Carian's esteem, as though the pirate's declaration had been referring solely to him. "Always a pleasure to greet our island brethren." He looked from Carian to Franco inquiringly. "Are you two ... acquainted?"

Franco muttered into his wine, "In a manner of speaking."

Carian barked a laugh. "Ha! Don't let the Admiral fool you, Captain. Our history ranges far."

Franco glared at him while Niko smoothed his hair, looking perplexed. "Well … allow me to welcome you, my Jamaiian fellow in the Guild, and yet …" Niko settled Carian a look of fatherly reprimand so obviously contrived that Franco wondered if the man hadn't spent some hours practicing it in the mirror. He placed a hand on Carian's shoulder. "I must say, it ails me that so few of your fellows could make it here tonight. I understand the logistical difficulty when Jamaii hosts but a single node—and of course there's your proclivity for traveling by ship. Now that I'm in power, we shall remedy this."

Franco couldn't be sure if Niko was referring to Jamaii's single node, the lack of support he received from the island's natives, or their love of sailing.

Carian spied a passing steward and spun awkwardly on one foot to snag a goblet from the tray with all the elegance of a spiraling spider monkey. He saluted Niko with the goblet as he resettled. "That'd sure be something to see, Cap'n."

"Ah well … you'll notice a plethora of changes now that I'm in power, my pirate friend. No doubt you'll want to test soon for *your* ring."

Carian snorted. "Why in Tiern'aval would I want to do that?"

Niko's smile dripped with condescension. He gripped Carian's shoulder again. "Why, we cannot have *untested* men traveling the nodes! This lack of structure has directly contributed to the realm's unbalanced state." He looked to Franco as if expecting his unquestioning support of this assessment. "You will hear more of the many improvements I have planned during my Address tonight, but the first reform to be enacted is no secret." He drew up tall to better convey the grandeur of his words. "Henceforth, no unringed Adept will be allowed to travel the nodes. Any Nodefinder wishing to do so will be required to test for his ring. Those who fail will—if accepted—train at one of the schools I shall be establishing … or I suppose at the Sormitáge," he added as a resentful afterthought, his tone implying the Sormitáge perhaps held its Adepts to a questionable standard.

Franco stared at him in horror. "However do you plan to manage this?"

Niko gave him a sagacious look. "I understand your reaction, my old friend—such necessary restrictions will be difficult to enforce. But let me reassure you, we've put much thought into the implementation of our reform. Of course, *you* needn't worry." He smiled and clapped Franco on the shoulder, rousing his repugnance once more. "Have you not claimed two Sormitáge rings, even as I?"

"Three," Carian remarked into his wine.

Franco shot him a warning glare, but the damage was done.

"Three." Niko affected a smile as his hand fell abruptly to his side. "Three?" His amiable veneer grew thin. "I did not remember it so."

"Bestowed upon him by the High Mage herself." Carian saluted Franco with his goblet. "The Admiral's got the rings and the certificate to prove it."

Franco seriously considered strangling him.

With some effort, Niko contorted his face into an innocuous expression. "Well, *well* …" He took a long swallow of wine—too long—and looked Franco over again as he lowered the goblet. Then came the painful spreading of lips that passed for a smile, and not a tooth of it sincere. "Well, now is the time to wear your rings proudly, Franco. I do hope to see you at my Address?" He appeared suddenly desperate to be away.

Franco managed an anemic smile. "I wouldn't dream of missing it."

Niko took his leave with haste.

When the Vestal had moved out of earshot, Franco clutched Carian's arm and hissed ferociously, "*What in the thirteen hells was that?*"

"Easy, Admiral." Carian's brown eyes were following Niko through the crowd. "This ain't my first pony show."

Franco cursed under his breath. His relationship with Niko depended on his ingratiating himself to the man, not showing himself a rival. "I'll never gain his confidence now," Franco snapped. "You might as well have announced our true allegiances as declare to Niko van Amstel that I have more Sormitáge rings than he does."

Carian shifted his gaze to Franco. "Forget Niko. We were never going to get anything out of that powdered nancy, and Devangshu knows all."

Franco blinked. "Vita?"

The pirate gave him a telling look. "I've learned a few things you need to hear."

"I—" Franco blinked and drew back. "Already?"

"You think the Great Master sent me along just for my stunningly handsome looks? Listen, you're hung between the devil and the deep blue sea here, Admiral. Everybody's got your name on their tongue, and plenty of 'em know you by sight. Me on the other hand …" and he shrugged his eyebrows meaningfully.

While Franco was pondering his point, Carian drained his goblet and pushed it off into Franco's hand. "Me and Vita got something we need to do. Just keep out of sight, savvy, Admiral? I'll find you after the, uh—" he cleared his throat significantly and grinned, "*Vestal's* Address." He ambled off.

Franco gazed after the pirate, trying to determine whether he should thank him or garrote him. Eventually he decided a high dose of wine was in order before either eventuality could come to fruition, so he refreshed his goblet and made an effort to blend in with the crowd.

Though Alshiba Torinin and her white Knights were still in the other room, the hair remained raised on the back of his neck, and he constantly felt the itch of eyes upon him. Franco had no illusions: someone was bound to recognize him again soon. Fortune grace him it wouldn't be the Alorin Seat.

When faced with the threat of torturous interrogation, any man might've thought to flee. Niko's portals offered a variety of paths towards escape, yet it never occurred to Franco to use them. For all he resented and loathed his oath to Björn van Gelderan, he was bound to it to the end of his days.

Which will be fairly soon, from the look of things.

A sudden tingling between his shoulderblades drew Franco's awareness, and he darted into the shadow of a statue a breath before Alshiba appeared in the gallery entrance. As the other guests broke into welcoming applause, Franco peered between the statue's legs and studied the Alorin Seat. She appeared as he remembered: a tall woman, flaxen-haired, beautiful if a little too thin in that willowy Avataren way. She wore a white, high-collared gown, and her blue eyes surveyed the room with keen deliberation. As Franco watched, her Paladin Knights filed in at her side. A nod from their mistress, and they fanned out into the crowd.

Catching his breath, Franco pulled back behind the statue and pressed his body close to the cold marble, heart racing. His eyes searched for some means of escape. A steward was just then passing, so Franco fell into step with him, shoulder to shoulder, hoping that from the back they seemed a pair. The steward cast him a curious eye, but Franco smiled broadly and nodded, and they turned together and headed beneath an arch into the servants' passages.

At an intersection of corridors, Franco peeled away, murmuring "Gratitude," though the steward seemed indifferent. Then he quickly lost himself within the maze of servants' corridors. Finally, when he was certain no one followed, he leaned back against a wall, pressed his head to the plaster, and exhaled a tremulous breath of relief.

He had to pull himself together. A confrontation with Alshiba seemed inevitable, and what in Tiern'aval was he going to say? She would want to know what had become of Raine, what had really happened in Rethynnea, where Björn was now, what his plans were ...

And whether these truths were bound to his tongue by magic or by honor, he wouldn't be able to voice any of them.

Franco was inventing some new curses when distant music caught his ear. Because its source lay further away from Alshiba, he followed its lilting stream through the maze of servants' corridors until one opened onto an elegant salon. Four musicians were performing on Caladrian *lira da gambas*, bowing rich tones out of the large, multi-stringed instruments hugged between their legs.

The rapid movements of their bows formed a raging melody that captured Franco's attention and drew him along on a river of tumbling notes. He stood in the shadows at the room's edge, letting the ever-developing harmony wash over him ... through him ... wishing he might've had the peace of conscience to enjoy it.

That's when he saw the man.

He stood leaning against the far wall with arms crossed. The long fingers of his right hand braced his jaw, while his forefinger idly stroked his lower lip in time with the music. Between his elegant clothing and his refined repose, he seemed the height of civility.

Franco couldn't say why the man had so captured his attention. It seemed as if his presence demanded his interest so completely as to have compelled it on the tides of *elae*.

As he stood watching the stranger, he noticed that his weren't the only eyes that lit upon the man and strayed away, only to return moments later. It seemed others, too, were drawn by some mysterious allure.

In that moment, the stranger turned his gaze directly on Franco—indeed, his eyes fixed so assuredly upon him that he could only have felt the heat of Franco's inspection and followed its trail right to him.

For a moment Franco felt pinned, caught like a boy staring unwholesomely at a lady's bosom, and a sudden unease beset him for no reason he could identify. Feeling unsettled by the man's gaze, he smiled uncomfortably and nodded a hello. After a tense pause, the man nodded politely in return, though he didn't immediately release Franco from his attention.

Then the musicians finished their tumbling concerto, and the salon erupted with applause. The stranger looked back to the performers, freeing Franco from the pinion of his inspection, and Franco drew in a breath of relief.

As the applause was settling, a steward appeared in a doorway across the room, rang a bell, and announced into the spreading hush, "My lords and ladies, please assemble in the Grand Hall for the Vestal Address."

A bubbling hum of anticipation followed this announcement, and everyone rose from their seats and started en masse for the doors.

The man of Franco's interest put one hand to his forehead and then swept it toward the musicians in an elegant gesture of appreciation. They bowed and smiled in return, beaming now. Observing the exchange, Franco imagined no acknowledgement held quite so much reward as one coming from that man.

Reaching the Grand Hall, Franco plucked another goblet from a steward's tray and took up an unobtrusive spot beside a column at the back of the room. From there, he had a clear view of the dais but remained mostly hidden from the sea of people filling in between him and the stage.

Sipping his wine, which tasted of rancorous anticipation, Franco cast his gaze around the wide hall, keen to any flashes of white that would indicate Alshiba or her Knights. Yet his attention kept returning to the stranger. Who was he, and why had he felt so drawn to him? He found his eyes constantly straying from their task, searching instead for the man who'd so captured his interest.

Suddenly a male voice said into his ear, near and close, "Excuse me ... but have we met?"

Franco nearly choked on his wine. He pushed a forearm across his mouth and turned to lock gazes with the stranger from the hall. "Your pardon," he somewhat gasped.

The man stood close enough that a swift dagger to the gut would've gone unnoticed between them. His eyes searched Franco's face intently. "You seemed to recognize me in the salon, but I can't place where we might've met." His manner was polite, his speech cultured, yet Franco sensed an unnerving disparity between his innocuous tone and his copper-eyed gaze.

"My error, sir. I ..." *Shade and darkness,* what *had* he been doing? "I mistook you for another."

"Ah." The man smiled, and in this conveyance his gaze softened. "That would explain it. Another then." It was his smile that held Franco captive now, for it radiated such compelling amiability as to melt away any fears Franco might've harbored—even to imply how absurd his suspicions had been. "I suppose introductions are in order then. If you will permit," and he held elegantly ringed fingers to his chest, "I am Immanuel di Nostri."

Franco blinked. "*Di Nostri*—the artist?"

The man made a humble nod. "I'm honored to find you know my work."

Franco stared at him. Immanuel di Nostri was one of the most famous painters of the Fourth Age. His masterworks graced every level of the Sormitáge's *Primär Insamling* museum, and he was rumored to have personally painted at least half of the university's Grand Passáge, which was inarguably the greatest artistic achievement of the time. But the artist hadn't been heard from since the wars—at least, not that Franco had been aware. He'd thought him long dead.

"*Thirteen hells*, di Nostri, I thought—" Franco stifled his outburst with a grimace. "Never mind what I thought." He stared somewhat ineptly at the man.

Immanuel smiled. "And you are?"

Franco realized he hadn't introduced himself in return. "I beg your pardon." He shook his head then, noting that he seemed to be doing naught but apologizing to the man. "I'm Franco Rohre."

Immanuel's copper eyes crinkled as he examined Franco over the rim of his goblet. "I've heard much talk of a Nodefinder with this name, often mentioned in association with a temple in Rethynnea and a certain fallen Vestal." He sipped his wine and then turned his gaze out across the room. "Depending on who is speaking, this Nodefinder has either the luck of the devil or is one incarnate." His eyes shifted back to Franco, innocuous but inquiring. "Perhaps you can say definitively which?"

"Only under duress," Franco muttered.

Immanuel chuckled. "So …" Taking another sip of wine, his eyes darted to the dais and back again. "You're a companion of the realm's newest Vestal?"

Franco grunted dubiously. "With a capital C."

"Close friends then," the painter quipped, keen to Franco's rather lackluster esteem for their host.

Franco inwardly cursed his imprudence, fearing he'd said too little and intimated too much. He remembered how Niko had boasted about being a patron of the arts. If Immanuel di Nostri depended on Niko for his livelihood …

His gaze darted back to meet the artist's and found the latter watching him compellingly. Franco looked away again with an uncomfortable swallow. "Niko and I were roommates at the Sormitáge, long ago, but …"

"But?"

Franco cast him a long look. Then he let out a slow breath. "But time makes heroes of traitors and fools of the wise."

"So sayeth the Immortal Bard Drake di Matteo." Immanuel raised his glass to acknowledge Franco's quote—or perhaps to note his adept maneuvering away from answering the question.

Hoping to direct the conversation elsewhere than his own activities, Franco held up his goblet in return. "I know your work from the Sormitáge, but where've you been since the wars? I confess … I thought—"

"Me dead?" Immanuel's eyes glittered. "After I finished my work on the Grand Passáge, I spent many years exploring, experiencing the treasures of the realm." He grunted then. "Would that I had spent those years in study at the Sormitáge instead."

"You regret your travels?"

"Rather the lost opportunity. But I've made good of it in recent months. I still have friends in the Sormitáge, and they've proven more than true in helping me recently." He added with a rueful grin, "I'll admit it's an odd experience, though, walking so oft beneath my own imagery … and without the opportunity to correct its many flaws."

Franco shook his head. "I saw none, surely."

Immanuel offered a smile of gratitude. "But what of you, Franco Rohre? What calls *you* to this gathering if not to congratulate an old friend?" His gaze and tone implied there could be numerous answers to this question.

Franco muttered into his wine, "The same as anyone, I suspect."

"Oh, indeed." Immanuel seemed to find this amusing. "Niko van Amstel has become quite the *patron*." He put the Veneisean accent upon the word, emphasizing its meaning. "I have spent many evenings here in the company of artists and philosophers," and flashing a shrewd look, he added, "as well as cutthroats and thieves, and men far worse than even these."

Most notably our host, Franco's conscience sneered.

For once, Franco was in accord.

"I see many such personages here tonight," the artist continued, gazing out across the assembly. "Do you think they all share your reasons for attending?"

Acknowledging his point with a pained look, Franco took another sip of wine and gazed out over the hall. On the dais, the Paladin Knights were assembling an honor guard in preparation for Niko's appearance. Franco watched the crowd in the room with ever-growing consternation.

"Your face betrays your thoughts, Franco Rohre."

Franco turned a swift eye back to Immanuel.

The artist gestured with his goblet, indicating the room at large. He leaned close as he murmured low into Franco's ear, "You see the web, don't you, my friend? Countless strands, each with its own wily spider." He angled Franco a meaningful look. "How many spiders do *you* see?"

Franco let out an explosive breath. "Too many."

"Just so." The artist saluted him with his empty goblet. "Too many."

Franco held Immanuel's gaze. "Then you hold no allegiances here?"

The painter's copper eyes glittered secretively. "I'm an artist, Franco. I but observe the world so as to capture its colors."

"Do you portray them all equally," Franco pressed, "or favor one over another?"

The painter laughed. "How careful you are—do you really think Niko van Amstel would take *me* into his confidence?"

Franco's eyes had but to sweep the artist once to concede his point. Niko loathed anyone likely to be more popular than himself, and Immanuel di Nostri possessed an effortless charm that Niko had no hope of matching.

Franco considered Immanuel for a long moment in silence then. A great part of him desired to confide in the painter. The man had admitted that he harbored no allegiance to Niko, and Franco's instincts certainly hinted that Immanuel was genuine in this statement. They'd barely met, yet Franco liked him.

Still, no matter how much he desired to trust Immanuel, he couldn't bring himself to do so. He wondered if he would ever be able to trust anyone again.

Turning away, Franco posed with some asperity, "So you've come here to observe the decline of the Adept race." He shook his head and cast the painter a rueful glance. "At least by your favored hand, our ugly end will be immortalized with its true complexion."

Immanuel frowned at this remark. "I'm dismayed to imagine myself as callous as you've just painted me, Franco, yet ..." he tapped a long finger against his chin. "The light casts many wavering shadows. How does one know which are true?"

Franco was pondering the meaning of this comment when Mian Gartelt appeared, plopping out of the crowd as if it had tasted a morsel of her and spat the rest out. To Franco's intense disconcertion, she saw them immediately.

"My Lord di Nostri! And … Franco. Why, I didn't see you there only moments ago, but … you two are acquainted?"

"Only just, dear Mian," Immanuel replied with cool civility.

Mian slipped her arm presumptuously through his and turned a vapid gaze up at him. To Franco, she seemed a fungus clinging offensively to the root of a majestic elm. "We are so blessed to have you back among us, my lord," Mian told Immanuel. "Do share with us your visions for your next project. You have taken on a new commission, have you not?"

Immanuel selected a full goblet from a passing steward. He held Franco's gaze over the rim as he replied in a tone thick with meaning, "A number of paths lie open before me."

Franco stared at him.

Whereupon a gong rang out, and the room fell silent for Niko van Amstel's Address.

FOURTEEN

"His narcissism is surpassed only by his rutting for adoration."
The Espial Franco Rohre, on Niko van Amstel

THE GRAND HALL broke into frenzied applause yet again. Niko van Amstel received his audience's admiration with a smile that made Franco's hands clench into fists. As Niko had been speaking, Franco had searched the crowd for faces that mirrored his own staid expression, his own barely concealed disgust. Too many were lifted to the dais with vapid adoration. Even knowing this lot had been hand-picked from the barrel of poor judgment, it still sickened him.

The applause at last quieted beneath Niko's paternal smile. On the dais, two rows of Paladin Knights now stood behind him, forming a resplendent backdrop for his speech. Niko raised his hands to the crowd, embracing them with open arms, with a smile that gleamed as white as the Knights' surcoats.

"My friends! A new day is dawning!"

Applause immediately erupted again, and a vainglorious Niko drank it in. Franco admitted the man certainly played well the part of the charismatic leader, what with his cap of blonde waves and ingratiating smile.

Niko held up his hands to quiet the room. "Ladies and gentlemen, friends, brethren of the Guild … thus far, I've told you some of the changes we can look forward to with my ascendancy, but now I must call to your attention a less pleasant truth."

The room went silent, all eyes glued to the tall, fair-haired man commanding the dais.

"My friends … too long have we wallowed in fear of what tomorrow would *not* bring, frightened for our children's future—for our very survival—living but as shadows of our former selves. Too long have those responsible for our race's decline gone unpunished!"

A chorus of agreement greeted this declaration, and Niko let it continue until the negative emotion became a palpable energy thrumming through the crowd.

"Our enemies flourish while we wither. They thrive in their bastard realm—*a product of the heinous rape of our own blessed Alorin!*—feasting on a stolen harvest, while *our* people struggle to right the Balance." Niko walked the dais with hands clasped behind his back and his brow deeply furrowed, the father troubled by his son's misdeeds. "Fewer Adepts are born to *us* each year, while T'khendar's inhabitants multiply, safe beyond their twisted nodes. Now, I must ask you, is this fitting? Is it *just*? Is it *tolerable* while even one more moon shines over our children's slumber?"

A rumbling erupted among the masses.

"Let me be the first to declare it." Niko planted his feet and faced the audience. "Let me tell you the truth none other will speak, and the answer is *no!* It is *not* just. It is *not* right. Our mother world should not succumb in an effort to feed the voracious hunger of its undesired spawn!"

The roar of outrage that greeted this sentiment made Franco's head throb.

"My friends," Niko called over the noise, using *elae* to fuel his voice now, "I give you my oath—even as I swore upon this ring to oversee the proper use of my strand—" and he held his oath-ring for the assembled crowd to see, "I swear to you that these atrocities *shall be ended!*"

The room erupted with thunderous applause.

Franco felt sick. His vision blurred with a future where events spun rapidly out of control—or perhaps it was his own head spinning from the toxic mixture of too much wine and defamatory slander of the people actually attempting to save their realm.

Niko's booming voice rose above the melee. "As your Vestal, I will do what should've been done three centuries ago! I shall call upon the forces of Illume Belliel to destroy the abomination that is T'khendar and see the Balance righted!"

The crowd went wild.

Franco had heard all that he could stand. Orders be damned—he wouldn't last another second in that room, at least not without inflicting bodily harm on Niko. With a glance at Immanuel, who stood listening with a frown, Franco set down his goblet and slipped unnoticed out of the hall.

He made his way quickly through the manor, despite his throbbing head and leaden feet. Niko's intent to destroy T'khendar seemed an unconscionable rending of all that he found noble. As he exited onto the patio, the staggering weight of this possible outcome and all of its ramifications crashed upon him. He braced hands against the stone railing and hung his head, trying to breathe through the combined pressure of his multiplying fears and the clenching fury in his chest.

"Franco?" Immanuel stepped out onto the patio behind him. "I turned and saw you'd gone and worried I was too late."

Franco lifted his head and gazed off across the lawn, jaw clenched. Desolation gripped him; the feeling reminded him too keenly of that moment three centuries ago when his entire path had changed. "It's been too late for me for a long time, di Nostri."

Immanuel joined him at the railing. "I once thought as you do." He glanced to Franco, and Franco saw understanding and compassion both in his expression.

"And how is that?"

Immanuel arched a resigned brow. "That our paths were as set as grooves in stone."

Franco flinched. He cast the painter a pained look and pushed away from the railing. "I can't linger here."

Immanuel followed him down the steps and into the gardens.

As they walked side by side, Franco shoved hands into his pockets and hunched his shoulders. His head felt like an anvil enduring a brutal pounding. "You came looking for me," he muttered, glancing at the painter. "Why?"

Immanuel met his gaze, but then he frowned and glanced away again, and for a long time the only sounds were the crunch of their feet on the gravel path. As they reached the lawn, Franco cast the artist a sidelong look of inquiry. "Well?"

Immanuel broke into a rueful smile. "Trust is an intriguing commodity, is it not?"

"I don't take your meaning."

The artist shrugged simply. "For me to answer your questions, and for you to answer mine, we need to trust one another, and yet ..." He gazed regretfully at Franco. "We have no reason to do so, even if we are free to speak our minds."

The unexpectedly familiar phrase recalled to mind the memory of another night, not long ago, when Raine had truthbound Franco before the First Lord. Franco had opened his eyes after the binding was laid to find both the Fourth and Fifth Vestals staring at him.

'I trust you implicitly, Franco,' the First Lord had told him. That statement itself had unnerved him more than Raine's binding. *'You are free to speak your mind. This truthbinding is only for your protection.'*

Raine had advised, *'You will find you can answer any question when offered of your own free will, but if the information is forced, coerced ... '*

'Then you will find my patterns there to protect you,' the First Lord had finished.

With the First Lord's words still echoing in cadence with the throbbing in his skull, Franco glanced to Immanuel again. He wanted to trust the artist—it would be a relief to be able to confide in *someone*. And yet ... he wasn't sure he even knew what trust felt like anymore. He certainly didn't trust himself with the sharing of secrets that might affect the Balance of the First Lord's game.

"Well, if it isn't the illustrious Franco Rohre!"

Franco came to a sharp standstill.

Belloth's bloody balls, this is just adding insult to injury ...

He clenched his teeth and turned to face the Nodefinder Demetrio Consuevé, who was coming across the lawn with four armed men spread out in a line behind him. Instinct drew Franco's gaze in the opposite direction, where five more men were approaching. All carried blades so dark against the night that they might've been folded of shadows instead of steel. *Merdanti.*

"This looks tediously familiar."

Franco turned Immanuel a look of sharp inquiry at this comment, but the artist merely shook his head.

"Franco, *Franco* ..." Demetrio approached with the moonlight limning the silver tracings on his baldric and the hilt of his rapier. As Consuevé neared, Franco saw a violet plume curled around his wide-brimmed hat. Beneath this dandified accoutrement, Consuevé sported the oiled moustache and goatee made so popular by the Archduke of Rimaldi, his liege, yet it was not as oily as his smile.

"I'm honestly surprised to find you here, Franco."

"Really?" Franco eyed the nine armed men even then surrounding him and Immanuel. "It seems a bit like you were expecting me."

Demetrio leaned on one foot and rested a hand rakishly on the hilt of his rapier. "See, now there's where you're wrong about me, Rohre. *He* said you'd try to slip away unnoticed from our little soiree, but I said, 'Rohre—he's a prudent man, cautious. He'd never be so stupid.'" Demetrio spread his arms, revealing dual daggers on a belt beneath his coat. "Yet here you are."

Franco gazed at him wishing he was armed, wishing his head wasn't such a torrent of agony, wishing he'd been better prepared in this moment to exact his anger against Demetrio Consuevé—Raine's truth, the man deserved it—but Fate had delivered him thusly. He'd seen neither hide nor hair of Carian and Devangshu, and their notable absence left him wondering what trouble the pirate was getting into. He hoped he was faring better.

To Consuevé, Franco said, "Who sent you for me? Niko?"

Demetrio twirled the corner of his moustache with thumb and forefinger. "Oh, we mustn't sully our newest Vestal's reputation by association with a name like yours, Rohre."

Franco grunted. "Dore then. I might've known."

Demetrio's teeth flashed in a cutting smile. They were very white in the moonlight. "He certainly knows you. I'm ashamed to say I doubted him."

Franco saw Consuevé as naught but an over-proud rooster perched atop the henhouse making noise. "As pleasant as this reunion is, Consuevé, what do you want?"

"Well, see, we have some questions for you. But first, let's address your friend here." His eyes swept Immanuel. "Is this the pirate we've been hearing so much about?"

"This is the famous painter Immanuel di Nostri," Franco growled before Immanuel could answer. "He has nothing to do with this. Leave him be."

"So he can raise an alarm and bring your friends—assuming you have any?" Demetrio barked a laugh. "You take me for a fool." He jerked his head to his men. "Bind them."

Franco felt hands grabbing his arms, forcing them behind his back. He gave Immanuel a fierce look of apology, but the painter seemed calm, unruffled, as Consuevé's men bound his wrists behind his back. Then they shoved a foul-smelling hood over Franco's head, and he saw nothing else for a long time.

Demetrio dragged Franco and Immanuel across two nodes and then crammed them in the back of a coach for an hour spent on a twisting road of torturous hills. When they finally pulled off Franco's hood, he blinked painfully against the light and looked around, trying to get his bearings.

They could've been anywhere in the realm, but the luxuriant architecture of the grand salon in which he stood hinted that Consuevé had taken him to the Cairs. Consuevé and his men collected around Franco with blades still held ready, their eyes watchful and alert. He wasn't sure what they expected him to do, being both weaponless and bound. Their obvious confidence in his talents would've brought a smile to his lips had his head not remained such a pulsating torment.

For the next turn of an hourglass, they stood facing a single, empty chair styled as a gilded throne. Demetrio and his men made crude jokes to pass the time while studiously ignoring Franco and the still-hooded Immanuel—ignoring, that is, save to deliver daggered glares of warning.

Finally, a painting on the far wall swung open, taking part of the paneling with it, and a procession of unusual characters emerged.

The man who led the group with a flowing stride walked tall and broad of shoulder beneath desert-styled crimson silks. Black cord bound his long ebony hair, which hung nearly to his waist, and three red-gold hoops adorned each ear. His strong forehead shielded dark eyes and accentuated the shadowed angles of his jaw. He might've been Bemothi for the coloring of his skin, but Franco decided that his height and build set his origins closer to Myacene.

A woman came next in the odd procession. She wore an elaborate headdress in the shape of two long-necked birds, and a pearl-studded veil that completely covered her face. It blended into the silken folds of her sunrise-hued robe, which was embroidered with colorful birds and flowers.

They were followed by a dark-haired man with kohl-lined eyes and a spider tattoo on his forehead, followed by two men dressed in wielder's blacks. Then a succession of bodyguards in red pantaloons emerged, and lastly, a bald, bare-chested giant with an enormous scimitar at his hip. He was *definitely* Avataren.

They must keep that one on a short leash, the voice in Franco's head smirked. Sadly, the effects of Niko's wine had worn off during their rough ride—inebriation had done little to help his aching brain but had at least muzzled the lunatic he rather ironically referred to as his conscience.

The leader sat down on the throne ten paces in front of Franco, leaned back, and crossed his legs with a rustling of silk. "Well, well, well ..."

Franco felt the man's eyes flowing over his skin, tasting of him with his gaze. But when the stranger's perusal of his person lifted to his face and their gazes met, Franco *knew* him with a certainty that stilled his breath. The power behind the man's dark eyes was too like that of Rinokh, who still haunted Franco's dreams. He couldn't now mistake the predation in a Malorin'athgul's gaze, nor the malevolent intent behind it.

"This then is the Espial Franco Rohre," the man remarked.

"The very one, my Lord Abanachtran," answered Consuevé.

The Lord Abanachtran turned and cast the woman on his right a critical look. "A shame your other quarry is not so easily claimed."

She bobbed a murmured apology, causing the tiny bells on her headdress to jingle.

The lord looked back to the assembly and waggled one finger at Immanuel. "And who do we have here?"

Consuevé yanked the painter's hood off his head. "The artist Immanuel di Nostri. Poor bastard has wretched timing."

Immanuel shook his head to flip the hair from his eyes and settled his gaze on their captors.

The Lord Abanachtran took one look at him and emitted a low chuckle that rapidly grew into bold, dark laughter. If the painter understood why his name had engendered this response in the Lord Abanachtran, his face revealed no sign of it. He remained, instead, remarkably self-composed.

Franco wondered what thoughts must've been tumbling behind the painter's cool, copper-eyed gaze and held a deep appreciation for Immanuel's collected deportment.

Finally the Lord Abanachtran's laughter faded, though his eyes still gleamed with malicious delight. "Let us proceed."

"My lord," Consuevé said with a bow. He turned to Franco. "Franco Rohre, you are charged with complicity in the destruction of Rethynnea's Temple of the Vestals and in aiding in the escape of Prince Ean val Lorian. Do you deny these charges?"

Franco wished Consuevé would at least remove his violet-plumed hat, which made it nearly impossible to take him seriously. He exhaled a sigh. "I can't speak about what occurred in the Temple of the Vestals for reasons that should be obvious, Consuevé."

"Truthbound," murmured the veiled woman standing beside the Lord Abanachtran. "Like the others."

The lord gave her a sidelong glance, either in acknowledgement or to convey his simmering irritation.

"Our lord doesn't care about the bloody temple, Rohre," Demetrio growled meanwhile. "Tell him where to find Ean val Lorian."

Franco eyed him irritably. So this then was their play. He well remembered Dore's unnatural interest in Prince Ean during their last misfortunate confrontation. This encounter seemed unlikely to fare any better. "I've no idea where the prince is."

"We *know* you serve Björn van Gelderan, even as the prince does!" Demetrio pulled his rapier and leveled the point at Franco's chest. "You disappeared from Calgaryn Palace while still employed by Raine D'Lacourte—"

"Technically I was never *employed*—"

"Don't *tempt* me, Franco." Demetrio pushed the rapier into the soft hollow of Franco's throat. "Dore has spies everywhere. He examined the reports, compared the evidence. We *know* you were Called in Calgaryn—summoned to serve beneath the oath Björn van Gelderan bound you with on Tiern'aval— and you answered that Calling with your soul, for here you remain, alive and well, while more honorable men have refused and died." With this, he moved the rapier's point to press over Franco's heart and said through a sharp smile. "You need confess to nothing."

"Very well, since you insist."

Demetrio bared his teeth in a snarl.

"You don't seem to understand the severity of your position, Franco Rohre," the woman noted from afar.

Franco shifted his gaze to her. "Perhaps you would kindly explain it to me, *khânum*."

She paused at the polite address of *madam* made in the desert tongue, and Franco saw that he'd surprised her. "You have a good ear for accents, Mr. Rohre. Mine is but a trace upon the common tongue. Nevertheless," she seemed to note in that moment the Lord Abanachtran's eyebrow twitching with impatience, "your situation is precarious. Answer our questions, and we may let you live. Deny us, and your end will be long and painful."

"Thank you for the clarification."

Demetrio growled an oath and pressed his rapier point more forcefully— and admittedly, painfully—into Franco's chest. The situation struck Franco as surreal, and for a moment he merely pondered it with morbid fascination.

Did any of these Adepts realize they served a creature whose sole purpose was the destruction of their very realm? Such depravity seemed outrageous to him ... until he remembered Dore Madden and recalled that some men could sink to incomprehensible lows … places so debased that they could hardly be called men any longer.

The Lord Abanachtran's gaze remained fixed upon him, and Franco felt his energy waning beneath the man's inspection. He wondered if the Malorin'athgul was somehow draining *elae* from his veins even then.

"Where can we find Ean val Lorian?" asked the lord in a low rumble.

Franco felt a thread of power lace into him, and his head exploded with pain. He doubled over and braced himself with hands on his knees. "*I don't know!*"

"We think you do." Demetrio watched him with a cold smile. "We think you know *much* more than you're saying."

"Read him," the woman ordered.

Franco closed his eyes against the pain still coursing through him. When he straightened and opened them again, one of the black-robed Adepts was standing before him. He pinned colorless eyes on Franco at the same time that his hand reached for Franco's face to take the truthreader's hold. The moment reminded him of the many times he'd watched Raine D'Lacourte questioning a man, though *this* truthreader wore but one Sormitáge ring.

Franco rarely found the humor in impossible situations, but he also greatly resented the imposition of these people, who seemed to think they had some claim to his person and his thoughts. Recalling his most recent truthbinding at the hands of Raine D'Lacourte, he gritted his teeth and flashed a humorless grin. "You'll be disappointed with what you find."

The truthreader smiled icily in return. "We'll see." He looked to Demetrio. "Hold him."

Demetrio's men grabbed Franco by both arms, and then a blinding pain shot through his skull. A truthreader could make his craft nearly painless, or he could rip through a man's mind like a scythe through wheat. Franco shut his eyes and clenched his teeth, forcibly swallowing back a cry.

For a moment, pain raged through his consciousness, and it took all of his mental strength to concentrate on anything but the fire of its passing. Had the Reading not been so agonizing, he might've found humor in the futility of the Adept's attempt to gain his thoughts. As if a mere single-ringed truthreader could break a truthbinding laid in by the Fourth *and* Fifth Vestals!

As was his wont, Franco sought refuge in retaliation. He forced coherent thought through the searing fire in his head and summoned images of the Adept attempting this mental rape. Gaining at last a clear picture of the man in his mind's eye, he proceeded to engage his imagination with images of the Adept's robes burning, his flesh melting.

The slightest intake of breath from his tormentor rewarded his effort. Franco opened his eyes to find the man scowling at him. He grinned and ground out through clenched teeth, "Going … well … so … far?"

The truthreader snarled a curse and dug his fingers into the flesh of

Franco's face and the fourth into his mind, not merely seeking to break through the wall that bound Franco's memories but using barbed daggers to do so. Thus followed a mental contest of wills, silent save for their gnashing grunts of effort.

Yet the deeper the truthreader probed, the more Franco felt the fourth collecting around him. His entire body was soon tingling with it, the hair on his arms electrified and standing on end. Close before his blurring vision, the truthreader's face grew redder, his grunts of effort more desperate. Sweat beaded on his brow and ran like tears down his temples.

Finally, the throbbing in Franco's skull grew so powerful that he felt it searing down his arms and legs as bolts of lightning through his veins. He knew he was losing consciousness the instant before it happened. Pain blinded him, and the world went white …

While Franco stood in the dark embrace of the black-robed truthreader, Pelasommáyurek gazed at his brother Shail. He'd never imagined, when he allowed himself to be taken captive, that Shailabhanáchtran would sit at the other end of Demetrio Consuevé's barbed hook.

How very interesting …

Franco was writhing tragically beside him when a voice intruded on his mind in the manner of communication he and his brothers were accustomed to using in the void.

Hello, Pelas. Shail's cutting mental drawl conveyed his delicious enjoyment at finding Pelas at his mercy.

Shail, Pelas's responding tone held cool indifference in return.

What are you doing here?

I might ask the same of you.

Shail's gaze shone with cold mirth. *You should not have allowed yourself to be taken. Why did you?*

To see what manner of creature lurked at the end of this snare.

Shail mentally *tsked* at him. *No vice closer courts disaster than curiosity.*

Speaking of misplaced fixation, why are you so concerned with Ean van Lorian? I noticed you sent Rinokh after the prince to his demise. I thought at first it was just an expedient means of ridding yourself of Rinokh, but now I realize it's a fervent obsession. Afraid, brother?

Shail's eyes flashed. He considered Pelas for a moment in silence, his gaze scrutinizing. *Ean val Lorian is but a pebble in our shoe, yet one I would remove when opportunity presents. But soon even he will be of no consequence, for Darshan raises an army of eidola at Tal'Afaq, and none from this plane can long stand before it.*

Pelas had postponed his intended visit to Tal'Afaq, but an entire *army* of *eidola*? That he had to see.

This game is beyond your depth, Pelas, Shail meanwhile warned. *Swim back to safer waters or lose your life to the waves. Should you surrender your will to me, I will allow you to continue life on this plane.*

Pelas barked a mental laugh. *Surrender my will to you? Can you be serious?*

Perhaps you mistake my offer. His tone dripped with threat. *Surrender now, here, or declare yourself an enemy.*

Pelas's eyes glittered with defiance. *I accept your challenge, brother. Let us see who will be the first to join Rinokh—*

A piercing scream shattered the silence, and the truthreader staggered away from Franco. To Pelas's surprise, he appeared to be the one screaming.

The Adept stumbled three paces backwards emitting that tortured shriek. Then he collapsed onto his back, pitching with convulsions. Pelas barely had time to process the curious event before the man jerked violently amid an ear-splitting snapping of bones and then stilled.

"Three bloody rivers!" Demetrio took a step towards the man but drew up short, uncertain, as he gazed in revulsion at the blood fountaining out of the Adept's every orifice. The other black-robed wielder and one of Demetrio's men both ran to the truthreader's side, but the Adept was quite obviously dead.

Pelas turned a curious look to Franco, who was slumped in the arms of Demetrio's men.

Shail demanded into the general commotion, "*Who* did this? What happened?"

The wielder straightened wearing an expression slack with awe. "Do you see, my lady?" he addressed the veiled woman. "The currents show the pattern of the working but not the signature of the wielder who cast it."

"Impossible," Shail growled.

"Nearly so, my lord," the woman agreed. She turned to him with a jingle of bells.

Pelas knew her from her reputation as much as her famous headdress. What he hadn't known was how deeply she suffered. He easily saw the darkness consuming her like an apple rotting at its core; *elae's* light had all but left her.

So my brother lays his bed with the Karakurt. Now that is intriguing ...

The Karakurt advised, "The difficulty inherent in the undertaking of hiding one's presence from the currents makes its craft more legend than fact."

Fury darkened Shail's expression, and he fixed his eyes on the wielder. "Explain these deeds."

The Adept held a hand to Franco. "It would seem the truthbinding upon the Espial held also some dormant pattern of protection, my lord."

Shail shifted his dark gaze back to an unconscious Franco and frowned. "Rohre did this?"

"Nay," said the Karakurt. "The wielder who truthbound him planted this seed, my lord. Rohre may have had no knowledge of the pattern at all." She walked towards Franco, and Pelas saw her face more clearly through the veil as she neared. She looked younger than her reputation made her, and was not unattractive, with the dark hair and features of the desert tribes.

She reached Franco and took his slumping head in her hand, lifting his chin. Pelas watched her look him over and then fix her hand across his face in the truthreader's hold. Whereupon he also noted the two Sormitáge rings on her fourth finger, partly hidden beneath a large ruby.

No doubt you keep that truth a guarded secret, Pelas thought. There were not so many female truthreaders in the land, and a female truthreader with her second ring could easily be identified from a search of Sormitáge records.

"What can you learn of him?" Shail rumbled.

After a silent moment of concentration, she shook her head with a jingling of bells. "This work defies even my skill."

Pelas arched a brow. *Especially with* elae *so far from your reach, my dear.*

She released Franco and turned to Shail, and Pelas noted the fear in her voice as she replied, "Whoever is protecting Rohre—whoever is protecting these secrets—is a worthy adversary, my lord."

Shail shifted in his seat, frowned, and tapped one finger against the arm of his chair. "The same man who hides Ean val Lorian from us?"

"Perhaps," she agreed.

"Who?" Shail's impatient tone conveyed his indignation. Pelas found the moment immensely satisfying, for his youngest brother was unused to being outwitted and out-maneuvered. "*Who* would have the skill to lay a dormant pattern within a truthbinding—one strong enough to kill anyone that challenged it, yet leave no signature upon the currents?"

The Karakurt walked a few paces with her thoughts and then stilled. She looked back to Shail amid a whisper of silk. "This is legendary talent, my lord. We must look for a wielder the likes of Arion Tavestra, Markal Morrelaine, or Björn van Geld …" The name gave her pause, and she aimed a swift look back to Franco. "Björn van Gelderan," she murmured then with dawning realization, her tone colored by awe, "The man Franco Rohre is reportedly sworn to."

"Conjecture," Shail groused.

She turned to him at once. "Rohre's sleeping mind is full of thoughts of the Fifth Vestal. I could not glean much else but this."

Shail eyed her skeptically. "Björn van Gelderan, the Fifth Vestal. A name from dusty texts." He frowned, grunted. "From all accounts, the Vestal betrayed the realm, and if recent rumors be true, he's returned to carry out Malachai's work and hasten the extermination of the race."

His gaze shifted back to Pelas and he added with meaningful menace, brother to brother, *I would count Björn an ally.*

"It wouldn't be the first time an enemy has purposely propagated misinformation, my lord," the Karakurt cautioned.

The black-robed wielder snorted. "Facts are facts, my lady."

Shail turned her a considering look nonetheless. "Björn van Gelderan …" He repeated the name as if tasting of its authenticity, but Pelas knew his brother was tasting possibility.

Until that moment, Pelas hadn't envisioned anyone from this world knowing of their true nature and purpose. Yet to think on it now, the very idea seemed naïve—to imagine *no one* knew of their existence? That no one would be working to counteract their efforts? It seemed folly beyond compare.

More the fools, he and his brothers. The price of their arrogance.

Still … it was a bit presumptuous to propose that Björn van Gelderan was actually an unseen adversary, working behind the scenes to thwart their efforts. The man had been gone from the realm for centuries, had he not? And all accounts placed him, as Shail had said, as one who might be counted an ally to their own cause.

"Björn van Gelderan aside," Shail remarked, "who else could've done this?"

She shook her head in a jingle of bells. "Of bracketed or rowed wielders in the known, Viernan hal'Jaitar counts among our allies, yet I daresay this working hangs above his skill. The High Lord of Agasan and others of the Empire might possess such talent, but it seems unlikely the Empress or her Consort would involve themselves in this effort. I know of a few others out of legend who could've managed it," and she added pointedly, "but *all* of them were sworn to the Fifth Vest—"

Suddenly she spun a look at Franco with a jingling of bells. "He's awake."

Franco regained consciousness the way one sometimes wakes from a dream, with reality and illusion blurred. He heard the Lord Abanachtran speaking while he drifted in and out of lucidity, but mention of the Fifth Vestal's name shocked him more fully aware. He listened then, eyes closed against the pain in his throbbing head, inwardly cringing as the woman spoke the truth so nearly.

Bitter regret filled him. To know himself responsible for alerting a Malorin'athgul to the First Lord's game …

"He's awake."

His bluff called, Franco opened his eyes and lifted his head. Only then did he see the truthreader splayed flat on the floor in a pool of blood. Franco stared.

"You see," said the woman, nodding towards Franco, "he didn't know."

"It matters little now," the Lord Abanachtran muttered. "He's useless to us if his information can't be gained. You know what to do, Consuevé."

Demetrio grinned at Franco. "Gladly." He twirled and lunged and stabbed his rapier into Franco's gut.

"*No!*" Immanuel gasped even as Franco uttered a pain-stricken exhalation and collapsed forward, hung between the arms of Demetrio's men.

Demetrio pulled free his slim blade. He looked at the crimson-stained steel and scowled. "Blast. I missed his liver."

"I did not say do it *here*, Consuevé," the Lord Abanachtran growled irritably. He settled his piercing gaze on both captives, and for a moment his eyes narrowed. "Traitors deserve a slow demise. Bind *Immanuel*," he emphasized his name with a sneer, "in the *goracrosta* and dump them together in a hole somewhere. I would each watched death's creeping shadow claiming the other."

Franco managed one last blood-tinged glance at Immanuel, who finally looked fretful, and then swirling darkness claimed him.

FIFTEEN

"He has not embraced life who does not every day surmount a fear."
– Dhábu'balaji'ṣridanaí, He Who Walks the Edge of the World

ALYNERI WOKE IN the early evening. She lay still beneath diaphanous layers of netting while the crickets sang and a passing breeze carried the scent of rain through the rippling tent walls.

For the first time since arriving at the Mage's *sa'reyth*, the lovely Jaya wasn't waiting at Alyneri's bedside with a meal and then a command that sent her tumbling right back into healing sleep. Looking around that time, Alyneri found in Jaya's place a claw-foot tub of steaming water.

She bathed and dressed in the gown Jaya had set out for her, its silk as rich in hue as the deepest wine, and then she stared at her reflection in a standing mirror as she combed fingers through her damp hair. A cursory glance showed a slender young woman with long, pale hair and lambent eyes, but closer inspection revealed dark circles beneath a haunted gaze and shadows that hollowed her cheeks.

Inside, Alyneri still trembled. The shock of her separation from Trell dominated her thoughts, and the wounds of their parting remained fresh and weeping no matter how many days passed. She found it so strange being in that place of lavish comfort, receiving the care of immortal *drachwyr*, while Trell lived in mortal peril, and Fynnlar ... well, Jaya had told her that Fynn would recover, but it troubled Alyneri that he hadn't yet woken, and that she hadn't been allowed to see him.

She felt a strange duality as she stared at her reflection, as if she lived two lives, or at least had two faces. In the way a river's smooth surface often concealed dangerous currents, Alyneri's own demeanor hid a riotous fear that rushed through the depths of her consciousness.

Jaya had repeatedly encouraged her to rest and recover, but how could she sleep when Trell might be dying? How could she lie idle when she should be doing everything in her power to find him?

Alyneri exhaled a tremulous breath. The truth was, she had nowhere else to go. But ... perhaps Jaya already had more news.

Alyneri set off to find her. After a confusing journey through the labyrinthine complex of tents, she finally found the Rival of the Sun sitting on a divan reading a book.

The *drachwyr* looked up when Alyneri entered, and her serene face lifted in a smile. "Ah, sweet Alyneri, how are you feeling?" Jaya set aside her novel and patted the cushion beside her for Alyneri to sit down.

"I slept again, thank you. I just ..." she bit her lip and slowly lowered herself onto the cushion. "Is there any news at all?" She pushed a trembling hand to her forehead and whispered, "I can't seem to stop shaking."

Jaya plucked at a strand of Alyneri's hair in a motherly way. "Let not your heart be troubled, *soraya*. Rhakar found Trell of the Tides once before; he will find him again. He is very good at finding those who are lost." Taking up Alyneri's hand, her oddly tangerine eyes widened and she observed gently, "My, but you *are* shaking. You must have more nourishment. You sacrificed so much of your own strength to save your friend—your pattern was terribly frayed."

"I would fray it again if it meant finding Trell," Alyneri whispered.

Jaya stood and tugged on Alyneri's hand to bring her to her feet. "Come. Some food will do you good." As she led her off, Jaya's face brightened. "Oh, but 'tis well you've awoken! For my brothers and sister return ere sundown, and they'll be anxious to speak more with you now that your health has been restored."

"And I them," Alyneri admitted. She had yet to see any of the others who'd greeted her upon her arrival at the sa'reyth, though she remembered them indelibly: the imposing and mysterious zanthyr named Vaile; the youth Balaji, who spoke with such command; and the compellingly handsome Náiir ...

Yet she couldn't think of them and not think of the circumstances that had driven her to seek their aid. Alyneri hugged arms to her chest. "Jaya, has Fynn woken yet?"

Jaya considered her quietly. Then she seemed to decide something. "Come. I'll show you why he sleeps so your mind may be at ease." She led Alyneri to a room that had been closed off with a black curtain. Jaya swept it aside and drew Alyneri just within.

In the center of the room, Fynn lay on a bed surrounded by an odd light. Alyneri looked around, trying to determine where the light was coming from, but it had no visible source. It merely hovered around Fynn in a pale nimbus while tiny motes seemed to dance within. Alyneri moved towards Fynn, but Jaya tugged her hand to remain.

"Don't approach too closely. He lies separate from us while he heals."

"Jaya?" a woman's voice coming from behind them held a note of alarm.

Alyneri turned to see a tall woman with flowing dark hair and brilliant blue eyes.

"Mithaiya." Jaya smiled brightly. "Sister, meet Alyneri d'Giverny, betrothed of Trell of the Tides."

Mithaiya cast Alyneri a fleeting look of welcome, but her gaze rapidly returned to her sister. "Jaya, what have you done?" Her tone sounded more accusation than inquiry.

"It's but a simple pattern."

"You've woven the third all about him!" Mithaiya peered critically at the nimbus of light surrounding Fynn and gave Jaya a sharp look. "You've timebound him, Jaya!"

"Only that he may heal within *days* instead of weeks." Jaya tilted her chin defiantly.

Mithaiya's eyes widened, and she hissed, "How is this not testing the Balance?"

Jaya arched an indignant brow. "If Phaedor can play with time, so can I."

"Only ever at *her* behest would he do such a thing!" Mithaiya's tone was rife with disbelief and disapproval. "Never on his own advisement."

"Think you really to lecture me on the motives of the Mage's zanthyr, Mithaiya?" Jaya tossed her head primly. "Next you will say he shares his mind with you."

"I'm not—" Mithaiya opened her mouth and shut it again. "I would *never* make such a claim." Her blue eyes returned to a sleeping Fynn, and a furrow marred her brow. "By the Lady's light, Jaya ... it's just so dangerous."

"The game progresses, Mithaiya," Jaya said unrepentantly. "It is possible you may have to take a side."

Mithaiya sucked in her breath with a hiss.

"But this is no fair reception for young Alyneri." Jaya patted Alyneri's hand while angling her sister a chastising look. "The youngling shouldn't be made to suffer our ancient bickering."

Mithaiya's tense expression abruptly softened. "You're right." She gave Alyneri a smile while her gaze conveyed apology. "You seem much restored since first I saw you sleeping." Her blue eyes flicked to Jaya. "I wonder now did my sister timebind you, too?"

"Blame Balaji's cooking if you must. I did only encourage her into enduring sleep. But come," she let the drape to Fynn's room fall closed and drew Alyneri off again. "We go to find nourishment for the frail flower of our Trell's eye. Have the others returned, Mithaiya?"

Mithaiya walked on her sister's other side. "Balaji and Náiir came with me. Ramu remains with the Mage, and Rhakar ..."

Alyneri caught Mithaiya's hesitation and her heart skipped a beat. She came to a sudden halt, tugging against Jaya's hand. "Did he—"

Mithaiya shook her head. "We've no more news of Trell, sweet one, only that he's been taken to Radov, or his wielder, Viernan hal'Jaitar. M'Nador has many prisons, however, and we cannot know which one conceals your Trell. The Mage's contacts must seek your prince now, for Tal'Shira lies beyond Rhakar's purview."

Alyneri pressed one hand over her mouth and gripped Jaya's hand fiercely with the other.

"*Vincal*, Mithaiya." Jaya gave her a scalding look. She tugged Alyneri into motion, and the three of them headed off again. Under her breath, she muttered, "Might you have waited for a better time to state this truth?"

"You would have me torment her with the secret, now she knows of it?"

Jaya cast Mithaiya a sidelong look. "I would have you be less transparent about its possession to begin with."

"She has a right to know these things. All mysteries are not for keeping."

Jaya rolled her eyes. "Try telling that to the Mage's zanthyr." She swept aside another curtain and led them into a large tent set with numerous groupings of sofas and armchairs. Alyneri was beginning to wonder if the *sa'reyth* had a limitless supply of rooms.

"When I *want* a lesson in futility I'll speak to Phaedor," Mithaiya remarked as she followed behind them. "From my own sister, I expect the light of reason."

"Back only minutes and already at it, I see," a male voice commented humorously.

Alyneri looked to one side and saw a man standing before a long table set with platters of food. She recognized the *drachwyr* called Náiir, whose eyes of wheat made her breath catch as they fixed upon her.

He finished pouring his wine and came across to them, and his sculpted lips twitched in a smile as he neared. "Can you two not mend your fences even to show kindness to a guest?" Reaching Alyneri, he plucked her hand from Jaya's grasp and looked deeply into her eyes as he kissed her fingers. "Alyneri d'Giverny, what a pleasure to finally meet you properly."

She felt herself go a little weak.

"But this is not your only name. No, not your true birth name," he continued, eyeing her with an elusive light in his gaze. "You have Kandori blood, if I'm not mistaken."

"My father ..." Alyneri whispered. Náiir had a way about him that quite stole her breath. "Jair Haxamanis."

Náiir's lips spread in a slow, seductive smile. "I knew we were related."

"That doesn't require much of a deductive leap." Jaya brushed past him and on into the room.

"Alyneri, Princess Heir of Kandori," Náiir continued, pinning Alyneri fast with that smile, which made her belly feel warm and her head light, "daughter to Jair and Melisande of Dannym, niece of Dareios, granddaughter of Jorin Haxamanis, son and heir of Vasudev, heir of Amlan, son of Giridhar, heir of Shrivasta, heir of Inesh, son of Samarth, heir of Muralidhar—"

"I don't see how you keep up with all these relationships." Jaya handed Alyneri a goblet, breaking the trance of Náiir's gaze. Alyneri gratefully accepted the wine. She needed it now for multiple reasons.

"You have your interests, Jaya, I have mine." Náiir looked Alyneri over with another sly and utterly intoxicating smile. "I'm fascinated by how one's seed can be so far reaching."

"I think you've assigned responsibility to the wrong causation," Mithaiya grumbled.

"Peace, Mithaiya." Náiir cast her a look as she seated herself on a couch. "I don't complain about your partaking of that pirate's loins upon every visit to T'khendar. I cannot help that my seed is prolific."

"Your ego is prolific," Jaya muttered.

Alyneri sipped her wine, grateful for its heat and the way it melted the sharp fear that lined her insides with frost. Then, too, Náiir's attention had a similar effect. She welcomed all of these sensations, for their distraction eased her mind. "You know much of the Kandori lineage," she said to Náiir. "Did you know my father?"

"In a sense." He smiled warmly at her. "We are related, you and I, if … distantly."

"Half of Kandori is related to you if distantly," Jaya muttered under her breath.

Náiir shot her a look over his shoulder. "And this seems troublesome to you why, Jaya?"

"I would you didn't fill young Alyneri's mind with your ideas and your talk."

"She could do worse than to gain from the immense wisdom of her paterfamilias," Naiir asserted with an arch of his handsome brow. "But I would know what stories she has heard of me," he added, shooting Alyneri a sudden grin. "Surely you find no harm in the sharing of tales, Jaya."

"Beyond fueling your unbridled narcissism?" She took a seat on the sofa across from Mithaiya and pulled her feet up beneath her like a cat.

"The Mage says we cannot love and respect each other if we do not love ourselves," an entering Balaji observed judiciously.

"*Thank you*, Balaji." Naiir flung a hand to his brother and a pointed look at Jaya.

"*I* would hear of Trell of the Tides," Jaya said with a lofty lift of her chin. Looking kindly upon Alyneri then, she patted the seat beside her. "For clearly he has found himself at last."

"Ah, well," Naiir remitted with a smile, "I can't argue with that." He made a debonair bow to Alyneri and walked her to Jaya's side.

Balaji approached carrying an empty goblet. "Do tell us Trell's tale, Alyneri, daughter of Jair." He handed the goblet to her.

Alyneri blinked as dark liquid swirled into the vessel. She lifted startled eyes to meet Balaji's gaze and found him smiling at her, though something about his smile more unsettled than encouraged her.

For a moment, Alyneri swooned. The idea that she was somehow distantly related to a Sundragon had her spinning, Náiir's attentions had her buzzing ... simply being the focus of such ancient creatures had her blood humming and her heart fluttering ...

Yet the glory of their attention helped push her fears from mind, and she tried to craft them a story worthy of their interest.

Balaji's wine tasted sweet and heady and brought color to her cheeks. Náiir brought her a plate of food. Then they all took seats and leveled their ancient eyes upon her.

So did Alyneri tell the *drachwyr* of Trell's travels to the west and of how she and he came to meet on Yara's farm. When she spoke of Trell rescuing her from the flooded river, Náiir shook his head and remarked, "Naiadithine has outdone herself."

"She challenges your own matchmaking, I do believe, Naiir," Balaji noted with a sharp grin.

"*Pshaw!*" Naiir scoffed. "A pretender! Why *I* have—""

"And Trell has learned of his birthright?" a new voice interrupted before Naiir could hijack them all onto a self-congratulatory tangent.

Alyneri turned. She hadn't seen the zanthyr Vaile come into the room, but the woman stood in the shadows, much as Phaedor always did.

"He has," Alyneri confirmed as the memory melted more of her fear. The moment when she'd told Trell his name remained immense and joyous.

"How did it come to be so?" Jaya asked with brimming excitement. "Tell us!"

So Alyneri continued the tale, speaking of the days of her recovery and of their ensuing time together. She ended with Yara's startling story about the blind Seer who'd read her future.

Whereupon Balaji chuckled as deep as distant thunder, earning a confusingly irritable glare from Jaya, and Náiir remarked in amazement under his breath, "*Isabel*. She is *so* much more daring than even the First Lord!"

"As reckless with her life as Arion ever was," Vaile agreed, but it acted as a sobering comment to the group.

Alyneri thought she must've misunderstood and worried that she hadn't. "Do ..." she had to work some moisture back in her mouth. "Pardon me, but ... do you know this Seer?"

They all exchanged looks, hesitating, and then into the silence, Vaile said, "She is Isabel van Gelderan, Epiphany's Prophet, High Mage of the Citadel."

Alyneri stared at her. She couldn't have been more startled if they'd told her Epiphany Herself walked the land. *Isabel van Gelderan! But ... ?*

She pushed her hair back from her eyes feeling awkward, like she'd become the brunt of a joke everyone else understood. "Then ... then Isabel didn't ... she wasn't …" She pressed the back of one hand to her forehead. Every account of the Adept Wars taught that Björn van Gelderan had murdered his sister Isabel and the other Mages in the Citadel on Tiern'aval. If that wasn't true …

"Isabel lives in T'khendar with the First Lord," Balaji offered. Then he added with a decadent sort of smile, "though you may have heard rumors to the contrary."

Rumors? Alyneri turned him a wide-eyed look and asked weakly, "Are all the histories wrong?"

"Only the ones written in this realm," Vaile remarked.

Jaya glared at her. Then she patted Alyneri's hand. "In time, *soraya*, all things will become clear."

"If time cooperates," Mithaiya said quietly.

This brought another shadow to their ancient eyes. Alyneri didn't understand the sentiment that hovered in silence among them, and she wasn't sure she wanted to. Anything that darkened the gazes of these creatures was likely to frighten her immensely.

"But this bodes well for you, sweet one," noted Mithaiya, breaking the silence and the haunting spell her comment had imposed, "and indeed, for all who cherish Trell of the Tides. For we knew already that the First Lord cared for him, and if he also figures into Isabel's path, we have likely not seen his end."

Alyneri didn't find this sentiment exactly heartening.

"So you left the farm of the old Kandori woman," Jaya prodded with a withering glance at Naiir, who grinned broadly, "and then?"

Alyneri took a deep breath and gathered her thoughts. "Then we went to Rethynnea, where Trell delivered the Mage's missive to his contact, as promised."

"And what did it say, this missive?" Vaile inquired.

Alyneri closed her eyes briefly and let out a little sigh. "It requested that Ghislain see Trell reunited with his family."

"Oh!" Jaya pushed hands to her cheeks. "How marvelous! I do love it when the Mage thinks of everything!"

"Whenever does he not, Jaya?" Naiir remarked.

The room fell silent again, with the others exchanging looks between them that were far too quick and knowing for Alyneri to understand.

But she did understand that thanks to the Agasi silver the Mage had given Trell, he'd been able to bribe Hadrian of Jamaii to save her from the odious Lord Brantley.

She continued the story then, speaking of how Trell had reunited with Fynn at Ghislain's home, how they'd returned to the villa and learned of the destruction of the Temple of the Vestals and Ean's disappearance.

To which everyone in the room fell confusingly silent *again*.

That time, Alyneri didn't let it go. "What is it?" She looked around at all of them with a sudden fluttering unease. "Do you know something of the temple? Of Ean?"

After a tense moment of silence, Balaji answered, "He is in T'khendar with the First Lord—or was when last we saw him."

Alyneri's heart filled with hope. "Then he's well? You've seen him?"

"Only briefly," Naiir said, "but Ramu has spent time with him."

"I sense something of his heart in yours," Vaile remarked then, pinning Alyneri with an arch look.

Alyneri dropped her gaze and flushed. "I ... loved Ean, once." She looked sheepishly around at the group. "But in my heart I'd already let him go before ... well, before Trell came back into my life."

"Of course." Jaya patted her knee and cast Vaile a look of barely concealed annoyance.

"And what is the rest of the tale, young Alyneri, daughter of Jair?" Balaji inquired. "There must be more yet."

"Oh yes." Alyneri felt relieved to return to her story and escape Vaile's discomfiting gaze. She continued telling them of Carnivále, Lord Brantley and her rescue by Trell and the pirates. This led directly to their recent travels ... and travails ... whereupon her voice floundered beneath a rising grief.

"Radov has Trell," Náiir remarked. Alyneri sensed a simmering fury in his tone and fire behind his gaze. "Until we know where he's being held ..."

"Even did we, Náiir," Mithaiya said curtly, "it's not for us to decide what's to be done."

Alyneri suddenly felt desperation grip her again. "But ... but why?"

"Because this is the Mage's game, *soraya*," Jaya consoled. She gave her a look of the deepest sympathy.

"We cannot take action because the game is in play," Balaji added by way of solemn explanation, "and we are not Players within it."

SIXTEEN

"If you would command anything—control or compel

anything—be willing to cause anything."

– The Fifth Vestal Björn van Gelderan

TANIS WOKE FEELING sore in a hundred places. He didn't know whether to thank Loghain for testing him in new and varied ways or to resent him for the same; nor could he understand why he could heal overnight from a beating by Fhorgs but still be sore from sword practice the next day.

He wondered if his unusual ability to heal had something to with the bond he shared with the zanthyr, though something in this answer didn't quite seem true. Still, he wouldn't have put it past Phaedor to offer him a reprieve from wrongful pain yet allow suffering when he felt Tanis had earned it with his own stupidity.

Outside, the barest hint of dawn tinged the fog, but much of the world remained dark. That particular creeping chill which often accompanied early morning had permeated the room. Tanis couldn't yet tell if the day would be born clear or overcast, but odds favored the latter, for while the Caladrian Coast boasted a more temperate climate than northern parts of the Empire, in the winter months it slumbered beneath cloud-blanketed heavens and lingering storms.

The lad lay in bed for a while letting his eyes recover from the sandstorm that seemed to have overtaken them in the night, and then for a while longer while he considered the effort it would take to cross the chilly room to reach his clothes. Normally Tanis would still be asleep during these nascent hours, but Loghain was due to depart with the dawn, and the lad wished to see him off.

Tanis really liked the Wildling. Over their days together, he'd come to appreciate Loghain's particular duality of genteel disposition and ghastly countenance. By the very nature of his being, the Whisper Lord challenged Tanis to look deeper and deny the validity of a judgment based on appearances.

The day before, after yet another bout of grueling sword practice—which activity, Tanis had learned to his dismay, the Whisper Lord apparently found more restful than rest itself—Loghain had shared dinner with Tanis and then joined him in his mother's game room. There, the Whisper Lord attempted to teach the lad strategy at Kings while chewing on a bit of ginger root to settle his 'perpetually tempestuous stomach.'

The game room's long gallery overlooked those razor-edged mountains of frost—the Navárrel. The snowy peaks had been reflecting the sunset back into the gallery as Tanis and the Whisper Lord sat to either side of an ornate marble Kings board.

Tanis had studied Kings with Fersthaven's Marshal, Master Lamory, a witty and charming man who played well; but despite the marshal's enormous patience, Tanis had never advanced beyond an elementary understanding of the game.

Oh, he'd grasped some of the basic tactics with ease, like the Pin and the Skewer and Back Rank Mating, but the further ahead a strategy required him to think and plan—as many as ten or twelve moves, some of them—the farther from his grasp the strategies slipped.

Loghain taught with as much patience as Master Lamory, and more often than not, his tolerant and didactic nature allowed Tanis success at applying his newfound strategies.

"But never expect such concessions from a Sundragon," the Whisper Lord had advised with a chuckle after letting Tanis take a play that a more competitive player never would've allowed.

It wasn't the only such warning Loghain gave Tanis regarding the enigmatic drachwyr, leaving the lad to wonder how a creature the size of a modest castle might engage in a game of Kings.

After teaching the lad a particularly vicious means of annihilating an opponent's guards, the Whisper Lord advised, "But if you ever play a Sundragon, Tanis lad, never use this strategy, for if you do, he will have your king inside of two moves."

That's when Tanis finally asked, "Sir, are you saying that Sundragons can really play Kings?"

Loghain barked a laugh. "I wouldn't be surprised to learn they invented the game!" But at the lad's obvious confusion, the Whisper Lord tilted his head sideways. "Don't you realize their nature, lad? They're of the fifth." When Tanis still looked blank, Loghain posed, "Like the zanthyrs?"

Now Tanis finally understood. "They can shift forms?" The idea opened an entirely new realm of speculation and wonder—as if dragons weren't intriguing enough already.

"Just so, lad. You're far more likely to see a drachwyr in the form than ever to see a zanthyr."

Tanis regarded Loghain wondrously. "I get the idea you know a number of them personally, sir."

"It has been one of my greatest privileges, Tanis."

A flurry of images bombarded him upon this confession, Loghain's thoughts coming loud and forceful as they carried the myriad faces of men and women who the Whisper Lord powerfully admired. One face stood out to Tanis, for he glimpsed it more than once: a handsome man with gloss-black hair and the bluest eyes the lad had ever seen.

Within these thoughts so unwittingly cast forth by Loghain, Tanis understood that these were individuals who had rallied to an immense shared purpose; and he sensed another cohesive element that he recognized as binding all of these faces together: a fierce and unwavering loyalty directed towards the blue-eyed man.

The lad was too bright not to make certain connections then, but this didn't mean he accepted them easily. "Sir …" Tanis fingered the marble knight in his hand, for he sensed he approached a subject rife with dangerous truths. "The blue-eyed man in your thoughts just now … is he the Fifth Vestal?"

Loghain lifted his golden gaze from studying the board. "Aye, lad." His expression turned grave as he considered Tanis. "But he's no one you need fear. Despite what you may've heard, the First Lord seeks naught but to save Alorin from those who would destroy it."

Tanis sensed no undercurrent of duality nor any attempt to dissemble in this statement, and Loghain's tone held such admiration and that Tanis felt only truth in his words. The lad had never experienced a situation where a man spoke a truth that violently disagreed with what most of the world believed … yet the lad knew the real truth was Loghain's.

Suspecting that further talk of Björn van Gelderan would likely take him far afield of any truth he was comfortable exploring, Tanis asked by way of returning them to more certain territory, "Are they only men, the … uh, Sundragons?"

Loghain tilted his head. "Why do you ask?"

"You said 'he will have you.'"

Tanis finally managed to make the move he'd meant to do ages ago, placing his knight to queen-four.

"Ah, so I did." The Whisper Lord eyed Tanis's placement of his knight with a hungry half-smile. "How very observant of you."

Loghain took Tanis's knight with a pawn—an outcome the lad had failed to predict in all his flurry over Sundragons and banished wielders. While Tanis was smarting from the loss of his piece, the Wildling offered, "I've met six Sundragons. Two are female, but the ladies will never play Kings. They much prefer the game of glass stones—Shari, as the Kandori call it."

Tanis shook his head somewhat glumly. He had no idea what to do now to make up for losing his knight. Much of his strategy had depended on it—a fact Loghain likely knew. "I don't know Shari," the lad said while vainly attempting to formulate a new plan.

"'Tis a game of strategy played with round pieces of colored glass—or among the princes of Kandori, polished rubies, emeralds and sapphires." He sat back with a smile while memories flashed through his thoughts. "T'were never deadlier opponents than Amithaíya'geshwen or Jayachándranáptra when either is intent upon winning a game of Shari, except ..." He pressed one leathery finger to his lips. "Actually, it may be more dangerous still when they let you win, for then they have settled a different sort of predatory eye upon you."

Tanis heard the thoughts Loghain's tongue had refrained from uttering and blushed.

The Whisper Lord shot him a wide grin. "I recommend you don't engage in board games with a Sundragon of either gender until you're certain of your mettle, Tanis lad."

Tanis assured him he had no intent of challenging a Sundragon in any capacity.

Loghain grinned even wider.

The night had ended with Loghain unsurprisingly taking the game and with Tanis really wishing he would've noticed that ruthless pawn before it destroyed his otherwise excellent strategy.

Now morning had come and Loghain would be leaving.

Tanis threw off his heavy eiderdown quilt and hurried to dress. Making his quiet way through the darkened villa then, he found Loghain seated at the long kitchen table, nursing a cup of tea. Across the vast room, the robust cook, Nathalia, was busily preparing breakfast while humming tunelessly to herself, and Madaé Giselle could be heard issuing orders from the bakery down a short hallway. Tanis smelled onions and eggs frying in Nathalia's iron skillet, but he was more interested in the plate of bacon on the table, for each piece was smothered in Madaé Giselle's prized bigleaf syrup, dark as molasses and sticky-sweet.

As Tanis sat down across from him, Loghain looked up and gave the lad his grimace of a smile. Tanis barely saw the Whisper Lord's gruesome features anymore, seeing instead the kind and considerate man beneath them.

"*Dal mogen*, Tanis," Loghain greeted in his own language.

Tanis didn't know the Tyriolicci tongue, but his truthreader's talent registered the thought behind the words and understood them to mean 'good morning.'

Tanis stifled a yawn. "And to you also, sir."

Loghain poured Tanis some tea from the pot on the table and smiled when the lad's next yawn escaped his attempts to hold it back.

"Lady of the Rivers take my eyes for they're a-tellin' lies!"

Tanis pushed a fist over his third yawn and looked over to find Madaé Giselle standing in the archway. She had a large crockery jar braced precariously between arm and hip and a floury handprint on her cheek. "What're you a-doin' up at this hour by the gracious heavens, Tanis lordling?"

"I ..." Tanis broke into another yawn. "... came to see Loghain off."

"Well, that's a-kind of you." Madaé Giselle came on into the kitchen, peered over Nathalia's shoulder to assess the eggs, and then set her jar down on a scrubbed wooden table at least nine feet long. She sighed discontentedly as she starting untying the waxed canvas lid. "I vow, that Dional had best find his *drogue* wolf today or it'll be nothing but dried beef for the household, and that's no decent fare for the lady's son!"

"T'isn't bad over toast, Madaé," Nathalia noted pleasantly.

"Don't be a-chiming in agin about it, Nathalia," Giselle squawked, giving her a sharp look. "We shan't be a-feeding the lady's son none of that goop your folk call gravy for his supper."

"It's mighty tasty, Madaé."

"Don't you listen to her, Tanis lordling." Madaé Giselle scoured Tanis with her gaze while busily retrieving bundles of herbs from inside the jar. "Nathalia's people aren't known for their culinary talents." She made a little spitting sound off to the side and then cast Nathalia another hawkish look.

"I guess Phaedor is still out with the huntsmen?" Tanis asked.

"As ever we can tell, milord." Nathalia came to the table with food in hand. "The Lord Phaedor isn't exactly forthcoming with his whereabouts."

"And what do you ken about it?" Madaé Giselle pinned Nathalia with a cronish eye. "I'll have you know, Tanis lordling, the Lord Phaedor was called away again ere the witching hour. Barely made it to his rooms, I vow, before Kendir was a-banging on his door. One of Dional's huntsmen was attacked by the dreaded beast. It lured Cyrt into some kind of a trap. Imagine a creature so smart and crazed at the same time! Cyrt may've lost a leg, or worse—can't say whether or not his lordship a-reached him in time, and we won't know 'til they all return."

"That won't be too soon, eh Madaé?" plump Nathalia noted.

Madaé Giselle grumbled something inhospitable and headed back out of the room, calling Nathalia after her.

Tanis dove in to his eggs hungrily and made a quick dent in the piles on his plate, yet all the while he remained acutely aware of Loghain's somber mood. A darkness accompanied the Whisper Lord this morning; obscuring mists shadowed his thoughts, and Tanis sensed grave truths hiding among shifting veils of regret.

"Where do you head now, sir?" the lad asked. He hoped he might draw forth the Wildling's usual jovial spirit.

Loghain glanced up from his tea. "To fulfill my duty, Tanis youth. Alas, time steals away, and ever must I chase it."

"You seem melancholy, sir."

Loghain gave him a regretful smile. "Duty casts a long shadow upon my path today. Would that I might linger here longer—in truth, if discipline did not itself require it, I might be tempted, for time within your father's spells passes differently than in the world beyond—"

"By the accursed light of Nuskat's grave!" Madaé Giselle came barging back into the room carrying an open basket of herbs. "It's all gone to blackspot!" She dumped the moldy vegetation on the prep table and glared reproachfully at it.

"What has, Madaé?" Tanis asked, half-turning in his chair.

"Heartleaf." She flicked at the offending leaves. "The last of my supply."

"That's a pity," agreed a returning Nathalia. She was laden down with bowls of vegetables. "Don't you need heartleaf for the pies I'm about to make?"

Madaé Giselle cast her a doleful eye. "You know I do, you impish tart. And now that *drogue* wolf's a-drawn off all my lady's foresters and not a soul around to gather more."

"I know heartleaf," Tanis said. "My lady used it often in poultices. I should be pleased to get more for you if you can tell me where it grows."

"Why y'are a love!" She beamed at him at first. Then she tilted her head and spied him shrewdly. "But ware, 'tis a hike east and north into the hills, for the stuff is rare enough in these parts. Two turns of the hourglass, mind, and that's with a span of good weather behind us to dry the path, which we don't have."

Tanis shrugged. "I've nothing to do until Phaedor returns." At least he didn't expect so. The patterns on his walls had remained quiet and dim, and he'd done more than his share of sword practice in recent days with Loghain.

"I'm heading that way for a stretch," the Whisper Lord offered. "We can hike it together."

"Suit yourself then." Madaé Giselle waved absently at them both. "But don't claim I put you to the task, should the Lord Phaedor take exception to the lady's son a-cavortin' in the hills."

"Mind you stay out of the forest, Tanis," said an entering Madaé Lisbeth.

Tanis rarely saw his mother's seneschal, but the diminutive woman never failed to make him nervous when she did appear. Even knowing she'd been his nurse when he was a babe didn't quell the sensation. It was like she knew all of his worst mistakes and reminded him of them with every inch of her gaze. He'd never known anyone who wasn't a truthreader to engender such a reaction.

Madaé Lisbeth set down her ever-present ledger on a counter and opened a high, glass-fronted cabinet full of folded linens just above it. "That *drogue* beast is giving our good huntsmen a turn for their efforts," she muttered with a shake of her greying head. She began taking out neat piles of tablecloths and placing them on the counter, ostensibly to be inventoried. "Last we heard, they thought it was making its way west, but I vow none of them know exactly where the creature is hiding."

"I'll be sure to stay in the clear, Madaé Lisbeth," Tanis promised.

"I suppose that's our cue then, lad," Loghain said with a quiet smile.

The Whisper Lord took leave of the household staff and especially thanked Madaé Lisbeth, but as they were heading out, Tanis remembered something and spun back to ask, "Madaé Giselle?"

She looked up from her work at the prep table. "What? Changed your mind already?"

"No, it's just …" he looked around, searching the kitchen with his gaze.

"What're you a-pining for, child?"

"I was just thinking I should take a knife with me, Madaé. Heartleaf is really hard to cut."

"A knife!" She shoved hands onto her hips. "Where's the dagger as obviously belongs in that sheath you're always a-wearing?"

Tanis gave her a pained look. "It's a long story."

She eyed him shrewdly, but she gave him a small butcher's knife to carry all the same.

Tanis parted ways with the Whisper Lord amid a bracing wind. The high plateau where their paths diverged offered a view up and down the coastline. South-westward, the distant cliffs vanished into fog, but to the north and east the grey-green hills of a great bay curved, its long, sandy beach a sickle moon beneath smoke-hued, sullen clouds.

Tanis watched Loghain trudging off into the misty hills until he passed from sight, then he continued along the path to find Madaé Giselle's heartleaf. Feeling somewhat disheartened by their parting, Tanis shoved hands in his pockets and slumped his shoulders while he walked beneath the oppressive clouds.

As the trail wound into the mist-drenched hills, the overcast devolved into fog and drizzle and the clouds settled down upon the land as if resentful of being roused in the first place. Tanis cast an annoyed look at the sky and pulled up the hood of his cloak.

Off to his left, dark swaths of forest clung like black moss to the steep sides of a ravine that dove many hundreds of feet into the land. He'd left the sound and smells of the sea far behind; now the air carried that particular musk of damp earth, wet rock, and moss.

As Tanis rounded a curve in the trail where a sheer incline emptied down into the forest on his left, a loud rumbling from everywhere and nowhere brought him to a precipitous halt. Instinctively, he moved closer to the rock face on his right and watched in awe and wonder as the trail just before him morphed into a mudslide that tore half of the hill down with it.

Tanis backed hastily away—but not quickly enough—for the path beneath him suddenly shifted and became fluid. In an instant, a mass of mud and rock had captured him up to his thighs and was carrying him on its tide, plunging relentlessly downward into the trees.

Wild wind stung Tanis's eyes. He threw an arm across his face as he plummeted beneath the forest canopy, terrified that the torrent would ram him into trees or boulders. Some low-hanging branches teased possible escape, but the clinging mud tore him forward before he could grab hold. Rough limbs scratched him while tree trunks blurred past.

And then, for all its intensity, the deluge just ... ended. The incline leveled out, and the landslide came to a sluggish halt.

Relief mingled with lingering fright as Tanis reached trembling hands for a near branch and dragged himself free of the heavy mud. A few harrowing minutes later, the boy sat adjacent to the mudslide, winded and shaken and drenched in filth, but otherwise unharmed.

Tanis spent a few minutes retrieving his composure, which had abandoned him higher up on the hill, and took deep breaths to calm his ragged nerves. Then he got unsteadily to his feet and looked around.

To all sides, the forest grew wild and dark. Fir trees black with moss blocked what little light the overcast allowed. He could barely see a hundred paces into the gloom. Directly above him, the hillside had sheared off to become slick and steep. He tried climbing it, but his feet simply sank as if into snow, and higher up the hill became nearly vertical—he'd never make it back up.

Tanis tried for the better part of an hour to regain the trail through the forest, but in every attempt, he reached a ridge where the land angled so sharply upwards that he'd have needed climber's picks to surmount it.

The adrenaline surge that had buoyed him upon the tide of mud soon abated, and now a sense of impending doom settled upon the lad. The mudslide had taken him into a valley on the north side of the trail—away from the path back to the villa. He couldn't just angle back the same direction in which he'd come, because all attempts ran him into that inaccessible ridge. Frustrated, Tanis reluctantly headed off into the forest instead, knowing all the while that he was heading in the wrong direction.

After about an hour of slow progress—wherein he slipped and slid through deep piles of leaves while being accosted by underbrush with a variety of spiny appendages—Tanis reached a creek. Though icy, the tumbling waters gave him a chance to clean up. He stripped off his clothes, waded into the water and rinsed everything thoroughly. His hands and legs were numb before he finished, and donning again his wet clothing seemed like adding insult to injury, but he took some small relief being free of the cloying mud.

As he stood shivering, staring at the stream and wondering what to do, Tanis remembered a story Fynnlar had told him once about a group of treasure hunters who got lost in the jungle but found their way back to civilization by riding a river. He decided to follow the stream and hope for a similar outcome.

He really wished he knew Phaedor's trick of conjuring fire while he walked, though, for his teeth were chattering despite the arduous trekking.

All in all, Tanis was not finding much to appreciate about his adventure.

The stream eventually became a waterfall that emptied into a crescent-shaped ravine, whose fern-lined walls fell away seventy paces to the rocky pool below. Tanis was forced to look for another path downhill, which took him deeper still into the forest.

The day lengthened, and the lad grew so cold that his feet and fingers ached. He decided to stop and attempt a fire, for he knew the night would grow colder still.

Tanis had learned much from his travels—first with Prince Ean and Rhys and later with the zanthyr, the latter of whom had advised him to always carry flint and steel. The lad had accordingly sequestered a bit of the stone in an inside pocket of his cloak, and he hunted around for a particular type of moss that he'd seen the zanthyr use often enough. Then he gathered wood. Once he got a fire going, he used Madaé Giselle's dagger to strip fir boughs to both shield his body from the cold earth and cover himself as the night deepened.

In this way did Tanis begin the evening: sitting fireside upon a bed of fir limbs, letting the heat steam away the damp from his clothes and boots. He had a supply of firewood that would keep through the night. He figured if he couldn't have food, at least he'd stay mostly warm.

He consoled himself with the knowledge that they'd be looking for him by now—at least ... well, if the hunters had returned and learned of his absence, the zanthyr would be well on his way to finding him.

But what if Dional and the others had spent another night in the forest? Surely *someone* would be sent in search of him ... wouldn't they?

Tanis imagined Madaé Giselle and Madaé Lisbeth at least would call for a search party, though the idea of these two ancient women trudging through the forest in the night was both sadly comical and a little frightening.

He tried for a long while to see if he could sense the bond that connected him and Phaedor—weren't you supposed to be able to perceive such things?—but he could claim no more awareness of the zanthyr's whereabouts than he'd ever been able to before.

When Phaedor had come for him in Rimaldi, the zanthyr said he'd just been waiting for Tanis's call. The lad suspected that 'call' was connected to the working of his talent, but he had no one nearby to work a Telling upon, and he didn't know how else to wield his gift that he might alert the zanthyr to his whereabouts.

Eventually these avenues became a little too frightening to ponder.

A morose mood and sharp hunger compounded his exhaustion, and Tanis was soon struggling to keep his eyes open. He tried recounting some of his mother's lessons, and this kept him alert for a while, but too soon his eyelids were fluttering again.

The lad had just begun to doze off when a sudden sense of alarm jolted him back to wakefulness. He scrambled to his feet, but then he just stood there listening to the darkness while his heart raced.

The forest lay quiet. Perhaps too quiet. He didn't expect to hear crickets at that time of year, but usually some nocturnal animals prowled the night—owls and bats and other such creatures.

Like drogue *wolves?*

The thought came with a sharp pang in the same moment that Tanis realized he wasn't alone. He snatched up his butcher knife and held it before him, but his hands felt clammy on the handle and his head too light.

Don't panic. Don't panic! What if it's just a raccoon?

Tanis took a deep breath to try to calm his racing pulse, but an imminent and pervasive sense of danger kept him far from calm.

What if it is the wolf?

Tanis pushed the hair from his eyes with the back of his hand and strained to see beyond his circle of firelight.

Surely a drogue *wolf is no less of a threat than a raving Malorin'athgul,* he reasoned, not entirely comforted in the correlation. He held his knife before him and assumed a fighting stance, balancing his weight evenly between both feet, knees bent. But he didn't feel the least bit brave.

Darkness enveloped the world beyond his fire-lit circle. Tanis listened for sounds from the deep, but all he could really hear was the crackle of his fire and the horrendously loud beating of his heart, which seemed to reverberate through his body as if it were a tower bell. He was scanning the darkness in a state of rising panic when the beast at last presented itself.

Tanis's senses screamed and his heart leapt into double-time as he watched the massive creature gliding from darkness into the light—head, shoulders and haunches emerged from the wall of night as if birthed by it.

Drogue *wolf,* his mental voice whimpered.

Twice the size of a normal wolf, this beast was born of impossibly high mountains and voracious winters—a *thinking* beast of cunning and intelligence.

And this one was clearly deranged.

Even had the wolf not held its head slightly tilted and sideways, Tanis would've known its illness from its thoughts, for they rolled upon a tide of madness. Tanis *felt* them, sensed them, even as he might know a man's thoughts—for all thoughts had force, whether they belonged to man or beast.

In one torrential rush, Tanis knew the virulent illness that drove the wolf to mania, as well as the crazed and vicious impulses that held the creature in thrall. He knew also that what remained of the wolf's true self desired only to leave this place—this forest that accosted his ears with its maddening hum—but he couldn't ... couldn't ...

The fever that ravaged the wolf was not unlike the terrible storm of Bethamin's Fire which had so destroyed the mind of the boy Piper.

The beast slung its snout to and fro while the muscles of its haunches twitched erratically. As it entered the edge of Tanis's firelight, the wolf bared its teeth, and a guttering snarl rumbled in its throat. The sound raised the hairs on the lad's arms and sent a shudder down his spine.

The wolf stopped ten paces away and faced Tanis. It seemed to see the boy for the first time, and when it did ...

With a sinking feeling, Tanis felt the beast's thoughts focus ... focus through the delirium—

Focus on *him*.

The wolf growled. Then it leapt.

Tanis dove.

It happened so fast. A desperate urgency gripped the lad and—

The world shifted.

The wolf ... *slowed.*

Tanis could think of no other explanation for what his eyes perceived. The animal appeared to hang in midair while Tanis slammed into the earth. He stared up at the hulking beast above, its razor teeth bared. But Tanis's motion and the motion of the wolf were no longer congruous—the two of them no longer traveled on the same thread of time.

Tanis pushed shakily to his feet and noticed that the motion felt heavy and his limbs sluggish, like swimming through the mudslide that had dumped him into this mess.

Still in the grip of that first instant of desperation, Tanis thought of what harm the wolf had caused, of what it would surely do to him if he allowed it, and the instinct to kill rather than be killed grew strong. He pushed his sluggish limbs until he stood beneath the wolf. Then he drove his knife towards the beast's throat.

It was all happening in an instant, yet Tanis knew each moment within that instant as intimately as if every ticking second existed for an eternity. The lad watched as his own blade inched closer to the wolf's throat, and then—

A shadowed ... *something.*

A bracing impact knocked Tanis sideways and stole his breath even as it broke the infinity into even smaller infinities—a second of time shattering into a thousand moments more—stretching this single instant beyond comprehension.

The lad felt himself flying ... falling, and he twisted to see Phaedor's dark form glide between himself and the wolf, the zanthyr's cloak floating in suspension upon the waves of endless time.

And the world started again.

Tanis hit the ground with jarring force. His breath completely left his lungs, and stars blanketed his vision. Tasting blood as he lay gasping for air, he watched the zanthyr catch the wolf's muzzle with both hands, swing the great beast around, and slam it to the ground pinned beneath him.

The creature exploded in fury. Dirt and leaves peppered the trees behind its powerful legs as clawed feet scrabbled for purchase. It growled a horrid, guttering snarl that raised the hairs on the back of Tanis's neck. But Phaedor was of the fifth; he sat as a vice above the wolf, still as stone, utterly immovable.

Frightened and shocked, Tanis pushed up and hugged his knees. He stared numbly at the zanthyr, drinking the air in little gasps. He realized that whatever he'd just done—*however* he'd done it—what the zanthyr had done to *join* him in that moment was exponentially more impossible.

As the lad watched, the wolf's struggling ebbed, and the beast finally calmed. Straddling the creature, Phaedor murmured something in a language that seemed to Tanis to be as ancient as the realm itself.

The wolf whined pitifully.

This plaintive whimper tore at Tanis, and he experienced a powerful pang of sympathy. He wondered why the zanthyr delayed putting the beast out of its misery and felt frustrated by Phaedor's uncharacteristic lack of compassion, until ...

Understanding dawned with a new shock spawned of sudden guilt.

Phaedor wasn't planning to kill the wolf. He was *Healing* it.

This moment of realization flowed into a lengthy and motionless silence, and Tanis—both altogether unnerved and powerfully moved—found himself perpetually checking to be certain that time yet flowed in its natural course.

The lad shakily reclaimed his feet. He took small comfort in brushing the dirt and leaves from his clothes and watching the pieces fall normally to the forest floor. An owl's hoot encouraged him, as did the sudden staccato of rising rainfall hitting the forest firs.

Finally, the wolf gave a different sort of throaty whimper, but this time its tone seemed submissive ... even perhaps tinged with contrition.

Phaedor released the beast and spun off it in one swift and graceful turn, and Tanis watched nervously as the animal sprang to its feet. The beast shook out its ruff and then the rest of its body, peppering the nearby trees with bits of mud.

Tanis stifled a latent shudder. He stood close enough to smell the beast's feral musk, but the wolf's thoughts were no longer loud enough for the boy to hear or sense, and its yellow eyes appeared altogether lucid as they locked upon the zanthyr's.

Phaedor nodded once.

The wolf snarled. Then it spun and bounded off, vanishing like a ghost into the curtain of night.

Tanis let out a shuddering exhale.

And the events of the night collapsed upon him. He pitched to his knees beside the fire, willing away threatening tears. No small part of the clenching feeling in his chest was the certainty that *he* would've killed the wolf while Phaedor had delivered its salvation. "What … what in Tiern'aval just happened?"

After a moment, Phaedor came and crouched down beside the lad. "Exactly what do you *think* happened, Tanis?"

He pushed palms to his eyes. "Don't torment me with questions now, my lord—*please*, I beg you!"

The zanthyr drew in his breath sharply. "It's not my intention to torment you, Tanis. Your perception and mine may not be the same."

Tanis hadn't thought of that. He dropped his hands and managed an uncomfortable swallow. His chest and throat were horribly tight. "I think … that time … shifted."

"And I would agree." Phaedor regarded the boy with an unwavering gaze. "Yet it is truer to say *you* shifted time."

"Yes …" Tanis abruptly leaned to brace elbows on knees and rest his forehead in his hands, feeling sick, "that's what I thought you were going to say."

It was one thing to dream of having special abilities—Tanis and his friend Tad val Mallonwey had often speculated on what it would be like to wield the fifth, or what sorts of magic they would craft of the fourth if they'd had the skill—but it was quite another thing to find yourself *shifting time* with no explanation or understanding of how you were doing it.

Phaedor left the lad to his confusion and used the time to gather some of the wood that had been scattered in the struggle. He tossed more logs onto the dying flames, sending up a shower of sparks among the smoke, and then tended the fire until it was blazing again.

Tanis sat up once the flames started scalding the top of his head. He looked over at the zanthyr to find him seated with an elbow draped over his bent knee, emerald eyes watching him, quiet and intense. The lad frowned. "What?"

Phaedor arched brows innocently. "I'm waiting for your questions."

Tanis grunted and sat back on his heels. "What's the point of questions? You never answer the important ones anyway."

The zanthyr regarded him steadily. "I could tell you everything there was to know in this world, Tanis—the whole of the *Sobra I'ternin*, should you wish it—yet this knowledge would be of no value to you without the foundation of experience against which to measure it."

He tilted his head to engage Tanis in this reasoning, holding the boy's gaze with his own. "How does one know courage if he has never known fear? Or trust if he's never known treachery?" He glanced to where the impression of the wolf's body remained in the soft earth. "How could you understand mercy had you not yourself just known its opposite—and felt the guilt that seizes within you still?"

Tanis dropped his gaze and clenched his jaw.

The zanthyr gave him a compassionate look. "Knowledge must be gained at its proper time, Tanis, that its *value* might be understood, that it might be given the correct significance based on one's experience—for you cannot say all facts are equally important, any more than you can say all men are compassionate, or all Malorin'athgul are evil."

Tanis frowned at this last association. Lifting his gaze back to the zanthyr, he drew in a deep breath and let it out slowly, feeling exhausted in body and mind. "All right, my lord. What would you tell me of what happened tonight?"

Phaedor cast him a droll look. "I would tell you that you are your mother's son. There are things you can do that others cannot." He cocked his head and regarded Tanis sideways. "Surely this doesn't surprise you."

Tanis thought of the way he healed so quickly. He'd assumed this quality was an attribute of the bond that bound Phaedor to him, but what if it wasn't?

The idea made him uncomfortable all over again.

"No, my lord," he admitted, accepting if not understanding. "I suppose this idea isn't new to me."

"Tell me now in your view, truthreader: what was it that you did?"

Tanis thought about it. He mostly just wanted the zanthyr to *explain*, but he also knew that protesting was a waste of his energies—especially when he was hungry and tired and cold and just wanted to go home. So he thought back to his mother's lessons, especially her last lesson and how it had begun like all the others, by his staring at a ...

His eyes flew back to Phaedor's. "The pattern."

The zanthyr's penetrating gaze seemed to hold the idea solidly in front of Tanis that he might better examine it. "Which pattern?"

"The other morning ... the day Loghain arrived, the pattern on my wall. It ..." he couldn't believe he hadn't connected it before, that he hadn't realized they were one and the same. "The pattern I used to start my mother's lesson the other morning ... it was the same pattern I saw Loghain use later that day. The ... the same pattern I must've ..."

"The pattern you used tonight."

Gulp. "Yes." Tanis pushed a hand into his hair and left it there, staring hard at the flames. "But ... how could I wield a pattern that I only just saw?" He lifted troubled eyes back to the zanthyr. "I'm no wielder."

The zanthyr nudged at the fire with a stick. "There are some few Adepts who have but to see a pattern to inherently grasp its use."

"Sure, if it's a native pattern of your own strand, but ..." A little late, Tanis picked up the undertone in the zanthyr's reply and gave him a sudden suspicious look. "*How* few?"

Phaedor grinned. "A very few."

Tanis grunted and rubbed at one eye. Something about that answer didn't seem to fit. It wasn't just that it startled him to think himself capable of a talent so rare—though it did. Rather, this explanation sort of slid off of Tanis's mind, like a too-big hat that wouldn't stay on. But Tanis was too tired to push the zanthyr for a better explanation.

Phaedor tossed his stick onto the flames and stood. "Come, lad." He gazed softly down at him. "You've done good work today."

Tanis frowned at him. "What's that supposed to mean?"

But the zanthyr merely held out his hand to help him up.

Tanis accepted and got to his feet. Strangely, at Phaedor's touch, the lad felt some of his spunk returning. "So, my lord," he asked as he brushed the dirt and leaves from his pants again while noticing resentfully how neither mud nor leaf dared cling to the zanthyr's clothes, "does this mean there are other things I can do? I don't suppose I could fly, could I?"

"I don't advise you try it, truthreader."

"What about conjuring fire? Can you show me that pattern?"

Phaedor arched a dubious brow. "Perhaps if ever I trusted you not to burn down the forest in the attempt."

While Tanis was leveling him an injured glare, the zanthyr extinguished the blazing fire behind them with naught but a sidelong glance and summoned a portal to deliver them home.

SEVENTEEN

"He who has a head of wax should not stand in the sun."

– A saying among chandlers

THE EMPRESS OF Agasan held court twice each month on a day known as Twelfth-day. For the High Lord Marius di L'Arlesé, this Twelfth-day was ending as most did: after a long, trying afternoon of diplomacy, bureaucracy and—as far as Marius was concerned—no small measure of ill-disguised idiocy.

"Ambassador Durith-Morgaine," the Empress's *elae*-enhanced voice interrupted both the tall man standing in oratory before her as well as the High Lord's thoughts. "Surely you don't presume to explain to me the fundamentals of economics."

Standing with his mouth caught somewhat agape, not unlike a trout snagged by a fisherman's hook, the tall ambassador flushed to the roots of his thinning brown hair and muttered a hasty apology.

Marius admitted that simply standing before the Diamond Throne could be daunting enough, even without the Empress's striking form gracing its cushion. The gigantic chair had been created by the wielder Markal Morrelaine during the Fourth Age—called the Summer Age—of Hallian van Gelderan's rule, in those sunny times before Malachai's violent storm and the wintry years that followed. Formed with *elae*, it dwarfed the other gilded thrones behind it and was positioned directly beneath the domed crystal ceiling such that the sun stayed upon it throughout the day. The entire throne sparkled so brilliantly that it made a man's eyes ache just looking at it.

Compounding this effect was the Empress herself, whose clinging dress of thread-of-silver was so encrusted with diamonds that it made her seem a universe of radiant stars against the upholstery of black velvet.

Because Durith-Morgaine still had not formed a suitable reply, the Empress continued in an unrelenting tone, "I needn't remind you, Ambassador, that Llerenas-Onstaz had its opportunity to unionize and chose against it—"

"Based on assurances from your Minister of Trade, A-Aurelia," the man stammered out the Empress's formal title, "who—who gave us his promise that our wares would find their niche in the marketplace."

Llerenas-Onstaz was an independent province located between Rimaldi and Ma'hrkit. Landlocked, they were in the unenviable position of bartering with richer, larger neighbors for the resources they lacked.

"But the unions have pushed us out of Rimaldi and Vaalden completely," added a shorter man who stood wringing his hands beside the ambassador. Marius couldn't recall his name, but he wore the Llerenas-Onstaz sash of the nobility in a diagonal stripe across his pale blue doublet.

"No one will buy our wares, Aurelia," the ambassador finished, "or even stock them in their stores. They're too afraid of the unions."

"The people aren't buying your wares, Ambassador, because your merchandise is poorly crafted." The Empress's *elae*-enhanced voice carried to the far corners of the vast hall, so that even the chamber mice in their subterranean lairs could hear her. "Inferior pottery that chips on first use, and ill-woven carpets that don't stand up to use aren't likely to fetch a copper in our civilized empire. Do not seek to blame the unions for Llerenas-Onstaz's floundering economy. The Empire isn't responsible for your failures of policy, and we don't subsidize ventures of enterprise."

Quiet but sneering laughter from the seated ranks of the imperial ministry followed these words, and both the ambassador and his noble companion flushed in anger, bowing their heads before the judging ministers and the perverse pleasure of the assembled nobility who had gathered in the vast hall.

"It seems cruel," the veiled Princess Nadia van Gelderan murmured from beside Marius. Their thrones were far enough behind the Empress's that low conversation could go unnoticed.

Marius turned her a considering look.

"They're a small province without the same resources as their neighbors." When she spoke, the princess's breath stirred the opalescent veil that covered her face, a long, diaphanous draping held in place by a circlet of emeralds, bright against the pale silk.

"Verily, Nadia," Marius agreed. "Membership in the unions would have offered them the expertise of traveling smiths and master craftsmen trained in cultural centers like Sfvat and Faroqhar, but for some reason their government refused the Empress's generous offer."

Now they were eating crow. The Empress would ensure these two chewed and swallowed every last bitter feather before offering them a morsel of help at double the usual price.

Nadia returned her gaze to the ongoing discussion. "It just seems cruel to me."

"Perhaps it is." Marius arched a resigned brow and let out a slow exhale. "Would that governing were more about *governing* and less about business, Nadia, but governments need income to function." He captured his daughter's gaze with his own, faint though hers appeared beneath the sheer layer of silk. "The people blame the government if the economy falters—by the Sanctos, they blame the government if the fish aren't biting. So the government becomes a clearing house for the Empire's trade. This is ever the way of things."

"Gaugin speaks in his writings about a utopia where equanimity reigns and the people live and work harmoniously as equals in a classless society."

"Gaugin is an idealist," Marius returned, "and like most idealists lacks that fundamental trait which would allow his ideas to become widely implemented."

"Pray tell me what trait that is, father?"

Marius turned her a wan look. "Practicality."

Nadia opened her mouth to reply, but Marius held a finger to his lips and guided her attention back to the proceedings of the court.

A new envoy was approaching with an assemblage of dignitaries in tow. Marius hoped this would be the last of them, for the day's proceedings had been long and the sun had already fallen below the goldline—that band of gilded statues that ran in a frieze along the length of the chamber's westerly wall, just below the high windows. The sun breaking the eastern wall's roseline marked the opening of Twelfth-day proceedings and falling beneath the goldline heralded its end.

The Lord Chamberlain stood from behind his ornate desk and announced, "The Lord Roric of Dalmain and his entourage." He looked to Lord Roric. "The claimant may approach the Diamond Throne."

Lord Roric nodded to the Lord Chamberlain and took a step forward. He bowed low. "Aurelia," he bade upon rising, "I come as a representative of the Archduke Tucane and the Court of Elders." He extended a rolled parchment to the Lord Chamberlain, who took it, read it over, and nodded to the Empress.

"Your credentials are accepted," came her throaty reply. "State your case, Lord Roric."

"Aurelia, I've come to request a renegotiation of the imperial tithe leveled upon Dalmain."

"A renegotiation of which tithe, Lord Roric?"

"The Adept tithe, Aurelia."

At this utterance, a hushed murmuring bubbled among the assembled nobility, which included ambassadors from every province in the Empire. Ambassadors from allied kingdoms were also invited to Twelfth-day proceedings, but only a few attended regularly.

"The imperial tithe is leveled fairly and equally among every sovereign province in the Empire, Lord Roric," the Empress returned. "Your Archduke's distant predecessor agreed to the tithe when Dalmain fell to the forces of the Emperor, my father, some two centuries ago. The then King of Dalmain chose to maintain his kingdom's sovereignty within the Empire's benevolent rule. The Empire sends trained men to defend your borders and stations soldiers along the imperial roads. Your cities know peace for the addition of our Red Guard to your Duke's peacekeeping ranks. The Adept tithe *is* the price of this peace and freedom."

"Yes, Aurelia, but the race was not dying at the time that these terms were negotiated. Hope remained that their numbers would recover."

"You speak of Adepts and our decline like a herd of cattle, Lord Roric." The Empress's tone had hardened measurably. "Is that how Dalmain views the descendants of the realm's most ancient race? Or is this merely your view?"

Lord Roric flushed. "I meant no disrespect, Aurelia. But to be fair," and he glanced at the men standing beside and around him, "we have so few Adepts to count among our people that they may well be compared to a rare breed of animal."

A sibilating discord of astonished murmuring hissed through the crowd at this.

The Empress rested an elbow on the arm of her throne and her chin atop her fingers. "I'm intrigued, Lord Roric." Her tone dripped with derision. "What terms does your Archduke propose?"

Marius shook his head with quiet disbelief as he watched the nobleman, who'd missed entirely the Empress's thrumming indignation, blithely steering himself and his Duke into a hurricane sea.

Lord Roric drew tall, apparently thinking he'd gotten the upper hand of the Empress with a smartly argued debate. "Currently, Aurelia, Dalmain is required to send Adepts equal to one percent of our population."

"Along with every other sovereign province in the Empire, Lord Roric," the Empress returned brusquely. "In exchange, the Empire sees those Adepts are properly trained and their talents tested during a ten-year term in the Imperial Adeptus. They return to Dalmain with well-honed skills."

"That may be, Aurelia, but with the tithe levy remaining fixed while Dalmain's Adept population declines, we have but few Adepts left to us until those others return."

"I don't see your point, Lord Roric. A constant flow of Adepts should be returning to you as they complete their tenure in the Adeptus."

"But they don't all choose to return, Your Majesty. Many take the skills we paid so dearly for them to learn and hire out to dukes and kings in other territories, leaving us worse off than before we paid the tithe to have our Adepts trained."

Muttering echoed through the chamber like distant thunder. Marius could see the Empress's benevolence deteriorating along with the daylight.

Lord Roric continued, unheeding, "Instead of one percent of our population, the Archduke proposes to send ten Adepts a year to Faroqhar for training."

"Preposterous!" rumbled the Lord Chamberlain, while the crowd broke into agitated muttering. Even the Princess Nadia drew in her breath sharply.

The Empress raised a hand for silence. Then she looked back to Lord Roric. "Since we are bandying over Adepts like Khurdish traders in the Bashir'Khazaaz, let us comport ourselves thusly. How much are these Adepts worth to your Archduke, Lord Roric?"

Lord Roric blinked. "I beg Your Grace's pardon?"

"How much are they worth?" The Empress waved airily. "Shall we put a monetary value upon their heads, or relate their value to the labor of common men?"

"A single Adept is worth many more men than one for one, Aurelia!"

She smiled coolly. "Very well. How many men?"

He exchanged an uncertain look of inquiry with the others in his party.

"Ten men?" posed the Empress while they deliberated. "Fifty? One-hundred?"

Lord Roric and his advisors continued speaking among themselves, and then he turned back to address the Empress. "A single Adept is easily as valuable to us as fifty common men, Aurelia."

"Let us be clear on our terms, Lord Roric. A single Adept, untrained, is worth fifty men to your Archduke?"

Roric glanced to his advisors, who nodded their agreement. "Yes, Aurelia."

"Is this to be any particular *kind* of men? Craftsmen? Soldiers? Common laborers? Need we specify which type, Lord Roric?"

Another glance to his advisors, and Lord Roric replied, "An Adept is worth fifty skilled men of any training. You see how valuable we believe them to be, Aurelia? How necessary to the Duke's service?"

"Indeed, my lord. You've made your case clear." She looked to her Lord Chamberlain. He readied himself with quill and parchment to take note of the new terms. She then returned her gaze to the envoy. "Henceforth, Dalmain may keep one Adept for every fifty of my soldiers that I withdraw from your borders. Let us begin with five Adepts in exchange for two hundred and fifty Red Guard."

Gasps of astonishment rippled through the crowd. Lord Roric paled.

"Dalmain continues to be plagued by Varangian raiders, I'm told," the Empress continued, her tone dangerously cool. "No doubt your Archduke will appreciate having more Adepts to fill the gaps in his rapidly dwindling ranks. I hear untrained truthreaders are especially effective at catching arrows with their chests."

The Lord Chamberlain clapped his mallet against the alabaster gong at his side, sending a deep, resounding chime through the massive hall and ending the Twelfth-day proceedings.

The hall erupted with discussion and chatter. Marius pushed out of his throne and descended the dais, but not before noting the look of horror upon Lord Roric's face and the shouts of the advisors now furiously encircling him.

The Empress and her guard led the way from the hall, and Marius found his place in the procession, grateful to be done with another trying day of what passed for diplomacy from the outlying provinces.

Once they'd gained the Empress's private antechamber, the Princess Nadia seated herself in a velvet-upholstered armchair and lifted off her veil. She settled colorless eyes on her mother, who'd taken up her usual position in the center of the chamber with arms outstretched while her attendants removed her courtly regalia.

Nadia frowned. "Aurelia, I don't understand why you were so hard on the ambassador from Llerenas-Onstaz. They're a small province with few natural resources."

"They should've taken my offer to join the unions when I first extended it," the Empress returned shortly.

"But they said the trade minister ill-advised them—"

"Nonsense. He advised them to unionize with the rest of the Empire, but they refused to accept our craftsmen into their guilds." She arched a disapproving brow. "If you'd been truthreading the man as I was, you would've seen the same."

The Empress turned to speak to her attendants, and Nadia took that moment to cast her mother a defiant glare. Seated across the room from the two women, Marius smiled at his daughter.

Nadia was the only one of his and Valentina's eleven children that even remotely resembled the Empress. The princess had her mother's coloring and eyes—not only their colorless gleam, but also their compelling depth. Nadia's eyebrows angled upwards to impart a fey appearance closer in likeness to her van Gelderan ancestors than her di L'Arlesé siblings. Though only ten and six, the willowy princess had inherited Marius's height and already stood as tall as her mother. All of these elements combined to give the princess a statuesque quality quite incongruous with her age.

"It seems petty," Nadia remarked with her colorless gaze still fixed on her mother. "The Empire has all and Llerenas-Onstaz little. Could we not afford to be merciful? Is the Empire so penurious that we could not have purchased some of their wares in a gesture of magnanimity?"

Valentina gave her an aggravated look. "Nadia, you have no idea what you're talking about."

"Then illuminate me, mother."

"I bade you attend Twelfth-day to *observe*," the Empress snapped, "not to question my decisions."

"Are my questions of so little value?" The princess cast her an injured look. "Shall I never have an opinion of my own or seek to learn why my thoughts are so ... so *wrong* in your eyes?" Nadia's brow furrowed. "Do you care nothing for me, mother?"

Valentina shot her an exasperated look. "Nadia, I endured eleven pregnancies to produce you and have spent the last sixteen years sharing my knowledge to give you a foundational understanding of the world *and* your talent. How could you imagine I don't care for you after all I've done to ensure your success?"

"Goodness mother ..." injury shadowed the princess's expression, "a simple 'I love you' would have sufficed."

Valentina put on a smile for her youngest daughter, but Marius imagined he could hear the Empress's teeth gnashing. Nadia had a unique aptitude for stirring Valentina's temper. When the two of them came together, they were naught but two nests of irascible bees looking for any opportunity to erupt.

"All right, Nadia," the Empress remitted, though her gaze remained diamond-sharp. "Let's address your question. I'm not subsidizing Llerenas-Onstaz because I expect their economy to collapse within the year, and any funds allocated to it now will have to be written off as a loss. The moment this collapse occurs, a flood of refugees will pour into Rimaldi and Ma'hrkit, spawning a host of new problems. At that point, the Empire will have no choice but to subsidize Llerenas-Onstaz—though I'm loathe to give any support to that bungling administration—but *that* is when I will show them mercy: when it is well and truly needed. When they're desperate. When I have the leverage to demand they make better decisions than they have in the past in exchange for my aid. Does this make it all clear to you now?"

"Abundantly," Nadia muttered.

The Empress smiled again, but her eyes remained hard, leveled on Nadia with uncompromising expectation. "Let us continue for a moment, then, to address the issue you took with my unwillingness to explain my decisions. I thought today's proceedings would've proven example enough, but it seems that I must put a finer point upon it. The United Guilds are threatening to strike. More Adepts are reported missing almost daily, and had you seen the lines of plaintiffs waiting stiffly in the halls outside the adjutant's office collecting dust like suits of armor, no doubt you wouldn't be here now demanding my precious time in explanation, but would instead have excused yourself precipitously to review your studies and find the basis of your own egregious misjudgment."

The Empress's attendants had removed her crown and jewels and were now attending to her diamond-studded gown. "And lest I leave any pressing matters unnoted," Valentina finished with a dramatic exhalation, "Marius assures me that Ansgar is planning another revolt." Her eyes tightened as she leveled a whiplash gaze upon her daughter. "Forgive me if I don't care to dissect my every choice and decision, Nadia, flaying the flesh of each for your obtuse inspection."

Marius inwardly winced at this cutting remark.

Nadia dropped her eyes, and her lower lip trembled. By the next breath, however, she'd regained her composure, and her gaze flashed back to meet her mother's, defiant and fierce. "I beg the Empress's permission to precipitously remove myself from the shadow of her unparalleled intelligence." She stood with a glare, snatched her veil back down over her face and stormed out of the room.

For a moment, the Empress stared perplexedly at the doors through which her daughter had just departed. Then she turned a frustrated look to Marius. "By the Lady, why must I produce such headstrong children?"

Marius gave her a shadowy smile. "The apple never falls far from the tree."

Valentina shook her head. "Sometimes it's more than I can bear, seeing all of my worst qualities reflected in my daughter-heir."

"She has many of your good ones, too."

"Has she?" Valentina arched a skeptical brow. "Children are cauldrons into which we pour all of ourselves in the hopes of creating some magical elixir that will somehow miraculously combine into a being with the best of our qualities and none of our faults."

"Like repels like, Valentina," Marius soothed. "Opposites attract."

Her gaze softened. "That must be why my love for you is so enduring, for you exhibit all of the patience and tolerance I find so lacking in myself."

Marius was opening his mouth to reply when a Praetorian entered carrying a red leather case.

Ah, good, the report from the Order.

First giving the Empress a look acknowledging her affections, he took the case wordlessly and opened it to read of the latest developments, hoping there was *some* breakthrough in the matter of the missing Sormitáge Adepts. Yet as he began to read, his eyes widened.

"Aurelia," he said, using the Empress's formal title in that setting. His gaze speared back across the room.

Valentina noted his look and commanded, "Leave us." The attendants departed, taking their assigned articles of clothing and jewels with them. Valentina now wore a velvet robe over the silk sheath that formed the base of her courtly gown. "What have you, Marius?"

"News from the Caladrian Coast and a remote valley ..." He gave her a significant look as she approached.

Her brows lifted, and she took the report from him. After a moment's scanning, she lifted her gaze wearing an expression of supreme triumph. "At last, I shall have some answers."

"Valentina—"

"I know, I know." She softened her interruption with a wry smile. "I shan't make the same mistake again, fear not. But you cannot hope to keep me from calling upon the zanthyr."

"I entertain no such notion."

She tapped fingertips against her lips in thoughtful silence. "It's a gift from

Epiphany that he comes now," she murmured after a moment. Then she looked back to Marius and flashed a rare grin, bright as her diamondine eyes. "I sense a shift in the Balance, my dearest love."

Marius didn't share her optimism. "I pray you are ri—"

Just then an imperial guardsman pushed through the Praetorians at the door. "High Lord di L'Arlesé!"

Marius turned sharply.

"Aurelia, Your Grace—" The soldier fell to one knee and bowed his head. "Captain di Alema requests the High Lord's presence in the Tower. It's a matter of some urgency."

"It had better be to interrupt me in the Empress's presence," Marius replied with a piercing look of censure. "What word does the captain send?"

"It's a—a man, Your Grace, a most … unusual man."

Marius cast a questioning look to Valentina, who shrugged. He turned back to the soldier. "Very well. Lead on."

"High Lord," the man replied with a smart nod. He straightened and led away.

As Marius exited the antechamber, Vincenzé and Giancarlo fell into step with him, and the three of them headed deep into the bowels of the palace along a route known by only a few. Eventually they arrived at the Tower, which was the primary dwelling of Agasan's intrepid intelligence service, the Order of the Glass Sword.

Down a maze of corridors, the soldier finally brought them to a holding cell. A host of black-clad guards stood outside its door of studded iron. "High Lord," greeted the ranking guard, "Captain di Alema awaits within." He bent and unlocked the door for Marius and then followed inside after Vincenzé and Giancarlo.

Marius swept into the cell. "What is it, Cap—" but sight of the prisoner struck him mute. The man chained hand and foot to the wall looked unlike anyone—any *thing*—Marius had ever encountered.

Captain di Alema snapped to attention. "Your Grace. Thank you for coming." A tall, dark-haired officer with blue eyes and a knife scar across his bearded chin, di Alema and Marius had battled countless threats together.

Marius turned him a look that spoke volumes. "You were right to call me, Captain. What—?"

But the question again froze on his tongue, for the prisoner just then started murmuring a rapid deluge of nonsense. The man appeared insane, shaking his drooping head from side to side.

The High Lord looked back to di Alema. "What language does he mutter?"

The captain shrugged. "We hoped you might know it, Your Grace."

Frowning, Marius moved to observe the prisoner more closely. *Sanctos Spirito but what a grotesque specimen of inhumanity!*

Bald and emaciated, the prisoner emitted a foul odor that made the filth of urine, feces, and unwashed men enjoyable by comparison. Huge patches of blistered flesh mottled his otherwise ebon-black body, while yellowish fluid oozed from fetid and charred cracks where natural skin and corrupted flesh met.

Di Alema noted Marius studying the man. "We thought they were burns, Your Grace, but—"

"No." Marius turned him a sharp look. "Not burns." He pulled a black-bladed dagger from his belt and pointed with it, careful to keep it out of the mumbling prisoner's reach. "Where the blackened skin touches pure flesh, the joinings are necrotic. Two forces are at work upon this man—opposing magics, if I'm not mistaken." He gave the captain a look of deepest concern. "This is Patterning at it most malfeasant."

"*Shala … bana …*" mumbled the prisoner, his head hung low. "*Shalabaaaaaah … shalabaaa-na …*" Abruptly he raised his head and shrieked, "*Shalabanaaaaaaaaah!*"

Marius tensed, cringing.

"I don't—" di Alema began.

Suddenly the prisoner threw back his head and sucked in a raw gasp. His eyes fixed unerringly on Marius.

The High Lord took a reflexive step backwards.

The man's eyes were appalling. The vessels of the left orb were so ruptured that it appeared a pale blue iris in a sea of blood, while the prisoner's right eye was the purest black from corner to corner.

The guards behind them cursed and di Alema hissed for order, but Marius stood rooted.

Dear Epiphany, what has been done to this man?

"*Shalabaaaaaaaah!*" the prisoner screamed. His one remaining eye bulged alarmingly.

Suddenly he sprang for the High Lord, straining to the ends of his chains, teeth gnashing and fingers as claws. A litany of spitting and feral snarls erupted from the depths of his chest, and despite his wasted condition, the thick chains looked like they might not be heavy enough to contain him.

Marius stared.

"That's why we have him chained, Your Grace," di Alema muttered. He gazed in dismay upon the snarling creature who was clearly a man no longer. "He's … it's … deceptively strong."

Eyeing the chains uncertainly, Marius worked the fifth into them until he was sure that the man would need the strength of ten horses to break them. Even so, he moved a few paces back. Di Alema joined his side.

"I would know everything you know, Captain," Marius muttered without removing his gaze from the gnashing prisoner.

Di Alema swallowed. "We found him wandering in the palace, High Lord."

Marius turned to him sharply. "*In* the palace? *Where?*"

"Outside the Hall of Rivers. As soon as the patrol called out to him, he turned … like this," and he indicated the frenzied, shrieking caricature of what had once been a man. "It took the entire patrol of six to subdue him and bring him here."

"*Shhhhhhaaaaaaaaal!*" yowled the prisoner in a high shriek, making di Alema flinch. And then, just as suddenly, his shrieking ceased. The silence, by comparison, was almost more startling.

The prisoner peered at Marius first with one eye and then the other, finally angling his head so that the black eye remained with its malignant gaze pinned on the High Lord.

In that moment, Marius became certain that someone *else* was watching.

He threw a net of the fourth over everyone in the room, protecting their thoughts, and the creature screamed again, this time with a decided undertone of fury.

"This being is not himself," the High Lord murmured. He held his pattern firmly in place while his unease compounded.

The prisoner started snarling what could only be curses from the stench of their tone. He bounded against his chains, snapping and biting, both eyes now open and fixed demonically upon Marius, emitting that guttural growl—

Then he simply slumped back against the wall, unconscious. The entire display was like a grotesque wind-up toy seemingly exhausted of its turn.

Silence filled the room.

"What … what happened, Your Grace?" Di Alema looked quickly from the prisoner to Marius.

"His thoughts were vile," came an unmistakable voice from behind them.

Marius turned to find the Empress standing in the portal.

Di Alema and his men instantly fell to one knee, pressed fists to the floor and bowed their heads.

"Rise, Captain." The Empress flowed into the room with her Praetorians in a silver halo around her. Marius exhaled a bit of the tension that had bound him, unexpectedly grateful for the reassurance of their presence. Valentina touched Marius upon the shoulder as she passed, a brief but loving greeting, and then walked to within arm's reach of the prisoner.

"*Aurelia*—" di Alema urged in warning, but Marius's swift look silenced him.

"Fear not, Captain," the Empress murmured without turning from her inspection of the prisoner. "I have his mind in thrall." As she reached to take the man's blackened chin in hand, three thin bands of gold gleamed upon her fourth finger, as well as two around her thumb. The Empress's skill with the fourth strand was such that she need but lay eyes upon a man to know or compel his thoughts; and there were few Healers in the realm more skilled, though the first was not her native strand.

Valentina lifted the prisoner's head with one hand and used her other thumb to pry back the lids of his eyes, studying each. Marius felt di Alema flinch beside him and knew only sympathy for the man. The workings of *elae* could be glorious when used toward constructive ends but utterly foul when crafted by a mind twisted with rank hungers.

The Empress placed her palm upon the prisoner's blackened forehead and concentrated, and there followed naught but the tense silence of alert men breathing and watching ... waiting.

Finally, she released the prisoner and stepped back from him. Her gaze moved from one chained hand to the next, studying each. After a moment, she chose his right hand and took it up for closer inspection. "Come, see."

Marius joined her side and looked down at the man's hand. The Empress's slender fingers appeared as pristine as white marble against the prisoner's rotting flesh, which was as blistered and blackened as a spitted boar roasted too close to the flames. Marius couldn't help but wish she might exhibit some measure of caution. Who knew what rancorous corruption was at work upon the man?

Resting the prisoner's tortured hand on her palm, the Empress pointed to a thin cylindrical bulge beneath the flesh of his first finger, just above the knuckle.

"What is that?" Di Alema asked, peering closer.

The Empress's eyes were as hard as the diamonds they so resembled. "I will tell you what it is, Captain. It's a Sormitáge ring."

Marius recoiled. "Who was he?"

"His name is gone even from his own mind," the Empress replied gravely. "But he was once a Nodefinder."

"Four bloody rivers!" Di Alema hissed. Then he remembered the company he was in and hastened to add, "Your pardon, Aurelia."

"An entirely appropriate declaration, Captain." The Empress released the prisoner's hand and shook her head, her brow furrowed deeply. "So do we witness the iniquity of *mor'alir* at its most contemptible." She turned to face di Alema in a swirl of velvet and silk. "Keep him under constant watch and alert me when he wakes."

Di Alema looked hesitant. "Aurelia ... forgive me—may I ask one question?"

She gave him an inquiring look.

The captain swallowed and lowered his gaze. "I beg your esteemed pardon, but it would ... it would seem the cruelest sort of torture to keep this man alive."

"His sacrifice may yet save the Empire, Captain."

Di Alema's gaze conveyed his confusion, but he bowed his obedience nonetheless. "Your will, Aurelia."

"Marius," the Empress murmured then, and the High Lord followed her out into the hall.

Valentina didn't speak again until they were back in the palace and surrounded by her Praetorians. "As startling as it is to see a man so grievously maltreated," she observed then, glancing at him, "I'm more concerned with finding those who harbor the knowledge to have performed such torment upon him."

"Unquestionably."

She shook her head and exhaled beneath a frown. "Not since Malachai's Shades ran amok have we seen such sinister and polluted use of *elae*. I would know who caused this corruption, Marius, but most importantly, I would know *why*."

Marius frowned. "You don't think the motive torture?"

"I think it was experimentation." She crossed her arms and walked with her gaze narrowed in thought. "Did it occur to you that we may have found one of our missing Adepts?"

"Unfortunately, yes."

Her colorless gaze flicked over him. "You know what must be done."

He grunted. "A general Questioning of Sormitáge maestros? Their indignant outrage will shake the university's very foundations, Valentina."

"Their dignity be damned. If someone at the Sormitáge is behind this, I will know who. Put the Order to the work—discreetly. Let our esteemed Endoge soothe any ruffled feathers."

"We're talking about *thousands* of Tellings …"

Suddenly the Empress stopped and turned decisively to Marius. "It cannot be a coincidence that the zanthyr Phaedor has returned to the Empire on the eve of this egregious transgression against the very nature of *elae*. I would ask my great-uncle's zanthyr for some explanation of these deeds, but until then, we'll do everything in our own power to learn of their source."

Marius frowned at her words. Valentina ascribed all manner of omniscient abilities to Björn van Gelderan's zanthyr. Even were the creature not impossibly disagreeable, Marius didn't trust a man who reported to no one, thought himself above all worldly laws, vanished for decades upon the Lady knew what task, and then reappeared again, unannounced and unaccountable, acting as if he'd never left.

But Valentina had her own knowledge of Björn's zanthyr, information passed down from her father, Emperor Hallian IV, who'd survived the Adept Wars harboring secrets shared by no other living man. These were truths Valentina would not divulge to Marius even after centuries of companionship, nor would she be swayed from her opinions of Phaedor.

While he had many misgivings about Björn's zanthyr, the evening was already too grim and his own spirit too exhausted to endure the argument that would inevitably ensue should he attempt to contradict her. So he replied, "I will dispatch a ship at once."

Valentina shook her head. "You go, Marius. I trust no one else to handle negotiations with Phaedor. I told you earlier that I won't make the same mistake again, and you well remember what happened when we last attempted to contact him in Adonnai."

How could he forget? An entire ship of Imperial Guardsmen had returned to the Sacred City with their arses handed to them via the flats of their own blades. Not a one could speak of what occurred save to say that the zanthyr was 'currently unavailable to the Empress.' By the time another ship navigated rough seas to reach that otherwise inaccessible portion of the Caladrian Coast, the villa's ephemeral visitor had vanished again.

"Use every means at your disposal to bring him to me. No request should be denied if it will result in his attendance here. I must speak with him urgently." Valentina searched Marius's gaze with her own. "You will go, won't you, *mio caro?*"

Realizing he'd forgotten to answer her, Marius ducked his head in a bow of acquiescence. "I live but to serve your will, my Empress, as ever."

"Depart tonight. As soon as you have put the Order to their task."

Sighing, Marius nodded.

Valentina leaned in to kiss him and let him taste of her gratitude. Lingering nose to nose, she murmured in her sultry voice, "Call the wind if you must. Sail swift."

Thus did the High Lord Marius di L'Arlesé take leave of his Empress to summon his fastest ship to sea.

EIGHTEEN

"A hero is no braver than an ordinary man, but

he is braver five minutes longer."

– The Karakurt

Thought simmered *at the edge of a mirror-dark lake whose waves were laced with crimson streaks of pain. It lingered there at the edge, too weary or too afraid to venture across those hazardous waters.*

"What a pathetic end," a man said.

Consuevé barked a laugh. "Can a traitor hope for more?"

Falling, falling …

Alertness flooded in on a tide of warning—

Franco's eyes flew open to darkness, and he sucked in his breath with a gasp. Hot, stabbing pain flamed in his gut like a poker straight from the forge. He attempted to move and found his hands still bound behind him. He lay still rather than provoke his injury further and tried instead to determine his surroundings.

Cold, damp air clung to his skin, thick with the stench of brine, while the roughness against his cheek could only be sand. The hollow echo of water lapping at stone filled in more of the image his eyes were denied.

"Before they bound me with the *goracrosta* … I managed a pattern to stop the bleeding, but you need a Healer … with more skill than I can claim."

Franco's heart leapt in his chest. "*Immanuel.*" Gratitude and guilt momentarily stole further words from his tongue. For all he regretted involving the painter in this farce, he feared a solitary death, no matter that it would've been his just due.

Then the artist's words registered. "Wait—you *Healed* me?"

Franco heard shuffling and then a grunt as Immanuel inched closer.

"Healing might be too ... generous." The artist's voice that time came near to Franco's ear. "Working the first strand is ... new to me."

Franco felt like he was caught in some sort of convoluted dream. "Immanuel ... are you a wielder?" His voice sounded strained and weak, much to his alarm.

Immanuel answered into the darkness, "Truer to say ... I've seen my share of first strand patterns ... and have some facility with their use."

Franco couldn't be sure, but he thought he sensed a strain of regret beneath the artist's words.

The crash of waves caught his ear, whereupon the absurd and desperate folly of their situation struck him. "Where are we?"

"A sea cave. The light may return before the sea ... if Fortune graces us. I think a cloud has passed before the moon."

"How long have we been here?"

"Nearly six hours, I suspect. The tide is returning."

As lucidity crept back, Franco noticed that his body was trembling, and his muddled thoughts finally connected the intermittent shaking with a deep chill that clung to him. It took effort to recognize the source. "Am I ... wet?"

"I'm afraid so, the—"

In that moment, the sky shed its veiling clouds and starlight speared down into the cavern through a gaping hole. Far above, and perfectly positioned in this jagged parting, a crescent-moon hung upon the lowest star of Cephrael's Hand.

Franco swore so heatedly that pain shot through him and stole his breath mid-curse.

"Yes ..." Immanuel murmured. "An ill omen to the superstitious. Consuevé and his men ... were laughing as they dropped us ... through the hole you see above. No doubt they expected us to drown ... but the tide was on the way out, and I ... managed to get us up onto this bank."

Franco realized only then that the artist was talking low and brokenly into his ear not from some desire for secrecy but because his voice was too weak to rise above a whisper. A sudden spear of guilt struck Franco. He clenched his teeth against his own pain and twisted his body until he faced the painter. He looked the man over then with what light was available to him.

Immanuel lay bound in coils of silver rope, which reached from a noose around his neck to lassoed ankles. His dark hair had come free of its queue and spread damply beneath his head, long locks encrusted with sand. In the sparse starlight, his handsome face appeared pallid.

"Are you injured?" Franco's eyes urgently searched Immanuel's person for a wound. It grieved him to imagine any harm coming to the artist. "Did they hurt you?"

Immanuel closed his eyes for the space of an indrawn breath. Even in such ignoble captivity, he maintained a startling elegance. "My infirmity comes from … this rope you see. *Goracrosta* is … brutal stuff. I'm … familiar with its use." He opened his eyes again as he added with a gritty, humorless smile, "You appreciate its qualities less … on the receiving end of its bite."

Franco forced back a heavy blanket of regret and fury and gingerly pushed up on one elbow to get a better look at the cavern. They lay on a slender strip of sand. To their high side sharp rocks collided with the sloping cavern wall. To the low side lay the incoming tide. Already the waves were lapping just a stone's toss from his feet.

He swung a look back to Immanuel. "How in Epiphany's name did you drag me out of the water? With your teeth?" He'd said it in jest, yet the artist merely gazed tragically at him. Franco gaped. "You pulled me onto land with your *teeth*?"

Immanuel smiled apologetically. "It was that or let you drown. Perhaps you'd have preferred the latter?"

Franco lay himself back down and exhaled a ragged sigh. It was hard not to let despondency overwhelm him. "I'd have preferred not to have involved you at all."

"A gracious gesture … yet as I recall, I followed you."

Franco clenched his jaw. He thought of a host of people he wanted to curse right then, but he knew he had only himself to blame.

You started down this path when you listened to Niko and followed him blindly into Dore Madden's hell.

And I've been atoning for it ever since!

Immanuel hadn't been far off when he'd asked Franco if he would rather have drowned. At least it would've finally put an end to the travesty he'd made of his life.

A wave of nausea came upon Franco, reminding him that he still had a hole in his gut, and he lay still while his injured abdomen throbbed sickly. On the bright side, his head at least felt numb. Numb and thick, so that thinking was as much a chore as moving his sluggish limbs.

He heard the waves increasing in volume. The rope binding his wrists was tight, swollen with seawater. There would be no slipping out of his bounds. Nor could he swim in his condition. At least not for long.

As he lay trembling with chill, he realized that the terror he felt at his impending death seemed somehow just, as if a penance overdue. "Immanuel," he said hoarsely, "I'm sorry."

The artist responded with a wry chuckle. "In a situation such as this … a little hope … would come in handy. I see that now."

Franco grunted. What was there left to hope for?.

"May I … ask a question, Franco?"

Franco turned his head to look upon the artist. Exhaustion pressed insistently behind his eyes, aided in its attempts to close his lids by the chill ice in his flesh and the loss of blood he'd sustained. But Franco forced himself to focus and blinked until the artist's face came into clearer view. "Of course."

Immanuel pursed his lips for a thoughtful moment. He looked somehow fragile lying there bound in silver cord, pale in the fall of starlight ... unearthly, like an *angiel* cast down from the heavens.

"My brother teaches that a man ... is destined to walk one path ... and one path only. For a long time ... I believed this. But now ... I wonder. I question ... I listen newly to old memories." He shifted slightly as if to seek a more comfortable position, but he could hardly maneuver within the tight silver rope, and a grimace crossed his face before he found breath again. "So here is my question ... do you know what it means ... to walk one's path?"

Franco thought immediately of Isabel and the wisdom she'd shared with him to this end. Yet Isabel's views required a sense of hope that Franco had never been able to muster. "Theoretically." A pained sigh escaped him before he could stop it. "A man's path is based on his choices."

"In your belief, is one's path ... foreordained?"

"In ... my belief," he nearly stumbled over the phrase, for he certainly couldn't claim to be a devoted practitioner of any faith—even Isabel's. A parade of countless mistakes passed through his mind, and he grumbled miserably, "For good or ill, you choose your own path. You make our own future."

"And what about the idea ... that certain men draw others into their paths ... even unconsciously ... others they will need to suit their ends? What is your view ... on this?"

Franco grimaced. "I think that view requires more faith than I could ever claim to possess."

Immanuel smiled quietly. "My last question ... ere we meet our Maker, Franco."

"Yes?"

"Does Björn van Gelderan defend the realm against the Malorin'athgul?"

Franco jolted violently at this unexpected question. Then he cursed as pain coursed through him.

"I apologize," came Immanuel's voice, low and regretful. "There was no easy way to ask it."

"What makes you think I know?" Franco cringed at his own shrill protest. He suddenly wished himself anywhere else than lying beside a man to whom he felt so indebted. For the span of an indrawn breath, he contemplated rolling his tortured body into the sea.

Immanuel answered softly, "You know."

Franco's gratitude to the artist filled him with obligation, but to share such a truth ... He wasn't sure why the question had elicited a feeling of betrayal, yet it had stunned him mightily. How did Immanuel di Nostri know of Malorin'athgul? *Why* would he know of them?

Desperation thrummed through Franco, and a forceful need to protect the

First Lord fueled a sudden vigorous return of stamina. "Why do you ask this of all things?"

"The answer is the price I require ... to save your life."

Franco barked a derisive laugh and looked around the dim cavern. "A postponement at best."

Immanuel closed his eyes and was quiet for a moment, as if summoning his strength. "*Goracrosta* can easily be severed ... by a Merdanti blade."

Franco gazed blankly at him.

"It so happens I have a Merdanti blade ... in my boot ... If you can release me ... I can free us from this place."

"*Shade and darkness*—why didn't you say something sooner?"

Immanuel arched a resigned brow. "I must be certain I can trust you."

"You *saved my life*. You don't think you can trust me?"

"Do *you* trust *me?*"

The question silenced Franco. He dropped his head back and closed his eyes, beset once more with a hopelessness that had long been an unwelcome bedfellow. "I'm not sure I know what trust even feels like anymore."

"Neither do I, to be fair ... but I've recently learned ... trust and faith ... they are different animals ... yet they amount to the same feeling ... the same sense of peril ... the same tumbling uncertainty. They require the same courage ... to brave the unknown."

In the relative silence that followed, Franco imagined he heard Isabel's voice whispering then, as she had once weeks ago, ' ... *you cannot care for nothing when you work so fiercely in support of my brother ...* '

Franco exhaled a shuddering sigh that sounded embarrassingly akin to a sob and gazed upwards at the heavens. He felt defenseless beneath the stars of Cephrael's Hand, stripped bare to the *angiel's* inspection.

The First Lord's words came floating back to him, '... *would that I had less personal experience myself ...* '

Franco shut his eyes against a sudden acute remorse. He'd never honestly contemplated what the First Lord had endured, what *he* had sacrificed, what *he* had overcome. For a moment, Franco tried to view things from the First Lord's eyes, but the difficulty in this task proved monumental—not because he couldn't assume or understand the First Lord's views, but because the man had endured so many centuries of sacrifice ... because he stoically harbored so many regrets ... so much loss.

Franco's exhalation that time caught deep in his throat. He didn't know how to trust Immanuel di Nostri, or even if he should, but he knew that he owed the First Lord a good deal more courage than he had thus far displayed. The Fifth Vestal had never sought the easy way, only the effective way, no matter the personal tragedy, no matter the loss of those he held dear. He'd proven that on Tiern'aval—and every day since.

Gritting his teeth, Franco pushed himself to a sitting position and looked down at Immanuel. "Yes."

The artist's copper eyes gazed curiously up at him. "Yes?"

"The answer to your question." He swallowed, still unable to believe he was saying it. "Yes."

Immanuel held his gaze for a long time. Then he seemed to collect himself and jerked his head towards his legs. "My boot … the dagger."

Franco felt the water lapping at his hip and turned to find the sea suddenly rushing in. "*Shadow take me—*"

"It will claim us both in a moment. Hurry, Franco." Franco hastened to maneuver his bound hands closer to the artist's feet. Immanuel added, "I cannot work … any power while bound with … *goracrosta*. We need the dagger …"

"I'm *working* on it." Between the awkward positioning of their bodies and Franco's numb fingers—never mind trying to feel his way sightlessly with hands behind his back—success was not so easily accomplished.

"You'll never … reach it … tha—" a sudden surge of the incoming tide washed away Immanuel's words as sea water flooded across their beach. The icy wave buffeted Franco, and he narrowly kept from rolling over, noting in the same harrowing moment that Immanuel's head was completely submerged. He made haste to help him, and together they managed to get him propped against the sharp stone wall, braced there by the swirling tide. The artist coughed and sputtered in the wave's retreat.

"Teeth …" the artist managed hoarsely.

Franco blinked blankly. "What?"

"Use … your teeth." He indicated his boot, submerged now beneath the swirling water. "And for sake of us both, Franco … don't lose that dagger!"

Franco muttered an oath and plunged his head beneath the waves. Water swirled around him. The current alternately tugged and pushed, lifted or dragged. Several times he was buffeted off his knees and barely held on by grabbing backwards onto the cording binding Immanuel.

The artist was coughing when Franco once again came up with only a spout of exhaled saltwater to show for his efforts. The sea was swirling around Immanuel's chest. There was no headroom on the narrow beach, but standing wouldn't have helped them in any case, for the chill waves were coming too forcefully now and would've readily swept a standing man away.

"I feel … a certain need … for haste," Immanuel gasped.

Franco gave him a look of apology and dove under again. Resolving to stay down until he found the treasured dagger, he hooked his legs around Immanuel's feet and nosed once again for the rim of his boot. He found it once and lost it as the waves lifted and nearly carried him away, but his foot remained hooked on the *goracrosta*, and he found his way back.

On his next attempt, his senses guided him better, and he thrummed with excitement when his lips and then his teeth felt the dagger in their grasp.

Clamping down on the dagger, Franco moved to rise, but now the water swirled farther above him. He lunged for the surface and came up with a gasp sucked in around the dagger clenched between his teeth. He spun around.

Immanuel had disappeared beneath the waves.

Shock and fear coursed through Franco.

Epiphany—pray don't abandon us now!

With the dagger's hilt gripped firmly in his teeth, Franco dove beneath the water. Perhaps the goddess heard his prayer, for moonlight in that moment shone down upon them, and Franco saw Immanuel's wavering form still wedged below. He prayed the man could keep hold of his breath.

Franco kicked to him and wrapped his feet around the other man's. Immanuel's eyes were open and his expression remained impressively serene though his gaze urged Franco to swift action.

Franco wedged his feet against the stones, gripped the dagger tightly between his teeth, and set to cutting. To his immense relief, the *goracrosta* parted quickly beneath the dagger's Merdanti edge. One, two, three turns of the corkscrew severed, the ends floating free. Franco dared not go up for a breath. Five, six, seven, eight—

A wave surged and tore Franco away. He tumbled in the surf, crashed his shoulder painfully against the rocks, was swept into a cauldron of swirling saltwater and spit back to the black surface again with violent disregard. He kicked above the waves and gasped and choked around the dagger between his teeth—the dagger he dared not drop. His wound was an aching torment all along one side, and the icy water had his head a throbbing agony again.

Keeping hold of the dagger despite his aching jaws while also not drowning was proving difficult. He had no way to safely transfer the dagger to his own bound hands. What's more, he didn't know if he'd succeeded in releasing Immanuel. In a desperate moment, he thought to look for leis or nodes—but of course Consuevé would've been careful to choose a cavern free of those particular routes of escape.

A wave surged behind Franco, and he helplessly rode its crest towards the cavern wall and its jagged rocks. His legs burned from fighting the swirling current, and exhaustion and hopelessness set in. In the last moment, Franco closed his eyes ...

Arms grabbed him into an embrace, and a force greater than the sea pulled him down, deep into the dark depths. To his dismay, another force wrenched the dagger from his teeth. He cried out at its loss, but then seawater was pouring into his lungs, burning and forcing breath. A silver light speared through the deep, reflecting in the dark waves ...

Franco gulped seawater and submitted to his end—

A sudden forceful thrust landed him on his hands and knees in airy darkness.

He sucked in a compulsive gasp. The air met with too much resistance, and suddenly he was vomiting seawater. The cold caress of a knife released his bounds while he choked and sputtered. Hands supported him, arms embraced him from behind, and several forceful squeezes later, he found a painful breath again.

Franco got back to his feet feeling shredded. He heard his own rasping inhalation echo in the void. It sounded pathetically like a whimper.

"The dimension of Shadow." Immanuel's voice came softly to his ears, softer than Franco's wheezing breath. The artist sounded restored without the magical binding of the *goracrosta*.

But Immanuel couldn't be merely an artist, could he?

"*Shadow*," Franco managed hoarsely. He extended a hand and felt around in the darkness until he found Immanuel's sleeve. He pulled the man closer then, pulled his own body closer to Immanuel. He summoned another painful breath. "Immanuel ... are you *fifth* strand?"

Silence. And then, "Yes."

Franco closed his eyes, fearing a sudden terrifying truth. "Are you ..." but the thought collapsed as his legs buckled beneath him.

Immanuel caught him in his arms—strong arms, a warrior's strength that belied his aristocratic build. "You're bleeding again." His voice filled with concern. "I have to get you help."

Franco wanted to finish his question—*such an important question!*—but heaviness was pressing him down ... down ... down into his own darkness, where even thought was too bright to be welcomed.

NINETEEN

"Let any man who begs understanding of the world first seek to know himself."
— *The Seventeen Pillars of Restoration,*
an excerpt from the assembled scriptures of Jai'Gar

EAN WOKE WITH a start.

Coming abruptly aware, he pressed palms to his eyes, then looked around. The dark green walls of the tent made shadows of the day's dying light, while beyond the open flaps, the sky flamed a vivid fuchsia with tongues of orange-red.

The prince pressed up to sitting and swooned. He threw out a hand to stabilize himself—*not a good sign*—and waited for the vertigo to pass, guessing what it meant that he felt so weak and queasy. He may have escaped the Labyrinth, but clearly he'd taken his time about it. To accentuate this thought, his stomach heaved an angry growl of outrage, and his head gave him an equally pounding unwelcome.

Regretting in every way imaginable the decision that had landed him the Labyrinth, Ean slowly got to his feet and shuffled stiffly from the tent.

Dorn looked up from tending their campfire as Ean staggered out. "Ah, Your Highness, 'tis well you've woken. The Lady thought you'd be back with us by nightfall." He took a heavy stick and pulled an iron pot from the flames. "Kept the stew hot for you in case she was right this time."

Ean lowered himself down beside Dorn and gratefully took the bowl he offered. Their camp overlooked a broad desert valley of sandstone towers and painted sands with a jutting mesa in the distance. "Where ..." his voice came in a rasp, and he had to work some moisture into his mouth. "Where are we?"

Dorn covered the pot and picked up his dagger and a stick he'd been whittling. "Close to the fortress of Tal'Afaq. Somewhere in southern Saldaria."

Ean lifted the spoon to his mouth but paused and frowned when he saw his hand shaking. "Dorn ... how long since we left Tyr'kharta?" *How long was I trapped in the Labyrinth?*

Dorn was prying at a notch marring the smooth end of his stick. He looked up under bushy eyebrows. "This is the fourth day, milord."

Four days!

No wonder he felt so lightheaded. Suddenly the bowl of stew seemed all that stood between himself and utter starvation. Mentally he attacked it with fervor, but actually he ate with deliberate patience. As he slowly chewed, he asked, "Where are Isabel and the others?"

"Looking for a way into Tal'Afaq."

Without me. Gods, what a mess I made of things.

Out of necessity, he paid some attention to his meal, but it was hard not to fret over Isabel, hard not to leap up to find her and assure himself of her safety. Of course, he had little right to worry—*he* was the one who'd been incapacitated for four days while the others cared for him and continued on.

Four days!

Oh the things an enemy could've done to him in that time—what *Dore Madden* could've done ... he shuddered to imagine. And what of Sebastian? What of Rhys and his loyal men still captive at Dore's whim? What horrors might they be suffering while he further delayed their rescue?

Inwardly, Ean cursed his brash stupidity, and if he was being perfectly honest, his *utter ineptitude*. Ramu had specifically warned him to stay alert for the Labyrinth!

He was naught but a child fumbling across a master's game board. Luck alone kept him alive. Luck ... and Isabel. And the zanthyr, and Creighton and a *host* of others. Wasn't it time he started being able to depend on himself?

Wasn't it time others could depend on him?

The image of Arion standing before the mirror seemed so indelible in his memory now. *That* man had been confident. Self-contained, clearly a force within the pattern. He'd been bold but never arrogant, for Arion had the talent to bring his promises to fruition. Ean now saw in himself many of Arion's same traits minus most of his skill. A galling state of affairs.

As he ate and the sun sank behind the escarpment, the ratcheting song of cicadas began filling the night, mingling with Dorn's whittling knife. The sky darkened to violet-blue and the air became crisp. Ean watched the stars appearing and experienced a sense of horror over the entire affair.

He handed his empty bowl back to Dorn. As the man was ladling out another serving, Ean asked, "Do you mind if I ask you a question, Dorn? About the night Isabel ..." But the words failed him in the end, for how did one really ask a man what it was like to be resurrected from death?

Dorn looked up under his bushy brows, considered Ean for a bit, and then shrugged. "It's a strange thing, milord." He went back to his whittling and continued as his knife shredded the wood, "I remember fighting you, I remember dying." His face pinched at this memory. "Then I knew nothing. I only realized that I'd been in darkness when the light appeared again." He stopped whittling and set his hands in his lap, and his gaze grew distant. "The light was the Lady, and she offered me a choice: to stay and find rest, or to come back and serve her, and you know ..." His frown deepened. "It was like I could see differently in that place."

When his silence deepened, Ean asked, "Differently how?"

Dorn glanced over at him. "I could see right from wrong like I never saw it before. Actually ... I'm not sure I ever saw it before, so I chose to come back and serve her." He shrugged and started whittling his stick again. "I daresay the others experienced the same."

Ean gazed wonderingly at him. *How many men truly get a second chance at life?*

Isabel's reply floated into his thoughts, *Everyone. Every day.*

Ean caught his breath. He set down his bowl and jumped up—actually, he took his time getting up so as to keep his dinner inside his stomach, but in his mind he jumped—and turned to greet her as she emerged from the trees with her men following close. She still wore her fighting blacks.

A deep tension inside Ean relaxed upon seeing Isabel whole and hale, and he exhaled a sigh of relief. "My lady."

"My lord." Isabel stopped in front of him and cupped his cheek with her hand, and he felt her hidden gaze inspecting deeply of him as only a Healer could.

Contrition swarmed him. "Isabel—"

She moved her other hand to place a finger lightly across his lips, leaving her staff standing upright beside her. Then both hands cupped his face, whereupon something snapped in her own heart and she clutched him into a fierce embrace.

"Come." Dorn waved at the other men while Isabel and Ean clung to one another. They moved past in silence.

Feeling her in his arms, knowing the danger he'd placed her in, Ean could barely contain the rage he felt at himself. He sensed in her thoughts the fear she'd had for him, concern that it had taken him so long to escape the Labyrinth when Arion had been able to dissolve the pattern in seconds, fear that he wouldn't escape at all ... but mostly he sensed her relief in having him back with her, and this filled him equally with joy and contrition.

Finally Isabel released him, took up her staff, took Ean by the hand, and drew him into their tent.

"Isabel ..." Ean began again as he ducked inside behind her, desperate to gain her absolution.

"What's done is done, Ean." She set down her staff and turned to him. "All that matters is what lies ahead." She nodded to the opening. "Close the flaps."

While Ean complied, Isabel sent the fourth into a lamp and then sat on a stool to untie the straps binding her legs and boots.

Ean stood by the portal, watching, admiring—shredding himself with blame—wondering how he could possibly deserve her ...

After a moment, he summoned the courage to ask, "Dore?"

"I let him go." She stood to undo the straps of her jacket. "I placed a tracing pattern on him though. After he fled my justice, he searched for and claimed your brother. We've been following them since."

"To Tal'Afaq."

"Yes." She discarded her jacket, stepped out of her pants, freed the laces of her tunic and let the material slide down her shoulders. It fluttered to the floor at her feet. "But I would speak no more of these things." She came towards him bound only in her blindfold.

Captured as ever by the mere sight her, Ean watched her gliding towards him limned in lamplight and thought this is what Isabel must truly look like, this being haloed in gold, formed of power and compassion and fierce beauty. But that was the only thought he had time for. Then his arms had enfolded her and his mouth was on hers and no other thoughts mattered for a long time.

Afterwards they lay with legs entwined and Isabel's head resting on his chest. He trailed his fingers through her unbound hair. As his heart was settling into a contented rhythm, Isabel said, "After we separated in Tyr'kharta and you went after Sebastian, I found the source of the foulness we'd both been sensing."

He turned his head to look at her better. "What was it?"

She pressed her lips together tightly and exhaled a slow breath. "The tortured remains of men—of Dore's experimentation." Her fury, tightly controlled, migrated across the bond, and something else ... something that left Ean unsettled without any understanding of why.

"The residue of the patterns worked there told the doomed men's story," she continued. "Dore has been experimenting with patterns that change a body's innate composition. Ean ... he's making Merdanti weapons out of men."

Ean jolted. *Thirteen hells!* Just the thought of such a thing ... "But wouldn't that kind of working kill a man?"

"Evidence of bindings hints at an answer." Isabel sat up and turned to look at him. "Ever Dore takes the chaste and corrupts it. My brother bound the Shades to him lest *deyjiin* claim those men forever, their very essence lost from the pattern for all eternity—true death, without the chance of Returning." She stood to claim a robe from nearby, wrapped herself in soft wool and tied the sash with a fierce exhale. "From my brother's desperate efforts to save the doomed, Dore derives dark inspiration. He kills men's bodies with perverse patterns, crafting them into monsters, and then binds their consciousness ..." She paused with fingers to her lips. "Not to himself," she decided then. "Dore hasn't the power to bind men's souls to this plane. Another must hold them here."

Ean shook his head, staring hard at her. "You think he's actually *succeeded* in this craft? Who would such creatures be bound to?"

Isabel pulled her hair across her shoulder and returned to the bed. The air had grown cold enough to see their breaths as she sank down beside him again. Her fingers absently captured a lock of dark hair and twirled it while her brow creased in thought. "My brother and I have long known the Malorin'athgul are hiding among Alorin's populace. They've had decades—centuries—to entrench themselves in the workings of Alorin's kingdoms and governments, long years to gain power. But only one of them shouts his identity through action and deed—boldly, as if he cares not whether others recognize his true nature."

Ean could think of only one man that fit this description. Had he not personally borne witness to the darkest of powers in a Marquiin's ravaged mind? Just remembering the moment, a cold chill skittered down his spine. "You speak of the Prophet Bethamin."

She leveled her blindfolded gaze upon him. "He is Darshanvenkhátraman, Destroyer of Hope, called Darshan by his brothers."

Ean sat up and pushed a hand through his hair. *This* was the man poor Kjieran van Stone had been sent to spy on? Gods above and below, had Kjieran any hope of surviving the encounter?

"Franco Rohre tells us that Dore Madden is sworn to the Prophet—to Darshan," Isabel said.

Ean lifted his gaze back to her. "Then you think … ?"

"Darshan must be involved in the making of these creatures." She exhaled and shook her head. "We don't yet know the mortal identities of the other two Malorin'athgul, Darshan's brothers, for they hide themselves well. But we have suspicions."

He caught the faintest pinching of her brow after this. "What is it?" He trailed the back of one hand along her arm. "Something else is bothering you."

She looked down at the lock of hair now tied in knots between her fingers and released it. The knots at once unraveled, likewise the tension in her brow, but Ean still perceived it in her thoughts. Whatever concern she harbored, she clearly didn't want to tell him.

"Isabel … ?"

He sensed her putting careful words to her fear, which only disturbed him more. What truth would require such delicate crafting?

"When I left to come with you," she finally answered, "my brother advised me, in his way, to take care that I knew where Epiphany's Prophet ended and the woman Isabel began."

Her words and tone roused a wary unease.

"Of course, I am certain of these things." She lifted her head and reached a hand to cup his cheek, reassuring him, for she remained as keen to his emotions as he was to hers. "But I think now that my brother meant something else in cautioning me."

Unsure where this was going, Ean pressed his lips into her palm. Her body called to his, and desire ever pulsed at her touch. Its beat was a welcome distraction from this topic in which he sensed a discomfiting truth. "What did he mean?"

"He meant for me to beware of blending my path with yours."

Now she had his full attention. "Isabel—"

"*I* cast the pattern that brought us here, Ean, but we were upon *your* path. In that sense, *you* should have fought Dore."

Ean gave her a look of frustration. "If I'd fought Dore without you, he would've killed me ... taken me, had his way with me." Ean suppressed the horror of that thought. His stupidity had nearly cost him his life—*again*. "If you hadn't been there, I would be dead."

"We were upon your path, Ean ... yet Dore is *my* wrong to right." Isabel shook her head and looked away from him, blindfolded yet seeing more than any mortal man. "And this is what troubles me. The woman Isabel might follow you anywhere, but Epiphany's Prophet has her own path to walk in this game— do you see? I fear my path unwittingly influencing yours, and it's so perilously important that it doesn't."

"It won't—*you* won't. I won't let you."

She looked back to him with a deep furrow between her brow. "This was the true meaning of my brother's warning. It's why he's kept his distance from you." She took his hand and interwove their fingers. Though he couldn't see her eyes, he knew they searched his face for understanding. "Like my brother, I must tread carefully, because yours is a path that skirts the fine edge of Balance, Ean, and three times dying for my brother's game is three too many."

She leaned and kissed him deeply, a glimmering of her own desperate heart. Then she pressed her forehead to his, and a tremulous sigh escaped her. "I don't want to be without you again."

Ean pulled her fiercely into his arms. He didn't trust himself to speak, for the idea of being without *her* nearly unmade him. He lay them back on the bed, tucked her head beneath his chin and stared off into the shadows, clenching his jaw as guilt clenched inside, at war with protest and desire. "I would die a thousand deaths for you, Isabel." Never had he meant anything more truly.

He felt her smile against his bare skin. "Sometimes you surprise me with the things you say. So like Arion ... yet so different."

These words brought an unexpected hollowness to his heart. He saw too clearly now the man Arion had been, and he knew he measured a good deal short of him. After a long silence, during which he argued with himself about the logic in asking what he meant to ask, he swallowed and eventually dared, "Do you miss him, Isabel?"

She tightened her embrace around his chest. "You've Returned. I need miss you no longer."

It should've heartened him, but he felt instead a pang of regret, for he saw suddenly—the way she spoke to him now wasn't the same as the way she'd spoken to Arion. The Isabel in Arion's memory even *felt* different; their bond had encompassed so much more.

Ean gritted his teeth. He hated himself for probing this topic, yet he couldn't let it go. "I meant ... do you miss *Arion*? The man you truly fell in love with."

She drew back from him with a gasp of surprise.

Ean somewhat blustered on, "I saw him—really *saw* him—for the first time while in the Labyrinth." Dreadful to be so envious of his own former self, but he wanted desperately to be *that* man, the one so coolly confident of his talents, the one who had claimed Isabel's heart for all eternity. He pushed a hand roughly through his hair. "I know his memories are mine," he admitted, casting her a look. "I know I'm the same *person*, Isabel ... but I'm not the same man."

Her brow furrowed as she gazed at him, and concern pulsed through the bond. Her following kisses reassured him, but they didn't convince him, and after a while she rested her chin on his chest. In the silence that followed, she trailed a finger along his collarbone and asked, "What did you remember?"

Ean propped an arm behind his head and looked down at her. The curtain of her dark hair seemed like night captured and bound against her pale skin.

"Dore had done something against you," he managed quietly. "I swore to follow him through eternity until I'd exacted vengeance in your name."

She arched a brow above her blindfold. "*You* swore, or Arion?"

He gave a slight smile, for he understood her point. "It felt like me."

Isabel sat up and slipped out of her robe. Then she settled back across his hips. Both the sight of her and the feel of her straddling him stirred him deeply. "In the morning we go to Tal'Afaq to rescue your brother."

Ean's gaze swept her form. "The morning is a long time from now."

"Yes." She pushed her hair back from her shoulders and leaned forward, pressing hands to either side of his arms. "You have a choice, Ean."

He looked up from her breasts reluctantly. "I do?"

"You can worry and fret over the man you used to be, or you can be *here*, now, with me."

His answering kiss proved there was no choice in this at all.

In the darkest hours of the morning, Ean lay with Isabel's sleeping form curled warmly against him while his thoughts dwelled on Sebastian. Since Ean's earliest days, his adoration for his eldest brother had known no bounds. One memory felt especially vivid, and Ean smiled into the night as he recalled it ...

Trell had wanted to explore the sea stack called the Devil's Horn, a massive outcropping of rock just off shore from their favorite beach.

"That's a bad idea," Sebastian had said. He'd been perched on a boulder with his knees drawn up, a pad of paper trapped between his legs and the point of a charcoal pencil. His left hand tied his ever-present string into knots while his right hand sketched a mermaid with deft skill. Ean could tell even from that angle that he was drawing her in a very unladylike position. "It's too far," Sebastian added. He frowned at his drawing and rubbed at the shadow beneath the mermaid's bare breast.

"It's not that far." Trell shaded his grey eyes with one hand and peered at the rock.

"I want to go," Ean said.

Ean had been eight years old, Trell twelve, and Sebastian ten and seven.

"I'm going," Trell said. He sat down to strip off his boots.

"You're staying," Sebastian muttered.

Trell squinted irritably up at him while pulling at his laces. "You're not my keeper."

"No, apparently I'm your warden."

"I'm going, and I dare you to stop me."

"Disobey and you'll be carrying me *and* my horse back to the palace."

"I want to go," Ean said again. "I'm a good swimmer."

"Take off your boots then." Trell flipped his black hair from his eyes and flashed Ean a grin. "Bet I can beat you."

"I doubt it. I swim better than you."

Sebastian assessed his drawing, blue eyes narrowed in scrutiny. "When I inherit the kingdom I'm having you both executed for stupidity."

"Ready-go!" Trell raced away.

Ean tripped-tumbled awkwardly out of his boots and rushed after him.

Low tide had just peaked, and the beach extended long before them as the boys raced. Even so, they still had to swim to reach the rock—apparently Sebastian had been right, for the mammoth rock turned out to be much farther than it appeared from shore—but eventually they gained their footing and proceeded to climb all the way to the top.

There they hunted for petrel eggs and watched the distant ships returning to Mieryn Bay and sunned themselves on spiny ledges streaked white with guano.

But the day got away from them, as days are wont to do with young boys, who are never very good at managing themselves much less the inexorable motion of time, and suddenly the tide was up and the boys found themselves stranded.

They wasted a good deal of daylight then throwing blame back and forth at each other, and more after that trying to agree on what to do. Both knew better than to risk swimming back to shore at high tide—not with the rip currents charging around the Devil's Horn. To make matters worse, the squall darkening the western sky looked like it was heading their way.

Ean was sitting with his knees drawn up to his chest, glumly watching the sun setting in a flaming pyre beneath charcoal skies and lamenting missing the evening meal—never mind the prospect of spending a frigid night atop a storm-washed rock—when he decided maybe Sebastian had been right and Trell's adventure wasn't such a fantastic idea after all.

That's when he saw the boat.

The sea waves were so high by that time that the little skiff vanished between the swells. "Trell!" Ean shouted. He spun his head to where his middle brother sat above him staring defiantly off to sea, as if turning his back on Ean would somehow prove it all Ean's fault, as he'd so many times insisted.

"Just leave me be about it, Ean."

"It's a boat!" Ean scrambled to his feet. "I think—it's Sebastian!"

Trell deigned to look. Then he jumped up and scampered across the spiny rock to join Ean on his ledge. The wind blew his dark hair into his eyes as he cast a narrow gaze across the sea. "You're right." He shoved hands onto slender hips and grunted. "Raine's truth, I never would've thought it of him—he's always such a bloody nesh."

"Come on." Ean tugged on Trell's arm and started climbing down.

The waves were churning into froth when they reached the waterline, and the wind was really up, whipping the sea into stinging spray. They held their hair out of their faces and watched with breathless anticipation as the rowboat bobbed into and out of view. Finally, Sebastian drew close enough that they could hear him shouting over the roar of wind and crashing sea.

"Jump!" he was saying, and he waved them forward when he didn't need his hand to row.

"Sod it," Trell growled, "he can't get any closer. We've got to swim."

"But ..." Ean cast eight-year-old eyes out over the crashing waves.

The belligerence in Trell's gaze softened with care. "Take my hand, Ean. Don't let go." Ean took it quickly and squeezed hard. "We jump on three."

And off they went.

A harrowing few minutes later, Sebastian hauled Ean and then Trell into the skiff. Then with Sebastian two-handed on one oar and both younger boys together on the other, they made haste to row away as fast and hard as they could before the waves sent them crashing right back into the rock.

Ean suffered the hard row back to shore enduring the painful silence of Sebastian's disfavor. He knew he'd be in for it far worse still once his mother learned of their little 'expedition into foolishness'—as Sebastian had reprimanded amid a slurry of curses the moment they were safely in the boat.

Even with 'tempting Fate so blithely' they almost made it to shore without incident, but then Cephrael's eye must've fallen ill upon them, for suddenly a wave caught the stern just so and cast them sideways into a reef. The shallow keel caught, and the next thing Ean knew the skiff had flipped and they were flying into the surf.

Ean came up sputtering and coughing. Sebastian surfaced just beside him, while Trell broke through closer to shore.

Sebastian was reaching for Ean when the young prince saw another wave lift the skiff off the reef and carry it towards them. He launched out of the water and onto Sebastian's head, plunging his eldest brother beneath the sea just as the wave crashed over them. Ean felt a searing pain lance across his back, and he gasped, sucking burning saltwater into his lungs.

Strong arms grabbed him and surged with him back to the surface, where he coughed and gasped around youthful choking cries. His eyes stung with tears, and his back burned so desperately he could barely stand to move, but that was okay, for Sebastian had an iron arm around him and was swimming for them both.

As soon as he could stand, Sebastian drew Ean into his arms and rushed him to shore. Ean's teeth were chattering, his body was shaking, and his back felt on fire, but his only thoughts were of his brother's heroic efforts.

"You sa-saved us!" Ean stammered.

As he was stomping out of the surf, Sebastian shook wet hair from his eyes and looked gently down at Ean in his arms. "I think you just saved me back there."

Ean rather imagined that he had. He didn't want to know what his flesh looked like after being so grievously misused by the skiff's keel, but better his back than Sebastian's skull. None of this would've happened if he and Trell had just heeded Sebastian's warning. "I g-guess I should be c-carrying your horse for you."

Sebastian pressed a kiss to Ean's forehead. "Tonight, little brother, I will carry you." And he had ... all the way back to Calgaryn Palace.

Sunrise saw Isabel and the prince on a precipice overlooking the fortress of Tal'Afaq. Ean wove the fourth to hide them from view of the distant guards while he studied the patterns of warding surrounding the mountain fortress. Turrets and watchtowers protruded from the rock face, but the bulk of Tal'Afaq extended back into the cliff, making use of a honeycomb of natural caves.

Ean found the Saldarian fortress impressive, but the dodecahedron of interconnected patterns surrounding the stronghold impressed him more. Each face of the geometric shape was itself a pattern, interwoven with all the others. Each pattern had its own purpose and had been carefully placed next to patterns of similar purposes, so that the entire sphere worked with seamless efficiency.

No man could pass through that barrier unnoticed. None could pass at all without working *elae*, and to work the lifeforce upon any of those patterns was to trigger a second layer of patterns concealed behind the first, and the patterns in *that* layer were uniformly deadly.

Ean shook his head. It must've taken decades to construct that shield of wards.

He clenched his jaw and tried to think of any possible way through it. That his brother likely suffered at Dore's hand, and he, Ean, was being prevented from rescuing him by a tangle of convoluted knots, its own sort of labyrinth … this made him all the more determined to reach him.

"What in Tiern'aval could require such protection?" he muttered to himself.

Isabel stood with her staff braced between her hands and a frown creasing her brow. "Craft most foul."

Ean grunted. "This would've taken years to create. I got the idea these creatures you spoke of were new."

"The *eidola* are not new," she said darkly, "just new to this realm, and Dore Madden has long wallowed in the muck of depravity. Before *eidola*, he made other monsters."

Ean heard multiple intimations in these words, but he had no images to give context to their meaning. "Is Dore in there?"

"I believe so, but I fear he won't risk open confrontation if he can help it. Dore prefers to let others fight his wars." She shifted her hands on her staff, turning it within her grip, the only indication of her impatience. "Can you see a way through the patterns, Ean?"

"No."

"Can you unwork them?"

The prince clenched his jaw. "No." Indeed, the complexity of interwoven wards was beyond his skill—at least without days of study beforehand.

"Did you search the nodes?"

Ean gave her a look, for he hadn't thought of that idea.

A Nodefinder saw nodes as Ean saw patterns—simply everywhere he looked—but the surest way of finding nodes when one wasn't a second strand Adept was to follow the currents. *Elae's* tides formed whirlpools over nodes and eddies over leis. One need only travel the river of the second strand to find them.

Ean called upon the currents using a pattern that would show him not only the placement of the nodes and leis but also the infrastructure of the fortress itself.

The currents followed natural channels, but like irrigation canals, if man dug new channels—rooms, passages—the currents would flow into those as well. Many patterns facilitated seeing these current paths, but few were as intricate as what Ean worked. He'd summoned this pattern as natively as he'd called upon *elae*. It might've told him something about his returning skill if he'd had time to consider it.

"I see only the one node inside the fortress," Ean said with a sinking feeling.

"I observed the same." Isabel shifted her hold on her staff. "Dore has the node as heavily warded as the fortress. What else do you see?"

Ean tried to stave off the hopelessness suddenly rising in him and focus on the task at hand. "I see …" He swallowed back a rising frustration. "I see many leis, but I don't see how they'll help us. We can't get to them."

"You violate the Fifth Law, Ean."

Ean grimaced. That pesky Fifth Law. *A wielder is limited by what he can envision.* Ean turned back to the currents and eddies that indicated leis. They lay deep inside the mountain's caves, perhaps not even in the fortress at all.

Isabel nodded towards them as if she saw them also. "What would a Nodefinder do to gain access?"

Ean frowned as he considered her question. The morning wind stirred in her long hair and rippled her cloak, giving an otherworldly cast to her form, like a being shaped of air and shadows …

"Ean, the fortress lies in the other direction."

His eyes crinkled with a smile. "Sorry." He took her hand and looked back to the fortress and the outline of bronze the currents were drawing of its depths. "A Nodefinder would put the leis to use for him," he said after a moment. He pointed towards a distant hill. "Those leis there. A skilled Nodefinder could reroute them to connect with the ones inside."

"Arion had his second row. That skill should be native to you, my lord."

Ean grunted and arched a rueful brow. Fate had truly turned him a blind eye to pit him forever against his own past genius. "I can't even *imagine* how to—"

"You can imagine it." She squeezed his hand. "The working should feel native, Ean. You've done it so many times before, and with far more difficult intersections than leis. *Imagine.* See what happens."

As ever, when Isabel commanded, memory surfaced. Images flickered like a shuffling deck of cards—years of lectures using words that no longer held meaning: the Greater Reticulation, the Lesser Tessellations, extratellurian cartography …

Suddenly an image formed whole and complete, and he saw a Sormitáge maestro standing next to an illusion of an icosahedron, pointing as he said, ' … *each is a node point in the Pattern of the World, each node hosting up to fifty-six ley lines within its matrix, each such magnetic channel capable of supporting twenty-four to the third power of leis …* '

The odd thing was, some part of him understood all of this.

Exhaling a slow breath, Ean squinted at the fortress. The rising sun had found it now, and the strong light shining so directly upon the stone stole all contrasting shadows, making the towers seem to lay flat against the cliff face.

Any shifting of second strand channels must begin with a study of the Pattern of the World—he didn't have to know second-strand Laws to understand this fundamental.

Ean let instinct guide him and willed himself to see the magnetic lines extending from the nodepoint deep inside that mountain. Patterns indeed native to him shifted and formed in his mind, became invested with *elae*, and grew into a geometric shape of intersecting lines. The leis shaped an intricate star pattern around the node, but many more lines connected this node to other similar star patterns—other distant nodepoints.

Ean floundered his way among the intersecting lines of kinetic power, mentally following each from one end to the other and back again. Trying to make sense of them was like tracing the individual branches of every tree in the forest canopy back to its roots—then memorizing each route. Once he finally found his footing upon these branching paths, he began to see how new connections might be formed.

The sun moved across the sky, bringing heat to the day. Isabel stood beside him all the while, holding his hand, never moving—not even seeming to breathe—only her hair or the edges of her cloak stirring with the occasional wind. She worked the fourth now to conceal them from view.

"There." Ean squeezed her hand while he continued scanning the multiple icosahedrons visible to his eyes. "I see how a connection can be made without destabilizing the pattern."

"Then let it be done, my lord, lest the day escape us."

As he assessed the glowing leis, deciding which he would move and how, the solution presented itself with startling simplicity. Using the fifth, he seared a path through the aether between two leis and then lay the second strand along it, the pouring of bronze into an earthen mold. A casing of the fifth sealed the new connection, binding it to permanence. Instantly the currents began to flow along the channel.

Ean stared, hardly believing he'd done it.

As he watched the currents surging along their new path, he couldn't help but wonder: how often must he have worked the second strand to have it feel so fluid in his thoughts, to have accomplished it with such ease? He hadn't seen the patterns as he'd worked. He'd merely envisioned the lines of connection between the two leis he meant to bind together. The First Law of Patterning gained a whole new meaning to him: *KNOW the effect you intend to create.*

Still, Ean perceived that countless years of practice and learning had gone into achieving this simplicity. A blossoming sense of pride filled him.

"It's done," he said, looking to Isabel.

"And done well," she agreed. She took up her skirts in one hand and her staff in the other. "Lead on, my lord. The path beckons."

TWENTY

"You cannot successfully determine beforehand
which side of the bread to butter."

– Madaé Giselle

TANIS WAS DREAMING of Pelas when the clinking of china disturbed
his sleep. He opened sandy eyes to find Madaé Lisbeth setting out his
tea service on a table by the fire. Darkness clung to the windows outside
his room, and the hearth had just been lit, for the flames were yet catching in a
grand snapping of crackling timber.

"Madaé?" Tanis pressed palms to his eyes. In the fog of lingering sleep, he
wondered why she was setting the service instead of Birger.

She turned him a smile over her shoulder, and the glow of a suddenly
flaming log illuminated her kindly face with light. "Ah, you're awake, dearling."
She straightened and pressed out her skirts. "Sorry to be so early with the tea,
but the Lord Phaedor needs you ready to go by sunrise."

Tanis shifted to sit up against his pillows. "Go?" He rubbed his eyes again.
"Go where?"

"I'm afraid it's time, dear."

Her tone more than her words brought Tanis fully awake. "We're leaving?"

"With the morning tide." She finished setting out his breakfast and came
over to his bedside. "I've laid out your things for today." She indicated the
darker shapes at the foot of his bed with a pat of one hand, "and Birger packed
the rest of your trunk last night after you took to bed. He's down readying the
carriage now. Giselle is preparing some special provisions for you—it's many
a day to Faroqhar by ship with steady winds; less if there's a wielder aboard as
can work the fifth—but the Lady knows a ship's fare is lean at best, and Giselle
knows *your* appetite." She added with a wink, "She'll be taking good care of
you."

Barely a week had passed since his encounter with the *drogue* wolf—not nearly enough time to do all of the exploring Tanis had hoped to do. He still hadn't found the pebble beach or gone to inspect the arches of the forest more closely. But worst of all, Tanis hadn't finished his lessons with his mother— surely he couldn't leave with so many unexplored patterns still on the wall!

Madaé Lisbeth stopped at the door and turned to look back at him. "What a handsome youth you've grown into, Tanis. I'm so very ... proud."

Tanis got the idea she'd meant to say something else, but her thoughts were suspiciously silent, as if she knew how to guard them from a truthreader.

"I've left a travel sack upon the chest in case there's anything else you'd like to take with you."

"Thank you, Madaé."

As she closed the door, Tanis fell back onto his pillows and stared at the flickering shadows on the brocade canopy above. *This is really happening.*

He'd forgotten all about going to Faroqhar. Why *were* they going to Faroqhar anyway?

Not that he didn't want to see the Sacred City, seat of the Empress of Agasan, but he couldn't bear the idea of leaving before he finished his mother's lessons. Never mind that he'd been many days now without another pattern glowing its welcome; he was sure more would come when ... well, when the time was right.

No, he decided, and the thought gripped him forcefully to bind his determination. *I just won't do it. I won't leave!*

Tanis threw off his covers, grabbed his heavy woolen robe, and somewhat stomped out of his rooms in search of the zanthyr.

He found Phaedor—for once—in his own chambers. Tanis stalked inside with all the aplomb of a slumbering bear cub tumbled from a tree, whereupon he announced, "My lord, I must speak with you this instant."

Phaedor was sorting weapons on a table. A dozen or more bundles wrapped in dark cloth were arranged before him. The only light came from the fire roaring in the great hearth. Its warming glow illuminated a circular span towards the chamber's center, leaving the distant edges in velvet darkness and highlighting the zanthyr's dark form as a great rent in the fabric of the room.

Phaedor's dark hair hid his gaze from Tanis's view, but the line of his jaw glowed in the firelight. He didn't look up from his task. "I'm listening, Tanis."

The lad came to a halt at the far end of the rectangular table and rested hands on the back of a chair. He took a deep breath of resolve. "My lord, I can't leave today."

"Indeed? Pray explain why, truthreader."

Tanis drew up tall. "To be frank, my lord, I'm just not ready."

The zanthyr lifted his head and spied him with an amused look. "Are you not?"

The undertone of Phaedor's reply caught the lad by surprise, for he perceived his implication. Abruptly the granite pedestal of his conviction morphed into a rickety attic stool covered in cobwebs and missing half a leg.

"Well ..." Tanis scrambled for something to hold his argument steady, "but my lessons!" His concerns came pouring out in a rush then. "My lord, if we leave, I'll never get to finish my studies with my mother. There are so many patterns on the walls that I haven't learned yet. If we depart now, I'll never have the chance to ... to study with her again." He'd been about to say *to see her again*, but the words wouldn't leave his tongue.

The first grey light of dawn now tinged the windows. Phaedor leaned both hands on the table and settled his gaze on Tanis, and the lad felt his emerald eyes penetrating all the way down to his heels. "Think you truly that these invaluable lessons are stored on the *walls*?"

Tanis opened his mouth to form a retort, but the words wouldn't form. Cast in such a light, the absurdity of this assumption struck him—never mind the implication in Phaedor's pointed stare, which conveyed the zanthyr's expectation that Tanis should be exhibiting greater intelligence than he'd managed thus far.

Suddenly the lad felt small indeed. His face heated with embarrassment. He wished he might drop his eyes but the zanthyr had skewered him with his gaze, so he rubbed at one eye and murmured, "You mean ... they're not?"

Phaedor rolled his eyes and straightened again. "The lessons are in *you*, lad."

Tanis stared at him with confusion swamping his thoughts. It seemed the whole room was shifting and oozing, walls and furniture morphing into unrecognizable new shapes. "But ..." Tanis decided he should sit and sank dispiritedly onto the chair.

The zanthyr cast him a droll look. "Do you really believe that your mother would send you off into the world without knowing everything you needed to know to find your path?" His tone was gentle but not without a hint of reproach. Phaedor went back to sorting his weapons. "No, Tanis. Her lessons are stored in your mind. You need only remember them."

Feeling utterly the fool, Tanis shuffled back to his rooms with none of the assertiveness that had driven him forth; indeed, the tide of fervent indignation had fled back to sea, leaving naught but drenched sands lying flaccid with chagrin.

Reaching his bedchamber, the lad placed his fingers lightly upon one of the patterns and idly traced its intricate design. *In my head? But how ... ?*

And then it finally made sense.

The way she never quite looked at him yet spoke as if he were right there ... These were *memories*. Memories of lessons his mother had given him when he was still a babe.

Tanis stood still for a long time with his hand on the silk paneling, overwhelmed by gratitude and love for his mother. That she would have cared so for him, that she could have seen to *prepare* him in such a … a magical way … it defied comprehension.

His throat tight, Tanis looked across the room to the wooden box his mother had so often paused to rest her hand upon. He'd never thought to open it, but now he knew that he must.

The golden wood chest had been lacquered to a high shine. Delicate and complex scrollwork of inlaid gold detailed the lid, while a band of sapphires demarked the parting. It was a lovely thing. Tanis lifted the cover on the hinged top until it held on the leather straps that secured it.

A folded letter lay inside with his name written on it in a flowing script. With the greatest of care, Tanis lifted the letter from the box and unfolded it. He read:

Tanis, my dearest son,

By now you must have come to know that these illusions are but memories of me, lessons that I gave you when you were too young to understand the words, but now that you have facility with language, they become clear.

As you discovered, I locked each lesson in your memory with a pattern. The patterns I painted upon your walls were triggers for these early lessons. There are more lessons to be remembered—for I have given you much knowledge that it may assist and protect you when the need arises. Don't be surprised if the dappled sunshine upon the grass wakens a new understanding. All things are composed of patterns, and their echo can be sensed in everything we touch and see.

I hope you will not think it vain of me that within these patterns I placed some small illusion as well, that you might better remember my face in the retelling. It was only my wish that you would remember me; and with the idea—the hope—that you also would want to remember, I crafted a little magic on behalf of us both. I pray you will forgive me this indulgence.

It seemed his mother had known his desires before he did. Gratitude gripped Tanis in a powerful hold. His mother's lessons became even more special now that he knew these were actual moments they'd shared together once, and again. There was something profound to him in this connection … how his past and his present were bridged across a wide span of years. The recent lessons seemed to have married his infant past—which previously had no existence at all—to his adolescent present, so that an important piece of his younger self found its place within the whole of who he was.

Smiling quietly, Tanis went back to the letter.

I've left you something of mine. No doubt you will recognize the little amulet I often wore. I'm sorry to disappoint you in the knowledge there is no magic within it. It won't call the wind for you or make you invisible to your enemies, but it was special to me, and I wanted you to have something that I loved in the hope that you might find it dear as well.

Tanis set down the letter and looked deeper into the box. It held four leather-bound books wrapped in worn ribbon, and two small velvet bags. Tanis opened the first bag and emptied its contents onto his palm. Twenty or so thin gold rings tumbled out. Each was sized for a man, and each band was etched with intricate designs.

In the second bag, he found his mother's necklace.

The silver amulet, no bigger than his thumb, looked much like a seal of wax—and indeed, on its other side, Tanis saw that a stamp had been pressed into the metal, a circle crossed by three intersecting lines forming the A of the *iederal'a*, the ancient symbol of the Adept race.

The chain was long enough to slip over his head, so Tanis donned it and placed the little amulet inside his tunic, liking the sensation of it next to his skin. His mother had said there was no magic in it, yet he felt somehow closer to her for having it around his neck.

Going back to her letter, Tanis read:

The journals belonged to your father. He wanted you to have them. Alas, you will not find his life's story upon these pages, nor even much of his rationale for the choices he made. His journals were ever a repository for his thoughts, sometimes jumbled and senseless, some-times profound; they were a place where he could reflect on lessons and friendships, on philosophy and theories new and bold.

These bequeathed to you were written during his early years in the Sormitáge—a carefree time in his life, before duty, love and sacrifice became an inseparable part of him.

If at times his writing seems cagey, his descriptions of others vague,

I suspect it is only that he knew even then that men would be looking to him, watching to see what he would become; and though your father was proclaimed to be many things, it was never said that he was cruel.

You are little yet at the time of this writing—just eighteen scant months of life have we shared, you and I; yet I believe there is much of your father in your build, and of me, perhaps, in your heart. You have your father's coloring and features, but I expect that now if you look within the mirror, you will see a little of me in your eyes, and of both of us in your smile.

Know always that I love you.

Tanis set down the letter and pulled out the four journals. They were each bound in worn black leather and tied with braided ribbons that might've once been violet but were now faded to brown. An intricate, looping pattern adorned each leather cover. It seemed to have been stamped into the leather, but Tanis rather wondered if *elae* instead had been used in the crafting.

He longed to open the notebooks and spend the day reading each of them from cover to cover, but the sun was well and truly rising, and any moment now Madaé Lisbeth would no doubt call him to depart.

Still, Tanis couldn't quite bring himself to put the journals down. Here was a lifeline to his father, a repository for his own private thoughts and even written in his own hand—and he'd wanted Tanis, his son, to have these things!

Until that moment, Tanis hadn't realized just how desperately he sought to know his father. Through his many recent lessons, his mother had become nearly as real in memory as she'd been in life, but his father ... the man retained an almost ghostlike quality in Tanis's memory—naught but a voice in a distant dream.

Here now, in his journals, was proof that the man had lived, that he was not merely a figment of Tanis's imagination nor simply the shadow that crossed the zanthyr's face upon an unfavorable recollection. Suddenly, his father's journals were more precious to Tanis than anything he'd ever owned.

Realizing he'd been clutching them to his chest for some time, Tanis reluctantly set them down.

Though he knew he'd reached the end, he still looked back to the letter wishing more might somehow appear. But there was only her profession of love and beneath it, a pattern embossed in the parchment, its impression just visible.

Tanis traced the imprint with his fingers until he felt sure he would never forget it. Then he read the entire letter again.

Finally he folded the letter and replaced it within the golden wood box. A part of him wanted to take it and the box along, but he knew if he did, it would become worn with time and reading, her lovely handwriting faded or smeared, the pages torn. But here … left within the mansion, it would remain protected by his father's spells, kept as pristine as the day his mother set quill and ink to the page.

The journals he took with him, placing them inside the satchel that Madaé Lisbeth had so cunningly left behind. Then he dressed and said his goodbyes to the room of his youth.

An hour ago, he'd been anxiety-ridden at the thought of leaving his mother behind; now, he knew he carried both of his parents with him … and that he always had.

It was still early when Tanis took leave of the villa staff. Madaé Lisbeth and Madaé Giselle hugged him quick and hard, and Nathalia smiled and handed him his bag 'for the road.' Then he and Phaedor were climbing into an open carriage with Birger at the reins and heading off west, past the stables and the servants' quarters, along a grassy track toward the sea.

The day had dawned fair, a good omen for any journey, and though the winter wind was brisk off the water, it carried a hint of spring. Tanis pulled his cloak closer around him and enjoyed the warmth of the sun.

Sitting across from him with arms outstretched along the back of the seat, the zanthyr gazed off to his right, over the open water. The sea breeze blew his raven hair back from his face, while the sun goldened his profile. Tanis thought if ever a creature had been made in the image of a god, it was Phaedor.

Smiling with the contemplation of what the zanthyr would probably say to this idea, Tanis asked, "My lord, where are we heading?"

"To Vesper Harbor. It's your family's private mooring and the only place for a hundred leagues where a ship can safely anchor."

This news made Tanis unexpectedly fluttery inside. "So there really is a ship?"

"I said as much a moon ago, Tanis."

"You say a lot of things. Twice a thing for every one thing you say, most of the time."

Phaedor cast him an amused eye at this.

Tanis narrowed his in return. "Are we really going to Faroqhar, my lord?"

The zanthyr shifted on his seat, turned his gaze fully on the boy, and remarked with an infuriatingly bland smile, "I suppose we shall have to ask the High Lord Marius di L'Arlesé as to the destination of his ship."

Tanis gave him a long, flat look.

The zanthyr just grinned until the boy turned away, shaking his head.

Their road traced the top of the cliffs and offered an unrestricted view of the open sea, which sparkled almost too brightly to look upon. The horses kept an even pace under Birger's steady hand, and gulls cried their morning song to the distant accompaniment of the waves. Tanis knew he would miss this place, but he no longer felt sad to be leaving; he just wished he might've found that beach.

Remembering the dream where he'd heard that sound led his thoughts back to his mother's letter. He thought about that feeling of connectedness he now shared with her, and he wondered if he would've felt so close to her if he'd known all along that her lessons were merely his own memories—if graced with a little magic to make their recollection more vivid. He didn't think he would've felt the same.

It was the first time Tanis truly saw a value in taking things as they came ... in allowing the curious and inexplicable events of his life to unfold in their proper time, without demanding to know what's next, without needing the constant reassurance of understanding, only trusting that whatever came next was the next thing that needed to come.

The lad's gaze shifted back to Phaedor and he sighed. "You were right, my lord."

As the zanthyr turned to look at him, the wind blew his hair across his brilliant green eyes, and he flipped it out of his way with a practiced toss of his head. "Verily?" He eyed Tanis with the shadow of a smile. "I am most intrigued to learn what could've happened to make it so."

Tanis frowned at him. "I have decided," the boy returned, settling him a disapproving look, "that there are some things we need to learn in the time we're meant to learn them, and knowing them sooner would ... well, it would lessen them somehow, lessen the importance of them in our eyes."

Phaedor's emerald gaze sparkled like the sea. "Found your mother's letter, did you?"

Tanis's mouth dropped ajar. "If you *knew* about the letter, why didn't—" Then he stopped himself, for of course he knew why the zanthyr had kept the letter secret. The lad puffed out his breath and turned his gaze toward the sea again. It was going to take some practice, this letting things just ... come.

Which made Tanis wonder ...

"My lord, does everyone have but to walk their path and things will just fall into place as though ... as though it was all figured out ahead of time?"

"Nothing is preordained, Tanis. If it were, Balance could not exist."

Tanis frowned. "Balance is based on what then? Our choices?"

"Of course."

"That seems too simple," the boy muttered.

"Sometimes the choices are simple," the zanthyr reasoned, "but predicting where each choice will lead? Therein lies the game."

Tanis crossed arms and settled the zanthyr a disagreeable look. "You haven't actually answered the question, you know."

Phaedor folded his hands in his lap and propped a booted ankle over his knee. "Very well." He fixed his gaze upon the lad. "The majority of people in this realm tread the fringes of the Great Pattern leading inconsequential lives. Be they tailor, soldier, merchant or king, their choices change nothing in the larger image woven in the tapestry. They live their lives disconnected from events quite beyond them, never knowing there is a greater pattern and never needing to."

"So in your view, a *king* leads an inconsequential life?"

"Most of them, yes."

"King Gydryn?" Tanis pressed.

The zanthyr arched a raven brow. "You would gain your answer faster, truthreader, if you managed fewer interruptions."

Tanis closed his mouth.

"Within the pattern itself walk the Players—those men and women whose choices ultimately shape the future of the world. For them, each choice *is* important. What may seem an insignificant decision to leave one's home in the early dawn could mean the beginning or the end of things a century later—oh, yes," he confirmed, noting the lad's surprised arch of brow, "the game of Balance is not to be entered into cavalierly, for once a man becomes a Player—once he places his foot upon a thread which impacts the shape of things, *forever* will that thread be his to walk."

Chills striped Tanis upon this declaration. He well remembered their first day together and the zanthyr's explanation of where they were headed: *We walk upon your path, Tanis.*

The lad's eyes flew to Phaedor's, and the zanthyr acknowledged his new understanding with the smallest of nods.

For some reason, this information made Tanis think of Prince Ean and how so much of what had happened during their time together seemed to hinge upon his choices. "Prince Ean must be walking a very important strand then," Tanis observed.

Phaedor looked back out to sea. "Ean has but one strand of the pattern to weave. The choices he makes will determine the strength of that strand. His thread is not necessarily more important than any other's, for it takes every thread to form the pattern. It is the pattern as a whole that's important." He turned and settled Tanis a telling look. "And the pattern as a whole is governed by Balance."

Tanis nodded his understanding—for he really did understand this concept now. The zanthyr's explanation brought new ideas into perspective, shaping a pattern within Tanis's own mind which had ever before been out of focus. It was only a shallow beginning, he knew, but Tanis could imagine himself one day being willing to tread deeper into the unfathomable subject of Balance.

Just not that day.

The carriage reached the bottom of a winding hill and leveled out just above sea level. There, the trees grew tall, protected by jutting cliffs. As they passed a break between the trees where a trail wound down towards the water, Tanis heard a familiar sound and caught his breath. "Wait! Birger, stop!"

The dutiful valet-turned-coachman drew rein upon the team, and the horses and carriage came to a smooth halt. Tanis practically threw himself off the seat and sprinted down the path through the trees. Moments later, he emerged upon a beach.

It was a tiny cove, barely large enough for a single sailboat to safely anchor between rearing grey cliffs streaked white with guano. Between the cliffs, dark waves broke on a short, shallow beach comprised of egg-shaped stones.

He'd found the beach from his dream at last.

Tanis walked across the stony shore listening to that sound ... the incredible sound of churning sea and rolling stone, dual elements married forever in a perpetual ebb and flow. It was exactly the sound he remembered, so true that he could almost hear his mother and father's conversation again. A cloud moved off the sun, and strong rays shone down upon the protected span of sea cove, illuminating its depths so fully that the water gleamed the truest topaz blue.

Tanis grinned so broadly his cheeks began to ache.

He felt the zanthyr coming up behind him just before he saw his shadow on the beach. "This is Cora Cove," Phaedor said as he neared. "Your mother came here often."

Tanis turned to him feeling utterly elated. "Because she loved it?"

"Because your father loved it."

Tanis arched brows over widening eyes.

Phaedor hooked thumbs into his sword belt and gazed out over the water. "In this place, your father said he could feel the fifth in all its grandeur. He claimed it poured forth from the rocks and the water, from the wind and waves. He could feel it in the stones shifting beneath the tide and in the endless rocking of the sea."

Tanis looked up at the zanthyr as he said these things. Phaedor seemed ever the dark statue, marble-hard yet of profound grace, a pillar rooted to the bedrock of the world. In that magical place, Tanis sensed grave power collecting around the zanthyr, as if he called it to himself simply by being.

Phaedor pointed to the break between the cliffs. "The sun sets between those two points, setting flame each night to the radiant water; and on a calm, clear evening when the sea is still, the heavens form a mirror, casting endless reflections of themselves." He let out a pensive breath. "In such times, Tanis, one feels removed from this world. To be upon this beach and feel the tides of the fifth rise and fall ... it is sometimes not unlike floating in the endless spaces between the realms, of a kind with planets and stars." Giving Tanis a solemn look, he admitted, "The fifth is strong here, and your father sensed that."

In the silence that followed, Tanis absently moved closer to the zanthyr. They stood for a long time listening to the crash of the surf against the tumbling stones, to the wind whispering through the trees and among the long, grey-green grass. Tanis thought perhaps he too could feel the ebb and flow of *elae's* elusive fifth strand. In fact, the lad was so enchanted—as much by the experience itself as by sharing it with the zanthyr—that he might've opted stay there for hours, or at least until hunger drove him forth, had he not been expecting a ship and a journey ahead of him yet that day.

So when the zanthyr turned to go, Tanis followed in silence, careful not to disrupt the tranquility, choosing to leave the magical Cora Cove unchanged in any way, even should it only be from the power of words.

But once they were on their way again, the boy was quick to ask a question that had been brimming for a while. "My lord," he said as the carriage started off with a lurch, "is not the fifth strand strong everywhere in the realm?"

"A reasonable assumption," Phaedor noted as he settled back into his seat, "but think again upon it, truthreader. Your sense of the fourth strand comes from the constant process of thought. Everywhere in this realm, someone is thinking. Even the thoughts of dumb beasts, no matter their banality, yet have force. But the fifth …"

He summoned a dagger from wherever he kept them magically hidden and balanced the razor-edged tip on his pointer finger. "The fifth, lad, is trapped in inanimate things. In stone and earth and molecules of air, in the rolling hills and tempestuous seas … in the languorous flight of the stars and the constant clutching of the jealous moon.

"Much of the power of the fifth is dormant until called into a higher order of motion. We know these things have elemental power trapped within them, but until the fifth is roused from its near static state and channeled, it is often difficult to sense." He handed Tanis the dagger and then settled him a look of inquiry, testing his understanding. "Places like Cora Cove *are* special, Tanis, for they remind us that there is vast power lying idle and still, sleeping all around us."

"I can see that, my lord." Tanis looked down at the dagger in his hands and wondered how much power lay dormant within it. Merdanti, like all of Phaedor's blades, this one was similar to the dagger he'd given Pelas, but slightly longer and with a fuller down the center.

Tanis made to hand it back, but the zanthyr waved him keep it. "For that empty sheath you're always wearing."

Tanis hesitated. "Another enchanted dagger, my lord?"

"Yes, its magical properties include the ability to fend off an enemy, providing it is used for its intended purpose."

"Which is?"

Phaedor gave him a bland look. "As a weapon."

"So I shouldn't give it as a peace offering to the next Malorin'athgul I meet?" Tanis grinned tartly as he put the dagger into the sheath at his belt.

"I do not recommend it, truthreader."

The dark undercurrent in the zanthyr's tone struck Tanis still with his hand grasping the hilt. It was one of those times when he wished he could swim deeper into Phaedor's thoughts that he might understand why he felt the words so ominous with foretelling—and then was really glad that he couldn't.

Tanis swallowed, finished securing the dagger in its sheath, and tried not to think on what Phaedor's comment might mean.

Vesper Harbor, as it turned out, lay just around the cliff west of Cora Cove, but they had to climb another mountainous hill to gain access to it. So it was that Tanis's first view of the harbor came from on high. He gazed out over a great half-moon bay whose waters were as dark blue as the sea beyond the bordering cliffs. A long stone quay extended out into the deep water. At its edge, two men were unloading trunks from a wagon.

As Birger began their descent down towards the shore, Tanis observed a single sailboat at anchor with some slight disappointment, for while lovely, it would need considerable renovation to resemble an imperial cruiser. He was just turning to ask the zanthyr about the matter when the tip of a mast came into view above the jutting rocks of the westernmost peninsula, followed soon thereafter by the bow of a ship.

On round the head came a three-masted imperial *draegoon*, easily eighty paces in length, sleek and fast with red sails bulging. Just the sight of it filled Tanis with excitement. He watched open-mouthed as she glided into the harbor, and he gasped with delight when her thread-of-silver on white foresail caught the sun. The Imperial Diamond Crown shone forth from its center, the personal crest of the Empress of Agasan.

It hit Tanis then. This ship belonged to the *Empress of Agasan*, and it was coming for them.

Tanis's coach reached the quay just as the ship did. The crew began throwing bow and stern lines to the men on the dock, and a general scampering ensued. Tanis watched the experienced men wrap the ship's lines around the mooring bollards and tie them off with a certain hitch that Tanis had seen Pelas use many times during their sailing expeditions together.

As the ship's crew were extending the gangplank, Phaedor motioned Tanis on down the quay. They reached the end just as the dockhands banged the massive walkway down on the stone. Somewhat awe-stricken, Tanis looked up the plank to find a tall man standing at the other end.

Flowing, shoulder-length black hair swept back from his forehead, while his patrician nose and classic line of jaw promoted his august bearing. Wearing a long, sky-blue coat over a white silk shirt and black pants, he seemed the quintessential Agasi nobleman.

"Tanis, I believe the High Lord means to disembark," Phaedor murmured.

Tanis realized he *was* kind of blocking the way, and with a hurried apology, he stepped back from the foot of the walkway. As the High Lord descended,

Tanis observed his carriage and commanding presence as much as the ten gold rings he wore, one on each finger. He came to a halt before them on the dock, at which point Tanis noted the slightest tinge of grey at his temples, but this only served to deepen his distinguished air. Truly, Tanis had never met a man so clearly born to rule.

"Your Grace," the zanthyr greeted with a polite nod. His tone was uncommonly respectful. Only the slightest hint of irreverence laced it.

"Phaedor," the High Lord returned with a slight frown. His voice was deep, his tone terribly polite. "I confess, I didn't expect to find you so ... easily." He glanced at the pile of trunks and then looked back to the zanthyr, and only because Tanis was studying him so closely did he notice the flicker of confusion that crossed his brow. "Are you ... heading somewhere?"

"I'm taking Tanis to Faroqhar. The boy's mother would like him to spend some time in the Sormitáge."

"Indeed, indeed." The High Lord's frown deepened as he looked inquiringly then to Tanis.

"Tanis, may I present the High Lord Marius di L'Arlesé."

The lad bowed. "I'm honored to make your acquaintance, Your Grace."

The High Lord harbored an unrelenting furrow between his ebony eyebrows. "Forgive me," he said, turning his gaze back to Phaedor and then around the empty bay, "but ... where is your ship?"

The zanthyr was playing with one of his daggers. He sent it spinning and made it flip three times before catching it by the point. "Oh, we imagined one would be along eventually."

"How convenient that mine happened to be passing by."

"Yes, it is most fortuitous, Your Grace."

Marius stared at Phaedor for a long moment of indecision. "Am I wrong to suppose you would not be unwilling to accept the hospitality of my ship in taking passage to the Sacred City—being that we've passed no other ships within twenty leagues?"

"Tanis and I would be pleased to accept the Empress's hospitality for our travels to Faroqhar. As you've so observantly noted, Your Grace, we're all packed and ready to leave at your leisure." Phaedor motioned to the gangway. "After you?"

"No." Marius frowned and stepped aside. "By all means ... after you."

"As you prefer." Phaedor swept up the gangplank with his raven cloak floating at his heels, and Tanis was left standing beside the High Lord, who looked mightily conflicted.

"Your Grace," the lad said quietly, "may I ask a question?"

Marius turned him a startled look—as if he'd forgotten Tanis was standing there. "Hmm? Oh—oh yes, what is it?"

"I was just wondering ... how long ago did you decide to come here?"

Marius did a double-take on the boy, whereupon his hazel gaze became piercing. "Five nights ago the Empress commanded me hence."

Tanis exhaled a sigh. "Would you believe me if I told you the zanthyr knew more than a moon ago that you'd be coming here on this very day?"

Still frowning, Marius looked back to his ship, where the zanthyr was now standing in conversation with the captain. "... I believe that I would." He continued to stare at the zanthyr while the men finished loading the trunks aboard. After a while, almost more to himself than to Tanis, he murmured bemusedly, "I came here anticipating a battle."

"He will ever do the opposite of what you expect, my lord. It suits his temperament to be disagreeable in every way."

Marius looked slightly startled, as if Tanis was a statue that kept unexpectedly speaking. "You seem to know him well."

"As well as anyone can," the lad returned with a shrug. "Phaedor is perceptive to the way others receive him, and he responds to their perceptions ... calculatedly."

"You say," the High Lord grunted, frowning.

"He will only let you see of him what it pleases him to, Your Grace." Tanis looked back to Phaedor standing aboard ship and observed quietly, pensively, "His motives are his own ... but you won't find a truer ally, nor a person more devoted to the realm's survival."

The High Lord really stared at Tanis then. "Is that so, truthreader? And how is it that you—a lad of ten and six at best—claim such uncommon knowledge of this immortal creature?"

Tanis dropped his gaze. "I'm not sure, Your Grace." He rested a hand on the dagger at his belt, but the contact only reminded him of how much he missed Pelas, so he released it again. Glancing back at Phaedor uncertainly, the lad caught his bottom lip between his teeth and muttered, "I think it may have something to do with the fact that he bound himself to me."

"Tanis," the zanthyr called at that moment, his deep purr-growl floating down from above.

At which point the lad gave Marius a fleeting smile and hastened aboard, leaving the High Lord staring after him in stupefied silence.

Tanis loved the sea, but passage aboard an imperial *draegoon* was a very different experience from his intimate sailing with Pelas. The naval captain barked orders, and the sailors scurried to comply upon the instant. Yet for all the noise of brusque commands, the crew operated smoothly. It seemed a well-run ship.

As Vesper Harbor was vanishing behind the head, the High Lord joined Tanis and Phaedor at the bow.

The High Lord fascinated Tanis. It wasn't just that he seemed to embody the ideal of nobility, father-figure, and king all in one; or the way that competence preceded him as his herald, but his presence commanded one's attention—much like the zanthyr's—and Tanis couldn't help staring at him.

The High Lord came to stand beside the zanthyr and turned at the railing to face him. "Is it true, what the boy said? You're bound to him?"

The zanthyr was staring out to sea. "You doubt the veracity of a truthreader, Marius di L'Arlesé?"

"Not usually, no, but ..." He turned a bemused look to Tanis and then back to the zanthyr. "But ... may I ask why?"

"Ask him," Phaedor replied, indicating Tanis with the slightest twitch of one eyebrow.

Frowning, Marius looked to the lad. "Why did he do this thing, lad?"

Tanis leveled an annoyed glare at the zanthyr. "He promised my mother he would protect me, Your Grace."

"Your mother," the High Lord repeated, staring at him, his hazel eyes intense. "Who is your mother?"

Tanis sighed. "I don't know her given name, but my father called her Renaii."

"I see," said the High Lord, though he clearly did not.

Tanis lifted his eyes to meet Marius's gaze, noting how the fine lines around his eyes made his countenance seem all the more dignified. "Perhaps you might tell me something of her name, Your Grace. A ... friend of mine said it was a term of endearment, like a nickname."

Marius seemed to be considering Tanis with a deep fascination. "Renaii translates to *light of my soul*. Our mythology claims the *angiel* Cephrael named his sister thusly. A nickname, like your friend said, but one with meaning."

"Would a husband refer so to his wife, Your Grace?"

The High Lord regarded him carefully. "He would, if he held her in regard above all others."

TWENTY-ONE

"Shallow men believe in luck. Strong men see only cause and effect."
– The Agasi wielder Markal Morrelaine

THE THING FRANCO first noticed upon waking was the absence of pain. He opened his eyes to a bright blur. He felt muddled, confused as to where he was versus where he had been. It was difficult to string his thoughts together; shifting images like veils masked his memory, preventing focus, denying rationality.

"Franco?"

He heard the voice, deep for a woman's, and thought he ought to have recognized it, but he couldn't place it. Thinking at all required too much effort.

A form hovered over him, dampening the too-bright air. He blinked at a face in shadow, framed by a halo of spun gold.

"Am I ... dead?" he barely heard his own rasping whisper. Surely the ethereal form standing between himself and the light was a guide to the afterworld.

A hand pressed against his shoulder. "No," she replied with a smile in her voice. "You're very much alive."

She moved her hand to his forehead, and cooling energy spread forth from her touch. He felt it sinking into his skin, swirling through the breath in his lungs, flowing through his veins—a sensation not unlike immersing his body in a pool of cool water—and everywhere the energy passed, he felt renewed. The stream of *elae* invigorated him, and in only moments, lucidity returned.

As the Healer removed her hand from his forehead, Franco blinked and focused on the angel of his recovery.

Alshiba Torinin straightened above him.

Oh Gods—

Horror lodged in his throat, and his heart leapt into a frantic rhythm urging flight. A sense of being trapped clenched within his chest.

Get a hold of yourself, man!

Raine's truth, his wits were all that would save him now. He pushed to his elbows and looked down at himself. He wore only a pair of thin linen breeches secured by a drawstring at his hips. Where Consuevé had stabbed him, just below his ribs, showed an irregular circle of new pink flesh.

Alshiba walked across the room towards a chest. "You had quite the ordeal, I'm told." A declaration, though her tone indicated she expected further explanation from him.

He managed a swallow as he followed her with his eyes. Only then did he notice the silent specter that was her truthreader standing against the far wall. The blonde man wore white from head to toe, but the silver crest embroidered on his doublet marked him unmistakably as a Paladin Knight.

Franco spun a look around the large, elegantly appointed bedroom, observing the walls upholstered in blue silk, a line of tall doors open to brilliant daylight, and a breeze fluttering in the drapes. Trying to calm himself, he asked, "Where are we, my lady?"

"At Niko's estate."

Franco pushed one palm to forehead and tried to blink away the cobwebs of unconsciousness that clung to him. Why in the name of Cephrael and everything unholy had Immanuel brought him *back* to Niko's and right into the hands of Alshiba Torinin? It seemed the cruelest twist of Fate.

Alshiba poured wine into a crystal goblet and brought it over. She bent and helped him sit up, and placed the wine in his hands while she put pillows behind his back for support. Then she straightened and looked down at him, watching … waiting for some response.

His eyes lifted to her. She wore her white-gold hair in a swirling crown of braids that accentuated her angled brows and upward sweeping cheekbones. Her Avataren features formed an angular symmetry that achieved harmony with the power in her aqua-eyed gaze.

Franco looked away again with a swallow. That palpable sense of desperation bade him guzzle the wine as if it were his last; yet Franco drank slowly, taking the opportunity to collect himself. As he lowered the goblet from his lips, he exhaled a measured breath, though he felt a realm away from calm.

"I'm grateful for your Healing, Your Excellency," he managed then, stalling for time to gather his wits.

"It was a near thing. A miracle Signore di Nostri reached me when he did."

For a regret-filled moment, Franco wished di Nostri might've left him in the cave to face his end beneath the stars of Cephrael's Hand—t'would've been a kinder one than he was likely to receive from Illume Belliel's interrogators. A sick feeling came to his stomach, and he risked another glance at the stone-faced truthreader. The Paladin Knights—wielders all—weren't chosen for their compassion.

Alshiba asked, "Have you no recollection of the night?"

His eyes darted to her. "A vague one … Your Excellency."

She took hold of a chair and drew it to his bedside where she might sit and view him eye to eye. She smoothed her white gown beneath her as she sat and settled her aqua gaze upon him. "Let me tell you what I've learned."

Franco stared at her in silence while his heart pounded a thunderous alarm.

"While I was Healing you, Signore di Nostri told a horrifying tale." She eyed him inquisitively as she said this. He knew her to be a shrewd judge of character, and though born to the first, she was as adept at reading the truth in a man's gaze as any Adept of the fourth. Never mind the *actual* truthreader across the room.

"It's unfortunately easy to believe that Demetrio Consuevé took you captive to achieve his own ends." Alshiba pressed her lips in a tight line and shifted her gaze, narrowed in anger, out the windows, as if piercing the distance to spear Consuevé even then. "I continue to receive troubling reports of him and expect Niko—now that he has been given the power to act—to take the man in hand without recourse, especially after this petty act of vengeance."

"*Vengeance*," Franco choked out in surprise.

She looked back to him. "What would you call it, Franco? Immanuel di Nostri—who I have no cause to suspect—claimed before my truthreader that Demetrio accused you of alliance with the Fifth Vestal and had you forcibly read. Vigilantism is as unwelcome in this age as the foul murders of our kind still taking place around the realm, the evidence of which you yourself have witnessed."

Franco grimaced at this reminder. What they'd found at Mark Laven's remote Malchiarri estate would forever haunt his dreams … a floor two inches thick with blood …

"Demetrio acted without sanction," Alshiba continued, "without trial or impartial adjudication from a panel of peers. Can there be any question of his vengeful intent?"

"… No, Your Excellency," Franco somewhat gasped. Could he be interpreting her correctly?

"And when, under coercion, the truthreader failed to elicit the forced confession Demetrio sought from you, he placed you *and* di Nostri—in all innocence—to find your deaths in a sea cavern. But not before putting six inches of steel into your gut to mitigate his aggravation." She eyed him steadily. "Is that how you remember it?"

Franco sat in stunned silence. Could it be possible? Could she be intimating his … *innocence*? Franco dropped his gaze back to his wine and murmured nervously as he took a sip, "More or less."

"As ever, Franco Rohre, you hide from me behind a curtain of humility."

Franco's eyes flew back to her. "No, Your Excellency, I—"

"Di Nostri told my truthreader how you saved him from sure death, how you miraculously found a portal out of the cavern, how you barely managed to return yourselves here, to Niko's home from which you'd been so brutally abducted, before collapsing into unconsciousness."

Franco forced down the wine caught in his throat, for her words chilled him. Immanuel di Nostri had risked dangerous half-truths before the Alorin Seat's truthreader? *Why?* Moreover, *how had he gotten away with it?* This knowledge unsettled Franco, for he knew that di Nostri harbored his own secrets which had yet to be accounted for.

He lifted his gaze back to find her watching him quietly, intently. "I ... don't know what to say, Your Excellency." For all he'd made it this far, he feared at any moment she would ask him the truth that Demetrio had failed to uncover, the truth of his allegiance to Björn van Gelderan.

Alshiba gazed steadily at him for a long time, long enough to make Franco immensely uncomfortable. It was all he could do to keep from squirming beneath her astute inspection. Then she lifted a finger to her truthreader. The man pushed away from the wall and approached, bent his ear to her.

Franco closed his eyes. This was it then. This was the end.

He heard Alshiba murmur something, and then ...

Franco's eyes flew open. The Knight was inexplicably walking *out* of the room. When Franco looked back to Alshiba, her gaze was aimed so forcefully and unerringly upon him that he recoiled back into the pillows.

The truthreader left, shutting the doors.

"Franco." Alshiba's gaze held him fast. "I will not ask who you serve."

Her tone elicited a responsive pang of guilt deep in Franco's chest. He couldn't look away—her eyes speared him body and soul.

"But I would know this: who truthbound you?"

Unbelieving, Franco's eyes darted to the door, towards the truthreader who'd just left, and back to her. "You're not going to have me Questioned?"

Her expression in response to this stabbed into his heart, so full of fury, so filled with bitter regret. "To what end? Another truthreader shedding our race's last blood upon the stones? Oh, yes," she added at his slack-jawed look, "di Nostri told us about that."

Abruptly she stood and walked away from him, and Franco saw in her stance, in the tense set of her shoulders and the clenching of her jaw, that she was holding herself carefully in check. Somehow he didn't think the frustration she battled had anything to do with him.

After a moment, she turned him a look over her shoulder. "I was hoping you would willingly tell me." She gave him a fleeting smile, rife with bitterness. "If I know my oath brother, he always leaves a window for a man's honor to make an appearance."

Franco swallowed. He got the distinct impression that when she'd said her oath-brother, she wasn't speaking of Raine D'Lacourte but of Björn. Yet astonishingly, it *was* Raine who'd truthbound him.

He couldn't believe the relief he felt. To be able to confess even one truth seemed a blessing beyond measure. "Your Excellency ... t'was Raine D'Lacourte who laid the truthbinding."

She spun with a hand pressed against the hollow of her ribcage. "*After Rethynnea?*"

"Yes."

She practically threw herself upon his mercy then, rushing back to his bedside and grabbing his hand. "Raine lives? He's safe?" Her other hand clenched his shoulder tightly. "Franco, you must tell me what became of him."

The urgency in her voice, in her pleading gaze, made Franco's breath catch in his throat. "I ..." He felt his obligation to her weighing heavily, for he owed her his life now. What *could* he tell her? "Raine is safe. He ... works still to right the Balance."

She didn't like this answer, he could tell. She withdrew slightly, though one hand remained upon his wrist. "Why hasn't he contacted me?"

Franco grimaced. "I feel sure he'll reach out to you as soon as circumstances allow."

Her gaze hardened, and he saw her jaw set as if to level her considerable will against him. Her hand upon his wrist suddenly felt an iron band shackling him to the truth. "He's with Björn, isn't he? In T'khendar?"

Alshiba's gaze skewered him, dual shafts extending right through his body into the pillows, the headboard, and the wall beyond. He doubted he could've lied even if he'd found the courage. "Yes."

"Willingly?"

Franco closed his eyes. "Yes."

She hissed an oath and tore away from him.

Franco opened his eyes to watch the force of her anger propel her across the room. Reaching the windows, she lifted a hand to the glass, and Franco saw that it trembled. She gazed outside for a long time then ... silent, tense. Threads of anger floated in the air around her, fine tentacles charged with power. He mustn't forget she'd gained her first row of Sormitáge rings—a wielder in full— long before she assumed the Alorin Seat.

For all the power she likely commanded, she cared not to hide her mind, or apparently her feelings, for a twisted expression of pain marred her features. It was well known that Björn had been her lover while he'd sat the Alorin Seat. His betrayal of her personally far surpassed merely appearing to switch allegiances.

"My lady ..." Franco murmured wretchedly. Two words, yet they were his apology and confession in one.

She gazed out the window with her distress so naked and apparent to him ... it was excruciating to witness.

This woman had suffered more confusion and heartbreak than even Franco could conceive of. Forced to take up her lover's discarded banner and lead the realm in Björn's stead, she had done so—yet the nature of Björn's loss didn't even allow her to grieve him as a vanquished hero. Instead, she must continue forward through the centuries never knowing why he'd betrayed her.

Quite unexpectedly, Franco's heart reached out to her, for once stricken more by another's torment than his own. Had Alshiba in that moment demanded all, he would've told her.

Finally, she pressed her forehead against her hand upon the glass and whispered in a wavering voice, "I don't know how much more of this I can endure."

Perhaps some of the rapport she'd established with him during his Healing remained between them, for Franco felt he knew her mind. He set down his goblet and got to his feet. He'd expected dizziness and was surprised at the strength he found in his limbs.

Franco went to her then—indeed, her desperation captured him so compellingly that he imagined he would've crawled to her if his legs hadn't held his weight. He took up the hand she clenched so tightly and with the motion of his thumb opened her fingers to reveal her palm. He caressed her hand without presumption.

At his touch, she turned her eyes to him, glassy with unshed tears.

He held her gaze. "What would you have of me?"

The words left his mouth as if without his volition, making him wonder if she'd worked a pattern compelling his troth. But *no*, he was simply seeing who Alshiba Torinin really was, glimmerings of the woman who'd claimed the First Lord's heart long ago.

She blinked in surprise, and dual tears streamed down her cheeks. Her brow furrowed as she stared at him, and her voice came breathlessly in response. "What could you possibly say that would make sense of any part of this?"

The suffering in her tone found an echo in Franco's own soul. He hadn't expected her to bare her feelings to him with such candid trust—Raine's truth, he'd expected anything of their meeting but this.

Yet even were these his secrets to tell—even were he free to speak them—he would surely need more time than either of them had to explain it all to her satisfaction. He shook his head apologetically, still holding her hand. "I fear nothing I could say would sound to your ears as anything but folly, only ..."

She searched his eyes with her own, which seemed startlingly beautiful in their grief. "Only?"

"Only ..." he exhaled a slow breath. She deserved *some* truth, didn't she? "The Citadel ... the deaths of the Mages, T'khendar ... none of these are as they seem, my lady."

He'd expected her to reject him, to pull away in anger or disbelief, but she gripped his hand tighter instead, latching onto even the small hope he offered. "Then what are they?"

"Lies obscured in shadows ... misdirection."

"For what possible aim?" Her voice betrayed her desperate desire to understand.

Franco swallowed. *Am I really about to say this?* How few souls knew these truths. "To buy us time, my lady."

He saw it in her eyes then, the dawning of an understanding. "Time for what?"

Franco held her gaze. "To prepare to fight them."

"*Malorin'athgul,*" she breathed, her eyes widening as she reached this conclusion. She withdrew her hand from his and pressed it to her abdomen. Then she stared at him for a long, tense silence. Finally, she exhaled. "I believe you."

Franco very nearly gaped at her. Even having made the confession with honest intent, he'd never imagined she would actually accept it.

She moved away from him, walking slowly across the room, gathering her composure with every step. "Then ... by your estimation, Björn works to Alorin's aid?" She turned him a look over her shoulder.

"Assuredly, my lady."

There's a certain text, the mad voice in Franco's head sneered drolly. Well ... he would *have* to be insane to have entrusted such truths as he had just confessed to Alshiba Torinin, especially with Niko van Amstel now pinned to her skirts. Yet ... he couldn't help feeling he'd misjudged Alshiba all these years. The First Lord had once loved her deeply, after all.

But he *didn't see fit to tell her these things ...*

Franco exhaled a measured breath. Wondering at his sudden loyalty towards Alshiba—so unexpected, so startling—he realized the feeling had begun when he saw that an Adept's life meant more to her than discovering the truth—even though that truth might lead to answers she'd been denied for over three centuries. It was testimony to a surprising integrity and strength of character. He didn't think—had their roles been reversed and Raine D'Lacourte had stood before him instead—that the outcome would've been the same.

For the space of an indrawn breath, Franco wondered why the First Lord had excluded Alshiba from his confidence.

Alshiba laid a hand on the back of an armchair and turned to face him. She gazed for a time at the oath-ring that glimmered on her hand, and then she lifted her eyes to him. "What do you know of the oathrings, Franco?"

He gave a little shrug. "I know you can use them to contact each other, but beyond that ... ?"

She arched a sardonic brow. "Yes, they're supposed to facilitate communication between Vestals, but either the power doesn't extend into Malachai's realm or Björn has done something to compromise it, for I've been unable to reach any of them there." She shook her head, her lips pinched tightly. "Tell me, Franco ... you've seen my oath-brothers: Björn—*and* Dagmar I would assume?"

"Yes." He couldn't believe how freely he admitted it to her, albeit not without due pangs of consternation.

"What color are their rings?"

The odd question gave him pause. "Why …" he frowned. "They look exactly as yours, my lady."

Her gaze bored into him. "Exactly? You're sure?"

Franco recalled the day before, when he'd faced both Vestals and received his orders. *Gods and demons* but it seemed an age ago already. He recalled clearly seeing both Vestals' oathrings gleaming upon their fingers.

He approached Alshiba and took up her hand to gaze into the azure stone. Lifting his eyes back to meet hers, he confessed, "I believe yours is slightly more blue than the First Lord's—but it is hard to say. It may just be the light."

She latched onto this with alacrity. Her fingers curled around his hand, preventing its release. "Björn's is darker? Clouded?" What was it in her tone? Fear? Fury?

"No, my lady." Franco dropped his gaze. He felt vaguely embarrassed, for he suspected her motive now for this line of questioning. "The First Lord's ring is nearly diamond-clear."

Alshiba snatched her hand from his grasp and pressed it across her mouth. Then she turned away. After a moment, he heard her whisper, "It is not the light."

Her anguished tone pierced his heart. "My lady …"

"T'khendar has wooed three of my Vestals now, it would seem," she hissed darkly, "a gluttonous mistress." She spun a fierce look over her shoulder. "I pray the end justifies the means."

Franco knew not how to reply to this, so he held his tongue.

She considered him for a time in silence. Then she gave a forceful exhale. "So … where do we go from here, Franco?"

Franco bowed his head. "I wish I knew, my lady." He searched vainly for any words to reassure her. "I know this must sound … impossible, but …" he lifted eyes back to her, "we're on the same side."

"*We.* You refer, of course, to yourself and *my* three Vestals." The acrimony evident in the small laugh that escaped her made Franco cringe. "Fine. Then you tell me, since we're all such allies, why did you attend Niko's fête?"

Franco's stomach did a little flip at the question. Her probing gaze held him fast once more, and he swallowed, too aware that no binding hid this truth from her inspection. He couldn't help but wonder if she was testing him now, challenging the fragile trust they'd just established.

He couldn't quite dismiss the irony in the moment. He'd told Immanuel di Nostri that he couldn't remember what trust felt like. Now he was entrusting some of his deepest secrets to a woman with the power to become their gravest obstacle … or their greatest ally.

Franco drew in courage with his breath. "The First Lord and the Great

Master are both concerned about your appointment of Niko van Amstel to the Vestal seat. They sent me to learn …" *Thirteen hells*, there was still so much he couldn't tell her, "… his plans."

She considered him quietly, her gaze now unreadable. How quickly she could draw in her feelings, keeping them contained behind a remote and impenetrable shield. "And you, Franco? Are you equally concerned by this?"

After a moment wherein every emotion he'd ever felt on the matter rushed forward to speak up and was banished to silence, Franco replied, "Very."

She nodded, frowned. He followed her gaze as she turned to look across the room to the doors and whatever waited beyond them. "Perhaps we should speak more of these things in the coming days. You will attend me, won't you? To share what … you can?"

He looked back to her sharply. He still couldn't quite process the abrupt turn his path had taken, so dramatically afield of his fears. "Then …" He looked at the bedroom doors again. "I'm free to go?"

She gave him a quizzical look. "For what crime should I be holding you? I'm not in the habit of arresting Adepts simply because their allegiances appear to disagree with my own. If you've done aught else against the *Sobra's* canon, some transgression against Alorin itself, feel free to confess it now."

Stricken mute, Franco shook his head.

Alshiba called for William, her truthreader. At once he opened the doors and stood in the portal, attentive to her need. "Let him come," she said.

William turned and nodded to someone in the other room. Then he stepped aside to admit Niko van Amstel. Franco only just stifled a pained wince.

"Franco, *Franco*!" Niko approached with open arms, and Franco stiffened as the man embraced him. Niko pulled away to take Franco by the shoulders, his blue eyes wide with concern. "I cannot convey how horrified I am by this turn of events. To think you experienced such an egregious indignity while a guest at *my* home—it appalls me! And Consuevé! The fiend!" He squeezed Franco's shoulders. "I will see him called to justice. This I swear to you."

Franco stared wordlessly at him.

"Your Excellency," William said to Alshiba in a pointed tone.

She turned him a brief look. "Yes, I understand." To Franco then, she said, "We're expected soon in Illume Belliel. Franco, I would we had the leisure to discuss this more, but time continues inexorably on with or without our consent." She reached into a pocket of her gown and withdrew a ring, which she extended to him.

Franco looked over the silver band engraved with patterns. It was wider but otherwise not unlike his Sormitáge rings. He lifted puzzled eyes back to Alshiba

She offered in reply, her tone dripping with an irony all too apparent to him, "You see … Niko has named you for his deputy." She continued on as Franco gaped at her, "Even had he not presented you for his choice, I would have pressed him to pick you, for Raine trusted you and spoke highly of you to me." She held his gaze significantly as she finished in a tone nine layers thick with meaning, "I will place my faith in you to do what must be done to restore Balance to the realm. Do you accept this appointment?"

Reeling, Franco stared at her while a thousand reasons advising against this action warred with all the reasons he must. Isabel's words came at once to mind: *'When a vision of the path ahead opens to us, Franco, we must not shy from it. Fate draws the shortest distance between two points.'*

Feeling a powerful sense of kismet at work—one which he both resented and feared with all his soul—Franco slid the ring onto his middle finger. The band expanded to fit over his knuckle and then shrank snugly back again to hug his flesh. He swallowed as he looked back to her. "Your will, my lady."

Alshiba looked to Niko. "You were wrong, you see?" When Franco lifted an inquiring gaze to her, she explained, "He believed you would refuse."

Niko managed a thin smile. "He continues to surprise me."

"Franco, I will contact you soon," Alshiba said. She looked to Niko. "We must depart."

Niko extended his hand to Franco, who took it out of necessity. "I look forward to the great work we will do together, my old friend. The house is yours, should you care to linger. My seneschal will see to your needs. Help yourself to anything you require." Then he nodded farewell and followed Alshiba and the truthreader William out of the room.

Well ... that was unexpected.

Franco pushed a hand through his hair and sank down onto the nearest chair. In his stillness, the strangeness of the circumstances collided with disbelief. Events so outrageous, so unpredictable—and frankly, unprecedented—that he was suddenly certain Fate *must've* had some hand in it, for however else could one explain such an ironic twist of his path?

He thought back to that moment in the cave when he'd first seen Cephrael's Hand glowing above. At the time, Franco had imagined it would be his last moment on this earth. Then everything had changed—as if looking upon Cephrael's stars had transported him to an alternate universe where enemies were allies.

As much as he wanted to, he couldn't now deny the unnatural feeling of Fate's hand working His will upon his life. He could sense it when he let himself, a sort of tension in the air, as if to herald an approaching storm. He could almost feel the threads of the pattern reaching out for him, binding him to a new course.

In times before, he would've sought to drown the feeling in drink, as if in finding him dissipated, Fate might look for a better candidate. But today was not yesterday, and for better or worse, Franco understood now that he was bound to the First Lord's game for eternity.

It wasn't lost on him that crossing paths with Immanuel di Nostri had been a turning point that brought him to this very future. He just wasn't sure yet if the moment had opened upon providence or purgatory.

Immanuel di Nostri ...

Thirteen hells, he had so many questions for the man! He'd never felt so confused, so unsure who to trust. He'd been half-hoping Immanuel would still be there when he'd first woken, but clearly the artist had told his tale and left.

Abruptly Franco groaned and pushed both hands to his forehead as another realization inserted itself on his thoughts: somehow he was going to have to explain all of this to Dagmar and the First Lord!

Franco fell back against the chair and exhaled a forceful breath. Would that Immanuel really had left him in the cave. Drowning seemed far preferable to the torture of such confession.

Grimacing, Franco got to his feet, but all the while he readied himself for travel, he knew, somewhere, Cephrael was laughing.

TWENTY-TWO

"Every man is the architect of his own fortune."

– Dareios, Prince of Kandori

THE MOMENT EAN stepped off the leis into the tunnels of Tal'Afaq, a pervasive sense of wrongness accosted him. It radiated from the dark cavern walls to permeate the air and collect in shadowed corners where it multiplied. Ean had experienced a similar wrongness in Tyr'kharta—Isabel had named it the call of Balance seeking to be righted, and he'd eventually equated the feeling with his brother's torment—but Sebastian's captivity comprised only a small part of what attacked his senses now.

Crossing the node beside him, Isabel's fingers tightened on his arm, and her lips formed a thin line. As Dorn and Lem stepped off the leis behind her, she murmured, "What do you see?"

Ean turned his gaze back to the tunnel ahead and the roiling tides of *elae*. He clenched his jaw. "Corruption."

Never had he seen the currents in such a frenzied state. What should've been golden appeared darkly veiled, and huge swaths of the tide carried a tar-like discharge that churned the fifth into a curdled, violent flow. More unsettling, these same currents carried the charred detritus of the first strand as a coating of ash. Ean knew instinctively that Dore Madden stood behind this desecration, yet to actually *see* it …

The part of him that had been Arion roused in fury at such wrongs committed with the lifeforce. Leveling a piercing gaze on the path ahead, he summoned the fifth, took Isabel's hand in his, and led them forward into the core of Tal'Afaq.

Patterns of warding repeatedly barred their path, but these were not so complex as the patterns around Tal'Afaq's exterior. Ean unworked them easily.

The tunnel narrowed to a bare crevice, and Ean began feeling as if the entire force of the mountain bore down upon him. The light shining through the splice at its end reassured him of their path, however, and soon he was stepping out onto a wooden walkway. He turned to help Isabel, and then they surveyed their surroundings—

Ean bit back a curse. She'd told him Dore was making monsters, but ...

The walkway hugged the cavern wall a good twenty feet above the floor, where the bodies had been laid. Chains of braided silver rope bound each man—what had once been men—to shackles in the floor, though it hardly seemed possible for animation to fill such wretched remains. They were alive in some capacity—Ean would've sensed this even without seeing the horrid, violet-grey effluvia they excreted to pollute *elae's* currents—but no hint of the first strand touched them. Whatever dark life fueled them, it was not of *elae's* aspect.

Easily fifty of these creatures were suffering through different stages of transition. Their collective moans sounded a low wail, a tower clock's inner cogs chinking off time's slow decay; with each second passed, a hair's width more of suppurating flesh expired, leaving a blackened husk as the gravestone of their humanity. For the flash of an instant, Ean feared Sebastian might be down there among those poor wretches, but then he sensed the first strand pattern still vibrant upon his brother, leading elsewhere.

Isabel withdrew her hand from his. In contrast to the leashed fury that fulminated around him, she held so much of the first strand that she nearly glowed with it. Great funnels of roseate light spiraled to comply with Isabel's summons, and when she walked away from him, they trailed behind and around her like gossamer wings.

"Go," she said as she walked with slow deliberation, her mind focused and already distant. He'd brought the woman Isabel into the cavern with him, but it was Epiphany's Prophet who walked away. "Find your brother."

"Isabel—" He knew her strength, yet he worried for her safety.

She turned her blindfolded gaze to him. "These creatures must be destroyed before they can fully transform, Ean. Once the pattern of changing is complete, only immolation or a Merdanti blade can end their torment."

"We'll stay with her, Your Highness." Dorn stepped forward with a hand on his blade. "You'll not see harm come to the lady on our watch." He spoke with such reverent determination, Ean couldn't help but believe him. Still, he lingered a moment longer, frowning with concern as he watched Isabel descend wooden stairs to the cavern floor.

He cringed as she walked among the chained then, and clenched his teeth when he saw her bend and lay her hand on the rotting flesh of the nearest one. A terrible compassion furrowed her brow. The doomed man shuddered violently and then went still, and the violet effluvia ceased its pollution of the currents. Isabel moved to the next man.

Ean swallowed and turned away.

He preferred not to think on this antipathy—the use of the first strand to take life instead of imparting it, even to end such an unconscionable imprisonment. He felt her abhorrence and grief through the bond they shared, but he knew she wouldn't flinch from her task, nor be swayed from her path, until all such creatures had been claimed unto death ... until the horrific imbalance of their degraded existence had been righted.

Ean carried the resonance of Isabel's deep emotion with him as he headed off. Her mourning grounded his resolve.

Above the *eidola's* chamber, Ean found a giant, multi-leveled cavern outfitted as an armory. Smoke formed an acrid haze above the workers, lingering until a wielder's pattern swirled it languidly upwards and away. On the cavern's far side, rail cars filled with ore stood before the mouth of a manmade tunnel, while other cave openings hosted scaffolding, ropes, or twisted, unsavory-looking stairs for use in delivering the treasures reclaimed from the earth.

Yet for all of this, the creature standing across the distance most claimed Ean's attention. Fully transformed, this *eidola* patrolled a high walkway circling the cavern. Of deepest black from head to heel, it appeared a shadow made corporeal. Blades in leather straps were its only raiment, yet it walked like a normal man, with hands clasped behind its back, while its unnatural gaze swept across men and forges and weaponry with equal dispassion.

Dispassion? Could such a creature *show* emotion? Could it even feel it? With morbid fascination, Ean wondered if its Merdanti face would reveal the same pliancy as a Shade's chrome-reflective flesh. Suddenly determined to see its expression as he destroyed it, Ean abandoned the thread he'd been following to his brother's location and headed around the cavern's edge towards the *eidola*.

Had Isabel been with him, she might've dissuaded him from this choice. Or had he been thinking of the woman Isabel instead of the actions of Epiphany's Prophet, perhaps he would've chosen to seek his brother instead of abandoning his path. But Isabel's emotions were resonating along their bond as she continued upon her dark work of salvation. Seeing one of the defiled creatures upright and hale, Ean couldn't help but act in kind.

The fifth amassed around the prince as he stalked the *eidola*, while the currents passing away from him smoothed and went dangerously flat. Keeping to the shadows, the prince stole around the edge of the walkway. His mind had gone as motionless as the currents that hovered in his vicinity, a deadly calm, yet his heart pumped a righteous cadence.

He sensed eyes on him as he stalked his prey, but a glance around revealed only himself and the *eidola* upon this high path, and the creature's attention was angled at the working men below. Ean pushed a buffer of still air before him to dampen his approach, and as he neared the creature, he drew his sword in silence. He came up behind it and took the first steps of the *cortata*, making a slow turn as he lifted the blade to strike.

The creature came alert. It spun and caught Ean's descending wrists with both hands, stopping his downward blade, and a snarl like a viper's rattle escaped its throat. It was alarmingly strong.

Ean wrestled against it, trying to free his hands from its grasp. For a moment, obsidian black eyes met his, and in that instant, Ean saw not the *eidola* but the Marquiin he'd freed from Bethamin's malicious hold. They were the same eyes, no doubt concealing a similar virulent compulsion ... chained by the same mind.

Ean lashed out ropes of the fifth to bind the creature, but the lifeforce simply slid around the *eidola* like water over oiled canvas. Ean could no more make a binding stick to it than he could free his hands from its granite hold.

The *eidola* forced Ean back, towards the walkway's borderless edge. The first vestiges of fear hung like a fringe upon his thoughts; its prudence would've better served him before he'd begun upon this new course. Now he could do naught but finish what he'd started.

Ean clenched his teeth, put all of his weight into his heel and pivoted. It felt like lifting a mountain, but he funneled *elae* into his intention and yanked the creature off its feet. The *eidola* flew into the cavern wall, taking Ean's blade— and Ean himself—with it. Stone shattered beneath its body, and a thunderous crash reverberated through the chamber.

As they both struggled back to their feet, still wrestling for Ean's blade, the prince finally had the intellectual wherewithal to let go and withdraw the flow of *elae* that wakened the sword. The blade crashed to the floor as if magnetized to the earth's core, and the creature went down with it. Ean made a hammer of his foot with the fifth and kicked. The *eidola* flew in a backwards arc and slammed down and through the wooden bridge to crash into the ledge beneath. It dislodged a cascade of barrels that had been stowed there. These in turn started an avalanche of debris that rained down on the workers, calling all eyes upwards in alarm and launching a general commotion on the cavern floor.

Ean grabbed his sword and ran to where the *eidola* had fallen. Men were shouting now and pointing up, while others tried to extinguish a fire that had started when several barrels crashed into an open forge.

Once again, Ean cursed his own cataclysmic stupidity. Couldn't he make any decision that resulted in less than pandemonium?

How long before a host of guards claimed him and then moved on to find Isabel? The very idea made him weak. His only hope now was drawing the *eidola* back into the caves and disposing of it there. He would have to trust to the currents to find his way out again.

A swift glance showed him a path. He sheathed his sword, took a running leap and flung himself off the walkway. Pushing the fifth to propel himself, he crossed the distance easily. His hands caught a drape of netting, and he climbed to the wooden scaffolding above.

Heart racing, he cast a look back at the *eidola*. The creature had regained the walkway and was staring up at him. Even as he watched, it took its own running leap.

Ean ran for the tunnel opening midway along the high bridge. At the far end, a figure suddenly dropped down from a ledge above. He barely gave the man a glance, only noting with relief that he wasn't another *eidola*, and turned sharply into the tunnel.

Too soon, Ean heard feet pounding behind him. As he ran awkwardly through the dark, he reached his mind beyond his view and called the wind, then cast it back through the tunnel. But the effect was pale for lack of wind to fuel it, and the feet continued their pounding pursuit.

Frustrated, the prince tried making the stone floor molten as Arion had done at the Citadel, but this complicated working required too much of Ean's concentration, and he released the intention with naught but a dull ache in his head to show for the effort.

The tunnel soon opened into another cavern, dimly lit by a few scattered torches, where the cave floor fell away into an abyss. Narrow ledges rimmed this hole, with a worn rope for the only handhold. Ean decided it would be as good a place as any to make his stand.

He turned to face the dark cave mouth and drew his sword. His chest rose and fell with his breath, but long gone was the inner cry of vengeance that had lured him off his own path. Now he knew only remorse and determination— remorse for the brash and idiotic impulse that he'd allowed to overwhelm his reason; and determination that this grave misjudgment wouldn't be his last play within the First Lord's game.

The *eidola* slowed its pace as it neared the end of the tunnel. To Ean, it seemed a demon emerging out of the depths, this time with its own blade held ready. It would be this test then that determined the victor. Ean made his mind calm, raised his sword, and rushed to meet the creature head-on.

Their blades clashed in a reverberation of enchanted steel. The creature moved fast and struck hard with bone-jarring blows. It drove Ean backwards towards the abyss, and in a narrow moment that left his heart pounding, the prince came close enough to its edge to see the stalagmites like daggers lining its base. He drew *elae* through the *cortata* and forced the creature back, gaining vital distance if not the upper hand.

Indeed, the *cortata* fueled Ean's blade while *elae* fueled his stamina, but he quickly saw that the *eidola* suffered not the limitations of mortal men. Ean could defend against it so long as *elae* fueled his strength, but if he continued too long, he would eventually drain himself of the ability even to hold the lifeforce.

The untenable nature of this truth lent a certain desperation to Ean's thoughts, and while he worked to maintain the steps of the *cortata* against the *eidola's* pounding blows, so also he mentally strove for some inspiration to overcome it.

Hope drained as he felt his energy siphoning off with every swing of his blade. Thoughts of loss began accosting him—nightshade fears, deadly to his resolve—and in this desperate state of mind, he resorted to what he knew best.

He spun out of the *cortata*, drew every inch of the lifeforce that he dared, and channeled it into a lashing current. Lightning flared through the chamber and into the *eidola's* Merdanti blade. Enchanted steel melted in a molten, mercuric rush. Then the bolt shocked through the *eidola* and blasted it backwards into the cavern wall.

The concussion sent Ean staggering—for he'd forgotten to stabilize himself against it. He spent a dazed moment recovering from the working, ears ringing. He pushed a palm to his forehead and felt *elae* draining out of him in a chill exodus. It was a good thing he didn't need the lifeforce to do what he intended.

The prince pushed after the *eidola*, who was half-sunk into the cavern wall and laboring to rise from beneath the rubble. Ean fell to his knees and slammed his hands against the creature's chest while his mind sought the patterns that bound the *eidola* to its golem halflife.

His consciousness speared into the creature's mind and went streaking through the storm of its thoughts, seeking the pattern he knew he would find deep within that malevolent hurricane. He sought it as a ship's pilot seeks an island's darker form through the night—instinctively, letting his mind guide itself towards that powerful marker.

The *eidola's* black eyes flew open, and its hands shot out and grabbed Ean by the throat, but though the pressure on his neck blinded him, his inner eye remained focused.

There!

He found the pattern twining among countless others—menacing forms with devastating purpose—but only one of them held that glow of extant power.

He barely noticed as the *eidola* lurched to its feet, barely realized he was no longer drawing breath. They entered into a desperate race, with Ean seeking the pattern of the *eidola's* beginning and the *eidola* seeking an end to his. The creature had just lifted the prince off his feet and was walking towards the abyss when Ean found the pattern's beginning and yanked with all the force of his will.

It didn't budge.

Bound with the fifth! He looked frantically for a secondary pattern interwoven among the one that bound the *eidola* to life.

Ean felt blackness stinging the edges of his consciousness. The woozy sensation of floating kept distracting him—likewise the pain in his neck and skull. He wanted only to surrender to the feeling of sleep and kept having to recall his consciousness to the task. He finally managed to take hold of the ends of both patterns, and with his last desperate ounce of effort, he set them to unraveling.

The *eidola* halted, stricken immobile with arms extended and Ean's inert form hovering over the abyss. As the patterns continued their rapid unraveling, it let out a shrill and inhuman keen.

Ean jolted back to awareness and grabbed onto the *eidola's* wrists. He swung his feet for the edge while he gasped for breath, but even as the malevolent life drained out of the thing, the *eidola* maintained its monstrous lock around his throat.

The creature's death cry blended now with another's rage, distant and powerful. The sound scraped along Ean's physical and mental ears like his breath scraped along his throat. A final spark flared and died in the *eidola's* eyes.

Then they were both falling.

Desperation clashed violently with a hopeless fear. Ean watched the edge escaping out of reach and knew he'd failed, that the creature was going to pull him down into death—

An iron hand clamped around his wrist.

Gravity wrenched the *eidola's* inanimate fingers from Ean's neck—sharply and not without claiming some skin in their passing. Then Ean was hanging painfully by one arm watching the creature fall. Seconds later, the shattering of rock reverberated in the cavern.

The iron hands holding Ean hauled him back up over the edge. The prince found his footing and looked up into the face of his rescuer.

A man of striking countenance gazed back. Seeing Ean stable on his feet, he tilted his copper-eyed gaze to assess the abyss where the *eidola* had fallen. "Well ... that's one way to be rid of them."

Ean sort of staggered away—from the edge as much as from the stranger. He shakily retrieved his sword from the cave floor and looked back to the man as he slowly straightened, pressing a sleeve to staunch his bleeding neck. "Thank you." His voice sounded hoarse, strained. A host of questions and uncertainties spiraled in his thoughts—*who ... how ... why?* Reason delivered no rationale for the stranger's presence, and even intuition held its tongue as to his possible aims.

The man seemed to understand receiving wariness where gratitude would've suited better, for he delivered the barest twitch of a smile. "I'd been following that *eidola* when you appeared to challenge it. I admit I was ... surprised at your valor."

Ean braced himself against the cavern wall. His neck and head were a throbbing agony, while the rest of him suffered latent trembling as the flush of adrenaline bled away. He leaned his head against the rough stone and closed his eyes, too weary in that moment to face his own stupidity. "That's a diplomatic way of saying what a fool I was."

"But perhaps ... a noble one," the man agreed with more gentleness than Ean deserved. He looked him over then. "Who is this noble fool, I asked myself when I saw you going after the *eidola*. You're not one of Dore Madden's sycophants—that's apparent—so who, how, why … ?"

At this echo of his own thoughts, Ean looked swiftly back to the stranger. He certainly didn't look the part of a villain—Raine's truth, he looked like some foreign duke, what with his elegant, thigh-length coat and long raven braid and aristocratic manner. The prince admitted that odder things had happened to him.

Ean felt a measure of his composure returning with his breath, and with this a resurgence of purpose, the resonance of his own true path—the real reason he'd come to Tal'Afaq. He pushed unsteadily off the wall.

"Dore Madden holds my brother captive. I came here to claim him, but …" he paused as the truth of his stupidity once again threw itself in his face.

The man eyed him curiously. "But you saw the *eidola* and thought it would be a fair diversion in the meantime?"

Ean's gaze hardened. "I saw it for what it was: an egregious aberration of *elae*, binding a living body unto death and a man's mind to a monster's."

"Ah …" The stranger's copper eyes scanned Ean speculatively. "Then you see far more deeply than I gave you credit for, noble fool."

Ean waved his sword at the man by way of sheathing it. "And you?"

Mystery hinted in his gaze, much like the zanthyr's own. "My brother spoke about these things to me." He walked slowly towards Ean. "I hardly believed him, so I came to see if he spoke the truth. When I laid eyes upon these *eidola*, however … when I saw deeply of their nature, of the thread of compulsion that binds them, as you said, to a monster …" His expression flickered through what might've been irony. "I've killed two thus far. You claimed a third. I'm told a fourth remains. Perhaps we will make quick work of it together."

Ean shook his head. "I must find my brother." Dropping his gaze, he added resolutely, "I was wrong to seek this vengeance now."

"I see."

Ean looked back to him. He searched the stranger's eyes with his own, finding no guile, only sincerity, and something more … "You saved my life, and I owe you for it, but my brother—"

The man lifted a hand. "Perhaps …" A smile twitched in his features, undecided of the final shape they meant to express. "Perhaps I could aid you in securing your brother's safety. Then we might talk of repayment of debts."

Ean felt an immense sense of relief mingled with a sudden welling gratitude. He extended his hand. "I'm Ean val Lorian."

The man paused with his own hand half-extended, and something crossed his expression, but then he completed their greeting and took the prince's wrist in his iron grasp. "Well met, Your Highness. I'm Immanuel di Nostri."

Ean's first strand pattern pulsed a strong beacon to his brother's location, but he was forced to travel a circuitous route to reach him. In this, Immanuel's companionship proved a boon. The man had recent knowledge of the caves and twice guided him around hazards that would've cost him time in retracing his steps and risked further unnecessary exposure.

They were following a tunnel when they heard sounds of many running feet. They pressed themselves against the wall and watched a dozen men fly past the end of the tunnel with swords in hand. Ean worried they were headed in Isabel's direction and wore a pained expression as he watched the guards pass by.

Immanuel eyed him quizzically. "Something I should know?"

Ean shifted his gaze to the man. Then he sighed. "I came with another. She's ending the lives of the *eidola* still in transition."

"Ending the *ei*—" The man looked truly startled. "That's a bold calling."

Ean rubbed his palm against one eye. "She is dauntless on her path."

Immanuel considered him upon this utterance, his gaze intense. Then he silently motioned them on.

That time Fortune's eye had been upon them, but only moments later she must've blinked, for the next storm of men barreled *into* the tunnel they were following instead of past it. They took one look at Ean and Immanuel and let out a uniform cry.

Ean had his blade out in time to cut down the first of them. Then he dove into the *cortata* and devastated three more. But Immanuel ...

Ean had wondered, when he saw that Immanuel carried no blade, how he'd managed to overcome two *eidola*, but watching him spin from assailant to assailant, ripping the swords from their hands and flipping them to stab back into their own chests ... well, he had his answer.

While Ean watched, fascinated, Immanuel plowed through the squad of guards and left no man standing in his wake. Ean found a grave beauty in the way Immanuel moved—no, the way he *flowed*—through the mass of attacking men. Ean had only ever seen such glorious equilibrium of motion in creatures of the fifth ...

It struck him even as he had the thought.

Gods above and below ... could he be any more obtuse? Ean pushed a palm to his throbbing forehead and wondered how close a truth had to be before he saw it—must it bite him in the nose?

He didn't need to study the currents to secure this truth—though he should've done it before he gave the man his hand in friendship—but he did, finally, just for the sake of belated prudence.

As Immanuel slew the last of their assailants and turned to him, Ean saw only an earnestness and intelligence in his gaze—and his presence upon the currents like a glowing star.

Immanuel discarded the last of his pilfered weapons as if an inconvenient burden. His eyes tightened slightly as he noted Ean's expression. "What is it?"

Ean pulled on his nose. "I was just … admiring your skill with a blade."

Immanuel arched a brow. "I've no doubt you could do it too, the making of one's flesh as stone so as to counter any blade save Merdanti. It comes naturally to children of the fifth, like you and I." At the prince's startled look—startled, for twice the man had now spoken the most recent thought on Ean's own mind—Immanuel smiled. "Yes, I see it in you, all over you." He waved absently at him. "The fifth is as alcohol, telling tales in your every exhalation."

He motioned them on through the tunnel then. But Ean couldn't get the images of Immanuel battling out of his mind. The way he'd spun and stabbed and flung blades without even looking …

"You fight as if with eyes in the back of your head."

Immanuel cast him an amused look. "Surely you fight with the same sense? The fifth binds you and I to everything around us, like water, alerting us to the smallest ripple in the pool." He cast Ean a sidelong look and a somewhat perplexing smile. "For lifetimes I lived indifferent to the workings of *elae*. But I've recently been remedying studies long overdue, and now I watch the currents as often as I watch my back for the daggers of my brother's spies."

Ean frowned. "Your brother … who told you of *eidola*. You're at odds?"

Immanuel considered him a moment before answering, "One might say our purposes are currently misaligned."

They moved on, but as they came towards the end of an upward-sloping cave, the sounds of men floated to their ears. Immanuel ducked down next to the cave's mouth, and Ean joined him at the edge, which overlooked another cavern thirty paces below.

A score and ten men were preparing for battle. They were arming themselves with a greasy sort of efficiency, boasting base insults, and naming off the deeds they would accomplish to exact their revenge on 'the invaders.' The thought of such men getting anywhere near Isabel roused Ean's violent protest.

"Perhaps we should do something about them, eh?"

Ean met Immanuel's gaze inquiringly.

He shrugged. "I wouldn't want such men chasing down the 'she' who accompanied me, were I in your shoes."

Ean gazed at him in wonder. Was the man reading his thoughts, or just somehow a kindred spirit that thought the same thing at the same time? Either way, the prince felt an unexpected and immediate kinship with the man.

Immanuel turned a narrow gaze back to the Saldarians. Ean could see the wheels and cogs of his intelligent mind whirring with perfect synchronicity. "It suits me to disrupt activities here, and we must cross this cavern in any case." He spared Ean a smile. "Would you care to join me in showing these men some humility? You have my oath it won't compromise your brother's rescue."

Ean looked back to the Saldarians. "There's near thirty of them down there—all well armed."

Immanuel seemed not to understand his point. "What purpose would it serve to attack unarmed men?" Upon which inquiry he launched himself over the wall. Ean watched him drop twenty feet to the ledge below and land soundlessly in a crouch.

It inspired him to do the same. Twenty feet whirred by in a flash, and he landed on a buffer of the fifth beside Immanuel, his heart racing with the exhilaration of what he'd just done—a very zanthyr-esque feat. He couldn't help the grin that escaped him, nor the small glow of pride.

A wielder is limited by what he can envision.

Immanuel straightened to his full height. Then he whistled.

The Saldarians turned, and the room fell silent while disbelief bloomed into anger. Then the men were rushing them. Immanuel went flying into the melee.

Ean stood for a moment, caught by wonder, watching as Immanuel tore two blades from his attackers, flipped the swords to switch his hold from blade to hilt, and stabbed them right back into their owners' chests—all in the breath of an instant. Then he was ducking, spinning, snaring more weapons and flinging them off again with deadly accuracy ... As nature wasted nothing, so did Immanuel display an economy of motion, so simple and yet so elegant, like those great predatory cats formed of muscle and stealth.

Immanuel clearly needed none of Ean's help to clear the room of thirty men. He'd merely included Ean because ... well, Ean suspected the man thought it would be fun to battle side by side.

He launched off the ledge after him.

Ean gained no joy in killing, but knowing what these men would do to Isabel if they caught her ... well, he didn't exactly mind it either. And he had to admit, as they moved back to back cutting a formidable swath through the mass of Saldarians, exchanging a knowing glance here and there, or a fierce grin, it *was* exciting fighting with Immanuel at his side.

TWENTY-THREE

"What you call impossible, I call a challenge."

– The Adept wielder Arion Tavestra

AFTER FINISHING OFF the Saldarians, Ean and Immanuel hastened out of the caves into the fortress proper. They were climbing a long, narrow staircase cut into the rock when the first strand pattern attached to Sebastian resonated so violently in Ean's mind that he caught his breath. Then he launched up the remaining stairs two at a time.

The stairwell opened into a long passageway. Smooth sandstone led away left and right beneath an arched ceiling of mosaic tiles. Partway down the corridor, a black-enameled door marred the otherwise empty wall, and Ean knew that he would find his brother through it.

He emerged into the hall with his blade held ready and Immanuel close behind him. Ean scanned the passage for patterns, and finding none, he moved to the black door. Yet even as his hand reached for the latch, he paused. Then he stepped back.

"Do you see something?" Immanuel peered intently at the lacquered wood.

Instinct guided Ean towards the wall. He leaned flat against it and gazed sidelong, scanning the face of the door, and there it was: a gossamer pattern too thin to be seen except from an oblique angle.

"How predictable you are, Dore Madden," he murmured. He shifted his gaze slightly to see all of the pattern, found its beginning and ending and unraveled it with a thought. Then he looked to Immanuel. *"Now* we go in."

A flicker of intent dissolved the iron lock. Black sand came pouring out of the keyhole as Ean pulled open the door to reveal a dim landing. Stone steps skirted the outside edge of a curving wall lit by slotted windows—clearly one of Tal'Afaq's exterior-facing towers. Ean glanced at Immanuel and then started down.

At the very bottom, they found Sebastian.

Ean thought he understood anger. He thought he'd known rage. The fury he'd experienced upon discovering the web of compulsion that bound his brother had been beyond measure.

Yet none of those moments had prepared him for the wave of fury that broke across his heart as he descended through an opening in the tower's lowest floor and came upon his brother.

They'd strapped Sebastian naked across an iron block. His wrists and arms stretched tight above his head. Silver rope stretched his ankles out behind him and anchored into bolts in the floor, so his overtaxed shoulders held the brunt of his weight. His back bore the marks of a vicious lashing, but his hands … Ean's eyes shied away from their mutilation.

He hardly realized he stood frozen on the steps until Immanuel's hand on his shoulder recalled him to the moment. Ean felt so many conflicting emotions he could barely find a coherent thought.

Immanuel's gaze took in Sebastian's broken form and then returned compassionately to Ean. "I'll wait just above. Call if you desire my help in any way."

Ean looked back to Sebastian and swallowed. Then he forced himself down the last few steps.

The currents flowed smoothly around his brother—this savagery had been the work of human hands—but Ean still studied their tides before approaching, lest he fall into some final trap. Then he rushed to Sebastian's side and laid a hand on his dark hair, damp with sweat.

Sebastian's eyes fluttered open.

A lump formed in Ean's throat, and his heart beat a rapid cadence, for he saw not the veil of corruption that had bound the creature Işak, but his brother Sebastian gazing back at him.

Sebastian managed a humorless smile, fleeting and full of pain, and then the whisper, "… knew you'd come."

Ean pushed back a shattering feeling of grief. "I had to."

Another smile flickered across Sebastian's face, ironic … rueful. "I dreamed of you … of us." He winced. "Almost made it all worthwhile … to have that memory back … after so long."

Ean scanned his brother's broken body, wondering how best to free him. He tried not to stare at Sebastian's mutilated hands, but his gaze kept straying back to them. "Why?" he found himself murmuring, not really meaning to say it aloud.

Sebastian closed his eyes and laid his head against one arm. He spoke with a singular weariness of spirit. "Dore knew my hands were the one part of myself I didn't abhor." He managed a grim smile and added with a twitch of his brow, "He had to whip that out of me."

Ean looked his brother over again, fearing for him on so many levels. "If I release you—"

"Just *do* it, Ean."

The prince drew his dagger and severed the *goracrosta* binding Sebastian's wrists. He exhaled a tormented groan and collapsed onto his knees.

While Ean attended to the bounds at his ankles, Sebastian laid his forehead against the iron block. "When I was lying there in the snow above Tyr'kharta," he murmured, his raw voice muffled, "I wondered what would be worse: to know who I was … to remember everything? Or to remember nothing, only having that terrible sense … that something vital had been taken from me. Whatever you ripped out of me … after that, I remembered all."

Having freed his ankles, Ean knelt at his brother's side and leaned to see his face. "And the knowing was worse?"

Sebastian turned his head and looked at Ean with a gaze lashed by unspeakable memories. "No. It was knowing and being so helpless that I couldn't abide." He grimaced again. "Help me … to sit."

Ean moved to aid him, for it was clear Sebastian couldn't lift his arms on his own. With Ean's help, Sebastian leaned sideways against the iron block and slowly drew in one knee to his chest and then the other, hissing as the effort strained the broken flesh of his back.

Resting his head against the iron block, he lifted blue eyes to meet his brother's horrified gaze. "When I saw you in Tyr'kharta …" He closed his eyes for a brief moment, as if to deny the memory. "When we met in Tyr'kharta, I believed nothing could save me, but whatever you did there …" Sebastian met Ean's gaze again. "You did the impossible. If there's any chance you can do what you claimed, I …" his voice broke, but he finished, "I … would rather die trying than spend another moment … bound to this hell."

Ean bent his head to capture again Sebastian's gaze, which had drifted on tides of pain. "When you recover from this … will you try to kill me?"

Sebastian flashed a bleak smile. "Probably. But not today. Today you're safe. I'm too weary even for Dore's compulsion to lift its head." He drew in a shuddering breath, and as he exhaled, he cast a despairing look at the stairs. "I remember those steps."

"A long climb," Ean agreed. "Would you choose to walk them?"

Sebastian closed his eyes and his brow constricted. "Today, little brother … I think I'll let you carry me."

Immanuel straightened off the wall as Ean came up from the flight below carrying Sebastian. His copper eyes widened. "Ah … Dore's wielder." He shifted his gaze quickly back to Ean. "Things become more clear to me."

Ean nodded dispiritedly towards the long flights of steps rising above them. "Will you lead?"

He seemed to collect himself. "Of course."

Sebastian soon passed into unconsciousness. Ean used *elae* to fuel and buffer their ascent, but the effort cost him. His head pounded with every step gained, and he felt continuously drained, as if *elae* merely flowed into and out of him again without replenishing his stamina.

They were nearly to the top before Ean heard men approaching from the final level above. He took the moment to lean his shoulder exhaustedly against the wall.

Immanuel turned him a look of deep concern. "Perhaps you should leave this battle to me?"

Ean barely found the energy to nod his agreement.

As the clamorous Saldarians came bursting through from the floor above, Immanuel's copper eyes narrowed, and he asked without turning, "Might I use your sword, Ean?" Then he added upon noticing Ean's questioning gaze, "They're learning, do you see? This crew carries Merdanti blades."

Ean turned his body to give Immanuel access to his sword. "It's—"

"Sentient? Yes, I know." He drew the Kingdom Blade from its scabbard with a sober flourish and lifted the weapon before his nose as he turned to face the oncoming Saldarians. His gaze tightened. "With your permission, Ean …"

"Please, Immanuel."

He ran up the steps to meet the Saldarian horde, and Ean did his best to keep pace. Beneath Immanuel's sword, men fell as trees to a cutter's axe, each pitching over the side of the narrow steps, bodies landing as fallen tree trunks on the stone floor forty feet below. Immanuel felled the last man with a blade through his heart and with a kick sent him tumbling to join his companions in death.

As the door came in view, Ean sought Isabel along the bond—only to perceive her presence surprisingly close. He realized that she'd done as he'd meant to do and had already followed the bond in search of him. There were certain benefits to loving a woman who could see into the future.

The moment Ean emerged from the tower with Sebastian in his arms, Isabel came around the near corner with Dorn and Lem close behind. Ean's soul sighed with relief.

Immanuel had been holding the door for Ean's exit, and now he closed it and moved around into Isabel's view.

She halted abruptly.

Immanuel stiffened.

The air in the space between them grew instantly charged and then went still, like the sea stretched flat between two successive squalls.

Immanuel turned Ean a sharp look as if to ask, *your other?* At Ean's nod, the man returned his gaze to Isabel and took three slow steps back. Then he placed a hand across his heart and gave a solemn bow. "Isabel van Gelderan, High Mage of the Citadel, I bid you good afternoon."

Isabel stood still as stone. A conflicting storm of emotion thrummed around her, both confusing and unsettling, but after a taut silence, one corner of her mouth twitched upwards in an almost-smile. "Immanuel di Nostri. To think, all this time ..." She shook her head. "How could I not have known?"

Immanuel shrugged inconsequentially. "You never gave me a second glance, my lady—but why should you have?" He placed his open palm across his heart. "I was merely a painter, one of many littering the Sormitáge's halls, and you the High Mage." Then he smiled and added with a nod to another sort of truth, "But then, too, I'm adept at hiding my nature."

"So it would appear."

Ean shifted his hold on his brother's inert body, bewildered by this conversation but even more so by Isabel's reaction. She stood braced as if expecting a storm but spoke almost with familiarity. The currents massed around both her and Immanuel, though neither called them to bear against the other, yet Ean sensed a grave truth was being batted back and forth between them. And threaded throughout all of this was Isabel's sense of immense conflict.

They were easily twenty paces distant, but Immanuel took another step away from Isabel. His copper eyes looked her over appreciatively then, making Ean flinch. "There are a great many people who would pay dearly to know you survived the Citadel, my lady."

She arched a brow above her blindfold. "There are a great many who will pay dearly because I did."

She and he held each other in silence then, somehow reading of one another. The moment drew out long enough for Ean to grow uncomfortable with the energy passing between them.

Finally, Isabel murmured, "You've chosen a path?"

"I ..." Immanuel frowned. Then he cast her a look of appeal—most surprising and unexpected.

Isabel's fingers tightened around her staff. "You are no longer yourself, Pelas," she remarked then, using a name unfamiliar to Ean, "not wholly."

Ean spun a look at Immanuel.

His face constricted. "No, my lady. I'm not."

The passage seemed to darken, but Ean couldn't tell which of them was muting the light.

Isabel turned her staff in her hands, kneading the enchanted stone. "What will you do?"

His gaze flicked away and back again. "I will once more seek my brother and demand that he free me from the chains of his will." Then he frowned, and his simmering anger set the currents churning away in waves. "That failing," he murmured tightly, "perhaps I will seek out *your* brother and ask him to do what mine would not."

She stepped towards him with sudden urgency. "You should come with us now."

Immanuel took a quick step backwards. He seemed startled by her invitation. He opened his mouth to speak and then closed it again and rubbed his jaw instead. "I … cannot. Don't you see … ?" He tilted his head as he held her invisible gaze. "I cannot know what other compulsions Darshan might've placed upon me. I can't trust my own mind, nor my decisions … my every thought is suspect."

Ean started violently at this admission. *Darshan? His brother?* He turned a furious look of betrayal upon Immanuel.

"Do not be quick to judge, Ean," Isabel advised quietly, though she herself stood amid a hurricane storm of uncertainty, just as he did. "The currents reveal the truth."

"And what truth is that?" Pelas inquired. His gaze had never left her.

She pressed her lips together tightly. "Darshan will never release you. Pelasommáyurek, *come* with us." Such ominous portent laced her tone that Ean felt this entreaty hit him like a punch to his gut. Isabel wouldn't be this insistent unless she'd looked down the path ahead and seen something that disturbed her greatly.

But quite aside from Isabel's foresight, the prince had his own perceptions, and he sensed something between Isabel and Pelas—some future—that made him cold inside.

The matter was decided for them when the ratcheting rattle of an *eidola* interrupted the silence. Ean spun a look over his shoulder to find one of the creatures stalking towards them leading a host of men.

Shade and darkness! And he with Sebastian to carry … ?

Immanuel hastily replaced Ean's sword at his hip, saying low into his ear as he came close, "I hope one day we'll meet again, Ean." Then he turned to face the *eidola* and placed his body between it and the others. "Go," he murmured, settling a predatory gaze upon the creature. "This one is mine."

"Hurry, Ean." Isabel clearly sensed his hesitation. "The path narrows."

Ean gave Immanuel one last searching look. Then he followed Isabel, his head swimming amid a sea of future storms. His bond with Isabel had somehow dumped him onto a path of the Sight, and it had him in its grip now and was shaking him as an angry child torments a doll.

Ean heard battle break out behind them—Immanuel undoubtedly engaging the *eidola*—and then men were shouting and feet were pounding in pursuit. He spared a glance to see the host splitting itself around the grappling pair, swarming past them into the chase.

Isabel motioned them around a corner and called a sudden halt. "Dorn, take Sebastian." While Ean handed his brother to the larger man, Isabel moved her staff in an arc and raised an invisible field of the fourth wall to wall. Those chasing would perforce careen through it, for only the currents revealed its presence. That done, she motioned them all forward in haste and told Ean as they rushed on, "You've got to get us out of here, my lord."

This went without saying.

Yet as Ean tried to focus on some possible escape, nameless fears attacked him. His head felt a bucket of ash, full of charred bits of things that might become—

Isabel grabbed his arm and forced him to a halt. Then she took his face in both hands. "Come back to me." Abruptly she kissed him hard, and as her mouth lit fires of desire to burn away that cold, prescient sun, so too her mind embraced his, twining through the bond, pulling him back from that omniscient path that wasn't his to walk.

Just as abruptly, she pulled away. "Focus on *this* moment, my lord, or none of us will have a tomorrow to shape to our desires."

Ean stared at her for a breath longer. Then he gave her another rough kiss and grabbed her hand to keep her close. "I have an idea." He drew her with him as he set off down the hall. "But I'm not sure how to make it work. You'll have to help me remember."

They speared ahead, while behind, the men chasing them ran through Isabel's pattern and came to a halt. Argument broke out among their ranks, for each man swore he'd seen the enemy running in a different direction. Soon Ean could no longer hear their harsh voices, only the unsound of *elae's* rushing tides.

Ean led them onto one of Tal'Afaq's crenellated towers. While Lem watched their backs, Ean tugged Isabel towards the tower's edge. Relief flooded him as he looked upon Dore's patterns of warding, for his suspicions proved correct.

"Look there." He pointed to the invisible web, knowing Isabel saw it in her own unique way. "The inner pattern-web is the dangerous one, but it's a lacework of holes." He could almost draw a straight line from the tower where they were standing to the ridge where he and Isabel had observed the fortress that morning. "The outer shell is the one designed to set off alarms of warning, but they're alert to us now anyway. If I can take us through the hole in the inner web, we'll make a clean escape." He searched her hidden gaze with his own. "*Can* I do it, Isabel?"

She traced a thumb across his lips, while a brooding smile hinted on hers. "You helped my brother fashion a new realm from the womb of Alorin's aether. I imagine you could make stairs of the air with ease."

Ean blinked at her. "*I*—?" Then he shook his head, not so much denying the truth as saving it for later inspection. He turned a discerning gaze upon the space between their tower and the distant ridge, his heart racing, acutely aware of the short span of time he had to effect their escape.

Isabel said low into his ear, "In your mind, when breaking free from the Labyrinth, you realized you could be at any place within it or exterior to it."

He gave her a startled look, for he hadn't told her how he'd escaped the pattern, yet she spoke only the truth.

"You could be anywhere within your mind that you chose to be," she continued, hastening past his surprise. "So is it the same in this world. You must cast your awareness across the distance. Place an anchor of your attention here and another anchor atop the far ridge, and claim all of the space between. *Own* it—even as you have owned me." And she emphasized this idea with images of their bodies intertwined, conveying the full concept of her meaning. "It is the same feeling of possession, of dominion," she murmured low into his ear. Thus she coaxed his memory through the veils of death. "All of that vast expanse must be yours in which to build your bridge."

She spoke to him of the Fifth Esoteric: *Absolute Being must equal the scope of a wielder's concept of effect.* He recalled his lesson with Ramu and a hall encased in ice. Definitely a mistake he didn't want to repeat.

Ean drew in a deep breath and summoned his resolve. Then he summoned the fifth. Its touch burned, for his mind had already been singed by overuse that day, but he focused his concentration and made his attention into a spear. He cast this spear of awareness forth with such speed that the ridge solidified within his perception almost instantly—Ean had to overcome his own startled response to keep from losing hold of it as soon as he'd claimed it.

He anchored his awareness there, as Isabel had bade him, and cast another anchor beneath his feet. Then he sought to form the bridge. In his mind, he saw it clearly, yet making it of air … it felt too insubstantial.

Though theoretically the pattern of air should hold them, he didn't trust his skill, and he knew that without complete certainty, the working would fail. Where he struggled lay in the aspects of air. It willingly filled every available space, yet it resisted assuming any form. Ean frowned out across the arid vista, which offered little except rock and sand.

Sand …

He smiled. Lifting his sword to use as his talisman, as the focal point for this powerful working, he called the wind towards him and made it spin—faster, harder. Soon these spirals were pulling sand upwards through their funnels, fueling his bridge. He held the intended shape in his consciousness, and the sand filled it with form.

Before him, a great bridge began to coalesce, conforming to Ean's vision, its leading edge a roiling, dun-hued wave tumbling forth towards the high ridge, molding an ever-lengthening and elegant arch behind.

"Your Highness, they're coming," Lem urged.

"And we're departing." Ean didn't remove his gaze from the bridge spanning the miles between him and the ridge, but he held a hand for Isabel to step first upon his knee, then upon the merlon. He joined her there in a single leap, and together they stepped upon his shimmering bridge of sand.

Though he'd been certain it would hold them, he still felt a glow of pride when his feet found solid footing. They rushed then, with Dorn carrying Sebastian and Lem bringing up the rear.

Ean didn't look back until they all stood once again upon firm ground—many minutes later. Then he released *elae* and his intention—which was all that had been holding the bridge in place, a rather frightening truth to ponder—and sand rained down upon the plains.

Ean swooned.

Isabel caught one of his arms and Lem the other, even as she hissed, "Ean!"

Doubtless he deserved the scolding in her tone. Between his battle with the *eidola* and his constant holding of the currents to aid his view—never mind the miles-long bridge of sand he'd just built to secure their escape—he'd done more with the lifeforce in a single day than in all the weeks of his training with Markal.

Elae draining out of him now felt like it was pulling him inside-out. His mind had become so sensitive to the elemental fifth that he could perceive the far reaches of the horizon. The expansive sensation gave him vertigo. He had the heady impression of being squashed as gravity pulled him towards the earth's core, while the vast spinning of the celestial globe hollowed his insides. Even the pressure of the air felt painful upon his skin.

Ean pushed palms to his throbbing forehead and was oddly grateful that they didn't sink into his flesh. "I'll be all right." His voice sounded hoarse … distant. "I just need … to rest a bit."

"Five hours," Dorn said.

Ean dropped his hands and cast the man a tormented look, though he couldn't help noting, with both gratitude and a hint of envy, the ease and gentleness with which the big man held Sebastian's unconscious form.

"Five hours?" Sebastian needed much longer than this to heal, and Ean suspected he did also.

Dorn twitched his head towards the fortress. "It'll take them about five hours to get here. Three on horseback."

"Three," Isabel said, her voice tight. "Then we must make good use of it."

Pelasommáyurek caught the *eidola's* wrist in both hands and spun, twisting the creature off its feet. He used momentum to lift it high into the air and turned a tight circle before releasing his hold. The creature flew across the corridor and smashed into the wall with a gratifying shattering of stone.

Unfortunately it wasn't the stone of its own body, but that would come in time. Pelas was enjoying the fight for now. In his mind's eye, he imagined he fought Darshan, and it lent a certain satisfaction to the encounter.

Pelas stalked towards the *eidola* as it struggled up again. Such golem creatures felt no pain, but their minds could become muddled rather easily. It gained its feet before Pelas reached it, but instead of attacking him, the creature scrambled off down the corridor.

Pelas grinned and dove into the chase.

No creature in Alorin challenged him physically—at least none he'd met, though he imagined that perhaps a zanthyr might prove a fair adversary. The *eidola* at least came close to being a worthy opponent—that is, if he restrained himself from using his power. In the very least, fighting it held a certain therapeutic value; it required little thought and provided enough physical distraction to allow his mind to wander unmolested along the paths he'd been recently exploring.

The *eidola* turned a sharp corner and dove into a twisting stairwell. It smashed each lamp as it descended in a rush, pitching the narrow tunnel into darkness. Smart. Such creatures were only as intelligent as the men they'd once been, as intelligent as any mind warped and twisted by *deyjiin* could be.

Pelas called the currents to light the way and descended after it.

He rather liked using *elae*. Until Tanis's startling revelation about his fifth strand nature, Pelas hadn't known he worked the lifeforce innately. Now he understood much better—not only his own workings but also those of his brothers.

How long had they been in collusion together against him? How long had they been using *elae* while exhorting its evils, jading him against his own nature, occluding truth? Doubtless since their arrival in Alorin. Darshan had no concept of hypocrisy, and Shail justified himself to no one.

Pelas's lips curled in a humorless smile as his feet made a rapid cadence on the steps. What a motley crew they were, the three of them—and Rinokh ... poor doomed Rinokh, too disconnected to realize he'd been standing in Shail's way.

He heard the *eidola* burst through a door somewhere below and hastened to catch it before it got too far ahead, but as he emerged into the corridor, something struck him from the side.

He spun, and a net of silver rope curtained over him. Heavy weights along the net's edge bore him to one knee, while the *goracrosta* sucked *elae* from his grasp. Pelas endured a moment of dizzying disorientation. Needles stabbed him everywhere, and as the *goracrosta* nullified *deyjiin* in his veins, he felt himself growing weaker.

Pelas gritted his teeth against the stabbing sensation in his flesh and turned his head to see the *eidola* standing beyond a line of men, and beside him, Dore Madden.

Realization cut sharply in his thoughts. *Ah, no ... how foolish I've been ...*

"Bind him in it," Dore commanded with a cadaverous grin.

Pelas felt webs of compulsion falling across his helpless mind. He could sense *elae* still, but it lay beyond his reach, as insubstantial as lamplight. Unable to resist, he fell to hands and knees, and then to his stomach. He looked up as Dore approached.

The wielder looked gleefully down upon him, veritably slavering. The unhealthy lust he exuded roused disgust enough in Pelas to momentarily overwhelm even the *goracrosta's* sharp bite. Dore Madden was naught but a carrion bird, hungering with such decayed desires that it couldn't even stomach the dead until the corpse had rotted beyond recognition.

Dore's flickering tongue licked across his whitened lips. "Oh, how the mighty have fallen." His eye twitched with what might've been a smile, but Dore deigned no expression unless it inspired dread. He spun away, and his next words floated back on a tide of foreboding. "Take him to the Prophet."

TWENTY-FOUR

"None are more righteous than a sinner reformed."

– Cassius of Rogue

THE ROYAL COUSIN Fynnlar val Lorian couldn't decide whether his near death had transported him to Elysium or the Fields of Punishment.

On the one hand, he was a prisoner at the end of a node with no hope of regaining Alorin save by the grace of some infernal dragon—or worse, a zanthyr. He couldn't move an inch without sensing some immortal creature watching him, no doubt imagining a new way to broil and eat him ... or just eat him.

He fancied himself possessed of a certain indigestibility—what with all the wine he'd consumed, surely his flesh had become pickled. He might've told them so to curtail any culinary interest, save that he didn't want to put the idea *into* their heads on the off-chance they hadn't actually thought about eating him yet.

It doubly grated on Fynnlar that he owed his life to a zanthyr, even if she was impossibly buxom and leggy. Never mind that she wouldn't give him the time of day now that she'd pasted him back together again.

Then there was Alyneri, who'd never been more confusing. One day she'd be impossibly morose and burst into tears if he so much as looked at her. Then on the next she'd be following that zanthyr Vaile around all the day and glaring at him for only doing what he did best—which was to say sitting idly and getting drunk ... or perhaps it was more accurate to say working hard at getting drunk. Yes, that had a nicer ring to it.

Vaile, Fynn had learned, was the steward of the First Lord's *sa'reyth*, which really meant she had license to kill anyone she chose. Fynn thought it a bit careless of the First Lord, considering how indiscriminate zanthyrs were about killing people, but this didn't explain Alyneri's attachment to the woman.

The one time Fynn had followed them to see where they went on their excursions, he'd found them in a clearing doing some kind of slow, spiraling dance. When they saw him watching, they'd leveled him dual glares of such reproach that he'd scurried back to the safety of Balaji's attentions and not emerged again for several days.

On that bright note—and the only boon he could find in all of this, really—Balaji had made him the beneficiary of an endless supply of wine for tasting and testing.

In truth, Fynn preferred Ramu's wines—Balaji's were a tad sweet for Fynn's palate—but Ramu was rarely about. Moreover, whenever the Lord of the Heavens did make an appearance, he always watched Fynn with the sort of knowing gaze that made him worry about his future, and that was rarely a pleasant contemplation.

The parting of drapes drew Fynn's gaze, and he roused from his ruminations as Balaji walked in with a goblet in hand. "And how are you faring this fine morning, Fynnlar, son of Ryan?"

Fynn scowled into his empty goblet. For any morning to be considered fine, it must necessarily not include a reminder of his imperious father. He raised his goblet dispiritedly. "Fill what's empty, empty what's full, and scratch where it itches. That's my motto."

"It seems to me a very pragmatic outlook on life." Balaji switched out the goblets in Fynn's hand. "Your logic is incontrovertible."

Fynn eyed him narrowly, trying to decide if he was mocking him, but the youth who was 'older than the sun' merely regarded him with a bright smile. Fynn saluted him with his new, full goblet and took a long swallow of wine. He decided he liked Balaji—inasmuch as he was of a mind to like any creature that could squash him with one toe.

Balaji watched him with a hopeful gaze.

Fynn made a show of swishing the wine around in his mouth and sucking in air across his tongue in that incredibly annoying way of true connoisseurs. None of these treatments made the wine less sweet, but beggars couldn't be too choosy or their benefactors got offended and found someone else to benefact ... benefice? *Whatever.*

"Well?" asked the *drachwyr.*

Fynn waggled his hand from side to side. "It's still a bit sweet to be a Volga ... but it has nice fruit and a complex finish." He'd heard one of those pompous Solvayre critics say that once. The Agasi far surpassed even the Veneiseans when it came to snobbery and pretention. "Of course ... I'll need to consume it all to appreciate its full body and flavor, the subtlety of which alters as the wine airs."

Balaji's eyes twinkled. "I'm not sure the wine has much time to breathe in your goblet, my new friend Fynnlar, but it is a fine day for tasting and making wine."

Fynn raised his goblet in salute. "Whenever is it not, He Who Chases the Shadow Edge of the Heavens?"

Balaji arched an amused brow. "You have somehow managed to include all of our names together this time."

"Oh?" Fynn frowned. "He Who Walks With the Bosom of the Sun?"

"Now you have confused me with my sisters."

Fynn made a face as he scratched his unshaved jaw. "If you didn't have such bloody long names we mortals might be able to remember them properly."

Balaji smiled and took a seat across from Fynn. "Our names were bestowed upon us by our Maker. We might've picked differently if given the choice."

"By your Maker ... you mean like *the* Maker?"

"The Father of All, yes."

Fynn drank more wine. "Who was your mother then?"

"As much as we could be said to have a mother, it would be this fair realm, my new friend Fynnlar."

Fynn frowned. "Are you speaking metaphorically? Because when vague, philosophical metaphors and I meet on the street, I just keep walking—unless they're sexual in nature, in which case I like to stop and buy them a drink."

"You display uncommon wisdom in this."

Fynn drew back a little. "I—what? I do?"

Balaji crossed his knees and reclined in his chair. "To stop and smell the flowers, as they say, is to truly partake of the many experiences this life has to offer. When a man is become too busy to enjoy the life he leads, one must ask why he leads it at all."

"Much better to be a follower, I always say." Fynn belched and motioned with his goblet. "That way you can see where the edge is before you walk off it."

Balaji sank his chin onto his hand and cast Fynn a winsome smile. "Truly, you are a fount of wisdom."

Fynn grinned accommodatingly. He wondered why Alyneri said Balaji made her nervous. Fynn found He Who Walked the Horizon of Whatever to be the most amiable of all the man-eating creatures he'd met so far.

"Balaji?" Náiir stuck his head into the room. Then he saw Fynn and gave him a smile. "Oh, good morning, Fynnlar, cousin of Trell."

Fynn belched and held up his cup in greeting.

The Chaser of the Dawn looked back to his brother. "You might want to come moderate the tempest."

Balaji arched a brow. "So early?" He motioned to Fynn as he stood. "Come, my new friend, Fynnlar. We must see what excitement the day is providing."

Fynn roused from his chair. "Alas, I fear my cup runneth empty."

Balaji cast him a look over his shoulder as he followed Náiir from the room. "I do bid you gaze again."

Fynn looked into the goblet and saw the bottom quite clearly. He was just opening his mouth to say so when a sanguineous liquid began swirling up until it nearly touched the brim.

Fynn sighed. If Elysium existed, the gods there would have such miraculous goblets—only their endless supply wouldn't be dependent upon a dragon's magnanimous disposition.

When they reached the tempest Náiir had spoken of, the blue-eyed *drachwyr* Mithaiya stood on one side of an argument fomenting clouds, and the zanthyr Vaile stood on the other filling them with lightning. Whatever language they were speaking, they sounded to Fynn like two cats throwing a hissing fit inside a rain barrel.

Behind Mithaiya stood a motley crew of certain misfits led by none other than—

"Carian vran Lea!" Fynn stalked over and threw his arms around the pirate, not even caring that he nearly spilled his wine in the process.

A grinning Carian took him by the shoulders and looked him over. "Fynnlar! About time you dragged your lazy arse out of bed."

Fynn scowled. "Oh sure. I only had a few seven-inch spikes through my gut. Nothing to concern you. I didn't nearly die. No need to write."

"But I heard that a zanthyr Healed you." Carian's eyes traveled up and down Vaile's form where she now stood in a boiling silence, thanks to Balaji's intervention. A gleam came to his eye. "I definitely would've taken advantage of that."

As if hearing him speaking of her, Vaile's emerald gaze shifted to them. Carian waggled his brows saucily and gave her a suggestive grin. She looked away again with withering indifference.

"Yep. Lots to take advantage of there." Fynn drank his wine. "I see you escaped T'khendar then. Balaji said you were having quite the frolic when he saw you last."

Carian grinned lustily over at Mithaiya, who was glaring at Vaile while Balaji spoke soothing words in a foreign tongue. "Balaji doesn't know the half of it, mate."

"So what *are* you doing here, vran Lea?"

Carian shifted his gaze back to him. "Oh, Rohre and I were on an assignment and got separated. We'd agreed to meet back here at the *sa'reyth*. Word is the Espial left the fête with a painter," his gaze gleamed with mischievous insinuation, "so there's no telling how long you'll have the benefit of my excellent company. So, Fynnlar …" he grinned, "are you finally ready to pay me that money you owe me?"

Fynn snorted into his wine. "Vran Lea, you know perfectly well I only pay my enemies, and then only when there's mortal threat involved."

A big man wearing a navy kilt separated himself from the group standing behind Mithaiya. He had the most massive calves Fynn had ever seen on a man—as opposed to, possibly, a bear. As he neared, he looked Fynn over with colorless truthreader's eyes. "Friend of yours, Carian?"

The pirate held out a hand. "Gannon Bair, may I present Fynnlar val Lorian, a wanton reprobate and by far the best man for the job."

"Job?" Fynn scowled at him. "I have my hands full as it is."

Gannon eyed him skeptically. "Doing what, may I ask?"

Fynn glared at Carian. "Why'd you bring him? You know perfectly well how terribly truthreaders and I get along."

"Carian tells me you have no moral compass," Gannon said.

Fynn straightened his shoulders. "I had one once, but I found it was greatly hindering my dissolute and aimless wanderings. I think I left it somewhere in Agasan. If you're looking for one, my lord father keeps extras in a drawer. He'll sell one to you for the special low price of your eternally indentured soul."

Gannon shifted his stance and rested a hand on the dirk at his belt. "I've heard of Prince Ryan. He's well-respected."

"Uh-huh," Fynn grumbled, "among *reputable* people. Look vran Lea—whatever this job of yours is, I can't just leave. I'm doing very important work for He Who Caws in the Heavens, but more importantly, my cousin is still missing."

Gannon looked up at him under his heavy black brows. "And just how are you contributing to the search effort?"

Fynn raised his goblet. "I drink every hour of the day to Trell's continued health." To Carian, he added, "My libations may be the only thing keeping him alive—have you considered that?"

Carian grinned across Fynn's head at Gannon. "See what I mean?"

Gannon grunted. "It is no great mystery why they get along."

"Who?" Fynn spun a look between them. "Are you trying to involve me in some conspiracy? Because I only participate in conspiracies on Tuesdays. I find otherwise they dramatically cut into my loafing time."

"It appears to me your entire life is loafing time," Gannon noted.

"My point exactly."

Carian grinned. "This'll be good for you, Fynnlar. A little nourishment for your responsibility-starved soul."

"Look at the pot calling the kettle black."

The pirate puffed out his chest. "But I'm a changed man."

Fynn grunted sympathetically. "Relationships with women—or, I suppose, dragons—will do that to you. That's why I choose a different one every time—women that is, not dragons." Fynn gestured with his goblet in emphasis. "Otherwise they attempt to bind you down with 'I love you' while they're bleeding your pockets dry of everything *you* love."

"But an oath to the First Lord is more binding still," Gannon remarked with a penetrating stare.

Fynn eyed him uncertainly and drank his wine. "Look … you're both wasting your time on me. I've proven myself to be incorruptibly corrupt—even more than you, vran Lea—oath or no oath. Besides," he glanced over at a scowling Vaile, "I'm not so sure you won't be kicked out of here in a couple of minutes."

"*Nah.*" The pirate waved away the suggestion. "Mithaiya expected a battle, but she says Vaile will come around. We just need a little space to plan our rebellion."

"Rebellion?" Fynn perked up.

Carian grinned and waved over two more of his companions. They slipped away while Mithaiya was talking with one hand on her hip and the other flung towards the next valley. She looked imperious, while Vaile remained stormy.

As the two men neared, Carian indicated the first of them, a tall Bemothi who walked with an aristocrat's practiced disdain. "Fynn, this is the Nodefinder Devangshu Vita."

Fynn nodded to him.

Carian then indicated the other man, who had a mop of red hair and deep-set eyes like onyx beads. Fynn had never seen him before, but he had a guileful look about him, which of course made Fynn like him immediately.

"And this is Kardashian."

Fynn perked up at the name of the infamous thief. He pressed a hand to his heart and bowed his head. "It's an honor."

Kardashian grinned.

"So ..." Fynn sipped his wine and eyed all of them over the rim. "What's this all about, vran Lea?"

Carian jerked his head at Kardashian. "Show him."

The thief opened a satchel at his hip and pulled out an enormous tome. Fynn did a double-take from the book to the satchel and back again. There was just no way a thing so massive could've been hidden in there.

Kardashian unwrapped the suede cover to reveal a gilded leather volume with a well-known seal engraved on the front. Fynn moved closer for a better look, not believing his eyes. "Is that what I think it is?"

"The Vestal Codex," Carian remarked, and there was more than a hint of pride in his tone.

Fynn turned to him sharply. "How in Tiern'aval did you get your hands on that?"

"We borrowed it from the Guild Hall in Rethynnea."

"*Borrowed.*" Fynn's eyes widened. "Surely D'varre kept it locked in his vault."

Kardashian snorted derisively. Fynn looked from Kardashian to Carian and back again. "You two *stole* the Vestals' sacred manifesto?"

They boasted happily culpable expressions, and Kardashian said, "Niko's speech provided the best possible diversion we could've asked for. The Guild Hall was all but deserted." He spoke with a heavy Dheanainn accent, making all of the vowels sound longer and rounder.

Fynn sipped his wine. "Who's Niko?"

Gannon muttered, "A rat in the wheat."

Whereupon Devangshu growled, "We're going to stop Niko's plague before it spreads."

Fynn eyed all of them speculatively. Then he looked at the book under Kardashian's arm. "Stop him ... with that?"

Carian grinned. "Knowledge is power, Fynnlar."

Fynn looked back to him. "If D'varre discovers you have that book—"

"Why do you think we brought it here, mate?" Carian clapped him on the shoulder. "Besides, it's D'varre who should be readying to meet his Maker, eh?" He eyed Fynn knowingly.

Fynn frowned at the memory of Rethynnea's Guild Master. D'varre had double-crossed them. He was to blame for their ambush in the Kutsamak and ultimately the three spikes Fynn had gotten through his gut. The worst part was Fynn had been forced to pay the man up front.

"D'varre ..." The name made the wine taste sour on Fynn's tongue. "He owes me a refund, which I intend to take out of his hide."

Carian's brown eyes gleamed with the prospect of sweet retribution as they held Fynn's gaze. He wrapped an arm around Fynn's shoulder. "Let me tell you about our plan." He smiled triumphantly at the others as he steered Fynn away.

Fynn motioned frantically to Balaji as Carian was dragging him off. He pointed inside his empty goblet and made a pleading face conveying his desperation. As his wine was magically refilling, Fynn turned back and regarded Carian seriously. "Just so we're clear, vran Lea, I can only commit on Tuesdays."

Alyneri stepped on her right foot, immediately pivoted to her left, and brought her hands together above her head. She took another step and spread her arms and sank into a wide crouch that pulled the soft leather pants she wore tight around her knees. She leaned her weight into her bent right leg and extended through her left as she rose.

Another step. She brought her hands together as if holding a sword. Over her head she lifted, slowly, precisely, making a mountain's peak of her arms before sweeping them swiftly apart and spinning into a sideways lunge. Her right leg extended straight as she crouched that time, and she brought her left hand down to touch the earth. She pivoted low, switching balance from left to right, and rose with her sword arm thrusting.

Elae sang in her ears as she continued the steps of the *cortata*. She'd never experienced anything like this sensation. Her body felt as light as air yet connected to the earth in some profound way. The more she flowed through the steps that formed the *cortata's* pattern, the more she felt magnetized to an even larger pattern beneath her ... as though with each new step she bound herself to the Pattern of the World and it to her. She felt threads of power grasping and supporting her, lifting and fueling her ...

A Patternist might've explained how the *cortata* worked, describing the purpose of every curve and swirl and what it accomplished on a metaphysical level—someone like her uncle Dareios Haxamanis, who read patterns with the same facility as he read truth in a man's thoughts. She hadn't seen Dareios since she was a child, but the thought of his smile reminded her of her father, Prince Jair, and both faces warmed her heart.

She needed that warmth. As the days drew into weeks and they'd still no word of Trell, Alyneri increasingly felt hollow inside. The waves of fear continuously crashing over her had carved a cavern in her heart, and every day deepened its darkness.

She'd needed something to focus on, something to anchor her and prevent her from worrying herself mad. She'd hated feeling so afraid all the time.

Wanting to be free of this fear had drawn Alyneri to Vaile. She remembered coming upon the zanthyr one day while walking the hills. She'd been immediately flustered, and a simple comment from Vaile had elicited a torrent of confessions. Something about Vaile's knowing gaze—so like Phaedor's, though softened with surprising feminine compassion—made Alyneri feel an overpowering need to tell her everything.

Vaile had stood in silence and listened to all of Alyneri's outpourings—her infatuation with Ean since she was a child, falling in love with Trell, and how desperately she hoped that Trell could love her back; how she'd betrayed him by keeping the secret of their childhood betrothal out of selfishness …

These confessions led to her deepest desires: to travel the world while honing her craft, to study at the Sormitáge and learn Patterning, to become a great Healer and *contribute* something to their world. Finally, she told Vaile of her experience with Phaedor and what she'd seen of him when they'd Healed Ean together.

All of this Vaile heard in silence. Then her emerald eyes had swept Alyneri, discerning but unreadable, and she'd spun on her heel and commanded Alyneri to follow. Startled, Alyneri had obeyed.

Thus had begun her lessons in the *cortata*, in swordplay, and—to her heart's joy—in Patterning. Alyneri never would've imagined such a predatory woman had a motherly side, but she'd never conceived that the dark shadow that was Phaedor had a star of divinity burning inside him either.

Vaile taught Alyneri swords with flawless competence, combining the study of swordplay with the dance of the *cortata* so that Alyneri had been immediately able to wield a blade that would otherwise have been too heavy for her to lift. After a week of practice, Alyneri had made enough progress that Vaile let Alyneri use her personal blades to learn—sentient Merdanti weapons!

Now Alyneri worked diligently from sunup until well past sundown running through her forms. When she and Vaile practiced together, the days felt longer still. Alyneri suspected that Vaile worked *elae's* third strand to lengthen the days so she might progress more quickly in the time allotted. Neither of them knew what the next moment would bring, only sharing in the unspoken understanding that the instant they received news of Trell, everything would change.

Learning to pattern challenged Alyneri more than anything she'd ever done in her life. Vaile was teaching her to do amazing—*startling* things. Yet for all of this, she'd found the *cortata* the most surprising—this practice, requiring total concentration, pushed all fear from her thoughts. It made her arms feel powerful enough to break bones—or at least to wield Vaile's Merdanti blades for hours unending. Learning it had offered benefits beyond her envisioning.

And for all of this, Vaile asked nothing in return.

Alyneri had been so surprised by the zanthyr's compassion, *so* surprised that the words had actually escaped her quite unexpectedly while they were taking a break one day.

Vaile only laughed at her. "We zanthyrs are …" She smiled quietly, and her emerald gaze took on the glint of mystery. "Well … we're a private sort of race, but that doesn't make us entirely uncaring. Just … *particular* about who we invest our time in." She turned Alyneri a meaningful look at this.

Alyneri blushed and dropped her gaze.

Vaile regarded her thoughtfully. "Mankind … you think the fifth strand races so mysterious, yet you are none of you truly as you seem."

Alyneri looked back to her. "What do you mean?"

Vaile arched a brow in faint challenge. "A zanthyr has but one life. You have many. When you look at us, you see *us*. But when we look at you … we see only a shell for the immortal being. We might've known you many times with different faces, different names. You live out your countless lives behind innumerable masks, leaving the discarded shells of lifetimes on the path of years behind you."

Vaile was full of such philosophy. The zanthyr looked upon the world with a deep introspection and remarked upon what she saw with a candor often as poignant as it was disturbing.

Usually Vaile joined Alyneri early with a meal to break their fast together, but on that morning the dawn light pooled into bright midday and the zanthyr still hadn't arrived. When hunger became too insistent, Alyneri returned to the *sa'reyth* to see what had become of her teacher.

She didn't find Vaile, so she went in search of Balaji. She'd noticed that one or the other of them could always be found in residence. Vaile was the *sa'reyth's* steward, Balaji its peacekeeper.

She found He Who Walks the Edge of the World in the *sa'reyth's* open-air kitchen. Rarely were the canvas walls of this massive tent lowered against the world. Balaji lorded over the kitchen as his kingly domain, and it ever stood open to receive, like its host.

When Alyneri arrived, the youth who was older than the sun stood at a long, wooden table slicing eggplants into thin strips. Alyneri leaned against a tent pole and watched him with a smile. She'd never seen a man with lovelier hands, or fingers more dexterous and skilled. Every motion Balaji made held a certain grace. But this could be said of all the *drachwyr*. Fifth strand creatures didn't move across the world—they flowed.

Something in Balaji always reminded her of Phaedor. To be certain, their manners were entirely opposite—Phaedor stood as remote as Balaji was engaging—yet the *drachwyr's* life-essence resonated with Alyneri in a similar way. She wondered what she might see if ever she were to share a Healer's rapport with Balaji. Would his soul glow as brightly as the zanthyr's had?

She hadn't been standing there but for a few heartbeats when Balaji glanced over his shoulder and cast her a smile. "Good day to you, Alyneri, daughter of Jair. I hope you've been enjoying this fine morning."

She managed a smile. "As best I can."

He motioned with his knife towards a stool. "Sit. I have just the thing to help you."

She obeyed, and he brought her a plate of dates and figs, along with a stew of spiced pheasant sweetened with currants and honey. After she thanked him with the acknowledgement that it was indeed just what she needed, she asked, "Do you know where Vaile is?"

"Our intrepid steward is in the next valley setting up a new compound." He looked up at her under his brows, which lifted to humorous points on each side of the noble's peak that defined his hairline. "We had unexpected arrivals this morning. Among others, an acquaintance of Fynnlar's—and yours, I believe. The pirate Carian vran Lea."

For a split-second, Alyneri wondered if the pirate might know something of Trell, but then she remembered that Jaya had told her Carian had been in T'khendar and couldn't possibly know any more of Trell's whereabouts than the rest of them. It was difficult keeping track of where her once-companions were and what they were all doing. She heard but whispers of Ean, and only her faith in Phaedor kept her from fearing for Tanis. Meanwhile, life at the *sa'reyth* felt disconnected from everything real, and everyone she cared about remained so scattered to the four winds …

"I didn't know the pirate well, but it will be nice to see him again." She took up a fig. "But why has he come here?"

"He and several Companions—as in the Fifty Companions—are upon a mission for the First Lord. At least, this is the argument they made for wanting to use his *sa'reyth* as their headquarters."

Alyneri drew back slightly. "And Vaile agreed to that?"

Balaji chuckled. "Not exactly. Hence the establishment of another compound nearby. It seemed a fair compromise to settle the tempest that raged this morning between Vaile and Mithaiya, though I don't doubt the solution gained in the compromise had been my sister's true intention all along." He waggled his knife at her. "Never let my sisters' seeming innocence fool you— they are both as crafty as they come."

Alyneri wouldn't have used the word 'innocent' to describe either of Balaji's sisters, though both had been exceptionally kind to her.

But hearing about Carian made her frown—or rather, the understanding that the pirate now served Björn van Gelderan just as Ean, Vaile, Phaedor, and all of the *drachwyr* apparently did. She felt excluded from elevated company for lack of an oath. It all remained incredibly confusing.

"Vaile has taken you under her wing, I see." Balaji sent her a smile as he chopped. "What adventures have been filling your shared days lately?"

"She's ..." Oddly, Alyneri found the truth somehow hard to confess. She desperately desired the skills Vaile was teaching her, yet learning such things still bumped up against some old sense of impropriety—unwanted feelings ingrained in her by the disapproving glares of northern nobility.

Well ... it was time to be finally free of their disdain, wasn't it?

Alyneri straightened her shoulders. "Vaile is teaching me."

"Ah, and a fine teacher she is. What is it you're learning?"

"Swordplay."

Balaji's knife stilled. "Is that so?" He started chopping again, and after a moment he looked up at her under his brows. "Has she taught you the *cortata*?"

Alyneri nodded.

"You've crossed blades together?"

She nodded again.

He stopped chopping, spread his hands and pressed them against the table. His eyes of pale wheat settled upon her while an odd stillness settled across the day. "Alyneri, daughter of Jair ... has she given you *her* swords to use in your practices together?"

Something in the way he looked at her, in the sudden silence of the world as he asked this question ... Alyneri's heart began fluttering. "Well ... yes. She has me practicing with them."

He arched a brow and returned to his chopping. "Is she teaching you other things?" That time he aimed a sidelong smile her way, but it didn't banish the threads of tension that rippled through the air now.

She pressed her hands between her knees. "Some."

"Patterning?"

Alyneri swallowed. "Yes."

Balaji scraped his knife across the table, sweeping the cut vegetables off into a bowl. He reached for a bunch of tomatoes as he inquired idly, "And is she teaching you the fifth?"

Vaile had every right to teach her, and Alyneri had every right to learn it, yet suddenly she felt as if they'd been upon some illicit craft.

Stop it! You're being so foolish! Balaji was only being kind in making conversation. Nothing in his manner held the least reprimand or disapproval.

Alyneri straightened her shoulders and tried to recall her composure from where it cowered at the far edge of the meadow. "She's taught me patterns from several strands, including the fifth, but we're still at the beginning of this instruction. Patterning is more complicated than I ever imagined."

"In the beginning it always feels that way." He smiled kindly at her. "In her teachings of the fifth, I hope Vaile is instructing you to use more discretion than she herself observes. Indiscriminately working the fifth strand is the surest suicide."

Alyneri smiled and dropped her gaze, remembering well those lessons. "She's admonished me *ardently*."

"*Khoob*, that is well for the sun."

Oddly, Alyneri felt as if the waters of their conversation had calmed and it was safe to climb back in. She took a few bites of her stew and chewed contemplatively while Balaji diced tomatoes with quick, deft strokes.

"Balaji?"

He looked up from his dicing with an inquiring smile, and Alyneri felt a flush come to her cheeks. How could a man be so amiable and yet so deeply stirring at the same time? And for all that, he barely looked older than herself! She felt ridiculous at how nervous he made her—far worse than Náiir, even though the latter stole her breath with his candid gaze and disarming smile.

"I was wondering …" She drew a swirl in her stew with her spoon while butterflies fluttered in her stomach. "You said once that you and the others weren't Players in the First Lord's game."

"Yes, just so."

She frowned. Then she looked up at him. "I guess I don't really understand what that means—or if I do, I don't understand why."

Balaji considered her for a moment. Then he wiped his hands on a cloth at his belt and came and took a stool across the worktable from her. As he settled, he placed a tomato on the scrubbed wooden top and reached for a bowl of unshelled filberts from further down.

While Alyneri watched bemusedly, he pulled the linen cloth from his belt and spread it across the table before him. "Imagine with me, Alyneri." He lifted both ends of the cloth and pulled it tight. Then he released it and left it suspended in midair. "This is the tapestry of life," he said, capturing her eyes with his own, "the field onto which the First Lord has directed his Players."

She watched him curiously.

"Place now our Players upon this field," and he nodded to the bowl of nuts.

She put a few nuts at various points on the cloth.

"Notice how each Player makes an indentation in the fabric."

"Yes, I see that."

"This is the effect of a Player in the game, as opposed to pieces or pawns, who make no dent in the tapestry of the game. Each Player is like a small well. Any pieces near him will fall into his well, and he can direct these pieces to carry out his intent."

He directed her gaze to the cloth overall. "Notice how the fabric has many wells, but none pull too strongly upon the others?"

"Yes."

"Balance works in this way. The right Players on the field at the right time create balance. Each Player in his actions pulls upon the fabric, but if he's working towards the same objective as his teammates, his actions won't disturb the other Players or upset the tapestry of the game. Now ... move two of our Players together."

She did so, placing a nut close beside one of the others.

"See the indentation now? The way the well of these two Players tugs more strongly at the others?"

She nodded.

"Like a game of Kings, Players need to remain on their own squares. The more Players you bring together, the deeper the indentation in the fabric, the more they begin to pull the game out of balance."

"That makes sense, but ..."

He smiled inquiringly.

Her brow made a little furrow as she tried to think it through. "But what happens if the tapestry itself becomes unbalanced?"

"Advantage slides to the other side."

"Oh ... I see."

He smiled. "Now place the tomato upon our field, our tapestry of life."

Giving him an odd look, she did so. The fruit sank into the floating cloth and pulled all of the nuts into its well.

Balaji held her gaze intently across the cloth. "This is us, should we step upon the field."

She drew back as if slapped and stared at him. "But ... why?"

Balaji settled elbows on the table and clasped his hands. "We're of the fifth, Alyneri. It birthed us, and it binds us to the realm with invisible threads of force. This connection gives us great power—some might say unbridled power, though that conclusion reveals a certain ignorance."

Alyneri motioned to the tomato in its well. "But it seems that by stepping on the field, you would make everything move in your direction. You would compel Balance to your will."

He gave her an acknowledging smile. "Yes *everything*—the good and the bad. We cannot step upon the field without creating that push and pull. Repercussions may not come immediately, but they will come. Balance doesn't always snap back in predictable ways. It can sometimes throw back at you the things or people who were far across the field. It can throw people onto your path who otherwise wouldn't have crossed it at all, simply because you stretched its limits just a fraction too far."

Alyneri exhaled a slow breath, understanding much more than she ever had before. But other things still made little sense to her. "The impact of stretching the Balance too far, I see, but I don't understand why Balance affects you more than it affects others."

He let the cloth float down and leaned forearms against the table as it settled. "We're immortal, Alyneri. The fifth strand races aren't meant to walk the tapestry of mortal life. That tapestry is too frail and our power too strong. We could as easily destroy the world as save it."

"But I thought you learned to measure your actions against how they affect the Balance? Mithaiya and Jaya speak of it constantly."

He sat back and gave her a considering look. "This cloth, our field," and he waggled a finger towards the linen on the table, "imagine it covered in cobwebs. My siblings and I … we skirt the fringes, taking care not to disturb the webs. Some paths we can follow for a time, wandering carefully between the gossamer strands casting only a slight tremor." He moved his finger around the filberts on the cloth to demonstrate this idea. "But were we to walk directly onto the field, the cobwebs would cling tightly to us. Our every step would stretch them, twist them, cause some to bind anew with others or to tangle and break."

Balaji picked up a nut and let it rest in his open palm. He gazed at it quietly. "Balance clings to us like cobwebs, Alyneri. We hover on the fringes of the First Lord's game taking action where and when we can." His eyes moved back to claim hers significantly. "But our every step must be inspected with the utmost care."

Alyneri exhaled a slow breath. "If you're not meant to walk the tapestry of life, why are you here?"

Balaji closed a fist around the nut and shifted his gaze off into the meadow. "You might say we *drachwyr* are the keepers of Balance—not as Cephrael, who wages judgment as Fate." His gaze shifted back to her, pointed and intense. "Balance clings to us like it clings to the Malorin'athgul, our immortal opponents in this game. It stretches between them and us like the cloth you just saw. We're anchors at two ends of the spectrum. Our existence keeps the fabric of Balance tight."

"But doesn't that mean …" Alyneri pressed fingertips to her lips. "Are you not just as powerful? Couldn't—"

"Yes, I know where your mind would lead you." His eyes tightened slightly. "These are difficult concepts to express. The idea of us as anchors conveys but a fraction of who we are, yet for purposes of your understanding, it must suffice."

He stood and moved the nuts back into their bowl, one by one, as if each carried within it a delicate but dangerous secret. "If Malorin'athgul and *drachwyr* met in combat, Alyneri, the world would be torn apart." He picked up his tomato and gathered his cloth. Pale golden eyes looked back to her. "Superior force will not decide this game. It is much too complicated for such mortal solutions."

Alyneri heard a chord of meanings in the word *mortal*: short-sighted, ignoble, moronic … .meaningless. A host of such words might've been substituted, for Balaji had said them all as he'd spoken the one.

Her mind was reeling from all he'd told her—*so* much of such significance, yet she had to wonder … *why*.

Why had he told her? It wasn't like these creatures to offer their knowledge freely. The realization made her feel suddenly cold.

She watched him replace the stool and return to his table, and her apprehension grew with every breath, such that at last she braved quietly, "Why have you told me this, Balaji?"

His gaze shifted back to her as he picked up his knife again. His smile told her much, but his eyes told her more, for they were not smiling. "Some paths are aided by this understanding, Alyneri, daughter of Jair."

Alyneri's breath caught in her throat. "… *My* path?"

Then his eyes did smile as they shifted to look past her. "Ah, but look who comes."

She turned over her shoulder to see Vaile approaching.

The zanthyr nodded to Alyneri as she came inside the tent.

"How goes everything with the pirate?" Balaji asked Vaile. He started dicing his tomato. "The Mage would be vexed if Carian accidentally fell upon your blade."

"I'm well aware of it, Balaji." Vaile chose a couple of figs from a bowl and lifted her gaze to meet Alyneri's, but when she saw the look on Alyneri's face, her smile faded and her brow arched considerably. She arrowed a look at Balaji. "What have you been telling her?"

The day darkened as if a cloud had passed before the sun, yet the sun still shone brightly beyond their tent.

Balaji arched a brow as he continued his chopping. "What have you been teaching her?" He lifted his gaze to her significantly.

Vaile's eyes narrowed like a cat's.

Just when Alyneri thought she could see clouds fomenting, the darkness evaporated as if it had never been. Vaile arched a defiant brow and ate her fig. Balaji smiled and returned his attention to his tomatoes.

Alyneri had expected some kind of battle, yet it appeared to be over before it had begun. She had no understanding of the accusation so evident in the exchange, nor how or why it had resolved. But as she departed with Vaile to resume her practice, Alyneri couldn't help wondering at Balaji's last comment and what price she would eventually pay for the knowledge he'd bestowed upon her.

TWENTY-FIVE

"Trust in Jai'Gar, but tie your camel."

– A popular caution among nomads

THE ADEPT WIELDER Viernan hal'Jaitar clasped hands behind his back and paced a lengthy square around the four lion statues demarking each corner of the hall. With every step, his thoughts grew darker, his gaze narrower, until all he saw was the shroud of his fury.

The chamber where he paced offered as much privacy as could be found in the Palace of Tal'Shira—safe at least from the Prophet's Ascendant spies. Hal'Jaitar trusted Bethamin about as much as he trusted a Valdére viper. Radov might've made his bed with that lunatic, but hal'Jaitar had no intention of sleeping under the sheets with the two of them.

He didn't believe in coincidence, but he did believe in Cephrael, Fate's Hand, uncle to Angharad and Thalma, the desert goddesses of Fortune and Luck. In Viernan's several centuries of life, he'd many times witnessed the *angiel* Cephrael throw His dice to the utter ruin of anyone who'd waged against Him.

His detractors to the contrary, Veirnan considered himself a prudent man; he wasn't apt to gamble on unwinnable scenarios or place a bet solely on the long neck of the underdog. And he most assuredly would not knowingly pit himself against Cephrael. Only a fool claimed no fear of his gods, and Viernan hal'Jaitar was no fool.

Yet ... it seemed he had somehow angered one of them—Thalma, Angharad ... Cephrael. How else to explain the turn of the game?

'If it was Cephrael delivered me to your doorstep ... you can be certain He had his reasons ... '

Trell val Lorian's comment still had hal'Jaitar reeling, and even more so after recent events. He misliked admitting it to himself—and would never deign to admit it aloud to others—but he feared it was no coincidence that no sooner had the lost prince appeared than had vanished an entire company of elite Talien Knights, along with Viernan's wielder Kedar, the Prophet's creature in Kjieran van Stone, as well as the King of Dannym and all of his knights.

No trace of the company, which had set out from Tal'Shira bound for the location of their parley, had been found or heard from again. Their considerable tracks ended suddenly in the middle of the desert where the sands had been scoured clean.

And of his scheme so carefully designed, his trap so artfully constructed ... had any of it come off as planned?

Radov's company had broken away as expected and the Ruling Prince returned in secret to Tal'Shira, but what of the deaths hal'Jaitar had organized to follow? Of the parley site, only charred cloth remained—tents, stores, even a week's supply of drink ... all burned to tarry sludge.

For the fate of the parley tents, he might've blamed his counterpart in the Akkad, Rajiid al'Basreh, or the Emir, Zafir al Abdul-Basir; but Viernan didn't believe al'Basreh had the resources or the wherewithal to eliminate Kedar, the King of Dannym and his men, and an entire company of Talien Knights potentially within the same span of hours.

Unless the Emir's Mage had worked his unwelcome hand ...

"There are no coincidences," Viernan groused under his breath, "only players acting beyond one's purview of the board."

A zanthyr had told him that once. The only piece of advice any of the creatures had ever offered that proved worth the effort of gaining it. Hal'Jaitar loathed zanthyrs nearly as much as he loathed Marquiin, truthreaders and gypsies, though not necessarily in that order.

"Hmm? What?" Sitting on one of the low couches across the room, Prince Radov roused from his stupor. "Did you say something, Viernan?"

"Yes, Your Grace."

"Oh." The prince frowned at the empty glass in his hand, whereupon he seemed to determine that it was, in fact, empty. He stuck his nose inside and took a long sniff as if to discern what spirit the glass had once contained—as if he'd drunk anything but that vile absinthe since he'd made his pact with the Prophet many long moons ago. "Well ..." Radov turned the glass upside down and watched a drop make laborious progress towards the rim. "What was it?"

"What was what, Your Grace?"

Radov shot him an irritable glare. "Whatever you said, Viernan."

"I was merely remarking upon a philosophical observation of fact, Your Grace."

Radov harrumphed. "Philosophy. A colossal waste."

"Yes, Your Grace."

Abruptly the prince launched unsteadily off the couch. "A ruler needs to know tactics! Swordplay! *Some* politics—it's true, you must admit the knowledge a necessary evil, Viernan. A prince has only enemies." He narrowed his gaze and surreptitiously peered around the empty hall. "Enemies who claim to be friends—those are the ones to watch with a hawk's keen eye, Viernan, mark my words."

Radov looked down at his feet and observed meticulously, "And a prince has enemies whom he pins beneath his toe by might and power; enemies he subdues through bribery and villain—ry," he wavered slightly on his feet, "and coercion. And enemies on the battlefield!" He shoved his hand to the sky as if it wielded a sword instead of an empty glass, "which a clear head and strong—" he paused, pushed a fist beneath his ribcage, belched and grimaced at the taste it brought to his tongue, "—sword … will righteously … overcome …"

Radov slumped back onto the couch again.

Viernan eyed the intoxicated prince with barely veiled contempt. "Poignantly put, Your Grace."

He'd considered monitoring the prince's consumption of the absinthe, but a sober Radov held no greater appeal to him. At least keeping the prince in his cups dampened his volatility.

"They're all against me, Viernan. You know I speak the truth."

Viernan cast him an intolerant eye. He wondered at what point his role had degraded from a prince's wielder to a drunkard's nanny; from Spymaster to chaperone, nursemaid and shepherd. "Who is, Your Grace?"

Radov waved his glass airily and whispered faintly, "… All of them."

Viernan returned to his pacing.

He found many distressing problems in the missing company. Had Kjieran succeeded in killing the King of Dannym? Had Kedar succeeded in killing them both? Had all somehow inadvertently fallen to the Saldarians dressed as marauders, who hal'Jaitar had sent in as a third contingency to divert and disrupt the lines to give Radov's company time to break away?

What had been the outcome of that battle?

Or … had the regiment been ambushed by Abdul-Basir's raiders? Or by his Sundragons? Or his Mage?

And why had hal'Jaitar's scouts found no trace of any of them?

The loss of Radov's knights could be overcome, but Kedar's loss truly stung. Competent wielders didn't grow as fruit, ripening from bud to delicate flesh in one or two seasons. Wielders had to be forged, tempered, honed and tested, a process that often required decades of dedication. Those of questionable moral fiber who were also talented in their craft were rarer to come by than a sentient Merdanti blade. Corrupting new ones took years!—years he didn't have with a war still on his doorstep and an inebriate prince valuable only for the recourse of his royal name.

And if the King of Dannym had somehow survived …

Hal'Jaitar clenched his hands more tightly behind him. Instinct whispered that Gydryn val Lorian had somehow gotten the better of him.

Belloth take those damnable val Lorians.

Hal'Jaitar's eye twitched. Trell was proving surprisingly resilient to torture—either that, or he really had been suffering from amnesia all this time, like he claimed. Viernan recalled the eldest prince, Sebastian, being equally obstinate under the knife. Now it appeared the youngest, Prince Ean, was becoming a beleaguering problem for Dore Madden.

One had to admire the val Lorians at least for their tenacity, though their other common traits rankled. Viernan couldn't abide honest men. What was *honor* in the end? A word.

Viernan would've liked to kill Trell—he would've liked to have done the deed personally—but Trell's comment about Cephrael ... hal'Jaitar had perceived no glibness in its utterance. This bothered him immensely.

If the Prince *had* somehow gained the *angiel's* favor, as he'd intimated, then killing him could have *personal* consequences. Balance clung like a death shroud to those who walked in the light of Cephrael's stars. Viernan was accordingly loath to cause some disturbance that might draw the *angiel's* attention to himself.

But Trell val Lorian posed a dilemma.

Viernan still hadn't discovered where Trell had been for the past five years, and this he *had* to know. His Shamshir'im network traded in secrets. It galled Viernan to think some other network had protected the secret of Trell's survival all this time. But more to the point, who else knew that Trell val Lorian lived, and what had they done, or could they do, with this information? The wrong others knowing of Trell's survival could spell disaster for his prince and their kingdom. Moreover, Viernan couldn't be certain that Trell wasn't a spy.

It all came down to the truth of his past. Viernan *had* to know what Trell had been doing since escaping death in the Fire Sea.

Since Trell proved less than forthcoming with answers, Viernan had questioned the Saldarian, Raliax; interrogated him within an inch of his skin—perhaps it was truer to say *inside* an inch of his skin—to determine what had really happened upon the *Dawn Chaser* five years prior, when Viernan had first tasked the Saldarian with Trell's death.

Hal'Jaitar admitted a truthreader would have proven helpful during that questioning, for Raliax's agonized shrieks and screams had somewhat limited the coherence of his answers. Nonetheless, hal'Jaitar had put some pieces of this puzzle together, and he misliked the picture that was forming.

Raliax claimed the prince had known nothing when he'd questioned him aboard the *Dawn Chaser*. Yet something in his description of those proceedings ... hal'Jaitar was certain the young prince had been truthbound, which might account for his later amnesia. It also meant he daren't truthread Trell now to learn what he'd been doing for the past five years, for it could drive the answers he sought into further occlusion.

But a truthbinding powerful enough to make a man forget his entire existence indicated a Sormitáge trained Adept. Worse, it implied that King

Gydryn had already held Prince Radov in suspicion ever before he sent his middle son from Calgaryn.

Could the Northmen have suspected M'Nador's duplicity all those years ago? And if so, what had Morin d'Hain and his spies learned in the intervening years?

Most unsettling was the idea that Gydryn val Lorian *knew* of Radov's duplicity and *had come to this parley in spite of it.* This would imply the King of Dannym possessed far more guile than hal'Jaitar had given him credit for. It would mean rethinking all of their conversations, every interaction …

He saw but a single solution to finding out what Trell knew … one he'd been hoping to avoid. Hal'Jaitar shifted his shoulders irritably, but it wasn't the silk that suddenly chafed.

When Jai'Gar had seen fit only to bless Viernan with a useless daughter, he'd cursed Huhktu, the God of Bones; but an education with the Sorceresses of Vest had made his previously willful offspring pliant, malleable and endlessly resourceful in fulfilling his wishes.

People were no different from any other animal. With enough force, enough pain laid in, even the most wayward of wills might become tractable.

Still, he trusted his daughter as much as he trusted a Sundragon, which was to say not at all. How could he trust a woman educated by whores in the vilest aspects of an Adept's craft?

Oh, Taliah was imminently *useful,* but she'd been eternally tainted, deflowered and corrupted into a wanton harlot, the integrity of her nature fractured into shards that could never be reassembled. Some workings of an Adept's craft lay beneath even Viernan hal'Jaitar's dubious morals. Taliah worked all of them.

Abruptly hal'Jaitar spun and walked to a line of heavy, dangling cords. Pulling one, he waited for the hall's sculpted doors to open. When they did, a black-robed Shamshir'im stood in the portal.

"Fetch Taliah to meet me in the prince's cell."

The man bowed wordlessly and departed.

"Hmm … what?" Radov roused with a start. "What did you say, Viernan?"

"Nothing, Your Grace. I will see you in the morning." He motioned to the guard standing in the doorway, and the man moved to escort Radov back to his chambers and his waiting absinthe.

A hard slap to his face shocked Trell back to awareness. He blinked to orient himself to his surroundings, and only then did he realize that the room had changed since he'd slipped into a pain-induced unconsciousness. Trying to focus in the dim, wavering light, he saw two indistinct shapes hovering over him.

His life had become a sequence of disjointed, agonizing interludes with huge gaps of darkness in between. Without anchors such as meals, or seeing the sun rise and set, he'd lost all semblance of the passage of time. He might've been in hal'Jaitar's dungeon for a fortnight or a year—he had no way of knowing. Nor could he tell how long they let him recover between bouts of torment. His brain, often deprived of oxygen and always of proper nourishment, had shut down such non-essential functions as coherent thought.

He heard voices speaking above him.

"… bade me use only barbaric means of questioning him, father," a female voice was saying, "what did you expect—"

"I expect *results*, Taliah!" a male voice snapped. Trell recognized hal'Jaitar's acerbic tone as much as the accent of his vowels. "I expect my interrogators to get my questions *answered* regardless of how sophisticated or crude their tools."

"Yes, father." Taliah bowed her head and pressed her lips together in a thin line.

"Ah …" Trell felt the knives of hal'Jaitar's gaze settle on him. "The prince returns to us."

Trell could barely make out hal'Jaitar's dark eyes among the shadows of his black *keffiyeh*.

"I offer you one last chance, Prince of Dannym," he murmured. "Tell me all, and I will let your end be swift."

"… *amnesia* …" Trell managed a raw whisper. It was the only answer he ever gave, no matter their questions, no matter what they did to make him scream.

A man develops ways of enduring pain, of becoming inured to it … or perhaps, if not inured, at least accepting of the way of things. Trell had learned to let the pain consume him without protest, without fighting it; perhaps … he'd like to believe he'd found a way of surrendering to the pain without surrendering to the one administering it, but it was hard to say what really happened in those moments of intensity when even thought fled from his screams.

He'd spent many hours thinking through these ideas in the early days of his captivity, of his torture, when he'd clung to honor and his own promise of eventual retribution. Now he simply clung to life and the single word: *amnesia*. It explained everything, and nothing, and he could still utter it no matter how swollen his lips or tongue …

"It's all he ever claims," Taliah remarked churlishly. "I've used the instruments of your instruction and Healed him each time to suffer anew, but he never offers anything beyond this word."

"You haven't made him scream emphatically enough!" Hal'Jaitar's voice cut like a whip. "You must put him into *your* control, Taliah. You should have broken him by now."

"Because an intelligent man screams doesn't mean you've broken him, father." Taliah's tone remained respectful. Her voice sounded a soft and delicate melody against hal'Jaitar's percussive outbursts. "Perhaps for an ignorant man it would be so, one with little to hold onto but brute defiance. A scream then means you've pulled from him the only crutch he clings to." She placed a hand on Trell's brow, still damp with the sweat of their last encounter. "But this one is far too sophisticated." Her hand stroked the hair from Trell's eyes, petting it gently back, yet no kindness lay in the act. Her motions, like her voice, remained oddly detached. "A scream from him means only that in that moment his pain was intense. An intelligent man requires more sophisticated torture."

Hal'Jaitar looked Trell over, and his lips formed a tight line. "Very well ... do what you will with him."

Taliah made a little gasp.

"I must have *answers*, Taliah."

"Yes, father—oh, yes!" She turned and waved to someone—Trell couldn't see who and cared not enough to move his head to do so.

"He must be relocated elsewhere from this place," hal'Jaitar groused. "I won't have you sullying my dungeons with stains upon the currents that shout your illicit workings to the world."

"Yes, father." Taliah waved to her men. "Come, come—take him."

Hands closed around his body, pain seared through Trell, and he gratefully surrendered to darkness.

When he next woke, light burned his eyes. He blinked in the brightness, eyes watering.

He felt surprisingly whole and pushed up to sitting to better look around. They'd moved him to a rectangular, windowless chamber of white stone, well lit by a massive iron chandelier hanging from the arched ceiling. Besides the cot on which he lay, the chamber held no furnishings, only a raised marble platform with chains set into either end.

That looks rather unpromising.

He pushed his legs over the side of the cot and looked down at his body. Pale circles lined the flesh on the inside of his arms. He vaguely recalled being nailed to the stone wall—an early torment—and suffered a latent shudder at recollecting the moment. But other than these scars, he found the flesh of his bare chest and arms surprisingly unmarred, especially considering what he'd endured.

Someone had washed him during his most recent unconsciousness, and now a pair of shalwar covered his legs, held up by a drawstring sitting low around his hips. He tried to remember how he'd come to that room, and why, but his mind recalled only cold and darkness and fiery pain. Days or weeks—he still didn't know—blended into one long incident without a clear beginning or end.

Trell pushed a hand through his hair and eyed the platform and its manacles. Clearly hal'Jaitar wasn't done with him yet. He had to wonder if the man ever would be.

Trell slumped back against the cold stone wall and let his hands fall to his sides. It was so odd, this existence, filled with equal portions of hopelessness and grief, defiance and resignation.

He supposed his years on the front lines had in some ways prepared him for captivity. Soldiers lived every day with the knowledge that each moment could be their last, and commanders rarely went into battle without understanding what fate awaited them should they be captured by the enemy, much less the acceptance of their own potential death in the battle.

At certain times in his short though successful military career, Trell had imagined a life of imprisonment. A man didn't live long on the front lines without coming to grips with such possibilities. You made a sort of pact with Death when you went to war, choosing him as your ultimate opponent on the field.

A grating sound from the far side of the room drew Trell's gaze, and he turned his head to see a portion of the stone wall swinging inward. Through the parting came Taliah hal'Jaitar.

Trell remembered *her*—even if the things she'd done to him remained blessedly blurred. He equated her with pain now on an existential level. His pulse automatically quickened, his muscles tensed, readying to fight.

Yet fighting was both impractical and all but impossible. Taliah had already proven that she could use his life pattern to incapacitate him, and the two hulking brutes that entered behind her seemed more than capable of doing the same with elbows and fists.

Taliah stopped in front of him. "Hello, Prince Trell."

Trell looked up and met her gaze. He'd never felt such aversion to a woman before; but then, he'd never had a woman repeatedly torture him, either.

Taliah was as diminutive as they came, fine boned and flat chested—a fact easily noted since she wore a dress cut nearly to her navel. She seemed the frailest of creatures; that is, until one looked into her eyes and saw that actually the girl Taliah had died long ago. Something dead inhabited her body now, animating her corpse with empty life like some horrific marionette.

Trell was determined to tell her nothing, to give her nothing of his own free will. It had become his personal crusade. He suspected they were used to such behavior from prisoners—seasoned inquisitors ate defiance on toast. But he had nothing else to cling to but what free will he possessed, little more than he might collect in dirt from between the stones of his cell.

"I see that my Healing took well," Taliah remarked as those dead eyes looked Trell over. "We should begin anew. My father is impatient for your information. Stand up."

"I'm fine where I am."

Her gaze hardened. "You can stand on your own, or I can make you stand."

"Then make me."

Taliah pursed her lips and looked to the hulks. They grabbed Trell by the arms and hauled him to his feet. He hung there between their arms.

"This would go much easier for you if you merely cooperated," she complained with a hint of petulance.

"I somehow doubt that, Taliah."

Setting her lips in a line, Taliah motioned to the hulks, and they dragged Trell to the platform. He struggled, but vainly. The two men had the strength of ten, and without much difficulty they'd stretched him on his back, flat against the cold marble. One pulled his arms overhead to fasten the manacles around his wrists, while the other spread his legs and clamped irons around his ankles.

"Perhaps I should explain how things have changed," Taliah noted as the hulks were shackling him.

Trell just stared at the iron chandelier and gritted his teeth, preparing himself. Things seemed just about the same to him.

"I lost my virginity to a man like Ghan," Taliah said, shifting her gaze to the hulk who was tightening the chains, stretching Trell's arms painfully over his head. "He tied me, much as you're tied now, and raped me until I was torn deep inside and my blood soaked the sheets. Then he turned me over and repeated the process with my backside." She gave a little smile, confused and embittered. "I was nine."

Trell stared at her. "Blessed Epiphany ... why?"

She shrugged, a mere twitch of slim shoulders. "This is how the Sorceresses of Vest initiate new members to their Order. It's impossible to see both paths of Alir until one has found a place of neutrality."

The hulks finished their work, and Taliah walked around the platform testing the tautness in the chains. Though Trell hadn't asked, she told him, "The Vestian Sorceresy believes every Adept has two potential paths; we call these the Paths of Alir, the heart-light. An Adept is called to whichever of the paths sings most loudly in the depths of his or her heart." She placed a hand on his ankle, and then yanked the chain tighter.

Trell sucked in his breath with a hiss.

"The light path is called *hal'alir*, and the dark path is *mor'alir*." Taliah tightened the other ankle with a similar painful outcome. "Either path is a valid pursuit, but once chosen, only one can be walked. To choose *mor'alir* is to abandon *hal'alir*. A *mor'alir* Adept, such as myself, might still Heal, but only when Healing crosses the *mor'alir* path. You see," she added with a regretful little smile, chilling beneath her empty eyes, "once a Healer has taken the blood of men unto herself, her soul will forever bear its stain."

She pulled on the chains holding his arms over his head, and seeming to find them tight enough, nodded to the hulks. They left and pulled the wall shut behind them.

"Most initiates chose which path they will follow."

"And you chose *mor'alir*," Trell growled, teeth gritted against the pain of joints already strained.

"Oh, no," she said from behind him, "my father chose for me. I was only nine. How could I know which path sang in my heart?" She stopped beside his head and trailed her nails lightly down the underside of his arm, tracing a line from scar to scar. "You're a beautiful man. I hated harming you. This way will be much better."

Trell couldn't imagine how. His hands were already going numb, and she hadn't even started on him yet. Dread tasted sharp on his tongue.

His shoulders were cramping where they pulled so tightly against his head, bringing an ache to his jaw, but he managed to ask, "Why not … employ a truthreader?"

It seemed too obvious a solution for stealing a man's secrets, perhaps too civilized for Viernan hal'Jaitar—yet the man was Sormitáge trained and knew the Adept craft. Trell had many times wondered, while in the throes of some new agony, why if hal'Jaitar had wanted the truth so desperately did he not use an Adept uniquely designed by nature to ferret it out.

"My father distrusts Adepts of the fourth," Taliah answered idly. She trailed her nails now down Trell's chest, tracing the muscular depression from breastbone to navel. "He knows too well how truthreaders are taught duplicity, how they circumvent their inability to lie with half-truths and practiced double-speak." Her fingers tugged at the drawstring of his shalwar, loosening the cloth around his hips. "But my father believes you were truthbound before Raliax found you at sea. He wouldn't risk another Reading on you, even did he trust the Adept performing it. No," she concluded, "my methods will be more effective."

With that, she climbed up on the marble platform and swung her leg across his hips, coming to rest atop him. For all Taliah revolted him, still his loins stirred traitorously beneath her warmth.

"My father thinks me a whore." She pushed back her long, dark hair and swept a stray piece from her eyes. "He rarely lets me use my own methods on his prisoners. He doesn't really trust me. But you've driven him to a desperate position. For that, I thank you."

Seeing those dead eyes staring down at him, her petite body pinned to his hips, Trell had the sudden unwelcome realization that the torture she'd inflicted upon him so far had barely skimmed the surface of possibility.

Taliah leaned forward and rested her hands to either side of Trell's raised arms. Up close, her large, dark eyes held flecks of green. He searched her gaze for some shadow of humanity but found only desolation's shadow.

"I walk the path of *mor'alir*," Taliah whispered. She leaned in and gave him a soft kiss. "You will soon walk it with me. In this we will be bound, Trell, Prince of Dannym, to walk together to *mor'alir's* end."

"You'll have to drag me, Taliah. I'll walk nowhere willingly with you."

She ran her hand along his face, pinned between muscular arms, and smiled sadly. "You still think you can resist my working, but this is because you have only what we've done so far to compare it against. A body's pain might be fought with the mind, but where can you retreat when the mind itself burns?" The smile returned to her lips, though it didn't touch those hollow eyes. "Let me show you what I mean."

She rose above him on her hands and knees, then leaned to plant a kiss upon his brow. At the touch of her lips, his head exploded.

Such pain as he'd never experienced flamed through his entire body, *so* much pain that he couldn't breathe, couldn't think, couldn't do anything but arch in a shuddering scream, silent for lack of breath to fuel it.

The blinding agony lasted an eternity in a minute's passing. When she released him from her punishing kiss, he fell back against the marble in utter, desperate relief. Every muscle cramped as he sucked in a shuddering breath.

She planted little kisses on his mouth and stroked his hair. "My father would know where you've been since the *Dawn Chaser* sank beneath the waves. Do you wish to confess?"

Trell tried to focus through the tears leaking from his eyes. "… amnesia …" he managed, giving her a gritty smile.

She smiled in return, slow, with a cat's self-satisfied mien. "I'm so glad you said that." Taliah sat back and pressed her sex against his loins. Her hips made slow circles, her thighs clutching and releasing. "The sorceresses prefer to interrogate their male prisoners with their penises sheathed inside them. It seals the connection in a manner that simple contact cannot possibly compare to. My father doesn't want me using this method on you, for he fears that you might make me with child. He doesn't really understand what I do."

Trell barely did either, but what he was starting to understand made him cold inside.

"It's my hope that we might walk the path of *mor'alir* together for *many* days." She pushed her hands against his chest and closed her eyes as she ground into him. "Sadly, none can resist the path for long."

Still wracked with pain from her last kiss, Trell knew only disgust and revulsion for the fey thing writhing lasciviously atop him.

She opened her eyes and smiled. Then she leaned in with another kiss. While Trell screamed—aloud that time, his raw pain rebounding in the stone chamber—Taliah moved her lips to whisper at his temple, "You see … the path of *mor'alir* breaks all men."

As Trell would soon discover, she was right.

TWENTY-SIX

"He knows the rules like the back of his hand … and pays them like attention."
 – The Second Vestal Dagmar Ranneskjöld,
 on Björn van Gelderan

AN IMPERIAL SHIP offered landlubbers little in the way of idle enjoyment, so during the long hours of sailing, when Tanis wasn't reading his father's journals, the zanthyr put him to work with combat sparring and sword practice, running him relentlessly through his maneuvers or his forms for hours at a time.

Sparring on the foredeck with the ship keeled hard to port, Tanis strained just to maintain his balance, much less fend off the zanthyr's tireless attacks, and when Phaedor called for the *cortata* or the *ta'fieri*, Tanis's growing skill was well and truly tested.

All those days, the High Lord watched from afar with his hazel eyes pinned unerringly on Tanis. The lad could tell Marius harbored an intense curiosity about his and Phaedor's relationship … about him.

Of course, Phaedor never asked why the High Lord had actually sailed five days to claim him from a remote stretch of the Caladrian Coast, and Tanis knew better than to broach the subject with either of them.

The High Lord did not intrude on their company until the wind died on the third day. Noon approached, and the sun strode high and warm. They'd been sailing steadily southwest with the wind for all of that time. Tanis suspected they'd have crossed all of Dannym and most of Veneisea by now had they been following that coastline, yet the vast reaches of the Empire of Agasan still spread endlessly before them. He noticed the change in the weather with each passing day; the wind no longer held winter's frost but spring's warming breath, and the sun felt heavier and hotter upon his back.

Tanis had stripped off his cloak one day and his vest the next. That morning he wore only a chestnut tunic of fine-spun linen with cuffs embroidered in gold, and dark blue britches rolled up to his knees. He was standing barefoot running through the *cortata* sans sword—which Phaedor often had him do to keep him centered on the motions themselves instead of on his blade—when he noticed the wind die and the sails fall slack, and the ship leveled out.

The crew immediately started searching the sea with their eyes, squinting beneath upraised hands, but even Tanis could tell the wind had abandoned them. The deep blue waters lapped languidly at the bow as the ship slowed on her course, and all around the ocean became as glass. Far astern, Tanis could see the wind-line rippling the water.

The captain eventually came forward to where Tanis had been working through the *cortata*. The captain was a big man, and he filled his naval uniform well. Tanis had noticed that when not wearing his officer's coat, the captain's arms writhed with ropy muscles as like the lines he'd likely spent a lifetime hauling.

That day, the zanthyr was sitting against the bulwark with one arm draped across his knee, watching Tanis quietly with his green eyes keen to the slightest misstep, while the High Lord stood several paces further forward, frowning at the sea.

"Your Grace," said the captain, calling Marius's attention.

The High Lord turned.

"What would you have us do? Wait for the wind, or …"

Marius considered him. "No," he said after a moment. His gaze strayed to Phaedor and lingered before returning to the captain. "I will see what can be done."

"Thank you, Your Grace." The captain bowed and retreated.

Marius looked to the zanthyr. Tanis could tell that the High Lord wasn't sure how to treat with Phaedor, though clearly their acquaintanceship had endured the mutual centuries. The lad had no recourse to the High Lord's thoughts, however, for the man's mind was as closed to him as the zanthyr's own—although Tanis had the sense that the barrier protecting the zanthyr's thoughts was far thicker than the barrier protecting Marius di L'Arlesé's. Yet there was not really any point in theorizing on how deep the barrier was; if you're staring at a granite wall, past a certain depth, it is simply impenetrable.

Perhaps at last realizing that the zanthyr might go on not noticing him indefinitely, Marius pressed the fingers of one hand to the railing and turned to the zanthyr. "I would call the wind for the captain … unless you would do it?"

Phaedor tossed the hair from his brilliant green eyes and settled them on the High Lord. "Speak plainly your desires, Marius di L'Arlesé."

Marius's brow pinched slightly, the only indication of the confusion he seemed always to experience in dealing with the zanthyr. "Would you call the wind for our ship, Phaedor?" He held a hand to the sea and shrugged resignedly. "I could do it … but not as effectively as you."

"Flattery hardly suits Your Grace."

Marius shook his head. "I've never been one to overlook the chance to improve my craft by observation of its mastery in another."

Phaedor moved to his feet in one swift and graceful motion that brought him up close to the High Lord, nearly nose to nose in fact. "Indeed, I have observed this about you, Marius di L'Arlesé." He gave him the slightest of nods and an even slighter smile, yet it was acknowledgement enough to make the High Lord arch his brows.

Then Phaedor moved to the bow, and only heartbeats later the breeze began to stir in the sails.

Tanis couldn't see any patterns of the fifth flashing, for the zanthyr worked the fifth innately and used no patterns to compel it, but the lad had no doubt that the High Lord understood the working from watching its story on the currents.

As the ship began to keel to starboard, Marius walked to the high side and leaned against the polished wood railing. Tanis went to stand beside him. It bothered him to see this man, who was so wonderfully courteous and genteel, standing humbled or confused in Phaedor's shadow. Not that anyone could outshine the zanthyr, but it was a bit easier to bear if one understood Phaedor's motives.

"He taunts you, Your Grace," the lad offered after a moment of standing in silence at the High Lord's side.

Marius arched a brow by way of resigned agreement. "I don't know what he hopes to have from me."

"I don't suppose to know it either," Tanis admitted, laughing at the very idea of such presumption.

The High Lord turned and leaned sideways against the railing to better look upon Tanis. "You've traveled with him for how long?"

"Since the harvest months, off and on. He joined our company south of Chalons-en-Les-Trois, but I met him first when he brought Prince Ean to Fersthaven—that's Her Grace's home—for Healing."

"I see." Marius spent a moment considering Tanis then, and the boy returned his gaze with dutiful attention. The High Lord's amiable and gracious manner helped Tanis feel comfortable in his presence despite this intense inspection. After a while, Marius said, "I admit there is something in your features that is familiar to me, but try as I might, I cannot place it. How many years have you?"

"Ten and five, Your Grace." His sixteenth name day seemed ages away yet, and at this point he somewhat feared reaching it. Some of the implications the zanthyr had been hinting at were decidedly ominous.

"You're tall for your age."

Tanis looked down at himself. Was he? It had been so long since he'd really looked at himself, and when he did manage to end up in front of a mirror … sometimes he hardly recognized his own features.

"And you were raised where?"

"In Dannym, Your Grace, as a ward of the Healer Melisande d'Giverny. I assisted her daughter—at least until I began training as a truthreader."

"You speak excellently of our language for one so young."

"Thank you, Your Grace. My mother taught me Agasi in my youth."

Marius cast him a look of bewilderment at this. "And you were trained in your craft by whom?"

"King Gydryn's truthreader, Vitriam o'Reith, started my training. I also learned from the Fourth Vestal while he was staying with us in Rethynnea—"

"The Fourth Vestal was *staying* with you?"

"Yes, Your Grace, during Prince Ean's convalescence, but I learned the most from …"

The High Lord's attention was fixed raptly on him. "Go on."

Tanis gave him an uneasy look and rubbed at one eye. "Well … I suppose it's truest to say that most of my training I received from my mother."

"Your mother was a truthreader?" Marius latched onto this bit of information with alacrity.

"Yes, Your Grace."

"Your mother who taught you Agasi, whom your father called Renaii."

"Yes, Your Grace."

Marius frowned at these perplexing facts. His gaze drifted towards the zanthyr. "And how does the elusive Phaedor fit into this puzzle?"

Inextricably, Tanis thought. He was grateful that the High Lord's question had not been directed at him, thus he was not compelled to answer it.

Marius looked back to him. "Do you seek to solve the mystery of your parentage, Tanis?"

"No, Your Grace."

The High Lord drew back in surprise. "You don't?"

"I *do*," Tanis amended in a suddenly small voice, "but I don't think it would be wise to pursue it—for me to pursue it."

The High Lord displayed a formidable frown upon this revelation. After a moment, he remarked, "You are an unusual boy."

As a means of escaping the High Lord's further speculation, the lad asked, "Your Grace, what is the meaning of the rings you wear?"

Marius flipped his hands back and forth to look upon both sides and the thin gold bands that adorned each finger. Now that Tanis could see them closely, he realized he'd seen such rings before.

"These are Sormitáge rings." Marius arched brows and made a self-deprecating grunt. "Doubtless this means little more to you. Such rings are relics from the Fourth Age, a greater Age. I wonder if they have meaning anymore."

"Do not let him fool you, Tanis," came the zanthyr's deep voice, and the lad looked up to see Phaedor joining them. The wind still blew steady and sure. Indeed, they might've been moving faster now than the entire trip thus far.

"To wear a ring on each of ten fingers means the High Lord has gained the revered status of a rowed wielder, a master of the Laws and Esoterics of every strand. He is one of the few living wielders who can work the fifth—and work it well."

"What others do *you* know?" Marius affected a casual tone, but Tanis saw the tightness around his eyes and sensed a deep disquiet underlying this question.

The zanthyr undoubtedly sensed it too, but he merely held the High Lord's gaze with his eyes glinting in shadowy amusement.

Marius gave him a tense look. "You are a singularly infuriating creature."

Tanis cast Phaedor an annoyed glare and then asked, "Why do you feel such rings have little meaning now, Your Grace?"

"Ah, well ..." Marius sighed and leaned back against the railing. "The Sormitáge is rife with young Adepts hoping to gain their rings and the opportunities such opens to them. Yet I often wonder if they've truly gained the status at all, for no Mages remain to oversee the trials, only Sormitáge maestros heretofore unschooled in the rigors of such examinations." He looked to the zanthyr, and a shadow fell across his gaze. "Another tragedy of Malachai's war."

"How is that?" Tanis asked.

The zanthyr flipped the hair from his eyes. "The Hundred Mages conducted the trials for the wielder's rings, Tanis. They traveled readily between the Sormitáge and the Citadel but claimed allegiance only to higher law, to that of the *Sobra I'ternin*. They were governed by an elected council of their peers, the foremost of these being the High Mage of the Citadel, Isabel van Gelderan."

"And they were slaughtered on Tiern'aval," Marius added tightly. "By Björn himself, if the Vestals are to be believed."

"With the Mages went the knowledge to gain the rings," Tanis surmised, feeling a sudden permeating sense of loss that he couldn't quite explain.

"Far more than this, lad," the zanthyr said. He pulled out his dagger and began flipping the blade, catching it by the point.

Marius eyed him disagreeably. "The Hollow Years following the Adept Wars—as those decades have come to be called—witnessed a huge gap in the generations. Young Adepts too innocent to have gone to war abutted the eldest Sormitáge maestros, who had maintained and protected the Sormitáge during Malachai's siege. As years drew on and fewer Adepts Returned, we survivors saw our race dying. Many of the eldest grew bereft of hope. They ceased to work the Pattern of Life and retired into their autumn days, taking their knowledge with them. Only a handful remain who knew life before the wars."

"Like yourself, sir?"

"Yes," the High Lord groused, "I linger. But I was never a maestro. I have neither the talent nor the training to teach."

"All might instruct if the desire survives within them," the zanthyr observed. He cast Marius a pointed look from among his wind-tossed curls.

Tanis let out a slow breath. "I didn't realize so much was lost—I mean ... I knew the grave loss of life, but ... *knowledge*, too ..."

"Yes, young Tanis." Marius's expression was grave. "We ken but a thimbleful of what once was a sea. In his madness, Malachai swore to wipe us from the earth. His war began it. Björn ensured its eventuality on Tiern'aval."

Tanis heard this statement and felt confusion over it. Since speaking with Loghain, certain information had found its place within his understanding and thereafter would not be dislodged again. Tanis no longer believed the Fifth Vestal was culpable for all of the things people blamed him for—the statements held no resonance of truth. Still, he'd never dare say such a thing outright to the High Lord of Agasan.

Instead, the lad asked, "What really happened at the Citadel, Your Grace? There's a thousand stories, but ... I wonder if even one is true."

Marius glanced to the zanthyr as if to give him opportunity to illuminate the vacuum of unknowns. The zanthyr yawned.

The High Lord returned his gaze to Tanis. "No one knows, lad. The only survivors of Tiern'aval are those Adepts known as the Fifty Companions, and they've been truthbound against speaking of what they know—even of who truthbound them." His gaze flicked once more to Phaedor as if to catch the zanthyr disproving this statement somehow by a roll of the eyes or perhaps a twitching brow. When Phaedor merely stared neutrally at him, Marius added with a disappointed frown, "Everything we know of the Battle of the Citadel came from Neralo di Romani, who was the Imperial Historian at the time."

The zanthyr remarked, "Alshiba's account. Not Raine D'Lacourte's."

The High Lord turned him an uncomprehending look. "You think Raine's would be different?"

Phaedor arched a sardonic brow. "It might be now."

To which allusion Tanis saw the High Lord veritably grinding his teeth.

The silence that followed felt deep and forceful. For many minutes, the only sounds Tanis heard were the splash of the hull through the waves, the creak of masts and rigging, and the wind in the sails. Then Tanis could stand no more the feeling of hopelessness radiating off the High Lord. The words came into his head almost as if planted there by someone else.

"All isn't yet lost, Your Grace," Tanis offered into the quiet of Phaedor's wind. "Perhaps such time will come again when men may study the fifth in safety in the east and those of the west might once again learn from maestros who do not fear its use."

Marius shot him a startled look. He opened his mouth to reply and abruptly shut it again. He searched Tanis's colorless eyes with a look of wonder and finally replied, "The Empress has expressed the same sentiment, Tanis of Giverny."

"Oh, I wasn't born in Giverny, Your Grace," Tanis corrected, not really paying attention to what he was saying, for his own thoughts were ranging far in the future, drawn there as if his prophetic words were carrying him swiftly down the strands of time. "I was born here, in Agasan."

"Tanis," the zanthyr cautioned, giving him a look of warning.

Tanis roused from his musing to find Marius staring hard at him. "You are one of the Empress's subjects?"

"The boy is subject to no one." Phaedor took Tanis by the shoulder and marched them away from the bow, and that marked the end of all conversation with the High Lord Marius di L'Arlesé.

TWENTY-SEVEN

"Gods have their own moral code."

— Morin d'Hain, Spymaster

EAN SAT UP as the sun was setting. He felt odd, disoriented. He pushed palms to his eyes, which didn't seem much restored for having rested for several hours, and looked to his brother, who'd been laid out prone beside him with a cloth draping his hips. Isabel had made strides in Healing his back, but his arms and shoulders sat oddly, and his poor hands clearly had not yet been tended to, beyond being immobilized around a simple splint.

"I've bound him into unconsciousness until we can help him further."

Ean turned to find Isabel standing between the open flaps of the tent. His gaze softened to see her. "*Thank you.*" He looked down at Sebastian again, and concern marred his brow. "What of his hands, Isabel?"

She shook her head. "Every bone in both hands is shattered. He'll need to be in a stable place before I reset and Heal them all, for he cannot be moved after that for several days." She brushed a stray strand of dark hair from her face, and her brow pinched slightly, perhaps in concern, certainly with sympathy. "It will be the work of more than one Healer to set him to rights, Ean. I know where to go to see to his welfare, but it will take too long overland. You must make a bridge."

Ean closed his eyes and stifled a groan. The thought of making another of those bridges, and the feeling he'd experienced afterwards ... Resigning himself to doing whatever she asked of him, Ean looked back to her and noticed the expression on her face. "Isabel ..." He climbed to his feet and went immediately to take her shoulders in his hands. "What is it?"

She turned from him and moved out of the tent. Puzzled, he followed her in silence, away from camp and to the very edge of the canyon. Sunset flamed the broad sky and painted the rock towers in variegated shadows, but Ean saw only the shadows upon Isabel's brow.

He took her by the shoulders again and turned her to face him. "Whatever is bothering you …" he searched her face with his gaze, wishing for the thousandth time that he might look into her eyes instead of at the fold of silk that forever shut him out—Arion had not been so denied. "Isabel … please tell me."

Silence lengthened between them, and both the mystery and the perception of her inner turmoil gave vent to his own fears, but then her brow relaxed somewhat, as if with resignation.

"To know one's future is to become the effect of it," she told him quietly. "This is a proven fact. You saw today how deadly bright shines the sun of foretelling, and you experienced but a fraction of its power reflected from my thoughts, many times diluted." She turned slightly away from his gaze to face the vista again, but at the same time she leaned into his embrace, so he would know she wasn't denying him.

"When a man is told the path of his future, he nearly always falls prey to it. He sets it in stone with his will, with his belief, even unwittingly so. But the future is *not* set. Our paths are not laid in stone, and though their overall direction isn't easily shifted, a man changing his mind at any point can alter his path."

"I understand this, Isabel."

She turned to him. "Do you?" She exhaled her dubiety and looked back to the view. "All paths are not created equally, nor are all Players in the game of equal value to the achievement of the goal. Only certain threads in the tapestry suggest its design. There are many ancillary pieces, many pawns on both sides, many threads that merely fill the tapestry's open spaces. These pieces, these minor threads, are still valuable to the whole, but a loss of one, a misstep of one, doesn't change the shape of things."

She leaned more closely against him and he wrapped both arms around her, though he felt less protective than desperately possessive, and he wondered at the sudden premonition that brought such uneasy feelings to mind.

"Then there are those whose every choice weaves its thread through the pattern, the great tapestry that is my brother's game. Your choices, *my* choices … our strands are thick, Ean. We bind many, many threads to us."

Ean pressed his lips to her hair. "Please just tell me what you fear, Isabel."

She shook her head and sighed, and he both felt and heard a terrible uncertainty in her exhalation. "I fear that my path is influencing yours."

This is what he'd been sensing in her, why he clung to her with such instinctive desperation. "What are you saying?"

"I fear that my brother was right. I fear if we continue forth together, my path will too strongly influence your thread."

"*No.*" Ean spun her to face him. "I won't believe that."

She removed his arms from her shoulders and stood her ground. "We were in a remote fortress, yet you crossed the path of a *Malorin'athgul*." The name came out in a hiss.

Ean pushed both hands through his hair, frustrated, not understanding why she kept insisting on this point. "But they lie upon *my* path, Isabel—"

"Not Pelas."

Ean dropped his arms and stared at her. "Then whose path does he cross?" He saw it in her expression then—or at least perceived it in the shadows of her thoughts. His heart became a sudden lump in his chest. "... *Yours?*"

She held him fixedly in her hidden, yet somehow scouring, gaze. "The point is that Pelas should not have crossed *your* path, Ean. Not yet, in any case."

Rising protest made Ean's breath come faster. He searched his mind for any rationale—anything to explain the day's events and make her see what folly she suggested to ever think of leaving his side. "You said ..." he threw out a hand, searching for the words, "you said every choice changes a man's path. Couldn't *Pelas* have recently chosen—"

"Yes, choice is central to Pelas's path," she cut him off tersely. "I know your mind, Ean, what you would propose to me: that there is merit in your actions, that Pelas helped us—indeed that the currents proved him an ally, at least for today. And you would be correct in all of this."

She walked a few paces away to stand with her arms crossed and her back to him. "Yet this being is *not* our ally ... not yet, if ever," she added, "and while it *is* valuable to put a face and name to another of our enemies, it is of the utmost urgency that your paths not cross again." She turned a look at him over her shoulder.

Ean refused to face the truth she was presenting him, so he asked instead, "Immanuel—*Pelas* ... he isn't like the others, is he?"

"Yes and no." She exhaled forcefully and looked back to the view. "Today I saw his path for the first time—that is, what one can see of its potential, for these creatures are not made within Alorin's fabric. Their paths are as fluid as the sea." She pursed her lips in a tight line, her brow furrowed. Then she shook her head. "We must go. Even now the line of men approaches."

The prince saw beyond her then, saw what she'd been observing: a cloud of dust rose along the distant ridge—men on horseback.

He took her arm as she moved to depart. He felt naked without her, so he spoke with the same honesty. "Don't leave me, Isabel. I'm not whole without you."

Her brow softened, and she rose to plant a soft kiss on his lips. "We are bound, you and I." She paused with her lips close, letting her breath mingle with his own. "You will never be without me."

Ean frowned as she withdrew, for her words held dual meaning, depending which word one emphasized. He chose the optimistic interpretation and followed her back to camp.

They made their way to the node they'd first arrived on in their initial chase after Dore Madden, when Ean had still been unconscious in the Labyrinth. Though the men from Tal'Afaq surely pursued them, they rode with care to protect Sebastian, whom Dorn carried before him on his mount even as the zanthyr had once carried Ean.

All the while, the prince brooded over Isabel's words, wondering if he cared at all to exist in the world without her. He might've put the time to more productive use, but his brain seemed incapable of any other thoughts.

The node lay amid a crumbling temple on a hill overlooking the ruins of an ancient city. It had probably been a place of great beauty during the Cyrene Empire's heyday, but the temple's once-lustrous marble had grown dull and pocked with age, and the nodecourt had become little more than a repository for rubble. Yet the node functioned the same whether decorated with the ornate temples of civilization or marked with a single stone, or none at all.

While Lem held the horses at the ready, Isabel drew Ean to the edge of the node. Splintered columns surrounded the nodecourt like the teeth of an ancient beast, giving Ean the uncomfortable sensation of walking into its maw. He'd been unconscious when Isabel had first brought them through the node, and he admitted a certain distraction at seeing the skeletal ruins of the city, which spread below and around them brokenly, ringed by the rib bones of city walls.

"Ean, we haven't much time," Isabel said, recalling his attention from the graveyard view. "The men of Tal'Afaq will doubtless pursue us here."

He looked to her, still feeling the echo of his fears. They lingered in the back of his mind with a heavy sort of dullness, like the morning after too much drink. "What is your will, my lady?"

"Take my hand," she offered, extending it to him, "and I'll show you."

Ean entwined his fingers within hers and brought her arm close, drawing her hand up against his chest where he might brush his lips against it. Through this tactile connection, Isabel shared her vision—*imposed* it, rather, upon his consciousness.

Ean no longer saw the nodecourt but a geospatial rendering of the Pattern of the World. The entire spherical grid of the Greater Reticulation glowed before him, ley lines connecting to nodepoints and welds forming a complex geometric solid.

"We stand at this nodepoint," Isabel said, making one point glow more brightly than the others, "and we need to reach this one." Another point, not connected to the first via any of the intersecting lines, also glowed. "We haven't time to travel overland from node to node. You must bridge them to take us in a single step."

Ean frowned. She made it sound so simple, but instinct told him it would be simple in the way the Esoterics were simple—broad statements about hugely complex topics, reduced to their axiomatic essentials and then generalized from there. As in, not the least bit simple.

Yet all he said was, "How do I do this, Isabel?"

"You must stand upon the Pattern of the World and bridge these points with your mind. You must use the second strand, not the fifth, for it is kinetic energy, not raw elements, that connects these points on the grid of the world; yet you'll find a certain affinity in the kinetic energy of the second strand *because* you're an Adept of the fifth. The pattern won't reject you as it would another." She pointed to the connecting lines in her illusion. "The ley lines are magnetized to polarities—but you don't need to understand the properties of inductance and magnetic fields. All you must know is that to bridge one node to another, a conductor must exist—*you*. The resulting induction from existing fields will pull us across."

"The essence of simplicity," he muttered.

She squeezed his hand. "You once crafted welds whole cloth out of the aether. You and Malachai and my brother *built* T'khendar's magnetic grid. You can do this, Ean. Do not let the idea of it daunt you. Any Nodefinder with his second ring can do this."

Ean's mind remained a blank. "But I have no rings."

She dropped the illusion of the grid and turned to stand before him. "Arion had twenty."

Ean clenched his jaw. It was always Arion whose name returned to haunt him. "If he was so magnificent, how did he fail so utterly?"

Isabel caught her breath sharply. Ean sensed an immediate change in her manner. "*This* is why the veil remains closed to you." Her whispered words announced her sudden understanding. "Whatever happened on Tiern'aval, you think you *failed*."

Ean gazed at her in frustrated silence. *I did fail!* He knew this with every fiber of his being, though he had no idea what he'd failed in.

He saw a crease form between her brows. "Arion was my brother's closest friend. Björn confided in him, he taught him things no one else knows. You *must* remember this knowledge, Ean."

Ean dropped his chin to his chest. "I want to, Isabel. I'm trying—I don't know why it won't come."

"Because you clearly fear the truth of Tiern'aval and cannot forgive yourself for it."

The blunt declaration hit Ean like a slap to his face. He clenched his teeth, knowing that sting of truth even if he understood nothing else. He lifted his gaze back to her. "Then what really happened?"

Isabel's frown deepened, so also her impatience to be away, but Ean couldn't get past it—something in this area of his past concealed a truth that plugged all memory beyond it. He knew he'd not find the knowledge she required of him without this answer.

Isabel placed both of her hands on his chest and turned her hidden gaze up to him. "*Ean* ... don't you see ... you're the only one who knows."

His mouth went dry with sudden foreboding. "... What do you mean?"

She smoothed the suede of his coat with one hand while the lines of concern marring her brow grew longer. "My brother claimed responsibility for the deaths of the Citadel Mages, but their blood stains others' hands."

Ean took a reflexive step backwards. "What are you saying—that ..." *thirteen hells!* "... that *I* killed them all?" He felt suddenly unstable on his feet and stumbled a few steps away to brace himself against a fallen column. He hung his head between his arms then and tried to stave off the swarming feeling in his skull, but his breath came too shallowly, and the world continued its sideways skid.

"The battle at the Citadel began with a failed coup," Isabel said quietly, compassion and concern adding a blue tinge to her tone of blackest regret, "surely this memory has returned to you by now ..."

Ean remembered—first the memory he'd regained in the Labyrinth, then that of his dream from months before, where he'd stood in that cavernous hall holding a bloodied sword beneath the dome he'd shattered, facing a pair of gilded doors but seeing only the faceless forms of traitors hiding beyond them. And he recalled ...

"You took those who were loyal to you," he murmured, recalling it as truth now instead of just a dream, "and I went into the hall to bring lasting justice to Dore Madden and the other men—Mages—responsible."

"Yes."

Ean straightened and turned to her. "What happened?

Isabel was hugging her chest with one hand pressed over her heart. "When the battle was finally done and Illume Belliel's Paladin Knights had been vanquished, my brother went in search of you. He found the bodies of the traitor Mages ..." and here she caught her bottom lip between her teeth, her brow furrowed with an eternal sorrow, "... but of Arion, he found no sign. Ean—" She approached and took both of his hands firmly in her own, looking up into his eyes. "Whatever truth there is to be uncovered, it lies upon your path. You're the only one who knows what happened in that room."

Ean stared at her while feelings, impressions ... perceptions fluttered through his mind, memories as birds trapped in a windowless chamber, seeking desperate escape. He saw himself in battle, saw the faces of his vengeance take form, saw his dark blade flashing through veils of the fifth ... and finally a face—*the* face from his many earlier dreams, ones that had come during his Awakening ... a face he'd tried to forget.

And throughout all of this—regret ... regret ... *regret.* It rang in these impressions as if a canon against which he'd measured all action.

"Arion didn't die on Tiern'aval." He heard himself confess these words, though his breath seemed too thin to support speech. This memory had come to him more recently, when he'd faced the doors of Tyr'kharta's hall and seen the Citadel's doors instead. With both images superimposed, so had returned the knowledge that Tiern'aval hadn't been Arion's end. Yet ... where *had* Arion died? This truth still hid from him.

Isabel pressed a hand to his cheek, and he lifted an agonized gaze to her. "Memory will come in time. Let it come, when it does. But for now we *must* away. I can feel Dore's men nearing, but more importantly, your brother needs Healing, and it cannot be done here."

Ean nodded, swallowed, collected the shards of his composure. If he'd built the welds of an entire realm—enduring all of the forces such activity entailed— he could certainly stand upon the pattern of this world for a few heartbeats.

Resolved at least to try, Ean took Isabel's hand. "Call the others."

He focused while she did so, closing his eyes to everything except the feeling of the currents. When he opened them again, he'd summoned the pattern to reveal *elae's* tides in their fullness. He saw how the currents swirled like water in a drain in the center of the nodecourt, and he drew Isabel with him as he moved towards that vortex.

Ean wasn't sure what he'd expected when he stepped upon the node itself—a sensation of vertigo, some uncomfortable tingling, perhaps—but casting himself onto the Pattern of the World felt more akin to diving into the raging rapids of a river of lava in flood.

The fury of this power could not be described. Nothing in the living world matched it—no hurricane, no cyclone, no tidal wave even approached its violence. If all such storms that had ever been were simultaneously combined and channeled along a single current—*then* one might approach the sheer voltage raging forever through the pattern.

Ean felt like he was being ripped apart.

"You must become the conductor!" Isabel's voice was an urgent command, but he hardly heard her for the roaring in his ears, like a waterfall surging and churning inside his skull, drowning breath, drowning thought ... *You must become the bridge between the points.*

Ean reeled in the onslaught. It felt like being unmade ...

Isabel's voice sounded distant, as if she called from a far hill. "Ean, you must do this. You *can* do this! Ean—they're *coming* ... "

Necessity recalled him to himself, but it recalled something more. For now he felt the Pattern of the World inside him, as if it had imprinted on every part of him, and he realized he'd felt this before ... this remaking of himself within the Pattern of the World, only that time it had ... *saved* him?

Memory surfaced, bringing knowingness and understanding of what he must do. Ean cast his awareness through the pattern, seeking the node of their destination. He flowed with that tide, riding the raging rapids, until he saw the beacon for which he searched. Finding it, he thrust himself *into* it. Another dive into another fiery pool, but now he understood they were both eddies in the same river, though no waters connected them. He would become that connection.

Like opening the tap, Ean drew upon the energy of the node he stood on and then directed it to where another version of himself floated in the eddy of the other node. Instantly he felt a force pulling violently at him, tearing him away. He resisted it and firmly anchored his awareness in both eddies.

Streams of light invaded his senses, and for a moment he felt as if part of him stood in both places at once, or as if his body had expanded to bridge the entire distance between them. He had some sensation of others, shadowed forms, more impression than substance, moving past. Then he could resist the forces raging through him no longer. One end slipped with a violent snap, and the world exploded into spiraling light.

Ean woke to the clamorous ringing of bells, which spawned an eruption of children's voices chattering excitedly in a language that sounded like the desert tongue. Ean thought he heard the word for 'hungry' and definitely the word for 'stupid' shouted more than once.

White netting draped the canopy bed in which he lay. Turning his head towards the voices, he saw doors open to a balcony covered in vines. The breeze that stirred the silk curtains already held spring's coming warmth. Across the room, Isabel's knapsack rested on a chair, but of his lady love, he saw no sign. Ean swung his bare legs over the bed and rose, noting in his nakedness that someone's care had erased the vestiges of battle and his brother's blood from his skin.

Across the room, a green kurta embroidered with gold thread hung from an armoire beside shalwars of the same expensive silk cloth. Woven gold slippers rested on the floor beneath these. On a table near the doors waited a domed silver platter, the fragrance out of which—wafting as it was across the room and directly into his nose—roused an impatient growl from Ean's stomach.

A host of questions paraded through the prince's head as he dressed and ate. Then he headed out of his room to seek some answers—

And drew up short in front of a boy crouched in the passage.

Dark-haired and brown-eyed, with the sloping nose of the desert tribes but a very impish chin, he looked up as Ean appeared in the doorway, flashed a devilish grin, and bolted from seating into a sprint without assuming any of the stages in between. Belled anklets jangled as he ran.

Ean followed him—or at least the sound of his passing—through grandiose halls of scalloped archways and ceilings painted with brilliant arabesques, past vast rooms tiled with spiraling designs, and finally beneath a spectacular mosaic arch in the shape of peacock tails. Beyond this, a grand, golden hall awaited. It's walls and groin-vaulted ceiling were entirely covered in swirling, gilded patterns. The only straight edges were those that led the eye upwards.

Ean caught sight of the boy halfway across the wide hall, heading towards a group of three men. They were all dark-haired and caramel-skinned, like the boy running towards them.

The tallest of the three stood shirtless with his arms extended. The other two men were securing a framework of gold chains around his torso. The framework resembled a cuirass in shape and hugged the man's muscular form. Even from afar, Ean saw patterns inscribed along the metal straps and on each gold plate where the chains connected.

The boy was talking excitedly in the desert tongue as Ean neared, whereupon the man in the center lowered his arms and turned with a smile. His white teeth shone against his caramel skin, gleaming almost as brightly as his colorless eyes. He wore his black hair short and his jaw clean-shaved—a strong jaw, with a deeply cleft chin—while black brows angled humorously over his tell-tale truthreader's eyes. In the center of his forehead he bore a black tattoo, intricately patterned, which spiraled along the line of his brows. A large teardrop ruby dangled from one ear. It occasionally caught the sunlight pouring down from the hall's high windows.

He opened arms broadly to the prince. "Ah, Prince Ean val Lorian, awake at last! *Salam, khosh amadid.*" He pressed palms together and gave Ean a polite nod—not quite a bow, but almost.

Ean recognized the form of respect as one used regularly among the Kandori nobility—which would also explain the man's bow, for it had been just deep enough to mark them as equals.

"*Salam, zohr bekheir,*" Ean returned, mirroring the other's bow. Straightening, he looked at the other two dark-eyed men and back to the smiling first. "I confess my ignorance. I don't actually know where I am."

"But of course, you are in Kandori," said his truthreader host, opening his arms again to the room at large, "and this is the palace of Andorr, ancestral home of the Haxamanis family. My home."

Ean had only a rudimentary understanding of the Kandori princedoms, for the lineages and hereditary successors to Kandori's nine royal houses were confusingly complex, but if any one house could be said to rule over the others, Haxamanis would be it. Alyneri had been birthed of that line, the only daughter of Prince Jair.

Ean regarded his smiling host. He was indeed in royal company. "Then you're Dareios."

Dareios pressed both hands to his heart. "*Khaneh shomast.*" *My home is your home.* He extended a hand towards the two men standing with him, whereupon Ean noted, among his other jeweled rings, the two thin gold bands on his fourth finger that proclaimed his Sormitáge training. "This is my cousin Bahman and his brother-by-marriage, Naveed. They assist me in my workshop."

"Your workshop?"

"Yes, I like to tinker with things—such as this vest, for example, an invention of mine which harnesses the power of the fourth to protect the wearer from his enemies."

Ean imagined such a device would prove valuable protection when you stood to inherit the realm's greatest fortune. No doubt the Kandori prince suffered many covetous factions seeking his life.

"But I must apologize for the informal nature of this meeting." Dareios mussed the hair of the young boy, perhaps seven years of age, who stood at his side. "This little scamp was meant to bring us to you when you woke, not the other way around."

The boy grinned broadly.

"He was at least easy to follow," Ean offered with a friendly smile.

"Ah yes. The bells." Dareios cast the boy a look. "He wears them because he makes so much mischief."

Ean thought of himself at that age and smiled. "The bells help keep him out of trouble?"

"Heavens no, but at least this way we know where he's stirring it up."

Dareios looked to Bahman then, who handed him a kurta of blue silk embroidered with gold. Putting this on over the odd metal vest, he noted Ean's gaze and grinned. "No doubt you've never seen the likes of this contraption. Here, I'll show you how it works." He extended his jaw and motioned to it with a waggling finger. "Hit me."

Ean blinked. "I beg your pardon?"

"Yes—yes," Dareios waved Ean to come at him.

Ean cast him a dubious look.

"I'll do it," Naveed said enthusiastically. He drew a curved dagger from his hip and struck at Dareios.

The dagger skimmed harmlessly off the air a hand's span away from the Kandori prince, but the resulting rebound against Naveed sent him spiraling through the air.

Dareios arched a triangular brow as the man landed in a tangle. "Now that is interesting." Then he shoved hands on his hips and barked a laugh. "Good thing you resisted the temptation, Ean. You saved me the necessity of an embarrassing apology."

Across the way, Naveed pushed up to hands and knees and shook his head.

Dareios stroked an eyebrow with his forefinger. "The second strand induction pattern should've handled that field refraction."

"Could be a problem with the flux constant across the field," Bahman said.

Dareios shifted his eyes to him. "Some error with surface normal calibration."

The man nodded. "I'll check the pattern alignment and make a new plate." He went over and looped his arm around his brother-by-marriage and hauled him to his feet. He slapped him good-naturedly on the back as they headed off together.

Dareios swatted the boy on the bottom. "Go help them."

He trotted off with a jingle-jingle-jingle.

"He is your son?" Ean asked.

Dareios watched the boy go wearing a slight frown. "My great-nephew. My wife and I had only daughters." Abruptly he pressed palms together, touched fingertips to his forehead and then lifted prayerful hands to the heavens and shook them at the ceiling. Ean couldn't be sure if this gesture was meant to convey to the gods his frustration or his contrition.

Dareios looked back to Ean, and wisdom and humor both danced in his eyes. "The Kandori believe princely souls are born of the gods. There is a story that says that when a royal prince and a woman mate on earth, the Goddess Inithiya must mate with her god-brother Huhktu in case a child is conceived of the union." He rubbed at one eyebrow. "Far-fetched, I know. With all the rampant sex of the royalty in this world, Inithiya would never get a moment's separation from her brother's loins. Then again, time has different meaning to the gods." He shrugged. "Perhaps it is true after all."

Ean smiled. "Far be it from me to question what a god can do."

"A wise answer, Prince of Dannym." Dareios gave him an approving nod and a grin. "The story goes on to warn that if a prince of Kandori lies with too many women, Inithiya may become vexed with him—for the Goddess of Spirit has better things to do, after all, than be harem-girl to the God of Bones—and in return, she may send the over-enthusiastic prince only daughters, that he might understand better the terrors of being a father of beautiful girls." He pressed palms together and thumbs to his forehead. Then he shook his head, lamenting, "This, Ean … this has been my certain fate."

"It doesn't seem such a terrible end to be blessed with beautiful daughters." Ean meant this sentiment, yet even as he spoke it, he realized that he couldn't conceive of a life so normal as to make a home with Isabel and fill it with children. This truth bothered him deeply.

"Yes," Dareios agreed meanwhile, eyes dancing, "but twelve of them?"

Ean chuckled. He could only imagine trying to corral a dozen Kandori girls, all no doubt with Alyneri's headstrong spirit.

As if to chastise Dareios's lack of gratitude for the blessing of many lovely daughters, a growl came from between two of the triform columns, and Ean looked over to see an enormous wildcat arching its back in a stretch. It pushed its haunches out behind it and then padded soundlessly towards them.

Ean felt his hand instinctively reaching for a sword that wasn't there. "Is that—"

"That is Babar." Dareios looked somewhat pained. He rubbed at one eyebrow again. "She makes a general nuisance of herself and claims all property as her own, as cats and wives will. Would that I could keep bells around her feet as easily as around young Sarosh's, but Babar is far less obedient than my nephew." He clapped a hand on Ean's shoulder. "Fear not, however. Babar prefers the meat of my enemies."

"That's … fortunate." Ean watched the cat settle at Dareios's feet and begin licking her paw, which entailed a necessary spreading of lengthy, razor-sharp claws. Sitting, her tawny head lay within easy reach of Dareios's fingers, so he dutifully scratched between her ears. Ean couldn't help but wonder exactly what criteria the wildcat used in deciding who was her master's enemy and if an animal could really be trusted to make that assessment on its own.

Dareios shifted his gaze to Ean, and his expression sobered measurably. "No doubt you will want to see your brother. Come." He led away, and after a few steps, Babar stood and followed on silent paws. "When I checked on them last, your Isabel and my sisters were about to begin resetting the bones in your brother's hands." He cast a Ean sidelong look. "You're blessed to have the dead returned to you … nearly whole."

"Is he? Whole, that is?" Ean thought of the web of patterns encasing his brother's mind and suppressed a violent burst of fury. He'd sworn to free Sebastian from that net, but he had yet to determine how to go about it without killing him in the process.

Dareios must've heard this thought—Ean hadn't exactly been guarding his mind, though he reminded himself to do so thereafter, for it was only polite when in the company of a truthreader—for the Kandori prince offered, "That is why she brought you to me: in the hope I might be able to help you."

Ean turned to him. "How is that?"

"It's my specialty. I'm a Patternist." Ean must've looked blank, for Dareios added, "Like mathematics, patterns are their own language. Every curl, every angle, every intersection—they all speak to purpose and action."

Ean stared at him. "You speak the language of patterns."

Dareios pressed a ringed hand to his chest with a humble smile. "I am … one of the best."

When Ean reached his brother's room, Sebastian was stretched out on a long table. His dislocated shoulders had been carefully set and bound in linen, and now a host of beautiful women draped in colorful silks were carefully aligning his fingers within the frame of two plaster molds. Once the bones were set properly, the women staked each finger between needles stuck into the still-soft plaster. Isabel worked among them, checking their progress and murmuring quietly in the desert tongue. She clearly hadn't slept.

Ean couldn't look upon her without feeling an immense sense of pride and wonder. In this life he hardly knew her—though he *knew* her instinctively in so many fundamental ways, yet much about her remained a mystery to him. In every respect, life with Isabel was an adventure, each day revealing to him some new quality of hers to be explored. She was as the wide sea; he could never delve all of her depths.

Yet now, seeing Isabel brought an uncommon heartache and a heaviness to his thoughts, for he could no longer look upon her without experiencing the fear of losing her. Almost worse was knowing he'd felt that fear before.

To keep from dwelling on those soul-shadows, Ean asked in a low voice, so as not to disturb the Healers, "Where did they get the molds for his hands?"

"I believe they used yours, Prince of Dannym." Dareios cast him a wry smile. "My sister Ehsan said of you while you slept that if Death himself had come calling, he would've had to wait for you to waken."

Ean grimaced. "Please don't tell me that was four days ago."

"Last night," Dareios replied with a curious look.

Isabel lifted her blindfolded gaze from her work and came over to them. She took Ean's face in her hands and kissed him, and ran her thumb over his lips as she withdrew. In that moment, brief though it was, Ean knew only Isabel—her touch, her smell, the feeling of their bond resonating ...

Pulling away, she gifted Dareios with a smile. "I see he found his way into good hands."

"As did this one," Dareios replied, nodding to Sebastian. "He looks hale compared to his state upon your arrival."

Isabel turned a slight frown back towards the sleeping prince. "We're finally resetting his fingers. In some cases the bones were so crushed that I needed to rebuild them before they could be reset." She pushed a strand of hair from her face and exhaled. "It's been a long night, but we have hope for his recovery."

Feeling a surge of gratitude and affinity that was nearly overwhelming, Ean drew Isabel into his embrace and murmured into her hair, "You are a miracle."

Isabel hugged him in return. Then she drew back and settled her hidden gaze on both princes. "Be ready. As soon as he wakes, I'll call for you."

She returned to the others.

Dareios put a hand on Ean's shoulder. "Join me for the noonday meal?"

As Ean soon discovered, the palace of Andorr was a massive fortress comprising many palaces, gardens, courtyards and temples. It crowned a mountaintop overlooking rich farmland, which in turn lay pinned between the palace and a tangle of stark, white-capped peaks that demarked the joining of the Dhahari Mountains and the Iverness Range.

Easily the most opulent structure Ean had ever seen, Andorr boasted as many jeweled panels, screens and doors as colorful frescoes and arabesques. Not a wall had been left unadorned—one would think the Kandori gods would be offended to cast their divine gaze upon naked plaster—nor could such an ornate palace suffer the indignity of a simple arch. A single arch, column or minaret became three, their sides fluted, scalloped or otherwise embellished so as to dazzle the eye. Either that or confuse it, for the ornate decoration upon walls, floors, columns, ceilings and every other available surface dizzied and boggled the mind.

"There is beauty in design, and there is beauty in simplicity," Dareios observed as they walked. "This is my home, so of course I notice its artistry not at all." He cast the prince a smile. "Every day I trod the university's Grand Passáge during my years studying at the Sormitáge, I walked with the same wonder as lies within your gaze. The Grand Passáge is a miraculous masterwork of art—one of the true marvels of the Fourth Age—the last great work to be completed before Malachai's scourge hit the Empire."

Ean had but the fuzziest recollection of the Grand Passáge—Arion had walked its corridors while its ceiling was under construction, and Ean had some sense of its grandeur if no clear picture of it. "I hope to visit the Sormitáge one day."

"Yes, you must. I haven't traveled extensively in Avatar, but in the Middle Kingdoms or the Empire, no city approaches the glory that is Faroqhar, birthplace of the *angiel*." Then he added with a flash of pearly teeth, "Or so the Agasi claim."

They took their meal in a breezy pavilion on the very edge of the mountaintop, overlooking the valley and the razor peaks of the Dhahari. As they were sitting down at a table draped in azure cloth, Dareios pointed to the many dishes laid out before them and rapidly listed off their names—*baba ganoush, fesenjan, ghormeh sabzi, fattoush,* among a litany of others—none of which Ean had any familiarity with, so he tried them all. The wildcat, Babar, claimed a spot in the sun and cleaned her striped and spotted fur while they ate.

Though he had many questions for his host, Ean remained in a tumultuous state of mind. So much had happened in so little time—only a handful of days had passed since he'd left T'khendar, since the First Lord had refused his oath and he'd learned that his loyal men were being held to lure him.

Every day Rhys and the others remained in captivity twisted a barbed arrow further into Ean's heart, but after encountering Sebastian ... Never mind Ean's own love for his eldest brother, but *thirteen hells*, Sebastian was still heir to the Eagle Throne! How could he choose any path but the one towards his brother's salvation?

Sensitive to Ean's state of mind, Dareios ate in quiet contemplation, giving the younger prince an occasional glance but otherwise not intruding on his thoughts. There were benefits to making friends with truthreaders. One need never explain the troubles that plagued one, for some thoughts spoke loudly enough on their own.

Ean admired Dareios for his tact as much as for the effortlessness of his manner. Ean found it daunting enough trying to meet everyone's expectations of him based on the name he'd claimed in another life, but add to this being constantly surrounded by ageless Adepts whose depth of experience imparted wisdom beyond their seeming years ... well, it only heightened his sense of inadequacy.

Yet unlike Ramu or the First Lord, Dareios put him at his ease. From the first moment when the Kandori prince had greeted Ean with parity, he'd felt relaxed in his company. With his generous smile and knowing gaze, which ever danced with subtle humor, one couldn't stand before Dareios of Kandori and feel anything but welcome ... and a little awed. He had to wonder, what was it like being the heir to the Kandori fortune—rumored to be the greatest fortune in the realm?

"Not so glamorous as you might imagine." Dareios cast Ean a smile across the table. "Your pardon, but you're free with your thoughts, Ean. I cannot help sometimes but overhear."

Ean cast him an apologetic look. "I forget to guard myself. It's all still new to me—and yet ... not." He frowned.

"You struggle with the Returning. My troubles—if they might be called troubles, which many would name ungracious of me—lie in the opposite extreme."

"How is that?"

Dareios ran a finger across the tattoo between his brows. "This is the mark of the *Khoda Panaheh*. In Kandori, to work the Pattern of Life is to seek divine favor, Jai'Gar's blessing, His permission, if you will, to remain upon this earth and do service to Him through the fair and honorable use of *elae*, which is His gift of godly power to mortal men. We tell many stories of how man first gained this power, but all of them end with the branding of the *Khoda Panaheh*."

He angled his chair away from the table and extended his feet towards the mountains, settling clasped hands in his lap. "As you will discover the longer you remain my guest, Ean, a great many of us wear this mark." He searched Ean's face with his crystalline gaze. "So I ask you, how can one *inherit* anything when the sires and the heirs live equally long lives?"

Ean blinked. The idea had never occurred to him.

Dareios scratched his head. "Sometimes the sires will linger for centuries, watching generations of their progeny mature and fade or choose to walk the pattern and join their ancient father in immortality; while other heirs decide to live but a single lifetime and move on, passing the torch to their chosen. But the former occurs more often than the latter—for many of us are born as Adepts, and it is in our nature to seek an understanding of our gifts, which understanding often requires longer than one mortal lifetime to acquire."

He looked up under his brows, and a thoughtful crease formed between them. One hand lifted to trace the edge of a silver knife lying beside his plate. "Subsequently the heirs linger, generation after generation, stacking up like firewood. We continue the tradition, of course, naming the heirs for each generation, though in truth there are often four or five others in any given house who might boast an earlier claim." He gave a resigned shrug and met Ean's gaze. "We are something of a dime a dozen, the Kandori heirs."

Ean considered him in wonder. "With such wealth, it would seem ... well, you'd think there would be more ... discord in this arrangement."

"Ah, yes, well ... there's a story to that." A grin spread across his face. "As you will discover, Ean, we have a story for everything, in Kandori." Abruptly he leaned across the table, laying a jeweled hand on the silk. "But tell me of your brother's condition—Isabel said you saw into his mind. Let us speak of what you know, and then we'll go to my lab and see if we can begin to unravel the tangled chains of his imprisonment."

TWENTY-EIGHT

"Count not what is lost, but what is left."

— Jayachándranáptra, Rival of the Sun

ISABEL REMOVED HER hand from Sebastian's forehead. It was done. The Healing was complete.

She set her hand in her lap and exhaled slowly, letting the tension of countless hours of working the lifeforce bleed out with her breath. She'd mended Sebastian's dreadfully frayed life pattern, making it whole again. It shone brightly in her consciousness as she withdrew from rapport.

She'd done what she could as well to aid his older wounds—the crippled leg that caused him such pain, an easing of the scar that marred his cheek—but this man carried wounds no Adept could Heal ... soul-cleaving wounds that had sliced gaping rents in the fabric of his being. Even if Ean succeeded in extricating his brother from Dore's treacherous patterns, Sebastian would still face his own path to full recovery of himself.

Isabel turned to the Healers standing around the bedside, seven in all. She observed their faces, young and aged, so calm and yet so watchful, their hope quietly concealed behind lovely dark eyes and beneath the shadows of the embroidered and jeweled scarves, *chaadars*, that covered their hair. Each of the women shone brightly to her *elae*-fueled eyes, rose-hued and vibrant, with the rushing currents of the first crashing around them as the sea against island rocks. Many of these women she'd known since the womb. Now they were Healers of considerable talent, the rocks of their own shores.

Isabel smiled. "It is done."

They broke into joyous clapping and kissed and hugged one another. Perhaps Sebastian's life had not been in danger, but the effort to restore his body's integrity had required no less of them than that life-or-death commitment.

Isabel stood, signifying the end of their work that day, and the women as one moved to depart. As each Healer passed, Isabel pressed her palms together and bowed. *"Sili ye naeghd beh aez haelva ye nesyaes."* *One day is worth two tomorrows.*

In turn, each woman finished the traditional exchange, saying in the Kandori tongue, *"May tomorrow know the joy of today."*

Then Isabel was closing the door and returning to her chair to wait for Sebastian to wake. It wouldn't be long. He'd been trying to surface from her enforced unconsciousness for the last several turns of the hourglass.

As she relaxed back into her chair, Isabel pressed steepled fingers to her lips and let her thoughts range far. She saw a path—so thin it might barely be considered a path at all, more a trail through the grass of uncertainty, the shadow of Fate's indifferent passing. Yet such trails could become paths ... with the right encouragement. Seeds planted along these trails drew new creatures of opportunity to their nascent buds, and once those buds bloomed, many more foraging possibilities would come, leaving their mark upon the trail, the footprints of promise.

She dared not directly influence Ean's path more than she already had—Cephrael knew she'd done too much as it was. Her brother had been wise to warn her. Ever he displayed a nearly omniscient wisdom, so impressive when he found these truths merely through a study of the currents, while she must tread far upon the paths of possibility to see them. He was an easy man to admire, her brother, though a hard man to love—hard, because he would and had made any sacrifice for the sake of this game, and he expected the same unwavering dedication from those oathbound to play it with him.

Sacrifice ... Isabel pressed fingertips to her brows. She feared what floated beneath sacrifice's desperate lake, far below the waves. She couldn't see its shape yet, but she sensed it hovering there, and for Epiphany's Prophet, sensing it was enough.

Isabel exhaled another deep sigh, strained by the ache of conscience. Balance forbade her any deeper involvement on Ean's path, yet she yearned to assist him. It was such a test of her discipline not to lay her hands upon Ean and rip away the veils of obscurity that prevented him from knowing his true self, from having the answers that were tormenting him so. Yet ... such a working would hopelessly violate the Balance in *his* life. It would mean his ruin, and perhaps the ultimate ruin of all.

She knew what lay at stake, but it didn't lessen her guilt. The woman Isabel saw in Ean the reflection of the only man she'd ever loved, while Epiphany's Prophet knew that Ean's talents would be desperately needed—*all* of his talents—if they were to have any hope of winning the game.

Winning ... such an odd description for the denouement she and her brother sought to this conflict.

Across from her, Sebastian began to surface from his own shadowed depths.

A low sound escaped him; not quite a groan, more his body's acknowledged awareness that what once had been painful, now ached no longer. His lids opened slowly, blinking, once … twice. He made to lift his hands and found them strapped to the plaster molds—a necessary precaution for a few days more, to be certain his finger bones were fully hardened in their restored shape.

"Do not." Isabel leaned to place a hand on his arm and press it back before he strained too hard against his gentle bonds. "The plaster is merely to protect your hands."

Blue-grey eyes opened fully and settled upon her, striking eyes—so like Ean's in shape, yet so different in the attitude they conveyed. Sebastian's eyes had seen too much harm; they couldn't but reflect the impression of experience. "You're a Healer?" His voice came hoarse, a bare whisper.

She moved to bring a goblet of water to his lips, and he drank.

"Thank you," he managed better then. His eyes scanned his own body, seeing hands taped and pinned, gauze-enwrapped shoulders, "… for all of this."

Isabel set down the goblet and sat back in her chair. "Your brother would see you whole. This is a beginning."

"My brother …" He frowned deeply at first, but then the slightest of smiles softened his expression. "To see him so … little Ean …" A light came to momentarily banish the shadows in his gaze. "I never imagined my littlest brother would one day come to my rescue." Abruptly the shadows returned. "Or that I would try to kill him for it. How improbable, the paths of Fate."

"Cephrael's hand weaves, and His choices are mysterious to us, for we cannot see the larger pattern He shapes."

He turned and assessed her shrewdly. "You help him—my brother. You're his wife?"

"We are bound to each other's paths."

"That sounds ominous." He looked around the room, noting high windows and the mountains beyond. "Where has he brought us?"

"Kandori."

He frowned. "Wasn't there … I seem to recall a Kandori prince in my father's court." Then he gave a rueful shake of his head.

"Perhaps you recall Prince Jair," she offered. "He married the Healer Melisande d'Giverny, who birthed a daughter, a Healer, Alyneri."

Sebastian brightened. "Betrothed of Trell."

Isabel nodded. "We are at the home of her uncle, Prince Dareios."

"Why?"

"Because Ean will need Dareios. As will you."

He considered her for a time after this statement. She felt his intelligent gaze assessing her, assessing his surroundings. This was a man used to perceiving danger in every breath. "I sense a new presence in my thoughts, intervening … bringing an uncommon peace. You?"

She nodded.

He seemed to infer her reasoning, for he didn't ask why she held his mind in a binding of her own, but no doubt he'd made note that she could.

"So ... what now, my lady?"

Isabel decided she liked Ean's eldest brother. Without Dore's lunacy twisting his thoughts, he had a quick mind and a discerning disposition. Time then, to seed her nascent path. "Ean risked everything to rescue you."

Sebastian winced at this. His countenance revealed a deep weariness, as if every day spent in the agony of Dore's thrall had shaved a decade from his future, leaving his life spent at the bare age of twenty and eight. After a moment, he leaned his head back against the bed. His voice ached as he murmured, "You think I'm unworthy of his aid."

She placed a hand on his arm. "All good men are worthy of help."

He looked swiftly back to her. "Am I a good man?" He grunted and looked off again. "I hardly know who I am ... and I've only glimmers of who I used to be."

"A man might say such at any moment in his life. We remake ourselves every day, with our every choice and action."

"A fine sentiment, my lady, but not so easily accomplished when your mind belongs to a madman."

Isabel recognized power in Sebastian—great power for a mind so imprisoned. If only his freedom could be gained as expeditiously as she'd restored his hands ...

Sebastian considered her as she thought on this, and his eyes narrowed with his inspection. Abruptly he latched onto the truth. "Whatever you're doing—this intervention that's allowing me such clarity of thought ... it's only temporary, isn't it?"

Isabel nodded.

Sebastian clenched his jaw. "So ... the moment you remove your working ... out comes the ravening madman, intent on doing Dore's bidding. Is that where we stand?"

She nodded again.

He frowned as he considered their predicament. "Can't you just keep doing whatever you're doing?"

"I dare not, for a multitude of reasons, not the least of which is the unhealthy number of bindings already compelling your thoughts. But this is only part of the issue we face, Sebastian."

He cast her a wary look. "What's the rest of it?"

"Dore has set his patterns with the fifth, as you know. Ean has the ability to unwork such patterns, but not without studying them with care, and the complexity of the patterns Dore has implanted on your mind will require deep inspection."

Understanding dawned in Sebastian's gaze. He gave her a fleeting and bitter smile. "Therein lies the rub ... I see. The moment Ean approaches me, I'll be compelled to kill him. Not exactly an atmosphere hospitable to study."

"Yet ... there is a way."

His eyes flicked over her. "So we come to it at last." His gaze narrowed. "I take it I won't like this idea, else you wouldn't have engaged in such preamble before presenting it."

Isabel cracked a smile. "Your wit does you justice, Prince of Dannym. It is guaranteed you won't like it."

"You have me at your mercy, my lady. By all means, let's hear this hideous suggestion."

Isabel lifted a bag from beside her feet and drew out a coil of silver rope.

Sebastian's expression darkened.

Isabel set the *goracrosta* down on her lap. "Not what you were you envisioning?"

"I was thinking more along the lines of padded shackles and a warded room—perhaps this room. Comfortably contained ... with a nice view." He cast an agonized look at the goracrosta. "I'll find ill comfort in the thrall of that dreaded stuff. Have you any idea what Dore—"

When he couldn't finish, only turned away with his jaw clenched, Isabel put a hand on his arm again. "There is another reason for using *goracrosta*, Sebastian. Two reasons. Will you hear them?"

Tormented eyes looked back to her. He nodded.

"First, though the *goracrosta* won't prevent Dore's compulsion, it *will* prevent your using *elae* to carry out its demands. This places you and Ean on equal footing, for he will not use the lifeforce to harm you. Second, I believe Dore is capable of tracking you through the bond he's placed in your mind."

Sebastian closed his eyes. After a moment he whispered, "I fear you're right."

"The *goracrosta* will confuse this, prevent his being able to trace you here."

His gaze flew back to her. "I would have to wear it *constantly*—" his voice broke, and he bowed his head, jaw clenching again.

Isabel wasn't insensitive to his plight, but she dared make no misguided concessions of mercy. "Can you trust yourself, Sebastian? Say it's so, and I'll release you now."

He cast her an anguished look. "You know I cannot."

"We want only to *free* you, but until we can trust you not to act against us in this endeavor, what other choice have we?"

Sebastian exhaled a slow breath. "None, my lady. Very well, I'll wear the rope, but just answer me one thing."

She nodded for him to continue.

The sudden desperation that came into his gaze tore into her heart. "*Can he do it? Can Ean free me?*"

Isabel sat back in her chair. She saw her tiny trail broadening as it led into the future. "If he knew all he has ever known," she began, "unquestionably. But he fears this knowledge, Sebastian. There's much you don't know about your brother, about his Return. He's afraid to remember the deeds that lie upon the path behind him, yet if he cannot forgive himself for these actions, he'll never fully regain his identity. You must help him."

"Me?" he looked astonished. "How?"

"Help him to find these truths and face them."

"How will I do that with *goracrosta* around my neck?" He sounded desperate.

"There will come a time, sooner or later, when the moment will be right." She paused to let this sink in.

He stared at her in silence. Then he nodded once and looked down at his hands. "Will you bind me here? Now?"

She heard the fear in his voice. Isabel stood and gathered her things. "In a few days, after you've rested and have the use of your hands again—a hint of freedom to balance the *goracrosta's* bite. Also, soon we must speak of Ean's men and anything else you can tell us of Dore's activities—tit for tat, I'm afraid, Sebastian. Ean would merely free you, but he thinks only with his heart." She paused at the door, sighed, and the hint of a tragic smile graced her lips. "He has ever been so."

Sebastian gave her a wondrous look. "Who are you, my lady?"

She turned a look over her shoulder and settled her blindfolded gaze upon him. "I am Isabel van Gelderan."

He nearly choked, and his eyes went round. For a space of several breaths, he seemed unable to summon words. Then he managed hoarsely, "Nothing scares Dore Madden—*nothing*. Except your brother ... and you."

"Dore escaped my brother's justice on Tiern'aval." Isabel's tone held a steel honed by centuries of sacrifice. "He will not escape mine."

Sebastian shook his head, still wide-eyed. "For all our sakes, my lady, I pray you're right."

"So do I, Sebastian. Good night to you," and she took her leave.

TWENTY-NINE

"Don't talk to me about heartache. Don't tell me about sacrifice.

None of us hold a candle to what he's endured."

— The Adept truthreader Cristien Tagliaferro,

on Björn van Gelderan

A DAMP DAWN FOUND Sebastian val Lorian standing shirtless on his balcony watching the day breaking against the Dhahari range. The thunderstorm that had raged all night was moving off to the north, leaving a trail of broken clouds which the dawn blessed now with its golden kiss. The snowbound peaks also reflected daybreak's blush, and between the rose-gold sky, the deep violet clouds and the light blooming along the mountains' crest, the morning seemed full of promise. For the first time in nearly a decade, Sebastian was looking forward to the day.

Well … perhaps t'was truer to say he held an anticipation that wasn't entirely bleak. For every grain of hope placed in the sack that was his fate—what few kernels he'd scraped loose from the path of an uncertain future—he carried a score more stones of regret. The bag remained torturously heavy.

Sebastian placed his bound hands on the railing, feeling the heavy plaster supporting them, and thought back to the recent revelation: *Isabel van Gelderan is bound to my brother, and Ean to her.*

Whoever could have imagined it?

He knew only a little about the woman who'd been the Citadel's High Mage—Raine's truth, he'd thought her dead from Dore's lunatic spoutings—yet Dore clearly feared her with a fervor bordering on insanity. This gave him some clue to the power she commanded, but her Healing told him more. His leg no longer ached, though the rains had lashed all through the night, and the scar on his cheek had faded to a thin line. Even had he been inclined to believe anything Dore said—which was quite the opposite—he would've noted Isabel's uncommon compassion in these acts.

But even more revelatory was Isabel's fourth strand working, which somehow intervened between Dore's compulsion and his own mind. Her miraculous intervention was allowing him a clarity of thought he hadn't experienced since N'ghorra—indeed, he'd forgotten what it felt like to think without the vitriolic specter of Dore Madden tainting his reason.

This freedom was worth any cost to him—well worth the numbing pain of *goracrosta*. He maintained his outward reserve, but he was reveling in the freedom to think his own thoughts, even for just a few days.

However ... through this clarity, Sebastian's intelligent mind made discomfiting connections, fitting the pieces that were Isabel and her brother Björn into a puzzle with his own brothers and the Sundragon Şrivas'rhakárakek. Thinking all of this through had kept him awake the last two nights—so, too, his guilt over his involvement in what was becoming a tragic farce, Dore's idea of comedy. Epiphany help anyone so ill-fated as to become the puppet in one of Dore's *tragedies*.

A knock on the door drew Sebastian's attention, and he turned to see a woman entering. Draped in a crimson sari banded in jeweled emerald and gold circles, and with a matching *chaadar* covering her dark hair, she seemed a *djinn* gliding through the room towards him, a vision born of magic.

She joined him on the balcony, pressed palms together and bowed with a smile. "*Sobh bekheir,* Sebastian, Prince of Dannym."

Sebastian caught his breath at this address.

Lowering her hands, she cast him an inquiring look. "Is something wrong?"

The shadow of a frown pinched Sebastian's brow. "I'm afraid your greeting took me off guard, my lady."

One corner of her mouth curled upwards as if to draw his gaze to the humor dancing in her blue eyes. "I merely said good morning. A curious offense."

Thinking of his two brothers and the shackles he now believed bound the three of them to oddly connected paths, Sebastian replied, "We are a curious brood, the princes of Dannym."

Her gaze swept him, and he thought he saw a glimmer of appreciation in the smile she smothered. "I am Ehsan, Princess of Kandori. I've come to assess the state of your healing for the Lady Isabel."

"Then I submit to your inspection, Princess." He turned to face her fully and held out both hands, bound in their linen gauze.

The smile danced in her eyes again. "This inspection will require a deeper delving than that, Prince Sebastian."

The barest tightening of his gaze conveyed his disconcertion at this repeated address. "Do you prey upon my sensitivities, princess?"

"Nay," she laughed, "merely your insecurities. Come." She waved him follow her back into the bedchamber and bade him sit upon a chair.

He did so, and she moved close to lay ringed fingers on his head. Looking up between her arms, his gaze followed the lines of jeweled bangles like vambraces stacked around her wrists, up across the sweep of her ornate sari, to a wide collar of precious stones that concealed the graceful line of her neck and hid the curve of collarbone that he would've found so alluring. He wondered if she slept in all that jewelry, and then he *wondered …*

She cast him a chastising look beneath one arched eyebrow—perfectly formed with just the slightest impertinence in the aspect of its angle. "And how did you sleep?"

He held her gaze. "I don't sleep, Princess."

She closed her eyes to sink into the Healer's rapport. "Then what do you do with the night?"

He sighed. "Most of the time, I just wait for it to be over."

She made her inspection of his life pattern in silence. Then she removed her hands and stepped back to look down gently upon him. "But now you've come to Kandori, and my brother and yours will see what can be done to bring peace to your dreams."

I would settle for any kind of dreams so long as they didn't reek of Dore Madden.

She held out her hands, palms open. "*Now* you may present your hands for ministration."

He noted the gold band of a Sormitáge ring on her thumb as he placed one heavy hand in both of hers. As she unwrapped the bandage, he asked, "Princess Ehsan?"

She looked up under her brows with the hint of a smile. "Prince Sebastian?" Then she laughed. "Why do you grimace so? It is your name."

He held her gaze. "How do you know the Lady Isabel?"

She lifted a slender shoulder in a dismissive shrug. "Long has my family served them."

"*Them.* You mean Isabel and Björn van Gelderan?"

She arched a brow as if to ask, *who else would I mean?*

He gave her a look as if to reply, *you tell me.*

She removed the last layer of gauze binding his hand to the plaster. "Lift your fingers."

He was almost afraid to do so, for the memory of their shattering remained so vivid as to impose the image upon his mended flesh and send pain shuddering through him again. But he wouldn't have her observe such cowardice, so he did as she required.

Each finger lifted cleanly, responding to his will, wholly restored. He clenched his jaw and looked back to her, but his eyes burned with gratitude as much as anger for the deed, never mind it was now undone. "Good as new." The words sounded nearly a curse.

She motioned him to place his other hand in her care, but she made no remark upon the bitter fury in his gaze.

When both hands were unwrapped and inspected, Ehsan pressed her palms together and bowed. "I will let the Lady Isabel know you're ready."

He stood and bowed to her in kind. "*Mamnoon*, Princess." *Thank you.*

Her eyes swept him again, and though he couldn't be sure, he thought they lingered for a heartbeat's pause at his linen pants hanging loosely from his hips. Then her blue eyes lifted and fastened on his, she gave him the slightest of nods, murmured, "*Kahesh mikonam*, Prince of Dannym," and departed.

Day had fully claimed the world by the time Isabel came to Sebastian's room carrying a bundle of folded clothes. Her arrival drew tension through him like knotted cord through wood, each node splintering as it passed. The moment was nigh when he would lose his hold on the peaceful reality of his own thoughts, and he already craved what would soon be lost again. More than he feared the *goracrosta's* numbing pain, he feared this ... this loss of himself.

"My lady." He came to his feet as she was shutting the door, "is there ... ?" But he bit back the words with an inward curse. Of course there was no other way, else they'd be following it. Why could he feel so courageous in the midst of a battle and so craven as he faced its beginning?

"*Sobh bekheir*, Prince of Dannym." Isabel nodded a hello. She wore a long tunic and pants cut in the Kandori style, and gold slippers carried her soundlessly as she moved across the room to set the clothes on his bed.

He watched her as she passed, for he had a boon to ask of her. "My lady, before you remove this binding of sanity ... if it's not too much to request, might I ... I would like to see Ean." *I just want to look upon him with my own eyes, just once with my own unadulterated eyes ... before he becomes my target again.*

"Ean wants this also," she replied gently, though he got the distinct impression she was responding to his unspoken thoughts. She turned to face him. "Sebastian, we're still looking for Ean's men. Have you any idea where Dore would've taken them?"

He pushed a hand through his black hair and sank down on the edge of his chair. "One of his castles I'd assume."

The barest tilting of her head revealed her surprise. "How many castles does Dore Madden have?"

A shadow crossed Sebastian's gaze. He tried only to answer her question without picturing the places themselves. "Many, my lady, and all of them pestilential warrens, breeding grounds for the ... vilest experimentation."

Isabel drew in her breath and let it out slowly. "Have you names? Locations?"

"I will give you a list—what few I know of." He moved to a near desk and quickly scratched out the names. Seeing his own hand drawing the quill across the page, however, brought a lump to his throat. Just days ago, he thought he'd be incapable of holding anything ever again.

As the ink was drying, he returned the quill to its stand. "Şrivas'rhakárakek." Sebastian looked up at her under his brow. "I released the Labyrinth upon him and he followed me across two nodes ... but he never ... he didn't bring harm to me." He searched her hidden gaze for some understanding of this mystery.

A slight smile hinted on her lips. "If you successfully released the Labyrinth on Rhakar, you took the point, Sebastian."

"Very well, my lady, but my question is, why did he follow me if not to seek retribution—to claim a point in return, as it were?" He blotted the paper and offered it to her, but as she made to take it from his fingers, he held it firm a moment longer. "Was he searching for Trell? Is that why he first came upon us in the Kutsamak?"

"Yes."

Sebastian dropped his gaze. Then it was as he'd suspected. The truth seared his heart with branding blame. Releasing the paper into her hand, Sebastian sank down on the chair behind the desk. A desperate guilt clenched him. "Does Rhakar search for Trell still?"

She nodded.

He leaned to rest elbows on his knees and pressed his head into his hands. After a painful silence in which he endured the flagellations of his own conscience, he said in a strained voice, "*I* sent him to his death."

Her brow lifted. "You cannot know Trell has reached the end of his path."

"I know Radov."

A moment later, he felt her hand brushing his hair, calling his eyes to meet her blindfolded gaze. How she saw him through the opaque cloth, Sebastian couldn't say, but he'd no doubt that she *saw* him, through and through.

Isabel stroked his hair gently. "You know Radov," she murmured, "but do you know Trell?"

Her words called to mind the image of his noble brother, humbled on his knees yet smiling enigmatically, promising another meeting even as Sebastian turned his back on him. Could Trell have known him on some level even as Sebastian had—instinctively, as if their shared blood sang a song of recognition?

Sebastian had been shattered by that meeting. Seeing Trell had splintered the walls of Dore's dam around his thoughts, opening a deluge of memories to make a mud of conflicting truths. But Trell had seemed confident, his composure unshakable.

Yes ... he supposed he did know enough of Trell to believe him capable of surviving even Radov's worst. After all, Sebastian had survived it, at least ... life imbued his body still. This was survival of a sort, though he loathed every moment of his current existence.

"You can reclaim your life," Isabel murmured, stroking his hair gently, "so long as the will to do so survives within you."

Her hand found his cheek, and he caught it suddenly and held it there, pressing his face into her palm. Her gentleness, her deep understanding ... she immobilized him. He felt a vessel stripped bare with nothing to offer but a ravaged hull. After floating for so long in the brackish hell where Dore had moored him, he almost couldn't bear the calm, clear waters of Isabel's compassion.

"Come, Sebastian." She touched his chin meaningfully, and though he dreaded it, he moved to his feet before her.

From her pocket, she withdrew two pieces of silver rope, intricately braided. Sebastian held out his hands, but despite his best efforts, they still shook. *Goracrosta* had been one of Dore's favorite torments. The things his twisted imagination had done with it ...

"I'm ready," he somewhat gasped.

She looped the first length around his wrist and pressed the two ends together, sealing it with a thought. "*Elae* permeates life—at all times, in all ways. *Goracrosta* cannot keep *elae* from flowing through you, it only restricts you from casting it outwards from yourself. We've chosen the lightest weave to spare you as much discomfort as possible." She released the ends, and he saw they'd reformed an unbroken cuff. It was lovely, in a horrible way, like having a viper coiled around his wrist.

And yet ... the pain wasn't as terrible as he remembered. Achingly cold, yes, but the stabbing pains, the fire in his flesh, the unrelenting agony that usually came with its touch ... these sensations were absent.

"One controls the effects and intensity of *goracrosta* through the pattern of its weave." Isabel wrapped the second silver viper around his other wrist and pinched the ends to seal them. "The Sorceresses of Vest intended the rope to be utilized thusly—providing infinite application—but most often it is kept in its basest form, for few outside of the Blackshard Circle know the weaves to control it."

He stared at her. "Someone *invented* this torturous stuff?"

"The Vestian Sorceresy believes pain holds the same value as pleasure." She released the second cuff and took up both of his hands. "The Quorum's magi created *goracrosta* to honor their gods; the Sorceresy perfected it so as to enslave them."

Isabel turned both of his wrists so the backs of his hands rested in hers. She caressed his open palms with her thumbs, and a soothing sensation spread along his arms, chasing away the *goracrosta's* bite.

His eyes flew to hers.

"It may last two turns of the hourglass," she offered, sounding apologetic, "but when it fades, any Healer can restore it. As you'll learn, the palace of Andorr has many Healers." She touched a hand to his cheek and gave him a sad smile. "Such suffering ..." She paused, and her silence conveyed everything words could not. "Such bravery in the face of it. You're among family now, Sebastian. None would add to your misery."

Sebastian dropped his gaze and turned away. "Isabel …"

How deeply her compassion pierced him! He'd endured the worst of Dore's demonic urges, but this … ironic to be so undone by a woman's gentle touch; ironic, too, that one binding imprisoned him while another set him free. His life had become a patchwork of ironies.

He gripped the back of an armchair while guilt gripped his soul. "Thank you for your encouragement," he murmured tightly, "but I don't deserve it."

"The only crime pinned to your soul, Sebastian val Lorian, is being born the son of a king and heir to a coveted throne. All else is Fate's doing."

He lifted her a look and growled, "Who will bear the guilt if Trell dies from Radov's hate? Cephrael won't carry it to his funeral bier."

"Don't deceive yourself, Sebastian." Isabel's tone pierced him with its censure. "Cephrael carries the weight of all."

Only with her stinging reprimand did he remember he wasn't merely speaking with his brother's beloved but with Epiphany's Prophet. Sebastian pushed a hand over his heart and bowed his head. "My lady, I beg your pardon."

"Granted. Come now, get dressed. Your brother awaits you—anxiously," and with this last, she darted a smile in his direction, and he knew he'd been forgiven.

Ean walked the wide, decorated halls of the palace of Andorr with Dareios on one side and the wildcat Babar loping soundlessly on the other. The cat seemed to have taken to his personality, or else to his scent, for she stayed close to him as they walked and had watched him with uncomfortable intensity all the day and the night before, claiming a worktable for her prime observation post while he and Dareios had studied in the latter's laboratory. Ean wasn't sure how he felt about being the subject of inspection of a predatory cat large enough to eat a small child.

With Dareios's assistance, Ean had flipped through books of fourth strand patterns, most of them in the compulsion category, memorizing their details. Dareios hoped this familiarity would help Ean in reconstructing the web of patterns Dore had used on Sebastian. Until Ean could view all of the patterns together in their polyhedron matrix and study their interrelationships, he had no chance of unworking the compulsion binding his brother. This dilemma consumed his thoughts.

And there were other factors to take into consideration, ones he never would've landed on without Dareios's expertise. Ean had let the truthreader work a Telling upon him, whereupon the Kandori prince had recalled Sebastian's mind as Ean had seen it—what few chances he'd had as he'd battled Sebastian in Tyr'kharta, and then later as he'd carried his brother from Dore's stronghold.

Dareios had seen patterns within patterns. The things he'd told Ean about these patterns had left him restless and disturbed.

"Darayavahush!" A woman's voice came sharply from behind them, further down the palace's wide corridor.

Babar made a low growl, and Dareios winced. Coming to a halt, he took a deep breath, smoothed his features into patience, and turned with a look of polite inquiry. "*Sobh bekheir*, mother-of-my-heart." He pressed palms together and blessed her with a bow.

The woman who approached looked to be in her middle years, but her age was likely misleading, for the tattoo of the *Khoda Panaheh* stood out on her forehead. She wore the tunic and loose pants called *shalwar kameez*, richly patterned in peacock colors, and a *chaadar* covered her long grey hair. Her earlobes sagged from the weight of ornamental earrings, while a jeweled collar of connected stones covered her neck and shoulders. Her bracelets nearly reached her elbows.

Dareios gave his mother a chaste kiss on the cheek. "You bless my palace with your sun, Mother."

"Of course." She received his affection with her dark eyes pinned on Ean. "Please introduce us, Darayavahush."

Dareios did, introducing his mother, Niga. Ean bowed and made the proper respects.

Niga looked back to her son. "You've been hiding here in the Moon Palace keeping your guests from us and denying them the splendor of the Sun Palace."

Ean didn't think more could be done to increase a palace's splendor short of building walls out of precious stones and mortaring them with diamond dust.

"Only in respect for their needs, mother," Dareios replied. "Their time is short."

She arched a brow. "And our wisdom is too long. Is this your meaning?"

"Why would that be my meaning?"

Her dark eyes flicked over him with a mother's venerable scrutiny. "Very well, your sisters and I will visit you here. The Moon Palace is not so large, nor so comfortable, but we will make do," and she added with a sweep of dark eyes over Ean, "in respect for your guests' needs."

Dareios placed a jeweled hand over his heart. "It would be my honor to host you and my sisters, mother-of-my-heart."

Ean admired his equanimity.

Niga seemed skeptical of it, but she gave her son the benefit of the doubt. "Look shortly for our arrival. It will be good for us to spend some time with Magdalena."

A shadow came to Dareios's eyes upon this pronouncement. "You will know her gratitude."

Niga nodded brusquely and departed.

Babar growled. Dareios frowned after her.

"Magdalena?"

Dareios darted a glance Ean's way. "My wife. She is ... unwell, else I would've introduced you." He turned and resumed their walk to meet Sebastian.

"I hope you won't think ill of me for keeping you isolated from my relatives," Dareios said then, eyeing Ean askance. "Kandori is an odd place, and we Haxamanis are an odd people. I have more women in my life than I care to deal with, all of whom, in their extreme, unparalleled wisdom, consider themselves in parity with me." He sighed. "I've been remarkably unsuccessful at dissuading them from this view. Would that some scripture might declare my innate superiority, but I've found nothing yet to prove it—at least," and he cast Ean a wry smile as he finished, "not anything they will accept."

Ean thought of his difficulty just dealing with Alyneri and felt a deep empathy for the Kandori prince. "And what of your daughters?"

"Ah, I married them off as expeditiously as possible. In that, at least, I had some say." He cast Ean a smile that faded with his wandering thoughts. "When Magdalena was well, she patrolled the harbors of my life, requiring the proper fees for entry and exit and shuffling my mother and sisters into appropriate berths with competence and grace. Alas ..."

Babar came up beside Dareios and placed her head within reach of his fingers. He stroked her with a pensive frown as they walked. "My wife is from Ma'hrkit. We met at the Sormitáge. My father would've preferred me to marry a woman of the sands, but the moment he met Magdalena, he understood my love for her." A contemplative smile came to his lips with these thoughts. "Still ... he warned me."

Ean turned him a look. "Of what?"

Dareios's expression reflected years of love as well as the regret that now limned those memories. "It's rare among my family to meet someone who hasn't worked the Pattern of Life. We're descended from immortal *drachwyr*. Following the example of our First Father and Mother and working the Pattern of Life ... this is considered both a duty and an honor for any heir in the royal lines." A tragic smile flickered across his face. "But my wife ... she doesn't trace her lineage back to dragons. Our stories and tales were meaningless to her—oh, she enjoyed them, but of their lessons, she took little heed. To the Kandori Adept, choosing immortality is a sacred calling, yet my wife would live but one lifetime. She says a dozen daughters and a scant seven decades with me is enough. Now she seeks the Returning ... and I will soon be without her."

"Dareios ... I'm so sorry."

He cast Ean a resigned look. "Thank you, but such kindness is unnecessary. Our Sire and First Father Náeb'nabdurin'náiir has been centuries without his beloved Amardad. Life goes on, in Kandori."

He gave Ean a considering look then. "But perhaps you'll understand why a man like me chooses to live elsewhere from the bulk of his relations, though I miss my father's regular counsel, I admit. But I've a wife who's determined to die and a mother who refuses to and eight sisters who would each have me as their lackey." He grimaced and shook his head. "No, the Moon Palace is a much safer place. If my brother Jair were alive, he'd be living here with me, make no mistake. Jair had no head for the politics of women."

Abruptly he frowned and looked to Ean. "But you ... you have some experience with daughters of the sand. My niece, Alyneri?"

Ean gave him a telling look. "If Alyneri is any example of Kandori women, then yes."

"And how is my niece?"

Ean shook his head. "I wish I knew. We separated in Rethynnea."

"I confess my own failure to keep appropriate tabs on my brother's daughter." Dareios stroked a triangular brow absently. "I was hoping the val Lorians could do better than we, but I cast no blame upon you for it. We Haxamanis are descended from *drachwyr*. We can't be expected to fit solidly into some mortal human mold."

Abruptly he pushed a hand through his short hair. "Ah, but my sisters use this excuse to try my patience endlessly, while my mother assumes it as the basis for the criticism of my many faults." Darting a rueful grin at Ean, he added, "and inversely her explanation for any irreconcilable fault of her own." He pressed palms together and raised them to shake at the heavens, adding a prayer in his own language.

They left the wide palace halls to proceed down a long colonnade passing between courtyards. The morning cast gilded light onto the pink marble paving stones and outlined the fluted columns' easternmost edge.

In his mind, Ean ran through the conversation they'd just had, and something occurred to him. "Dareios, why didn't your father marry off your sisters?"

Dareios was casting a solicitous look up at the clouds gathering above the palace. "The scriptures grant emancipation to Kandori Adepts who gain their ring. My sisters were all Sormitáge-trained Healers before my mother began considering proper husbands for them, and by then it was too late." He added with an irascible frown, "Doubtless this had been her plan all along. Now my sisters each have the right to choose their own husbands in their own time." He shot Ean a tormented look. "A few have. Most seem content to meddle in my affairs. Ah well ..." he exhaled a resigned sigh and shook his head. "At least my life isn't dull."

Ean was just pondering this idea when something flew out of the shadows with a whir. He drew back stiffly and simultaneously summoned *elae*, but the weapon rebounded off the force-field around Dareios's golden vest and went clattering across the marble tiles. Babar chased after it.

Ean held the fifth in a cloud of power, his senses on full alert, but Dareios just grinned and held out his hand to a form that materialized out of the shadows of a column. It was his cousin Bahman, smiling from ear to ear.

"Well done, Bahman!" Dareios shook his hand enthusiastically.

"It was the flux differential," Bahman said. "Just as you thought."

"Excellent, excellent." Dareios placed a hand on his cousin's shoulder and started them walking again. "Just a few more tests, and we'll be ready to make delivery. Let the Kagan's agent know His Highness will have it soon."

Bahman nodded and jogged off.

"Then ..." Ean scratched his temple and pointed to the gleaming gold framework extending beyond the rolled sleeves of Dareios's kurta. "The vest isn't for yourself?"

Dareios laughed. "Heavens! Why would anyone bother to assassinate me?"

Ean frowned, feeling suddenly foolish. "*Not* because you're heir to the realm's largest fortune?"

"Along with eight others from my generation?" He arched an amused brow. "And six from the generation before them, and we might continue counting all the way back to the fortune's eldest heir, Mirza Parviz, who some say still lives in a cave in the Dhahari. As the story goes, in his extreme old age he's actually become a dragon. But I can tell you, from what I last saw of him, this story likely stems from the state of his breath and the inhuman flatulence he can produce after a meal of falafel."

"I see," Ean murmured, though he really didn't.

Dareios clapped a hand on his shoulder. "My inheritance isn't riches, Ean, it's the life it allows me to lead."

"Then the fortune doesn't exist?

"Oh, it exists." Dareios gave an emphatic grunt. "Takes all of us to manage it, to be frank, but wealth has a way of making slaves of its heirs." He cast Ean a serious eye, as if probing Ean's understanding with his colorless gaze. "Some men spend their entire lives protecting their inheritance, coddling and hoarding it like rodents, never leaving their extensive grounds for fear of what will happen if they remove their eyes from the stonework. But a man who covets his own wealth pays a heady price, in the end. If there's one story all Kandori children know, it's that one."

Then he flashed a grin to banish the sobriety in this sentiment. "But of course, Kandori children know all of the stories, as any of them will happily prove if you dare to ask them and have days to spare ..."

That's when Ean saw Sebastian.

Sebastian gazed at his brother from across a sand court. Ean emerged from the shadows of a pink marble cloister while talking to a tall man of such dress and stature that he could only be a prince of Kandori.

Yet Ean ... amazingly, his littlest brother seemed well paired with the Kandori prince. The set of Ean's shoulders, the way he focused the whole of his being through the sharp point of his gaze. It made Sebastian smile to see that his brother had come into his own so potently. And to see Ean without the poison of Dore's compulsion … Sebastian drank it the vision greedily, thirstily.

Ean turned as if feeling Sebastian's eyes upon him. He spoke a word to the Kandori prince beside him, and then he came around the sand court towards Sebastian. Isabel touched Sebastian's arm, a gentle encouragement. Thus did he walk to meet his brother, for the first time in years looking upon him without eyes colored by a false enmity cruelly imposed.

As they both rounded the edge of the court and faced each other along its length, Ean extended his stride until he was nearly running. A flurry of uncertainty beset Sebastian as the distance shortened between them, but then Ean was pulling him into a fierce embrace. The strength in his little brother's arms was fueled by a desperation that echoed in Sebastian's own heart.

"They told us you were dead!" Ean voice sounded strained and tight. "Else father never would've ceased looking for you. But we never named you, Sebastian." The words sounded as choked as Sebastian felt in hearing them. "We never let you go."

Sebastian clutched his brother in silence, trusting his actions to convey what his voice could not. They clung to one another while clouds moved across the sky. Then Ean pulled away. His eyes were glassy, like Sebastian's own.

Unfortunately, tears wouldn't restore what had been taken from them, nor vanquish the terrors of the intervening years. Yet just looking upon his littlest brother, so grown, so … accomplished, it brought warmth to places in Sebastian's soul long frozen by apathy. Ean had their father's eyes—eyes all three brothers shared—but Ean's held a peculiar cast that only Patterning imparted. You saw it in a man when he knew he could change the shape of things made by his gods.

Sebastian was seeking words to greet Ean when his brother shifted a tense gaze to Isabel.

"There is something else you should know, Sebastian," she said then.

Sebastian reluctantly abandoned his study of his brother's face to give Isabel his attention. "The good news never ends." The words came out more bitterly than he'd intended, but one couldn't make sweetwater when all one had was salt.

"We have reason to believe now that Dore has planted specific patterns within your consciousness with destructive intent, snares and pitfalls intended to react to aggression aimed against the patterns of his compulsion."

"They're especially attuned to the fifth strand," a male voice added, and Sebastian turned to see the Kandori prince had joined them.

Ean opened his palm to the arriving prince and greeted him with his gaze. "This is Dareios, Sebastian. He's been helping us resolve how to free you."

Sebastian felt a growing unease. "But if you can't work the fifth …" He'd been counting on Ean being able to easily subdue him by binding him with the fifth.

A stream of curses ran through his head. He shifted his gaze back to Isabel; it would be but moments before she removed her pattern of intervention and thrust him back into mindless fury.

Sebastian looked around at the others. "Very well. How do we make this work?"

Isabel nodded to the Kandori. "Dareios has a plan."

Looking indecently pleased, Dareios clapped his hands together and rubbed them briskly. "We solve this in the way of our forebears, my fellow princes, as in times before man learned to tread the paths of magic."

Sebastian gazed at him blankly. "What way is that?"

Dareios's handsome face split in a grin. "Why, hand-to-hand combat!" He motioned to the sand court behind him.

Sebastian swept a dubious gaze over Ean's form. "We're going to *wrestle*?"

Ean shrugged.

"And you expect you'll pin me?"

The first hint of a smile shone in his brother's eyes. "I *am* spry."

"And I've got at least thirty pounds on you, little brother."

"Which will make you slow."

Sebastian grunted. "We'll see." He looked back to Isabel with skepticism pinned to every feature. "You expect this will work?"

"It is the best solution we've found. If you have another, Sebastian, please share it with us."

Sebastian ground his teeth. "No." He turned back to Ean. "And what if I pin you? What's to stop me from taking your life as Dore's will commands?"

"Isabel and I will do our best to prevent your bringing lasting harm to Ean," Dareios replied, "without equally bringing lasting harm to you ... or to ourselves."

Sebastian arched a leery brow. "Tell me one last time why Ean can't just read me now, while I'm—*Shade and darkness*, while I retain some *semblance* of myself?" He heard the raw despair in his own voice and stifled a grimace, grinding his teeth instead.

The other three exchanged glances, whereupon Isabel answered, "Many of the patterns Dore implanted lie dormant until invoked by circumstance."

"Unless they're actively in use," Ean added, himself sounding grim, "I won't be able to see them. If I can't reconstruct the entire matrix, I won't be able to free you—though I'll unwork anything I find, if I think it won't harm you. From what I've seen of your mind already, Dore interwove many strands of the fourth within your consciousness. I have to be able to find the fifth strand pattern that binds all the compulsion patterns together and holds them in place. To do this, I must be able to reconstruct the entire matrix."

Sebastian closed his eyes and focused all his will on trying to stifle his frustration and imminent fear—fear of harming his brother, and a *dreadful* fear of returning to that tortured imprisonment where he barely knew himself.

"So the plan," he began slowly, letting his gaze fall in turn on all assembled, "is to revert me to a raving lunatic, release that lunatic on my youngest brother, and simply *hope* I don't kill him before he finds the necessary patterns locked in my head?"

"You have the right of it, Sebastian." Isabel's tone brooked no more discussion. She lifted her blindfolded gaze to the heavens, clouding now with thunderheads. "Let this be done. The day grows darker by the second."

"Ne'er a truer word was spoken, my lady," Sebastian groused.

Dareios opened his arms. "Come, my princes."

They followed him onto the sand. Dareios stopped in the middle of the court and used his foot to carve a line in the earth. He motioned the brothers to either side of it. "If you will both remove your kurtas ..."

Sebastian drew the tunic over his head and handed it to Dareios. Ean did the same.

Sebastian studied his brother as he would any opponent then. He'd been right in estimating the differences in their frames. Whereas his younger brother sported the broad shoulders and smooth muscle of a man barely beyond his teens, Sebastian's frame had been thickened and hardened by his years in N'ghorra. They were both of them lean, however, both of a height with each other.

"Ready yourselves," Isabel murmured. The implication in her tone held more ominous portent than the storm brewing over their heads. Tension bound all four of the Adepts like a strung cord tightening with every breath. Then Sebastian felt a lifting, as if a cool breeze through his consciousness. In that moment, his soul screamed.

In the next, madness descended.

Ean stood bare-chested before his brother and contemplated the coming confrontation with mixed emotions. On the one hand, he yearned to have Sebastian restored to him and was willing to go to any extremes to achieve this. On the other, he didn't imagine the process was going to be pleasant for either of them.

"Ready yourselves," Isabel murmured.

Ean hardened his resolve, but still he flinched when he saw the darkness return to his brother's gaze—it was like watching Sebastian being erased before his very eyes.

With his next breath, Sebastian launched at him.

Ean ducked to meet him and they locked heads, arms and shoulders bracing as their feet made a fast circle in the sand. His brother had weight on his side, as he'd promised, but Ean's reach was longer. He dug in his feet to keep from being overpowered.

In those first moments, Sebastian tried repeatedly to shove him down, hands grappling for purchase on Ean's limbs. Ean just tried to maintain his locked position, shoulder to shoulder, and keep the bulk of his body out of reach—for he both needed and used every moment of contact to study his brother's mind. What he found horrified him all over again, for now he understood better each pattern's purpose.

Sebastian's mind hosted a honeycomb matrix of fourth strand compulsion patterns. Ean scanned each pattern in the matrix while also looking for the tell-tale symbology Dareios had been schooling into him. Here a pattern made to deny any thought Sebastian had if it ran counter to Dore's earlier compulsion; there one that told Sebastian he had no true thoughts of his own; one insisted any action he took without Dore's approval would be disastrous, and another enforced pain if he dared to disobey. One specifically sought positive emotions such as hope and twisted them into apathy. Still others imposed brutal illness if he failed to comply. And in every pattern appeared the central combination that ordered Sebastian to obey Dore in all things.

Ean felt sick. This wasn't merely compulsion forcing a man to do things against his will, this was *nullification* of his will entirely. To be so imprisoned day in and out, unending ... he could barely comprehend such a hell.

Suddenly Sebastian growled and dropped a hand to grab for Ean's leg. Ean's foot slipped in the sand, and he went down on one knee. Sebastian was at him instantly, using the full force of his weight to bear Ean to the ground. Ean struggled to regain both feet, straining to the full extent of his power. He dared not work the fifth, not even to fuel his own strength, not with Sebastian so close and those patterns in his head set to react against the fifth.

With a grunt of effort, Ean made it back to his feet. The brawl would've been exciting if there wasn't such desperation in it. If his brother got a firm hold on his neck, he could break it before anyone could stop him—he was strong enough to do so. Worse was how murderously he pursued this effort, his gaze veiled with a darkness that seemed almost inhuman.

Ean sensed that Sebastian was fighting the compulsion too—for all the good it did him. Yet as he grabbed hold around Sebastian's neck again and their eyes met, Ean saw the glimmer of his brother suffering beneath this overwhelming subjugation of his will. The moment broke his heart.

Thunder sounded above them, and a chill rain started falling, skewing their hold on each other. Ean attacked his brother with renewed determination.

He slipped free of Sebastian's hold and darted low to grab his waist. Sebastian twisted, and Ean's arms slid down his hips to lock around his leg instead, knocking him to hands and knees. Sebastian scrambled on all fours, but Ean climbed up his leg and caught his hips again. They fell then, spinning in the sand, and Ean at last pinned his brother beneath him. He launched fully into his mind while Sebastian growled and cursed and swore to end him in brutal ways, but Ean hardly heard him now for the whipping wind and the roaring of *elae* in his ears.

Ean spun his mind around Dore's matrix, memorizing it for Dareios's later inspection and study, but as he began a second pass in search of that fifth strand pattern of binding, he spotted a distant pattern disconnected from the primary compulsion. Like a thread caught upon a thorn, only a tiny bit of it fluttered free of the blackness hiding it. Ean latched onto this thread with alacrity. It took but the breath of a thought to begin its unraveling.

Beneath him, Sebastian stilled abruptly.

Thinking little of the thread he'd pulled, Ean sought again the pattern of the fifth that held the matrix together. Deep he pushed his mind into his brother's captive consciousness, fast he sent his mental gaze swirling in and out of the matrix. So engrossed was he that when Sebastian began writhing beneath him, Ean hardly registered his outcry. Yet no matter how deeply he probed, how many singular paths he followed—tracing each and every pattern in the matrix from beginning to end—Ean couldn't find the only pattern he truly sought.

Some part of him heard others shouting, but he was so intent. He knew he had to be close to finding it! So he pushed harder. His intention became a spear working its way deeper into the meat of Sebastian's consciousness, until—

A tidal force repelled Ean from Sebastian's mind and likewise propelled his body into the air. Ean flipped head over heels and landed in a backwards sprawl on a cushion of the fifth, his head just inches from the stone steps, stunned nearly to the point of blacking out.

It took many seconds to right himself. As his breath returned and he realized he was still floating in midair, he shook off his daze and blinked to focus on the form of Isabel across the court. She stood with one palm facing him and her staff pointed at the marble beneath his back, holding him just shy of disaster while the storm's rising wind tore at her clothing.

Then the truth finally registered. A sick feeling beset Ean, and he looked to his eldest brother to find him curled in a fetal ball in the damp sand.

Some part of Sebastian was aware enough to realize that Dore's compulsion felt different now. Since last he'd faced Ean in combat, his brother had unworked a host of patterns binding his thoughts. He'd believed these patterns had bound only his memories, but he saw now even with what dim awareness he possessed that having those memories restored had also restored a part of himself.

This did not make it easier to resist Dore's compulsion. Verily, resistance was impossible—his body would merely continue to comply despite any thoughts to the contrary. It was almost worse having this conscious awareness, watching as if a distant spectator, helpless while his body betrayed him, while traitorous hands sought his brother's neck.

The part of Sebastian that recalled himself recognized Ean's presence in his mind, even as it realized the absence of the usual necrotic taint that was Dore's awareness, which forever tasted of bile. Then he remembered the *goracrosta* and felt a surge of gratitude for its bite—if only it had some ability to dull the compulsive entity now running his body. Alas, he watched himself attempt to capitalize on his brother's misstep and force Ean to the ground, still just as helpless to stop this dramatization as Ean apparently was.

Thunder sounded, and rain opened upon the world. Sebastian's hands grew slippery, while the *goracrosta's* icy sting intensified. The demon that had hold of his mind ignored this pain like it ignored everything else—everything but the command to slay Ean val Lorian and stand over his body until it grew cold in death.

Then, the unthinkable: Ean slipped free of his grasp and dove for his hips. The real Sebastian watched with bated breath, hardly daring hope his brother could pin his demon-possessed body, yet in but a few swift moves, he'd done just that.

Ean speared into his mind with fervor then, and though Sebastian felt this intrusion painfully, yet he welcomed it. The entity that had hold of his body scrambled and swore and promised a litany of painful deaths to his dear youngest brother, but Sebastian, lurking in the shadows of his own mind, held the anguished hope Ean would yet succeed.

He felt Ean circling like a hawk in his mind, felt the heat of his inspection and his probing mental gaze, and then he felt Ean pause … and something else, like a sudden tugging at a loose thread. Sebastian tried to tell him to leave that thread alone—that it was knotted and hidden for a reason. Yet Ean worried at it until he had it firmly in his grasp, and then he pulled.

Pain flared like the sun.

For a moment Sebastian saw only vivid, agonizing light. Then the pattern of occlusion dissolved like a dam made of mud, and the floodgates of memory opened. Sebastian thought at first he was the water washing through his mind, for the rage on its rushing tide stole his breath. But as the water continued pouring forth in a deluge of vivid recall, Sebastian realized he was the dam being slowly unmade, his fragile foundations obliterated by the raging waters of true memory.

And the story the waters brought back to him …

Long Sebastian had believed that Dore bound him before leaving N'ghorra. As the first of his true memory returned, however, Sebastian saw this for a lie and understood—Dore wouldn't have denied himself the joy he experienced in subjugating a free man to his will.

But it was learning the *way* this had been done that so shattered Sebastian's hold on reality. He experienced all over again the horror, the agony and the unparalleled shame of those early weeks of his bondage. For Dore had not merely bound him in those months of captivity, he had *broken* him.

Delighting in every moment, he'd held Sebastian with straps of the fifth and raped him repeatedly, until he'd felt the man's domination from soul to loins.

No words could convey the horror of this rape. Reliving all those months, *re-experiencing* that agony, even the sensory pain of it coming back in brutal force ... Knowing now what had been done to him, it nearly broke Sebastian all over again. His soul screamed.

The entity running Sebastian's body cried out with the pain of these memories, but the little part of himself who remembered it too nearly, curled into a ball and willed itself into death.

THIRTY

"What is bred in the bone will not leave the flesh."

–An old Nadori proverb

VIERNAN HAL'JAITAR MADE his way through the secret passages of the Shamshir'im feeling unnerved. He'd just left a meeting with his prince and the Prophet, and the latter's allusions during their meeting had immensely unsettled him.

Hal'Jaitar felt certain that the Prophet knew what had become of his pet truthreader Kjieran van Stone—and possibly Kedar and all the rest as well— while Viernan remained mired in the mystery. Too, the Prophet seemed to have some vendetta against him personally, which made Viernan fear what Bethamin had learned of Kjieran's experiences in Tal'Shira.

Had the truthreader told him of Viernan's attempts to kill him?

It chafed on the Consul that Bethamin's spies might tread deeper paths among the realm's secrets, or that Bethamin's information network might extend further than Viernan's own. Had the Prophet been merely mortal, the Consul might've handled this inconvenience in a multitude of ways. But the Prophet Bethamin wore his inhumanity in every motion, gesture and turn of his gaze, and hal'Jaitar would've been a fool not to fear him—or at least not to fear the power he so indiscriminately wielded.

The Consul misliked uncertainty in dealing with an enemy.

He clearly didn't understand enough of Bethamin's origins, but he sensed that attempting to learn more would elevate their mutual disregard to open conflict. The kingdom would suffer then—or rather, Radov's rule and the power this offered hal'Jaitar would suffer—so he dared not provoke the man.

But it infuriated him no end to dangle at the Prophet's mercy.

Reaching the Shamshir'im compound, he swept inside his offices to find another unwelcome guest.

"Father." Taliah rose from her chair.

Of course she wore that harlot's gown. In exchange for a king's ransom, the Vestian Sorceresy had promised to make a wielder of his useless daughter but had returned a whore in her place—*Huhktu's ashen bones*, he despised those damnable witches.

He seated himself behind his desk and speared Taliah with a scrutinizing gaze. She might at least properly clothe herself in the presence of her own father, but she'd traded honor for a witch's gimlet eye and unpropitious power. "You have news of the prince?"

"Yes, father." She crossed her arms self-consciously across her chest and dropped her gaze. "I've assembled all of the pieces of his past."

He sat back in his chair. "Very well. Proceed."

So she began.

While Taliah spoke of early truths he already knew, hal'Jaitar ruminated on the ill manner in which she'd gained this information.

An inquisitor exhibited a clean sort of honor in bleeding a man for his secrets with iron and steel and flame. Every man who stepped upon the field of battle expected this end should he fall into enemy hands. Since time immemorial, men had used coarse and bloody torments to wage a hard form of justice—intemerate justice, inasmuch as both sides engaged in similar practices.

But to wield *elae* as torture ... hal'Jaitar found this a disgraceful affront to all wielders of proper training. Not that he wouldn't resort to such means when circumstances required, only that he would never have sullied his own hands in the sordid practice.

In any case, Taliah had gotten the entire fantastical tale from the recalcitrant prince, beginning with Naiadithine's intervention in the Fire Sea and ending at last with the ambush that brought Trell finally back to M'Nador, full circle.

Yet in having the full picture, hal'Jaitar felt only more disturbed. The prince was clearly favored not only of Naiadithine but also of the Emir's Mage and his Sundragons.

Dore's Saldarians had reported a Sundragon tracking their party through the Kutsamak and all the way to Doane. Had he been, in fact, seeking Trell val Lorian?

Viernan admitted a certain disconcertion at this idea; it seemed a logical conclusion, but one that held unsettling ramifications. Viernan knew well of the Sundragon Şrivas'rhakárakek. He would not easily give up his search for Trell val Lorian, and thanks to Raliax's bungling ineptitude, that search would lead Rhakar to M'Nador ... to Tal'Shira ... and directly to hal'Jaitar.

Viernan hissed at this prospect.

And what of the Emir's Mage and *his* apparent interest in Trell?

Hal'Jaitar had only heard rumors, but rumors often held a shard of truth. If Björn van Gelderan was indeed masquerading as the Emir's Mage ... well, Viernan already had his hands full dealing with Radov's war against the Emir.

He had no intention of fomenting new contention with immortal wielders and drawing their gazes directly to himself in the process.

The Consul knew he'd best rid himself of the prince forthwith. Still, he feared drawing Cephrael's eye by killing the man himself.

He looked back to Taliah, who stood with downcast eyes waiting for her orders. "We should be done with him."

She drew in her breath sharply. "*Father* …" She dared lift her eyes to meet his.

Viernan's daggered gaze swept her in challenge. "You disagree?"

"It's only …" she dropped her eyes again. "Respectfully, father, the prince sent his Healer to a *sa'reyth* where the Sundragons are known to reside. By now they must know he's in our possession. If you claim his life … will you not also earn their wrath?"

Hal'Jaitar shifted in his chair. "He cannot stay here." Not with the Prophet lurking about. Not as a lure for Sundragons or—Jai'Gar forbid—Björn van Gelderan himself.

Taliah stared at him with palpable anticipation. "Then … ?"

"Take him to Darroyhan."

Her face lifted with delight. "And he's mine to do with as I will?"

Viernan eyed her with barely veiled disgust. "So long as he never lives another day of his own free will, I don't care what you do with him."

Taliah reclaimed her solemn demeanor at once, but she couldn't conceal the gleam in her eyes as she bowed and departed.

Well and good.

Hal'Jaitar sat back in his chair and folded hands in his lap. That had ended more providently than he'd envisioned. He would let Taliah deal with Śrivas'rhakárakek, Cephrael and all the rest of them. Fate was her problem now.

THIRTY-ONE

"A man is insecure upon his path until he has honed

his instincts on the whetstone of choice."

–Isabel van Gelderan, Epiphany's Prophet

HAVING BEEN MANY times to Calgaryn, a city of respectable size and beauty, and to Rimaldi, which surpassed even the Cairs with its ornate, gilded palaces and elaborate parks, Tanis was expecting something of similar scale from Faroqhar.

Morning had barely dawned as they closed in on their destination, and a still sleepy-eyed Tanis positioned himself as close to the bow as possible so as to have the first view. Yet as the coastline began enlarging before them, starting with the two snow-capped peaks that Tanis at first thought were clouds and growing into a mountainous landscape covered with buildings that clung to the steep hills, he began to see that he'd somewhat underestimated the Sacred City.

And the view kept expanding.

They passed four large marinas sporting forests of masts like bleached trees before they reached Iaspian Bay and the really big ships.

"Valdaccio to starboard!" called the ship's first mate, pointing toward the so-named harbor, and the crew hit the decks to make ready to take them into port. Tanis had never seen so many ships in his life. He wondered if all of the craft that ever sailed the waterways of Alorin were not at this moment moored or berthed in Iaspian Bay.

They sailed past galleys from the southern islands, Free Cities' caravels, huge Bemothi galleons and crimson-hulled carracks out of Avatar. The captain called for the oars as they entered a mammoth channel, and the sailors began stowing the sails while below-decks the rowing team kept a steady cadence.

Closer inland, a massive, crenellated wall blocked the channel. As their ship approached the wall, an iron portcullis rose between the two guard towers. The

Imperial Red Guard manned the walls while steely-eyed archers peered down. The guards appeared to salute Tanis as the ship sailed underneath, and it took the lad a heartbeat's startled pause before he realized that the High Lord was standing just behind him.

Beyond these high walls and their imposing towers lay the imperial fleet. Tanis had never seen one of the Agasi *dregondar* warships, but Fynn had spoken of them, and they looked every bit as formidable as the royal cousin had described.

Finally they neared a majestic structure of white marble that dwarfed even the temples of Rethynnea's Avenue of the Gods. From the colonnaded façade, a long, wide staircase led down to a jetty, where a row of imperial banners flapped in the breeze.

Two dozen Red Guard awaited there in glistening splendor. Their silver armor sparkled in the bright morning sun, while their sanguine cloaks tossed and snapped in the wind. Halfway up the steps, two men lounged with legs outstretched. They looked to be dicing.

As the ship was maneuvering towards the jetty, Phaedor came to stand on Tanis's left. The zanthyr took in the Red Guards awaiting them and arched a brow above a shadowy half-smile. "Reinforcements, Your Grace?"

The High Lord looked a little pained. "Moral support, I rather imagine. Valentina recalls well the returning state of the last ship we sent in uninvited search of you." He nodded towards a soldier at the front of the ranks, a dark-haired officer. "As well does Captain di Alema, who made the journey."

Phaedor's cool-eyed gaze fell upon the captain. "Di Alema struggles with darker dreams now than any I gave him."

Marius cast him a sharp look. Clearly the High Lord knew exactly what dark dreams the zanthyr was referring to. "Indeed," Marius murmured after a pause. "The very reason I braved the unknown hazards of Vesper Bay in search of you."

Tanis caught a sardonic undertone in his words, but the rapid images his troubled thoughts conveyed were frighteningly incongruous with this levity. Tanis knew enough of Marius di L'Arlesé by then to understand that the wielder let not his thoughts be read save by his own accord. He wanted them to see these horrifying things.

The zanthyr held the High Lord's gaze. "And the currents?"

Marius pursed his lips in a tight line. "I would know what your sight reveals, for I can make no sense of them."

"What *do* you see?"

The High Lord shook his head bleakly. "Darkness. Shadows, where none ought to prey. Like and unlike *deyjiin's* taint in the dark days of Malachai. Whatever its source, it emerges from Kjvngherad and rides the tides to Faroqhar and beyond, a permanent stain."

The zanthyr eyed him circumspectly. "You believe the Danes plan a revolt."

"I do."

"No doubt you are correct."

Marius exhaled a frustrated sigh. "Mayhap *you* can convince the Empress. Without proof, Valentina will take no action."

"Her Sight reveals nothing?"

Marius gave him a heated look. "Her Sight is as clouded as the currents. We are both of us blinded."

"*Ah ...*"

In that single moment, Phaedor had the whole of it—Tanis saw it in the slight tilt of his head, in the sudden quiet of his gaze, in the way his eyes narrowed with introspection and then focused sharply with understanding.

As if sensing Tanis's perception of these things, the zanthyr placed a heavy hand on the lad's shoulder. Something about the gesture seemed unhappily portentous.

"I would know what you—" Marius began, but in that moment the ship came alongside the dock and crewmen started scrambling to secure the mooring lines.

Soon the zanthyr was guiding Tanis to disembark. They headed down the gangplank and collected at the base of the walkway while the High Lord spoke with Captain di Alema and the crew began unloading Tanis's trunks.

The zanthyr noticed the lad watching the two men dicing on the steps and murmured into his ear, "They are the High Lord's men—his great-nephews, though centuries distant. The tall one is Vincenzé and the shorter Giancarlo. You can trust them even as Marius does."

Tanis thought it an odd thing for the zanthyr to say, and he didn't like the implication—why should he need to trust anyone with Phaedor at his side? Still, the thrill of anticipation filled Tanis too fully for such thoughts to pierce and hold, and he visually explored his new surroundings with an appreciative gaze.

First, he noticed how massive the buildings of this port were compared to other cities, how each marble facade—with its countless columns, friezes and statues all swirled together with innumerable quatrefoils—was so ornate that one's attention could easily drown in its detail. How men had swarmed from nowhere and everywhere to attend the Empress's ship. How the Red Guard stood at such immobile attention with their uniforms sparkling in the sun. How blue the sky seemed, how large the trees, and how green the hills behind the white buildings.

The High Lord concluded his briefing with the captain and turned their way. "Phaedor," Marius approached with swift steps, "the Empress left word for you to attend her upon arrival." His tone betrayed the faintest hint of apprehension.

Tanis suspected that all the days they'd spent aboard ship together had been in anticipation of this moment—or perhaps in denial of it—when the truth of intentions must be faced. The lad joined the High Lord in looking expectantly to the zanthyr, himself feeling the mounting tension that suddenly extended in taut threads among those listening. Even the men upon the steps had paused their game and were now alert and watchful.

Phaedor replied in his deep purr-growl, "I will attend the Empress," to which Marius visibly relaxed, and Vincenzé elbowed Giancarlo in the ribs and flashed a victorious grin.

"But," added the zanthyr, the single word eliciting a distressed look of alarm from the High Lord, "I must take Tanis first to the Sormitáge and see him properly enrolled."

Marius looked dismayed at the idea of such a delay. He cleared his throat. "With your permission, I would take the boy under my protection in your absence—that is, if you trust me to see to his welfare."

The zanthyr made a show of pondering this idea, but Tanis knew him too well to be fooled by the show—Phaedor had been expecting this outcome all along. Tanis couldn't be certain, but he got the idea that the zanthyr had just accomplished some kind of coup. Certainly his gaze glinted with triumph.

"Well, lad," Phaedor posed, "do you accept the High Lord's protection?"

Tanis was so embroiled in trying to figure out just what the zanthyr was up to that he almost forgot to answer.

"Tanis?"

"Oh—*oh*. Yes, of course. I'm honored, Your Grace."

"I will give you a moment then." Marius gave them a polite nod and walked to speak with his men.

Tanis felt a little confused as he watched him go. Something was happening here—that much he recognized, but he lacked the understanding to pair all the pieces with their proper opposites. When he looked back to the zanthyr, it struck him that they were parting, and a grave unease flooded him.

"My lord ... why do I feel like this is goodbye?"

Phaedor regarded him gently. "You must walk your path, Tanis. We have ever been upon it."

"But ..." Tanis felt a too-familiar sensation in his chest. "But what about you? Must you now walk yours without me?"

"I'll be waiting when you return. But come." He motioned them towards Marius and his men. "The High Lord awaits you, as the Empress awaits me."

When they rejoined Marius, with a confused Tanis now wondering at the zanthyr's cryptic comment—*when I return from where?*—the High Lord placed a hand on Tanis's shoulder and told Phaedor, "I will see him fairly tested and placed according to his skill."

"I would expect no less of you, Marius di L'Arlesé," Phaedor replied. Then he vanished.

Giancarlo hissed an oath, and Marius spun his head in search, but Tanis merely gazed upon the space the zanthyr had just vacated feeling the loss of his companionship as a sudden ache in his heart. "He does that a lot," the lad remarked, feeling suddenly small and unreasonably abandoned.

Marius turned him a faintly exasperated look. "I suppose … he's gone to the Empress?"

"He gave you his word, Your Grace." In Tanis's estimation, nothing more need be said.

The High Lord seemed to agree. "Then we shall keep to ours as well." He motioned to his men. "Tanis, this is Vincenzé."

Tall and broad-shouldered, Vincenzé bowed with a flourish of one arm and flashed a quick smile beneath bright blue eyes.

"And Giancarlo." Giancarlo stood shorter and stockier, with a cleft in his chin and mischief in his colorless gaze. Both were olive-skinned and somewhat rakishly dressed. Tanis liked them immediately.

"To the Sormitáge then," said the High Lord, and thus did they depart.

The next hour became a blur of grand edifices, soaring passages of gilt and marble, and more languages than Tanis's inquisitive ears could absorb. Yet the lad could no longer find that sense of excitement he'd first experienced upon making port.

Parting with the zanthyr had left him feeling unbalanced. It wasn't that he feared so much the indefinite path before him or how long their parting would be; rather he sensed that he was well and truly on his own. The zanthyr's many recent cryptic hints and warnings haunted his thoughts, especially the way Phaedor had looked at him when Tanis had cavalierly mentioned giving away his new dagger. He got the distinct impression that if he fell into the soup with another of Pelas's brothers, Phaedor wouldn't be there to pull him out of the cauldron.

Complicating the issue, Tanis wasn't at all sure he even wanted to enroll in the Sormitáge—it wasn't as if the zanthyr had *asked* him—and he certainly wouldn't have so readily agreed if he'd known it would mean leaving Phaedor.

Tanis could hear his new companions thinking about him … wondering, conjecturing. Tanis knew their questions—even had they not been obvious in Vincenzé and Giancarlo's expressions, their thoughts were loud enough: *Who is this boy? What makes him so special?* And the clenching question that even Marius di L'Arlesé couldn't quite conceal from him: *Why is Björn van Gelderan's zanthyr so invested in this boy's welfare?*

To get his mind off Phaedor's departure, not to mention Vincenzé's incessant mental theorizing, which wasn't always complimentary, Tanis asked the High Lord, who walked beside him, "Your Grace, what is involved in enrollment at the Sormitáge?"

Marius cast him a pensive eye. "Invocation Trials have just ended, so we'll request a special sitting for you."

"Forgive me, Your Grace, but I know nothing of these trials."

"Phaedor spoke nothing to you of Invocation?"

"He must've forgotten to mention it."

Marius really frowned at him then. "The trials are held to determine an Adept's level of ability, Tanis. Only then can you be placed in studies befitting your skill. With occasional exception, new students are typically assigned to Docian status, that is 'yoked to the honest study of *elae.*' Such Adepts wear the Docian collar until they pass the Catenaré Invocation Trials, usually a span of five to eight years."

"Eight years," Tanis murmured. It seemed a grisly length of time to spend memorizing his Truths.

As they neared a circle of tall pillars, Giancarlo tapped Tanis on the arm. "Ever crossed a *soglia're?*"

"No, sir, what is it?"

"A node made into a bridge," Vincenzé said, coming up on Tanis's other side.

"But one even you can cross, *cucciolo.*" Giancarlo mussed Tanis's hair.

"You sure landed a golden ticket, lad," Vincenzé observed with a grin.

"How do you mean?"

"Being in the High Lord's protection?" Giancarlo kissed his fingers and flung them to the sky. "There's no greater personage to open doors and opportunities. You could go anywhere and do anything in the Empire beneath his name."

Oh ... Tanis turned forward again, and his eyes became rounder as understanding dawned. No wonder the zanthyr had been radiating such triumph. It only made Tanis miss him more.

Then they were crossing through a series of tall statues to reach the middle of the court, whereupon they traveled three miles and arrived at their destination in a single step.

Emerging off the *soglia're,* Tanis couldn't help but stare up at the Sormitáge's grand edifice. The sun flamed the limestone, and the many statues decorating the pediment seemed ready to come alive in its glow. Beneath the mammoth portico that dominated the building's façade, pockets of students hung about, sitting or lounging on the long flight of fifty steps leading up to the entrance.

As soon as one of them spotted the High Lord, the rest seemed to instantly follow—like a silent signal passed among migrating birds. Tanis watched a stream of whispers travel speedily through the crowd of students, so that while the closest were still bowing and murmuring polite acknowledgements, the news of the High Lord's arrival had already flown into the university building.

By the time they reached the top of the torturous flight of steps, a tall, slender man in a violet robe was waiting for them. "High Lord di L'Arlesé." He gave a stately bow. "You honor us yet again. How may I serve you this day?"

"I've come to enroll a new student, Liam." Marius motioned Tanis in front of him and placed his hands on both shoulders. "Tanis, this is Liam van Gheller, Endoge of the Sormitáge."

The Endoge looked Tanis over in one quick sweep of colorless eyes. As he returned his gaze to the High Lord, the barest hint of a frown furrowed his aging brow. "Let us attend to your needs in my chambers, Your Grace. If you will permit me?" and he motioned them inside.

They followed the Endoge into an immense atrium. The entire place was awash with frescoes, cornices and elaborate sculptures, but even this display of opulence didn't prepare Tanis for the dome they next passed beneath, or the endless passage the dome opened onto. Wider even than Calgaryn Palace's famed Boulevard, its immense ceiling appeared as a river of color and gold extending into infinity.

Everyone they passed—be they student, docent or maestro—scattered like birds to make way, despite there being room enough for an entire military procession to pass abreast. Tanis was grateful for Marius's notoriety, though, for with all eyes pinned to the High Lord, no one in the least noticed the nameless boy walking in his shadow.

As Marius walked at the Endoge's side, his thoughts vacillated between the mystery of Tanis's origins and the still-unresolved disappearances of Sormitáge Adepts, of which Malin van Drexel's remained the most pressingly disturbing. Though the forum lacked privacy, necessity and his recent absence urged him to speak.

"Liam, how proceeds the investigation?"

The Endoge cast him a troubled look. "The interrogation of the maestros continues with astonishing discretion, Your Grace, doubtless aided by the fact that all who are read are truthbound to silence about their Questioning before departing the interrogation room."

"I knew you would be most adept at handling the matter, Liam."

"Thank you, Your Grace. Unfortunately, nothing has yet come to light, save some minor indiscretions—and some not so minor," he added with an intemperate frown, "but we're attending to each accordingly. As much as I shudder to imagine one of our own behind these disappearances, it pains me almost more to continue forth with no hint of the cause."

Marius cast him a furtive eye and asked in an even lower voice, "And the missing volume from the Archives?"

The Endoge shook his head, his lips pursed tightly.

Marius worked the muscles of his jaw and gazed forward again. He knew he had to be missing some important clue in all of this—but what could it be?

As they were climbing a flight of wide marble stairs, the Endoge broke their mutual silence by offering, "In regards to our earlier conversation, High Lord, and your interest in any exceptional students, there is another to which I might call your attention. He's recently gained his Nodefinder's ring at only fifteen and shows extraordinary promise."

"To be certain. Tell me of him."

"The boy is Felix di Sarcova della Buonara."

"*Another* Sarcova son?"

"The youngest of the nine—this one is from the fourth wife, I believe." The Endoge pressed a finger thoughtfully against his lips. "Buonara ... yes, number four. The boy is quite naturally talented. He also seems to have a penchant for finding his way into places he doesn't belong—extreme even for an adolescent Nodefinder—no offense to Your Grace."

The High Lord arched a wry brow. "I recall a number of transgressions while exploring my craft as a youth, Liam. An absence of good judgment and common sense *is* a natural failing of second strand sons."

"Nor are these qualities lacking merely in second stranders, Your Grace," Liam admitted, "though I fear Felix's failings may extend beyond his innate nature. That is, I suspect the boy of a lack of self-discipline when faced with certain possessions of value that do not, strictly speaking, belong to him."

Marius gave him a hard look. "A thief?"

The Endoge sighed. "We have as yet been unable to prove he's stolen anything from within the *many* restricted spaces where he's been caught." He sounded disappointed. "But this only makes me more suspicious. Why risk expulsion if not for the purpose of thievery?"

Marius could think of quite a few reasons, but he said only, "You've truthread him, of course."

"The boy has an uncommon ability to vacate his mind completely."

Marius arched brows at the Endoge's uncharacteristically dispirited tone and suppressed a smile. "I must meet this boy."

"Pray keep him in your sights, Your Grace." Liam gave him a weary look of caution. "For all his ability, I'm not sure we shall be able to recommend him to the Guild."

"I'm astonished to hear such despondency from you, Liam. What has the boy done to so erode your faith in the efficacy of this 'perfect educational system,' if you will forgive my quoting you?"

"Near-perfect, Your Grace," the Endoge corrected. Then he sighed. "I remain in the deepest mystery as to how the Sarcova boy is finding his way about the university's restricted spaces. Three weeks ago, Maestro Helsing came upon Felix in his wine cellar, which is trace-sealed and bound with the fifth—a bit excessive for a wine cellar, I'll admit. Nevertheless, the point is that the boy found his way inside."

Marius turned him an amused look. "What was his explanation?"

"He said he fell in."

"Did he?"

"As impossible as it sounded," Liam remarked sourly, "I couldn't find another truth within his consciousness to contradict his statement."

They turned down another long passage wide enough for fifteen horses to walk abreast and proceeded beneath its ceiling of luminous art. "A week ago, the Imperial Curator caught Felix after midnight in the Ancient Weapons wing of the *Primär Insamling*. The cases were undisturbed, else I would've had to expel him instead of imposing a fine and penance of fifty hours in service."

Marius chuckled.

The Endoge continued restlessly, "Not a day later, Felix disrupted the entire Physical and Theoretical Sciences wing when he appeared atop the dome of the astrological observatory across the quad—"

"On *top* of the dome, did you say?"

"Veritably, Your Grace," Liam grumbled sourly. He speared Marius with a piercing look. "The boy even has the audacity to claim to have walked the highest levels of Kha-Faelling Tower."

Marius barked a surprised laugh before he could stop himself.

The Endoge wore a look of withering malcontent. "Even *I* haven't seen the highest levels of Kha-Faelling. The nodes to those levels have been twisted for centuries."

"Yet you truthread him and uncovered … ?"

"I read him within an inch of his life," scowled the Endoge, leaving little question as to the result of the interrogation. "And then, just yesterday, Literato N'abranaacht found the boy snooping in his own locked office and nearly took his head off with a saber before he realized the boy was a student and thus need be accorded a certain measure of restraint."

"N'abranaacht," Marius murmured, his faint Calabrian accent sounding the name *NAH-brah-nokt*. "I don't think I've met the literato. What's his specialty?"

"Oh, he's become quite the talk of late. He's an Arcane Scholar recently returned from Myacene with some … well let's say some *interesting* patterns and artifacts that have created quite a stir. The Order of Sobra Scholars is reviewing them as we speak."

"Intriguing. I'd be interested in a report when they've finished their study of his findings."

"Most assuredly. I should be pleased to arrange a meeting with the literato if you so desire it."

"At a later time, perhaps, Liam."

The Endoge gave a courteous nod of acquiescence. "Of course, Your Grace."

The Endoge's office spanned two stories, the main floor of which contained an enormous library. Tanis had never seen such a collection of ancient-looking books, with many set behind glass cases or otherwise on protected display. Upon arrival, the Endoge, Marius and Giancarlo immediately vanished up a curving staircase to the second level and the Endoge's private study, leaving Tanis with Vincenzé.

Feeling a bit out of sorts—said feeling being compounded by the anticipation of whatever testing Invocation would require—Tanis lowered himself onto a long, upholstered bench and pressed his hands between his knees.

"Nervous?" Vincenzé sat down beside Tanis and gave the lad a grin.

Tanis turned him a considering look. Vincenzé was exceptionally vocal in his thoughts—so vocal that Tanis had begun to wonder if the man was testing him somehow, as if he wanted Tanis to hear him. Tanis saw something of the character of a devious cat in Vincenzé, and the lad was chary of being swatted with a claw. "Should I be?"

Vincenzé flashed a wider grin. "That depends."

"On what?"

"On a lot of things."

Tanis frowned at him. "Like what?"

"Well ..." he gave him a sly smile, "you know ... students don't usually get admitted outside of Invocation. The maestros want their pupils raised in straight little rows, all neat and tidy like a line of graves. Admitting a student outside of Invocation disturbs their morbid sense of order."

"That would be fine with me," Tanis muttered. He would just as soon have returned to the zanthyr's side—if only 'his path' would divert in that unlikely direction.

Vincenzé arched brows. "You're not hoping to gain your rings, truthreader?"

Tanis gave him a level look. "I don't think a few gold rings make the wielder, do you?"

The man flashed another grin, but there was agreement in it for all it was taunting as well. Vincenzé leaned back on one elbow and extended long legs out before him. "So tell me, young Tanis, how did you come to travel with the zanthyr Phaedor?"

With the question, Tanis felt a sudden compulsion to tell Vincenzé his entire life story—all about how the zanthyr had brought him to Fersthaven and how he was bound to him—when all Tanis would have intended to speak about was their quest with Prince Ean.

A sudden suspicion took root on the heels of this, and Tanis darted a glance at Vincenzé's hands. His left sported a large, engraved carnelian ring that might've been a family heirloom, but Tanis saw that upon his right hand, Vincenzé wore an unmistakable gold band on each of his middle three fingers.

Tanis met his gaze neutrally then. "Are you testing me, sir?"

Vincenzé barked a laugh. "So you know the taste of compulsion, do you? And do you know, too, how much it tells me that you could so easily resist it?"

"Not as much as you hoped it would." Tanis easily plucked that thought from Vincenzé's mind.

Vincenzé laughed louder that time. "Well noted!" His blue eyes looked Tanis up and down again with appreciation.

"You're a Nodefinder by birth, are you not, sir?"

Vincenzé nodded.

"And you've worked the Pattern of Life?"

This time the man looked genuinely surprised. "Right again. How … ?"

"Your thoughts are very loud, sir. It doesn't take much skill to hear them."

Vincenzé regarded him admiringly. "Even so? What other secrets have you gleaned from my outspoken skull?"

"Only that you're quite willing to use whatever skills with the lifeforce you possess to gain some answers out of the 'zanthyr's boy.'" Privately, Tanis still suspected that the man was purposefully shoving such thoughts his way.

Vincenzé pursed lips as he gazed at Tanis. "No wonder you don't trust me, eh? I suppose that's a hazard of poking around in a man's head—"

"I wasn't poking!" Tanis protested, glaring at him.

"—without the context of his perspective to frame them," Vincenzé finished. He sat up and gazed at Tanis with his dark brows furrowed. "My honest apologies, Tanis. Whatever else I might've intended here, I didn't mean to make myself a threat in your eyes. The High Lord is most curious about you—which curiosity you must admit is more than justified—and it's long been my duty to ferret out such answers on his behalf."

Turning back to gaze at his knees, Tanis let some of the tension melt out of his shoulders, but he still felt on edge—not from Vincenzé's prying so much as from some other discordant tone that seemed to have no source, only permeated every shadow and crevice of the room—of the entire university, now that he thought upon it.

"What did you mean when you said the High Lord's curiosity is more than justified?" Tanis had sensed something in the man's thoughts upon that statement, some underlying truth not quite voiced.

Vincenzé leaned back on his elbows again. "You know … the valley."

Tanis turned to look at him. "I don't know what you mean."

"You told the High Lord you were born here, in Agasan, but he construed that you meant the valley where his ship made port." Vincenzé arched a brow. "Did you not mean it so?"

Tanis shrugged. He hadn't meant to say it at all. "It's true. I was born at the Palazzo di Adonnai." No use denying it now.

"*Precisamente.*" Vincenzé cast him a knowing look, cocking his head slightly sideways to emphasize his point. "It's quite mysterious then, your being here. *Capisci?*"

Tanis still didn't understand him. "Why is that mysterious?"

"Surely you've heard the stories of the Valley of Adonnai? Tales of that place are like ghost stories to children back home in Caladria. It's legendary."

The statement had an ominous ring to it. Tanis had no idea what to make of this news. "What … do they say?"

"Well, to be clear, most people don't believe the valley exists, and as far as anyone outside of the imperial family is concerned, it doesn't. Lots of stories claim that people go in search of the valley and never come back. Some say if you sail too close to its coastline, Wildling sirens will pull you onto the rocks. Others claim the valley appears and vanishes with the seasons. Most of the stories say something about magic, that you can only find it if you know where it is … that sort of nonsense." He grinned. "You know how stories are, but some parts must be true, *eh?*"

Tanis sort of stared at him. "Do the stories say anything about … about who owns the valley?"

Vincenzé angled him a knowing look. "It doesn't exist, remember?" Then he frowned. "But someone must own it, *eh?* Or once did, I suppose. Doubtless the High Lord would know if the lands were ever associated with a House or titles. As Adept bloodlines have died out over the centuries, so have their holdings often been lost. The Empire has shrunk in more than just its Adept population."

Vincenzé sat forward and rested elbows on his knees. "And then there's the zanthyr Phaedor," he muttered, unheeding of Tanis's dismay at all of this information, for the wielder was consumed now by his own thoughts. "I can't tell you all the stories I've heard about *that* creature. Admittedly, most people wouldn't know his name, but those within the Empress's counsel, such as the High Lord, know it a mite too well."

"Phaedor is a force within the pattern," Tanis said.

Vincenzé looked at him sharply. Then he stared in silence long enough to make the lad uncomfortable. Finally he scratched his head. "You do know who that creature serves, don't you?"

Tanis understood quite well who Phaedor served, and he didn't think Vincenzé knew the half of it. But he didn't want to talk about the zanthyr, for in his over-sensitive state, it only made him sad.

Fortunately, Giancarlo at that moment came skipping down the stairs, and Vincenzé looked up to address him. "*Yeh cugino, che y'presa coso lungo?*" *What's taking so long?*

"The Endoge is talking to the High Lord about the van Drexels." Giancarlo threw himself into an armchair across from the long bench where Tanis and Vincenzé were sitting. "The family is claiming restitution from the Sormitáge and demanding that all of the maestros be truthread about Malin's disappearance."

"Who is Malin?" Tanis asked.

"He's a Maritus truthreader," Vincenzé muttered absently while frowning at his cousin.

"What happened to him?" Tanis asked.

Giancarlo turned his dark eyes to Tanis. "He went missing."

"The third Adept in a series of recent disappearances," Vincenzé added. "His family claims he was kidnapped."

"As does his roommate, Felix di Sarcova. He says Malin was heavily involved in researching for his thesis and never would've left of his own volition. The family says the same."

"*Was* he kidnapped?" Tanis asked.

Giancarlo shrugged. "Who can say? He vanished without a trace—no evidence, no ransom, nothing on the currents, just ... *nothing.*"

"See, that's the real problem." Vincenzé turned to Tanis. "Malin had his Maritus bracelet."

Tanis gave him a blank look.

Giancarlo laughed. "Until you've gained your ring, truthreader, you'll either be cuffed, braceleted or collared."

"Every collar, cuff and bracelet are fashioned of *elae* with multiple patterns ingrained within their metal. An Adept can't leave the university grounds without triggering alerts in a variety of places."

"Not even on the nodes?" Tanis asked.

Vincenzé shook his head. "The nodes into the Sormitáge are twisted, lad. You'd have to be at least a fourth-ring Nodefinder to have hope of unraveling them—*Sancto Spirito*, you'd practically need to be the Great Master himself."

"Not if the Nodefinder was born with a variant trait," Tanis pointed out.

Both of the men gave him a powerful look at this, and Tanis realized the idea hadn't occurred to them.

As if to assuage the unease Tanis's remark had engendered, Vincenzé said, "Students with variant traits are required to register with the Office of Recondite Scholars."

While Giancarlo murmured, "Any working of that sort would surely have appeared on the currents. The High Lord would've seen something."

"Only if he was looking for it," Tanis pointed out.

"If not the High Lord then the Order," Giancarlo returned, apparently unwilling to believe that an idea posited by a fifteen-year-old boy had not already been explored by his betters.

To Tanis, news of missing Adepts seemed a grim herald. The lad had too much acquaintance with Adept kidnappings—Ascendants plucking them unwitting from their villages, Pelas abducting Healers for his own dark desires, and even Loghain, who claimed traitors in the First Lord's name.

Yet, Tanis didn't think Malin's disappearance was related to any of these causes, which indicated yet another predator on the prowl for members of an already dying race. Tanis alone of those in the room knew how a body might travel in a way that left no trace on the currents, but the names of those who might accomplish such an act comprised a short list.

The lad rubbed at one eye and looked off into the library, feeling uneasy.

"What is it?" Vincenzé leveled his bright blue eyes on Tanis, moving his head as if scanning Tanis's thoughts with the motion. "You know something, *eh*? I can see it in your face."

Tanis turned him a beleaguered look. The man was too perceptive by far. "I know disrelated things, but *you* know more than you've said. Who is the prisoner in the Tower?"

Vincenzé's thoughts had been very loud in proclaiming the existence of this unnamed abomination—visions that closely echoed those the High Lord had so thoughtfully gifted to them while coming into port. Only Vincenzé's thoughts, in contrast, hinted at some relation to the missing Malin van Drexel.

"How does he know about the prisoner?" Giancarlo booted his cousin in the shin.

Vincenzé turned a glare at his cousin to a frown at Tanis instead. "He claims he's not in my head, but I think he can't tell the difference."

"You should guard your thoughts," Tanis grumbled.

"I *do*, truthreader." Vincenzé gave him a telling look. "But you push past them."

"I'm not *pushing*—"

"Never mind." Vincenzé held up his hand with a slight smile. "It tells me something of you, *eh*? So I am pleased. To your question: the man was an Adept. Something was done to him, something very foul."

"*Lui un lunatico.*" Giancarlo made wild hand motions and waggled his head.

"Crazy," Vincenzé agreed, "but frightfully strong despite looking like he ought to be on his deathbed. He was relentlessly truthread, but his mind is gone."

"Gone?" A sudden chill skittered along Tanis's spine, an unwelcome reminder of a dark, cold room and the hopelessly destroyed mind of a boy named Piper. "What do you mean ... gone?"

"The Empress said he couldn't even remember his own name."

"He just kept howling indecipherable syllables," Giancarlo added.

Tanis swallowed. He suddenly had that feeling again ... the one that had first gripped him when he watched Pelas sitting in a café in Rethynnea, enveloped in his personal darkness.

"What were they?" Tanis hoped beyond hope it wasn't what he imagined. "What did the words sound like?"

"*Shalabaaaaaah,*" yowled Giancarlo suddenly in a near-perfect mimicry of the madman. "*Shalabanaaaaaaaaah!*"

"Thank you, Giancarlo," came the High Lord's voice unexpectedly, "for that incredibly accurate recounting."

"High Lord," Giancarlo said with an accommodating nod and a grin.

"Shalabana ..." Tanis repeated slowly. He lifted troubled eyes to the High Lord.

Marius frowned at him. "What have you, Tanis youth?"

Tanis swallowed. "Nothing, Your Grace." He managed a meager smile. "Just a memory of someone I'd rather forget."

"Very well then. The Endoge has decided to conduct your Invocation personally to better expedite your admission. He will see you now."

"Yes, Your Grace." Tanis pushed to his feet and walked with heavy steps of apprehension up the stone stairs to the Endoge's private study.

THIRTY-TWO

"The peril shadowing every talent is the lure of playing with it for pride."
—Liam van Gheller, Endoge of the Sormitáge

THE ENDOGE WAS seated behind an ornate desk of bleached alder when Tanis entered his office. The older man looked up and waved the lad on inside. The Endoge's colorless eyes appeared wise but unreadable. Without his floppy cap, his bald pate shone in the lamplight. Being also clean-shaven, his grey, tufted eyebrows stuck out rather dramatically.

"Welcome, Tanis." The Endoge stood and walked around to greet him with an outstretched hand.

Tanis clasped hands with him nervously.

"You have a firm grip. Always a good beginning." The Endoge motioned him towards a grouping of armchairs near a long window. "The High Lord tells me you've been training with the zanthyr Phaedor."

Tanis wondered how many other zanthyrs these people knew that they need always refer to Phaedor by name, but he answered, "Yes, sir. He is my guardian."

"When you're finished with your schooling here, you won't need protecting. Come, take a seat."

Tanis slowly sank down onto the edge of the indicated armchair while the Endoge relaxed into one directly across from him.

"I imagine you're a little apprehensive right now."

Tanis nodded.

"You needn't be. All Adepts are admitted here providing they have proper sponsorship."

Sponsorship? Tanis immediately fretted this news.

"With the High Lord Marius di L'Arlesé as your sponsor, of course, you needn't fear for acceptance." The Endoge settled into a more comfortable position in his chair. "Invocation is merely our means of ensuring an Adept is placed accurately according to his skill. It wouldn't do to put an upper level student into classes for those who can barely sense the lifeforce, nor the latter into an applied lecture on the Esoterics." He eyed Tanis inquisitively at this, ostensibly gauging whether or not Tanis knew of the aforementioned Laws.

"Yes, sir," Tanis said when he realized the Endoge was waiting for some kind of response.

"With this in mind, you and I may proceed with the same understanding: that hoping to *impress* me is of no value; providing the answer you *think* I might desire is unproductive; seeking in any way to *escape* an answer by subterfuge is not only futile but also detrimental. The value of Invocation is in discovering how much you know and how much you *don't* know. Do you agree to follow these stipulations of Invocation?"

"Yes, sir." Tanis felt like he was back in classes with Master o'Reith, who always gave the impression that Tanis had done everything wrong ever before they began a lesson.

"And how old are you?"

"Ten and five, sir."

"How long have you been training in your gift?"

"I—" But Tanis realized he couldn't actually answer that question. There was a truth within it that he couldn't speak, couldn't find within his own understanding. So he answered instead, because it was all he could manage, "I started training with Vitriam o'Reith almost two years ago, sir."

"Very well." The Endoge clasped hands in his lap. "I find it singularly unhelpful to ask a student what he *thinks* he knows. Invariably the student thinks he knows far more than he actually does. We will therefore begin with a test that tells me much of your previous study, for the task encompasses many skills. Stand before me now, Tanis."

Tanis did so.

"You may place your hand in the proper position upon my brow. I will think of a memory, and I would have you tell me everything within it that you see. Begin."

Tanis placed his hand in the truthreader's hold, careful to position his fingers properly across the Endoge's brow, and entered rapport with the older man.

Immediately he saw a scene unfolding before him. At first the images were confusing, for he encountered many layers of memory and had to sort through them all. But his mother had taught him how to do this, so he set to work.

First he worked to find the time and place the Endoge was remembering—it was a memory of a time he was truthreading a boy.

Then Tanis found the images belonging to the boy within that same memory.

Next Tanis had to sort out the memory belonging to the woman who the boy was telling the Endoge about, as the boy recounted *his* memory of a story the woman told him.

All of these remembered images were jumbled and mixed, and the sorting process involved assigning the many pictures to the right person's thoughts.

Tanis's mother had taught him how to sift through a layered memory. He hadn't had to work with quite so many layers before, but the technique remained the same. Thus, with meticulous inspection, Tanis eventually got all of the images properly sorted, and the vision became clear: in the memory, the Endoge was truthreading a boy, who in turn was recalling a conversation with his mother.

"Tell me what you see from this memory, Tanis youth," the Endoge murmured, eyes closed.

Tanis took a deep breath. "From your thoughts in this memory, sir, I can tell the student had caused some recent trouble. You were hoping to find out more about him to better understand him. He submitted to a Telling. One of the moments you contacted during the Telling included a conversation that had taken place between the boy and his mother, where his mother laughingly claimed that his father was an avieth."

"Is there more to this Telling?"

Tanis considered this question.

His mother had taught him that truth has a certain resonance. If one looked for the resonance, a truth could be read even in the latent memory of another. Theoretically, and if the memory was clear enough, Tanis ought to be able to read not only the boy's thoughts about what his mother was telling him, but the truth or falsehood in her words at the time she spoke them. Though the boy himself wouldn't have been able to recognize a truth or a lie simply by its resonance, nevertheless the resonance of truth—or lack thereof—would still have been perceived, even did it pass into his consciousness beneath his awareness at the time.

The nature of the fourth strand made such latent readings possible. All thoughts have force—energy—associated with them. This energy is captured in the memory, and with it is also captured all of the images and perceptions associated with the initial experience.

When a truthreader contacts a memory of another, all of the original perceptions captured in that memory become the truthreader's own. The actual energy is not transferred—Tanis's mother had tried to explain how a transference of energy would require doubling the existing energy, none of which Tanis truly understood—yet the memory *was* copied in the sense that it became the truthreader's experience as well.

Tanis didn't actually understand the physics behind all of this, and his mother had informed him that the magical laws describing latent memories were contained in the Esoterics—which automatically told Tanis that they were hopelessly incomprehensible—but he knew enough to *do* the working, even if he couldn't explain its process fully.

To answer the Endoge's question, Tanis concentrated and looked deeper into the scene, using his own mind to read the boy's memory newly instead of depending on the Endoge's memory of it, because the Endoge's recollection was colored by *his* conclusions.

This was both like and yet unlike choosing a different way to cross a stream. The stream still flowed the same course, like the memory, but on one side of the stream, the memory appeared as seen through the filter of the Endoge's thoughts; on the other side was the actual memory.

Tanis had to find the actual memory.

It took all of the skill his mother had ingrained in him to find where the path branched—that smallest of cuts in the mental fabric where the Endoge's recollection diverted from the actual memory transferred from the boy.

Instead of following the Endoge's side of the memory stream then, Tanis instead crossed to the other. This was not so easily done. The actual memory was deeply wrapped within layers of energy, all of which had to be transcended. Tanis at times had to make his mind both hard enough to pierce these veils and yet diffuse enough to seep through them without rending the slightest thread.

The Endoge had been correct in stating that this was a test of *all* of his skill.

When Tanis at last found the true memory—the boy's own memory, not the Endoge's recollection of it—everything came into brilliant color.

The lad hadn't realized the images he was seeing were dulled until that moment, but he couldn't mistake the change. He explored the scene then for himself, and he looked for the truth in the mother's words. And then he knew.

"There is more, sir," Tanis remarked at last, hearing his own voice as if from far away. "The student thinks his mother is lying, but she believes it to be the truth. She knows her son won't believe her, however, and is using this as a means of hiding behind the truth, as it were. Yet it *isn't* true, in the end," Tanis added, almost sadly, for it would be a fine thing to have been fathered by an avieth.

Tanis retreated from rapport then and removed his hand from the Endoge's forehead. The older man opened his colorless eyes, and though he was very good at guarding his thoughts, there was certainly a shadow within his flinty gaze that might've been astonishment.

"Tell me, Tanis," said the Endoge as Tanis sat back down across from him, "with whom did you study?"

"With Vitriam o'Reith in Dannym, sir, and the Fourth Vestal for a time in Rethynnea—"

"The Fourth Vestal?" He stared at Tanis. "This is no small thing, to have studied directly with Raine D'Lacourte."

"Yes sir," Tanis murmured.

"And have you any other teachers you failed to mention before?"

"Well … most of my training came from my mother."

"She was a truthreader?"

"Yes, sir."

"Very well. Have you studied your Truths?"

"Yes, sir."

"All of them?"

"Yes, sir."

The Endoge gave him a considering look. "You do know that most truthreaders enrolled here do not complete their initial study of the Truths until they've gained their Catenaré cuff?"

"No, sir. I didn't know that."

"Very well. You're clearly schooled in Readings and Tellings. What about truth-bindings?"

"Yes."

"Compulsion?"

Tanis swallowed. "Yes."

The Endoge drew back with a frown. "And have you studied the Laws of Patterning?"

"Some of them."

"Indeed?" he asked skeptically. "Which some?"

"The first, the fifth, the twelfth, the sixth, the fifteenth … a few more."

"In that order?" the Endoge asked, eyeing him intently.

"Yes."

"And the Esoterics?"

"Only up through the eleventh, and only in theory."

"And what is the Eleventh Esoteric?"

"'A wielder is limited by what he can envision himself envisioning,'" Tanis quoted.

"And the Fifth Esoteric?" the Endoge pressed, looking dubious despite obviously knowing that Tanis spoke the truth in all things.

"'Absolute Being must equal the scope of a wielder's concept of effect,'" Tanis said at once.

"Which means?"

"It builds from the earlier Esoterics, sir." Tanis worked hard to remember his mother's complicated lessons—there was a reason the Esoterics were so-named. "The First Esoteric states that Absolute Being is the entire concept of actuality, meaning that Absolute Being is form, material composition and position in space as modified by time. The Second Esoteric tells us that patterns lie within the boundaries of Absolute Being. The Fifth Esoteric seeks to further clarify that a wielder must envision the entirety of Absolute Being to properly effect change."

"And what does that *mean*?"

Tanis broke into a rueful smile. "I think it means, for example, that if you hope to change a lump of rock into a chair, you have to be able to conceive of everything that the rock *is*, and where it is, and how it interacts with the fabric of space-time surrounding it, as well as everything that the chair would be—it's entire form—and how it would interact with the surrounding space." Then he remembered something important that his mother had explained many times, and he hastily added, "But the Esoterics deal with things conceptually, sir; that is, you can't sit there trying to change a rock into a chair and think through all of this linearly—you have to grasp the entire concept at once."

"Remarkable." The Endoge regarded Tanis for a long time in silence then, and the lad couldn't tell if he was pleased or unhappy or fretful or disgruntled—but obviously many thoughts were swirling behind his colorless eyes.

Suddenly he seemed to rouse from these deep thoughts. He sat forward and held out his hand, palm up. "I would that you might show me these lessons of yours."

Tanis eyed him uncertainly. "Which lessons, sir?"

"The ones where you learned such esoteric skills," the Endoge replied with a meaningful smile.

Tanis had already noticed that the Endoge wore three rings on his fourth finger and more than likely didn't need the contact to read Tanis's thoughts; that he'd offered his hand was simple courtesy.

There was no avoiding it, so the lad took the older man's hand that the Endoge might enter rapport with him.

"Now ..." the man murmured, closing his eyes even as Tanis shut his, "show me these lessons."

Tanis felt the Endoge's firm hold upon his hand, but the older man's skill with the lifeforce was so deft that Tanis perceived only the merest whisper of his presence in his mind—that the lad noticed it at all was only because he was looking for it.

Dutifully, Tanis sent his attention back to the first of his mother's lessons, to that day when she appeared beside him so unexpectedly. From there, he let his mind drift forward, touching briefly upon each subsequent lesson. He didn't realize how many of them there had been, but somehow he'd packed more than a year's worth of lessons into a single month.

No sooner had he reached the final lesson on timeweaving, however, than something released—like a clasp upon a treasure chest—and suddenly images were pouring out, the golden memories of *other* lessons that hadn't yet been triggered into recollection by a pattern upon his wall. Now they flooded into Tanis's mind, unrelenting, and within every image came the sure knowledge of an entire lesson.

And there were *hundreds* of such lessons. *Years* of lessons.

Tanis felt deluged by them, swamped and flooded ... a tiny doll riding the wave's tumbling crest, only just remaining afloat by some mere chance of Fate.

And throughout, the whisper-thin presence that was the Endoge drank it all in.

When the deluge had exhausted itself, each lesson finding its place within the whole of Tanis's understanding—completely without his conscious thought, denying all explanation and leaving the boy reeling—the Endoge's presence in his mind became a blinding light seeking further answers.

Still struggling to comprehend the experience, Tanis bobbed helplessly on the waves of his own confusion while the Endoge pried into the private rooms of his mind. Yet when the man sought to open the golden wood box that contained the treasured letter, Tanis started back to awareness and slammed the door upon his thoughts with such force that the Endoge actually recoiled.

The lad understood the older truthreader's angry response; he observed as the Endoge beat repeatedly upon the door of his inner mind. But the lad wouldn't allow him into that room again, no matter how intense the fire of the Endoge's determination; no matter how blunt the force of his battering skill. Tanis sheltered behind a door of granite as solid as the zanthyr's own, and there was no chinking it, much less getting past it.

Either with indignation or the fervent insistence of his curiosity, the Endoge became ever more furious to see what lay behind that door. Finally, when Tanis could sense the man tiring and knew it would become dangerous for him to persist, the lad cast the Endoge the thought, *Sir, the knowledge behind this door is not for you or anyone else to know. It is my own, and my mother's, and you haven't been granted the grace of this truth.*

The Endoge stilled at this, though his mental presence remained strong. And then, abruptly, he withdrew and released Tanis's hand.

The lad opened his eyes and shook out his fingers; he looked uncertainly at the older man.

Sweat soaked the collar of the Endoge's robe, and his bald pate glistened with it. He sat in his chair wearing a gritty expression. Tanis could see that their brief mental battle had disturbed him greatly.

Abruptly he pushed to his feet and walked to a sideboard, where he poured himself a glass of wine and drank it swiftly down. Turning to Tanis, he said in a low voice, "I apologize, young man. I saw something within your memories ..." He looked into the empty bowl of his goblet and shook his head. "I should not have pressed you so. It is quite a deplorable display of ill manners. I'm grateful that your skill allowed for self-protection." Looking up again, he added regretfully, "It isn't often that I'm denied."

Tanis summoned his composure from its place of hiding beneath his chair. "What's next, sir? Have you more tests for me?"

The Endoge gave him an unlikely grimace. "Lord and the Lady, no." Suddenly he pinned Tanis with his gaze and asked with a passionate curiosity, "Tanis youth, who is your mother?"

Tanis felt the threads of a Telling binding him, forcing him to answer, but he had no answer to give—at least not the answer the Endoge was seeking. "All I know is that my father called her Renaii."

The threads of the Telling resonated such that they both felt the truth in this.

The Endoge dropped his gaze and looked away.

"Is there some problem, Liam?"

Tanis turned to look around the back of his chair and found the High Lord standing in the doorway. He seemed every bit the elegant image of royalty in his thigh-length dove-grey coat with his hair swept back just so. And his thoughts radiated such concern for Tanis that in that moment the boy realized if he couldn't have the zanthyr's sure companionship, the protection of Marius di L'Arlesé was not a poor substitute.

"Tanis," said the Endoge, looking pained, "might you wait for the High Lord downstairs?"

"Of course, sir." Tanis nodded to Marius, and the High Lord moved aside to let him pass.

"What happened?" Marius's demand came fiercely the moment Tanis was out of earshot. "When the currents went awry—"

"I bear the fault, Your Grace." Liam poured himself another goblet of wine and arched a rueful brow before partaking of it. "I apologized to the boy."

"*You* apologized?" Marius turned a look over his shoulder toward the stairwell Tanis had vanished down. "I feared the boy had done something—"

"Oh, he did," Liam assured him with sudden vigor. He wandered back to his chair, sat down and exhaled heavily. "I pressed him while in rapport, Your Grace ... and he shut me out utterly."

Marius stared at him. "A boy of fifteen?"

"Verily." Liam's gaze strayed toward the unlit hearth as he sipped his wine. After a moment he asked, "Are you aware, Your Grace, of the Order of Emridala?"

"A vague recollection. They were engaged in experimentation with the first strand."

"Not just the first. Will you join me, Your Grace?" The Endoge indicated a chair across from him, and Marius moved to take it. "The Emridala operated on the premise that a young mind learns more rapidly than an aged one. Members of the Order started instructing their youth at eight months of age."

"Valentina began Princess Nadia's training at the age of two years," Marius noted, frowning thoughtfully at the comparison. "What results from the Emridala studies? I cannot recall."

"They discovered that while information might be placed in the mind of a youth, the child seemed to lose access to it after a certain age. It was as though a curtain were pulled across all such lessons. Even when contacted again with the help of a Reading, the lessons remained garbled, perhaps stunted by the lack of language at the time it had been taught. Inevitably, in the rare case when such lessons *were* remembered with clarity, the child was incapable of application."

"So they failed," Marius concluded.

"The Emridala were unsuccessful." Liam lifted his colorless eyes to meet the High Lord's. "Tanis's mother was not." He raised a hand in response to Marius's arched brows. "I make no implication that the child is a product of the Emridala, Your Grace. I only relate that Tanis was similarly taught from the earliest of ages. Yet where the Emridala failed, the lad's mother succeeded in spades."

Marius gave him a sharp look. "How successful?"

Liam arched brows as if to reply, *you have no idea.* "The boy seems to have a firmer grasp upon the initial Esoterics than some of the first-ring truthreaders I've known. He worked a Telling and pulled a latent truth from a *third-hand* memory." The Endoge looked in bemusement at the High Lord. "I'm in the unusual position, Your Grace, of needing to place Tanis with the Devoveré Thesis students, simply because I'm afraid it would draw too much attention to the boy if I let him test immediately for his ring."

Marius sat back in his chair and stared wordlessly at Liam. After a moment, he inquired, "Who is the boy's mother—surely you recognized her?"

Liam shook his head. "That's the strangest part of all. Tanis clearly recalls his mother in their lessons—this knowledge resonates in his recollection. Yet when I looked in upon those same lessons in his memory, I saw no one."

Marius rested his chin in hand in utter fascination.

Still clearly shaken by the experience, Liam pinned Marius with a telling look and repeated, "He *shut me out,* Your Grace. In my enthusiasm to understand how the lad's mother had so skillfully taught him, I sought too deeply into his secrets. In that moment, he imposed a barrier that I couldn't break, even using every craft available to me."

Marius glanced to the three rings Liam wore on his fourth finger and felt a thrill of excitement pass through him. It had been centuries since an Adept was born with such ability—could it mean the Balance was finally shifting?

No wonder the zanthyr has such an interest in the lad. If only …

Marius finally realized what man Tanis reminded him of. He, too, had been a vibrant talent. Marius searched his memory for another who might make the same connection; alas, he could think of no one in Faroqhar who had known the man.

Except the zanthyr. But no assistance would be found in that quarter, to be certain.

Even so … at best, Tanis could only be a distant relation; yet if that man had any extant bloodline at all, Marius would pay dearly to know of it.

Shelving these thoughts for a later time, the High Lord pushed to his feet.

"I promised to see Tanis fully enrolled and the hour grows late, Liam. In which Hall will you place him?"

The Endoge stood as well. "The younger Maritus and Devoverés reside in Chresten Hall, Your Grace, only ..."

"Yes?"

The Endoge frowned. "I'm suddenly of the unwelcome recollection that there are no rooms available in Chresten, unless ..." his colorless eyes flicked to the High Lord's. "I hesitate even to ask, but would Your Grace be averse to placing Tanis in Malin van Drexel's room? I'm afraid his is the only empty bed in Chresten."

Malin van Drexel.

Marius's every sense crawled with a sudden sense of kismet.

He knew that when the *angiel* Cephrael worked His hand upon the realm, the fabric of the Great Pattern vibrated. A lucky few could perceive that vibration. The even more fortunate had learned to recognize it—Marius among them. He'd long ago stopped questioning his instincts when he sensed the *angiel's* involvement—in such a time, for good or ill, the only course was to continue on.

The High Lord held the Endoge's gaze. "No, Liam, I don't mind your placing Tanis in Malin's room."

"I do apologize again, Your Grace," the Endoge murmured. "I will see to it at once."

Marius sent Vincenzé and Giancarlo to help Tanis get moved into Chresten Hall and himself went quickly to join the Empress. He knew her mind, knew where she would be taking the zanthyr, and his instincts were rewarded upon his return to the palace, for he learned that she and Phaedor were already en route to the Tower and their unusual prisoner.

Arriving outside the chamber where the prisoner had recently been quartered, the High Lord looked to the line of Praetorians standing before the doors. "Is the Empress within?"

"Yes, Your Grace." The lead Praetorian bowed and stepped aside.

Marius traced an intricate pattern in the air to release the trace seal and sent the fifth into the doors to open them. As he walked within, Marius felt his ears pop, and he shifted his jaw slightly to clear the sudden pressure from a host of layered wards—a necessary discomfort endured for everyone's safety.

Dominating the center of the chamber stood a stone slab to which the prisoner had been chained. As Marius approached, the zanthyr's dark form was bent in inspection of the prisoner, while Valentina, standing beside him in a beaded gown of silver, stood as brilliant as a captured star.

The Empress turned at his approach. "Marius." There was much said in her tone ... and in her eyes as she looked upon him.

"Aurelia." Marius bowed in reverent greeting. He gained her side and looked upon the unconscious prisoner, who was six times enfolded with iron manacles.

"He fell into a trance while you were at sea," Valentina murmured.

The zanthyr appeared to be engaged in deep inspection of the man. He stood with eyes closed and one hand upon the man's forehead. The High Lord walked to the other side of the table, opposite the zanthyr, and frowned down at the prisoner. "The necrosis seems to have spread." He glanced up at Valentina.

"We've learned much about what was done to him since you left, Marius. We've attempted to reverse the process, yet in vain, for his flesh continues its transformation."

Indeed, the man's bare flesh had become almost entirely black. He might've been formed of stone as ebon-dark as the deadly Merdanti blade strapped to the zanthyr's hip. In the few spots upon his person where natural flesh remained, it showed red and suppurated. What had at first appeared a leprous affliction now proved some parasitic form of necromancy.

This thought had just occurred to Marius when Phaedor opened his eyes and removed his hand from the man's head. His gaze remained fixed there, his expression intense.

"Well?" asked the Empress. "I would know what you learned of him."

Phaedor lifted his gaze to her. "I learned that you've been keeping him alive and in so doing have allowed the pattern to spread."

Valentina shook her head. "We had little choice. This man is our only link to whoever worked such foul craft upon him."

"No doubt you will discover that soon enough."

Marius bristled, but Valentina replied only, "What would you have us do?"

Phaedor held her gaze. "Kill him—while you still can."

Marius gazed at the zanthyr with his teeth clenched. It would do no good to argue, debate or protest—this he knew. Phaedor only ever said what it suited him to reveal. Marius drew breath to convey his displeasure—or at least remark critically upon the zanthyr's obdurate nature—but Phaedor preempted his comment with an upraised hand and a warning flash of emerald eyes. "Say no more in this creature's presence."

The Empress frowned. Her gaze swept everyone in the room, but it lingered longest on the unconscious prisoner. "Let us retire to my chambers to speak more of these matters."

As the three of them walked amid a cloud of Praetorians back to Valentina's apartments, Marius couldn't help but wonder why Phaedor had really come to Faroqhar. The zanthyr only ever acted upon his own motives, which seemed wholly unknown to anyone except the Maker, yet Valentina trusted the infuriating creature to the extreme limits of Marius's patience. While she obviously honored some agreement with her departed father, Hallian IV, *he* had no obligation to place any faith in Björn van Gelderan's zanthyr. Phaedor was the most elusive man Marius had ever come into contact with, and likewise the most difficult to understand, command or influence. That he was going along with Valentina's wishes so compliantly made Marius highly suspicious.

Reaching the Empress's chambers, Valentina took a seat and turned her gaze to the zanthyr. "You must know that my Sight—"

"Is clouded." The zanthyr pinned her with his emerald gaze. "If you would know why you cannot see the path, seek ancient names long hidden, much feared. One is harbored in the head of that man, your prisoner. It is all he knows."

"He spoke nonsense syllables only," Marius said, staring at him. He liked not at all the threat lacing the zanthyr's words.

Valentina turned the High Lord a concerned look. "Perhaps they were not nonsense?"

The zanthyr gazed darkly upon her. "And the word?"

"Shalabaanaaatra," she said. Abruptly she lifted her gaze to Marius. "It is like a resounding shout, without end, this word, stretching from creation to infinity. It has neither beginning nor ending in his thoughts, encompassing the entirety of his mind."

"Shalabaanaaatra," Marius slowly repeated with a frown. Giancarlo had just been speaking this word to the boy Tanis, but Marius didn't know how the subject rose between them.

"You do not recognize it?" Phaedor asked Valentina. "Too long have their names been hidden from the world if Hallian, your father, spoke nothing of them to you. Or perhaps if I say the *Qhorith'quitara*, you will recall."

Valentina sat back in her chair. "Can it be," she said in a low voice fervent with disquiet, "that you speak to me of *Malorin'athgul?*"

The name sent a shock coursing through Marius. He looked up under his brow at Valentina. "The first volume of the *Qhorith'quitara*," he said, low and fierce. "It's the book Malin van Drexel removed from the vault. It still has not been found—*Sanctos Mordaani*," the curse escaped him like a hiss of foretelling, for he should've seen the same connections.

"So you begin to see," the zanthyr murmured.

"I see a picture, but it makes no sense to me." Marius shook his head and went to pour himself a glass of wine. "Assuming Malorin'athgul do exist," he remarked then, too unsettled by the idea to discount it outright, "how would they have entered our world?"

The zanthyr pulled out his dagger and fingered the blade. "What's done is done. Seek instead to learn what games they are upon, for one of them surely plots against you."

Marius's frustration bristled. "If you know so much of their activities, speak plainly."

The zanthyr turned him a cool eye. "Where was this man, your prisoner, uncovered?" He tossed the dagger idly, making it flip three times before catching it by the point.

Marius's expression darkened. *Damn the creature for knowing so much and revealing so little!* "He was discovered wandering the palace halls."

"Adepts materializing, others vanishing ..." Phaedor flipped his dagger again. "It would appear your security is showing its holes, High Lord."

Marius gritted his teeth. "You tell me how they're traveling the realm without leaving traces on the currents!"

Phaedor caught his dagger fiercely between fingers and thumb and cast Marius a severe look of censure from under his brow. "At least in following this line of inquiry you would be asking the right questions."

Valentina traced her lips with her forefinger. "I don't understand ... what would Malorin'athgul have to do with the Extian Doors?"

"The Extian Doors?" Marius blinked at her. Then, noting her expression, he repeated again, more emphatically, "*The* Extian Doors?"

"Or a fair representation of them. The Order reported while you were at sea: the Extian Doors were raised in Köhentaal—raised, they believe, on the eve of Adendigaeth."

Marius swiftly looked to observe the zanthyr's reaction to this astonishing news, but as usual, the creature gave no indication that he cared one way or another. Marius shook his head in bewilderment and looked back to his Empress. "*How*—and for what possible reason?"

Valentina grunted. "I'm more concerned with *who*. The list of wielders with that kind of skill is short indeed." She shook her head, and her gaze became clouded with uncertainty. "Would that the Sight had not abandoned me. Instinct says Markal had some hand in it, but ..."

Marius downed the last of his wine in a gulp. It flamed in his empty stomach as he growled into the cup, "I would happily interrogate Markal if only I could lay my hands on the man."

"You need only brave the nodes to T'khendar to find him, Marius di L'Arlesé." The zanthyr flipped his dagger again and caught its point on the tip of his finger. "He's been there six moons or more."

Marius gripped his goblet in his fist. "*How, by the Lady*—?"

"Prior to this, Markal slept under your nose for three centuries, a hermit in the hills of Talieri."

Valentina's chuckling formed a soothing balm for Marius's rigid displeasure. He looked over to find her laughing. "The energies flooding *elae*'s tides coming down out of the Geborah mountains would've washed any hint of Markal's presence out of the currents. Oh, you *are* a brilliant man!"

"Why tell us now?" Marius couldn't cleanse the irritation from his tone. "The knowledge is of no use with the man languishing a realm away."

Phaedor arched a raven brow. "What you do with the information, Your Grace, is hardly my concern."

"Certainly not anymore!"

"Peace, Marius." Valentina looked to him. "I would see the doors with my own eyes—"

"Oh, Valentina, you can't seriously think—"

She raised a hand to quiet him. "My heart tells me Markal had some hand in this, that they're not the legendary gates to Annwn and this is merely an elaborate hoax, but Marius ... what if it isn't? The *Sobra* speaks of the Extian Doors as being raised by Cephrael himself. You know the mythology."

"Yes, *mythology*—"

She cast him a telling look. "They would not be the first things to emerge out of legend into our world."

Marius gritted his teeth and held his tongue. Much as he'd like to argue with her, he had no firmer ground to stand his logic upon.

"My Sight is dying, Marius." She searched his gaze for understanding, for agreement. "The currents carry a taint unlike anything seen in history, our race totters on the fringe of extinction." Her voice, husky and deep, resonated with her deepest fears. "What if these *are* the real doors? What if they herald the end of days?"

"More likely the Danes had some part to play in it. Köhentaal is but a stone's throw from their border." Marius gave her a look rife with frustration and then turned to the zanthyr. "Phaedor, surely you don't subscribe to these doomsday theories."

"Nothing is assured," the zanthyr murmured, which of course was no answer at all.

Valentina stood and walked to Marius. She placed her hands on his chest and looked up at him. "*Mia caro*, would *you* trust the eyes of another man to tell you if the doors are true?"

As the High Lord gazed into his Empress's eyes, he knew he would lose this battle. "No." He dropped his gaze in submission. "No, I would not." Abruptly he looked back to her. "But Köhentaal lies at the furthest rim of the Empire, Valentina. The territory is dangerous—"

"I will accompany the Empress to Köhentaal."

Marius spun a heated glare at the zanthyr.

Valentina nodded to the efficacy of this idea, effectively sealing the matter. "It would be a boon to have you there to speak of what you see in their construction."

"Your will, my Empress," Phaedor said with a quiet nod.

Marius ground his teeth. He loathed this turn of fate immensely—how could he place his Empress at the mercy of a creature of such ambiguous allegiance? "It's a journey of many days, Valentina," he protested, feeling strained by events spiraling out of his control—and infuriatingly into the zanthyr's, it would appear. "Permit me to accompany you as well."

"No, Marius. We cannot both depart the capital. If I haven't returned by Twelfth-day, you must hold proceedings in my stead."

The zanthyr settled his gaze upon the High Lord, and his emerald eyes gleamed meaningfully. "We shall both take care for the treasures in our hands, Marius di L'Arlesé."

THIRTY-THREE

"There is a finite law: what a man can't do, and what a man can do.

And then there's what a wielder can do, and that is infinite."

–The Adept wielder Arion Tavestra

THIRTEEN HELLS! EAN threw up his hands and stalked across the sand court where he pushed palms to tired eyes and tried to quell his frustration.

Beneath a blustery overcast, an illusion glowed in the air behind him. Taller than a man, the hovering icosahedron of interconnected patterns cast wavering shadows throughout the pink marble courtyard. He'd brought Dore's pattern matrix to vivid life through a deft working of the fourth, meticulously reconstructing each pattern for inspection.

For all the good it had done him.

Clenching hands into fists, Ean ducked his head and growled, "I know it has to be there, but I'll be damned if I can find it."

Dareios sat at a linen-draped table cluttered with the remains of their recent meal. He propped one gold-slippered foot across the opposite knee, rested an elbow on the table and traced the line of his jaw with his forefinger while his colorless gaze assessed the matrix. A slight tightening around his eyes was the only indication of his perplexity. "If these patterns weren't so offensively vile, I might congratulate their maker on his deviousness."

Ean turned him a look across the court. Three days ago his brother had lain nearly where Ean was now standing—he thought he might still imagine the impression left by Sebastian's coiled form as they'd lifted him onto a stretcher and carried him away—and he had yet to resurface from that moment. Ean had no idea what he'd done or how much harm he'd brought upon his brother. Isabel could only tell him that Sebastian appeared to suffer from some mental trauma. She could do no more than keep his body comfortable while his mind recovered. If it could recover.

Three days, and still Ean had come no closer to finding the pattern of the fifth that bound all of Dore's patterns into permanence.

"It *has* to be there." He glared at the floating sphere. It was less a geometric shape with twenty flat sides than a three-dimensional puzzle formed of dozens of interconnected patterns, like snowflakes crossing through each other, or an ornament of intersecting lace panels. Every pattern had countless joining points, places in one pattern that mirrored other patterns, points where they intersected in purpose and design. These mirror points allowed otherwise disparate patterns to cross in symbiosis.

Ean cast Dareios a tormented look. "Why can't I see it?"

"That *none* of us can find the fifth in this construction is not a testament to our inadequacy but to its maker's ingeniousness." Dareios extended a jeweled hand towards the hovering matrix. "It's there, Ean. We have merely to continue our search and study with patience. Haste will only further obscure the truth we seek."

"Spoken like a scholar," Ean grumbled.

"Argued like a soldier," Dareios returned with a wink.

Something poked at the table's linen from below and the wildcat Babar tumbled out with an edge of the linen caught in her mouth. Between teeth and claws she nearly dragged the tablecloth off the table and half the china with it.

Dareios nudged and hissed at her in his own language. The cat flattened an ear. "*Go*, Babar!" He made a shooing motion with his hand and leaned to stare at the animal. "Go beleaguer your mistress, who likes you more than I do."

Babar stared at him for a moment more. Then she twisted with another harrowing tug of linen and scampered off.

Dareios sighed and sat back in his chair. "I vow, that animal is far more vexing than the problem facing us. Yet they are similar creatures—patterns are creations formed of thought and intention, and they live, even if only for a brief instant, every time a wielder casts them forth with purpose." His gaze shifted back to Ean, who stood now with hands shoved in his pockets and a scowl on his face. "Perhaps a break from this task would do you some good, Ean. Your brother's condition clouds your thoughts. I'll stay and keep at our study. As you know, I but live to solve such problems, whereas for you, they tend to be—"

"Daunting?" Ean posed disagreeably. "Tormenting? Agonizing? Exasperating?"

Dareios grinned. "I was going to say tedious, but as you will."

Ean regarded him for a moment in silence. Then he grunted. "You have it?" and he motioned to the illusion. Dareios would need to take over its rendering to keep the illusion in place.

The hint of a smile danced in the truthreader's eyes. "I think I can manage it, Ean."

Ean nodded and left him.

Isabel stood with hands pressed to the railing of her balcony. A blustery overcast clung to the Dhahari mountains, those razor peaks ripping shreds out of the clouds as they passed. The grey sky appeared featureless and flat, yet the lack of color in the sky brought out the color in the earth: the green of the valley, the darker blue-green of the mountain firs, the pale gold of fields and the hills bathed in russet gauze. Some people hid from this kind of day, making false light indoors to remind them of the sun as if lessened by its absence, but Isabel saw promise when the sky slept.

She preferred to contact her brother beneath a roofless sky, come wind or rain or snow, for she loved the wind in all its many forms, even as she loved storms and the sea and the twirling heavens on a clear night. She could lose herself in them for hours just listening, her ears attuned to their starsong, her mind seeking to know their language.

In these elemental entities, whose dispositions and whims appeared so incomprehensible and capricious to most, Isabel saw magnitude and purpose. Elemental forces ever reminded her of her brother.

It was a small ritual, finding a place to stand beneath the open sky and a moment of solitude in which to cast her mind across the endless void to find her brother's thoughts, but she respected what small ritual she could manage. Ritual gave a deeper context to her connection with her brother and added a sense of devotion to the act, which she appreciated. For she *was* devoted to him—to him and to their mutual game, knowing that upon this rested the future not just of Alorin but of all the Realms of Light ... and possibly those of darkness, too, though she'd put little attention towards their future if Alorin fell. No doubt her brother had considered them. His gaze was as like the heavens; little passed beneath it unobserved.

Lifting her chin to feel the wind caress her skin and stir her hair, Isabel relaxed and expanded her mind and sought the space of her brother's thoughts. Quickly she sensed him—for the realm of thought lay above the physical and followed not its laws. Time, space and distance ... these aspects cast no shadows over thought. A single thought could exist eternally in an instant, or be known by all no matter how disparate their locations. Finding her brother's mind, Isabel inserted her presence with a gentle chime of greeting.

Ah, hello, sister ...

Björn's mental voice held a certain resonance that always warmed her. She sensed he spoke with others in T'khendar in that moment, but her brother had ever been capable of carrying on multiple conversations simultaneously. Just one of many reasons she admired and adored him.

What news, Isabel?

It had been many days since she'd updated him, yet it took but the space of a few quiet breaths to communicate all, such was the alacrity of thought.

She'd always sighed at the inefficiency of translating and congealing thought into ideas, ideas into symbols, symbols into sounds, and then the reverse on the other end—sounds decoded back to symbols to ideas to the purity of conceptual thought—this process repeated endlessly …

Language had become so ingrained that even truthreaders fell prey to it, when in fact they heard not the 'language' of another's thoughts but simply the complete thought itself, its full concept gleaned and duplicated, often in picture form. Truthreaders could communicate with thought alone, easily and simply. It astonished her how few of them realized this on their own.

In return for her news, Björn updated her on affairs since she'd left T'khendar. Much had happened in a short span of time, though this didn't surprise her. The game was accelerating, the most powerful pieces being put into play. It only followed that the interchange upon the board would intensify.

I sense your restlessness, Björn said into her mind. *What troubles you, Isabel?*

She cast a mental sigh. *I'm troubled by Ean's path.* It often surprised her how readily she confessed her fears to her brother … even when she denied them in her own thoughts … or in her heart.

Why?

It has become fluid.

The breath of a pause filled the space of his mind—an eternity in that communication form. Then: *I was afraid of that.*

You were right to warn me.

I don't enjoy being right at the cost of your happiness.

I could never be happy if my happiness endangered the game.

In acknowledgement of the deeper implications of these truths, she felt an ethereal caress, like a stroking of her hair. *Ma dieulle, tan cyr im'avec,* his mental voice whispered.

Y dama avec'im, she replied lovingly, and withdrew from his mind.

"What did he say?"

Isabel turned to find Ean standing between the open patio doors radiating frustration. She dropped her hands from the railing and moved to join him inside just as rain broke lightly upon the world. "Much has happened since we left. The game moves quickly." She closed the double doors behind her. "I told Björn the names of the fortresses Sebastian gave to us. He'll have his network investigate, looking for your men. Cephrael willing, we'll know something soon of their location."

Ean nodded wordlessly and looked away; she saw his jaw clench.

Isabel sighed. Seeing only the power that resided within him, she forgot sometimes that Ean was still so young in his new life. She might expect him to mold the waters of the sea into a ship to carry them, but she couldn't expect him to maintain an immortal's practiced stoicism when he felt stymied at every turn. He needed her so desperately, yet she now believed she was the wrong person to help him on his path.

"Ean …"

He spun her a fierce gaze, beautiful for all its intensity. If he only really knew what he was capable of … She walked to him and placed her hands on his chest. He wrapped his hands around hers tightly. "I know your mind," she said gently.

His jaw tightened. "My brother lies beyond my reach. My men equally so. Every day that passes takes them further from my grasp."

"Your path has never been so fluid."

"You say that like it's a bad thing."

Isabel slipped her arms around him, and his arms enfolded her at once. No matter the distance between their hearts—an unwanted distance caused by diverging paths—he never pushed her away. "That your path has never been fluid before, this is what troubles me."

"More fluidity would appear to mean more opportunity."

"Yes, but opportunity for what?"

Oh, that he might see what she foresaw, that she might share with him the fears that plagued her, but it wouldn't serve Ean to know any more than he'd already gleaned from her troubled thoughts—indeed, he'd gleaned too much already.

She pulled away and placed a hand on his cheek, letting her fingers scrape the scruff shadowing his chin. The lines that connected his cheekbones to his jaw were wonderfully alluring to her. She would've loved him if he'd been buck-toothed and deformed, but she didn't deny an appreciation that her true love had Returned as a handsome prince instead.

She watched him searching her gaze—or attempting to, beneath her blindfold.

"You say you know my path. But I don't know yours. It's enough to drag me under just worrying for Sebastian and the others. This specter of future that hangs over me since Tal'Afaq feels like a cloak choking me at every turn." He clenched his jaw and turned his eyes from her. "I cannot think of losing you, too, Isabel."

Isabel sighed. "This is the problem with glimpsing the future. It changes in the now what has yet to be. You become the effect of something that hasn't even happened, provoking its eventuality."

He opened his mouth to protest, but she placed a finger across his lips. "Instead of living and making choices in that moment, about that moment— enjoying or hating or elating in that moment, but knowing you are in *that* moment—you make choices based on some perceived future that might not have come to pass, except for the fact that you're already—consciously or unconsciously—making choices to bring it into being. This circular cause is how Seers lose themselves."

Ean frowned at her. "Isabel … I know what I saw."

She could barely endure the truth in his words. She traced her fingers along his unshaved jaw. "I have to walk my path, Ean." She added quietly, even knowing what the words would do to him, "You once said the same to me."

She saw the shock in his expression, followed by contrition beyond measure. A host of emotions flickered across his face, and then his gaze hardened. He bent and swept her up into his arms.

"You want me to be in this moment?" he growled into her ear, his voice rough. "Your will be done, my lady."

And he took her to the bed.

Rain lashed the windows as Ean lay with Isabel's long hair spiraling across his chest and her legs entwined with his. One arm held her close, keeping her near, while the other draped overhead, elbow bent, an oblique expression of the duality he felt in that moment—possession and dispossession, contentment interlaced with frustration. Increasingly it seemed he was ending up in bed with her in some haphazard attempt to announce his claim, to possess her in whatever way she allowed.

He wondered if she knew he recalled those moments when last they'd parted, the conversation she'd hinted at. He'd dreamed that confrontation once, but in the months since, those incorporeal dreams had grown the flesh of true memory.

Ean had once thought Isabel had been the one pushing him away; but looking at those memories now, he knew that in truth he'd been steadfast on his path, only he *wanted* to be uncertain. He'd wanted not to leave her—he'd sought vainly for any reason to stay, one that overshadowed oath and honor. He'd *wanted* to believe that life with her was more important than anything else, more important than the game … but he couldn't.

He'd told her as much. To her credit, she'd understood, even though he couldn't understand now. Now she *was* more important than anything or anyone—certainly more important to him than a game he could barely comprehend.

He knew she lay awake, so he said quietly, "I remember asking you how long we would be apart. You didn't tell me then because you said you didn't want to frighten me. Did you ever tell me?"

After a long silence, she answered, "Yes … on Tiern'aval."

Ean closed his eyes, but still the regret found him. Somehow it would've made it so much easier to accept his choice if he hadn't known what it would mean. But he had, and he'd still chosen to die for the First Lord's game. "Three hundred years?" his voice sounded embarrassingly high. "You told me we would be apart for *three hundred* years?"

"Yes."

"You saw all of my deaths in between?"

She pushed up on one elbow and with a finger against his chin turned his gaze to her. "What dark places your mind treads, my lord."

"I naught but stumble in darkness without you, Isabel." He clenched his teeth and shook his head and looked away from her again. "I feel like in all the centuries we were apart, I naught but stumbled in darkness."

He heard a strange noise escape her and turned back. "Are you *laughing* at me?"

She tried and failed to suppress a smile.

Ean cast her an affronted look. "You think I'm overreacting. Well ... I'm not." He slung himself off the bed and paced across the room, spearing a glare at her along with the complaint, "I'll have you know my reactions reflect an eminently appropriate degree of desperation."

"Ean—"

"I'm trying to play a game I barely understand, Isabel. I'm trying to be *worthy* of you, but—" He stilled and sliced fingers through his hair, letting out a growl. "I have no idea what I'm doing." Abruptly, he came back and sank to his knees beside the bed, entreating her with his gaze. "I *need* you. I have so much yet to learn—or at least to remember—and the stakes are so high. I'm clearly not the hero this role requires."

"Ean, you do yourself an injustice."

He moved to sit beside her, took up her hand, and pressed his lips to her palm. "Maybe I was such a hero, once," he admitted. Odd echoes of that perilous duality which had so possessed Arion accosted him suddenly, a clenching sense of purpose interwoven with regret. "Maybe I can be again someday." He took her other hand and rubbed his thumbs across her palms, resisting the urge to pull her closer. He lifted his eyes and searched her hidden gaze. "But without you beside me, Isabel, what hope do I possess?"

She regarded him quietly. "The Kandori have a saying: a man who complains that the sun rises and sets fills his belly with air."

"Which means what, exactly? Kandori proverbs are about as comprehensible as the Esoterics."

She withdrew her hands from his and stroked his hair back behind his ear. "It means that complaining about things one cannot change is a waste of time." When Ean bristled, she continued quickly, "It *also* means that we must learn to make the best out of any circumstance, *and*," she added as he opened his mouth to protest, "that the man who accepts his path reaps the greatest rewards from it."

"So you're saying I should just accept this and let it go?"

Isabel answered gently, "You're expending a lot of energy in protest of something that hasn't happened yet—energy that would be better expended elsewhere."

"I know what I perceive, Isabel."

"You perceive my confusion, Ean, but you fill the space of this unknown with your own fears."

Ean frowned at her. Then he set his jaw and frowned off into the night. He felt as if every mistake he'd ever made somehow clung to him still, and that his past failures were somehow endangering everyone he loved. Fear for his brother and Rhys mingled like shadows with his perception that Isabel intended to leave, and his guilt over mistakes he could no more remember than amend. The result was a tormenting black sea of frustration.

Rather than face those impenetrable waters any longer, the prince stood and sought his clothes.

Isabel turned her head to watch him dress. "A woman could only be flattered by such a dramatic display of devotion."

Ean poked his head through the neck opening of his kurta and paused. "The woman Isabel … but not Epiphany's Prophet?"

She arched a brow above her blindfold and exhaled resignedly. "Epiphany's Prophet would say this display shows a lack of faith in one's path."

He shoved his arms through the sleeves and tugged the tunic roughly down. "I wouldn't say my path has proven exactly trustworthy, Isabel."

Her brow furrowed as she regarded him. "It isn't the path that leads you astray but the choices you make upon it." When Ean said nothing to this, merely clenched his jaw and continued dressing, she asked, "Where will you go? The hour is late."

"Dareios is probably awake in his lab. The man never sleeps."

"He is a scholar in the guise of a prince."

And I'm a fool in one.

"Ean …"

He grimaced, knowing she'd caught the thought. "My brother sleeps like the dead." He tied the drawstring on his *shalwar* and glared up at her under his brows. "As you said, it'll do me good to expend my energies on a situation I might actually be able to do something about."

He turned his back on her concerned frown and left.

THIRTY-FOUR

"We all have within us the potential to be gods."

– The Fifth Vestal Björn van Gelderan

E AN SPENT THE rest of the night with Dareios until the man himself
sought sleep a couple of hours before dawn. Then the prince walked the
palace halls in silence and darkness, embroiled in thoughts far darker
still. He eventually found his way back to the courtyard.

The sand lay damp and silvery beneath a clearing sky just shy of daybreak.
Ean slipped out of his shoes and walked to the middle of the court. He looked
up at the stars and let the night's lingering chill drain the emotion from his
limbs. He stood there for a long time.

Eventually he wandered the court tracing lines in the damp, heavy sand
with his bare feet. He didn't recall when he began walking through the *cortata*.
The Adept dance of swords merely came upon him as a natural course, the way
a man will sometimes hum as he walks or works, hardly aware of the tune he
casts into the day, yet kept company by the sound. So did the *cortata* comfort
Ean as might an old friend, easing his thoughts—indeed, erasing all thought
beyond the motion required in the dance, his entire mind focused on carving
the *cortata's* pattern through position and movement and line of limb.

Day broke upon the world. The sky brightened to rose-gold, and the clear
morning brought a still, cool calm, one mirrored in Ean's mind as he finished
the *cortata* sequence for the fourth time and started anew. His feet followed
channels through the sand now, each time passing in the same sweep or curve,
carving the trough deeper. It pleased him to move with slow precision, to know
he formed each angle of the pattern perfectly in every moment.

As his mind had begun to settle, Ean realized that he'd long depended on
this dance to clear his head. Arion had worked the *cortata* thousands of times,
perhaps in the tens of thousands, and had counted upon it not merely in battle

but to vanish any thought that lingered against his will. No wonder the motions were so second-nature to Ean—he could've done it blindfolded and backwards.

As the sky lightened to blue, Ean became vaguely aware of people walking beneath the colonnades bordering his cloister—servants, adjutants, women draped in colorful, flowing silks—but none of them disturbed his concentration. He'd gained such focus that he could move through each position perfectly and still perceive the happenings in the world around him. He felt distant from his body, as if his mind had wandered into the far heavens and now extended all the way to the dome of the horizon in every direction.

When he finished his fifth pass through the sequence and lowered his arms, applause floated to him from the colonnade, and he turned to see three women in colorful *saris* clapping their hands, dark eyes smiling beneath the jewel-encrusted *chaadars* that covered their hair. He smiled and bowed, recognizing Dareios's two sisters standing with another woman he didn't know.

This woman pointed admiringly to the sand and said something in her Kandori dialect.

One of the sisters—her name might've been Yasmine—translated to Ean, "She says you missed your calling, Prince of Dannym. She has never seen a man who can paint with his feet."

Ean looked down at the channels his feet had carved in the sand. Then he frowned. He retreated from the sand court to stand atop the stairs and gazed down at his creation.

He'd always conceived of the *cortata* as a pattern in three dimensions formed of feet, body and arms. He held this pattern in his mind when he worked the forms—he'd hazard to say he knew the *cortata's* pattern more instinctively than any other. Yet he'd never seen it as he was seeing it now.

Looking down upon the sweeps and swirls carved so deeply into the sand—two-dimensional instead of three—he saw a portion of the pattern he'd never glimpsed before. Always he conceived of the pattern in its full concept—that is, three-dimensionally—yet this two-dimensional segment was a cross-section sliced through the pattern's core, like an orange cut in half …

Ean shoved palms to his temples and stared, wide-eyed, as realization dawned. Could it really be that simple?

He called the fifth and in three steps had launched himself to the roof of the nearest walkway. The women gasped, but Ean heard only the sweet song of resolution singing in his ears. He found his footing on the tiles and turned to face the sand court. Then he called the illusion of Dore's matrix into being.

He might've remained upon the steps and merely turned the illusion to see it from a new angle, but he didn't trust himself in such reconstruction. As he'd never seen the *cortata* from above—in the thousands of times Arion had worked it, he'd never viewed that representation of it—so Ean could not easily conceive of Dore's pattern from any other angle than the one he reconstructed from studying Sebastian's mind. But he *could* call the matrix into being and then change *his* position relative to it.

The morning lengthened and a crowd began to gather while Ean studied the matrix, walking from rooftop to rooftop all around the courtyard. In the middle, his illusion glowed like a captured sun. He'd formed it larger than before so he could see each loop of every pattern with perfect clarity.

He was still standing on the roof when Dareios arrived. Ean felt like they'd only separated a short while ago, though the day had seen at least three turns of the hourglass.

Dareios stood on the steps, rested hands on his hips and craned his head back to view the prince atop the roof. "What is it you're doing up there, Ean—besides entertaining my sisters?"

"Come and see, Prince of Kandori." He summoned the fifth and spared a moment's thought to mold his intention. Rainwater swirled from rooftops and columns, from gutters and puddles among uneven tiles, to form a staircase of glistening dew.

The onlookers gasped. Some clapped.

Working the fifth in this way came naturally to Ean, as naturally as a truthreader gleaning veracity from another's spoken words. He needed no patterns to change the shape of elements that would easily take any form, nor to command them from one static state to another. Such workings were native to him, intrinsic to the way he thought, and they left little trace upon the currents. Forces already acting upon the world—gravity, inertia, kinesis—these responded to his whim, shaped as easily as clay beneath a potter's hands. Ean needed only to form his intention—a clear idea of what he wanted to accomplish—and focus his will to make it become.

Dareios inspected the glistening staircase. Then he set one tentative foot on the first step, testing the integrity of the stairs now extending to the rooftop where Ean stood. When the stair held his weight—water bound into a solid by gravity's force reapplied from all sides—he broke into a broad grin and began ascending. The onlookers erupted with mad applause.

"Long have the years been since a fifth strand Adept made himself known by action and deed," Dareios commented as he climbed. "A great long while."

Ean turned him a look as he gained the roof. "This pleases you?"

Dareios watched the staircase fall into rain behind him. His eyes danced as he looked back to Ean. "More than a little."

"Would that everything came to me so easily." Ean returned his attention to the pattern. "But the day is much brighter than when you and I parted. Look," and he nodded to the matrix, "I think I've found it."

Dareios arched brows. "The fifth? Where?" He turned his colorless gaze to the illusion.

"You must assume the view from above. Look down ... look for the flat planes dissecting the vertical lines, a two-dimensional pattern hidden among the others."

While Dareios studied the illusion, Ean swept his hair back from his face with both hands. "I have to give Dore his due. This is brilliant."

While he'd been studying the pattern, the ghost of a recollection had come to him—a remembered conversation—Dore Madden's grim-featured face nose to nose with Arion's and the declaration, both promise and warning, '... *your talent with the fifth is nothing compared to what I can do ... '* and behind this, Arion's thought—his concern at the time—that Dore would put the whole of his devious intelligence towards malevolent aims.

"I see what you mean." Dareios walked along the roof just as Ean had, peering down at the pattern. "Rather than encase the entire matrix within the fifth, he's built the matrix *around* his fifth strand pattern." He made a complete circle of the rooftops, studying the pattern from every side.

He beamed as he rejoined Ean. "Well ... shall we go break it apart?"

They moved from the cloister to Dareios's laboratory—much to the disappointment of the assembled princesses, who'd made quite the morning of watching Ean cavorting atop the roof—and spent the remainder of the day extracting the fifth strand pattern from Dore's matrix.

Because so many other patterns connected through it, Ean had to meticulously separate each pattern, one by one. As they pulled each pattern apart from the whole, Dareios both drew its two dimensional representation on sheets of clear glass—the parchment of a Patternist—and formed his own illusion of the singular pattern and left it floating. By midafternoon, Ean was passing through floating patterns just to cross the room.

When Ean struggled to separate a pattern from those connecting through it—often due to unfamiliarity with the pattern in question, making it difficult to know what threads among that jumbled intersection belonged where— Dareios would work a Telling to see the original pattern again as Ean had first seen it in Sebastian's mind, and in this way he would help Ean extract it.

By early evening, they'd isolated the fifth strand pattern of binding and nearly all of the other patterns in the matrix. Those still missing were the ones Dareios called deadfalls, patterns Dore had placed to prevent anyone from working the fifth to attack or otherwise deconstruct his binding.

Ean had the most important piece in the fifth strand pattern that held all the other compulsion patterns in place, but he couldn't go in and unwork it with those deadfalls still active. They would have to be addressed first. He suspected the deadfalls—like the fifth strand pattern that had eluded him for so long—were hidden within other patterns.

As night blanketed the world and Dareios excused himself to visit his wife, Ean sank down on a stool, leaned back against the table's edge and rested clasped hands atop his head, letting his elbows hang. His eyes ached, and his head felt full of wool. He hadn't truly slept in days. Ean thought it ironic how some cosmic power seemed to hold him and his brother on the extreme opposite ends of the spectrum: Ean couldn't sleep, and Sebastian couldn't wake.

Or maybe he didn't want to.

Ean stiffened with the thought. He remembered walking the paths of the dead, remembered the hopelessness that had possessed him and the whispering voice that kept him from imagining any other existence. Yet when he'd lain for a week unmoving, walking those paths, the First Lord hadn't waited for him to find his own way out. He'd gone in and found Ean.

What if Sebastian walked those endless moors? What if he now traveled with that same melancholy voice murmuring doleful platitudes to degrade his hopes? Ean didn't know how to find the dead moors, but he'd be damned if he'd sit around and wait for his brother to give up.

He left the laboratory with purpose lengthening his stride and called the currents to light the way through the palace's dark corridors. He walked with his hands in his pockets, his head down and his thoughts ranging far. While his mind explored the problem of the deadfalls, his eyes observed how the currents of the fifth pooled and swirled around his legs. Then he suddenly realized what he was seeing.

And came to a standstill.

It was a particular aspect of the fifth strand that it magnetized to itself. None of the other strands displayed this attractive property. The fifth collected to Adepts of its aspect, who inherently thought in fifth strand patterns, and as Ean had so many times observed, the fifth collected *around the patterns themselves*.

Gods—how could he have missed this?

If he called the currents while looking into his brother's mind—essentially pulling them *through* his brother's mind—the currents should collect, even minutely, around the patterns of the fifth binding Sebastian's consciousness, thus revealing the deadfalls.

By Cephrael's Great Book, if he'd only thought of this before, he could've saved himself days of searching!

There were as many possible patterns to reveal the currents as there were Adepts in Alorin, but Ean knew exactly what patterns he would need to use to reveal the fifth. Arion had spent ages developing such patterns.

Ean set off again with excitement now hastening his pace. For the first time, he felt a measure of confidence—no, certainty—that he could follow through on his promise. He *would* free his brother!

Sebastian's room lay in darkness when Ean let himself in, but he needed no light, for the currents as he'd summoned them glowed so brightly as to cast shadows on the day. Yet their swift flow grew sluggish as they crossed his brother's sleeping form; there, the currents pooled in a lazy swirl before slipping off again, pulled back by the force of their own tides. Amid that eddy, the collecting currents became as ink, gradually darkened by the malice of Dore's matrix.

Staring for a moment at his brother lying as the dead within that inky pool, Ean inhaled his determination, climbed on the bed, and straddled Sebastian. He placed a hand to his forehead and formed the pattern to draw the currents through him. Yet when he released it into action ...

Something isn't right.

The pattern should've compelled the currents through Sebastian's form. They should've magnetized to him, but they were being repelled instead.

Then he had it: the *goracrosta*.

Ean drew his dagger and severed the silver rope binding Sebastian's wrists. He tossed the pieces away and summoned the currents again. This time they complied with his intent.

Sinking his thoughts deep into Sebastian's mind, the prince found and studied Dore's matrix. He didn't need it to be active now, for he knew its construction intimately. As Ean watched the currents flowing through the matrix, the fourth funneled in with a crystalline shimmer but left in a flow of darkness, like sunlight refracted through a crystal; yet instead of splitting the light into harmonic colors, Dore's matrix stained it with shadows.

The fifth still resisted flowing into the matrix, perhaps due to the latter's inherent polarity. Ean increased his intention, setting the entire force of his will to compel compliance, and ...

There!

The first of the fifth strand deadfalls lit with the faintest glow. Just as Ean had suspected, it showed a dim tracing within one of the fourth-strand compulsion patterns. Ean immediately sought its beginning and ending and set it to unraveling.

One by one, the deadfalls lit with a faint glimmer, and Ean unworked each. The more patterns he unmade, the brighter the others became, such that by the time he'd found and unraveled them all, the central fifth strand pattern that bound the entire matrix was glowing as luminously as the full moon in its brightest arc.

A surge of elation thrilled through the prince. Now, *finally*, he could fulfill his promise. He dove for the pattern of binding and cast his mind as a spear. But the moment that spear-point touched the fifth strand pattern, Sebastian's entire body convulsed—

And he woke with a gasp.

His hand flew up and grabbed Ean's neck before he even came fully alert, while webs of the fourth struck out for Ean's consciousness. Ean seared them from the aether in sudden alarm and threw up a shield of the fifth around his mind, but he couldn't so easily dispense with the hand choking his throat. Too late, he realized his error in removing the *goracrosta*, for now Sebastian had both his full faculties with *elae* and the compulsion to kill him in forceful effect.

Already seeing flecks before his eyes, Ean cast another spear towards the pattern of binding, but the pain of Sebastian's choking fingers disrupted his concentration and skewed his aim.

Now Sebastian came fully alert. He surged up to grab Ean's throat with both hands, forcing the prince desperately backwards. Waves of compulsion bombarded Ean's mental shield.

Pinned to the mattress beneath Sebastian's throttling hands, the prince felt a vessel being sucked beneath the waves of a storm-washed sea. He would only survive so long as his mental shield survived, and that would fail the moment he lost consciousness. His own fists hit impotently against Sebastian's strength.

Do not counter force with force; channel it.

The Fifth Law of Patterning pierced like a ray of sunlight through the storm befuddling Ean's thoughts—Arion's experience coming to his aid—and a pattern imposed itself upon his consciousness. It took three attempts to craft it correctly and hold it in his mind, but when he felt another wave of compulsion hit him, he released it.

Sebastian ripped backwards and away from him as if caught on the end of a fisherman's line.

Ean watched his brother's body sail across the room and slam into the wall, shattering a lamp in the process. He'd known his second strand pattern would convert Sebastian's compulsion into kinetic repulsion, but he hadn't imagined it happening with such force.

Ean rolled quickly off the bed and came up with a hand splayed in a shield of the fifth, instinctive to Arion's style. Now both mind and body were protected. So, too, he cast a web of the fifth across the door that no one might interrupt them and come to inadvertent harm.

"Sebastian ..." Ean pushed a hand to his tortured neck as his mind madly sought some solution. "It doesn't have to be this way."

Sebastian was pushing up from the floor, and he lifted his eyes and pinned them darkly on Ean. The prince saw no hint of his brother in that gaze, but surely Sebastian lingered somewhere in those shadows, brutally imprisoned. He didn't want to harm him, but he couldn't see a way back into his head without subduing him, nor a way to subdue him that spared him from harm. The worst of it was he'd been *so* close!

Sebastian regained his feet. Ean searched his brother's face, but when only the black gaze of Dore's puppet gazed back, Ean got the sinking feeling that his princely brother hadn't returned from sleep at all. He'd only succeeded in rousing the demon.

Sebastian pushed the back of one hand across his bleeding lip, his eyes murderous. "You shouldn't have removed the *goracrosta*, Ean."

"Yes, I see that now."

The currents were collecting around Sebastian, indicating he called them into a pattern. In their encounter in Tyr'kharta, Ean had shown Sebastian that he could unwork patterns before they were released, so Sebastian now hid his working from Ean's view. Whatever else Dore had done, he'd given Sebastian the skill to hold an iron screen across his thoughts.

Ean saw the pattern flash as Sebastian released it, and he instinctively strengthened his shield while the room exploded around him. Wood, plaster and glass ripped through the chamber. The poster bed flew into the wall. The balcony doors tore outwards off their hinges, and needle shards of flying glass shredded the drapes. The concussion knocked Ean off his feet, but he rolled with its force and came up in a crouch. His shield of the fifth held firm.

The second explosion, coming on the heels of the first, concussed directly against Ean's shield and sent him flying backwards again. He threw a cushion of the fifth behind him and flipped over it, regaining his feet uncertainly.

Thirteen hells!

What a mess he'd made of things!

Sebastian approached. With every step he threw another concussive bolt of the fourth. Ean gritted his teeth and held his shield firm, but in truth, he clenched his teeth against his own stupidity.

How easily he might've made the stones open up to swallow Sebastian, yet Ramu had made it clear that wielding the fifth in combat meant pitting himself directly against Balance in an unwinnable contest. Ean had discounted Ramu's advice once before; he wouldn't do so again. But this left both of them wielding the fourth, and in this they were uncomfortably well matched.

Blast after blast rebounded against Ean's shield, driving him backwards across the balcony. The prince had a vast repertoire of his own patterns to use, courtesy of Arion, yet these would only destroy Sebastian, and what Ean most needed was another glimpse into his mind. He needed him closer, not blasted into oblivion, as Sebastian was continually attempting to do to him.

For every step forward Sebastian claimed, Ean took one in retreat. He was nearing the railing and the very edge of the palisades, where the cliffs fell away two-thousand feet to the plains below. One blast hitting him wrong and he would fly over the rim of the world.

Oh ...

Do not counter force with force, channel it.

The same law could work to his aid again.

Suddenly seeing the shape of a desperate plan, Ean prepared himself, prepared his intention and his patterns, summoning and holding as many as he could while also keeping his shield in place.

Right before he released the first of them, he managed a painful swallow and the weak-hearted thought, *Are you really doing this?* But Arion had been reckless in a carefully considered way, and it had served him well. If Ean couldn't regain his abilities—*all* of them—he might as well give up now.

A wielder is limited by what he can envision.

Ean would envision greatness in himself.

With Sebastian's next blast, Ean released the first of his patterns to rechannel Sebastian's fourth   strand energy into his own intent. The concussive force of the collision of patterns propelled him backwards, up over the railing. At the same time, Ean threw a lasso of the fifth. It caught around his brother and yanked him off his feet after him, so that they both catapulted over the edge of the world.

Ean pulled on his lasso, and Sebastian's body slammed into his, setting both of them to spinning. They tumbled in a tangle through a rush of wind, his brother's face twisted with unreasoning rage as they clung to one another. Then Sebastian wrapped his legs around Ean's hips and went for his throat, while Ean dove for his brother's mind.

Sebastian still held his shield in place, but Ean knew the corridors of his mind almost as well as his own. He threw another intention towards the ground while simultaneously rushing along those mental corridors seeking freedom.

Sebastian's fingers felt as claws around his throat, his legs a vice around Ean's hips, and every spinning revolution pulled painfully first one way and then the opposite as gravity dragged them greedily towards the earth.

While Sebastian's snarling features grew blurry, Ean sought the foundation pattern of his mental shield. Desperately spearing through the maze of his brother's mind, he finally found it and ripped it to unraveling. The pattern disintegrated into mental ash.

Sebastian roared, but the wind stole his fury. His fingers tightened around Ean's throat, and blackness encroached upon the prince's tearing eyes. Their spinning fall flung Sebastian down and Ean up, round and round. Somewhere in one of these revolutions Ean saw the ground rushing up to meet them, but he was committed: they would both die in this attempt, or both survive it as brothers.

Mentally Ean clung now to Dore's matrix even as Sebastian clung to Ean's body in their plummeting gamble with Fate. Ean tried again to form that spear to penetrate the fifth strand pattern and unwork it, but too soon the ground took shape beneath them. Sebastian, now on top, raised his head and—

They hit.

And bounced on a pillow of air created by the intention Ean had cast at the outset. But he'd misestimated the force of their fall. The cushion flung them high again, but it also flung them apart, even as the ground exploded beneath it. A geyser of rocks and dirt bombarded Ean as his body spun out of control. He threw a field around his brother to protect him, but then he was slamming into the side of the crater his working had just formed. His arm crunched in a sharp flare of pain, and he tumbled roughly down inside the crater's shell.

For a few frozen moments, he knew only pain. Then awareness surged back. He sat up abruptly, choking and coughing and spitting bitter dirt from his mouth. His throat felt so raw he could barely draw breath, and one arm hung useless at his side. From the sharp pain in his chest that intensified every time he attempted to inhale, he suspected he'd broken a rib.

Gathering his wits, Ean called the currents to light the now dust-filled night and saw his brother lying face down about ten paces away. He half-crawled, half-stumbled over to him. Ean couldn't find the energy to care if Balance claimed him anymore—so long as he made good on his promise first.

With a desperate will formed of raw determination, Ean wrapped a binding of the fifth around Sebastian and climbed atop his inert form. He shoved his good hand across his brother's eyes and mentally dove into his mind. The demon that possessed Sebastian's body roused at once, but Ean knew it now for what it was—naught but a greedy dragon guarding a sacred treasure. Well ... Ean would be the prince who slew it once and for all.

No spears this time. Ean focused the force of his entire being at the pattern of binding, found its beginning and end, and cast a roiling flame into that minute place of separation. Not merely content to release it to its work, Ean mentally guided it through the entire pattern from both sides at once until those dual channels of raging fire met in the center and—

The pattern exploded.

But not just the one pattern. A chain reaction spread like wildfire through the entire matrix. Beneath him, Sebastian howled murderously, with pain and fury intermingled in his hoarse scream. At first startled by the mental flames surging up around him, Ean finally realized the patterns had been designed to combust and take Sebastian's mind along with them.

Desperately then, he dove into that blazing inferno, feeling its heat as acutely as if he'd truly rushed through a forest fire. Even feeling himself burning, he pushed through the choking detritus of disintegrating compulsions seeking his brother's life pattern. But reaching it was truly like trying to find his brother's body in a flaming forest. He could barely see, barely breathe. His own mind felt on fire, connected as it was to Sebastian's own, and all of the pain his brother endured, he experienced as well.

Finally, he saw a light glimmering through the smoke and flames, and he speared towards it. Terrifyingly, his brother's life pattern was already fraying, so Ean wrapped a lifeline of the fifth around it, wrapped *himself* around it, but then he could do no more than huddle there while the matrix burned. He felt it as trees combusting on all sides, concussions buffeting and blasting him with searing heat, some so violent as to nearly knock him into unconsciousness along with Sebastian.

It didn't occur to him that shielding his brother's mind with his own could've resulted in the matrix claiming both of their lives, but it wouldn't have mattered even if it had, for Ean could walk no other path than the one that gained his brother's freedom.

He imagined himself and Sebastian huddling there in that forest of exploding trees, where wildfire raged all around and burning smoke choked the air, and he held tight to his unconscious brother, sheltering him with his mental body, using every ounce of *elae* he could summon to keep them coolly protected against the raging onslaught, himself barely clinging to consciousness, until …

The fires waned. No more trees exploded—none were left. The mental air began to clear. Finally Ean dared lift his mental gaze and saw only the starry heavens of Sebastian's mind—*free.*

Gingerly, so carefully, Ean slowly released his shield around his brother's mind, released the patterns of the fifth with which he'd bound his body. He opened his real eyes and looked down on his brother's form, on his face smeared with dirt and blood. Aside from knowing he still breathed, Ean had no further sense of him.

Fear gripped him in its own chokehold—for *oh*, he'd taken such chances! The prince drew in a tremulous breath and lifted his eyes to the sky—and to the seven stars of Cephrael's Hand. Ean managed a painful swallow as he stared up at them. Ever the constellation seemed to shine upon some portentous moment of his life.

Ean pushed the hair from his eyes with a trembling hand. His body felt stretched as thin as old linen, while his head felt too full, like a bin of chaff, dense yet still empty. His shoulder and arm throbbed, his side burned, but he really only felt the ache of his heart.

Had he succeeded … or had he failed?

Ean was just wondering if he should try to reach Isabel when Sebastian's eyelids fluttered. Ean's breath halted in his throat and he stared, waiting …

Sebastian opened his eyes. Red-rimmed. Bloodshot. For a heartbreaking instant, Ean couldn't tell who stared back at him.

Then Sebastian blinked and looked slowly around. "*Shade and darkness,* Ean …" His hoarse groan seemed to encapsulate Ean's entire existence in that moment. "What did you *do* to me?" A muffled choke that might've been a laugh escaped him.

Emotions at once both wonderful and overwhelming flooded Ean, too precious to put into words. He grabbed his brother up into a fierce embrace.

"*Gods above* … you did it …" Sebastian choked out a bare whisper and clutched Ean tightly in return. "By Cephrael's Great Book, Ean—*you did it!*"

Ean clung to his oldest brother in life as he'd clung to him amid that raging inferno, yet now he knew only the searing heat of happiness. He felt Sebastian shaking in his arms and experienced anew that heartbreaking compassion for all his brother had endured.

But Sebastian wasn't crying—he was shaking with joy, his shoulders wracked by silent laughter that finally burst out of him, bold and wonderful.

Soon it had overtaken Ean as well, and their foreheads fell together, hands gripping the back of each other's necks, until such joyous tears had washed the dirt from their faces.

Years later, the Kandori would tell a story of two godly brothers who'd fallen from the sky in battle and then laughed at their folly amid the crater made by their anger.

Hugging his brother, laughing and grinning so wide that his face hurt, Ean cast forth the thought: *Isabel, it's done!*

He couldn't be sure, but he thought he heard her smiling reply, *And done well.*

THIRTY-FIVE

"From Chaos we were spawned, and to Chaos we shall return."

–Excerpted from "The Prophet's Creed,"

The Book of Bethamin

DARSHAN WATCHED AS they brought his brother Pelas before him bound in woven chains of *goracrosta*, his face hidden beneath the curtain of his long, dark hair. Darshan's expression revealed none of the fury that seethed inside, none of the betrayal he'd felt upon learning what Pelas had done—an entire crop of *eidola* destroyed! He'd known Pelas would find some way of excoriating him for the compulsion he'd worked upon him, but he never imagined his brother would fall to such treacherous lows.

Darshan hardly knew how to interpret the feelings that raged inside him, tumultuous and intense, causing physical sensations he'd never before experienced—not even at Kjieran's faithless duplicity. As he watched Pelas being forced to his knees, compounding emotions formed new worlds within his consciousness; gasses of condemnation met the dark stars of betrayal and combusted in an ever expanding nebula of fury. He *would* bring Pelas under his control. His brother would be *made* to obey or be destroyed in the process.

They'd forced Pelas down so he now lay prone before Darshan with the tip of a spear aimed at the base of his skull. His arms and wrists were bound tightly behind him in an elaborate system of slipknots that connected to the *goracrosta* collar around his neck, so that the slightest motion tightened the noose. Dore could make torture devices of the most common of objects, but his work with *goracrosta* approached an art.

Darshan's gaze swept his Saldarian guards and lingered a heartbeat longer on Dore Madden, who seemed inordinately delighted. He wondered what torments the man had waged upon Pelas while in transit from Tal'Afaq. He'd bidden his brother be returned to him unharmed, but Dore could find shades of grey even within a mandate that was utterly black and white.

"Leave us," Darshan commanded darkly.

Dore whisked the men from the room.

When he and his brother were alone, Darshan bent and helped Pelas to his knees. His brother sat back on his heels and stared at him in silence. His black hair hung loose about his shoulders, and his copper eyes were condemning, but otherwise he seemed to Darshan a living example of the mold of perfection their Cosmic Father had shaped them all within.

Darshan stared at Pelas for a long time feeling that nebula's continuing combustion. It infuriated him that his brother could remain so composed while he suffered such incinerating anger. As Darshan studied Pelas's calm face, his own constricted and warped, emotions flickering through his gaze with each newly combusting star.

Then he backhanded Pelas in a violent exhalation.

Pelas flew sideways across the marble tiles. Darshan stalked after him and kicked him hard. Pelas exhaled a grunt as his body lifted into the air, and another as he hit and rolled upon landing. His face distorted with pain.

Darshan kicked Pelas repeatedly then—wildly, with rage fueling his savage motion—and every time his foot connected with his brother's body, he felt another star exploding. Somewhere along the fringes of the vast expanding cosmos, entire planets were being annihilated.

Finally, Darshan grabbed the noose around his brother's neck and hauled him to his knees. He held him there while he beat him, exacting the measure of his fury in each brutal blow. He beat Pelas until his flesh split and his lips bled, until he showed some remorse.

Except Pelas refused to.

No matter how brutally Darshan struck him, Pelas made no sound, and the accusation in his gaze never relented.

Suddenly the fury became too overwhelming. Rage exploded out of him in a thunderous shattering of the fifth. Stone cracked—the air itself cracked. Darshan punched his brother down to the tiles. Then he hauled him up and punched him down again. Pelas fell each time bearing his pain in silence, only his eyes revealing his burgeoning hate.

Finally, Darshan slammed his foot into his brother's skull. That time Pelas did cry out. He flew sideways like a broken doll, rolled upon landing, and his head bounced against a column. He lay motionless.

Darshan's anger abated abruptly. For the space of a heartbeat he feared ... but no, these bodies were imbued with their immortal essence. Fists alone—even his own powerful ones—could not affect lasting harm. Pelas had only been stunned. Darshan saw his brother's eyes focus after a moment, and then he drew in a shuddering gasp.

The instant's fear had done what Darshan's pummeling fists could not, however; it had bled his anger, draining the well of his fury into a bitter sludge.

Darshan's bare chest lifted and fell with his rapid breath. He spun away from Pelas and forced composure, lest the hammer of his anger drive a wedge even further between them. As his mind settled, the exploding stars of the nebula dimmed. Combustive gasses still mingled in deadly proximity, but without a spark to ignite their reaction, they became inert.

He looked to where his brother lay helpless, bound and collared, his dark hair a liquid splay of ebony across the marble floor. *By Chaos born*, he loved Pelas! As much as he might be said to know anything of love, he knew it for Pelas. Why couldn't his brother understand that his every act proceeded from this endearment, from his unbridled *care* for him?

Darshan drew in his breath and let it out again, tasting the metallic remnants of his anger as a tang upon his tongue. He would try once more to reason with Pelas, though he held out little hope for success.

"Why must you force my hand like this? You test my forbearance to the utmost with your flagrant misbehavior."

Pelas slowly elbowed himself up to his knees. He shook the hair from his eyes, spat blood from his mouth, and settled an unyielding gaze on his older brother. "You started this, Darshan."

"*I*—" Darshan spun to him, instantly fuming. *Pelas* had begun it by spending centuries playing with colored mud and engaging in mortal dalliances, their divine purpose abandoned!

But Darshan would not suffer another argument over his brother's petty grievances. "What's done is done—and in your best interests. You would do well to accept what cannot be changed."

Pelas spat blood from his mouth again. "Then we have nothing to discuss."

"We have *much* to discuss." Darshan leveled his brother a piercing glare.

"Those *eidola* were bound to me."

Pelas snorted. "Enslaved is more apt."

Darshan's expression darkened. "I felt their loss each time one expired—with each fragile soul ripped from the bosom of my awareness."

The faintest disbelief lifted his brother's brow. "A few *eidola*—"

"FIFTY!" Darshan roared, and the air raged with his fury, blasting past Pelas, sending his long hair shooting back from his battered face. "*Fifty eidola!* Purloined! Destroyed! Claimed by you—*blood of my blood*—into permanent death!"

For a moment Pelas looked taken aback. Then some kind of understanding came to his gaze, and his lips slowly curled in a smile. He broke into quiet laughter.

Darshan bore his mirth in simmering silence, determined not to lose his temper again. Exacting his anger only seemed to bolster Pelas's obdurate will.

But his brother's laughter grated. When he could bear it no longer, he ground out, "Care to share the source of your humor?"

Pelas sobered. He gingerly shifted his jaw from side to side, as if testing its integrity, then tilted his head up to meet Darshan's gaze. His eyes were cold. "I doubt you would find the same amusement in it."

Darshan clasped hands behind his back lest they lash out at his brother of their own accord. "I would you might see reason," he remarked with frustration pulsing in his tone. He started pacing before Pelas's kneeling form. "Think, Pelas—think what we might accomplish together!" He turned him a look of appeal. "If we were united in purpose."

Pelas arched a contemptuous brow. He looked down at his body, bound in *goracrosta*, and winced as the noose tightened—triggered by his movement. Already his neck bled beneath the abrasive silver rope; a growing stain darkened the collar of his shirt. He lifted a disbelieving gaze back to his brother. "*This* is how you entreat my cooperation?"

"I would have preferred a more civilized approach, but you forced my hand when you murdered my children."

"Your *chil*—" Pelas choked on his disbelief.

Darshan turned to pace back in the other direction. "If you won't see reason, Pelas, I must resort to more disagreeable methods. I confess, I find them less palatable, though Dore assures me of their success."

"That wretched creature feeds you poison with his every breath."

Darshan cracked a bare smile. "This ... this is the difference between us." He approached Pelas until he towered over his kneeling brother. "*I* exploit the adoration of these creatures to forward *our* purpose. I use their squabbles, the petty bickering of inconsequential kings, to make great gains along *our* objectives, and I let these doomed creatures make what they can of their inconsequential lives beneath the auspices of my will." Abruptly he bent and grabbed Pelas by the throat, pushing his nose a mere inch before his brother's. "But in all of this, I am *never* deceived."

Pelas glared blackly at him. His deep hatred seemed an inverse reflection of the bond they'd once shared, long ago, when all they'd known was the void of unending space and the violent yet infinitely sublime rush of unmaking.

Still clutching Pelas's neck, Darshan moved to his knees and pressed their foreheads together. "Oh, Pelas ... *Pelas* ..." he whispered. He felt his breath brushing against his brother's mouth, even as he sensed Pelas's throbbing pulse and tasted the tang of his anger on the electrified currents. "You've abandoned our purpose. I don't know how you became so wayward, so utterly lost. But all the protection we have in this effort lies in staying true to our divine cause." He pulled away and cupped his brother's face with both hands, searched his gaze with his own. "Should we stray from our path, the vengeance of our enemies might be waged against us. If we betray our Cosmic Father, Pelas, he'll exact his justice in retribution."

"There is no justice in this, Darshan." Pelas's eyes were cold. "Only your own petulance."

Darshan brushed his thumb across his brother's swollen lip, bringing a new welling of blood. He leaned in to cleanse it with a kiss. Their lips met, and Darshan ran his tongue across his brother's mouth, tasting salt. They had acted as one in the void. They must be as one again.

He let his lips linger against the corner of his brother's mouth, their exhaled breath mingling. Darshan stroked Pelas's dark hair. "Can you not see I must save you from yourself?"

Pelas jerked his head free of Darshan's hold. "I know your twisted sense of compassion."

Darshan felt a welling sorrow and let it linger. Grief only enhanced the righteous sense of duty that now gripped him. "No, dearest of my brothers," he replied, moving back to his feet, "it's you who have twisted from the faithful path onto the road of iniquity." He looked to the doors at the end of the hall. "Come."

They opened to admit Dore Madden, followed by two pairs of Ascendants carrying heavy gold poles set into marble bases.

Pelas's gaze narrowed. "More compulsion, *brother*?" The word slapped Darshan with its contempt.

Darshan regarded him sadly. "We are past the point of simple cures." He grabbed the noose around Pelas's neck and hauled his brother off, deaf to his strangling cries. He dragged him all the way onto the balcony, out into the open night.

There, he slung Pelas to the stones, bare beneath the starry heavens, where he lay gasping ragged breaths. A storm would've been more fitting for the working Darshan intended, but he could call the lightning out of a clear sky as easily as from a tumultuous one.

Dore directed the Ascendants to set the poles to either side of where Pelas lay. He struggled to rise, but Dore took hold of the strap connecting his wrists and collar, and twisted. Pelas choked with a shudder and abruptly stilled, his head caught at a strange and awkward angle.

"There now." Still holding the strap of rope twisted taut, Dore bent and stroked Pelas's head. "You remember what I can do with this, don't you?"

Darshan misliked the hungering in Dore's gaze. "Release my brother and move away, Dore Madden, unless you would feel the sky's fire in your own blood."

Dore gave Pelas a lustful look. Then he sucked in his breath across a thrusting tongue and released him to stand back.

Lying on his side, Pelas looked to the gold poles. "What's all this?"

Darshan felt Pelas's apprehension flowing crisp on the currents. It pleased him to know his intractable brother would soon learn obedience ... thrilled him to imagine their working together anew.

Pelas must've caught some inkling of his thoughts—even through the *goracrosta*—for his expression darkened measurably. "What is it you attempt here, Darshan?" His tone assumed more accusation than inquiry.

Darshan glanced at Dore, who nodded and licked his lips. Every cell of the man radiated wicked delight. But of course, Dore thrived on making helpless victims of the strong.

"Our power was given us to carry out our *purpose*, Pelas." Darshan shook out his hands and opened his arms, bare save for the bands of gold circling each bicep.

He could taste the power in the air from fingertips to tongue—ever *elae's* fifth strand collected around him as readily as their own *deyjiin*. Pelas's presence only added to its potency, though his brother would have no recourse to either power, not bound in *goracrosta*. Thus were gods made as helpless as mortals.

"You have abused this gift," Darshan continued while his awareness roamed the heavens searching for lightning's magnetic surge, "trifled with it, adulterated it, wasted it on frivolous pursuits; and thereby you have endangered your own eternity. Even compulsion couldn't curb the base desires of frivolity that have apparently overwhelmed your judgment. Therefore, I must protect you from yourself."

Pelas turned a sharp look from Darshan to Dore, to the poles on either side of his body. Dore had begun unwinding an iron shackle from around each marble base, and now he and the Ascendants opposite him began attaching them to Pelas's bound ankles and wrists. His brother's eyes went wide. "You can't—you can't *possibly*—"

"Oh, it's quite within my means, I assure you." Darshan knew his brother's mind; he tasted the tang of Pelas's fear rising on the currents. "I will sear the ability to work our power from your mind. No more will you know the sweet kiss of *deyjiin*. Never again will you betray our power with the harlot *elae*. Both will be denied you evermore, Pelas."

Darshan found the lightning and with an inhaled breath, he called it down upon his brother. It struck one pole and immediately leapt to the other, catching Pelas in between. His brother convulsed. Blood frothed where clashing teeth bit through his tongue, and with every undulation, the *goracrosta* constricted and released.

As the first wave drained away and Pelas lay gasping and shaking, Darshan gazed tragically, regretfully upon him. "Remember, dear brother, you brought this on yourself. What I do now ... I do for your salvation."

He called forth the lightning in an unrelenting stream, and the storm lasted for a long, long time.

PART 2

*"All paths may wind again towards the light if
hope survives the long night between."*
- Isabel van Gelderan, Epiphany's Prophet

THIRTY-SIX

"Men might be driven to despicable acts under the banner of noble intention."
– Zafir bin Safwan al Abdul-Basir, Emir of the Akkad

TRELL STOOD AT the window of his room gazing out at the endless blue sea and the sloop making its way into the island's harbor. The harbor boasted a single jetty where they received food and supplies each week, for the only thing Taliah hal'Jaitar sowed on that barren rock was hopelessness.

He wasn't sure what he'd expected when the mutes had shoved him, hooded and bound, into a skiff and aimed the prow north. Taliah hadn't been forthcoming with her plans for his future, and he hadn't asked her because it hadn't mattered.

All night the brutes had rowed. Then came the morning sun rising over a gilded sea, and the dot of an island in the distance. It had grown into a swath of volcanic char. The high end of the island towered a hundred feet over the water, while the low end sloped into a rugged escarpment that vanished at high tide.

And the towering fortress of Darroyhan clung to every inch of it. Forged of sharp coral and bleached rock, its highest towers scraped the clouds, while the lower towers, like the one where Trell had been housed, were stacked fat and rugged to do battle with the sea.

Darroyhan might've been constructed to provide a refuge for M'Nador's Ruling Prince should he ever have need to flee the princedom. It lay just north of the trade route between Tal'Shira and Vest—Trell had ascertained that much from watching the ships passing in the distance—and would've provided a strategic location for naval warfare.

Perhaps that remained its intended purpose. Trell only had access to a small portion of the fortress—barely more than the one tower that overlooked the jetty—so he couldn't know what other uses Taliah, her father Viernan hal'Jaitar, or Radov had for the place. He did know that the walls were patrolled by Nadoriin, that a Talien Knight oversaw its upkeep, and that the servants who interacted with the ships coming and going all had their tongues cut out—whether this indignity had met them before they came to serve at Darroyhan or because of it, Trell didn't know.

As he'd sat in the boat on that first morning watching the formidable fortress growing larger, he hadn't been sure why Taliah was taking him there. Now he understood that she'd brought him there to break him.

The first day she'd given him a room, new clothes, even ordered him bathed and shaved for her pleasure. That night, she'd called him forth and bidden him sit down at the table where her servants had set a fine meal. She let him eat the entire meal without saying a word, and when he'd finally set down his fork, she'd smiled.

Then she'd caused him such gut-wrenching pain that he'd vomited up everything he'd just consumed. As he'd crouched on hands and knees gasping for breath, she'd come and stood over him, just short of his own filth staining the marble floor. "Do you understand, Prince of Dannym?" Her voice chimed like sharp crystal. "You will do nothing ever again without my permission."

Trell had felt as if she'd reached into his stomach and turned it inside out. He pressed the back of one hand against his mouth and looked up at her. "Does that include breathing?"

She smiled sweetly. "Yes. But I give you permission to continue that for a while longer. Now, clean this up." She turned and walked away.

"With what?" he'd called after her.

"You have a shirt."

It had been one of her more pleasant lessons, upon reflection.

Beyond his window, the sloop rounded the jetty, and the dock men headed out to receive the ship, accompanied by a pair of soldiers.

Trell heard a latch click behind him and felt the air stir as his bedroom door opened. He didn't turn to see who'd come in. He didn't need to.

"You will go to help the men unload the supplies today," Taliah said as she entered.

"Why?"

"Because it pleases me to watch you work."

Trell turned her a look over his shoulder. "As you wish. Shall I go as I am, or do you prefer to dress me differently?" His tone held the respect she required, but his eyes smoldered.

Taliah's lips curled in a smile. She came across the room and planted herself in front of him. He stood a head taller than her and might've strangled her with his bare hands, save that he knew she could kill him faster and more painfully than he could accomplish the deed in return.

She reached one hand to cup his face. "I know I haven't broken you." She stroked his cheek and gazed into his eyes, yet she might've been training a dog or a horse. She certainly didn't see him as a man. "I know you think there is still hope, Trell. But you and I walk the path of *mor'alir* together now. On this path, hope is only a reflection from *hal'alir*, the sunlight glinting on the surface of the waves while we sink further below. It may call to you, but in the end, you will discover that you cannot reach it."

Trell removed her hand from his face. "Would you like to pick a new shirt for me, Taliah, or should I go like this?"

She pulled away from him with a little pout. "Wear your cloak." Then she turned and stalked out.

The ship was tied and the men had begun unloading by the time Trell reached the dock. He was heading out to join them when a flat blade caught him across the chest. He turned his head to look into the hard, unforgiving eyes of one of the Nadoriin soldiers, a captain by the rank on his surcoat.

"Put up your hood and keep it that way."

Trell held his gaze and did as he was told.

The sword lifted, and he moved on.

Reaching the ship, he set to helping the sailors unload their cargo, taking care to keep his hood up. The unloading took the better part of two hours. When he and the two sailors were finished, a pile of crates occupied half the dock. No doubt he would spend the rest of the day hauling it all inside by himself, but at least such labor gave him something to do and kept Taliah away from him.

Trell had just loosed the bow line when one of the sailors let out a cry. "Wait!" He'd found one more crate.

Trell stuck a foot on the boat's edge and leaned to receive the crate from the sailor, an older Nadoriin with gentle eyes. But just as the man was placing the crate in his hands with a grateful smile, a wave surged and lifted the boat. Trell lost his balance and toppled onto the deck in a tangle of crate and limbs, and his hood fell back.

"Sorry! Sorry!" The sailor hurried to help Trell to his feet.

"*Mamnoon*," Trell murmured in the desert tongue, smiling thanks to the older man. He pressed palms together and bowed. "*Enshalah Jai'Gar baray barekat biareh.*" May Jai'Gar bring good blessings to you.

The older man's eyes widened with his smile, and he answered in kind, "You speak so well of our language. I—" but whatever he'd meant to say, the crossbow bolt stole from his tongue. It struck him just below his sternum and sent him crashing backwards into a pile of empty crates.

Trell spun in shock even as the other sailor yelled a furious protest.

The soldier standing on the dock repositioned his crossbow to aim at the sailor. "Speak another word and share his fate."

The younger man clapped shut his mouth, but his brown eyes welled with rage.

"Speak of what you've seen," the guard growled at the sailor, indicating Trell with a flick of dark eyes, "and you'll know the sting of the Shamshir'im."

The sailor went pale.

Trell couldn't blame him. Viernan hal'Jaitar's network of spies and assassins wasn't known for tolerance and compassion.

"You." The guard motioned to Trell. "Get on with it."

Trell slowly picked up the crate and stepped from deck to pier. The surviving sailor hastened to unhitch the stern line and pushed the boat away from the pylon. As the sails filled and the sloop pulled away from the dock, Trell set down the crate and then sank down on it. He watched the ship until it passed beyond the jetty. Then he rubbed his forehead and closed his eyes.

A man had lost his life solely for the crime of seeing his face.

Dropping his hand, he turned a look towards the fortress and the retreating guard and wondered if Taliah had meant for something like this to happen.

Ever she played such games with him: cruel, twisted exercises meant to disturb him, to unravel him, to discompose and antagonize and unnerve him, to shatter the cage of his conviction.

She wanted to change the shape of his mind.

He should've broken by now—had he claimed even a shard of the self-pity that was his due, he would have—but the acts Taliah undertook to break him were no worse and no better than any prisoner of war could expect.

And he *was* a prisoner of war, no mistaking it, so he'd assumed that identity and likewise the understanding of the horrors that would come with it. He believed nothing Taliah or anyone else said, he trusted nothing they did, and he made no decisions about himself, no matter what Taliah made him do, for her every act was intended to humiliate and shame him. She *wanted* him to hate himself.

She could cause him enormous pain. She could make him do nearly anything she desired. But Trell knew instinctively that she would only succeed at degrading him if *he* took the first step down that path.

That night she let herself into his room, as she often did.

Sometimes she came in the night to hurt him. More often she came to use him. Taliah could twist his life pattern to make him do most anything she desired, even to coax an erection out of his body in spite of his unwilling mind. On such nights, she would often use him at her leisure—and then she would make his erection so pronounced and agonizing that he would finally beg her to release him, too.

She would make him work for it then, reminding him with every thrust how he had succumbed to her will.

That night she slipped into his bed and draped her leg over his hips, smooth skin gliding along his flesh as he lay on his side. Trell liked to imagine a viper had just slithered into bed with him. The vision kept him grounded to reality.

"You let your hood fall back today," she whispered. Her tongue probed the outside edge of his ear.

He kept quiet. Sometimes snakes left you alone if you remained still.

"Why did you do that, Trell? You knew what would happen to those poor men."

Did he? He supposed he might've guessed if he'd thought the scene out beforehand. Taliah's tactics were perverse but rather predictable.

"Two lives." Her tongue probed the backside of his ear and caught in the hollow at its base. Then she took his lobe between her teeth and bit down. "Two men whose blood is on your hands." Her teeth slid slowly off his earlobe, scraping his flesh.

His eyebrow twitched. "Two?"

She pulled his shoulder to force him onto his back and climbed atop him. The moonlight limned her naked form and made her dark eyes bright. A demon would've been more welcome company.

"Two men, Prince of Dannym." Her hand reached between his legs while her mind clutched his life pattern. He felt her working both hand and mind and fought against the tide of arousal, but he could no more resist her demands for pleasure than he could her demands for pain.

She sheathed him inside her and exhaled a delighted sigh. "The one who died today." She began moving her hips in a slow gyration. "And the one who will die once he reaches port."

Trell gritted his teeth. "Why wait?"

"We cannot be seen to kill the sailors who service our island, or none will dare to make the voyage."

Trell closed his eyes and turned his head away rather than watch her take her pleasure out of him like an animal to be pinned and milked. "The one who survived will tell the tale."

"Ahh ..." She pushed her hands to stroke herself and threw back her head as she ground atop him. "Precisely why ... he will be killed after he reaches port."

Trell offered the nameless sailor a silent and grave apology.

When she was finished with him, Taliah laid her bony chest across his and kissed his mouth. He'd trained himself to endure her kisses by imagining the head of a cobra swirling around his tongue. A soldier became still and obedient in the presence of such kingly snakes, or he didn't live long in the Kutsamak.

Taliah pushed up on her elbows and ran her fingers along his collarbone. "I'm very pleased with you tonight."

Trell tensed beneath her. "Why?"

"To bring needless harm to others is the beginning of the *mor'alir* path. In Vest, Adepts will be given a blade and instructed to kill. A child may gut a grown man, a woman slay a child, or a man his own mother … the sorceresses' choice varies. The doomed have only their innocence in common."

And all of you, your inhumanity.

"I didn't harm those men on purpose, Taliah."

She chimed a laugh. "It doesn't matter. Knowingly or unknowingly, the path is the same."

She slid off him then, and a moment later he heard his door click shut.

Trell sat up in bed and gripped his sheets in clenched fists. He should've known better than to engage in any discussion with her. She always found a way to leave a stinging barb beneath his skin, that he might worry and work at it until he'd made a weeping sore.

He pushed out of bed, walked to the windows and threw them open. Then he leaned both hands against the jamb and breathed deeply of the scent of the sea. If he couldn't cleanse his body of Taliah's touch, at least he could purge the air they'd shared from his lungs.

Believe nothing. Trust nothing.

He wanted to ignore her, but her words had caught him, just as she had known they would.

Taliah had become adept at finding the cracks in Trell's moral compass and working some toxic thought between them to corrode the gears. Would that she'd known nothing of him at all, but in their weeks together, he'd too often laid helpless while she'd taken apart and inspected the turnings of his mind. She knew him well enough now to understand where to place her stakes so as to disrupt the cogs of his certainty.

He *would not* walk the *mor'alir* path. She knew this. That's why she'd said what she said.

But he couldn't let those words go uninspected. *Was* the path the same whether he knew it or not? He'd caused the death of an innocent man. Whether through carelessness or neglect or succumbing to trickery, he *was* responsible. Trell thought of the old sailor's smiling eyes and felt guilt clench in his chest.

He hung his head while his hands made fists against the wood. Yes, he'd caused that man's death. Likewise, in a way, his friend Graeme's, whose life had been claimed first by a Nadori arrow meant for Trell and next by the River Cry; and the holy man Istalar, who'd pushed Trell free of a collapsing cave that he might find his way back to himself.

Was he any less responsible for their deaths or any more responsible for the sailor's?

Didn't a man choose the path he walked?

The Emir certainly believed so. The scriptures of Jai'Gar taught that a man has free will to walk the road of the righteous, and the Emir believed that a man confirms his choice with every action and decision. Faith in the scriptures inspired him to form the Converted, to offer men of all races a chance to choose a new and righteous path, no matter how entrenched they'd become along their existing one.

Trell straightened. He drew in a deep breath and exhaled a sigh, letting the tension drain from his shoulders and the guilt from his chest.

He'd been a military commander—a part of him always would be—and as such, he claimed responsibility for every life lost beneath his command. Jai'Gar willing, one day he would have an opportunity to atone for all of them.

Trell sat on the windowsill and slung a long leg over the rim to hang outside the tower. Far below, the ocean foamed over rocks of razor-edged basalt. At high tide the sea battered against the tower's very foundations. If he'd been a gambling man, he might've tried his luck with the waves. Naiadithine had twice kept him safe while a guest in her realm. She might protect him again.

Then again, she might let him die just to demonstrate his own foolishness. Gods were fickle that way.

He leaned his head back against the jamb and looked up at the stars. The chill night air raised gooseflesh on his bare arms and chest, but he welcomed the sensation. It held an odd sense of freedom in it.

The constellation of Gorion the Archer hung low on the eastern horizon, while Sepheune's Trident blazed at its zenith. He recalled a different night, some few months ago, when he'd sat beneath the stars of the First Lord's *sa'reyth* sharing a drink with the Whisper Lord Loghain. How long his path seemed between then and now, and how convoluted it had become. And yet …

He scanned the sky. Then he grabbed hold of the jamb and leaned precariously out of the tower window to gain a wider view of the heavens. One slip and he'd have met the rocks, but he knew the constellation had to be there …

Finally he saw it, still low in the west and nearly hidden by the curve of the tower: Cephrael's Hand.

Ah-ha. There you are. Trell pulled back inside and leaned against the wood again. One corner of his mouth curled in a smile. *I thought you'd be watching.*

When he'd said goodbye to Alyneri on that fateful night in the Kutsamak, it had all been so clear—the promise of his path, the Mage's plan suddenly outlined in stark simplicity. Trell still recalled the moment when he'd glimpsed the future and past touching in a circle of promise, but he could no longer recall exactly what he'd seen. Too many dark days and nights of pain blurred the vision now. But he remembered seeing the Mage's plan, remembered how it had flashed before his eyes as if the heavens had opened and bathed him in the light of prescient understanding.

'If it was Cephrael delivered me to your doorstep, Viernan, you can be sure he had his reasons.'

Trell smiled to himself at this recollection. Had he really made such a bold claim to Viernan hal'Jaitar?

The vision from that night had faded, and with it the singular sense of purpose he'd once known. Though he couldn't recall anymore what he'd glimpsed beneath those skies, he remembered the *feeling* of it. He remembered what it felt like to know he figured into the Mage's plan.

And it had made him realize that Cephrael had been watching the night he took the first step on his path. The *angiel* had been watching when events brought Trell back into Radov's hands, full circle as it were. And Trell had no doubt the *angiel* was watching him still.

He had to wonder, too … if during all of that time he'd been upon his path, as the Emir would say he had, no matter how twisting its route … what made him think he wasn't upon it now?

'… *the Mage has taken a liking to you* … ' Vaile's words, spoken the day they'd met, *'and that is lucky, too.'*

Taliah would have him believe Fate had abandoned him to her, but what if it was the other way around? He had to believe he still had some role to play in the Mage's game—the idea just *felt* right.

Maybe he was clinging to senseless hope, as Taliah proclaimed. Or maybe he was trusting his instincts. Whether or not anyone was looking for him, whether he had any hope of ever knowing freedom again, he still had to live by the same code.

He had inspected Taliah's logic and found it wanting.

Yes, he'd made a foolish choice in not wondering why Taliah really wanted him out on the docks that day. The old man had made a poor choice in looking on Trell's face instead of wondering why this stranger had taken such care until that time to keep his hood low.

Perhaps, of the three of them, the remaining sailor would make a better choice and think the situation through, even as Trell promised himself he would do a better job from there on out.

This was his path now. He had to walk it to know where it led.

Feeling finally free of Taliah's cloying scent and noxious thoughts, Trell returned to his bed. The stars of Cephrael's Hand moved in their silent arc across the heavens, following a path charted by the gods. Traveling west to east, they passed above Trell's open window, and he slept soundly beneath them all the night.

The sailor Hafiz hurried down the shadowed alley, feeling the press of the high stone walls too nearly akin to a bare, earthen grave—the one that would no doubt be waiting for him if the wrong people recognized his face. He looked both ways before crossing the street and entering the Al-Nefaru café, which dominated a corner across from the Souk Marmadii, the long, covered market adjacent to Tal'Shira's central-most square.

Hafiz hurried through the outer café and down a spiral stair into the bowels of the restaurant. Hovering above the long rows of tables, a haze of scented hookah smoke blurred the headier fragrances of cardamom, cinnamon and saffron into one inseparable bouquet. The hum of conversation from hundreds of mouths formed another haze, this one of sound, which obscured individual words in the same fashion. Looking nervously around, Hafiz made his way among the tables and down a narrow hallway in search of a specific room.

Most dared not even whisper of this room, though all the sailors of Tal'Shira had heard of it. Hafiz had spent the last of his coin bribing the captain of the *Ha'azali* into telling him which café actually housed the room. He'd risked his life even asking about it, but Hafiz was a marked man already. If the information he held could keep him alive—if it could keep his family alive—he had to sell it.

And everyone knew when you had dangerous information to sell, only one man in Tal'Shira could be trusted to buy it.

Hafiz rounded a corner and came to a sudden halt, for there before him stood the infamous blue-lacquered doors.

'*You knock once and once again, and you enter, and you kneel, and you wait.*'

These were the instructions for contacting Thrace Weyland.

Simple enough, yet Hafiz hesitated. He looked over both shoulders. He wetted his lips, spread his fingers and then clenched them into fists at his sides.

Every Talien Knight, every soldier, and every spy in the princedom wanted to personally present Thrace Weyland's head to Viernan hal'Jaitar. Countless bounty-hunters were after him. Mercenaries, too. Rumor even had it a zanthyr hunted for him. Hal'Jaitar had promised that whosoever removed Weyland's head from his shoulders would be copiously rewarded from this life into the afterlife.

Yet for all the people hunting him, for all those who knew his name, no one had ever been found who had actually *seen* Thrace Weyland. Even those who were rumored to have dealt with him couldn't say they'd laid eyes on the man himself. It was most mysterious.

Of course, a wise man didn't actually go about claiming to have sold secrets to Weyland—not if he long wanted his head to remain attached to his body. But rumors were like mist. They had no clear source, nothing stopped them from spreading, and only the sun of truth could evaporate them.

Hafiz stared at the blue-lacquered doors like they were a rearing viper splaying its hood. Finally he wiped sweating palms on his stained shirt, shook out his hands, and then knocked once and once again.

One of the doors swung silently inward.

Hafiz poked his head through the opening and then moved on inside. He passed through a dim room full of empty crates into a parlor hazed by apple-scented smoke. Cushions of various colors and fabrics were scattered across the layered rugs that covered the earthen floor. Finely woven tapestries decorated three of the room's walls, while a wine-hued curtain draped the fourth. Several large alabaster urns lined that wall as well.

And in one corner beneath a patterned awning, an old Nadori man sat cross-legged and puffing on a hookah.

Hafiz looked around the room. Then he looked at the old man again. The latter hardly seemed more than an old beggar, the kind that hung about the markets making foul jokes to ruff up a man's pride while a gamin crew of pickpockets robbed him blind. The old man's skin was as dark and leathery as a shoe too many times repaired. Sprigs of shorn white hair stood out from his knobby skull like bristly sea grass. He appeared so ancient that even parts of his beard had abandoned him.

"Ye one of them's as come to kneel and wait?"

Hafiz started at the old man's voice. "Y-yes." He wiped his palms on his shirt again. "That is, yes."

The old man gestured towards a cushion with the mouthpiece of his pipe. "Might as well sit down. Last one was wait'n a while."

Hafiz sat.

The old man puffed on his hookah and watched Hafiz with the milk-white eyes of the nearly blind. After an immensely uncomfortable silence, during which time Hafiz began to worry that the old man was reading his mind, or assessing his future, or otherwise casting some ill-conceived curse upon his house, Hafiz said, "Do I just … wait here?"

The old man took a long draw on his pipe. "Ye knock once and once again, and ye enter, and ye kneel, and ye wait." He quoted the custom in his dry, raspy voice. Then he cackled. "But *you* ain't kneeling, is ye?"

Hafiz abruptly shifted to kneel on the cushion.

The old man harrumphed. "So … ye buyin' or sellin'?"

Hafiz pushed hands against his knees and regarded the old man uncertainly. He was beginning to suspect the stranger was Weyland's agent, as unlikely a candidate as he appeared. "I'm … selling."

The old man cackled again. "Better be juicy." He puffed on his hookah. "He don't pay silver for rumors and smoke, and ye take yer life in yer hands wastin' his time."

"I saw this with … my own eyes." Hafiz dropped his gaze as guilt made a fist in his chest. He'd done nothing when it happened, but he was doing something now.

The old man puffed on his hookah, and the silence lingered and lengthened. Pipe haze filtered lazily across the room, teasing Hafiz's nose, blurring his vision. Long tendrils of smoke curled and unfurled like snakes. Hafiz began to see shapes in their motion, stories unfolding …

"… What?" whispered the old man. His voice barely disturbed the nearly hypnotic silence. "… What did ye see?"

"... A prince." Suddenly Hafiz shook his head to clear the haze from his thoughts. He blinked. Then he narrowed his gaze suspiciously.

The old man looked unimpressed. "Lots of princes in M'Nador." He puffed on his pipe.

"This one wasn't Nadori, but he spoke our tongue." Rumors of a missing northern prince who spoke the desert tongue had been circulating the docks for weeks. Every sailor knew Thrace Weyland would pay for word of him.

The old man set to hacking and coughing and finally hawked up a lump of phlegm, which he spat into a copper urn. He returned to puffing on his hookah and eyed Hafiz shrewdly through the haze. "Yeh? Must've been Kandori. Lots of princes in Kandori, too." He gummed his mouthpiece from the left side of his mouth to the right. "Where'd ye see him?"

Hafiz swallowed. "Darroyhan."

The old man removed the pipe from his mouth. He stared for a moment at Hafiz. Then he replaced the mouthpiece between his gums and set to puffing again. "I know who ye *think* ye saw ... but speaking our tongue is no proof."

"I've heard the rumors."

"Ha!" The old man spat. "Everyone's heard the rumors. He *wants* them to hear the rumors. How else will people learn what he'll pay to know? *Nyeh.*" He gestured with the pipe again, pointing it at Hafiz. "Speaking our tongue is no proof."

"They killed my uncle!"

The words left his tongue haphazardly, both a curse and a confession. He clapped a hand over his mouth and begged the gods to forgive him.

The old man looked him over circumspectly. "Go on then. Let's hear this story."

Hafiz pressed palms together and murmured a silent prayer to Huhktu, asking the God of Bones to look kindly upon his uncle in the afterlife.

Then he pushed hands to his knees and told the old man his tale. His voice broke when he spoke of casting his uncle's dead body overboard, of offering his bones to the sea. "I prayed to Inithiya to take his spirit," he hastened to add, as if the old man sat in judgment on his piety, "and I prayed to Naiadithine to give him a place in her court."

The old man scrunched his rubbery upper lip nearly into his nose as he peered at Hafiz. He gestured with the mouthpiece of his pipe again. "Why do ye think they let ye go, if'n ye really saw who ye saw?"

"There are rumors enough about Darroyhan already. Few captains willingly sail there."

"Rumors are good for a sailor's business. More rumors, more money."

"Hal'Jaitar pays for the distance from port to port, not for the bravery it takes to get there."

The old man spat at Viernan's name. "Ye think they mean to kill ye then?"

Hafiz nodded. "I worried they would take me as soon as I made it back to port. So I waited until I had the tide. Then I secured my rudder on a seaward course, dove overboard and swam the two miles to shore. My cousin smuggled me in through the city gates, and I spent my last copper seeking ... well ... you."

"*Me*," the old man snickered through toothless gums. "I ain't him. But he'll hear this news and pay ye well for it."

Hafiz exhaled a cry of relief. He might've wept had he not already forsaken so much of his honor that day.

The old man arched a wispy white brow. "Ye got a family?"

Hafiz nodded. "In Minara." It was the harbor town south of Tal'Shira where he'd been raised.

The old man motioned with a bony finger towards the alabaster urns. "See that 'un with a camel on the front? Open it up and take out what ye find."

Hafiz cast a curious glance to the urns. Then he stood and did as he'd been bidden. Reaching deeply inside the largest urn, his fingers met with a velvet bag. It felt heavy when he lifted it. *Very* heavy. Hafiz drew it out and turned to the old man.

"Well? What ye wait'n for? Open it."

Hafiz untied the cord and looked inside. Then he blinked and pulled the bag wider. His mouth fell open.

"Best get yer family out of M'Nador, Hafiz of Minara." The old man puffed on his hookah. "I'd head out while the Ruby Road still holds true and a man can travel unmolested into the west."

Hafiz hastily retied the bag and shoved it inside his shirt. "Yes. Yes, I'll do that."

"Don't delay."

"No. I won't delay."

The old man frowned at him. "Well—get off with ye!"

Hafiz fled, but he kept his hand across his heart. Across his heart ... and across the fortune in Agasi silver pressed beneath it.

Thrace Weyland watched the sailor Hafiz run out and then fell back against his pillows. He let out an explosive breath. As the outer door closed with a click audible only to his ears, he dropped the illusion of the old man. The hookah pipe fell from a mouth slack with surprise. Then he launched to his feet.

By Cephrael's Great Book!

Thrace swept aside the drapery, worked a trace seal upon the door it concealed, and hurried down the tunnel behind it.

When he emerged from a door at the other end, he looked like a boy of fifteen with a truthreader's colorless eyes.

It was one of life's little ironies that illusions came so naturally to truthreaders, that those most capable of finding and speaking truth were so equally capable of concealing it from others.

Not that crafting believable illusions was simple. Like any talent, it had to be cultivated, the required skills honed, and a repertoire of characters studied, collected and exhaustively mimicked. One couldn't simply throw on another man's face and expect others to believe it, no matter how closely this borrowed visage resembled the other man's. Mannerisms, accents, speech patterns, the way a man walked or laughed, even which curses he used ... all of these traits had to be imitated for the illusion to hold true, for it to be widely and uniformly *believed*.

Thrace Weyland was an accomplished illusionist, and this skill had kept him alive in one of the most cutthroat cities in the realm.

Of course, being able to read a man's thoughts helped, especially when he was coming towards you in a dark alley. And no amount of lurking in another's man's head obviated using your own wits—as a case in point, Thrace Weyland certainly wasn't his real name. Truthreaders unequivocally made the best spies, a fact Raine D'Lacourte and his Brotherhood of the Seven Swords could well attest to.

Historians liked to hold up fifth stranders as the most powerful Adepts— mainly because Malachai had made such a mess of things—but when one looked at all the skills that came naturally to truthreaders—illusion-crafting, mind-reading, telepathy, and harvesting the combined energy of thought to foment wicked explosions—really, who needed the fifth?

Thrace didn't blame Radov and Viernan hal'Jaitar for hating truthreaders. The whole 'he can't lie, he's a truthreader' colloquialism ironically failed to illuminate the truth. No one knew better than a son of the fourth strand how easily a man could learn to lie—by substituting one question for another, by deliberate misinterpretation, by offering different information than what was requested, neither providing an answer nor telling a lie.

A truthreader who didn't learn such double-speak wasn't long for this world. A man who could say only *exactly what was* tripped haplessly into a multitude of social *faux pas*: the duchess who expected compliments where criticism would've been better suited; the prince used to fawning flattery no matter his repellent manners; the lord who wanted his indiscretions kept discreet; or the king with an eye for another's lands.

When you could read a man's thoughts as easily as his expression, learning to slip around the truth wasn't duplicity. It was survival.

Thrace ducked into a basket-weaver's stall in the Souk Marmadii and waved to the owner as he passed through. When he emerged on the other side, he was a fat, bearded merchant who walked with a limp. He hailed a pedicab and paid the boy five *reale* to take him to the palace.

Long before the cab reached its destination, Thrace had moved on again, but before the night was through, he'd sold the news to operatives from five intelligence agencies and penned a letter to the man he personally served.

The First Lord would've paid him more than all of the rest combined, but as Thrace placed the letter in the hands of the one who would deliver it, the promise of Björn van Gelderan's thanks was payment enough.

They'd found Trell val Lorian at last.

THIRTY-SEVEN

"Once bitten, twice shy. Twice bitten—a bloody fool."

– The royal cousin Fynnlar val Lorian

RHYS VAL KINCAID, Captain of the King's Own Guard, knew he was dying. Every breath he drew felt like knives in his lungs. Moving required more effort than he could summon, since the greedy cough that was ravaging his chest stole most of his energy for its bidding. He'd walked out of Tyr'kharta and into the fortress of Ivarnen, but now it was all he could do to lie still. The illness denied him breath and sleep equally, such that he would stare for hours unending at the stones of his cell, coughing with every inhalation, wishing Death would make up his mind.

The others had watched him helplessly—Brody, Cayal and Dorin. They'd given him the mold-eaten straw pallet and themselves slept on the filthy stones and regretted every day that this was the most they could do for their captain.

In the beginning, defiance and hope had buoyed them all. While the wielder called Işak had held them in Tyr'kharta, they'd still believed Prince Trell would somehow escape and come for them. Brody had whispered stories of Fynn's exploits and filled the men's heads with such talk that they'd been sure the royal cousin would appear any hour, despite the grievous wounds he'd sustained before they parted ways in the Kutsamak.

Then, when they'd learned they were being held as a lure for Prince Ean— *Prince Ean!* Who'd risen as if from the dead and vanished into thin air ... or if the zanthyr was to be believed, across a node to T'khendar, which in Rhys's view amounted to the same thing—the men had spoken with pride and wonder. They'd known it was only a matter of time before they were freed.

But then the wielder Işak had come to see Rhys in his cell, and everything had changed.

That was the moment Rhys forsook his honor. That was the moment he gave illness reign, for he'd compromised the only thing he truly had to protect himself in those dungeons.

I should've told him!

He'd recognized his prince. There was no getting around it. He'd recognized his voice from the beginning, but he'd told himself ... he'd told himself Prince Sebastian was dead—he had to be, for what other alternative explained his eight-year absence?

Oh, there were many gruesome explanations, when Rhys later thought upon them ... afterwards, when it was too late. *Then* he'd finally summoned the courage to consider where Prince Sebastian might've been all those years. Every answer he landed on made him cold inside.

What tortures his prince must've undergone! What horrendous forges they would've needed to melt down King Gydryn's shining firstborn and reforge him into the ignoble man called Işak'getirmek.

Ignoble ...

No. Prince Sebastian carried no ignobility—not any more. Too well Rhys recalled the moment the man had come to him in his cell, so obviously devastated and seeking understanding ... not even knowing his own face. In that one brief meeting when Rhys might've helped him, instead, he had denied his prince.

Whatever his prince had done, whatever had been done to him ... as far as Rhys was concerned, he carried no shame, for Rhys claimed it all as his own.

Rhys stared at the ceiling and labored to breathe and wondered if this day would be the day he died.

Three times he'd failed his king by failing to protect his sons: Ean in Rethynnea, Trell in the Kutsamak, Sebastian in Tyr'kharta. This was why the illness had found purchase in his body—why he regretted the deference the men had continued to pay to him. He would rather have died than live with the shame of these failures.

His one grace ... the one blessing he could find in any of it, was that where he'd failed, Prince Ean had not. Rhys hadn't known at the time why they'd fled Tyr'kharta in the night. Now he did.

Prince Ean had come for them at Tyr'kharta. He'd come for them, but he'd found a lost brother instead. Prince Ean would've recognized his brother; and unlike himself, Prince Ean would've had the courage to do whatever he must to save him. Rhys had no doubt in his mind this was what had occurred.

The captain smiled in the darkness of his cell.

Prince Ean ... how reckless he was. How utterly incautious with his life. But he'd always been so. And Prince Sebastian ... their Majesties' firstborn had been ready to lead nearly since he was old enough to walk ... as careful and considering of his actions as Ean was devil-may-care.

A memory of the princes came back to Rhys suddenly, a memory long lost—or perhaps buried beneath the tide of grief that had overwhelmed them all upon learning of Prince Sebastian's death … his *supposed* death …

Rhys and Prince Sebastian had been sparring in the palace's practice yard. Rhys had seen over thirty winters and the prince barely seventeen, but the young man had mastered his sword forms and had the strength to carry off quick feints and fast advances. Oh, when they locked blades, it was no contest—Rhys easily overpowered him—but in the dance of swords, when footing and form was the sport of the day? Well, Rhys couldn't let down his guard for even a moment or the prince would have him.

Rhys remembered that contest so well. Prince Sebastian had feigned weakness to draw him in, only to put him immediately on the defensive with a sudden fervent advance. The prince's blade had flashed in the spring sunshine, his gaze determined and focused beneath his sweat-dampened raven hair. He'd forced Rhys nearly to the line before the king's swordmaster, Thale, had rung the bell for pause. Rhys had been so proud of him as he'd lowered his blade.

"T'was a bit showy, Your Highness." Thale walked across the sparring ground towards them, rubbing at the fringe of salt and pepper scruff he called a beard. "Successful in this venue, but in battle, you'll want to save your energy."

Prince Sebastian turned to him. "I used the Randolph maneuver like you showed me."

"Yes, but it's intended for use when you have assailants before and behind you."

"I was imagining they were, Sir Thale."

A smile twitched in the corner of Thale's mouth. "In a spar, you fight what's there, my prince. You'll have shadows enough haunting you in a real battle. Don't get into the habit of making them up yourself."

The prince considered this and then nodded. He looked back to Rhys. "Again?"

"Perhaps a break," Thale said, with eyes on the captain.

Rhys nodded his appreciation. What his prince lacked in experience he made up for in stamina, and it was an unseasonably hot spring.

They'd retreated to the shade of a tent and a table of refreshments. Across the yard, the younger princes, Trell and Ean, stood side by side in the archery range, firing off arrows at a straw form. At eleven, Trell stood a head taller than Ean at seven, but both princes were all bone and lean muscle and not half an inch to pinch on either of them. The bows they were using were a bit too large—much too large for Ean. Most of their arrows flew wild of the mark, but they were clearly having fun, which was about all you could hope for with that pair.

Prince Sebastian leaned against a tent pole and watched his brothers while his left hand tied his ever-present piece of string into knots. As Rhys came up beside him, Sebastian shifted his gaze with a contemplative smile. His expression reminded Rhys so much of the king—they were two of a kind, King Gydryn and his firstborn, as close as a father and son could ever hope to be.

"What do you know of the desert races, Captain?"

Rhys sipped chilled wine. "I know they seem only to want to fight each other."

"Father is talking of sending me as his ambassador on the upcoming peace mission." Sebastian turned with a faint frown marring his brow. "I feel like I know so little of their culture ..." His gaze strayed back to the archery yard, where his brothers were now shouting at each other.

"Surely you've studied—"

"Oh, Master val Priven has tomes about the Akkad." He waved a hand for emphasis of this point. "All about their history, the various tribes, their panoply of gods ... but I feel like these are just words on a page. If I'm to treat with these people, mustn't I know more of them than just the names of their dead kings?"

"You need know which end of your sword to lead with, Your Highness," Thale said from behind them. "Their culture knows little but war."

Sebastian turned him a look over his shoulder. "I think that view is part of the problem, if you'll forgive my so saying, Sir Thale. The Akkad isn't a culture of barbarians. Even the briefest glance at their literature speaks to this truth."

Abruptly the young princes came barreling through the tent.

"You did!" Prince Ean yelled in his seven-year-old voice.

"I did not!" Prince Trell put the table between himself and his younger brother and glared at him. "You missed 'cause you're a poor shot."

"I'm better than you!" Prince Ean dove under the table and scrambled towards Prince Trell, who spun and streaked away across the yard. Ean nearly knocked down Thale as he erupted out from under the table in pursuit.

Thale stared irritably after the boys while brushing wine from his coat.

Sebastian smiled. "Who were you saying were the barbarians, Sir Thale?"

The swordmaster turned him a mordant eye. "I shall be speaking to Master val Priven as to his handling of your brothers, Your Highness. A proper teacher would have those boys collected and upon their studies."

Prince Sebastian grinned. "You'd have an easier time corralling a pack of weasels."

Thale pushed his hand in one last disgruntled sweep of his coat. "I quite agree in that regard." He walked to join his prince and Rhys at the edge of the tent. "To address your earlier comment, Your Highness, I cannot speak to the learnedness of the Akkadian culture, only to their propensity to solve conflicts through bloodshed."

Rhys grunted.

Prince Sebastian frowned at both of them. "Father says Prince Radov is somewhat difficult to treat with ... that he's not known for his diplomacy."

Rhys grunted heartily at that, also.

Thale arched a resigned brow. "I would say His Majesty has the right of it."

Sebastian drew in a thoughtful breath and let it out slowly. "My father thinks theirs is a conflict of ideologies, the Nadori and Akkadian peoples. He says that finding resolution when basic beliefs are at odds is difficult even under amiable circumstances."

"His Majesty is ever wise," Thale said.

Just then Sebastian's attention was drawn back to his brothers. Rhys followed his gaze in time to watch Prince Ean climbing a high trellis with the alacrity of a squirrel. He gave barely a glance around him before he launched himself through the air at Prince Trell. Had he missed, he would've landed flat on his stomach and probably broken a few ribs, but his diving aim appeared to be better than that of his bow arm, for he landed squarely on his brother, and they both tumbled into a pile of hay that had been arranged for target practice. The bales collapsed on top of them.

Muffled squealing followed.

A smile twitched at the corner of Prince Sebastian's mouth. "I'd best go dig them out." He headed off across the yard.

"Let me call Master val Priven, Your Highness," Rhys offered.

Sebastian turned and opened arms to the captain as he continued walking backwards. "No need, Captain. If I can be a successful agent of peace between my two brothers, helping the Akkad and M'Nador find mutual ground should prove simplicity itself . . ."

Prince Sebastian ... he'd been such a bright star in their lives. How dark the world had seemed afterwards, without him.

Rhys wasn't sure why he had remembered that conversation out of the many they'd shared. Perhaps it was because that was the first time he'd realized his prince's conscientious and considerate nature, the first time he really saw the king's reflection in Sebastian's ideas. How he'd loved him! Even as if his own son ...

And how treasonous he'd been to deny him in Tyr'kharta, no matter how different he'd become.

Rhys coughed in the hard straw and stared at Ivarnen's moldy stones and wondered with every set of footsteps in the corridor if Death was finally coming for him.

He'd already come for his men.

Death in the guise of Dore Madden. Death in the guise of a demon with eyes like polished onyx. They'd come and claimed Dorin and Cayal and Brody—Dore Madden with his cadaverous frame and demonic eyes, and the demon itself, looking hellishly more alive than Dore.

It had spoken while the men were being chained together, told them what lay in store. *'You will become as me,'* it had said in that ratcheting, inhuman voice.

Oh, they'd fought then, his brave men, but in futility.

And all during the grim display, Rhys had lain dying on his pallet and watched Dore Madden. The man had muttered like a lunatic, but Rhys had heard his words and understood.

Prince Ean had taken something very precious from Dore, and that something was his brother. He'd freed him from Dore Madden's patterns and compulsions—the man had muttered vehemently on this point. And now Madden was punishing Prince Ean by turning honorable men into demons, setting up another trap for the prince in Ivarnen and holding Rhys as lure.

But ... Prince Ean had freed his brother!

Somehow ... somehow Prince Ean had saved the man from the darkness that had possessed him in Tyr'kharta. Rhys had hardly heard anything after this understanding sank in. Just the idea of it made him smile, even as he'd coughed into the bloody straw.

His men had each looked at him as they were being hauled out of the cell, their eyes full of fear and regret and contrition—things all noble men find in themselves in the end—but in their eyes, too, had been the unquestionable shadow of accusation.

Our prince abandoned us.

Oh ... Rhys knew what fear was whispering to his men, but now he understood, even if they did not. As he'd stared back, he'd denied the men this charge against their prince, even knowing they were going to their deaths and this would be the last exchange between them. He wouldn't accept their unspoken blame. He wouldn't accept even that they'd offered it. He would take the memory of honorable men with him when he died.

Rhys had watched his men being hauled away to endure unconscionable torment, but somehow the only feeling he could find was vindication.

Prince Ean had done what Rhys had not, and he'd unknowingly saved Rhys in the doing. For the captain could rest easy now, knowing his princes were together. He wished he might've looked upon the two of them just once, side by side, but he knew Prince Ean would be too smart to walk into another trap.

Prince Ean hadn't come for them, in the end. Rhys hoped he never would.

THIRTY-EIGHT

"The heavens cannot tolerate two suns, nor this realm more than one master."

– Shailabanáchtran, Maker of Storms

ISABEL DREAMED A true memory …

The Citadel's Grand Ballroom was a whirl of glittering chandeliers and colorful silk as the orchestra's enchanting music drew ever more couples into the dance. Isabel stood to one side sipping wine from a crystal goblet while she surveyed the room.

Arion and Björn had vanished somewhere—as was their wont—abandoning her to a never-ending procession of would-be suitors. Isabel denied them all graciously and watched in silence as they retreated from her presence wearing quiet looks of dejection.

Then her eyes fell upon a man in a suit of dark silk, stark against his pale blonde hair. She didn't think *he* was coming to ask her to dance.

"My lady." He pushed a hand to his heart and swept the other aside as he bowed to her.

She nodded to him in reply. "Dore Madden." Her eyes looked him over. "I'm surprised to find you here."

He bristled. "All were invited."

She knew he took offense at everything—he was like a sea urchin, all poisoned barbs. "And all are welcome, but such frivolity is not your usual choice of entertainment, I suspect."

His boiling dark eyes assessed her while his mind tried to skim the surface of her thoughts. He had as much hope of penetrating her shields as he did of becoming a Vestal, but Dore Madden was every bit as brazen as Arion—without a hint of Arion's charm. "I noticed you're not dancing either." His tone inverted her words back against her as if an insult.

"There is as much pleasure to be gained in watching as in dancing, I often feel." She smiled to ease his indignation. "Perhaps you feel the same."

His dark eyes swept her again. "Arion shouldn't leave you alone. If you were mine, I would never leave you alone."

Isabel could only imagine—but she tried not to. "Important men are burdened with important matters."

Something vicious and hungry flashed in his eyes at this. "Better I am unimportant then."

She blinked and drew back. "I would hardly describe you so."

"And how would you describe me?" He nearly glared at her in challenge.

Isabel considered him. Dore and Arion had many times butted heads—they were as opposite as night and day in every imaginable way save one: like Arion, Dore had a brilliant mind ... perhaps too brilliant for his own good.

"Your work in researching the Ninth Esoteric has gained the Council's eye." She hoped her smile might defuse the misplaced ire burning in his gaze. "You've gained your first row and bracketed the next. Endless possibilities lie open to you."

Dore held his fingers out in front of him to view the fifteen thin gold bands he wore. His expression darkened. "All, I suspect, save the one I want."

Isabel wondered in that moment what he hoped to achieve by this conversation—a rare opportunity to speak with her. It bothered her immensely that he might've crossed the world merely for the chance to engage with the High Mage of the Citadel beyond the ritualistic interplay of Invocation Trials.

Isabel tried to look encouraging. "A rowed wielder has many paths open to him."

"None that end in the Mage's Council."

She caught her breath, her mouth forming an *oh,* unuttered beneath her disbelief.

"I'm as qualified as any," he pressed on, dark eyes alight now with fervent purpose, "and more than some—Jasyn ryn Tavenstorm has but one row."

She finally found her voice beneath the pale shavings of surprise. "Having one's first row isn't the only qualification for the Council of Mages, Dore."

"What qualifications am I lacking?" It was nearly a hiss. Indeed, such vehemence emerged in this demand, she felt a viper had just struck at her.

The room seemed to darken while Isabel held his gaze ... or perhaps looking too deeply into Dore Madden's eyes simply drew one also into the darkness that perpetually lurked there—echoes of *mor'alir.*

Still, he wasn't unjustified in his query, for he had talent aplenty and passion to make up for whatever skill he lacked. *Such* energy possessed Dore Madden ... yet often as not, he directed this considerable energy towards destructive endeavors.

Ever the two paths of Alir lay split before Dore's feet. He walked with his left foot on one path and his right foot on the other. In the flash of a moment,

Isabel saw the Hundred Mages split thusly if ever Dore Madden gained their ranks, and she vowed never to allow that vision to realize.

Perhaps because words so obviously failed her, Dore leveled her a look of seething resentment. "Some have begun to whisper, my lady."

Isabel had the disturbing sensation in that moment of being sandwiched between two darkly shadowed beings, both of them reeking evil. She resisted the urge to look over her shoulder to see if indeed another lurked there in wait. Instead, she sipped her wine. "One cannot walk the Sormitáge halls without breathing in whispers; the air there is thick with speculation and rumor."

"These speculations have teeth, my lady. They speak of corruption, of Mages walking the path of *mor'alir* ... of dark patterns—*inveteré* patterns—in use."

She stared at him. Foreboding raised the hair on her bare arms—but that's exactly what he wanted, for her to feel threatened. She wouldn't grant him that boon. "Teeth are harmless on empty air, Dore Madden. One must give them something to cling to first ..."

The dream shifted.

Veils of shadow passed before Isabel's dreaming eyes like sheets of rain streaming across the plains. She no longer saw memory. Now she saw only darkness. Out of it rose a creature more magic than man. It approached her with eyes as black as its thoughts and opened its mouth—wide, wider. Out crawled *eidola* like cockroaches. They swarmed across her, laughing with Dore Madden's voice.

She turned to look where they were running and saw the lights of a castle on a lonely mountain. The *eidola* milled around its base, black as midnight water, their numbers growing as the thing behind her continued vomiting them endlessly out, until they surrounded the mountain in a writhing sea, until she floated helplessly among them. Four grabbed her and pushed her below the waves, and she saw that each one wore Ean's face, now black as ebony.

Their numbers grew into a tidal wave that broke free of the shore and bore down across the surrounding land, burying towns, razing cities. She rode helplessly within the tumult, one of the many, until the wave crashed over a man—a statue—a god—he stood immobile as the *eidola* broke over and around him, but her hair caught in his stone fingers. Tangled ... tangled in his hands, in his arms, tangled ...

A crushing waterfall of images freed her from his arms. She fought to breathe beneath the onslaught—fought to remember each picture, for even then Isabel knew this was no dream—until the images exploded in a geyser of fire and roiling smoke, into boiling clouds of violent madness.

Suddenly she stood across from the statue again ... shaking, freezing, staring into eyes that reflected a storm of light and shadow. Helplessly she walked to it. Her clothes dissolved beneath its gaze, and then *she* was dissolving, becoming as vapor …

A knife flashed to her throat …

She felt herself splitting, rending, and she saw …

Isabel woke. She sat up in bed and pushed a trembling hand across her mouth. It had been long years since her dreams reeked of foretelling.

She knew the room stood empty even without looking for Ean. He rose with the dawn now—if he made it to bed at all—to work with his brother, teaching him freely what Dore had only compelled.

Dore …

Her own words echoed in memory: *'Teeth are harmless on empty air, Dore Madden. One must give them something to cling to first … '*

Isabel pressed her lips together tightly. If only she'd known that she was foretelling her downfall—giving Dore the key to accomplish it, in fact.

… one must give them something to cling to …

And he had. *Oh*, it had been a bundle of lies, but so artfully crafted—ingeniously so—expertly designed to attack the Mages' own insecurities, and with just enough truth to cast a shadow that clung to her name. They had believed it because they *wanted* to.

Isabel exhaled a sigh and pressed her hands to her cheeks. She hadn't been in the habit then of traveling the paths of the future. Back then she'd trusted to her dreams to come when they would. But she'd learned since that Prescience was a fickle mistress, revealing her secrets where and when she pleased, and she didn't often please to tell her Seers what they would be pleased to know.

Isabel had sworn never to make that mistake again. Now she walked the paths of the future as often as those of the present—perhaps more so.

Isabel exhaled a tremulous sigh. In the long years since that conversation with Dore, she had many times wondered if their lives might've been different if she'd only looked into Dore Madden's mind instead of maintaining a distant propriety … if she'd trusted to Arion's warnings, or taken action earlier to involve her brother. Would Arion have lived? Would Malachai have kept his sanity? Would the Citadel still have fallen?

But while the woman Isabel wondered, Epiphany's Prophet had walked the mist-shrouded paths of time, and she knew … she *knew* there had been no other way.

If they'd met the Malorin'athgul on the playing field at the turn of the Age, before the Adept Wars or even shortly thereafter … even had Arion still lived … all would've fallen and their cause would've been lost. Every sacrifice would've been for naught.

Now the images from her dream floated before her vision, demanding inspection. When she viewed the images separately, she only nebulously understood them, but when she viewed them as a whole, her path stood illuminated with painful clarity.

She'd been upon that path when she'd allowed naivety to blindfold her to Dore Madden's plans, and she remained upon that path now, blindfolded to all but her Sight, when it was leading her once again to utter ruin.

Isabel pressed fingers to her temples, willing away the dull throbbing behind her eyes that often accompanied a foretelling of such intensity. Or perhaps its source lay deeper, in the wave of protest coming on a tide of fear.

Rising from a bed grown cold without Ean's warmth, she took up her robe and donned it as she walked to the balcony. The Kandori day had dawned bright, though winter still vied with spring and blew a chill breath across the world. The breeze clutched at her robe and tangled her hair as she placed her hands on the railing.

Isabel had never felt such duality in her own path.

Yet in truth, there was no duality of path, only duality of desire. What Isabel wanted had always come second to the path walked by Epiphany's Prophet. To choose any other route would be to deny a duty as native to her as the lifeforce itself. But her *heart* ... she had a woman's heart, not a Prophet's, not a god's ... and she feared how many times it might be shattered and still find its way back together again.

Closing her eyes, Isabel sought her brother's mind.

Sister of my heart ...

His mental voice felt such a welcome balm after the disturbing dream. Tears sprang immediately to her eyes.

Isabel ... ? His thoughts turned wary with concern. *What happened?*

A dream. She pressed her blindfold against her closed lids to stem the tears. *I must show you.*

Isabel meticulously recalled every moment of the dream—as she'd trained herself to do—until it all lay before her brother's mental eye.

He was silent when she finished. He knew as well as she did what it meant.

More tears escaped her, and she smudged them from her cheeks with both palms. *If even one can be salvaged,* she posed into his stunned silence, *is it not worth any price?*

She sensed his disconcertion on the other end of their bond and knew the twisted expression his face would reveal. *But at such cost, Isabel!* His mental voice mirrored all the regret she already felt in her heart. *Can you truly pay it?*

She clenched her teeth while a desperate fear gripped her soul.

There's always another way, he offered, though he sounded uncertain, an alternate path unclear to either of them.

Perhaps ... she agreed, for in theory it was true—one always had a choice, *but at what tumbling consequence? We've seen the ramifications of forcing new paths away from the one extending before us. Those new branches have rarely led to satisfying outcomes.*

To put it mildly, he admitted, though she heard only sorrow in his tone. *Isabel ...*

He stroked her hair, an ethereal caress, and then embraced her in the same manner. She felt his arms around her, warm and strong, heard his voice whisper into her ear, *Oh, dear sister ... I am so, so sorry ...*

She cast him a mental nod, for words failed her utterly.

Ma dieulle, tan cyr im'avec, he whispered lovingly as he withdrew.

Y dama avec'im.

Isabel exhaled a shuddering breath. Then she returned inside and prepared herself to face the rest of the day ... and all of the days thereafter.

The currents swirled around Sebastian's sight in funnels, in streams, in whirlpools and massing clouds of gold, bronze, rose and silver. Abruptly an eddy appeared in the shimmering fourth strand and he swung his sword for it. The blade sliced through the stream but to no effect. Ean's pattern still hit him in the face like a wet towel.

"*Blaarg.*" Sebastian shook his head and cast an irritable look at his littlest brother, who was standing across the marble-tiled court. "This isn't working."

Ean's hopeful expression faded. "No. Clearly not." He looked to Dareios, who sat in a chair at a linen-draped table where their morning meal stood untouched. "What do we do? He needs to be able to catch the patterns on his blade, but if he can't see them ... ?"

"Most of us can't see them, Ean." Dareios's colorless eyes sparkled with humor.

Ean looked back to Sebastian and frowned. "You're watching the currents like I showed you?"

"Yes, but Ean ..." he pushed a hand through his raven-black hair and turned blue-grey eyes off towards the mountains visible beyond the open-ended courtyard. Day had been upon them for three hours, and already Sebastian felt drained. They'd covered what seemed a months' worth of practice in those few hours, yet Ean pushed him relentlessly, and Sebastian did his best to keep afloat, for he felt the pressure equally.

They both harbored guilt over Rhys and his men remaining in peril of their lives—if they still lived at all, which Sebastian feared unlikely—but their guilt emitted from opposite poles. Sebastian had placed Rhys and the others into Dore's hands, but Ean had left them there when he chose to rescue Sebastian instead. They both bore this guilt, bore it together as brothers, yet sharing the burden in no way lessened the weight of the load.

Sebastian returned his attention to the problem at hand. "I can see the currents. I can even see when you're working something with them, but I can't see the pattern itself. It's like ..." he shrugged as he held his brother's gaze, "swiping at shadows."

"Ean, might I suggest you come and break your fast—" Dareios broke off his comment to lift up the linen tablecloth and nudge at the wildcat Babar, who was lurking beneath it.

She hissed and swiped at him with one dangerously sharp-clawed paw.

He dropped the tablecloth on the cat and turned to Dannym's two princes wearing an expression of resigned acceptance. "Wildcats and women ... I cannot decide which is more infuriating." Then he sat back in his chair and crossed his knees. "But you two have done miraculous work already this morning. I would say you've earned the respite of a meal—brief though it shall no doubt be if Ean has his way." His eyes teased Ean with their humor, but his words cast a tiny shadow of reprimand in reference to Sebastian's still somewhat fragile mental state.

But Sebastian understood why Ean worked them so hard. Dareios couldn't know the guilt they faced together.

Ean looked back to meet Sebastian's gaze. Ever Sebastian saw self-reproach in his brother's eyes, even as Ean no doubt saw the same in his. Sebastian bore far more guilt, however, for his brother Trell's imprisonment also weighed upon his conscience.

Yet in all fairness, he rather imagined you couldn't measure guilt. Whether a lot or a little, even the smallest drop felt as heavy as the realm upon your shoulders and as vast and boundless as time itself. How did one quantify something like that?

Ean exhaled beneath a furrowed brow. "I just want to try one more thing before we stop. I have an idea."

Sometimes it would strike Sebastian in the oddest moments that his little brother was teaching him how to wield *elae* far more adroitly than Dore had ever managed. The thought always made him grin.

Ean arched brows inquiringly. "What?"

"Nothing." Sebastian waved his sword in an idle motion. "Let's try it, whatever it is, this idea of yours."

"Then you'll eat—promise me," Dareios chided.

Sebastian turned him a grin. "I can think of several who'd be better suited as nursemaids, Dareios of Kandori."

Dareios's eyes danced with humor. "No doubt many of my sisters would agree with you, Sebastian, but somehow I wonder if you'd find yourself quite so carefree beneath my sisters' ministrations."

Sebastian thought of the Princess Ehsan and the way she'd looked at him and wondered at the implication in Dareios's tone.

Ean waved to Sebastian to join him, then started across the courtyard towards Dareios. "I'm going to need you for this. He needs to see it as I see it."

"Ah ..." Dareios stood and walked to meet them.

The truthreader had many times proven invaluable in bridging Ean and Sebastian's minds—for Sebastian remained too sensitive to Ean's mental presence to share minds directly with him. The touch of Ean's mind felt like a sword straight from the forges, too hot for Sebastian to bear, while Dareios's expert mental touch might've been a breath of wind if Sebastian felt it at all. Through the Kandori prince, Sebastian and Ean were able to connect.

Dareios held out his hands, and the brothers each took hold of one. "Very well, Ean, show me what you would have Sebastian see."

Sebastian closed his eyes.

It never failed to amaze him, looking into Ean's mind. Depending on what his brother focused on, the view varied greatly—from starry expanses washed with luminous color to rushing waves as like riding upon a sea of gold.

That time, as Dareios opened a channel into Ean's mind for Sebastian, he saw the rushing currents of *elae*.

"Sebastian, can you work something?" Ean's voice sounded far away, though he stood but a pace in front of him. "Perhaps the fifth strand shielding pattern from yesterday."

Wondering what Ean was up to, Sebastian dutifully called the pattern into view and cast it forth. Had he actually put it into use, he would've held it in place. Releasing it merely cast a momentary shield before his body, which quickly evaporated.

But as he released it, so also he saw it through Ean's thoughts.

Amazing! His brother really could see the pattern exactly as Sebastian had formed it in the exact moment of its forming. It was an exciting experience, seeing it from both sides.

Yet what he saw next …

"Ean, what is it you do?" Dareios's voice was low, curious.

Ean's mind had become a swirling vortex of golden light. To look upon it … it was as if he'd dived directly into a pattern … or perhaps into the fifth itself. Sebastian felt swept along on a raging current while light streaked painfully by. He plunged beneath waves of gold and came up mentally gasping, singed yet oddly elated, helpless against the swirling current while craving its overwhelming embrace.

"*Ean* …" Dareios's tone conveyed a sudden unease.

"Don't worry …" His brother's voice came low and calm, but clearly from a place of deep concentration. "I'm almost there …"

Suddenly a pattern exploded into view before Sebastian's mental gaze—brilliantly glowing and viciously bright, painful as staring into the sun. Sebastian cringed and would've jerked out of rapport had not Dareios been squeezing his hand so tightly.

"That's it!" Ean sounded triumphant. Abruptly the vision vanished. Ean had closed off his mind.

Sebastian blinked open his eyes. When the spots finally cleared before his vision, he noticed Dareios staring at his brother.

Ean noticed also. "What's wrong?"

"Ean ..." The truthreader looked stunned. He released their hands and pushed both of his to smooth back his dark hair. "*That* ... you ..." He waved one hand wildly. "You just ... *deduced* the pattern of your own variant trait!"

Ean rubbed at his jaw. "Is that bad?"

"It's unheard of! It's *never* been managed before. It's—" Shock apparently kept stealing the words from his tongue. "It's *phenomenal.*" Dareios gripped Ean by the shoulders. "Have you any idea the value of this pattern—or how dangerous it is?"

Ean blinked at him. "Dangerous?"

Sebastian grunted, for he had the gist of it already. "If Dore Madden had such a pattern, he'd be unstoppable."

Dareios cast him a telling look by way of agreement. "Wars might rage for *eons.*" Perhaps because Ean still looked confused, Dareios posed, "Think upon it: if every Adept in a battle could see what's coming at him? Patterns would fly like shuttlecocks back and forth across the lines in a never-ending volley." He released Ean's shoulders and exhaled a slow breath. "Many believe there's a reason so few Adepts are born with your particular variant trait."

Ean eyed him uncertainly. "What reason is that?"

"They believe too many Adepts like you would unbalance the realm."

"That's encouraging."

Dareios traced a finger along a triangular brow. "The Quorum of the Sixth Truth was comprised entirely of Adepts with your variant trait, did you know?" He dropped his hand and regarded Ean seriously. "Many believe the cataclysm that wiped their Order from the face of the realm was an act of Balance seeking to right itself. Never again have so many Adepts been born with that trait. Besides yourself, only two other men in the last half-millennia have ever been known to posses it."

"Who?" Sebastian asked.

Dareios shifted his colorless gaze to him. "Björn van Gelderan and Arion Tavestra."

Sebastian turned Ean a shadowy smile. "So ... *one* other, then."

Ean scowled at him. "Ha. Very ha."

Dareios traced one eyebrow again. "Would that I hadn't seen that pattern so clearly, Ean. I don't even trust myself with it."

"Consider it a sacred charge then." Ean turned and strode to the table, and Sebastian followed him. Dareios frowned after them both.

"Dareios, have you considered what would happen if I manage to get myself killed in the near future?" Ean looked up under his brows as he sat down in a chair. "Which I might remind you, I am very good at managing to nearly do."

Dareios walked to rejoin them, but he stopped short and frowned when he noticed that Babar had taken over his chair and now sat primly surveying her domain. "*Move*, Babar." He flicked a hand impatiently at her.

She hissed and flattened an ear.

In reply to which he sat down anyway, forcing her quite indignantly from the chair. She yowled a feline reprimand and scampered off across the marble tiles.

Dareios sighed as he watched her go. Then he turned his gaze back to Ean. "Now …" He sat back in his chair, folded jeweled fingers in his lap, and arched one triangular brow. "You were about to convince me why I should remain the repository for this insanely dangerous pattern."

Ean was peeling an orange. "Think upon it." He cast Dareios a dry smile, using the same tone and inflection Dareios had used on him just moments ago. "Isabel hasn't told me specifically why I'm so important to the game, but it doesn't take a great leap of logic to imagine it has something to do with this variant trait of mine. If that is the case and the pattern that allows me to see other patterns were to die with me?"

Dareios regarded him seriously. "I mislike the direction of this rationale, Ean."

"But you can't fault the logic in it."

Dareios worked the muscles of his jaw. "No. Sadly I cannot." His gaze shifted between Ean and Sebastian. "You would teach this pattern to your brother?"

Ean split the peeled orange and handed half of it absently to Sebastian. "Him and him alone."

"And I would—"

"Hold it in trust."

Dareios sank his chin onto one hand and considered him. "Would you submit to a truthbinding on your knowledge of this pattern? I would feel comfortable only if it remained a troth between the three of us alone."

"I would." Ean looked to Sebastian. "Will you?"

Sebastian exhaled slowly. He loathed the idea of letting anyone put anything into his head again, but he trusted Dareios, and he understood the danger of this pattern, even if Ean seemed cavalier about it. He shifted his gaze back to their host. "It would protect the pattern, too, wouldn't it, your binding? No one would be able to strip it from my thoughts."

Dareios nodded, an acknowledgement of both the truth of his words as well as Sebastian's grasp of the risks involved.

"Very well. I'll submit."

"*Khoob*, that is well for the sun. We'll attend to it after we break our fast." All the unease vanished from Dareios's manner then, the matter being resolved. He smiled and reached for his goblet with one hand and a piece of fruit with the other. "Tell me of your work with the Labyrinth yesterday. How did it progress after we parted?"

"Sebastian has the trick of it now." Ean cast him an admiring smile. "I last timed him at three and a half minutes to escape."

Dareios nodded appreciatively. "And Ean's time?"

Sebastian poured himself some wine. "A count of twenty."

"I still say it was eighteen." Ean gave him a hard look.

Sebastian grinned at him. "You weren't the one counting."

Dareios let out a low whistle. "Eighteen or twenty, that's a startling record." He shifted his gaze to Sebastian. "How many times did he escape that quickly?"

"Over a dozen. I stopped keeping track after a while."

Ean grunted. "Sore loser." Then his lips curled with the hint of a smile.

Sebastian eyed him dangerously. "A wise mouse doesn't antagonize the bull."

Ean cast him a flat stare in return. "Which one of us is the mouse in this scenario?"

To which a feminine voice remarked, "*Ah* ... ever it warms my heart to see such love between brothers."

Sebastian turned at Isabel's voice and pushed from his chair nearly in the same instant as Ean and Dareios.

She emerged from beneath a colonnade wearing a slim desert gown of emerald green. It clung to her curves and floated before her feet, much as her long chestnut hair floated around her shoulders, bound only by an ebony blindfold.

Ean took Isabel's hand and kissed her palm. Then he pressed it to his face and closed his eyes. "My lady," he breathed.

"My lord." She smiled radiantly upon him. Even Sebastian felt the glow of her attention. He got the idea her eyes would've been dancing beneath her blindfold and wondered suddenly at their shape and color. Then he wondered if she unveiled in the night, or if she hid her gaze even from Ean—a tantalizing, taunting mystery.

Isabel turned her head slightly to look at him in the way she looked at everyone without actually *looking* at anyone. Still, he put a tight lid on his thoughts.

"*Sobh bekheir*, Dareios, Sebastian." Her smile felt an immeasurable grace.

Ean still had hold of her hand and seemed unwilling to let go. "Would you break your fast with us, my lady?"

"If you desire it, my lord."

Ean helped her into a chair between himself and Sebastian.

Dareios retook his seat. "As always, Isabel, your timing is impeccable."

She smoothed the silk of her gown beneath her. "One must have *some* defining quality."

Dareios smiled and bowed his head. "My lady, the number of your qualities rivals all the jewels to be found in Kandori."

The group fell into easy conversation while they ate, for Isabel had a way of making every man feel the most important person at the table. Ean basked in the warmth of her near presence, of her hand in his, of her smile and her laughter and the sound of her voice. He tried not to dwell on the deep unease he sensed in her that morning. He tried to encourage himself with positive thoughts—by *Cephrael's Great Book*, he'd freed his brother from the worst imaginable abuse of magical bondage! And soon ... soon they would find and save his men as well. Ean had to believe in this, for thinking of any other outcome made him feel too desolate.

Yet for all of his attempts to hold onto the sun, somehow by the time the meal had ended, a grave shadow had overcome his thoughts and he was arguing with her again.

"... If you think force will be the deciding factor in this game, Ean, you have too narrow a view." Isabel placed her hand on his, but it hardly softened the sting of her words.

"I'm meant to fight them, Isabel. I *sense* that." Ean pressed his lips in a tight line and held her blindfolded gaze. "Tell me it isn't so, that you've looked down my path and see no such conflict at its end."

She drew in her breath and let it out slowly. "To look down your path isn't enough. I would need to look down theirs as well."

"And haven't you?"

Her brow pinched faintly. "It isn't that simple. The Malorin'athgul have no path within our realm. They only have purpose. I cannot easily see into their future because there's no path down which to follow their future steps."

"That can't be good," Sebastian muttered.

She turned to him. "You have the right of it, Sebastian, but it's worse yet. These beings are what we call vortices. The force of their will commands towards them the people and things they need to achieve their aims."

Ean felt a deep weariness beset him upon being reminded of this fact, a feeling of being doomed before he began—despite the fact that he'd begun this game centuries ago. He couldn't help wondering if he'd felt doomed then, too.

Sebastian settled Isabel a troubled look as he set his goblet on the table. "How do you possibly fight something like that?"

She arched a resigned brow. "You only hope to convince them to change their minds about what it is that they desire."

Dareios exhaled a heavy sigh and shook his head. "No easy feat."

Ean thought of Dareios's wife, who was apparently determined to die. The Kandori had his own experience from which to speak.

"Cephrael warned us in the *Sobra I'ternin*—he warned us this could happen." Isabel twined a lock of hair through her fingers and cast her hidden gaze out over the valley. A deep line furrowed her brow. "Cephrael had a better understanding of Balance perhaps even than our Maker did."

Dareios choked on his wine.

Isabel turned her face to him, and a wry smile hinted on her lips. "Blasphemy from Epiphany's Prophet—yes, I know how it sounds, Dareios, but hear me out. In his visionary state, our Maker created sometimes without imagining how each creation would ultimately evolve through countless millennia. But Cephrael knew that Balance was the greatest force in this universe, and that it couldn't always be predicted how Balance would shift to keep the universe ultimately aligned."

"Isabel …" Dareios stared at her. "Could I have heard you correctly? Are you implying you think the Balance shifted *first*?"

"That the Malorin'athgul found Alorin perhaps *because* it had shifted?" She sighed and shrugged slender shoulders. "The more I understand of them, the more I think it's possible."

She let each of the three princes digest this, and then Ean felt her mind shifting. What had been formless now aligned along a definite course, and he knew she meant at last to broach whatever had been so troubling her.

Isabel leaned forward in her chair. "Sebastian, I would that you might tell me if Dore has a stronghold near a lake, or perhaps close to the sea. A castle crowning a mountaintop."

Sebastian held her hidden gaze. "Ivarnen is such a fortress, my lady. It sits on a lonely mountain in the midst of the Enduil Estuary in Saldaria."

"A lonely mountain." She touched fingertips to her lips. "Yes … that is how it seemed to me." Her fingers stiffened suddenly and pressed against her mouth.

So acute were her feelings in that moment that Ean wanted to pull her close, to embrace her and swear to destroy any cause for her fear. Instead he clutched her hand. "What is it, Isabel?"

"Ivarnen." She looked to him. "That's where your men are being held."

Sebastian hissed an oath, and Ean turned an inquiring gaze to his brother.

"Ivarnen is a mountain fortress crawling with soldiers and surrounded by a wide moat of the sea." Abruptly he pushed from his chair and walked a short distance as if to hold off some grave disagreement. "There's no way in or out of Ivarnen save through one gate, or through a node Dore keeps closer than his favorite—" But whatever comparison he'd meant to make died on his tongue. He shook his head and turned them all a look. "It's the most heavily fortified of any of Dore's fortresses, and crawling with Saldarians."

"And *eidola*." Isabel sounded grim. "He's making them there, and I suspect many already walk its corridors."

Ean got the sense there was much more she wasn't saying.

Sebastian cursed and shot Ean a heated look. "Not with a hundred men could we do this, Ean. Not with five hundred."

'It should be a small task for a ringed wielder to take on a few hundred men ... '

For some reason Rhakar's comment came back to Ean and made him smile. Leave it to the *drachwyr* to reduce things to their simplicity.

Ean held his brother's gaze. "Then three will have to accomplish what five hundred cannot."

THIRTY-NINE

"Solitude is a wielder's surest companion."

– The Agasi wielder Markal Morrelaine

TANIS SAT LEANING against one column of a semi-circular arcade in the Sormitáge's *Giardino del Vento Ehst*. Across the mottled lawn, where splotches of brown betrayed winter's lingering kiss, Maestro d'Eleray stood lecturing to a group of Maritus students on the nature and use of latent Tellings. Tanis was only partly listening.

The wide silver band he wore on his fourth finger gave him the right to sit in on any lecture or class in pursuit of a maestro to sponsor him for his ring. But Tanis couldn't shake the feeling that his path had led him to the Sormitáge for reasons other than learning. The zanthyr had said as much—in his cryptic, elliptical way—pointing out that Tanis's mother had already taught him all he needed to know. But if that was true, why would she have wanted him to go to the Sormitáge?

This thought ever hovered in the back of the lad's mind, like a vagrant glaring from a recessed doorway. It stood as a harbinger of threat, whispering from the dark shadows of Tanis's thoughts where it kept ill company with apprehension.

It didn't help that his new roommate had managed barely a word of welcome and treated him instead with cold suspicion, or that people campus-wide observed him with their thoughts full of barbed and spiny speculations. Word that the High Lord was sponsoring Tanis had spread through the university like the wind, scattering a toxic pollen of rumor such that by the time Tanis had emerged for his first morning's lesson, every student was already poisoned against him.

Tanis had gleaned from the minds of those who could not yet control their thoughts that the population of the massive university seemed split into two factions: those who were certain that Tanis was a spy, and those who were sure he was the High Lord's bastard. Tanis might've answered any of them with the truth had they cared to ask, but students of all ages seemed more inclined to speculate about him than speak to him.

The most popular rumor among the *frites* claimed he was a spy for the Order sent to investigate the recent Adept disappearances. But *frites* were the least of his problems. The docents resented his placement as Devoveré for apparently random, petty reasons and stopped him frequently in the halls to inspect his ring. The literatos generally suspected he was reporting on them to the High Lord and gave him a wide berth, while the maestros eyed him circumspectly and guarded their thoughts. The diverse looks Tanis received as he walked through the Sormitáge halls might've been cataloged in a work comprising several volumes. Without the support of even his roommate, Tanis was feeling understandably lonely.

On the bright side, he'd managed to find the university's training hall, where instructors from around the globe taught martial arts and students paired up to practice with swords, mace, bow, or a plethora of varied weaponry. Even so, Tanis could only run through his sword forms so many times in one day. The instructors looked at him strangely when he tried to practice the *ta'fieri*, and his nearly flawless execution of the *cortata* sequence drew too much unwanted attention. So Tanis had taken to practicing his forms early in the morning or late at night and spent most of his daylight hours reading his father's journals.

As the sun climbed the sky that morning, casting the arcade's half-moon shadow over the lecturing maestro and his class, Tanis looked back to the passage in the journal he held propped against his bent knees. He'd read it several times already, but his father's words kept drawing him back the way one seeks the company of an old friend.

> *Today I reached a milestone in my training. I will write more of it in a moment, for indeed, the achievement marks the first of the rings claimed of my second bracket. Four more to gain my first row, and I intend to see it done before my twenty-fifth name day. From what I can tell, none will have accomplished so much at so early an age save the Alorin Seat himself. One day I hope to stand before him and swear fealty as a banner lord might swear to his liege, laying not pride of blood but ten gold rings at his feet in tribute.*
>
> *The contemplation of such a moment, as remarkable and long-dreamed as it is, yet pales in mind and thought when placed against the moment currently possessing me. For today I met the woman that I intend to spend my eternity with.*

As reward for today's achievement, my master arranged our meet-
ing and attended himself, though I suspect he imagined his role more
warden than chaperone. He said it was folly, this desire to meet her, to
speak to her beyond our heretofore stilted interactions.

He said beyond that forum, I was but one more stone on a beach
of shining pebbles, no more remarkable than a host of others. He said
she would not deign to acknowledge me even should I be standing
between her and the sun, casting my impertinent shadow upon her. He
called me a fool, but then he's always calling me a fool, and I'm always
proving him wrong. It's my greatest challenge to show this master of
cynicism how nothing is impossible.

He arranged our meeting in the Giardino del Vento Ehst. She stood
waiting beside the statue of the Custode della Verità Sacra,

Tanis looked up from his father's eloquent script and focused his gaze across
the lawn, away from the lecturing maestro, towards a distant statue. He could
just see it peeking beneath the marble archway that demarked a path through a
grove of linden trees. Perched on its high pedestal, the statue seemed nearly as
tall as the trees, though Tanis suspected this was merely a trick of perspective.
He turned back to his father's words.

Custode della Verità Sacra, Keeper of the Sacred Truth, whose
twirling form is captured for eternity in the Giardino del Vento Ehst.
One arm reaches to the heavens, the other lengthens gracefully behind
her, the folds of her stone gown flow like twisting marble flames.
Serenity imbues her features, cast in the everlasting light of the sphere
balanced so precariously and yet timelessly upon the tips of her gently
reaching fingers. She is the flame of truth, that resonance that perme-
ates all existence, as ephemeral and yet immutable as Epiphany must
be.

As my master and I arrived, the lady of my dreams stood before
the statue in quiet observation, her face uplifted to the sphere of truth
and bathed in dappled sunlight, seeming in that moment to me equally
as pure as the statue, blessed of grace, and utterly incorruptible.

My master made the introductions. Banal, unimportant. She spoke
quiet words of acceptance, but her eyes said so much more. I could not

contain myself. I fell to my knee and pledged my troth. I can barely remember what I said—the words came pouring out, overflowing my lips with hasty and incautious truths. She laughed when I'd finished and bade me rise—said we were making no knights today, but perhaps I could escort her in a walk about the gardens.

My master watched as she extended her hand to me, and his eyes were dark orbs of disbelief as I took it and looped her arm through mine. He stood speechless while we walked away, or else he held his tongue in respect of her. No doubt I shall feel the brunt of his displeasure in tomorrow's lessons and many more to come. Yet how can I regret a moment of the day? I walked with perfection beside me and left her side reluctantly, forever changed.

A shadow befell Tanis, and he looked up to find Vincenzé standing between him and the sun. The man had an uncanny ability to find Tanis no matter where he was on the vast university grounds.

"*Ciao*, Tanis," Vincenzé greeted as Tanis squinted up at him. He cast a blue-eyed glance over his shoulder towards the class and then back to the lad. "I cannot tell if I'm interrupting your lesson or a moment's idle reflection that would've been better spent in study."

"Not that it would matter in either case, I suspect," Tanis grumbled, for whenever Vincenzé came calling, he expected Tanis to drop everything and attend him in the High Lord's name. Still, while the lad felt slightly disconcerted in Vincenzé's company, the man had proven his only ally amid the inhospitable morass of gossip and rumor that he was forever trying to pole his way through.

Vincenzé slung himself down beside Tanis and leaned in to view the open pages of the journal. Tanis closed the book pointedly, to which Vincenzé grinned. "What's that you're reading?"

My father's most intimate recollections, Tanis thought, but he said only, "At the moment, a description of the *Custode della Verità Sacra.*"

Vincenzé lifted his gaze towards the distant statue. "Why not view it for yourself, *eh?*"

"Perhaps I will do that, sir. How can I help you today?"

Vincenzé chuckled. The two of them ever skirted around each other, much as the High Lord and Phaedor had done while still aboard ship. Tanis knew Vincenzé's mission involved bleeding him for personal facts to assuage the High Lord's endless curiosity, and he felt obliged to thwart the wielder if at all possible.

"The High Lord is asking how you're settling in so far. He would be reassured of your welfare and see that you've everything you require."

Tanis tied the ribbon around his father's journal and placed it inside the leather satchel at his hip. He didn't trust that Vincenzé might not know some pattern to read its words through the cover. "I haven't yet found a maestro to sponsor me for my ring, if that's what you mean."

"But that's not really at issue, is it, *eh cucciolo?* We both know you could test for your ring at any time. *Sancto Spirito*—the Endoge himself would vouch for you."

"So what *is* at issue?"

Vincenzé's eyes danced. "You tell me. You're the one who said the ring doesn't make the wielder."

Damn the man—he remembered their conversations too well. Tanis hadn't meant anything by that remark, yet Vincenzé found a way to use it against him.

The lad grunted and shook his head. "You think I'm a spy, too, don't you?" *Why must everyone think I'm a spy?* Even Pelas had been certain of it—though Tanis had come to love Pelas's epithet of 'little spy' and wished Pelas might've been there now to counsel him.

"You must admit the possibility based on the facts, young Tanis. Such a talent as yours, and already trained beyond your years ... none of us understand why you've come here."

Tanis exhaled a ragged sigh and leaned his head back against the column. *Neither do I.*

Vincenzé braced an elbow on one bent knee and extended his other leg in the grass. "Nonetheless, the High Lord swore to see to your welfare, and he means to keep that promise." Tanis caught a deeper meaning beneath this statement, but Vincenzé had uncommonly close guard upon his thoughts that morning. "Is your room to your liking? Any trouble with the Sarcova boy?"

"Felix has barely said two words to me." Tanis wished that truth didn't sting so—he'd liked Felix immediately and thought they should've been friends by now.

"Don't tell me." Vincenzé's blue eyes glittered with mirth. "He thinks you're a spy."

"You all do." Tanis frowned at the man. "You know, you're only enforcing the rumors by calling on me all the time."

Vincenzé chuckled. "No self-respecting spy would meet so obviously and openly with his handler."

"Explain that to the rest of them, will you?"

Vincenzé gave him a humorous look. "You could help yourself by actually attending a class." He waved nebulously at Tanis's posture and position. "This kind of loafing doesn't exactly help your cause."

"I'm *not*—" but he bit back his protest, for the man had a point. Tanis certainly didn't look like he was paying attention to the maestro's lecture. He *looked* like he was doing nothing of value, and he was bright enough to recognize that most of the time perception was nine-tenths of the truth. Still,

Tanis couldn't quite find the benefit in sitting attentively through a three-hour lecture on things he could do in his sleep.

Vincenzé pulled at a long piece of grass and tossed it absently away. He turned his gaze towards the lecturing maestro. "The High Lord is interested in your roommate, Felix di Sarcova. Like you, he's an exceptional talent. His Grace would know your perceptions of the boy."

Tanis gave him a hard look. "I'm not about to *become* what everyone is already whispering of me."

Vincenzé eyed him carefully. "You have the High Lord's sponsorship—a great honor. That should elicit your gratitude, young Tanis."

"The High Lord has my gratitude," Tanis returned evenly. "It doesn't extend to spying for him. Should he prefer to withdraw his sponsorship, I will happily rejoin Phaedor and we can be on our way."

Vincenzé grinned broadly at this—not the response Tanis was expecting. "You have an uncommon strength of character for one so young—even among truthreaders, who maintain their innocence longer than most." He gazed admiringly at Tanis then. "Do you see how much this tells me of you, *cucciolo*? No, you are no spy, *eh*—not for us, not for anyone, I think."

Vincenzé's gaze drifted to a group of blue-robed literatos just then passing on the path between them and Maestro d'Eleray across the lawn. He nodded in greeting, and the men bowed respectfully in return, but Tanis felt each of their gazes scraping across him.

When the literatos were gone, Vincenzé chuckled deeply and leaned back on one elbow. "Aside from dodging the daggered looks of literatos, what have you been doing since your arrival, Tanis? I assume you have spent *some* time attending lectures—you know," he waived airily, "in and around your secretive journal reading on art history."

In point of fact, Tanis had learned more from his father's journals than in any of the lectures he'd attended thus far, but Vincenzé's remark reminded him of a question he'd been meaning to ask.

He'd spent many weeks at the Villa Serafina, and during all those days his hair had curled around his ears, but in the fortnight since he'd left the Adonnai Valley, the honey-hued fringe had grown long enough to brush at his collar. Too, a shadowed scruff had sprouted along his jaw since he left the villa, but in all of his weeks there, not a tendril had grown. Tanis had immediately thought of his father's preservation spells, but he didn't understand how a spell placed on a house could possibly have impacted how quickly the hair was growing on his chin.

He glanced to Vincenzé's right hand and the three rings adorning it, marking his knowledge with the second, third and fourth strands. Their eyes connected as Tanis looked up again. "I've actually been meaning to ask you about something."

"Would this be something you heard in a lecture, or something from that mysterious book of yours?" He aimed an inquiring look at the satchel that concealed the journal in question.

Tanis frowned at him. Sometimes talking with Vincenzé reminded him of conversing with the zanthyr: half of everything the wielder said had some hidden meaning, and he always seemed to know when Tanis was keeping some truth from him.

Tanis flicked discontentedly at a blade of grass clinging to his pants. "Will you hear my question, sir?"

Vincenzé grinned. "To be certain."

"I was wondering ..." the lad cast him a considering look from beneath his brow, "how would one stop something from aging?"

Vincenzé drew up both knees and draped elbows across them, letting his hands hang between. "The obvious answer is the Pattern of Life."

"For a person. But what about for a thing?"

"You ask about preservation patterns, eh? The Sormitáge makes good use of them—from the paintings on the ceiling of the Grand Passáge to the treasured Archives."

"Those are third strand patterns, right?"

Vincenzé nodded.

"How do they work? Surely they're not pinned to every book in the Archives individually."

"They very nearly are. Any pattern increases in intricacy the larger the area and the greater the number of things within that area that a wielder intends to control. And when you're dealing with time itself ..."

"But could you cast a pattern over the Archives to prevent it from aging?"

Vincenzé plucked a stalk of long grass and munched on the end thoughtfully. "I suppose you could if you went stone by stone, wall by wall— but look, Tanis," he gestured with the grass stalk, waving it hither and yon, "if it was truly feasible, our ancestors would've constructed it thusly. To cast a third strand pattern across the entire Archives ... even should it be possible—which I entirely doubt—" and he aimed a pointed look at the lad, "well, it would mean trapping everything in the building out of time, eh? I'm not certain you'd even be able to reach the Archives under those circumstances."

Something about this explanation made Tanis fluttery inside. "What do you mean, you wouldn't be able to reach it?"

Vincenzé waved his grass stalk vaguely. "The building would be traveling in time differently from your own stream, eh? In fact, it'd not be traveling in time at all, while you continued on. You'd have to timeweave back to the exact moment in which the Archives last existed to find the building at all. And the working ..." Vincenzé let out a low whistle. "You'd have to be able to command copious amounts of elae as well as conceive and compel a host of interwoven patterns ... you'd be ripping more than a building out of time—do you see?"

Tanis was sure that he did.

Vincenzé's gaze became thoughtful as he further considered the concept. "Too, if you just kept the building trapped in time, *eh*, but not the land around and beneath it, the building might not age but the land would. So essentially, you'd have to be able to rip the entire *terra firma* out of time. *By the Lady*, what power you'd have to command!" He gave Tanis a look that spoke volumes. "That's more than just the third strand you'd have to be working, *eh*—and all the while fighting against not only the obdurate motion of time but the vast power of the pattern of the realm itself."

Tanis thought of the alabaster arches worked all over with patterns and the feeling of the third strand humming through them and went a little pale.

Vincenzé regarded him carefully. Then his blue eyes widened. "*Sancto Spirito*," he murmured with sudden understanding. "You *know* of such a working."

Tanis cast him an irritable look—the man was entirely too perceptive.

Vincenzé let out an incredulous whistle. "Where? Where have you known such a thing?"

"Can't you just pluck it from my head the way you've been getting all your other answers?" Tanis remarked churlishly.

Vincenzé laughed. "It's not so pleasant, having your thoughts on display, is it, *cucciolo*?"

"I wasn't reading you on purpose!"

The wielder's gaze softened. "I'm not in your head, Tanis. It's your face that betrays you—the honest face of an honest lad. But you must tell me now—the cat is out of the bag, *eh*? Where is it that you found this working?"

Tanis frowned. He understood now what his father had done in constructing the arches. What Vincenzé couldn't know, but what Tanis was now putting together, was that in all the time he'd spent at the Villa Serafina—on this trip as much as in his early life—he hadn't aged. His mother could've implanted ten years—*thirteen hells*, she could've given him a *hundred* years—worth of lessons while his baby body aged not a day.

Tanis felt more than a little dismayed by this new understanding. The idea of sharing any of it with Vincenzé ... well, guilt flooded through him at the mere suggestion of it. But then he realized that he probably only really knew a fraction of what had been done to create the working, and that telling Vincenzé about a preservation pattern wouldn't suddenly give the man a map through the impassible Navárrel peaks to find the protected villa.

The lad exhaled and looked up under his brow. "A pattern like you just described is in place in the Adonnai Valley."

"*Ho, ho!* Now that *is* something to know!"

Tanis turned and gazed off into the distance rather than endure the triumphant gleam in Vincenzé's eyes. He regretted bringing up the subject now. "Sir," he murmured then, hoping to direct Vincenzé's interest elsewhere, "could a variant trait give a person the ability to timeweave, even if he or she isn't third strand?"

Vincenzé looked the lad over speculatively, and Tanis felt certain he was trying to guess why Tanis was suddenly asking about *this* unusual topic. Finally, he plugged the stalk of grass back into the corner of his mouth and leaned on one elbow.

"*Theoretically*, I suppose it's possible. A variant trait accounts for Geshaiwyn being able to both change their features and travel the *leis*, and avieths are known to carry the variant trait that allows for timeweaving, but those are Wildling races already associated with the third strand." He narrowed his gaze thoughtfully. "Your question would be better addressed to one of the Arcane Scholars who specialize in this field of research."

"Do you know someone I could ask?"

Vincenzé shook his head. "The Imperial Historian is the one you want to speak with. He'll be able to refer you to the right scholar."

Applause echoed from across the way, and Tanis looked over to find that Maestro d'Eleray had ended his lecture.

Following the lad's gaze, Vincenzé clapped Tanis on the shoulder. "Come, *cucciolo*. Let's break our fast together—'tis the least I can do in return for the information you've given me this day."

Tanis slowly joined the taller man in standing and then slung the strap of his satchel diagonally across his chest. Inhaling a slow breath, he prepared himself—and his truthreader's sensitivities—to face the crowds. Already he was noticing looks from the dispersing students, and worse, Maestro d'Eleray's chilling stare.

Vincenzé *tsked* and muttered something under his breath in his native tongue. He glanced at Tanis out of the corner of his eye. "Ne'er there was a more exclusive community than what you'll find populating this campus, *eh cucciolo?*" He shook his head as he motioned Tanis off. "At every level, Sormitáge residents do naught but seek reasons to ostracize each other."

Beyond the gardens, they joined the masses of students passing along a wide foot-path connecting two of the larger lecture halls. Vincenzé nodded toward a group of students years older than Tanis, all of whom wore the grey and red coats of the Imperial Adeptus. "See those Adepts? The noble classes shun them because they come from poor families, sponsored instead by the Empress's benevolence. Each might be twice the talent of one of the blood, but without a coat of arms, they could well be begging on the street for all the fair notice they'll receive from the Empire's blue-blooded caste."

Next he shrugged his head towards a group of students sitting on the lawn. They were of varying ages and nationalities, but they all wore a wide gold cuff on their wrists. "And that lot—Catenarés. They'll segregate themselves and look down their noses at Docians with the same disdain that the Maritus students pay them in turn."

He indicated a group of younger students wearing torque-like gold collars. They were cutting across the lawn amid a hum of avid discussion that Tanis suspected included gossip about him.

"And those *frites*? They're outcast because they're … well, *frites*." Vincenzé exhaled a resigned sigh and rested a hand on his sword as he walked. "Maestros rarely associate with literatos—or Sanctos-forbid, a docent—even though the rest of us are hard-pressed to tell the difference between a literato and a maestro save that literatos rarely teach.

He adjusted his baldric as he commented, "The politics of families cuts another haphazard swath; likewise religions shared or shunned. And you'd need a year of solid study to understand the hierarchy among the scholars." He cast Tanis an apologetic smile. "The Sormitáge shoves everyone into some caste or another."

Their path opened onto a broad piazza dominated by a massive fountain sparkling in the noonday sun. Dozens of students were already crowding around it, and the hawkers were descending like flies—loudest among them was the one announcing hot buns and sausages.

As they passed a group of noble girls heading in the other direction, Vincenzé started chuckling. Tanis turned to him. "What?"

His eyes gleamed humorously. "Well they're not *all* staring at you with scathing glares, are they?"

"What do you mean?"

Vincenzé glanced over his shoulder towards the girls they'd just passed. When Tanis followed his gaze, he saw all three girls staring at him, though they quickly looked away when he caught their gaze.

"I think those three would've happily accepted your attentions, *cucciolo*."

Tanis looked to him in confusion.

Vincenzé laughed. "Why do you look so startled? You're a handsome youth—and you have the High Lord's sponsorship on top of those good looks."

Tanis didn't need to be reminded of that.

"Life might've been easier for you here if you were short and rat-faced, Tanis." Vincenzé eyed him consideringly. "The most universally despised man is the one who has no faults."

Tanis was pondering this logic as they headed down some steps. He noticed a crowd collecting around the entrance to a limestone building on the east side of the quad. A host of gold torques, bracelets and cuffs gleamed in the midday sun as students of all levels milled in animated conversation.

Vincenzé gazed curiously at the crowd, and shortly the cause for their aggregation presented itself, for the doors opened and a white-robed and hooded man appeared. He came to the edge of the steps to meet the press of bodies and a slew of shouted greetings and questions.

"Who is that, sir?"

Vincenzé's eyes narrowed as he gazed at the melee. "That would be the

Literato N'abranaacht, if I'm not mistaken. An Arcane Scholar." Vincenzé
sucked at one tooth. "He's become quite the celebrity of late."

Wondering at the tension suddenly threading through Vincenzé's thoughts,
Tanis observed the literato with interest. A sleek white hood covered his head
with only a wide, slotted opening for his eyes. The folds of the hood blended
into his silken robes, the iridescent cloth of which shimmered in the sun. Quite
in contrast to his elegant garments, the black hilt of a greatsword rose over his
shoulder.

"Why does he wear those robes?"

"He's a Palmer, lad."

"Is that a kind of Adept?"

Vincenzé gave him an amused look. "The Holy Palmers are one of the more
benign religious factions tolerated by the Empress."

Tanis frowned. "Is that why the students are so interested in him? Because
of his beliefs?"

Vincenzé barked a dubious laugh. "Not a chance." He placed a hand on
Tanis's shoulder and prodded the lad into the shade of a narrow lane edging
the piazza. "The Arcane Scholars are the Sormitáge's heroes, *eh*, always off in
foreign lands exploring treacherous caves and crumbling temples in search of a
particular treasure."

"What treasure would that be, sir?"

Vincenzé cast him a telling look. "Dark patterns. Lost works. Ancient
knowledge—*arcane* knowledge. Things lost in the storms of history or claimed
by time's greedy appetite. N'abranaacht is recently back from Myacene. His
journey was apparently profitable."

Something in Vincenzé's tone made the lad turn to him again. The wielder's
lips were set in a tight line, belying the mildness of his words.

Presently they came upon a tavern whose tables spilled out into the narrow,
cobbled street. There they shared a luncheon of *cinghiale* stew and plum
pudding, washed down by the last of the winter's heavy-frothed black beer.
Though simple, it was better fare than what he'd been eating in Chresten Hall's
dining room.

While they ate, Vincenzé told Tanis stories of himself and his cousin
Giancarlo during their childhood in Caladria. Most of the tales involved times
Vincenzé had won some bet, but Tanis suspected there were just as many stories
that Giancarlo could recount to the opposite outcome.

Finally Vincenzé pushed away his bowl, leaned back in his chair, and rested
clasped hands across his abdomen. "That's your problem, lad."

Tanis was eying the remaining bit of Vincenzé's stew and wondering if he
should ask him if he could finish it. "What is, sir?"

Vincenzé eyed him speculatively. "You don't fit into any caste." He
resumed the thread of their earlier conversation as if they'd never left it. "You're
neither poor, nor the prickly son of a merchant prince, nor carrying titles or a

noble's standard; rather being sponsored by the High Lord Marius di L'Arlesé himself—who has never sponsored a student to the Sormitáge, not even his own progeny," he added with an upraised finger and a pointed look, "—and therefore by extraction they suspect you more noble than their own elite and hate you for it. You skipped all the ranks up to the first ascension. You're not Devoveré but neither are you Maritus, wearing instead the Postulant's band, announcing to everyone that you arrived here ready to test for your ring. They can't even pigeon-hole you into one of the smaller outcast groups, for your Agasi is cultured, your coloring is fair, you're clearly not a Wildling, or—Sanctos-forbid—a Dane. You simply don't fit anywhere, Tanis."

You're telling me, the lad inwardly sighed.

And there lay the crux of the matter, the nagging suspicion that kept him up at night. Tanis believed he didn't fit into any caste because he wasn't *meant* to—because he'd come to the Sormitáge for some purpose other than learning. Yet what that purpose could possibly be … the mystery kept presenting itself for his inspection, but he had yet to find any answer.

He missed Phaedor's company, but even more, he missed the zanthyr's guidance. At least when he'd followed Pelas into peril that sense of duty had grounded him. Here he just felt alone. Tanis knew Vincenzé intended well, that his words were meant to reassure him that he'd done nothing to deserve the treatment he'd received thus far, but having these truths presented to him only heightened his sense of isolation.

He pushed back from the table. "I'd better be going, sir. Thank you for the meal."

Vincenzé cast him a tolerant look of farewell, but Tanis thought he might've caught a hint of pity within his gaze as well.

FORTY

"Colleges hate geniuses as armies hate heroes."

– Liam van Ghellar, Endoge of the Sormitáge

TANIS DREAMED …

    He and his mother sat on a blanket among the daisies. Before them stretched a long hillside overlooking the sea. The sun shone strongly from the south, bathing them in warmth, while the breeze planted cool kisses across his hot skin.

    His mother wore a wide-brimmed hat, and her colorless eyes were in shadow, though a bit of sunlight dappled her chin as she smiled at him. He saw himself in her eyes—a towheaded toddler clothed in linen pajamas and tunic, hems worked with gold. Looking down, he saw his pudgy toddler legs strewn with the detritus of daisies.

    Knowing only happiness, Tanis's little hand extended the pathetic corpse of one of his victims toward his mother. The yellow core held but a single white petal, itself somewhat mangled.

    His mother's bright laughter made music with the crashing sea. She impulsively drew him onto her lap and enfolded him within her arms, so that they both gazed out at the cerulean sea. Tanis felt her chin resting upon his head, felt the cooling breeze and the shade of her hat and her soft arms protecting him.

    "Ah, Tanis love, we must be sure to enjoy these moments." Tanis heard a wistful longing in her voice that he didn't understand, an ache that seemed to refute her words. It warned of long years of emptiness and longer strains upon her heart, emotions his young ears were too innocent to interpret or comprehend.

    His mother stroked his hair as she continued quietly, contemplatively, "There will be times when our paths seem to stretch endlessly on. Though impatience would guide us differently, we must use those seemingly endless stretches as moments of respite, times we might ponder our own questions and explore our inner truth."

She squeezed him gently, and he snuggled closer to her. His mother always smelled of warmth.

"You see, those are the times when Fate is not requiring greatness of us." His mother's voice seemed far away now, as if in her mind she was already exploring distant shores. "Let us not, however, be waylaid by such respite into thinking we are not still upon our path—and let no fears turn us from it—but let us have faith instead that when Fate requires our involvement again, He will present himself with action."

"Ma-ma," Tanis said. He held up the flower to her again.

She took it and gave him a kiss on his baby cheek. "My angel-heart," she whispered, her breath a caress upon his ear. "I love you so ... "

Tanis woke still feeling the touch of his mother's lips upon his cheek.

He lay for a while, letting his eyes adjust to the darkness of his room. Dawn's first light barely limned the edge of the curtains, and the chamber remained bathed in shadows. Somewhere in the depths of the room, Felix was snoring softly.

Tanis climbed from his bed and dressed. Then he jogged down to the courtyard while the air was still crisp and started moving through the *cortata* sequence with the slow precision the zanthyr had ingrained in him.

The Adept dance of swords was first and foremost a pattern, but one crafted with hands, arms and feet in synchronous motion with the mind. With or without sword in hand, it required concentration in the crafting—at least until its twists and turns became second nature. Tanis knew it instinctively now, but how well he'd be able to maintain it if he had to do it in an actual battle ... ? Well, he hoped he'd never need to use it, but the way the zanthyr had been talking ...

Whether Phaedor had intended his warnings in earnest or had meant only to scare Tanis into keeping up his daily practice, the outcome was the same. By the time the sun had risen above the campus trees and the university had come to life—the manicured paths beyond Chresten's garden courtyard now flooding with people—Tanis had worked three times through the *cortata*. As he finished his last low-crouching turn and straightened, he happened to glance up.

Felix was looking at him through the window of their third-floor room.

Tanis smiled and raised a hand.

Felix just stared at him coldly for a moment longer and then turned away.

Tanis let out a slow breath and gazed with furrowed brow at the now empty window. His most earnest advances, his most innocuous hellos, had only resulted in the other boy viewing him with open distrust. Tanis had hoped that maybe they would end up in a lecture together, so at least they would have something in common to talk about, but Felix was Devoveré. He wasn't required to attend lectures and had the freedom instead to pursue whatever path of higher learning most called to him.

Yet, Tanis didn't think Felix was upon a course of study—at least not one he could make any sense of. He never saw him carrying books or papers—not even journals for taking notes. Nor did Felix seem to keep to any particular schedule. When Tanis did catch a glimpse of the other boy around campus, he usually walked alone. Tanis thought surely they should've been compatriots for this reason if no other, for they both seemed isolated from the greater community. But Felix wanted nothing to do with him.

Gazing up at their bedroom window, Tanis realized that most of the university's students had long set off to greet the day's adventures, and it finally occurred to him to wonder how Felix spent his time.

When Tanis returned to his room, Felix was sitting at his desk hunched over a paper with pen in hand. Tanis only glimpsed a few lines of writing as he passed by—long lines of jumbled letters like some kind of incomprehensible code.

Tanis walked to his wardrobe and opened the doors. "I thought I might attend a lecture Monseraut Greaves is giving today," he offered with a glance at Felix, who remained intent upon his scribbling. Tanis took off his sweat-soaked tunic and donned a clean one. "Have you attended any of his lectures?"

Felix hissed a curse and crumpled up the paper into a ball. He ducked his head and growled low over his shoulder, "I can't concentrate when you're talking to me."

Tanis noticed several identical balls of crumpled paper which Felix had already shoved to the side of his desk. "Is there something I can help you with?"

"*No, Tanis—Sancto Spirito!*—can't you just leave me bloody enough alone?" Abruptly Felix scraped his chair back, grabbed his knapsack from the floor, shoved all the crumpled balls into it and stormed from the room.

Tanis stared after him in surprise.

When so many people view you with mistrust, the generality tends to obscure a more singular view. Otherwise it wouldn't have taken Tanis so long to wonder what Felix might be trying to hide from him.

But he was wondering now.

Taking up his satchel, he set off after Felix, intensely curious of a sudden to know where he was going. Felix had already reached the end of the hallway when Tanis emerged from their room, so the lad had to jog to close the distance. He heard Felix storming rapidly down the mahogany staircase, and he gained the mezzanine landing just as Felix was crossing the atrium's chequered floor towards the dining hall.

Tanis ran to catch up. Felix noticed him following and upped his own pace. Tanis watched him shove through the line crowding the dining hall's entrance, but by the time Tanis pushed between those same students who stood waiting for their turn at the buffet, Felix had vanished. Tanis stood in the portal gazing in frustration across the wide hall of tables crowded with heads, seeking one in particular.

A tall truthreader twice his age scowled at Tanis. "You're blocking the way, eh?"

Tanis turned and noticed the Adept standing there holding four mugs precariously balanced, and he moved out of his path with a murmured apology. He cast one more disappointed look around the room, but Felix had well and truly vanished.

There was nothing to be done for the day then but continue on with his intended plans, yet Tanis felt uncommonly disappointed, as if he'd missed a consequential opportunity.

Since he'd nowhere to be until after midday, Tanis stood in line for his breakfast and then found a table near the corner. While he ate, he read his father's journal. His father's long-stroked script told a new tale that day:

Lately, I've been having an ongoing and quite fascinating discussion with Benerio di Vangieri, one of the foremost Applied Patternists in the Sormitáge's Department of Metaphysical Sciences. He's spearheading research into reading the currents using fourth strand truth patterns.

Traditionally, the Seeings used to bring the currents into view are categorized in the Illusion band, but Benerio is using truth patterns as well. Combined, they elicit a resonance unlike anything I've experienced while reading the currents.

Benerio is excited about my idea to layer his designs with my first strand tracking patterns to create a singular pattern that reveals both truth and individuality of character—that is, to be able to see not only what was done but who did it. Once perfected, this pattern could be used to trace the workings of specific wielders from anywhere on the globe.

I've also begun experimenting with a layered pattern using the fifth to reveal physical detail otherwise impossible to see, such as the outlines of rooms inside a building, or the chambers of a beating heart.

This is the pattern so far ...

The next four pages contained patterns—one carefully penned diagram per page. It took Tanis several minutes of study to realize they weren't four separate patterns but *one* pattern viewed from each of four angles.

Of course!

Tanis hadn't realized it before, but he saw the logic now. Patterns weren't two-dimensional—at least ... well, most of them *couldn't* have been only two-dimensional. The more complicated, the more forces they sought to compel and control, the more dimensions they would have to occupy.

He thought about what his mother had told him of Patterning—how in order to wield a pattern, you first had to be able conceptualize it, to memorize it exactly. Then you had to be able to channel not merely *elae* but also your own *intention* into the pattern. This took practice, because it was quite a few things you had to conceptualize all at once.

She'd tried to explain how Patterning was its own language, which Tanis more or less understood. Just as one learned how a number was a symbol representing a quantity, or how a word represented an idea, patterns had their own representation: a potent combination of intent, purpose and action.

Tanis tried to envision his father's pattern as it would appear in three dimensions. Moving from page to page, he layered each piece of the pattern upon the next in his mind's eye, fitting the sides and angles and loops upon one another like a three-dimensional puzzle. As his mind traced every line and swirl, he wove the image into being.

It wasn't until the dining room went silent that Tanis looked up from his journal and received a shock. There, before him, hovered the pattern he'd been conceptualizing in his mind—he'd unwittingly crafted it as an illusion that everyone could see! The pattern glowed in an intricate, crystalline dodecahedron and cast refracted light on everyone nearby.

Abruptly he released the illusion and buried his gaze in his book, red cheeks burning. He felt eyes lingering on him far longer than was comfortable, and a hum of murmuring continued even after the eyes moved on. Most discomfiting were the thoughts left unspoken which nonetheless reverberated around the room unevenly, reverberating back to Tanis's perception. The general opinion seemed to be that Tanis was showing off.

Feeling suddenly most unwelcome, the lad gathered his things and hastened out of Chresten Hall.

Across campus, the lad walked with his eyes downcast. Shame sat heavily on his shoulders. Though it had been an honest mistake, a truthreader of his ability was expected to exhibit better control over his talent. The others were only justified in thinking ill of him.

The morning's losses had drained the shallow well of encouragement which Tanis's dream of his mother had replenished. Now frustrations and uncertainties flowed in to fill the vacuum. Tanis had never felt so alone, nor so lonely for lack of company.

Unable to push off the glum cloud that enshrouded him, Tanis let his feet find their own way across campus. He wandered for a while through the Grand Passáge, gazing up at the fantastical ceiling that stretched nearly half a mile, its length quartered by intersecting passages and gilded domes. At every corner, a marble sculpture fashioning some new creature erupted from the joining of walls. Sometimes fierce, often elaborate, each sculpture held an incomparable grandeur.

After a while, Tanis turned down one of the intersecting hallways and at last emerged onto a wide quad. He sat on the steps for a while watching the ceaseless flow of bodies in and out of buildings and along each path. He saw robed maestros and peak-capped literatos, sometimes in close discussion but more often trailing a cloud of students; Bemothi and Nadori Adepts distinguishable from each other by the styling of their garments and the way each assiduously avoided the other; and golden-haired Danes viewing everyone with contempt. He saw Veneisean Adepts from Queen Indora's Conscriptus wearing their sashes of bright tangerine, and myriad other races and nationalities in a never-ending flow. Every once in a while he would see the pearlescent robe of a Palmer passing like a star among the darker stream.

He recalled the wonder he'd experienced while walking Cair Rethynnea's Thoroughfare, how he'd been so amazed to see so many peoples from every walk of life. Yet the Sormitáge far surpassed even Rethynnea's diversity.

After a while, Tanis pushed to his feet and joined the flow, falling in a few paces behind a mob of young second strand *frites* who were twittering with the latest gossip. Apparently it had come to light that the Order was investigating the Adept disappearances and that they'd begun Questioning the maestros. This was quite the news. The young *frites* were all aflutter with speculation over who had been truthread and what other crimes the Order's operatives may have uncovered.

They were walking along a path bordered by towering maples just beginning to bud when the chattering *frites* turned between two statues and descended a mossy staircase set into the hillside. With nothing more important to do, Tanis followed them.

At least a hundred granite stairs ended at the wall of a massive amphitheater. The *frites* had all gone on through the columned entrance—Tanis heard the constant hum of their conversation echoing out of the interior—so he stayed on their trail, growing ever more curious about their destination.

He emerged into daylight again in a stadium built to host thousands. The frites had descended to the first circle of rows and were gathering along the backless marble benches that framed its center—and what a center it was!

Huge slabs of black and white marble formed the floor, which spanned at least two hundred feet. A maestro stood at the near edge of the chequerboard tiles with hands clasped before his grass-green robes. He waited with miraculous patience for the young Nodefinders to settle.

Then he said: "Welcome, welcome. Are we all here? Very well, let us resume. For any who missed yesterday's discussion, we've been covering the Unified Pattern. Now, as you have learned, second strand Adepts use but a single pattern—intrinsic to our innate composition—to travel upon the Pattern of the World."

He raised his arm, palm out, and the air began to shimmer at the tips of his fingers. The shimmering rapidly expanded into the illusion of a pattern, golden and complex, which turned slowly on its axis. In the light of the pattern's reflection, Tanis caught the glimmer of several Sormitáge rings on the maestro's fingers.

"This major pattern, called the Greater Reticulation, is constructed of fifty weld points," the maestro continued then. "Each of these points branches into ten to twenty-five nodal connections called the Lesser Tessellations."

The illusion shifted. One point grew larger while the others faded. New golden strands branched from this singular point in pyramidal fashion, forming multiple icosahedrons. The maestro explained while the illusion rotated, "Each node hosts up to fifty-six ley lines within its matrix. Each ley line is capable of supporting twenty-four to the third power of leis."

The original illusion altered again, with the single node shrinking back to become merely one point among the greater pattern, whereupon the maestro said, "The interconnectedness of the entire geopolyhedron of the Greater Reticulation must become second nature to a Nodefinder who hopes to reach the First Ascendancy and gain his Devoveré ring. You should all have begun charting the Greater Reticulation with Maestro Hunn in Extratellurian Cartography. See me after the lecture if you have not."

He dropped his arm, banishing the illusion, and walked to the forward edge of the tile he was standing on. "But the focus of today's lecture is on using *our* pattern—not to travel upon this miraculous geometric matrix, for which none of you are ready—but upon our *leis* court, here." And he motioned to the tiles spreading around his person.

Casting a compelling stare around the assembled Nodefinders to first capture their gazes and their attention, the maestro took a big step to his right. Tanis saw the flash of a pattern in his mind's eye, and the maestro appeared four squares to the left.

The *frites* all let out a whoop of excitement.

The maestro made a little bow, and the *frites* broke into mad applause.

Tanis smiled from where he leaned against the tunnel's archway. This maestro seemed experienced in handling such a young crowd of second stranders, who were notoriously hard to corral.

The maestro took a quick tour around the chequerboard court then, stepping hither and yon and vanishing and appearing randomly. The *frites* were all standing up and bubbling with excitement by the time he stepped off the court to let them have a go.

Tanis smiled as the *frites* bounded and cavorted then, gleefully vanishing and reappearing, sometimes right on top of one another with bumps and tumbles and shrieks of laughter. The amphitheater soon echoed with delighted squealing and shouts of challenge.

He'd heard a lot of talk about the ballgame called Quai—the observation and discussion of which was a favorite pastime for most Sormitáge residents—but until Tanis saw the *frites* bouncing from square to square, he hadn't realized this was the amphitheater where they played Quai each week. Every Hall had its own Quai champion, and a student could win or lose an entire month's tuition gambling on a single game.

Tanis watched the *frites* until the Nodefinders' repetitively flashing pattern was bombarding his consciousness with relentless repetition, whereupon he took his leave. As he climbed the steps, he noticed the maestro watching him with a tense gaze.

That afternoon, the Imperial Historian Monseraut Greaves gave a lecture on the origins of the Empire. Sitting in the back of the crowded lecture hall, Tanis listened raptly as the historian spoke of the Age of Fable and the times known as the Before, when chaos ruled Alorin with an iron fist.

It surprised the lad to learn that Adepts of those times knew nothing of the *Sobra I'ternin* or even of the strands of *elae*—that this knowledge came much later in the realm's collective history. He found it startling to hear that even today, some kingdoms of the realm—many in far eastern Avatar—refused to acknowledge the *Sobra's* truth and clung instead to the practices of a darker age.

Tanis thought immediately of Pelas's Fhorgs and their staunch belief in blood magic, which seemed naught but gruesome ceremony and superstition to the lad, yet which he'd seen them cling to with fervent faith.

But when the maestro started talking about the Quorum of the Sixth Truth, Tanis really got interested.

"The Quorum were a fraternity of fifth strand Adepts in Cyrenaic times, which we Agasi call the Before," the maestro lectured. "They thrived for centuries in times when no one even knew of the *Sobra I'ternin*, long before we had any codified structure like what you find in Adept life today."

He held his glasses away from his face as if to ascertain their clarity and then resettled them upon his long nose. "The Quorum weren't using the same nomenclature as what we use now," he told the room then, "but from what we can piece together from their recovered writings, they spent decades—*centuries* even—researching variant traits, cataloguing what each trait could do and exploring ways to pursue them."

A student in the front raised his hand. "What do you mean 'pursue' them, Maestro?"

The historian arched a bushy salt and pepper eyebrow. "I mean they were experimenting with impregnation and controlled breeding programs designed to produce specific variant traits in children."

A startled hum passed through the room at this.

"Yes ..." the historian noted the collective reaction. "Not something you would see today. But you must understand the circumstances in those times. Without the *Sobra's* guidance, everything we knew about *elae* came from the Quorum's research. Their knowledge was limited mainly to fifth-strand endeavors, yet they were the recognized experts the world over in matters of the arcane, and they were much sought after for their skills."

He turned and began pacing the room, hands clasped behind his back, letting his ample belly lead the way. "Those were darker times," he said with a frown. "Even so—can any of you imagine an organization of *hundreds* of *fifth strand* Adepts? Perhaps thousands? When today we strain to find even a handful born to that elusive strand?" He cast a telling look across the silent room.

Another hand raised, another question. "What happened to the Quorum, Maestro?"

He opened palms. "They broke apart. No one is sure what happened. Much of their documentation was lost in the cataclysm that shook the world five millennia ago—an event that most of you know as Cephrael's Blight. We have reason to think, however, that the Quorum may have *caused* this cataclysm, which nearly wiped out all life in the realm and cast most of civilization back into barbarism."

He stopped behind the central table that held books and other papers and rested a hand on its edge, as if the strenuous pacing had tired him. "It took another twenty-five hundred years to climb out of that uncivilized pit. It wasn't until Hallian the First came out of a cave carrying the book he claimed Cephrael put directly into his hands that civilization and the Adept gifts were truly restored.

"It was the Fourth Age of Fable into which Hallian emerged. It was a vicious time. Adepts lived hidden, in fear for their lives from the vindictive efforts of superstitious, bigoted men. The realm endured constant invasion— Warlocks from the Shadow Realms were a considerable threat, and kings employed zanthyrs to protect their holdings. It was a time of witches, mystics, demon sorcery and blood magic—which the Fhorgs of Myacene practice to this day. A dark time. No one understood *elae* and the Adept gifts or how to properly use them. We had no codification, only a vast panoply of practices based on conjecture and superstition, or upon the specious results of brutal experimentation."

"Maestro," another student asked, "what about Illume Belliel's Council of Realms? Did they not have jurisdiction in those times?"

The historian took off his spectacles again and cleaned them with a handkerchief. "The earliest record we have of the Council of Realms comes from a recounting of Björn van Gelderan's, when he braved the welds and their host of dangers to ultimately reach Illume Belliel."

He put his glasses back on and cast the room a grave look. "If not for the Fifth Vestal, we Adepts might still be fighting for the right to live free."

"I thought Emperor Hallian, not Björn, was the civilizing influence," someone said. The contempt in his tone came through loud and clear.

The historian eyed this student irritably. Tanis scanned the heads in the crowd, but he couldn't tell who the maestro was scowling at.

"We owe a great debt to Hallian the First," Monseraut agreed, though his tone contained a disdainful edge, implying the student's obvious lack of understanding as well as his ill manners.

"So Hallian comes out of his cave carrying the *Sobra I'ternin* and begins translating, teaching, codifying," the maestro continued. "He was the first translator of the sacred text—given the key to the understanding of its patterns by whoever put the document in his hands."

"I thought it was Cephrael," the same student remarked.

"And so it is widely believed—*believed* being the operative word, Eddard d'Ardenne," Monseraut added with a scowl at the Veneisean boy, whom Tanis still couldn't see, "by which one must infer that there exists a lack of sufficient proof to fully explain either Hallian's acquisition of the text or his initial attempts at translation." He huffed testily, muttered something that sounded indignant, and speared a beady gaze back into the audience. "Hallian used the *Sobra's* truths to drive the wild Varangians from his lands. With iron and blood and steel, he tamed the barbarism of the Fourth Age of Fable and ushered in the Fifth Age of Reason. Hallian's descendants are now the ruling elite of Agasan."

After the lecture, Tanis was feeling a bit aimless, so he found a bench in a quiet cloister and resumed reading his father's journal.

In recent entries, his father had been expounding on the Laws of Patterning and comparing them to the Esoterics. Tanis didn't always follow his father's reasoning, for he lacked the education necessary to achieve full understanding and application of these abstruse Laws. Yet the ideas alone sparked new worlds of thought.

That day, Tanis read:

It amazes me how two men can interpret the First Law of Patterning so differently. My master knows that 'a wielder is limited by what he can envision,' but he thinks of this law only in terms of how to combine and wield patterns. He sermonizes endlessly that two wielders, if left to themselves, might wield the same pattern for different purposes.

This is all fine, but I think he's entirely missing the point. I say patterns be damned—the only thing limiting a wielder is his imagination.

I would sometimes that none of us studied, for we only inherit the limitations of our teachers—in this regard, my master is correct. Teachers pass on their failures as much as their wisdom, a litany of things never to try because they 'cannot' be done.

Even when an instructor allows a student to attempt some new feat, the attempt remains tainted by the instructor's own dubiousness. This doubt colors the student's ability because it limits his imagination. He becomes the canvas bearing the dark marks of each instructor's doubt, marks that become chains binding him to mediocrity.

It might be most efficacious to give an Adept one fundamental and let him extrapolate the rest, especially among the more brilliant minds. The Adept of a particular strand has the ability to think in concepts. If he has one fundamental, he can jump to a plethora of new advances. Whereas if you teach him things, it restricts him to the parameters of what he's been taught.

Yet a student cannot be limited by what he doesn't know he can't do. Better he go and try and see for himself instead of never trying. The failures of one do not universally apply to all.

For some reason, these words made Tanis feel better about being able to timeweave. Perhaps his talent wasn't one most people knew about, or talked about, but that didn't necessarily make it unnatural—as he'd been thinking of it—just ... unusual. In his father's view, that would probably make it a good thing.

As he was pondering this idea, Tanis noticed a mass of people flooding into a lecture hall across the quad, so he joined them to see what was going on.

The lecture was well under way by the time Tanis made it into the hall, which offered standing room only. On stage stood a tall man dressed from head to toe in the silken garments of a Holy Palmer. Tanis recognized the same literato that Vincenzé had pointed out to him the other day, though he no longer carried his blade.

The literato was lecturing on a pattern that glowed in the center of the room. Three-dimensional, the illusion slowly rotated on its axis, showing all of the facets of the oddly irregular diagram, which disturbed Tanis on a fundamental level. It was all sharp edges where it should've been smooth and thorny barbs where you'd expect it to curve. It looked like someone had taken a rosebush and twisted it into knots. The literato was indicating parts of it here and there with a gilded pointer.

Something about the pattern hurt the back of Tanis's eyes. It was almost like he couldn't look directly at it but could only view its reflection, as if it had to pass through the lens and bounce off the back of his eyeball first. He blinked several times, but it didn't lessen the uncomfortable effect.

"As you can see," the literato said in a voice that was both deep and melodious, the kind of voice you simply felt compelled to listen to, "the connectivity of the integral quatrefoils follows the expectations of the Third Law ..."

The literato was explaining the pattern's purpose and use, but he might as well have been speaking Fhorg for all Tanis could understand him. The rows of scholars in the front apparently followed his talk, however, for even then one raised his quill to note, "But it seems to violate the First Esoteric, Literato N'abranaacht."

"Indeed, Maestro di Relisi," the literato admitted with a polite bow of acknowledgement, "for as you have noted, it does not within its design give us any indication of how to apply it towards Absolute Being. Yet lest we forget the Twelfth Law, the pattern need not be perfect, but the wielder's concept of it must be."

"But what's it meant to *do*?" a woman near Tanis whispered to the man standing beside her. They both wore Devoveré rings and looked about twenty and five, but Tanis wouldn't have made a bet on their true age.

"That's the incredible part," the man murmured in reply. He had a long, aristocratic nose and raven hair and reminded Tanis somewhat of the High Lord. "He's saying it has the potential to Awaken an Adept even after the window of adolescence has closed."

She drew in her breath with a little gasp.

"But it's clearly a dark pattern," the man continued with his brown eyes pinned on the illusion in question. "Dangerous. That's why you see all the *Sobra* Scholars in the first row. They're here to ascertain if the pattern can be trusted enough to experiment with it."

"A dark pattern." She gave a little nervous laugh. "You mean like a *mor'alir* pattern?"

"Be silent!" a balding literato standing beside them hissed with a glare. He pushed forward through the crowd to distance himself from them.

The man replied in a low voice, ignoring the huffy literato. "*Mor'alir* Adepts don't necessarily work dark patterns; mostly they work *hal'alir* patterns repurposed to destructive ends. You'll never hear of actual dark patterns unless you entertain an Arcane Scholar. Dark patterns are all they ever talk about."

"But why do they call them dark if they're not referencing the *mor'alir* path?"

After a round of shushes from others nearby, the man took the woman by the elbow and moved them out of the press of bodies, closer to the doors. Tanis followed, intrigued to hear the man's explanation.

"The actual term is *inverteré*," the man said then. "The slang term of 'dark' comes from the aspect of these patterns' function, which is akin to a shadow. Dark patterns sort of twist *elae* inside out. They corrupt it somehow. No one is sure why, even now, even with all the *Sobra* has taught us about the lifeforce. The *Sobra* Scholars believe such patterns cause *elae* to mirror itself, triggering refractions which injure the strand's integrity. We don't use them—and the Sormitáge doesn't teach them—because their results are unpredictable."

The woman looked back to the lecturing literato and inched up on her tiptoes to see over the heads of those in front of her. Then she settled back on her heels and frowned. "Marten, who would dare use a dark pattern to try to *Awaken* someone? If what you said about them is true ..."

He gave her a telling look. "If you thought you were an Adept long past your Awakening, wouldn't you go to any lengths to try to find your gift?"

She looked faintly horrified. Well, Tanis felt the same.

The man and woman left, and Tanis turned back to the lecture, unsettled by what he'd heard.

As he was making his way through the wall of people to find a clear view again, he spotted Felix across the crowd, standing next to a girl wearing lavender spectacles. She wore her dark hair collected into loose, looping braids in a style preferred by provincial noble families. Tanis believed the hairstyle had been invented for the specific purpose of ensuring such girls remained free of suitors.

No sooner did Tanis notice Felix than the latter looked over, noticed Tanis watching, and gave him a cold stare in return. Seconds later, the room broke into applause. Tanis glanced to the stage to find the literato bowing, and then everyone was up from their seats and a wave of people were pushing him towards the doors.

With some creative maneuvering, Tanis managed to keep his eyes on Felix and the girl, but by the time he cleared the line snaking out, they were far down the passage and about to turn the corner. Tanis shoved through a group of Maritus students in front of him—making no friends in the moment—and ran after Felix and the girl.

He saw them turn another corner, but by the time he reached the same corridor, the passage stood empty. Tanis rushed down it anyway, hoping to stumble upon them again, or at least catch a snippet of conversation to lead him in the right direction, but after taking several turns just on instinct, he found himself quite alone amid a warren of narrow halls. He wandered for an uncomfortable length of time, then trying to find his way back to the main passage, cursing Felix all the while.

Eventually he heard male voices approaching, and soon two men rounded a corner.

The first he recognized instantly as the Literato N'abranaacht—the man was, after all, quite unmistakable with his tall build beneath the flowing pearlescent robes. He'd donned his sword again, and this time Tanis was close enough to see etched silver patterns inscribed in the black leather baldric strapped across his chest.

The second man stood a head shorter than the literato. He had greying hair cut just above his shoulders, a hawkish nose and dark eyes beneath equally dark brows. Tanis recognized him from the recent lecture as the Maestro di Relisi, the one who had asked a question about the First Esoteric.

Maestro di Relisi saw Tanis first, and his bushy brows pinched together.

"What's this? What are you doing here?" He flicked a bony finger at Tanis. "Students are not allowed in these corridors."

"I'm sorry sir, I—"

"You're Maritus? Catenaré?" He looked Tanis up and down and his brows narrowed quite spectacularly when he noted Tanis's hand. He snatched Tanis's wrist then and examined the silver band on his finger. "A Postulant, eh?" His gaze flicked over him again with cutting severity. "What are you doing back here?"

"I ... think I'm lost, sir."

N'abranaacht chuckled. "Really, Paolo, you act as if the boy's some kind of spy."

Tanis turned him a sharp look, but the literato's brown eyes were gentle, smiling as they gazed down at him. He could see nothing else of the man's face—not even his eyebrows—only his darkly lambent eyes framed by pearlescent silk. Up close, the effect was slightly startling.

"Why don't I escort the lad back to civilization," N'abranaacht offered. He laid a hand on Tanis's shoulder. Something about the gesture, the imposed intimacy, made Tanis uncomfortable.

Maestro di Relisi scowled. "Nonsense. I'll call a docent."

"No need. I welcome the excursion." He looked down at Tanis. "You're in Chresten Hall, no doubt. It's near my apartments."

"But—" the maestro protested.

"It's no bother, Paolo. We can continue our conversation another day." His eyes smiled again, yet a flintiness within them left little room for argument.

The maestro made a bow, but his manner had cooled, and his tone lacked for warmth as he replied, "As you wish, N'abranaacht."

As Maestro di Relisi stalked off, Tanis exhaled a tremulous breath and gazed after him with a troubled frown. No doubt he'd made yet another enemy.

"That's a ponderous sigh for so young a personage," N'abranaacht observed. He looked quietly down at Tanis, but something in his gaze that time seemed not quite so friendly.

The boy wondered if he'd somehow offended him. "Yes, I ... well I didn't mean to interrupt, sir."

"A welcome interruption, in my view."

"Yes, sir, that was apparent—" Tanis caught his breath, wondering why he ever would've made so blunt a remark.

N'abranaacht seemed not to notice. He released Tanis's shoulder and motioned him down the hall. "Shall we?" Tanis dutifully fell into step with him. The literato walked so close at his side that their arms often brushed in passing. "So, truthreader, tell me your name."

"It's Tanis, sir."

"Tanis," he repeated in his melodious voice, rolling the lad's name across his tongue as if each consonant and vowel held a truth to be dissected and understood. There was something dangerous in the way N'abranaacht said his name … in having the man say his name at all.

Tanis looked up at him uncertainly, but the literato's eyes were still smiling. It was so incongruous, the dark, smiling eyes and gentle voice and the feeling Tanis got from the man, which was anything but amiable.

"And tell me, Tanis, why have you come to the Sormitáge?" Their arms brushed again in passing.

"I really don't kn—" Tanis clapped a hand over his mouth. He'd meant to say something else entirely, yet his tongue had quite betrayed him.

N'abranaacht chuckled again, but Tanis couldn't tell this time if it was in good humor or malicious amusement. Was the man somehow compelling him to speak these raw, unfiltered truths? If so, he was more expert even than Pelas, because Tanis felt no patterns at work—he *felt* no compulsion.

"You don't know why you've come?" N'abranaacht murmured. "How odd. Most Postulants come to gain their ring." Tanis could hear the smile in his voice as well as his dry undertone.

"Yes, sir." Tanis shifted uncomfortably and frowned up at the literato, wondering … "Are you an Adept, sir?"

"Alas, I am *na'turna*—a requirement, I fear, for Arcane Scholars. The university leadership believes the temptation would be too great to use the *inverteré* patterns we research, had we the necessary talent."

They exited the corridor through a side door and emerged onto a path that wound through a lengthy colonnade of elm trees. Night had fallen, but plenty of Sormitáge residents were still making their various ways hither and yon. Relief washed over Tanis to see other people. He'd begun feeling like no one in the world existed except him and N'abranaacht—an unsettling contemplation.

Suddenly the man's arm enwrapped Tanis's shoulder. The gesture appeared friendly and warm, yet Tanis would've felt more at peace with a viper around his neck.

"You are quite the enigma, young Tanis," N'abranaacht murmured in that gentle voice which was so at odds with Tanis's perceptions. The literato nodded politely to a pair of scholars passing the other way and kept Tanis tightly in the circle of his arm. "Tell me then, who sent you to the Sormitáge?"

"My mother wanted me to study here, sir." For once Tanis felt relief in being able to provide an answer that was congruous with his own intentions.

"Your mother?" N'abranaacht seemed displeased by this answer, as if he'd expected Tanis to say something else. "Who is your mother?"

"My father called her Renaii."

"Another peculiar response. Does she have no name beyond what your father called her?"

"I imagine so, but I—never really knew my parents. I was only two when we … parted."

Here again, Tanis would've liked to have answered differently—he would've liked not to have answered at all! How was the man forcing these replies out of him if he wasn't an Adept? Tanis sensed nothing of *elae* within or around the literato, yet if N'abranaacht couldn't be blamed for Tanis's uncharacteristically blunt responses, who or what was causing them?

N'abranaacht squeezed his shoulder gently. "I find you most intriguing, Tanis. It isn't often one meets an orphaned truthreader. Where, then, were you raised?"

This time Tanis tried very much to control his answer, to put form to his thoughts before the truth was surgically excised out of him, but again his tongue flapped with betrayal. "I grew up as the ward of the Duchess and Healer Melisande d'Giverny of Dannym."

"How curious. Who sponsored your studies here then?"

Tanis clenched his teeth and tried to hold back his answer, just to see if he could. He might as well have been trying to hold back a river in flood for all the words went flowing across his tongue anyway. "The High Lord Marius di L'Arlesé is my sponsor, sir."

"Indeed. That is no small boon."

Tanis was becoming well and truly frightened. Something was definitely being done to him—*worked* upon him—to force these answers. The fact that he couldn't even *perceive* the magic was one of the most terrifying experiences of his life. Worse even than his first encounter with Pelas …

Abruptly Tanis looked up at the literato. His brown eyes were smiling down at him, warm, compelling …

Tanis caught his toe on an uneven tile and skipped-stumbled several paces forward. He laughed nervously as he recovered, but he took care to stay slightly in front of N'abranaacht as they continued along. He could see the lights of Chresten through the trees. A watchtower beckoning to an exhausted, storm-stranded sailor could not have been more welcome.

He glanced back at the literato to give him an uneasy smile. "And you sir?" He hoped in part to turn the conversation away from himself and in part to assuage a sudden frightening suspicion. If N'abranaacht was truly not an Adept, the literato should feel nothing in Tanis's next remark and would only answer as compelled—but if he was something more … Tanis swallowed, put the entire force of his skill into forming the question, and braved, "Where do *you* come from?"

The barest tightening around N'abranaacht's eyes told Tanis what he needed to know. The man was impressive. If Tanis hadn't been watching so closely, he never would have noticed that N'abranaacht had felt his compulsion at all, for surely the literato's reply gave no hint of it as he answered patiently, "A place far from here, Tanis youth." He reached to place a hand on Tanis's shoulder, but the boy deftly avoided it. No way was he letting the man touch him again.

They reached the path to Chresten's doors, and Tanis lengthened his stride to put more distance between them before he stopped and turned. "Thank you for the walk, sir."

"Of course." N'abranaacht bowed politely. "I hope you will join me again some time, Tanis—perhaps … for tea tomorrow? I will send for you. You might tell me then how you came to acquire the High Lord for a sponsor."

Tanis had no intention of going anywhere near the man. "I … couldn't, sir. Not tomorrow." Not any day.

N'abranaacht closed the distance between them in a single step. "Oh, but you simply must." One finger caught Tanis beneath his chin and gently lifted the lad's gaze to meet his own. Every one of Tanis's senses screamed in warning. "Let's just say it's the price I require for my service to you tonight."

Tanis felt frozen—*literally* frozen to the stones. He believed he could not have moved if he'd tried. "That—that seems like two services given, sir," he stammered.

N'abranaacht's eyes smiled again, and this time they were decidedly predatory. "Oh … I think you will make it worth my while."

Then he released Tanis from his thrall and glided away into the night.

FORTY-ONE

"He's discarded the rigid cloak of law. Judgment suits him better."
– Ramuhárikhamáth, Lord of the Heavens,
on Björn van Gelderan

BJÖRN VAN GELDERAN, Fifth Vestal of Alorin, stood on his balcony gazing out over the realm he and his friends had made. The wind tossed his dark curls and tugged at his coat as it howled hungrily around the towers of Niyadbakir. Across the green valley, a line of low-lying clouds hugged the distant mountains, assuming their shape, while a storm pushed impatiently from behind.

No matter how often or how long he gazed upon it, Björn never became inured to T'khendar's wild beauty, nor forgot that this immaculate creation had been birthed through the minds of men. But the realm's beauty hardly consumed his thoughts that afternoon. The game progressed, and like T'khendar, it had changed through the centuries.

In the beginning, it had been like a match of Kings, full of strategy and planning, thinking twenty steps ahead, envisioning every possible outcome of playing this or that piece at a certain time, estimating consequences to the ninth hand of chance.

The game had grown since then. His Players now manned the field, weaving their own strands of the great tapestry. He saw the pattern taking shape at last, and while it was as he'd always envisioned, it had become so much more; for his Players made choices that added their own dimension and color to the tapestry, and many bound new threads to themselves in ingenious and even startling ways. Some Players were finding and using their own pieces—or forging them sometimes, whole cloth, out of the muddle of common man. He'd chosen his Players well and prepared them as best he could, but he could do no more now than let them play, as they'd been intended to do all along.

He admitted that the game now held a certain unpredictability.

This very capriciousness made it more exciting. The game had been in play long enough to have taken on its own life, its own personality. He knew now how the game itself would react, and he understood how to send it spiraling in new directions—well ... most of the time.

Björn's task in these times fell to prediction. To see beyond the next sunrise—the next many sunrises—and know what would be waiting upon that far horizon. No, not merely to know it, but to frame it himself, to bring into being the next swirls of the pattern he needed to shape.

To have that foresight, he had to understand his Players; he needed to know how they thought, what they feared, what they cherished, and what drove them to overcome; he had to know what choices would entice them and which they could resist—for if he could predict their choices, even somewhat, he could predict the next phase of the pattern, the next twist of each binding thread.

This wondrous tapestry that his game had become kept weaving itself into innumerable spiraling designs ... patterns within patterns; the contributions of others had formed a vast canvas upon which they painted the stories of their lives—each one individual, each one inspired, all of them interwoven, bound by purpose.

As Master of the Game, it fell to him to keep these many threads aligned. If he could succeed ... what a glorious masterwork they would all have created in the end.

A shadow came to stand beside him on the balcony—Dagmar, dressed in his characteristic black. The Second Vestal nodded to the far horizon and leaned elbows on the railing. Two Vestal oath-rings gleamed dully in the overcast. "Storm's coming."

"Evidence of our living realm." Björn felt the rising tide of the fifth tingling along his skin. "I remember the first time we made rain that wasn't yellow with sulfur. Malachi stripped down and danced in it."

Dagmar arched a humorous brow. "He always was a bit off his gourd, wasn't he?"

"I think we all were." Björn cast him a wry smile. "We rather had to be, didn't we, to imagine we could do something like this?"

Dagmar's smile faded. "Aye, brother."

Björn gave him a curious look. "What's on your mind? Something to do with this storm?"

"Nay, this one is natural enough." Dagmar turned and leaned back against the railing to better meet Björn's gaze—only he didn't look at him, but rather at a silver coin that he passed slowly between his fingers. "Rinokh succeeded again in sending an electrical storm through the Eye. This last storm left a tear in the aether an eighth of a mile long."

The Eye. That place where the barriers between the realms grew thin; where a wall of volcanic glass separated the fringes of Chaos from a ravine that eternally twitched with unmaking; and where the Malorin'athgul Rinokh malevolently hovered.

Björn exhaled a pensive breath. "We knew he would try—proof that this game won't be solved by force. Even were we to succeed in defeating Rinokh's brothers, they would merely join him on the fringes of the Realms of Light, seeking a way back inside … and they'd have all of eternity to find one."

Dagmar grunted. "The battle would be unending. A shame we can't unmake the immortal the way we unmade the shell he claimed in Alorin."

Björn arched brows by way of agreement. Then he glanced sideways at Dagmar. "You and Ramu repaired the tear without too much effort, I hope."

"The tear bothered me less than the fact it happened at all."

The First Lord looked him over. "Do you need more help?"

Dagmar flicked his coin into the air and caught it again. "Nay." He turned and leaned sideways against the railing. "Just thought you should know."

"Thank you."

"In other news, your contact in Illume Belliel says Alshiba still hasn't sought the Speaker's aid."

Björn turned him a look. "Light above, what is she waiting for?"

"Gods help me if I know. Franco apparently as much as told her he can travel to T'khendar and that you're holding her Vestals hostage here."

Björn cast him a sidelong grin. "Hostage?"

Dagmar shrugged. "Just passing along the conversation as it was relayed to me."

"Franco is in Illume Belliel with Alshiba?"

"Nearly every day since she thrust the deputy ring upon his finger."

"Keeping him close beneath her watchful eye."

Dagmar arched a telling brow. "I sometimes wonder she hasn't uncovered a way to listen in on Franco's dreamscape meetings with me."

Björn flashed a grin. "Doubtless she's tried."

Dagmar flipped his coin and caught it again. "Your contact says that Alshiba won't be able to gather more than fifty Paladin Knights to her cause."

The First Lord frowned. "Fifty isn't nearly enough."

"That's what I told him."

Björn rubbed his chin and considered his oath-brother. He couldn't be wrong about why Alshiba had elevated Nico van Amstel to become the new Second Vestal. Her motivations seemed obvious. But if his presumptions were correct, why was Alshiba waiting so long to take her next step? Unless …

Björn arched a brow as he saw a more subtle motivation come into focus. He considered where the path of this idea might lead and saw numerous threads spiraling off of it to form a beautiful new design.

The First Lord smiled and turned to Dagmar. "Perhaps I ought to go stir up some trouble."

"*You?*"

Björn leaned his hip against the railing. "Who better?"

Dagmar regarded him flatly. "*Anyone* would be better. *I* would be better. It's me she's trying to replace."

"Only because she had more second strand resources available—albeit insultingly inferior." He grinned at his next thought. "Doubtless, if Alshiba had some means of replacing me, she would've tried long ago. Besides," he clapped Dagmar on the shoulder, "what have we to fear with you to take over in my absence? None could wish for a stronger leader, my friend."

Dagmar gave him a look of blatant suspicion.

Björn laughed. "You've got to learn to accept a compliment without suspecting me of going off to martyr myself."

Dagmar watched him coolly. "Aye, brother, as soon as you can take one without turning it back around on the giver."

The shadow of a smile hinted on Björn's lips at this, and his eyes sparkled with humor. "Well enough ... there may be room for improvement in both of us." He nodded towards his study, and they headed inside together.

"Do you really think it's time to bring Alshiba into the fold?" Dagmar sounded less than pleased by the idea.

The First Lord cast a look over his shoulder as he passed through the open doors. "I guess we'll find out."

Inside Björn's study, the Second Vestal threw himself into an armchair and extended long legs dejectedly across the carpet. He followed Björn with his gaze as he walked towards his desk. "You know she's going to flay me alive."

Seated in a near armchair, Raine D'Lacourte looked up from the book he'd been reading. "Who's going to flay you alive?"

Dagmar gave him a look. "Alshiba."

Raine turned an inquiring glance from Dagmar to Björn, who was just sitting down behind his desk. "When is this momentous occurrence expected to happen?"

"When she gets here," Dagmar muttered unhappily.

Raine stiffened. "Alshiba's coming here?"

Björn shrugged. "We'll see."

"Don't let him fool you." Dagmar rolled his head around on the back of his chair as if already enduring Alshiba's flaying knife. "He's going to Illume Belliel to claim her."

"*What?*" Raine gaped at Björn.

Björn rested his chin on one hand and his elbow on the chair arm. "A one-man raid on the cityworld isn't exactly what I had in mind, Dagmar."

"But you do intend to go to Illume Belliel?" Raine looked confused. "I thought we were waiting for Alshiba to come to us."

"It appears she needs some encouragement."

Frowning, Raine rose and went to pour himself some wine. He turned with goblet in hand and gazed uncertainly at Björn. "If you're caught ..."

Björn chuckled. "Do neither of you have *any* faith in me? Have I become just the ghost of my own memory ... some ancient name of old to be invoked in a prayer?"

"More likely a curse," Raine muttered into his wine, "but I take your point."

"We have unquestioning faith in you." Dagmar motioned to Raine to pour him a glass and shifted disagreeably in his chair. "Just not in this game without you."

Björn shook his head. "You do yourself an injustice, brother."

"Possibly. But like Raine said, if you're caught—"

"If Illume Belliel succeeds in catching me, then it will prove that they've gained the knowledge to defeat our enemies. I would become merely," he waved an airy hand, looking for the right word, "... superfluous."

Raine choked on his wine.

Björn leaned back in his chair. He toyed with a crystal pyramid used as a paperweight on his desk. "Sadly, I don't think that will be the case."

In truth, he would've relished such an outcome. Yes, he lived for this game—he'd sacrificed everything for it—but if the game itself became unnecessary ... if the realms could be made safe without his involvement ... well, he would gladly have abandoned the whole affair.

He cast his gaze to include both Raine and Dagmar while his fingers traced the edges of the pyramid. "This thing we do isn't a sacred act to be carried forward in spite of all. We don't gain any righteous pinnacle for the sacrifices we've made or the trials we've endured ... we're not playing for the sake of having something to do, only to see something important done. If someone else were to accomplish the same end a better way ... our task would be complete."

Dagmar took the goblet Raine handed him and raised it. "To better men than us."

Raine considered Dagmar with a frown. Then he clinked goblets with him and drank.

Looking back to Björn then, Raine remarked, "I always wondered why you didn't tell Alshiba the truth." He walked over and slowly settled back in his chair. "Me, I understand." His gaze bore rueful apology. "But Alshiba would've done anything you asked of her."

Björn gave his oath-brother a tragic look. "Anything ... except the one thing I most needed her to do."

Raine frowned. "Which was?"

"To stay behind."

Dagmar grunted at the truth of that.

"But if you'd told her why—"

"There's no way she would've stayed, Raine." Dagmar gestured with his goblet. "You *know* how stubborn she is. She would've demanded to come with us."

"Who would've held the Seat then, Raine?" Björn searched his oath-brother's colorless gaze with his own. "You? *Seth?* Dagmar had to be here with me to repair T'khendar. It had long been the plan for him to return after we deposited the rest of you back in Alorin."

"Yes, enduring thanks for that, brother." Raine cast Dagmar a pointed stare. "We fretted over your disappearance for centuries."

"The twisting of Tiern'aval's weld didn't exactly go off as planned, Raine. I certainly didn't expect the whole bloody island to get ripped out of the realm." He grimaced into his wine and remarked before taking a sip, "I felt rather bad about that."

Raine frowned at him. Then he looked back to Björn and frowned at him harder. "It still seems an unnecessary risk to me, your going to Illume Belliel. I'm sure Dämen would agree."

Dagmar snorted. "Dämen is like an old woman with his worrying."

Björn ran a finger idly along the edge of his desk. "We always knew Illume Belliel would be the last piece. I think it's time to set it in motion. It may take some time to get that wheel turning." He lifted his gaze to his Vestals. "Maybe just time enough."

"You have a lot of wheels spinning already, brother," Raine remarked.

Björn smiled. "But I have you now to help keep them going."

Raine grunted dubiously.

Björn gazed upon his oath-brothers with a contemplative smile. Seeing them both there, knowing they played side by side with him in this great game ... warmth filled his heart. How humble these men—*great* men, by any standard, and far more capable than they gave themselves credit for.

Dagmar cleared his throat to gain Björn's eye. "You know the minute you set your foot on the field, all the Players will want your help."

Björn arched a resigned brow. "The minute I appear on the field, they'll all *need* my help." *Alshiba perhaps most of all ...*

He pressed his lips together at this thought. So much had been left unsettled between them. He had many wrongs to atone for, more than he could possibly ever make right. He sighed. "This will be hard for Alshiba." Then he shook his head and pressed his lips together. "Hard for us both."

Raine was regarding him seriously. "She's never stopped loving you."

Björn shifted his gaze to him. "Ah, Raine ... we've never stopped loving each other."

He rested his head back against his chair and lifted his gaze to the ceiling and the patterns frescoed there. Often he would let his eyes follow their whorls and spirals and feel his tangled thoughts begin to unwind. Now he let his wandering gaze pull at the threads of a love that was centuries denied.

Thinking of Alshiba and their time together recalled a familiar ache he'd suppressed for too long. Yet he couldn't help feeling it now.

How beautiful, the bonds of love. He could see these ephemeral threads connecting the Players on his field, binding them in unique and enduring ways, binding them across continents and even through time, through loss and heartbreak and betrayal. These special bonds forged their own glorious pattern above the tapestry that was his game, and the threads of that pattern were far stronger than anything simulated by men or magic.

Bjorn had known more sorrow, more loss, more betrayal and more sacrifice than any of his Players. He supposed he had a right to grieve. Yet a wielder learns indelibly that his thoughts sculpt what is to become. In his long years of life, Björn had seen too many times how his attitude changed the shape of things. Sorrow, grief, regret … these emotions weakened the threads that bound the game and introduced darkness into the pattern. There was darkness enough without his adding to it through self-pity.

His emotion, misplaced or wrongly channeled, could change the shape of the world. The cost of feeling these emotions was just too high. He couldn't afford them.

Björn exhaled a measured breath. His game had developed its own personality, but also its own peculiar energy. He'd learned how to read that energy like he read the currents, interpreting its swells and ebbs, the tugging of its tides, the mercurial, shifting currents of his Players as they shaped, framed and pulled the tapestry with their choices. He'd honed his senses to recognize particular surges that signaled new threads.

One such energy was cresting now. He felt it in the rising hair on his arms, in the quickening of his heart, in the slanting daylight and the sharpness of the air. And he sensed it in the threads binding him and his Vestals … in the threads binding them all.

He pushed from his chair. "Thus it begins."

Dagmar eyed him darkly. "Whenever you say that, the space between my shoulder blades starts twitching."

Björn's eyes sparkled with humor. "You really have no faith in me whatsoever." He headed around his desk.

Raine followed him with his gaze. "What will you tell her?"

Björn laid a hand on his shoulder as he passed. "The truth. What else is there to say?"

Raine's expression grew troubled.

Björn headed for the doors then, but just as he reached them, he turned with a final thought. "Dagmar … advise Franco to do nothing to betray Alshiba's confidence, even should it appear to mean betraying mine."

Dagmar regarded him soberly. "Your will, brother."

Björn smiled in gratitude and took his leave.

FORTY-TWO

"We hold the keys to our own prison cells. Fate is a careless warden."

–The Adept truthreader Thrace Weyland

THE DOOR TO Trell's tower room opened with a crash. He jerked awake to see one of the Nadoriin standing in the portal—the same guard who'd shot the old sailor. The guard pitched something at Trell. "Taliah says to put that on."

Trell sat up and caught the item out of the air. It turned out to be a leather collar with a small gold bell and a matching leather thong. Trell hooked his forefinger through it and held it up for the guard to see. "Pretty. And what will you be wearing?"

The guard pushed his hand onto the hilt of his sword. "She's waiting."

What he really meant was *he* was waiting.

Trell slipped his legs over the side of the bed, then looked up under his brows at the guard. Apparently the man meant to wait *and* watch.

No doubt Taliah had given that order as well. She spent her nights dreaming up new ways of humiliating him.

The thong had clearly been made for a smaller man. Walking turned out to be challenging. The leather constricted and chafed in the most uncomfortable places imaginable. He buckled the collar around his throat and followed after the Nadoriin.

Taliah was sitting at a long table in a loggia overlooking the sea when the guard ushered Trell within. Abalone tiles covered every surface, from vaulted ceiling to columns to walls, so that the easterly sun made the entire loggia gleam with pearlescent light. It was one thing he admired about the Nadoriin—even a crude fortress was outfitted as a palace.

Taliah smiled as she watched Trell approach, but her smile faded when her gaze shifted to the Nadori guard. "Go stand by the door, Captain Fazil—in case I need you later."

Both Trell and the captain knew this meant, *I want an audience and you're it.*

The Nadoriin glowered at her, but he did as he was told. Trell wondered if Taliah had taken hostage the life patterns of *every* person on that barren rock. He'd no reason to think he was the special exception, and the guards were unusually compliant considering the kinds of things she demanded of them.

"You shall serve me today, Prince of Dannym." Taliah sat primly back in her chair and folded hands in her lap, waiting.

Trell looked across the loggia to a table set with silver bowls and domed trays. He moved in that direction.

"On your hands and knees." Taliah gave him a little smile that in no way resembled the expression of anything living.

Trell chewed on the side of his cheek while he considered his options. He could refuse to allow her to humiliate him, but she would just use pain to first punish and then coerce him into doing whatever she desired anyway. In either case, he would end up on his hands and knees. What difference then to just do it now and skip the painful appetizer?

He got down on the floor.

She snapped her fingers beside her chair. "Come."

Trell forced a calming exhale and shuffled over to her.

"Stop." She held up her hand to halt him beside her chair. The she laid her hand on his head and patted softly. "Good boy."

Trell clenched his teeth.

"Now get my meal."

He did as he was told.

"Do you see, Fazil?" Taliah waved an airy hand as Trell was crawling towards the table of food. "Do you see how easy it is to make a man obey— even a princely one? A little pain applied in the proper order and place, and he becomes as a puppy eager to be trained."

The captain glowered blackly at her.

Trell made his way back to the table carrying the first of the bowls. He handed it up and returned for the next.

Taliah chose a grape from the bowl, popped it into her mouth and chewed thoughtfully. "Any Adept talent that exists falls upon both the *hal'alir* and *mor'alir* paths, Fazil, for all are harmonics of each other. For instance, Healers make the best torturers, as you have no doubt observed—and, I might add, incomparable courtesans. In Vest, truthreaders trained in illusions are sold as sex slaves for thousands of *reales*. But the paths are not restricted to Adepts alone. For instance, soldiers turned to the *mor'alir* path make delightful servants."

She reached down to receive the last bowl from Trell. "Thank you, sweet prince." She petted his head by way of reward, then caught a hank of hair and with one finger twined it idly around.

Trell drew in a slow, calming breath and reminded himself that being petted like a lapdog was the least of her imposed indignities.

"Because a man obeys," she continued, "doesn't mean he's broken—don't be deceived in this, Fazil. Obedience can be gained through any number of methods, but to break a man … this is to make him *want* to obey, to bring him to such a point of subservience that he seeks desperately his mistress's approval and will do anything to gain it. *That* is what it is to be broken." She took another grape and sighed as she ate it. "But gaining that most desirable state takes time—the stronger the temperament, the longer the path. Until then, gaining the man's obedience must suffice. It is the first step."

Releasing Trell's hair, Taliah took a strip of flatbread smeared with goat cheese and spread a jam of figs across it. "Men are no different than dogs, Captain, in the end. Obedience doesn't come naturally to man or beast, but with proper indoctrination, both become tractable and easily controlled." Her hand caught Trell's chin and pulled up his head to make him look at her. "Do you not agree, Prince of Dannym?"

In the flash of an instant, Trell saw himself launching to his feet, snaring her knife from the table and plunging it into her heart. He knew in truth she'd have him writhing on the floor before he could rise from his knees.

She squeezed his chin harder, and her gaze became sharper. "Don't you agree?"

"No."

She released his chin and drew back from him. "How not?"

He settled back on his heels and tossed his head to clear the hair from his eyes. "You don't control me, Taliah."

She laughed. "Of *course* I do. Look at you on your knees before me! Look what you wear for my pleasure—you, a prince." She leaned closer to him and stroked a finger appreciatively down his bare chest. "Think what you have done because I commanded it of you."

"By choice."

Her expression hardened, and she drew back again. "At *my* command."

"Which I chose to comply with."

"Because you've been *trained* to comply." Her tone snapped like a whip. She made him feel it too, all along the back of his thighs.

Trell sucked in his breath and said through clenched teeth, "I still made the *choice* to comply, Taliah."

"Because you understood there is no choice!" Abruptly she banished her displeasure, took up his chin again and shook it like a mother scolding a naughty child. "In the end, you will do what you're told because you understand what awaits you if you don't. It matters not the *reasons* you obey, so long as you do obey. The result is the same."

A hurricane raged in Trell's gaze, but his voice remained calm. "In the end, all you have to command is a man's willingness. You can never change that, Taliah."

A smile flickered beneath those dead eyes. "Oh, no ..." She leaned and kissed his mouth and let her breath mingle with his. "That is exactly what it means to be broken, sweet prince."

After she finished her meal, Taliah released Trell to his own devices—and clothes—as a reward for his obedience, but he knew she'd still be watching him. She would often leave him alone just to see what he would do with his time. If he gave her any hint that he cared for anything, that he enjoyed or needed anything, she would use it against him later.

He usually spent his free time out on the head on the island's south side, sitting on the rocks and counting the hours passing in the crashing of waves. He'd nothing to do there but think, but he'd long sought the silence of his thoughts when no other peace could be found; his head remained a sure refuge.

That morning as he was crossing the fortress yard towards the south gate, a commotion drew his gaze.

The pig trough had dislodged from the fence and the sows were pushing it violently around the pen, endangering the trough as well as the corral. The keeper watching them seemed unsure of the best course of action.

He had reason to be wary. Each of the dozen or so sows must have weighed several hundred pounds. If hungry enough, they could churn through a grown man's body in about eight minutes, leaving only teeth and a bit of hair to account for his ever having lived. But this lot looked well fed, if a bit rowdy.

Trell headed over and offered his help to the keeper, and together they corralled the pigs into a smaller pen while the keeper fixed the trough. All the while the man barely looked at him, adopting the diffident manner of peasants the world over, though he thanked Trell profusely when they were done.

As he headed beneath the gate, ignoring the hostile stares of the Nadoriin guards, Trell wondered how much these people knew of his identity. Taliah had many times imprudently named him Prince of Dannym before her mutes and Captain Fazil. Guards talked, and Fazil wasn't the only Nadoriin who looked upon him with a contempt that far surpassed disdain for a mere prisoner.

Trell wondered what the guards whispered among themselves. If they knew he was a prince of Dannym, then they knew they were holding prisoner the son of an allied king. What had they been told of him to justify such an act, or didn't it matter to such men?

These questions more intrigued than disturbed him; it was just that he knew *something* was being said about him because of the way the keeper had treated him. Trell had no more right to the keeper's deference than any slave, yet the man had offered it as if it remained his due.

The fortress of Darroyhan clung greedily to its island—in some cases, such as with Trell's tower, the land all but disappeared at high tide—but the south end hosted fingers of basalt that extended out into the sea.

Trell sat bare-chested on the foremost of these, letting the Nadori sun bake his skin and remembering how often he'd wished, during those sweltering days of entrenchment at the River Cry, that he might've stripped similarly down. But had he done so there, he'd as easily have caught a Veneisean arrow as the wind in his hair, which would've somewhat dampened any pleasure to be gained in the experience.

For part of the day he watched ships passing on the far horizon. For a time, he listened to the waves and tried to hear the song of the sea as Fhionna had taught him to find the song of the river; the sea sang a very different melody from the Cry, but Trell thought he heard Naiadithine's haunting whisper from time to time.

Mostly, he spent the day thinking.

Taliah would have him believe she'd usurped all power of choice—she tried diligently to make it appear so—but it wasn't choice that bothered Trell that day so much as the compromise he made of his honor in choosing to comply.

Thus far, his compromises had only affected his pride—if she thought she could break him by simply forcing him into menial labor and scanty apparel, she was badly mistaken. But how many more compromises would he be forced to make as their match of wills progressed?

For all intents and purposes, Taliah owned him. But he had to believe she didn't own his will ... that some investitures of his Maker were truly inviolate. It troubled him, though. How long would it be before compromise became a way of life? Before he stopped *choosing* to comply and simply did as she required, fully and wholly indoctrinated, his will buried or lost beneath a fear of overwhelming pain?

He *could've* chosen the route of pain that morning, for as long as he could take it, but he'd learned that she could make it last far longer than his capacity to endure. Then he would've been in agony *and* serving her on his knees. But would choosing pain have proven she hadn't broken him?

How did he determine where his will ended and hers began?

As the sun was falling in the west and pulling the tide jealously with it, Trell dove off the rocks and swam out to the break where a reef caught the waves. He could see five towers of the massive fortress from that vantage point; likewise the patrols manning its high, crenellated walls. They kept an eye on him, but they knew—like he knew—that he wouldn't swim past the reef. Beyond lay only miles of open sea, sharks and sure death.

But it made him wonder ... why did he cling to this life? What right had he to imagine he would ever escape it?

Trell dove beneath the waves and drifted there, gazing up at the wavering patterns of shadow and light that danced on the surface of the sea. If he couldn't escape, would he spend the rest of his mortal days fighting Taliah in a battle of wills?

He swam towards the surface and spat water from his mouth as he emerged. He doubted Taliah would find him as intriguing, or his cock as inviting, when his flesh was flabby and his bones gone brittle.

Not much liking that thought or where it took him, Trell rolled onto his back and let the saltwater buoy him weightlessly between sea and sky. The heavens above remained a deep, endless blue, more depthless than the ocean beyond the reef. He couldn't see the stars, for the daylight masked them ... but what fool imagined they weren't still shining?

Trell felt a wave rise and lift him, and the sensation made him think of Naiadithine as she'd carried him to safety on the shores of Kai'alil. He remembered little of his near-drowning, but he recalled her image in the shape of the waves, and he remembered her command.

Follow the water, Trell of the Tides.

He had no reason to imagine he would ever escape Taliah.

But he'd no reason to think his gods had abandoned him, either.

Trell rolled onto his stomach and swam back to shore.

He returned through the south gate into pandemonium. A quick glance around told the tale. The sows had torn the trough off the wall of their pen again, and this time they'd taken the stakes down with it. Nadoriin guards ran hither and yon trying to catch the pigs and going about it all wrong, while the Captain of the Guard, Fazil, whipped out his displeasure upon the poor keeper instead of letting the man do his job.

Trell hurried over and showed the guards how to use planks to round up and channel the sows into the other pen. Then he walked to the captain and the keeper.

The latter had fallen to his knees against the wall. His shirt lay in shreds across his bloodied back, and he screamed wretchedly with every lashing. Fazil raised his whip to cast another.

Trell caught the captain's arm. "He's had enough."

The Nadoriin jerked free and slashed again.

Trell caught the whip that time, feeling its sting as it lashed into a coil around his hand. He stepped between Fazil and the pig keeper, his gaze hard. "I said he's had enough."

The captain looked murderous. "He's had half of what he deserves." He yanked on the handle to free his whip.

Trell held firm. The braided leather pulled taut between them, tense as the thread that bound their mutual gazes. "Then I'll take the rest."

The Nadoriin's lip curled in a sneer. "*You'll—*" Then he must've realized

Trell meant it, for a malicious excitement brightened his expression. He kicked the keeper away and motioned Trell into his place. "Hands on the wall."

Suddenly wondering what lunacy had possessed him—did he *seek* pain now?—Trell tossed his shirt aside and pressed his hands to the cool stone. He closed his eyes, braced himself, and sought his soldier's practiced calm.

The first stripe of the whip landed with ice and fire. After five lashings, only the fire remained. But Fazil didn't stop at five. Trell clenched his teeth so hard he thought his jaw would shatter. Honor bade him take the keeper's punishment, but he only swallowed his screams out of pride.

"*Stop this!*" Taliah's fury shattered the air into shards.

But that wasn't all it did.

The captain gasped and dropped to his knees. The whip fell from his hand, and he toppled, twitching, onto his side. His face contorted in a gruesome rictus.

Trell pressed his forehead against the stone wall and slowly lowered his trembling arms. Just this motion exploded more fire across his back. Even breathing was painful.

Taliah released Fazil from the torture of her anger as she reached them. "What are you *doing*, Fazil?" Her voice cut like a crystal knife, sharp with incredulity and reproach.

The captain slowly pushed to his feet, his eyes murderous. "He's a prisoner and a *traitor*," he spat at her. "You treat him like a paramour."

"A traitor? A *traitor?*" She laughed at him. "How ripe. Did my father tell you that?"

The Nadoriin went ashen.

Taliah plugged her fingernail like a dagger beneath Fazil's chin and looked into his eyes. "Do you imagine I wouldn't know you report on me to my father, trying to prove yourself a worthy spy? But Viernan hal'Jaitar will not make you Shamshir'im. My father would cut out his own heart before he trusted a man like you with the secrets of his dark brotherhood." Her nail dug in beneath the cleft of the captain's chin as her eyes dug into his soul. She looked back to Trell. "Our sweet prince is no traitor. *We* are the traitors." She grabbed Fazil's jaw roughly and added in a hiss, "*And I will do what I please with my own property.*"

The yard had quieted during this display. Guards, servants—all stood rooted as if fearing Taliah would level her ire upon them next. Trell thought about turning away from the wall to face her, but he was fairly sure he couldn't stand up without its support.

He felt her fingers twining into his damp hair, and she murmured close in his ear, "You and I will have words later." Then she turned to the Nadoriin. "Fazil, you will carry Trell to the infirmary and see that his wounds are cleaned and salved. Report to me when it's done." Then she left.

Trell thought he could hear Fazil's teeth grinding, but the Nadoriin called for a stretcher, and he was gentle enough helping Trell onto it.

The two guards laid Trell face-down on a table in the infirmary, and then Fazil sent them to fetch an attendant.

As their footsteps were receding, the Nadoriin crouched in front of the prince. "Why?" A storm of confusion darkened his expression. "Why do you submit to the witch?"

Trell managed a snort of disbelief and whispered, "What would you have me do?"

Fazil's murderous gaze answered that clearly enough.

Trell closed his eyes. Such fire flamed along his back ... he could barely think. "I would *you* might succeed, Captain, for even my imagination has failed."

The captain said nothing for a long time. Trell lay with eyes closed trying not to think about the fire in his flesh, trying not to imagine what his back must look like to radiate such pain.

Finally he felt two fingers press gently at his shoulder. Fazil's. And next the words: "*Barat doa mikonam.*" *I will pray for you.*

Trell managed a nod.

The Nadoriin left. His departing footsteps mingled for a time with the attendant's approaching ones, and then the woman arrived with water and ice and cooling salve, and Trell sank into blessed oblivion.

He woke to a hand shaking his shoulder and looked up into the eyes of one of Taliah's mutes. The man extended a hand to help him sit up.

As he complied, Trell realized the fire in his back had faded to embers. Taliah must've Healed him while he lay unconscious. The skin of his back felt whole again, but every motion stung—doubtless meant to be a not so subtle reminder of Taliah's enduring displeasure.

The mute waved him to follow.

Trell looked down at his naked body. "My clothes?"

The mute motioned more insistently.

Exhaling in resignation, Trell pushed off the table and followed the man to attend his mistress.

Taliah sat waiting for him in the middle of a wide hall. Two men were on their knees before her, also naked, with their hands bound behind their backs. Recognizing them, Trell got a bad feeling about what this meeting would entail.

Taliah cast the prince an arch look. "This man," she said, indicating the pig keeper, "has explained what happened. Fazil has confirmed it. Both have been given a chance to tell their stories. I have sat in judgment and found their acts equally unworthy." Her gaze swept Trell, and an unwholesome gleam lit her dark eyes as she admired his naked form. "You will decide which one will keep his life this night."

Protest and concern flooded him. "If this is about my—"

"I have not asked your opinion yet!" She slapped him with her words and her power, bringing a hot sting to his cheek and an ache to his jaw.

Trell pressed his lips together tightly and forced his hands to relax at his sides. If he succeeded in making a fist, he feared what he would do with it.

Taliah held a hand towards the keeper, who was pale of face but staring fiercely at the floor. "This man failed in his duty. His pigs escaped and made havoc in the yard, damaging property and destroying stores. Fazil's men were forced to abandon their posts due to the keeper's incompetence."

Trell wanted to point out how such an act hardly deserved death in reprisal, but this wasn't about justice. It was just another of Taliah's games, another way of forcing him into her misshapen mold.

"Fazil," she said then, indicating the naked Nadoriin with a nod, "took it upon himself to damage my personal property." She looked back to Trell significantly. "Which of them shall live and which shall die? You will decide and carry out my will."

Trell drew in his breath and let it out slowly. "No."

Her eyes narrowed. "*Choose.*"

"I won't sit in judgment on these men, Taliah."

"*I* have already found them both lacking. That should be enough for you."

Trell shrugged.

She sat back and looked at him. "The keeper's pigs caused a fortune in damages. He cannot make reparations except with his life. This is our way."

"It isn't my way."

Taliah's eyes flashed in reproach. She sent a spear of power into his stomach and twisted it in fury.

Trell fell to one knee and pushed a fist to the floor for support.

"You have no *way*," she spat at him, "you are my property. I can make you kill them."

Trell looked up under his brow. His gut roiled with such stabbing pain that he had to gasp to reply, "You can make me *wish* I'd done it."

Frustration sent her out of her chair. "Why must you continue to fight me?" She glared furiously at him. "We walk *mor'alir* together! We're already *far* down the path, yet you persist in acting as if you stand at the crossroads! You have no choice in this, Trell. Accept it!"

Abruptly she moved to him and bent to cup his cheek with her hand. She brought her face close, her brown eyes so dark as to be nearly black. She might've been pretty if she'd retained an ounce of humanity, but Trell only saw a dead thing possessed now by a serpent's soul.

"Accept it, and I will free you from the pain." To encourage him, she made it worse. The blade that had been twisting in his gut now scissored violently from side to side.

Trell gagged on the pain. He braced himself on hands and knees and dragged in shuddering breaths.

Taliah took his head and pressed her lips to his ear. "Choose."

Trell clenched his teeth and shook his head.

Her hands tightened, nails biting into the thin flesh beneath his hair. "Pick one," she hissed, "or they both die."

It took the gravest force of effort to summon breath. He turned his head and met her gaze. "I won't become ... the weapon ... of your spite."

Her eyes grew agate hard. She shoved away from him and back to her feet and screamed madly, "You will be whatever I make of you! *Choose!*"

Trell pushed fists painfully into the tile floor and held her gaze defiantly. "You can demand it all you like ... my honor forbids it."

A little puff of disbelief escaped her, but then she smiled as if suddenly satisfied—never a good sign. "No, Prince of Dannym." She turned to reclaim her chair. "It is your *pride* standing in the way."

Taliah sat down again with a sideways sweep of her gown. "Pride has no place on the path of *mor'alir*. We don't seek that brazen light or its false brightness. Pride, arrogance, vanity and pretention ... these lie upon *hal'alir*. Humility, penitence ... these guide the *mor'alir* Adept."

Finally she released him from the agony of her distemper. Trell inhaled a shuddering gasp and fell onto his side, drenched in a wave of relief.

"Obedience, subservience, self-abnegation." Taliah gave him a quiet smile while her eyes licked lustfully across his form. "These are the qualities of a *mor'alir* Adept."

She motioned to her mute, and the man grabbed Trell under the arms, dragged him forward and plopped him limply before Taliah's chair. She hooked her pointed-toe shoe beneath his chin and forced him up on his knees. Her eyes sought his gaze. "Do you not see how the qualities you seek and admire—the qualities you find so *honorable*—lie on the *mor'alir* path? If you would truly know honor, Prince of Dannym, you will choose, as I have commanded of you, for you serve me now."

Trell clenched his teeth. Ever she attacked him with twisted logic, seeking to ensnare and corrupt him during tides of pain and weakness, when his resolve stood at its lowest ebb. "Then make of me your weapon—you'll still be the one killing them, Taliah."

"But the choice to *save* one will have been yours."

He flipped the hair roughly from his eyes. "An untenable choice."

"*Life* is untenable!" Abruptly she exhaled a frustrated breath and motioned to her mute. "Slay the peasant."

He grabbed the man by the hair and slit his throat.

Taliah turned her dead-eyed gaze on Trell. "One day you will give me similar obedience."

The certainty in her tone made him cold.

She flicked a hand to indicate Fazil. "Release him."

The mute complied, and Fazil got to his feet, but his lips were compressed in a tight line, and shame for his nakedness pinned his eyes to his feet.

Trell pitied him. A man like Fazil, who sought approval and honor, would shatter on Taliah's *mor'alir* anvil.

"Return to your post, Fazil," Taliah said, "but attempt again to gain my father's favor, and I'll keep you lashed to my table until you're *begging* to serve me, until the very thought of defiance is so far from your soul that you would rather slit your own throat than disobey." Her gaze licked over him. "Remember: you live free by my mercy and no other's."

Fazil nodded, unable to look at her.

She motioned to the mute, and he hauled the Nadoriin from the room.

Taliah looked back to Trell, who remained on his knees. Then she frowned. "Take the keeper and feed his body to his pigs. You can repair the stall while you're at it." She irritably waved for him to rise.

The muscles of Trell's jaw worked as he got to his feet. "My clothes?"

She cast him a cold smile full of wretchedness and fury. "You will be clothed in your honor, Prince of Dannym. Surely that is enough for you."

FORTY-THREE

"Be wary of enemies reconciled and of meat twice boiled."
— *The Hearthwitch's Handbook*

THE SAILOR HAFIZ slammed his glass down on the counter and waved to the barkeep. "Another!"

The man came over and refilled Hafiz's glass with a dark eye of disapproval. "Don't you think you've had enough, son?"

Hafiz grabbed the glass before the barkeep had second thoughts about it. "No." *Not nearly enough.* He didn't want to be sober for what they would do to him. Hafiz nursed his seventh serving of absinthe and lamented the wretched turn of his life.

He'd never imagined that his wife would refuse to leave their village, or that his mother would shame him for not avenging his uncle's death there and then. She'd castigated him and accused him of thinking that silver could mitigate the pain of her brother's death, but he noticed that she'd kept the coin after paying him thanks in ugly words. Both mother and wife had shunned him and humbled him and cast him from their home, that they might grieve for his uncle without the greedy hands of a coward staining his memory.

What else could he do then? They'd called him craven, and perhaps he had been in that moment when the arrow struck his uncle's heart, but Hafiz wouldn't become what his mother had accused him of. Some future day, he would meet her beneath Jai'Gar's heavenly pillars and prove to her that he'd died with honor.

He knew the Shamshir'im had to be looking for him. He just wished they'd be faster about it.

He'd made it easy for them, coming back to the Souk Marmadii and making big claims of having seen a prisoner on Darroyhan, telling stories to the drunkards in the bazaar, to anyone who would listen. He'd even once thought he saw the old man, Weyland's agent, listening for a while. Afterwards he'd ambled off, shaking his half-blind head. But by Huhktu's Bones! Hafiz had been shouting his story for two days and still no one had come to claim him. It seemed a cruel form of torture to make him sit and stew and contemplate the real torture ahead.

Hafiz downed the last of his drink and was just raising his glass to call for another when dark shadows befell him.

At last.

He spun to find two dark-robed and turbaned Shamshir'im standing over him. Only their eyes were visible between the cloth cloaking their faces, and those dark orbs did not look upon him kindly.

The barkeep took the glass out of his fingers. "You disgrace your house, Hafiz."

He turned the man a mad smile as the Shamshir'im dragged him away amid whispers and stares. *No, don't you see? I go now to bring it honor.*

FORTY-FOUR

"All men strain beneath the yoke of Balance.

It is a harsh and unforgiving master."

– The High Lord Marius di L'Arlesé

EAN AND ISABEL made love with desperation that night. Ean couldn't tell if it came of his apprehensions or hers, or a combination of both, but they each felt desperation's cold presence like a third lover with them ... between them ... sometimes embracing the both of them. That need to possess Isabel which had so often fueled Ean's passion of late felt suddenly an unwelcome voyeur, for he wanted less to possess her than to never let her go. He couldn't clutch her close enough, couldn't know her body intimately enough, couldn't taste her or touch her or penetrate her deeply enough. And Isabel ... she clung to him as though that night would be their last.

Ean sensed nothing of this idea in her thoughts—she had her mind tightly shielded—but he did sense a great loneliness where none had existed before. She refused to explain why she felt this way, though she didn't try to deny it.

When their lovemaking was done for a time, Ean held her close, her head on his chest and her hair draped across his body, legs entangled. For a while his thoughts wandered, but in the past few days, and especially that night, they seemed always to work their way back to one person.

"How did you know him, Isabel?"

Ean couldn't say what put thoughts of Immanuel in his head. Half the time now he suspected she put them there, knowingly or otherwise, because some thoughts bled across the bond even when she tried to keep them close.

But she seemed surprised by his question, so perhaps she hadn't been thinking of the man after all.

"In the corridor that day." Ean stroked his fingers through her long hair. "You knew he was one of them. Had you met him before?"

"As Immanuel di Nostri, I knew him," she admitted. Her voice came quietly, as if it had traveled a great distance to reach him from where her thoughts dwelled. "But he was careful to conceal his nature then. In Tal'Afaq he was not."

"But how did you know he was Malorin'athgul? How could you tell when I couldn't?"

She lifted her head and resettled it within the curve of his shoulder, so that he viewed her face in profile. "Few written works tell of the Malorin'athgul. Most who know of them beyond my brother's circle learned of them through the *Qhorith'quitara*. These are apocryphal writings that give the Malorin'athgul's—well, it would be most apt to say the writings relate their mythology and list their divine names."

"Is that how you knew Pelas?"

"I knew him from his description in the *Sobra'Iternin*."

"So the *Sobra* describes each of them?"

She turned and draped an arm and a leg across his form. "The *Sobra* is written in patterns, Ean." Her finger traced the line of his chest, while her brow formed a similar furrow. "It doesn't describe them in any human sense. Instead, it catalogues their life patterns. All who have looked upon those patterns have them indelibly imprinted in their memory, for they are not patterns one can ever forget."

"That's how you recognized him then ... from his life pattern?" While startling in its way, it yet seemed a rather benign explanation compared to the places his imagination had taken him. But it also threw into stark illumination how little he really knew of Isabel.

She'd *read* the *Sobra I'ternin?* The rumors spoke of Björn having completed its translation, but if Isabel had also read the entire work ...

It only made sense. Björn shared everything with Isabel; he wouldn't have kept important knowledge from her. Thus she'd become the High Mage of the Citadel, as powerful within her purview as her brother when he'd held the Alorin Seat.

And for all Ean knew ... well, Isabel still held the rank of High Mage, and Björn ... Ean didn't believe for a moment that the First Lord had abandoned his responsibilities as the Alorin Seat. Rather, he appeared to have transcended them into something larger.

"You're very quiet, my love."

Ean lifted his head and pressed his lips to her hair. As he settled back into his pillow again, he said, "I was just thinking how little I really know of you."

Her hand slipped further around his chest, and she drew herself closer, her body and hair like satin and silk against his skin. Her finger continued its slow tracing of his chest. "One day you will remember all."

"Will that be the day you remove your blindfold?"

Isabel stilled. Then she sat up and looked down at him. "Ean ..." she frowned in wonder. "I don't wear the blindfold because of you." She seemed genuinely startled by his question. "However did—?"

"I just assumed it was related to my ... failures."

A gentle smile lifted her features, and she leaned in and kissed him lovingly. "Ever you seek to claim fault for all—don't you see this bravery in yourself?" She touched his rough, unshaven jaw with a gentle hand. "So like my brother—the two of you would battle each other over who should bear the heavier burden of guilt."

Her smile and her kiss eased the sting of her words. Ean pushed a hand behind his head. "But if not because of me—Arion, I mean ... then why?" He cupped her face and traced his thumb across the silk covering her eyes. "You walk the world forever denied its beauty."

Isabel considered him in silence for a moment. Then she exhaled a measured breath. "I made a promise—*we* made it together, you and I. It makes sense to me that if you couldn't remember the moment, you would yet perceive the association."

"But what was the promise?"

She gazed down at him with sorrow branded like the Kandori *Khoda Panaheh* across her brow. Then she lay her naked form over his and let their bodies be draped in the cloak of her hair. As she rested her cheek against his chest, she murmured, "I allowed my eyes to deceive me once to fatal ends. I swore never again to walk the world blinded to the truth, blinded by mortal eyes."

At this description, a sudden memory sparked to mind, the image blurred with ... he realized the blur was a haze of tears. He saw his hands—Arion's hands—tying a blindfold across Isabel's closed eyes. Then he'd kissed her.

"I put it on you," he said quietly, and she nodded. "To wear always."

She nodded again, and her cheek felt wet now against his chest. Her voice came faintly, "But I would remove it ... if you asked."

Ean stiffened beneath her. He knew what such an act would mean even without fully understanding it. "Isabel ... you're scaring me."

She sat up to face him, legs straddling his hips. "There can be only truth between us." She reached for the dark fold of silk.

Ean sat up abruptly and caught her wrist. "Stop."

She drew in her breath, and her bottom lip trembled.

To see her so close to tears nearly undid him. "*Isabel—*"

She wrapped her arms around him and drew him close, and for a time, neither of them spoke. Finally, he heard her whisper, "In all my life, there has only been you."

Ean didn't understand what was happening, what had *happened.* Whatever prophetic dream had visited Isabel in the night, it had taken something vital from her.

He took her face with his hands and with his thumbs wiped away her tears. "I love you. I have always loved you." He searched her hidden gaze, knowing she looked into his eyes even if hers were denied him. "I could never love anyone but you."

She nodded. Her lips parted with her inhale, so fragile and yet so tormentingly beautiful. And in that moment, Ean's sudden rising need drew both of them into its embrace again.

The prince rose before the dawn and went to the Moon Palace's nodecourt to study and chart a path to Ivarnen.

The second strand governed a Nodefinder's ability to travel, but as Isabel had reminded him, Ean indeed felt within its kinetic power a certain kinship to the fifth. With the necessary patterns under his command, the Pattern of the World embraced Ean as it would embrace its own second strand Adepts.

As the prince stepped upon the node and opened himself to the rushing kinetic river, calling up the Greater Reticulation to study and plot, the prince marveled at how far he'd come even since arriving in Kandori.

His work with Dareios had solidified an understanding of patterns which he'd lacked while working with Markal in T'khendar; and the trials he had undergone, culminating in his gaining Sebastian's freedom ... these had reaped an odd and unlikely confidence he hadn't imagined he would ever feel. As he stood then upon the Pattern of the World with the rushing power of a planet's kinetic force pummeling through him, and *liking* it, understanding it, knowing he had the skill to channel and define it ... this heralded a magical and wondrous moment of identity regained.

By the time Sebastian joined him beneath a rose-gold sky, Ean had mapped the way and was standing on the node forging the last *leis* into place. He felt his brother's presence as he opened his eyes.

Sebastian offered him a copper mug steaming with mulled wine. It smelled spicy and divine. "Is this how you sleep now, little brother? Standing in a courtyard all night? A tragic waste to leave a woman like Isabel in your bed all alone."

Ean walked over to him and took the mug. "For all you know my one night might've lasted as long as twenty."

Sebastian grinned. "Yes, but could *you* have lasted for twenty nights?"

"An old man's question."

"An adolescent's boast." Sebastian laughed at Ean's withering look and draped an arm around his shoulders. He clinked mugs with him as he drew him off. "Dareios is calling for us. Last minute details before we launch upon your dangerously insane plan to get us all killed."

"Dangerously insane is what I do best." Ean let Sebastian draw him away from the nodecourt. His work there was done in any case. "What of my pattern? Are you comfortable with it?"

Sebastian gave him a telling look and then downed the last of his drink. "I have the pattern."

They'd practiced using the pattern derived from Ean's variant trait until an evening rain and exhaustion had driven them inside. But it had worked. Sebastian could see every pattern Ean threw at him.

Ean cast Sebastian a sidelong glance. He still felt wonder being near him again, still had moments of incredulity when he couldn't believe his beloved older brother was alive and standing at his side.

Sebastian wore his hair longer now than he had in their youth. Now his long waves teased beneath his cheekbones and curled around his collar. Now he had a thin scar as a reminder of the unimaginable horrors he'd endured. But his blue-grey eyes were just as engaging as Ean remembered from their youth, and his smile just as ready.

Ean realized he'd been staring when Sebastian quirked an inquiring brow at him. He cleared his throat, earning an amused look from his brother, and said, "The pattern has to become native to you. You need to be able to hold it in place and work a hundred others on top of it."

"I know. It will." Sebastian smiled. "Mayhap you should've given us those twenty nights for practice instead of using them to bed a woman."

"Hypocrite."

"Ah, the difficult choices of youth."

Ean cast him a wry smile. "This youth could take your head off with a thought."

"I guess I'm lucky he's my little brother and knows how best to treat his betters."

Ean arched brows. "*Betters?*"

Sebastian regarded him with a superior air. "Only one of us will be king."

Ean eyed him surreptitiously. "I think which one is still open to debate."

Sebastian's blue-grey eyes danced with mirth. He wrapped an arm around Ean's shoulders again and gripped him close as they walked. "If our father names you heir, little brother, I'll stand in line to serve in your court."

The prince held his brother's affectionate gaze for a moment and then dropped his eyes to smile softly to himself. How he admired Sebastian! And how resilient he'd proven in the days since his 'reawakening.' He'd endured unknowable torment—years of captivity and vilely enforced submission and the torture of not even owning his own mind. Ean had feared his brother's psyche would've been shattered; yet Sebastian had never shown a moment's darkness since the night they reunited as brothers in true.

In the privacy of his thoughts, Ean worried that Sebastian was still floating on the fair tides of freedom, but that the winds of his past would catch up with him eventually. He hoped his brother would be able to weather that storm. He planned to be there to see it through with him, if and when it hit.

Dareios and his two assistants were waiting in the lab when Ean and Sebastian arrived.

"Ah, my princes, *sobh bekheir*." The truthreader pressed palms and bowed his head to them. Then he waved excitedly at his cousin Bahman.

The latter lifted a tunic formed of gold chains and sculpted plates and brought it over.

Ean gave Dareios a swift look. "You're giving us your magic tunic?"

"No; no, this is a new model." He winked at them. "Bahman and Naveed have been working on it feverishly. I daresay they've improved upon my original."

Bahman stopped before Sebastian and extended the metal shirt to him. It looked similar to a shirt of mail, though less completely structured, with patterns inscribed on chest and arm plates and intricately woven chains.

"Wait—this is for me?" Sebastian turned a startled look around at the others. "But Ean—"

"Ean can shield with the fifth."

"Consistently," Ean amended, for though they'd been working on that pattern together, Sebastian still had a long way to go before he would be able to hold it effortlessly in place.

Dareios advised, "The mail is designed to protect against projectile objects—arrows, fast strikes and the like—but it won't keep a man from throttling you in close combat." He motioned again to the shirt Bahman was holding out for Sebastian. "If you will accept it?"

Sebastian aimed an accusatory glance at Ean.

Ean willed his gaze to convey all that he would have his brother understand. "I won't risk you—"

"I know." Sebastian quieted him with an upraised hand … and then a smile to soften his brusqueness. "I get it. And I'd be a fool not to accept." He turned a grateful look to Dareios, and then to Bahman and Naveed. "Thank you." He took the mail shirt and looked it over. Then he looked up at Ean under his brows. "This was your idea?"

Ean smiled. "I wish it had been."

"You may thank my sister Ehsan, Sebastian." Dareios's colorless eyes glinted with humor. "Or possibly curse her. We have yet to see how well it works." He eyed Sebastian quizzically. "It does intrigue me that she's taken an interest in your welfare." His tone implied everything his benign gaze lacked.

Sebastian looked slightly taken aback. "Your sister has displayed only the utmost propriety in our interactions, Dareios."

The truthreader rubbed at one eyebrow. "Perhaps that is the problem." He dropped his hand and frowned at Sebastian. "If I sent her to you dressed as a dancing girl, might you take her off my hands?"

Sebastian barked an incredulous laugh. "A Princess of Kandori? Why would she go anywhere with me?"

Dareios arched brows. "I believe you undersell yourself, *Prince* of Dannym. But matchmaking will have to wait for your return." He waved them towards the doors and moved to walk between them. Draping an arm around Sebastian's shoulders, Dareios added low in his ear, "Think upon it. Ehsan is a skilled Healer and the most beautiful of all my sisters—but don't let her know you heard me say it, or they'll all come nipping at my heels in indignation."

Sebastian chuckled.

"Of course, if Ehsan isn't to your taste, there are seven more where she came from."

Ean cast Dareios a reproving grin. "You're incorrigible. What would your mother think?"

"If she was doing her job properly, it wouldn't fall to me." He turned Ean a desperate look. "They've descended upon my palace, Ean. I must take steps." He glanced back to Sebastian and looked him over appreciatively. "And a handsome prince of Dannym is a most eligible choice."

Sebastian looked appalled by this description. He opened palms and offered a lament to the ceiling, "What world have I been reborn into? It hardly seems like the one I left eight years ago."

Dareios took Sebastian's hands and pressed his palms together instructively. "There. Kandori's gods only listen if you pray in this wise." Dareios rolled his eyes heavenward and exhaled a resigned sigh. "At least, this is what my mother in her infinite wisdom will tell you. This, she explains, is the reason all of my prayers remain unanswered."

Ean chuckled. "Because you're lacking penitence?"

Dareios's eyes danced. "I believe my lack of faith is likely the larger issue. Mind, it could have something to do with the fact that I pray every day for my sisters to find husbands and my mother prays for exactly the opposite, thus confusing our gods, who were never very attentive listeners to begin with. But as for Ehsan, Sebastian …"

As they continued down the hall, Dareios extolling his sister Ehsan's virtues in great detail while Sebastian stared straight ahead rather red-faced, Ean felt an overwhelming gratitude to the truthreader.

They were all trying to keep their manner buoyant; perhaps overly so in their need to feel a lightness where only a heavy, hollow anticipation lurked. Necessity demanded they find this felicity, for were any of them to think too deeply upon the coming night, the horrors they expected to face would only cloud their last hours and bring a sorrowful cast to the day.

It was foolhardy and reckless, their plan, but they'd reached no better solution, and Ean had promised on the night he saved Sebastian that he would only envision greatness in himself.

It was going to require greatness of a monumental nature to get out of Ivarnen alive.

Ean stood in the nodecourt watching the sun diving towards the palace walls. Sebastian stood behind him fingering the Merdanti blade that Dareios had placed in his hands earlier that day. They were waiting for Isabel.

Ean would've been content to wait forever—he would've been content to live out his life with her in Kandori and never leave—were he not so worried for his men.

Sebastian grunted. "It feels strange to me."

Ean cast him a look over his shoulder. They both wore the *drachwyr's* style of fighting blacks, with bindings at elbows, thighs and knees, but Ean didn't think Sebastian was referring to his clothes. "What feels strange?"

Sebastian held out the blade before him and eyed along its razor edge. "Having a weapon sing in your head."

Ean smiled and turned back to the node. In his mind he held the route they meant to travel. Part of him already felt far down those ethereal paths. "Sentient blades are far superior to dormant ones." He glanced over his shoulder again. "You'll get used to it."

"Dore never would've trusted me with a sentient weapon—and rightly so." Sebastian moved his blade through the first few motions of the *cortata*. "He never would've trusted me with the fifth—not with anything that I might've used to harm him ..." He lowered the weapon and his gaze darkened. "Or to escape."

Ean scowled at the stones beyond his feet. "Dore's concept of trust pertains solely to its use in manipulating others."

Sebastian glanced up under his brows ... frowned. "It's so odd. You clearly know him, but you can't *really* know him—it's like you truly are two people. On the one hand, you're just my little brother, but on the other you're ..." he made a circular motion with his blade and flashed a smile. "Well, as Dore would say, you're the magnificent Arion Tavestra."

Ean gave him a pained look.

Sebastian's gaze softened. "But I get it, Ean. I understand what that's like. I know the feeling of duality ... of having memories that don't and yet somehow *do* belong to you." He walked over and placed a strong hand on Ean's shoulder. "*You* saved me from that living hell." Sebastian held his gaze pointedly. "Not Arion Tavestra."

"You have the right of it again, Sebastian val Lorian."

Ean and Sebastian both turned at Isabel's words.

Ean tried not to frown as she came across the court dressed in her fighting blacks and carrying her Merdanti staff—since learning Phaedor had made it for her, the staff ever gave Ean the sensation that somehow the zanthyr lurked nearby, waiting for the opportune moment to appear and chastise him for some new stupidity.

Ean took her hand and drew her close. He tucked her head beneath his chin and murmured, "Now that you're here, I know we'll succeed."

Isabel drew back and cupped his cheek with her hand. "Your success has never depended on me, my lord. You only liked to imagine it so." She added with a slight turn of her head towards Sebastian, "For my benefit, I think, but a general need not be a gentleman."

Sebastian waved his sword idly towards Ean. "Only at heart, perhaps, for a lady deserves no less."

She arched a brow at him, but her lips hinted with humor. "Oh, you are both in league together already, I see. Very well. I submit to being treated like a lady."

Ean cast her a smile and captured her hand in his again. "There are worse offenses."

This brief respite of levity was all they could manage. It ended as Ean turned his gaze to the node. He exhaled forcefully, feeling the pull of the Pattern of the World as well as his conscience, as if both were already anchored in Ivarnen. Staring at the tiles of the court, he saw only the lines of power he meant to travel upon. "Ready?"

Sebastian came and grasped his other hand.

"Lead us on, my lord." Isabel squeezed his fingers and gave him a smile. "Valor calls her champion."

Ean opened himself to the currents and stepped on the node.

Swirling light blinded him, but he knew the channel he needed to find and sought it among the rushing brilliance. Down then, towards a new vortex they fell, surrounded by blinding lines like streaming stars.

Ean found the next channel before the first one ended, and he felt himself pulled in a new direction while the universe swam around him. He held tight to the others' hands, hardly realizing the ache in his cheeks came from the size of his smile, for he saw—he really *saw* it.

I can travel the Pattern of the World.

He found the last channel—the *leis* he'd forged with the fifth—and dragged them onto it before the current swept them past its tiny opening.

The next thing he knew, the Pattern of the World was behind him. It hadn't quite spit him out of its door—he could still feel it, like a raging river on the other side of a hill—but the noise in his ears had quieted.

Before him, a twilight world waited.

Sunset still flamed in the far west—it remained afternoon in

Kandori—but there on the far eastern coast of Saldaria, night's first stars were appearing.

"Well, that was … something." Sebastian extracted his hand from Ean's and shook it out. Ean *had* been holding on perhaps a bit tighter than was strictly necessary.

"Well done, Ean." Isabel moved towards the edge of a cliff overlooking a broad estuary. Twilight bathed the surrounding mountains in violet and turned the estuary's glassy waters darkly mercuric. "Where have you brought us?"

Ean reclaimed her hand and led her westward around the hill rising behind them. Eventually the view cleared and they looked out over a mountainous isle sitting in the middle of the estuary where river met sea. Lights burned within the massive castle that crowned the mountain's summit, and also along a tumbling wall that stretched to the water's edge. The effect was akin to a stone dragon huddling atop the mountain and trailing its tail down the back.

Sebastian exhaled forcefully. "Ivarnen."

Isabel gripped Ean's hand. "Do you see, Ean?"

"Verily, my lady." The currents washing away from the castle were churning with a darkness every bit as violent as what they'd witnessed in Tal'Afaq. "Dore's card of calling."

Isabel twisted her staff in one hand. "He's there."

"I expected he would be."

She looked to him, and he sensed a sharp urgency crossing the bond. "I cannot interfere. Not in this. Not again. The illusion we discussed is as much as I dare."

"I know, Isabel."

Sebastian cleared his throat. "My lady, we've got this."

Isabel turned and laid her hand lightly against Sebastian's chest. "Yes …" She ran her fingers along the baldric that held his blade and then pressed harder to feel the enchanted mail he wore beneath his coat. "I believe that you do."

Ean saw a brief flare as the sun fell finally beneath the curve of the world. "It's time." He led them down the side of the sandy hill towards the sea far below.

"Ean …" Sebastian called Ean's gaze back to him as he brought up the rear, but when their eyes met, he gave a frustrated exhalation. "Never mind."

Isabel glanced over her shoulder as they continued their descent. "What is it?"

Sebastian stared hard at the trail, obviously seeing something other than their feet. "I feel … I don't know … like something important is missing—some oath or vow or sacred troth that will doom us for lack of having spoken it." He gave her a rueful look. "We're heading into gods know what kind of hell on an insane quest, and I don't even have a lady's kerchief to stuff beneath my armor."

"You're not wearing armor," Ean pointed out from the lead.

"Near enough." Sebastian pulled at the golden collar partially hidden beneath his coat.

Isabel turned him an amused look. "If you say you desire to give an oath, Sebastian, do so."

"To whom, my lady? I get the sense your brother is the one who carries the burden of oaths."

She blessed him with an admiring smile. "Again ... you've the right of it."

Sebastian fell quiet for a time. Then he said, "I would give it, Isabel."

She glanced back at him. "And he would accept it, Sebastian, providing you knew what you were giving."

Yet he wouldn't accept mine ... Ean clenched his jaw. He didn't want to think on that memory. His own lack of an oath remained a wound that continuously throbbed, a reminder that he hadn't been worthy of pledging what he felt deep down was rightly his to give. He knew exactly how Sebastian was feeling.

Sebastian thought on this as they continued their descent. "I should know him." His words came softly, musingly. "I *would* know him—I mean, I will. I intend to, and yet ... I hardly feel I need to." He happened to catch Ean's eye as the prince glanced over his shoulder, and Sebastian's expression held boundless gratitude. "I know *you*, Isabel," Sebastian continued, looking back to her, "and I know Ean. I know what you've both done for me and what you've told me of your brother's game. I shouldn't desire to know more than that."

"If you do, he will provide it, Sebastian." Isabel stopped as they navigated a sudden drop in the path. Sebastian took her hand and helped her over the edge. She nodded him to lead on and said, "When you do meet my brother, you'll find that he's an easy man to admire but a hard man to love."

Walking silently in the lead, Ean felt this truth echo painfully in his chest, though he couldn't tell from which of his many losses the pain originated. Sometimes thoughts of the First Lord brought an ache similar to what he experienced around his missing oath, only ... deeper. The two felt connected somehow. He didn't know why.

"Why do you say that?" Sebastian asked meanwhile.

Isabel slipped her arm through his elbow. "One can admire from afar, but to love someone we need intimacy. Beyond admiring each other's strengths, we desire also to share our loved-ones' fears and failures—for our weaknesses and inadequacies append us to each other in critical ways." She turned Sebastian a pointed look. "Björn will never show you this side of himself."

Ean grunted at this. He recalled so well the torture of enduring the First Lord's benevolent gaze leveled in forbearance. He stopped at the next ledge and retrieved Isabel's hand from his brother's arm. He could only take so much.

Sebastian grinned at him.

Isabel kissed Sebastian' cheek and squeezed his hand, and said to him over her shoulder as Ean led her away, "Never will you meet a man more driven by purpose, Sebastian. People have said of me that I see the future along many paths, but my brother doesn't seek to know the future; he seeks to *cause* it.

"Ever he watches the threads of the tapestry to determine the ramifications of choice—both his Players' choices and his own. He's too many times witnessed his own failure bring death, even were that failure a simple crack in his composure." She pressed her lips together and shook her head. "One hairline fracture in my brother's self-control caused the Citadel to fall—at least, so he feels."

Ean opened his mouth to protest, but she headed him off.

"Yes, I know you blame yourself equally, Ean, but do you see how both of you strive to take responsibility for the entire game as if no other Players existed? As if none of them had any choice, and the only choice that mattered was your own?"

Ean clenched his teeth and held his tongue. Her correction, gentle though it was, echoed too closely Markal's caustic reprimands.

Looking over her shoulder at Sebastian, Isabel finished, "When you come to know my brother, Sebastian, do not look in him to find mortal failings. The maker of the game cannot afford the luxury, and it only weakens all of us to clamor for weakness in our leader."

The waves lapped languidly at the land when they reached the estuary's rim, which was part marshland, part sandy shore. With the tide in, nearly a mile of deep water separated them from the isle and the stone dragon called Ivarnen.

Sebastian came to stand beside Ean at the water's edge. "Remind me how you planned to get us across?"

Ean cast him a devious look. "That's the easy part." He formed his intention and stepped down upon the water, feeling it go instantly solid beneath his feet. Smiling, he cast a spear of the fifth through the water towards the isle, making solid what was fluid, binding molecule to molecule with thought and intent and just a little pinch of pride.

He watched the water forming into his nearly invisible bridge until he knew its far end touched the isle. Then he looked back to Isabel and held out his hand.

She took it and stepped down on the water that wasn't quite water anymore. Her staff clicked against the glossy surface as if against ice, and she set off in the lead.

Sebastian stepped down beside Ean with an arched brow. "Oddly, I don't recall your sharing this part of the plan."

"I don't like to brag." Ean set off behind Isabel with a grin on his face.

"Gloating doesn't seem to be beneath you though." Sebastian stomped a couple of times at the watery bridge. "And you're sure Dore won't see this working on the currents?"

"It's native to Ean," Isabel replied from the lead. "If you or I had compelled the elements thusly, Sebastian, Dore would instantly find the mark on *elae's* tides, but Ean is an Adept of the fifth. He would have to command far more of the lifeforce than this requires for the currents to show the working."

Sebastian shook his head and dropped his gaze to watch his feet treading on water that wasn't. "There's *so* much to learn ..." After a moment, a brilliant smile lifted his features.

Ean caught the look and smiled to himself. Every time he expected his brother to fall into melancholy at a thought, or to sink beneath waves of regret over everything that had been taken from him, Sebastian managed somehow to see the brightness instead.

Ean wondered if his brother knew how he admired him, how much of an inspiration he was. Between his own promise to look for greatness in himself and Sebastian's already living it, Ean was coming to believe he might one day actually achieve his goal.

FORTY-FIVE

"Talent is often developed at the expense of character.
The greater the talent, the more the mischief."

– Liam van Gheller, Endoge of the Sormitáge

T ANIS STOOD IN the shadow of a column along the Grand Passáge
watching his roommate, Felix, doing the same.

He'd woken that morning still unnerved from his encounter with
N'abranaacht the night before. It had shaken him on a number of levels, but it
had also roused a terrible suspicion.

Tanis had lain in bed for a while staring at a crack in the ceiling and wishing
he had someone to talk to … just anyone who could advise him. He'd thought
of asking Vincenzé, but he didn't think the Caladrian knew much about the
particular type of demons that were stalking through his thoughts, and the lad
just wasn't comfortable opening up to the High Lord or anyone at the Sormitáge
about his suspicions.

Eventually a scratching, snarling and occasional crackling had drawn Tanis's
attention, and he'd pushed up in bed to find Felix sitting at his desk alternately
scribbling and cursing. It seemed to be a habit of his.

Tanis had climbed out of bed and prepared to start his day, but all the while
he was washing up and getting dressed, he'd watched Felix crumple page after
page and shove the balls into a pile. Finally, Felix had hissed a heated curse,
gathered all the balls of paper into his knapsack, and barged from the room.

Tanis had taken up his satchel and followed. This time he locked onto Felix's
mental signature—why he hadn't thought to do so the last time, he couldn't say,
but with Felix's mental signature in mind, Tanis could track him anywhere.

In retrospect, the lad felt a mite foolish—he just wasn't used to resorting to
his talent to solve problems. But he made a firm commitment to do so in the

future. What was the point of having so much knowledge and skill if he never used it?

As he waited now behind the column with his father's journal in hand, trying to look inconspicuously bored, Tanis kept a firm lock on Felix's mental presence. He wasn't reading the other boy's thoughts—Felix had an uncommon, natural talent for guarding them—but Tanis could feel him from a distance in the way one senses another person in a room. He tried to stay far enough behind Felix that the latter wouldn't notice he was being followed. At least, that was Tanis's hope.

Thus far he'd been successful. Tanis had watched Felix creep from shadow to shadow, intentionally avoiding everyone's notice—he obviously had a lot of experience in skulking. Tanis had seen him several times fall in at the tail end of a pack of students and walk close enough to appear as part of the group to a distant observer, but not so close as to draw notice from anyone in the group. He never stayed with any one group for long. Before they perceived him, he would've darted away into another shadow or down a connecting corridor.

Why? Tanis shook his head with this thought. *What's he doing that he's so afraid of people finding out about?*

Several columns ahead, Felix moved off again into the flow of bodies along the Grand Passáge, which was ever as crowded as any boulevard in Cair Rethynnea, and equally as broad. Tanis slipped the journal beneath his arm and followed.

At the next dome, Felix turned off the Grand Passáge, headed down the Lord of the Forest corridor, then exited through a gallery connecting to another hall. Just as Felix was passing into the adjacent building, a host of red-cloaked soldiers wearing silver breastplates emerged. *Praetorians.*

Docents, students and scholars all stepped aside to let them pass, and in the general commotion, Felix disappeared.

Tanis inwardly ground his teeth. He could sense Felix still close by and quickly scanned the crowd. He thought he caught a glimpse of Felix's head through a window in the building at the end of the gallery and was about to set off after him when he realized the Praetorians were in the way.

Actually … they were coming right towards him.

With a great clanking of armored boots on stone, the marching soldiers encircled Tanis. The lad looked around at the steely faces of the men and felt suddenly small indeed. Worse was the wave of excited murmuring that spread through the crowd.

The foremost among the guards clapped his heels together and declared, "*Signore*, if you will please come with me."

Swallowing, Tanis nodded.

The soldiers turned as one and started back the way they'd come. Tanis thought he recognized a couple of the men as having been on the dock when he and the zanthyr had arrived in port, but he couldn't be certain. They all wore identical helmets with etched nose-plates and a stripe of bristling crimson feathers, and they each marched with the same intimidating presence.

At first Tanis wondered if this was N'abranaacht's idea of sending for him. Then he remembered that only the Empress could command the Praetorian Guard, and his hopes surged at the idea that perhaps they were collecting him on Phaedor's behalf. As the phalanx of Praetorians headed inside the building with Tanis firmly ensconced in their center, the lad happened to glance to his left. Felix stood leaning against a statue, wearing a decidedly self-satisfied smirk.

Several galleries later, Tanis was still puzzling over his roommate's expression when the Praetorians stopped before a sunlit courtyard bordered on three sides by tall limestone walls and on the fourth by the portico under which they'd halted. A marble-paved path led through the middle of a garden to a large fountain with a centaur at its gushing apex. The Praetorians spread out along the portico, and the leader motioned Tanis to proceed into the garden.

As confused as he was apprehensive, Tanis slowly descended the steps and headed along the marble path towards the fountain, which was large enough and loud enough to drown out the excited chatter of the crowd gathering behind the soldiers.

The centaur stood with a drawn bow and arrow pressed to a reclining maiden's heart. The scene appeared so realistic, the statues so lifelike, that Tanis worried the pair might've been turned to stone rather than carved from it. The maiden arching helplessly beneath the arrow's threatening tip wore an expression of rapture, but Tanis, looking into the empty eyes of the centaur, just felt apprehensive. The creature had an intimidating ferocity about it.

Rounding the back side of the large fountain, Tanis came to an abrupt halt.

A long marble bench curved synchronously with the fountain's sculpted edge, and a figure dressed all in white sat upon it. A circlet of emeralds bound the opalescent veil that obscured her features and her long dark hair.

"There is much to appreciate about this fountain." As the girl lifted her face to the centaur, Tanis could see the outline of her profile through the sheer silk veil. She pointed as she went on, "The feral centaur represents lust, an embodiment of unbridled passion—for life, for power, for riches. His lust is juxtaposed against the maiden's purity, which represents innocence stolen, ravaged by time, by experience, or by love's hardships. Yet within the maiden's expression, you see both fear and desire, reflecting our own inner struggle to fulfill the craving of our hearts."

Tanis didn't know how to respond to this. The last thing he'd expected was to receive a lesson on art appreciation from the Imperial Princess Nadia van Gelderan.

He knew a little of the princess—some from the zanthyr, but more from gossip around the Sormitáge halls. The Empress Valentina had borne eleven children to produce a female truthreader, who was immediately proclaimed her heir. Nadia was a fourth strand prodigy, like her mother and her truthreader grandfather, Hallian IV.

Beyond these facts, there were as many rumors circulating about Nadia van Gelderan as there had been about Prince Ean back in Calgaryn—from absurd whispers that she was actually a siren, to talk that her veil hid a deformity. But all of these rumors maintained that if Nadia lifted her veil to a man, he might as well be staring at the stars of Cephrael's Hand, for Fate would claim him soon enough.

Tanis finally realized he'd been standing there staring at her while she was waiting for a response. He looked to the statue with a slightly furrowed brow.

"I don't know, Your Highness. It's fierce. There is power in it." Tanis gazed at the sinews of muscle in the centaur's back and shoulders, along its up-bent arm. The creature looked so frighteningly *real*. "If I had to hazard a guess, I'd say a fifth-strander sculpted it with *elae*."

"That's very astute of you." Nadia indicated the fountain with a slender hand. "*Nessun and Dahlia* was forged by the Adept sculptor Lorenzo Dellanova, whose artful hands crafted many of the sculpture fountains decorating our fair city. Dellanova is one the best known artists from the *Illuminato Secolo*, that last wonderful century before the Adept Wars, when so many masterworks were created. Dellanova had many contemporaries, most notably the painters Raphe Nordskov and Immanuel di Nostri."

Tanis did a double-take.

The hint of a smile fluttered Nadia's veil. "I see you know these names."

"I'm familiar with … some of di Nostri's work," Tanis managed, feeling a sudden bare anguish descend upon him.

"Well, of course you are." She waved and made a little laugh. "Nordskov and di Nostri are credited with much of the masterwork that is the Grand Passáge."

Now Tanis well and truly gaped at her. He actually grew a little sick to his stomach. To think … all this time he'd been walking underneath that ceiling, awed by its majesty yet rarely giving the paintings the study they deserved. Suddenly he felt as though he'd been passing Pelas himself, day in and day out, without a single nod of greeting.

He swallowed and looked away from Nadia, trying to keep his expression neutral. Yet even could he have found his voice in that moment, he had no idea what to say to her.

Nadia noted his reaction with a curious frown. After a slightly uncomfortable silence, she looked back to the fountain. "The Empress would have me spend all of my waking hours studying political philosophy, but I much prefer the philosophy of art."

Tanis hugged his father's journal to his chest, feeling inordinately out of place and missing Pelas most desperately. "Forgive me, Princess …" Words failed him again, and rather than try to explain himself, he said instead, "I'm … I don't understand why you've called me here."

"You do not wish to discuss art with me, Tanis di Adonnai?"

This appellation made Tanis blink, for he'd never heard himself named in such a manner. "I ..." he frowned. "I ... would, should you wish it, Your Highness," which was true enough. Nadia was lovely—even with the veil this was apparent—and he'd no pressing business elsewhere, yet the entire encounter felt so odd. Did a person really just dally about idly discussing art with the heir to an empire?

Yet you've traveled with princes and the cousins of queens. You've sailed with the High Lord di L'Arlesé and trained in your craft with the Fourth Vestal.

The oddest part of this thought was that it wasn't his own.

He cast the princess a considering look.

Though her veil obscured the fullness of her expression, Tanis thought she was amused. She patted the bench beside her, inviting Tanis to join her. "The High Lord has never sponsored a student to the Sormitáge, you know."

Still hugging his journal, Tanis walked over and slowly lowered himself onto the bench a discreet distance from Nadia's person. He remained all too aware of the watchful Praetorians. "I don't think it was entirely his idea."

"The High Lord is not usually duped into doing things against his will."

"He wasn't facing a usual opponent."

She smiled wryly at this. "Whatever the cause of his sponsorship, Tanis, Marius di L'Arlesé is a most honorable man. He ... suggested I might converse with you, after a fashion."

Tanis immediately knew an untruth in this statement, though it was also partly true. He considered Nadia carefully then, wondering what the High Lord had actually said to her. Instinct whispered that the princess was upon some game of cat and mouse. Playing along for the moment, he thought in reply, *Only because Vincenzé failed to uncover anything useful in his probing.*

Nadia gave a little laugh. Tanis hadn't exactly pushed the thought over to her, but neither had he hidden it, much as she had likely done just moments before. Truthreaders were known to share the 'public' space of their minds with one another, especially among friends.

"You are not so innocent as the High Lord would have me believe, I think," the princess murmured, eyeing him with amusement.

Tanis drew slightly back. "The High Lord described me as innocent?"

"Not his words exactly," she admitted with a smile. "Vincenzé called you cagey."

Tanis grunted. "I hold him in mutual regard."

She really laughed at this. She leaned to lay her fingers upon his knee with a gentle grace. "Your candor is refreshing." She straightened and watched him quietly for a moment. "I confess my curiosity was piqued once I learned of you."

Again, Tanis caught something in her words, an underlying truth she kept closely guarded. His eyes moved to her hand and noted the Sormitáge ring she wore. He sensed the princess would be a strong adversary, should they meet mind to mind.

"So tell me, Tanis," Nadia continued as Tanis was wondering how best to treat with her, "why is the High Lord so interested in you?"

His eyes lifted back to meet hers. "His Grace didn't tell you?"

"Have you *met* my father?" she laughed, to which Tanis gave her an acknowledging smile.

Though she was clearly withholding things from him, Tanis perceived no threat from Nadia. In fact, her mental presence rubbing against his felt … nice. *Really* nice, like a gentle breeze off the mountain, or sunlight on his bare skin. So Tanis decided to trust her, after a fashion—or at least to trust his instincts about her.

He returned his father's journal to his satchel. "The High Lord mightn't be so interested in me were it not for my relationship with the zanthyr."

She drew back slightly. "The zanthyr. Could you possibly mean the zanthyr Phaedor?"

He settled her a level eye by way of reply.

She gazed at him in astonishment. "My mother has spoken of Phaedor to me. They're traveling together even now—I don't know where, and Marius won't say. But he's not sure she'll be back by Twelfth-day." She moved closer to Tanis. "What is your relationship with Phaedor?"

Tanis let out a long, slow breath. "He is both guardian and guide." He cast her a look and stood to walk towards the fountain. "The High Lord had many questions for me, but the zanthyr didn't want me talking about myself."

"Why? Why must you be so secretive?"

Tanis shoved hands in his pockets and stubbed a booted toe against the fountain's base. "I don't know. I don't have that much information even to share. But whatever Phaedor's reasoning, it's likely explainable by Balance—or at least unexplainable by that same rationale."

"Balance." Nadia gazed wide-eyed at him. Clearly whatever she'd expected to gain in her little game, it wasn't this. "You think … *he* thinks you can somehow affect the Balance in the realm?"

Tanis understood how remarkable—and ridiculous—it sounded. He felt the same way. "My mother said I have to walk my path." He gave a shrug and then turned and sat down on the fountain's rim. "I know that everyone's path isn't necessarily impactful, and I don't know that mine is either, but I know that the zanthyr is invested in keeping me upon my path." He added with a grimace, "*Really* invested."

Nadia pressed fingers across her lips. The space of her mind radiated wonder … and not a little fascination. After a moment, she took up the delicately jeweled hem of her veil and twined it thoughtfully among her fingers. "The Palmers believe that we all have a path, but while some tread a peripheral existence, others walk a thread central to the overarching pattern of the Maker's vast tapestry. Finding and knowing one's path is at the core of their faith."

Tanis frowned at this. It seemed odd to him that an Arcane Scholar like N'abranaacht would subscribe to such a passive faith. After a minute's thought, he looked to her again. "Why do they wear the robes?"

"Their robes are meant to be an inverse metaphor—the idea that we are all blind to our future, that we walk our path on faith, not empirical fact." She frowned at her own words. "I don't suppose they could really go around blindfolded, could they? Covering themselves from head to toe except for the eyes represents this inverse concept of walking blindly with faith along our paths."

Tanis pinned his hands between his knees. "It sounds benign enough."

She smiled. "They also believe fifth-strand creatures have no path."

Tanis found something in this comment unsettling. "Why do they think that?"

She leaned back on her hands on the bench. "It's complicated, but it has much to do with their immortality." Nadia regarded him quietly then while the only sound was the rushing roar of the centaur's fountain. Tanis returned her gaze, feeling oddly warm beneath her inspection. Nadia's smile disarmed him, and … well, she *was* lovely.

After staring into each other's eyes for perhaps longer than was advisable, Nadia dropped her gaze back to her hands. "You're not as I imagined you."

"I'm flattered to think you imagined me at all, Princess."

She laughed then. "I cannot believe Vincenzé called you cagey. I find you very … charming."

Tanis couldn't be certain, but he thought he saw the faintest blush come to her cheeks upon this pronouncement. He leaned and rested elbows on his knees. "Vincenzé pries." Then he tilted his head to capture her gaze with his own and gave her a smile. "You entice."

"I do *not*," she gasped, embarrassment coloring her tone. She pressed fingertips to her lips and gave him a blushing smile beneath her veil. "You're the one who opened your mind to me."

Tanis frowned, straightened. "I'm sorry … was that inappropriate?"

"You're just so *different*. I don't understand why Fe—" Abruptly she stopped herself, making Tanis wonder what she'd been about to say.

To fill the space of her sudden uncertainty, he asked, "Different from other truthreaders?"

She replied with a telling look. "From any Agasi I've ever met."

"Well, I was raised in Dannym."

She gave him a doubtful look. "It's just … most truthreaders I know are more guarded."

Tanis wondered what she was used to dealing with if she thought he was unguarded. His private mind had been closed to her from the beginning.

She must've caught this thought—not that he'd hidden it from her—for she said, "Exactly my point, Tanis. Most truthreaders I've met won't share even the common space of their minds with me."

Well, if Vincenzé is any indication of the way Agasi Adepts treat with each other, it's no wonder.

She laughed again. "Tanis, are you trying to sway my loyalties?"

Tanis cast her the quirk of a grin. "I wouldn't dream of it, Your Highness."

"Will you spend the day with me?"

The moment the invitation left her lips, Nadia looked as startled as Tanis felt. He blinked as he held her gaze ... but then he smiled. *Why not?* He had nowhere he had to be, and somewhere he very much did *not* want to be, and it certainly provided an indisputable excuse for denying N'abranaacht's expected summons.

Tanis stood and gave a little bow. "It would be my pleasure, Princess."

She eyed him quietly. After a moment, he felt her mental presence open to him, a clear—and surprising—invitation. He replied in kind, not merely to be polite but because he wanted to.

He'd known so few truthreaders, and none of them female save for what memories he had of his mother. He found Nadia's mental presence alluring, and every time she smiled he felt an odd sense of pride. As his eyes explored her face, observing the curve of her lips beneath her veil, he chastised himself for the thoughts that came into his head.

These he very much kept to himself.

Nadia stood and motioned to the path. "Shall we?"

He came to her side. It surprised him to realize he stood taller than her. "And where would you go, Your Highness?"

"I think you should call me Nadia." Her colorless eyes found his and shied demurely away again as they started off together.

Tanis wasn't sure how to interpret the meaning in her gaze. "I'm not sure that's a good idea, Princess."

She laughed. "You'll share the intimacy of my mind but not speak my name? We're practically holding hands, *Lord Adonnai.*"

Tanis glanced uncertainly at her. "I'm no lord."

"My father says the zanthyr named you heir to those lands. That makes you a peer of the imperial court."

She'd spoken so nonchalantly, yet the words hit Tanis like the bolts of a crossbow, each one right into his chest. He couldn't help wondering who the High Lord thought owned those lands. "Fine," he managed, looking away with a swallow. "I'll call you Nadia if you promise never to call me ... that ... again."

As they rounded the fountain, the Praetorians clanged to immediate attention, heels snapping and vambraces clapping across their chests with smart precision. Tanis eyed them nervously.

Nadia noted his reaction and placed a hand on his arm. "They would as soon harm my own person. You're under the High Lord's protection, remember?"

The Praetorians surrounded them as they ascended the steps—to the immediate hum of gossip from the crowd of onlookers. Tanis thought he recognized some of the faces as having been standing there as he'd entered the garden, and he marveled with some asperity that so many people had nowhere else to be. Fortunately, there seemed to be few *frites* among the assembly, which meant they had at least a few minutes before the entire campus knew the Princess Nadia had invited him to walk with her.

On the bright side, N'abranaacht would likely find out the same way.

"I thought we might tour the Grand Passáge before luncheon," she told him brightly. "I got the idea you'd never received a formal tour. You did say you'd put yourself at my disposal to discuss art at any time."

Tanis gave her a look. "I'm not sure those were my exact words."

Her colorless eyes danced beneath her veil. "Close enough."

For all that walking with the imperial princess garnered an uncomfortable surfeit of attention, Nadia proved knowledgeable about the plethora of art adorning the Sormitáge halls, and she provided an intriguing explanation of the incredible paintings above them.

Her tale of the Lord of the Forest and his love affair with the Lady of the Rivers, one of Agasan's oldest and most enduring legends, reminded him of a Kandori story Farshideh had told him about Naiadithine, Goddess of Water, and her lover Napaealath, God of Stone. Tanis remembered hearing the story as a child and finding certain moments within the tale when Farshideh's words seemed so clear, so perfectly *right*. Now he knew that experience as the resonance of truth. He found it wondrous that two diverse cultures could have such similar legends, and that the truth would chime so richly in both of them.

They took luncheon together in the walled garden of one of the residences reserved for the imperial family, a five-minute walk from the main administrative complex. Tanis felt relieved to be somewhere without a thousand curious eyes watching and interpreting his every move, doubtless reading into each raised eyebrow, smile or scratch of the nose. Even the Praetorians left them alone, which Tanis found surprising. Highborn ladies in Dannym were never without a chaperone, and certainly not while in the company of a young man such as himself. Well ... none except Her Grace.

Nadia caught him wondering at their lack of a chaperone as they were sitting down to eat. The table was draped in fine linen and covered with mouth-watering delights, but Tanis stood staring at the departing line of servants wearing a faintly dismayed expression.

Nadia laughed at him. "Just what do you think is going to happen, Tanis?" She swept her silk skirts beneath her and settled into her chair.

He turned her a suspicious look, for he'd caught a hint of deviousness breezing through the part of their minds they now openly shared.

"Something perhaps like … this?" and she drew back her veil. Crystalline eyes gazed at him, framed by dark lashes and eyebrows that angled upwards. Nadia had a fey look about her, reminiscent of Alorin's most ancient races, those which the van Gelderan line was said to be descended from.

Nadia settled an elbow on the table and rested her chin on the back of her hand, fingers draped delicately. "Tanis, I do believe you're staring."

Abruptly he cleared his throat and took his seat. "Forgive me, Princess."

"Very well, Lord Adonnai."

He glared at her, and she laughed. "Eat something, please." She motioned to the plates of food. "I hear the menu at Chresten leaves much to be desired."

Tanis arched a brow. "How did you know I live at Chresten Hall?"

She dismissed his suspicious tone. "Most Postulants do."

Tanis helped himself to several dishes and then sat back in his chair to look at her. She was still regarding him with chin on hand and a secretive little smile hinting on her lips. "Nadia," he said, holding her gaze, "are you flirting with me?"

Abruptly she straightened and the smile vanished, replaced by prim indifference. "Of course not."

Now it was his turn to smile at her, deliberately dubious.

She helped herself to some fruit from a large platter. "What were your thoughts on what we saw in the Grand Passáge?" she asked coolly.

"Ah …" Tanis took a bite of something on his plate, but his eyes remained on the princess. "So we're swimming back to safer waters, then?"

Her gaze flashed to his. "What were you expecting?"

"We practically held hands the whole way here, Nadia. You've unveiled your face to me. I suppose I expected something …" he paused, pursed his lips in thought, "I don't know … catastrophic."

Her eyes softened. "I see you've heard those rumors, then."

He shrugged indifferently.

Nadia plucked a grape. "Some are inconvenient." She placed the fruit in her mouth and chewed slowly. Then she looked up at him under her lashes, suddenly impish. "Some are expedient."

"I gather you know what they say about me, too." Though he was quite enjoying her company, he'd not forgotten she'd sought him out for a reason, and he suspected it had nothing to do with what the High Lord may or may not have said about him.

Her gaze clouded, and he knew he'd hit the mark. She looked away, and then her eyes flashed back to his, suddenly intent. "*Are* you a spy?"

Tanis crossed his arms. "Are *you* a siren?"

Nadia arched brows in surprise. Then she burst out laughing. When she'd recovered, she gave him a look of open affection. "Very well. So tell me, Lord Adonnai, are you working for the High Lord in *any* capacity?"

"No more than you are, *Princess*."

She fell back against her chair and gazed wordlessly at him.

Tanis leaned forward and rested forearms on the table, returning her gaze intently. After a moment, her mind brushed his again, a tentative advance. His smile broadened, and he let her take a deep draught of his thoughts in reply. Her eyes widened, but he felt her drinking in the energy of his mind all the same, and he watched appreciatively as her cheeks turned rosy and her eyes became soft.

"Tanis," she said almost breathlessly, "... are you flirting with me?"

"Without question, Nadia."

She exhaled a little laugh and cast her gaze away, but her enduring smile belied her, and she didn't withdraw from his mind. Soon her eyes sought his again. He felt her touch in a mental caress like the nudging of a purring cat, making him want to rub against her in return.

"Perhaps we should stop," she whispered, blushing furiously.

"Perhaps we should." He didn't look away.

If anything, her mental touch became stronger, a silent plea to listen not to her words but to the amazing and wonderful feelings crashing on the shores of his mind. He replied with a mental sigh of wondrous contentment.

"By the Lady," she whispered, her eyes glossy and skin flushed. "This is so ... *nice*. I've never—"

"Neither have I."

Tanis's heart was thrumming in his chest, and the rush of blood through his veins was causing an acute ache in every part of him. He could barely imagine the sensation of kissing Nadia when just touching her mind felt so heady. Self control—and a wide table—kept him rooted to his seat. Finally, with a great deal of effort, he drew his mind back from hers and exhaled explosively.

She gave a little sigh. The touch of her mind lingered longer, hovering at the edge of his. They were back to safely holding hands, but this time her mental fingers were well entwined with his own, and she seemed disinclined to let go. Which suited him fine.

Nadia dropped her eyes back to her plate. From their sharing of thoughts, he knew she felt as he did, that food was not the sustenance they desired.

After a lengthy silence in which they both eased their breath and recovered some semblance of decorous comportment, the princess murmured, "You seem so much older than your years." She glanced up under her lashes again. Her cheeks maintained their rosy hue. Likewise her lips, which had become deliciously flushed. He wanted to kiss them. *Dangerous thoughts.*

Tanis forced himself to eat something just to divert his attention from Nadia's mouth. "The zanthyr says knowledge ages you."

"Yes," she agreed, furrowing her brow slightly, "but it's not just that.

You're ... well, you're ..." Her eyes swept him appreciatively, as if she couldn't help herself, and then she cast a blushing smile off into the gardens.

He frowned down at his body and tried to see himself through her eyes. His shoulders had broadened during his months of training with the zanthyr, and his chest and arms cut a muscular edge. Certainly he'd grown taller in recent months as well. He might be as tall as Prince Ean by now. He knew his jaw had become more defined, and he often saw angular shadows beneath his cheekbones when he looked in the mirror.

He'd never wondered if girls thought of him as good-looking—flirting with girls fell somewhat low on his list of priorities—but he supposed they might. Nadia certainly seemed to, anyway, if told from the look in her eyes. It made him both a little uncomfortable and oddly proud at the same time.

In this wise, the day passed blissfully. They finished their meal—surprisingly finding an appetite for food—and then strolled the grounds together, talking and sharing, laughing often. Nadia had a quick wit, and her strength of spirit reminded him fondly and with a touch of sadness of his Lady Alyneri.

The princess shared stories of her upbringing and told him about her mother's love affair with her Protector, who became the High Lord and her Consort when Valentina claimed the imperial throne; Tanis told her of his travels with Prince Ean and spoke at length about the zanthyr. But no matter how deep the secrets revealed, no words could approach the intimacy they shared through their gentle and constant touching of minds.

When at last a Praetorian appeared, looking slightly embarrassed at the interruption, and told the princess it was time to return to the palace, Nadia exhaled a wistful sigh and nodded regretfully. Only then did Tanis realize the sun had fallen behind the trees and the day was almost done.

Nadia looked back to him, and he felt the heat of her closeness. They'd stopped just inches apart, close enough that Tanis might have kissed her by simply leaning his head—and desperately wanted to, but he couldn't presume. Everything within him was clenched tightly. The sensation thrilled him.

She searched his gaze with her own, and he heard her sharing the thought with him, *I don't want to say goodbye.*

He smiled. *Then don't.*

She turned a desperate look toward the waiting Praetorian. *I ... must.*

Nadia ... Even as his next thought occurred to him, Tanis knew the imprudence of it. It was daring, to be certain, and bold—*very* bold. Yet it was but a simple working and one that could be easily removed.

Though he saw nothing but audacity in proposing it to her, he couldn't help himself now that he'd thought of it. He let the idea unfold in his mind then, and as soon as it had fully blossomed to her understanding, Nadia's eyes widened.

"Really?" She retreated from the intimacy of their common mind to challenge his resolve. "Tanis ..." her gaze searched his with wonder and surprise. "It's such an intimate connection. You wouldn't be able to hide your feelings ..."

I don't want to hide from you. This simple truth yet held a profound significance to Tanis. Nadia made him bold. She brought out a side of himself he'd never known. He'd only just met her, yet she made him feel older, prouder, powerful in a way he hadn't imagined. Protective even, like the zanthyr, and he ... *liked* finding these traits in himself.

Tanis daringly took up Nadia's hand. After sharing so much from mind to mind, that simple physical contact felt electrifying. When he lifted his gaze to meet hers, he let his smile become suggestive, enough that he saw her blush beneath it, and he placed into the shared space of their minds, *It would be as we are now. I would be at your beck and call ... just a thought away.*

She caught her breath. He sensed anticipation fluttering within her; butterflies of apprehension and excitement. She caught her bottom lip between her teeth and gazed up at him, her eyes so lovely framed by her dark lashes. *But ... are you certain?*

He rolled his eyes. "Have you not seduced me all afternoon?"

"Me?" she gasped incredulously. Then she laughed, both in rejection and acceptance of this truth, her eyes dancing.

"Come then." He extended his hand towards her.

She drew back. "You want *me* to do it?"

"You're the ringed truthreader here."

Nadia arched a brow. "Any fourth-strander wearing a Postulant's ring should equally possess the skill to create a bond with another. You do it."

He gave her a look. "You want *me* to work a fourth strand bonding pattern on *you*—the Empress's heir." Tanis grunted and shook his head. "I can only imagine what the High Lord would make of that. Do you *want* me beheaded?"

She lifted her chin, and her eyes sparkled with challenge.

His gaze darkened. Then he grabbed her hand and pressed his lips to her palm—already having formed his intent—and in a breath it was done.

A bond was the lightest of patterns in the Binding classification. It forged a feather-light connection, like tacking two pieces of cloth together with honey; whereas bindings—such as what the zanthyr had done when he bound himself to Tanis—would be more akin to unthreading and reweaving the two pieces as one.

Bonds were simply forged and easily broken. The Empire used them readily among the Imperial Adeptus to assist in coordination among the ranks during battle, and Nadia had told Tanis that all of her Praetorians were bonded—so in a sense she'd put the idea into his head to begin with.

Tanis felt the pattern settling like gossamer around their minds, wakening a unique awareness of her, an essence that was vitally and singularly *Nadia*. He sensed her now, and the feeling made him imagine them lying together beneath the sun bathed in the other's closeness.

Nadia's lips spread in a slow smile. "My ... that was *expertly* done."

Tanis tested their connection by thinking, *Nothing less than perfection for you, Princess.*

Her eyes glowed with pleasure, and her vibrant emotion rebounded back to him so readily that they both burst into laughter at the same moment.

It *had* been expertly done, just as Tanis's mother had taught him. If he'd added a few extra layers to the working that they might feel more of each other than most bonds allowed, it was only because he thought Nadia would've wanted to experience that deeper connection too.

Nearby, the Praetorian cleared his throat.

Nadia turned the soldier an apologetic smile and stepped back a discreet distance from Tanis, but her eyes continued their bright dance as the two of them turned and headed off.

They parted ways in a piazza. Tanis stood by while Nadia departed, veiled once more, seeming an angelic apparition among her silver-plated protectors, a wisp of cloud surrounded by stars.

One day that will be me at your side, he thought, forgetting she could hear him. Her laughter floated musically on the actual wind, heard by his naked ears, and he suppressed a grimace of embarrassment lest all the gossips watching them note it.

Oh, it was very sweet, she said, and he could tell she was still smiling.

Tanis watched her go with a neutral gaze, but inside he felt warm and excited and outrageously thrilled. He couldn't believe he was actually courting the heir to Agasan's imperial throne. And though he imagined it would likely end badly, he felt surprisingly unrepentant and not the least bit afraid.

Farewell, Princess.

Lord Adonnai, she returned with an adorably prim edge to her tone that was wonderful for the fact he could perceive it. *Dare not stray too far. I may need to call upon you at a moment's notice.*

And I will come, he thought happily. Only that time he was careful to keep the thought to himself.

FORTY-SIX

"A man need not seek his path, for his path will

find him whether or not he wills it."

— Excerpted from *Footsteps with our Gods,*

A Treatise on a Palmer's Faith

ANIS ARRIVED BACK at Chresten Hall to a commotion outside his room. A green-robed maestro paced like a caged raccoon in front of Tanis and Felix's door while another man, possibly his clerk, stood in the opening. Tanis slipped past him with a muttered apology but stopped just inside, arrested by what he saw.

Two of the Sormitáge's Regiment Guard were industriously searching their room while Felix stood in the corner looking sullen. His calico hair stood every which way, and his clothes were rumpled.

Linens, clothing, Tanis's practice swords, books and random shoes lay scattered across the floor. One guard was searching Felix's desk. He was going through every drawer inspecting each item and showing it to the clerk. The other guard had upended Tanis's feather mattress and was searching beneath it. Their armoires and bookshelves had already been ransacked.

Finally the guard searching Tanis's side of the room flipped his mattress back into place and turned to the clerk. "Well, that's everything."

The maestro stuck his head into the room and glowered at Felix. "His knapsack! Check his knapsack! It must be there!"

The guard approached Felix and held out his hand. "Well then, hand it over, Sarcova. Let's have a look."

Casting the maestro a venomous glare, Felix shrugged the knapsack off his shoulder and thrust it wordlessly at the guard.

The guard loosed the drawstring and opened the satchel, but he frowned as he peered inside. "What's all this?"

"What? What?" the maestro stuck his head further into the room. "What did you find?"

The guard cast a curious look at Felix and extended the sack back to him. "Hold this while I have a look."

Felix glared blackly at him, but he held the knapsack open while the guard dug through the crumpled balls of paper stuffed tightly inside. The soldier pulled a few out, uncrinkled them and frowned at the long lines of letters filling every inch of space on each page. "There's nothing here but wads of paper, Maestro," he said after a moment. He turned an annoyed look at the scholar. "I think the lad's telling the truth."

Felix flung a hand into the air. "*Thank* you." He retied his knapsack and slung it back over his shoulder, looking vindicated.

"This isn't over, di Sarcova," the maestro snarled while the two guards filed out, muttering to each other. "I caught you red-handed!"

"Red-handed implies I had something in my *hand*," Felix retorted icily, "which I patently did not."

"You—you were in my chambers! You're a *thief*, and I intend to prove it!"

"Good luck with that, Maestro."

The man's face turned red as a beet. He stalked over and pushed his face nose to nose with Felix's. "You think you've fooled me? I'll have your head on a plate and your bloody ring too—and don't even think about requesting admittance to the Guild!"

Felix held his gaze, unflinching. "If I have such magical capabilities as you claimed to the guards, Maestro, why would I care about joining your stupid Guild?"

The man glared at him a moment longer. Then he spun on his heel and stalked from the room, shouting back, "The Endoge will hear of this!"

Felix followed him to the door and called after him into the hall, which was filling with residents eager for gossip, "Thanks for the visit, Maestro Lommeur! So glad you stopped by to talk about your incontinence issues. Wish I could've been of more help!"

He withdrew back inside and closed the door to the sound of snickering from the hallway. Then he turned a look to Tanis and frowned. "Sorry about … all this." He waved a resigned hand about the room.

"It's fine, Felix."

"No, really." Felix sank down into his chair, pushed elbows onto his desk and laid his forehead in his hands. "I'll clean it up."

Tanis walked over to the papers the guard had let fall and retrieved them. Smoothing one, he looked it over. Long lines of letters streamed across the page. It reminded Tanis of the word puzzles he'd loved solving as a child, where he would search for hidden words within a jumble of nonsense letters. Tanis had been good at such puzzles, for his mind had easily seen and recognized patterns from the youngest of ages.

As his eyes scanned the page in his hand, automatically searching for the patterns recognized in common words, his eye caught on an arrangement of letters altogether startling and far from common.

He lowered the page and looked over at Felix, suddenly unsettled. "*Felix* ..."

The other boy turned and immediately noted the paper in Tanis's hand. He scowled. "*Sancto Spirito*, Tanis." He launched out of his chair and snatched the page away. "Can't you just leave me alone?"

Tanis stared at him. "Felix, where did you learn that name?"

"What name? What are you talking about?"

Tanis pointed to the letters written on the third line. "*That* name."

Felix glowered and shoved the page into his knapsack. "Stay out of this, Tanis." He spun away, threw open the door and rushed down the hall, pushing roughly by the students still crowding the passage.

Tanis went after him. He latched onto Felix's mental signature again, and this time he didn't care if the other boy knew that he followed.

Felix stormed down three flights of stairs like all the demons of Shadow were chasing him. He burst through Chresten's doors and down the steps and went flying across the yard into the night. Tanis sprinted after him.

The boys were close in height, but Tanis had been diligent in keeping up his physical studies, and in the long stretch of open path he cut Felix's lead in half. Felix sped past the university buildings, spearing through the darkness like he'd run this gauntlet a hundred times. He leapt a hedge, half-slid down a hill, and rammed through a set of double doors into a lecture hall whose windows were dark.

The heavy doors slammed just as Tanis reached them, catching his elbow and shoulder with a sharp flare of pain. He shoved them open again and continued the chase, spotting Felix's dim form just before the boy vanished around a corner.

Tanis ground his feet into the tiles to propel himself as fast as possible. He grabbed the edge of the wall as he careened around it and headed down a long corridor lined in tapestries, which hung as darker shadows in the nearly lightless passage.

"Felix, wait!"

Just ahead, Felix paused in a spot of moonlight and swung a look over his shoulder. A twisted expression conveyed both triumph and anger. Then he turned and—

A pattern flashed violently in Tanis's mind, bringing him to a staggering halt. For an instant its brilliance blocked his vision—vivid and painful in its sharpness. When the lingering afterimage cleared and Tanis could see again, Felix was gone.

Tanis groaned in frustration and doubled over, pushing hands to his knees while he tried to catch his breath. As he stared at the empty corridor, reason came in with its soothing calm, and understanding dawned. The lad recalled his mother's lesson on variant traits as if she'd spoken it but yesterday:

'Nodefinders exist—equally rare—who have been known to travel upon twisted nodes that none should be able to follow.'

There had to be a node or a leis in the corridor. Just as he was wondering how he might find it, another of his mother's lessons came to him. He formed his intent as she'd taught him, and the node winked into view.

Tanis approached it curiously. The portal seemed shadowed somehow, not the brightly shining reflection his mother had described, and he assumed this to be a product of the node's twisted construction.

Still, Felix had followed it, and in so doing, he'd shown Tanis the pattern he used. It had been seared in Tanis's mind, as indelible as Loghain's pattern had been, which Tanis had then instinctively used to slow the *drogue* wolf's passage through time.

It never occurred to Tanis to question his decision to follow Felix across the node, or to wonder at the danger involved. As he had wordlessly followed Pelas from the café in Rethynnea, trusting somehow to his path, so did Tanis channel *elae* into Felix's pattern and take that fateful step.

A moment of swirling disorientation followed. Painfully brilliant light twisted with variegated shadows, giving him the sensation of falling, but then he found himself standing upright—if a bit woozy. He blinked to focus his *elae*-blinded eyes in the dim light of his new surroundings.

It must've been the greatest library he'd ever seen. Lamps burned low in sconces along the wall to his right. They gave off just enough light to chase the shadows from the corridors between the stacks, but not enough to illuminate the highest levels of the giant shelves. Above him, the vaulted ceiling was lost in shadows.

"Bloody Sanctos on a stake!"

Tanis turned in place to find Felix standing several paces away, gaping at him. "How in thirteen hells did you do that?" Felix's expression twisted from startled to frightened to furious. "Even a ringed wielder shouldn't have been able to follow me. The nodes are *twisted,* for Epiphany's sake!"

Tanis walked towards him. "You have to tell me about the name on that page, Felix." He fixed a firm gaze on the other boy, his voice low. "It's a very dangerous name to know."

"Whatever it is, how by Cephrael do *you* know it?" Felix started backing away in pace with Tanis's approach, mismatched eyes hot with accusation. "Did the High Lord send you after me?"

"By all that's holy, Felix," Tanis growled exasperatedly, "I'm *not* a spy for the High Lord!"

Felix halted like he'd been slapped. He stared at Tanis in silence, and his expression lost some of its certainty. "You couldn't say that so clearly if it wasn't true."

Tanis let out his breath. "No."

"Then—" Felix flung a hand in the air before pushing it through his hair again, keeping it lodged there. "For love of the Lady, why did the High Lord sponsor you?"

Tanis tried to keep hold of his patience. "The High Lord wanted a favor from my guardian." He kept his voice low, but inwardly he was grinding his teeth, for they might've had this conversation weeks ago if Felix hadn't been so intent on hiding his secrets. "My guardian in return elicited the High Lord's sponsorship that I would find a place here."

"That's all?" Felix sounded disappointed.

"Yes, that's bloody all."

Felix stared at him with his jaw shifted forward and his lower lip protruding slightly, as if he couldn't quite think through this perplexing news without crunching up his face in the process. After a minute of this, he remarked, "Some guardian you must have to be the kind of man the High Lord calls on for a favor."

Tanis exhaled a sigh, finally feeling like Felix wasn't going to bolt again any second ... like they were finding common ground. "You could say that."

"But that doesn't explain how in Belloth's bloody name you followed me."

Tanis glanced back at the node. He couldn't really answer that either. "I can just ... do things sometimes." He shrugged.

Felix stared at him, waiting for more. "What ... that's it? You just do the bloody *impossible*, follow me across a twisted node—*you*, who aren't even a *Nodefinder*—and just expect me to believe—"

"It doesn't matter what you believe. I don't care what you believe. Believe anything you like." Tanis stalked towards the other boy with a determined stride. "Just answer my question: how did you learn the name Pelasommáyurek?"

Perhaps the gravity in Tanis's voice finally got through to Felix, or perhaps it was the utterly uncompromising look in his colorless gaze, but Felix finally exhaled a dejected sigh, walked over to an armchair set against the paneled wall and slumped into it. He slung his knapsack on the floor between his feet, rummaged through it, and pulled out a folded page. This he handed to Tanis.

It appeared to be a list of names written in another's lean hand, not Felix's careful print. Many of the names had a line crossed through them, including one Tanis read with a pang of unease: Isahl N'abranaacht. As Tanis scanned through the rest of the names, a strange feeling beset him ... as if he knew them all somehow. In a moment he had it.

"These are all maestros and literatos."

Felix nodded. A haunted look had come to his gaze. Now that Tanis saw it for what it was, he realized he'd noticed it since their first meeting. Something had been deeply troubling Felix for a long time.

Felix handed him another page, also written in that lean hand. This was a list of letters written at random, side by side, similar to the other pages Tanis had seen Felix struggling with.

"I found those two papers in a book Malin had." It sounded like a confession, reluctant and apologetic and probably long overdue. Felix pushed a hand through his calico hair and fell back in his chair. "I think the long one is some kind of code. Malin loved codes—he was always making them up." He looked away and grumbled bitterly, "It would be just like him to conceal some vital information in a code that only a genius could decipher."

Tanis took one of Felix's crumpled pages and compared it against the one written by Malin, his colorless eyes scanning back and forth, automatically seeking patterns. "You've been trying to break it down and decipher it," he murmured.

"Yes—but Fortune curse me, I've gotten nowhere." Felix pushed palms to his eyes with a painful grimace.

Tanis squatted down to sit on the edge of the facing armchair. "Felix, what happened? Were you ... were you *with* Malin when he disappeared?" He could think of no other explanation for Felix having these notes—the investigators would surely have confiscated them otherwise.

"Yes," Felix whispered, still covering his face.

Tabling for a moment the mystery of how Felix had kept this information hidden, Tanis asked, "Did Malin tell you something? What happened to him?"

Felix slammed his hands down on the arms of his chair. "I don't *know!*" Tanis heard immense chagrin in this outburst, and beneath that, fueling the sense of desperation that bound Felix still, a deep fear that he'd failed his friend. Felix held a hand towards the distant dark with perplexity narrowing his gaze. "Malin was just there one minute and gone the next."

Tanis frowned. "Wasn't he a Nodefinder?"

"Yes, but not like me." Felix looked Tanis over sharply, his gaze still hinting of suspicion. "Not like you. Besides, I checked all up and down the corridor. Even climbed the stacks on both sides. No nodes, no leis ... there's just *no way* he could've vanished, but ... he did."

The hint of wary unease settled upon Tanis. "Did Malin tell you anything before he disappeared?"

Felix rolled his head around on the back of the chair agitatedly. "He'd been acting strange for a fortnight—I don't know, maybe longer. He finally told me to meet him here, said he'd found something no one would believe ... that he didn't believe it himself."

"What was it?"

"Burn me if I know! Malin was acting like ... like he expected something to come for him. You know, jumping at shadows. He said someone was hiding here or something ... I don't know. It sounded like he was in trouble. I thought ... well, I thought maybe one of the names on that list was his kidnapper."

Tanis looked the names over again. His eye stuck on Maestro Lommeur, who had so furiously threatened Felix in their rooms that night. That's when he understood. "You've been investigating them. All the names crossed off on this list?"

Felix nodded glumly. "For all the good it's done."

"That's a lot of names. You've inspected them all yourself?"

Felix worked the muscles of his jaw. "Not exactly."

Arching a brow at this ambiguity, Tanis went back to the list and looked over the rest of the names, but other than Maestro Lommeur's, only N'abranaacht's held any significance for him. He glanced up at Felix. "You said you found this list somewhere?"

Felix grimaced. He exhaled a ragged sigh and closed his eyes again. "Malin had this ... book, you see. Oh, he shouldn't have touched it—I *told* him that!—much less taken it from the vault. It was ..." he slapped his palm to his forehead again and ground out, "By the Blessed Sanctos of my ancestors— he was so stupid!—it was one of the volumes of the *Qhorith'quitara*, the apocryphal books of the *Sobra I'ternin*—a book of power, you know?" He dropped his hand to his lap again and exhaled a forceful breath. "I found that list of names inside the book."

"Was that all you found?"

Felix sighed dramatically. "... *No.*" He bent over and rummaged through his knapsack again and came out with three more pages like the one Tanis already held.

Tanis looked each of them over intently, whereupon that uneasy feeling became a raging river of alarm. "This is bad," he murmured, forcing a dry swallow. He looked up at Felix under his brows. "This is very bad."

Felix sat up and leaned towards him intently. "It's a code of some kind, right?" Then he threw up his hands and fell back in the chair again. "Curse me if I can figure it out."

The first thing Tanis noticed about the four pages of apparently random letters was the actual name hidden among them near the top of each page. Felix wouldn't have known these names—clearly he hadn't realized they were names at all—but Malin obviously had. Probably he'd discovered them in the stolen book, but this didn't explain ... .

Tanis frowned. Something had caught his attention, but it took a moment to realize what he was missing. He scanned the page beginning with *Pelasommáyurek* spelled out near the top. Then he saw another name he recognized several lines down, mixed in with other letters at random: *Kaye Lommeur*, the maestro from earlier that night. Something about them both ... what was it that his eyes saw but his brain couldn't quite grasp ... ?

Then he got it. Both names were formed with the same letters.

Kaye Lommeur. Pelasommáyurek.

It was an anagram—if an imperfect one.

Tanis's heart beat faster as he looked back to Malin's list of maestros and quickly scanned it, memorizing each name. Then he went back to the four pages Malin had written, each beginning with a name of a Malorin'athgul, and he searched for the maestro's names within the random letters. He started with Pelas's page, then moved to the one beginning with Darshanvenkhátraman. In both cases, the names from the maestro list appeared somewhere further down the page, hidden within the seemingly random letters.

Tanis lowered the pages and looked away. His pulse was racing, and his head felt tingly and tight. All of his senses were screaming in warning, for he understood what had happened here.

Malin had found the names of the Malorin'athgul. Then, at some point, the mind of a cryptographer had seen a pattern, an anagram, in a maestro's name. Whatever happened after this discovery, it was enough to scare Malin to silence—at least until the pressure to confess what he'd found became too great and he'd called upon his roommate.

But what name had scared him?

Tanis knew Rinokh was gone from the realm for good—the zanthyr had assured him of that—and Pelas ... he just couldn't believe Pelas was responsible for Malin's disappearance. He prayed he wasn't. Besides, 'Kaye Lommeur' was the only name on Pelas's list, and Pelas *that* man was not.

With a dry swallow then, Tanis looked to the third page in his hand, the one that began with Shailabanáchtran spelled out across the top. His eyes scanned across and down, line by line ... and there it was.

Isahl N'abranaacht. Shailabanáchtran.

Tanis went cold.

The pages slipped from his fingers, and he sank back against the chair and pressed a fist against pursed lips, stifling the groan of dread that was trying to escape. His instincts had hinted at it the other night when walking with N'abranaacht, but he'd been too fearful to admit it could be possible.

No wonder Pelas had avoided the Sormitáge during their travels together, despite his professed admiration of the place. He knew his brother was hiding here.

"... Tanis?" Felix's voice held real fear.

Tanis shifted his eyes to him. *Gods,* what should he do? Nadia had just told him Phaedor had gone with the Empress. He doubted he'd enough clout with the High Lord to make him believe such as this—not if Marius wasn't aware already of Malorin'athgul in their realm, which Tanis couldn't know, and especially not with N'abrachaacht's popularity.

The next wave of consternation broke over him as he realized that while he hadn't recognized Shailabanáchtran beneath his Palmer's robes, Shailabanáchtran had *certainly* recognized him. Now it *all* made sense.

Tanis covered his face with both hands and let out a tremulous breath.

"Is it that bad?" Felix asked in a small voice.

Taking a deep breath, Tanis tried to calm his racing heart. *Think! Think, damn it! What do we do?*

First, the evidence. He dropped his arms and looked over at Felix, who sat with his hands trapped between his knees, shoulders hunched. "Where's the book Malin stole? Do you still have it?"

Felix eyed him uncertainly.

Tanis had no patience for any more of Felix's secrets. *"Felix, do you have the book or not?"* his voice sliced through the room, spiked with compulsion.

Felix inhaled sharply. "Yes, I have it." He reached both hands into his knapsack, felt around a bit, and then lifted something out from the beneath the pile of paper. Crumpled balls tumbled to the floor, and out came a large book wrapped in suede. Felix held the book like it was about to bite him and handed it over quickly to Tanis.

Alarms all across the library sounded, a banshee's screeching.

"Shade and darkness!" Tanis pushed the book towards Felix. "Put it back in your knapsack—hurry!"

Felix recoiled like the book was a snake. "Are you crazy? I don't want that thing anywhere near me anymore! Put it on a shelf or something."

Tanis forcibly shoved it into Felix's hands. "They've got this entire place warded for *this* book, Felix. What if they can just as easily tell who's had their hands on it?"

Felix paled. "All right." But when Tanis stood there waiting impatiently, Felix's mismatched eyes narrowed. "Do you mind? Kind of a private activity here, putting it back again."

That's when Tanis understood. Turning away, he said, "The book wasn't just in your knapsack. The knapsack is your coach, isn't it?"

"You know," Felix growled, *"real* Nodefinders prefer the proper term: *stanza segreta.*" He hastily crammed all of the fallen balls of paper back into his satchel. Then he slung the strap over his shoulder and nodded to Tanis. "Hurry—this way."

They rushed down an aisle between two stacks, ears ringing from the screaming alarm. "Can't we go back the way we came?"

"No, trust me," Felix muttered. "You never know who might be wandering by. I have a faster route anyway." Felix turned at the end of the aisle and led Tanis on another chase through the maze of towering bookshelves, in and out of shadows.

Just as they were about to reach the front of the massive room, double doors burst open and a dozen red-cloaked Imperial Guards rushed in with lanterns held high. Four men followed, carrying staffs with some kind of protrusion at the end and wearing black cloaks marked with silver quatrefoils crossed with swords.

Felix sucked in his breath and yanked Tanis back behind the bookshelf. "It's the Order," he hissed. "They've got bright-eye bulbs on their staffs. If those things get a whiff of us, they'll flame to life." He slowly leaned to brave another look. "Okay, they've gone down the other row. *Hurry.*"

A tense silence cloaked the boys as they slipped across the corridor, and then Felix grabbed Tanis by the arm and hauled him towards a reading alcove. He ran them right into the wall, and—

Something cold and rough hit Tanis in the face, and he blinked in the dim darkness of a forest. Felix still had hold of his wrist and was dragging him through the trees while fir limbs scraped his arms and face.

As soon as they reached a clearing among the heavy trees, Felix released Tanis and started pacing a circle, hands on his hips, breath moving fast with disbelief. "What by my blessed Aunt Bruna was all *that* about?"

Tanis took it as a rhetorical question. He pressed his palm over the bridge of his nose and tried to calm his racing heart, which was thrumming with dire apprehension. "We need evidence," he murmured, "but ... I have no idea how to get it."

Felix spun to him. "Enough of this, Tanis—*talk*. What did you see on those pages? You went as pale as the moon."

After a moment, Tanis dropped his hand and settled Felix a look of pained resignation. "Is there somewhere we can sit down? It's ... kind of a long story."

They passed the night on a marble bench inside the Quai stadium, which happened to be only a short distance away from where they'd arrived.

First Tanis told Felix about the Malorin'athgul—at least as much as he understood of them—but this digressed into his travels with Pelas, and then an explanation of the zanthyr and a few of their experiences together, which culminated in his arrival at the Sormitáge. Finally he recounted his run-in with Literato N'abranaacht. All of this took much of the night in the telling.

The grey light of dawn was hinting around them, shifting the world from pitch black to mist and shadow, when Tanis finally walked Felix through the understanding he'd gained of Malin's discovery, ending with the anagram of Isahl N'abranaacht and Shailabanáchtran.

"I knew it!" Felix hissed. He slammed his fist onto his knee. "I knew N'abranaacht wasn't the saint he makes himself out to be." He cast Tanis a peevish glare. "You know I investigated him—or tried to. He caught me in his office and nearly took my head off with a sword. Who keeps sabers on their walls, by the all the holy *Sanctis*?"

Tanis gave him a telling look. "Immortal creatures with identities to hide."

Felix grunted. "And you really think he's the one who took Malin?"

Tanis blew out his breath between his lips. "Well I can hardly say it's certain—not without some digging—and digging anywhere near Shailabanáchtran is likely to get us both killed. But it makes sense."

Felix rubbed at the edge of the marble bench wearing a ponderous frown. He looked up under his brows. "The Order is Reading all the maestros, you know. The *frites* are all over it. Literatos will be next."

Tanis shook his head. "They won't find anything Reading N'abranaacht, Felix. He can hide his connection to *elae*—don't ask me how, but I'm certain of it. He's fifth strand, but they think he's *na'turna*. They won't even be looking for *elae's* mark within his life pattern—*shade and darkness*, who's to say he doesn't have a way of faking even that?"

"Nobody could ..." Felix began, but at the look on Tanis's face, he left the thought unspoken.

Tanis pushed a hand through his hair and gazed off into the grey dawn, a muscle working in his jaw. After a moment, he muttered, "Shailabanáchtran is about the deadliest adversary you could imagine, Felix. He's probably worse than you can imagine, actually." He frowned as something occurred to him, and his thoughts wandered. "I don't know ... I think fifth strand creatures have an innate facility with the other strands, like they can sometimes just tap into them without needing to know the patterns involved. There's a certain propensity to be able to work the other strands innately."

In fact ... if Tanis had been fifth strand, this explanation would make sense of all the mysterious things *he* could do. But he'd never heard of a truthreader being associated with the fifth, and he'd done nothing with that strand himself.

Still musing, Tanis thought of all the things he'd seen Phaedor and Pelas do. "Reweaving a man's life pattern from next to nothing ... being impervious to Tellings ... healing practically overnight ... working *deyjiin* as easily as *elae* ... placing compulsion on people without even trying ..."

Felix gave him an odd look. "You realize I have no idea what you're talking about now."

Tanis cracked a smile. "Sorry ..." He shook his head and returned his thoughts to their current problem. "It's just ... I know how Malin felt, harboring this secret. Being Malorin'athgul isn't something you can simply accuse someone of."

"I can get us into N'abranaacht's apartments if that would help."

Tanis thought about that for a moment. "How? On a node?"

"On a leis." Felix yawned. "... Since the nodes and leis are all twisted, the Sormitáge engineers weren't particularly careful about where they constructed their buildings. With a little research, I can usually find a leis leading most anywhere."

"Felix ..." Tanis moved his head to capture the other boy's gaze with his own. "How have you managed all of this for so long without being caught? I would've thought surely they'd have questioned you about Malin's disappearance."

Felix snorted. "Yeah, of course. But my dad's a truthreader, Tanis. I grew up with *eight* Adept brothers. You think I don't know there's a hundred ways to avoid lying while still not telling the truth?" Seeming suddenly exhausted, Felix collapsed back on the marble bench. "Besides, the captain of the Regiment Guard who was investigating Malin's kidnapping is *na'turna*. He doesn't know how to ask the right questions." He lifted his head to look at Tanis. "And you and I both know that the right question is everything."

"Wait ..." The statement gave Tanis an idea, and he blossomed, but then he saw the futility in it and wilted again.

"What?" Felix cast him a look.

Tanis rubbed his face with both hands. His eyes felt like a sandstorm had hit them, and his head felt thick and webbed with cotton. They'd resolved little towards how to reveal N'abranaacht for what he was, but at least they'd bonded over this mutual goal. Tanis supposed gaining Felix's trust showed some small progress for their night's work.

"I had a ... thought," Tanis said through a wide yawn, "... but I don't see how to make it work."

"So let's hear it."

Blowing out a heavy breath, Tanis fell back on the bench and let his arms drape to either side, mirroring Felix's exhausted pose. He gazed at the slowly brightening sky. "We'd need another truthreader—a *talented* one. Ideally Devoveré."

"I ... may know someone," Felix said after a moment. "I've had a truthreader sort of helping me with my investigation."

Tanis's attention was instantly caught, for just as Felix had the thought, he'd clamped down on his mind. The effect was as if he'd seen Tanis suddenly in the hallway and slammed the door in his face. Someone actually trained in guarding their thoughts would've been more subtle, but Felix had roused Tanis's curiosity instead of avoiding it.

Tanis decided not to press Felix on the name of his friend and said instead, "I missed an appointment with N'abranaacht yesterday, but I've no doubt he'll call me to have tea with him today."

"You can't go, Tanis," Felix muttered. "You said he recognized you."

"That's why we need another truthreader to show up instead. If the meeting is innocuous enough, N'abranaacht will be forced to maintain his show of benevolence." And if whoever went in his place was sitting across from the literato at a tea table, N'abranaacht would have fewer opportunities to establish that dangerous physical contact. It at least slightly lessened the odds against them.

"And while this ... doomed soul takes your place?" Felix murmured through a yawn.

"We investigate his rooms."

Felix abruptly pushed up on one elbow. "Tanis ... that's an excellent idea."

Tanis pressed his palms to his eyes and tried to squeeze the prickling sand of fatigue out of them. "So who's this truthreader you're so avid to keep secret from me?"

At this remark, Felix eyed him irritably, like a calico cat with its ears flattened. "See, this is precisely why people don't like truthreaders."

"What people?" Tanis lifted his head to look at him. "Guilty people?"

Felix gave him an affronted look. "*Private* people."

"Private people with guilty secrets," Tanis corrected. "If you don't want me hearing your thoughts, Felix, don't think them so loudly. Now, you were going to tell me about this truthreader ..."

"No I wasn't."

Tanis pushed up on one elbow to look at the other boy. "I could easily compel it out of you."

"But you won't, because you're not a bully, and because you know I'd report you."

Tanis balked. "*You'd* report *me?*"

"Just to get you out of my hair." Felix flashed a grin. "Without a second thought."

Tanis gave him long look. "You're kind of reprehensible."

"You try growing up with eight Adept brothers and tell me you don't have to sell your soul just to get the chance to eat your own dinner without fighting for it tooth and claw."

"Thirteen hells, were you raised in a cage?"

"Of rabid badgers." Felix sat up and stretched, yawned again. "Well ... I'd better get going."

Tanis did a double-take as the other boy got to his feet. "Going where?"

"We need another truthreader, right? So I'll have to go ... fetch one."

Tanis reluctantly pushed to his feet. "We'll go together."

"Forget it, Tanis." Felix grabbed his knapsack and started off towards the stairs. "This is one time you can't follow me."

"I can and I will, Felix." Tanis stalked after him.

A long flight of stone steps ascended to the top level of the oval-shaped stadium, but with the clouds now glowing rose-gold behind the colonnade crowning its rim, Tanis felt like they were climbing into the heavens. "Whoever this truthreader is will be putting themselves at grave risk," he said while watching the sky turn from grey to blue before his eyes. "I must be certain they're up to the challenge."

"I can assure you, *they* are."

"Felix, you're not hearing me." Tanis took his arm to draw his gaze.

Mismatched green and blue eyes peered back. "I won't send someone up against N'abranaacht unless I think they can come out of the encounter unscathed. You're not a truthreader. You won't be able to look for the abilities I can observe."

"This … person is Devoveré, Tanis. You're not even Devoveré."

"The ring does not the wielder make, Felix."

Felix frowned irritably at him. "Fine, but you'll have to follow the rules."

Tanis smiled and arched a brow. "This gets more interesting by the minute."

FORTY-SEVEN

"Walking with a friend in the dark is better than walking alone in the dark."

– The royal cousin Fynnlar val Lorian

ANIS AND FELIX stopped by their room to change clothes—Tanis didn't think it was a good idea to *look* like they'd been up all night, what with the alarms having gone off in the Archives as they had—and headed off again towards the node Felix meant to travel.

As ill luck would have it, their way took them past the Imperial Archives. A clump of *frites* stood on the lawn humming with gossip like a hive of bees, their topic no doubt concerning the host of Red Guard who stood watch in front of the building's entrance. A crowd of students, scholars and docents had gathered at the base of the steps, waiting for permission to enter.

Seeing a familiar face among the diverse groups gathered there, Tanis nudged Felix and asked in a low and somewhat urgent voice, "Can't we get to the node some other way?"

Felix scowled at him. "It'll take three times as long—"

Just then the man Tanis had noticed looked over, and his gaze fixed unerringly on the boys. Tanis blew out his breath. "Never mind," he grumbled. "He's seen us now." Tanis put on a friendly face and smiled at the man. He even managed a tentative wave, though nothing too eager or the other would wonder at it.

Vincenzé separated himself from a group of official-looking men—which included two of the black-cloaked Order operatives who'd come into the Archives with the Red Guard—and headed their way.

"Well, well." The wielder looked the boys up and down. Tanis was suddenly very glad they'd decided to change into fresh clothing. "You're up and out early, *cucciolo*. And who is this with you?" Vincenzé's blue-eyed gaze assessed Felix.

Tanis didn't believe for a moment that Vincenzé didn't know Felix on sight, but he played along. "This is my roommate, Felix—"

"—di Sarcova della Buonara," Vincenzé finished, but his grin seemed a little too hungry for it to feel pleasant in the receiving. "So you've made up, the two of you. Mended your fences?"

"I don't recall saying they were broken." Tanis nodded towards the gathering of guards and men. "What's happening?"

Vincenzé arched a sardonic brow. "Am I meant to believe you don't already know?"

Tanis frowned at him. "*Frites* talk, but that doesn't mean I know as much as you do."

Vincenzé eyed him circumspectly. "Nicely evaded, truthreader." His gaze skimmed shrewdly over Felix again, and Tanis had no doubt he was searching the other boy's thoughts for anything to use against them. Fortunately, as Tanis himself had discovered, Felix had a natural ability to vacate his mind ... as if he could truly sit for hours and think of absolutely nothing.

Perhaps coming up empty from his inspection of Felix, Vincenzé returned his gaze to Tanis. "An important work vanished from the Archives some time ago," he said then, putting a pointed edge on the statement. His thoughts placed Malin, Felix and the book into the same pot, but he clearly lacked the broth to combine them all into one ill-fated soup. "Last night it reappeared just as mysteriously."

Tanis scratched his head. "How did you know it reappeared?"

"Alarms, *cucciolo*." Vincenzé's shrewd gaze pinned Tanis beneath it. "The whole campus is warded to recognize this work and sound an alarm that even the High Lord will hear."

"Is that all?" Felix yawned. "Come on, Tanis. I told you it was nothing—just some old book only a maestro could care about."

Vincenzé's gaze shifted to him as sharply as an archer realigning his bow. "I didn't say it was a book that was missing, Felix di Sarcova." His blue eyes took on the hungry gleam of a cat with its paw on the canary's tail. "So how did *you* know it?"

Tanis thought for sure they were caught and was bracing himself for the worst, but Felix just yawned again. "So it *was* a book then. I suppose that's better than what the *frites* are all saying, that someone was killed."

Vincenzé eyed him suspiciously. "Blood may yet be spilled over it."

"Oh, it's that kind of book, eh?" Felix turned Tanis a grin. "Must be a work of dark patterns or blood magic. Or demonology, maybe." He shifted mismatched eyes to Vincenzé as if for confirmation.

Vincenzé's gaze narrowed. "You will not trick me into naming this book, Felix di Sarcova."

"No? Damn. I guess we can go then."

A nice idea, yet Vincenzé stood squarely in their path. He crossed his arms. "And just where could you be off to so early?"

"Evans Hall." Felix cast Vincenzé an impatient look. "You know, where my cousin lives? They have better food."

As if to attest to the veracity of this claim, Tanis's stomach growled loudly.

Vincenzé looked them both over for a moment longer, considering them with narrowed gaze. Though Vincenzé had his thoughts better guarded that morning, Tanis could tell he was trying to decide whether or not to detain them for more questioning. He had no real reason to suspect them, however—save his own all too perceptive instincts—and his thoughts loudly proclaimed his concern at angering the zanthyr by interrogating Tanis and thereby upsetting the High Lord in the process. "I suppose you should be on your way then," he said at last, but he sounded unconvinced of this decision. "I may call upon you later, Tanis."

"I'll be counting the minutes, sir."

Vincenzé eyed him once more and then stepped aside to let them pass.

When they were well out of earshot of the wielder, Tanis hissed, "Why'd you talk so much about the book, Felix? He's suspicious now."

"He was suspicious anyway," Felix grumbled. He pried at a hangnail with his teeth. "Besides, it would've made him even more suspicious if we didn't seem curious." He eyed Tanis askance. "Or at least if *I* didn't."

They walked for a while in silence with Felix picking at his thumb and Tanis worrying about how much Vincenzé could actually have guessed about their involvement with the book.

Finally Felix turned them down a path towards a distant building with the name *Evans Hall* carved into the lintel. Tanis's eyes widened. "You really were taking us to Evans Hall?"

"Of course. It's never a good idea to lie to a wielder, and even stupider to lie to one of the High Lord's men." He gave Tanis a wry look. Tanis thought Felix had never seemed more the disheveled cat back from a night's carousing, what with his gold-brown-auburn hair all awry and a fuzz of auburn scruff around his jaw. "You might not believe me," Felix muttered then, "but I don't actually have a death wish."

"You're right. I don't believe you."

Felix cracked a lopsided grin. He gazed contemplatively at Tanis for a moment. "You're different than I thought you'd be."

Tanis rolled his eyes. "If you'd given me even half a chance—"

"Tanis, see reason," Felix interposed, "how would *you* feel, knowing what I knew—carrying around one of the apocryphal books of the *Sobra I'ternin* in your knapsack, by the holy *Sanctis!*—knowing the High Lord's got the Order investigating—probably looking for *it* rather than Malin—and suddenly a truthreader your age, who's a bloody Postulant already and can probably read your mind as easily as his own handwriting, shows up to be your new roommate? Do you think you'd just blab about your entire life on a whim? Be all, 'Oh hello, let's be besty-best friends!' like some gabby girl?"

Tanis grunted, though his eyes were smiling. "I suppose not."

Felix observed him peevishly. "Oh, *you've* been so candid, have you, with all of *your* secrets? Like how in the thirteen hells you followed me across that node? Like that?"

"It's not the same—"

"Pot," Felix jammed a finger into Tanis's arm. "Kettle," he indicated himself. His mismatched eyes narrowed to dangerous slits.

Tanis grinned crookedly. "I concede your point, Felix."

"Good," Felix relaxed and looked forward again, "Because I'm hungry, and I don't share meals with wankers. Just ask any of my older brothers."

They climbed the steps to Evans Hall, and Felix pushed inside.

"Is your cousin the truthreader we're going to see?" Tanis asked as Felix was leading them down a narrow hall between a gallery and a line of docent offices.

"What? No. Phoebe's not even here. She's up in the north country visiting her aunt, probably getting knocked up by some flush-faced Dane."

"But you said ..." But then Tanis let go of the thought, because Felix had only told Vincenzé that his cousin *lived* at Evans, not that he—or in this case, she—would be there.

They made a quick tour through the dining room, collecting as many edibles from the buffet as they did dirty looks from the Hall's actual residents, then Felix slipped out a door that led toward the kitchens.

"So listen, Tanis ..." Felix passed a piping hot apple tart back and forth from hand to hand while they walked. "This ... person is likely to be a bit miffed at me. Actually, I may get utterly flayed." Felix tried to maneuver his mouth into position to take a bite of the tart without scalding his tongue, but ultimately gave up and put it in his pocket instead. "I was supposed to ... uh, show up last night, see ... but you know how that went ..."

"Right."

"Plus, this truthreader won't be expecting you at all. So let me do the talking, okay?"

"As you wish, Felix."

They exited Evans Hall through the kitchen yard. Felix opened the gate of the walled yard, but when Tanis made to walk through, Felix grabbed him by the collar of his jacket and hauled him behind a shed instead. He pushed a finger to his lips.

A moment later, footsteps came rushing through the yard, and the boys watched a man slip out the open gate.

"Amateur," Felix muttered. He nodded to Tanis then, and they went back inside the Hall.

Tanis still sensed a nervous energy in the other boy. Felix's eyes traveled everywhere now, and as soon as they exited Evans Hall, Felix pressed them quickly away into the trees lining the maze of campus paths. They came to a gazebo. Felix grabbed Tanis's arm and darted towards it like he meant to run them into the railing, and suddenly they were running down an alley between two buildings.

Felix drew them to a halt, leaned back against the wall, pulled the tart out of his pocket and set to munching.

Tanis considered him as he recalled the many pathways Felix had already taken him on. "You have this entire campus mapped in your head, don't you?"

"Of course."

"It must've taken years to travel and map all of this. How long have you known you had a variant trait?"

Felix grinned. "All my life." At Tanis's wondrous look, he said, "I have five Nodefinder brothers, Tanis. The *leis* in Sarcova Manor were twisted before I was born—the Lord Sarcova apparently misliked his children popping in and out of rooms randomly. He took special exception to their using *leis* to escape his justice."

"So you realized when you were a boy that you could travel twisted nodes, but you never told anyone?"

Felix arched a derisive brow at him. "How many people have *you* told?"

Tanis didn't know what to say to that, so he said nothing.

"Exactly." Felix sounded vindicated. "Come on then. The node's just over here." He led away down the alley, and one wall soon opened upon a small courtyard. Black and white marble pavers in the court were arranged in a particular pattern ...

"This is—"

"Yep, a nodecourt. Amazing what you can find forgotten around this place. Here, you'll need this." Felix handed him a bag from his knapsack.

Tanis looked at the cloth dubiously. It appeared to be nothing more than a common hemp bag, the kind used for carrying fruit or vegetables. "What's this?"

"Trust me. You want to wear that." Felix had his own bag in hand. "Go on, put it on."

Tanis arched a skeptical brow. "You first."

Felix shrugged and put the bag over his head. Tanis didn't—he wasn't about to traverse the Pattern of the World unprepared for whatever lay at the other end of the node.

Felix reached around and felt up Tanis until he found his forearm. Then, all but blind, he led them onto the nodecourt.

An intense disorientation pulled at Tanis—far more than anything he'd experienced thus far. In that split-second before they traveled, Tanis felt as if the entire Pattern of the World surged through him. Felix's hand remained firm around his arm, and in just a breath, the rushing sensation faded.

Tanis blinked and looked around. They stood in a vast bedroom, elegantly appointed in colors of the sea. Heavy aqua silk draped the canopy bed dominating one wall. The chests and armoires shimmered with nacre, while the ornate molding of the walls drew the eye upwards towards a colorful painting on the ceiling depicting mermaids and nymphs at idle play.

Felix was just standing there, looking very odd with the sack crammed over his head. Tanis got the idea from listening to his thoughts that he was waiting for someone to notice him. "Why are we—?"

"*Shhh!*" Felix squeezed his arm to emphasize his warning.

Far across the room, two sets of glass-paned doors stood open onto a wide balcony overlooking—*thirteen hells*, was that the city of Faroqhar? But to embrace such a view, they would have to be ...

"Princess?" Felix finally called in a tentative voice.

Tanis stiffened. *Princess?* He looked around the room again, and his gaze tightened. *As in the Princess Nadia van Gelderan?* His thoughts darkened. *As in—her bed chamber?*

Tanis felt her presence then, coming quickly from elsewhere in her apartments, and betrayal clenched around his chest. *Hello, Nadia.*

He heard her mental gasp, felt her sudden confusion. *Tanis? How ... ?*

He closed his mind to her with a snap.

A second later she rushed into the room and came to an abrupt halt. Her eyes found Tanis first—excited, confused—and then Felix, who remained hooded beside him. "Felix!" Understanding resolved her thoughts.

Felix pulled the hood from his head, already grinning, and bowed with an elaborate flourish. "Your Highness."

Tanis stood in a cloud of injured fury.

Nadia shifted her gaze immediately back to him. Though he'd closed his mind to her, his thoughts were obvious on his face. Nadia's expression became stricken. "*Tanis ...*"

Feeling betrayal's cold hand around his heart, Tanis turned with every intention of walking back across the node.

"Tanis—stop! *Please!*" she held out a hand to him. "I know how this appears, but it's ... it's not what you're thinking." Immediately she opened her mind to him, though he had closed his to her, and showed him the truth.

Images tumbled forth: Felix appearing in her room one night, her surprise, his falling to his knees in contrition begging forgiveness, promising his service in return; how sudden curiosity had overshadowed propriety.

Tanis felt the tension inside unclenching. He closed his eyes, exhaled a breath, opened his mind to her—to which she also exhaled in relief, both mentally and physically—and then opened his eyes again.

She was staring at him with a hand over her heart, and her eyes and mind held such happiness to see him that he couldn't help but return it in kind. His gaze softened. *Nadia ...*

Felix was staring at the both of them, turning his head from the princess to Tanis and back again. "*Sancto Spirito*, is one of you going to tell me what the bloody hells is going on?"

Neither spoke for a moment as they held each other's eyes, then Nadia's brow lifted ever so faintly. "Tanis is courting me, Felix."

Felix's eyes bulged as he gaped at Tanis. Then his expression turned sooty. He plugged a finger into Tanis's chest. "Forthcoming much?"

Tanis cracked a smile.

Suddenly Nadia's eyes narrowed. "Why *are* you here? Don't you know it's Twelfth-day, Felix? What if one of my attendants had been in the room?"

Felix grinned. "Then I would've vanished again as soon as she screamed."

Nadia arched a brow. "So you say. Or would you have begged her for your life like you begged me? Promised *her* your eternal troth?"

"Only if she was attractive." Felix nudged Tanis and flashed a grin. "She's got to have nice teeth, you know."

Nadia seemed offended. "Are you saying you only pledged to serve me because of my teeth?"

"Nay, Princess. I pledged to serve Your Highness because you would've had me beheaded otherwise."

She put a hand on her hip and arched her brow higher. "So this pledge to me is just some backwards form of extortion?"

"Maybe we should get to the reason we've come." Tanis looked to the open door. "Are we safe speaking here, Nadia?"

"*Nadia?*" Felix turned him a wide-eyed stare. "It's *Nadia* already?"

"It was that or endure her calling me Lord Adonnai."

Felix screwed up his face. "Calling you ... *what?* Why would she call you that?"

"We're safe speaking here, Tanis." Nadia turned to Felix looking imperious. "*You* might know all about him if you'd taken even a moment to talk to him, Felix."

Felix opened his mouth to protest. Then he shut it again and glared at her instead. Then he gritted his teeth. "Before *yesterday*, Princess, you'd never even met Tanis and now you're practically betrothed?" He flipped his auburn hair from his eyes. "The way I see it, you should be thanking me."

Nadia crossed her arms and stared narrowly at him. "Thank you."

"Why should Nadia be thanking you, Felix?" Tanis asked.

Felix's gaze flicked to him. "I'm the one who sent her to find out if you were a spy."

"You *sent* me?" Nadia's tone was dangerously cool. "I recall it was my idea—"

"*Your* idea!"

"—to see if Tanis was as suspicious as you claimed."

"I am terribly suspicious," Tanis agreed.

She looked surprised by his equanimity. "You knew?"

"I knew you weren't there because of the High Lord," he said with a soft smile, "but I never suspected Felix."

"Well, now that's all settled," Felix grumbled, "we've got a lot to tell Your Highness."

Nadia's gaze shifted from Felix to Tanis, considering them. "Come. I was just sitting down to eat." She aimed a forgiving smile at Felix and added, "And you look hungry." She spun primly and led away into the other room.

Felix and Tanis followed a few steps behind the princess. "So … you'll be the new High Lord one day, *eh?*" Felix fixed Tanis with an uncompromising stare and a finger pointed at his nose. "Just so we're clear, I fully expect a finder's fee."

FORTY-EIGHT

"Dare every day to be irreverent and bold."

– The Adept wielder Arion Tavestra

A QUARTER-PASSING OF THE hourglass saw Ean, Isabel and Sebastian reaching the isle of Ivarnen. An uneventful climb through the city's dark, cobbled streets brought them within view of the fortress's exterior portcullis, which remained open but heavily guarded.

Sebastian turned to Isabel. "You're ready with your illusion, my lady? I'll need a cloak—a black cloak."

Isabel's lips curled in a smile. "You're wearing it already, Sebastian. All is in place."

Sebastian's brow furrowed. "And Dore won't see this illusion on the currents either?"

"Never fear, Sebastian. Remember, you must act as if you're holding us in chains, for in their eyes you will be."

He gave her a serious look. "Yes, my lady." Then he set his shoulders and led them towards the gate, walking with a slight limp.

One of the guards immediately came out to challenge them. Beyond the gate, Ean saw a bailey full of soldiers.

Sebastian acted as if he was pushing back what appeared to Ean as a nonexistent hood, but the guard's eyes widened. "It's you." He lowered his sword minutely. "Haven't seen you in a while."

"Been away." Sebastian's voice came low, nearly a growl, reminding Ean with a chill of Işak—which was exactly the point.

Sebastian had been sure that the men guarding Ivarnen wouldn't know what had become of him—Dore shared no secrets, especially in failure—but he would have to appear to them as if still bound to Dore ... as if still Işak'getirmek.

Ean hadn't anticipated how much it would unnerve him to hear his brother once again speaking and moving with Işak's voice and manner. And if *he* felt so unnerved by it, what must it be doing to Sebastian to be acting the part? Abruptly he regretted that the idea had ever occurred to them.

"Who's this?" the guard motioned with his blade towards Ean and Isabel. Ean had no idea what guise of illusion Isabel was weaving over them, but he didn't doubt for a moment that the guard would believe it.

"Prisoners to be taken to the Advisor."

The guard looked them over with eyes like dark pools. "Got nothing on the docket about new prisoners. Nothing about *you*."

"I don't report to you or your docket, sergeant. I report to the Advisor, and these prisoners are for his attention ... from the Prophet."

The guard eyed him narrowly and sucked on a tooth. "How can they be from the Prophet when the Prophet's already here?"

Ean felt a sudden hollowness in his core. Darshan was in Ivarnen?

Sebastian countered with an angry growl, "*Stupid* man. The Prophet sent me to claim them to be interrogated. Now, stand aside. Or shall I *make* you move?"

"Yeah, I'll move." He sucked on a tooth again and cast Sebastian a stare full of malice and contempt. "But you'll take an escort with you to the Advisor."

Sebastian looked him over critically. "As you please—but see that your men keep their hands off my prisoners."

The guard looked him over again, taking special note by way of pause at his crippled leg, and his brow arched mockingly. Then he stepped aside to let Sebastian pass. He made a sound with his tongue and a motion to his men, and two guards fell in with them.

When they were through the second portcullis and out of view of the gate, Sebastian snatched one of the guards and pulled him close. "Go find out where the Advisor is and see if he's ready to receive me." He laced the order with compulsion and pushed the man roughly away. "Hurry."

The man ran.

Then Ean watched his brother silently change the man's pattern, installing a new compulsion that sent the guard to inspect the latrines instead.

Ean found a new level of respect for his eldest brother. He'd no doubt Sebastian—Işak—had been this man of brusque action and cold contempt. Yet even when so rigid and disdainful, even walking with a limp and with that scar flaming on his cheek, still he'd exuded a nobility that even Dore's degradation had been unable to fully erase.

They crossed the lower bailey amid the tang of forges and the scrape of men sharpening steel, surrounded by a host of soldiers, weapons, munitions ... clearly the men of Ivarnen were preparing for some kind of war. Ean wondered if they were preparing for him.

By the time they reached the far side of the lower bailey, rain had begun falling and the wind had picked up, bringing with it the acrid smell of heat and ash and the sour stench of hundreds of unwashed men. But these displeasing odors were fresh compared to the toxic reek on the currents.

They soon reached a set of long steps descending into a tunnel. Sebastian looked to the guard at his side. "The dungeons? Have you a key?"

The man swallowed. "Aye, but—"

"Perhaps you'd rather these prisoners await the Advisor's pleasure in his parlor? Shall we serve them wine and a hot meal while we're about it?"

"No—no, milord."

Sebastian held a hand pointedly for him to lead down the stairs. A long descent later, they reached an iron door, whereupon the guard fumbled for his key.

During the descent, the stench of *eidola* on the currents had grown thicker and stronger. By the time the guard got the door open, the sensation had become so overpowering that Ean almost failed to notice the tension held in his brother's shoulders, in the clenching of his jaw and the cording muscles of his neck. Sebastian was clearly struggling with an entirely different evil, and Ean's heart went out to him.

Isabel's hand caught Ean's, cautioning him to stillness.

The guard opened the door and led them into a dim stone passageway, dank with mold and roiling with a volatile energy. Ean had to shut his mind to the currents just to draw breath.

"My other prisoners," Sebastian growled as the guard was locking the door behind them. To Ean it seemed his brother was holding himself together by a thread. "Where are they being held?"

The man turned the key slowly and then looked back to him. "The ones from Dannym?" Something in his gaze. Ean saw it too.

In a split-second Sebastian had the guard around the neck and was shoving his body against the wall. Then came again that Işak-growl—"Tell me what you know,"—and the compulsion to encourage the guard's answer quickly along.

Ean watched Sebastian working these compulsion patterns with alacritous ease and felt a new sense of horror on his brother's behalf. How often he must've been forced into using them for such patterns to become so native—and how evil they *all* were ... Working compulsion of any kind crossed the path of *mor'alir*, and that was ever a dark and desolate stroll.

Watching Sebastian in this role broke Ean's heart all over again.

"It's just—they say—" The guard gasped for breath around Sebastian's clutching fingers. Ean knew too well their strength. "There's talk ... they were moved ..."

"To where?"

It wasn't Sebastian's glare that brought such fear to the guard's darting eyes. "Milord ... they took them to the caverns."

Sebastian stilled. Then he closed his eyes, and for a moment Ean feared he was going to lose his hold on this dreadful travesty of himself that he'd been compelled to wear for so many years.

Sebastian's hand tightened around the man's neck. "*Which* cavern?"

The guard shook his head wildly, eyes bulging for lack of breath. "It's not ... my post ..."

Sebastian let out a slow exhale. Then he turned them a look fraught with uncertainty and guilt.

"Do what needs to be done, Sebastian," Isabel responded resolutely. "The well of mercy in Ivarnen has long gone dry."

Sebastian clenched his teeth and looked back to the guard, whose face went suddenly slack with apprehension. He threw a pattern on top of the man, and the guard fell to the stones in a writhing, soundless torment.

Abruptly Sebastian fell back from him and spun away in horror. He pushed a hand to the opposite wall and hung his head. "It won't last long," he nearly gasped, indicating the pattern and its tortured subject. Then he lifted a desperate gaze to Ean. "It's—"

"What Işak would've done." Ean put a hand on his brother's shoulder and willed his gaze to convey all the compassion and understanding he felt in his heart. "I know, and we needed Işak to buy us entrance, but Sebastian ... let go of him now."

Sebastian's expression was so burdened with despair ...

"We'll find another way."

Sebastian stared at him with burning eyes. Then he straightened, sniffed once and nodded, and the persona of Işak fell away, discarded like a stinking cloak. "Right." Sebastian tugged on his coat and exhaled forcefully. "This way."

Two corridors later, they rounded a corner into a long passage of iron doors and nearly collided with a group of guards.

Sebastian turned Isabel a swift look, the question all too clear in his gaze, but she shook her head. Neither she nor Ean would ask him to don the mask of Işak.

But subterfuge wouldn't have helped them in any case, for instead of charging, the guards parted to make way for an *eidola*. It drew its weapon with a slow, ominous scrape and said in its rattling viper's voice, "Methinks you belong here not."

Sebastian exhaled an oath and took a reflexive step backwards.

Ean couldn't blame him. No words could convey the visceral horror of seeing such demons in the flesh—and realizing they could *talk*.

The creature started towards them.

Ean stepped in front of Sebastian. "Take the soldiers. Guard Isabel."

He walked to meet the *eidola*.

In the days since Tal'Afaq, Ean had put long hours of thought into how to face these creatures more effectively than he'd managed the first time. Time to put his theories into practice then.

First noting that this *eidola* held a mortal blade, not Merdanti, the prince used Immanuel's advice from when they'd fought together in Tal'Afaq and made his flesh as stone. He caught the *eidola's* descending blade in his bare hand and ripped it out of its grasp. Then he grabbed the creature and flung himself around it and up onto its back. He bound its body with his legs while he pushed hands to either side of its head and sought the pattern that bound it to life.

The *eidola* raged. It howled. It rammed Ean backwards into the wall, pinning him between the slab of stone and its stone body. Its hands grappled for Ean's head, but he had his arms extended to their fullest, his weight in his legs and the fifth all around him. He found the pattern he wanted amid the muck of the creature's mind, but he didn't just unwork it. He *ripped* it apart.

In that split-second moment as the pattern was tearing, while the creature still clung to life, something far larger and more powerful retaliated against Ean. A wave of vehemence launched towards him—

The *eidola* collapsed.

Ean recoiled mentally and physically and steadied himself against the wall, breathing hard. How horribly close he'd been to receiving the backlash of what had to have been a Malorin'athgul's unbridled fury. It had felt entirely too akin to Rinokh's rage on the night in Rethynnea when he'd nearly died.

The guards, too, stood stunned. Their eyes were fixed on the *eidola* lying immobile on the floor. They obviously expected it to rise again. When it didn't, they shouted and charged.

Sebastian passed Ean in a blur.

Ean spared a glance after his brother, but there were only six guards, and Sebastian had a Merdanti blade, Dareios's enchanted mail, and a pattern of the fifth to protect himself. Ean would've insulted him deeply if he'd tried to help.

Isabel came up and pressed a hand to Ean's forehead. "What happened there, in the end?"

Ean gave her a look. "Darshan happened."

"You'll be more careful next time." She ran her fingers lightly across his temple, along the line of his jaw. Ean felt oddly like she was memorizing the shape of his face.

The last of the guards fell to Sebastian's blade and he swung a look over his shoulder. "Ean ..."

The prince nodded. He took Isabel's hand and they moved on together.

They met four more *eidola* along the way. Ean destroyed each of them and departed their minds before that malevolent force could latch onto him, but each almost-meeting with that forceful presence disturbed him immensely.

He learned that whoever—*what*ever—had made these creatures, the same pattern had been used to bind all of them to life. By the time he faced the fourth creature, Ean found the pattern of binding within a heartbeat, and two more saw it ripped apart.

At an intersection of tunnels, Isabel stiffened and squeezed Ean's hand. He motioned to Sebastian to stop and turned to her. "Tell me."

She pressed her lips together, radiating alarm. "My path ..." She looked away, down the darkened tunnel. "My path leads to the left." He saw her swallow, felt the tension binding her. "I can sense them ... *hundreds* of them."

"*Eidola?*" His voice sounded pathetically faint.

She nodded.

Ean held her hidden gaze. "But we're not here upon your path."

She shook her head in acknowledgment of this truth.

"Right." He looked to his brother, who was watching them warily. "Then we go forward." So they headed off again, away from the branching tunnel and the army of *eidola*.

They'd barely gone twenty steps, however, when a voice echoed from everywhere and nowhere. *"Ean val Lorian ..."*

Both princes drew up short.

"That's Dore's voice." Sebastian spun a look around the tunnel.

Ean reached to still his brother's hand upon his weapon. "He cast it upon the currents. Wait ..."

"Ean val Lorian ... I know you've come to me at last to answer for your crimes. Bring my wielder back to me ... and see your men returned."

Sebastian hissed an oath. "What kind of fools does he take us for?"

Something in this question reminded Ean of Pelas's remark in Tal'Afaq. A tragic smile flickered on his lips. "Noble ones, I think."

"Seek me ... and ye shall find ..."

Ean exhaled a slow and determined breath.

"Ean," Sebastian's eyes widened. "You're not seriously—"

"It's what we came here to do. He's just making it easier for us."

Sebastian arched brows with high dubiety. "You and I must have *very* different ideas of what that word means."

"Hurry," Isabel whispered.

Ean gave her a look, wondering and worrying at the hurricane he perceived in her thoughts. He tightened his hand around hers and moved into the lead, following Dore's trace upon the currents.

The way took them from the dungeons to the upper levels of the castle. They were upon a winding spiral stair when Isabel stopped them again.

Ean turned to her, feeling dismayed. "What now?"

"Something ..." She shook her head, caught the corner of her bottom lip between her teeth, and exhaled a slow breath. "The paths have shifted again."

"Like in Tal'Afaq?"

She looked to him. "Like Tyr'kharta."

Somehow that seemed worse, though he wasn't sure why.

"Something isn't right here."

"Much isn't right here, my lady," Sebastian said.

"I concede your point, Sebastian, but this is different." She twisted her staff in place before her feet.

Ean felt her emotion through their bond. If he hadn't known her better, he would've described it as panic, but this was Isabel ... to imagine her feeling such a thing was inconceivable.

"What is your will, my lady?" Sebastian asked.

Her hands tightened on her staff. "Lead forth with care, my lords."

Sebastian grunted. "So sayeth the *angiel* as her knights head into hell." He drew his blade, held it before him and moved into the lead. "I knew Dore was making monsters, but ..." He clenched his jaw and aimed a look at his brother. "When you spoke of these creatures to me, Ean, you called them *eidola*. You didn't say they were demons."

"They're not demons." Ean pushed a hand through his hair. "They're just ... men bound to one."

"They'll be demons in my dreams," Sebastian groused.

They finally gained the landing where a single, dim lantern hung above an iron door. Instinct made Ean grab for Sebastian's arm before he could touch the latch. "Wait." He gave his brother a look of caution.

"There's nothing on the ... what are you doing?" Sebastian looked at Ean oddly as the prince pressed his head to the wall to examine the door from an oblique angle.

"No," Ean murmured. "The currents never show Dore's traps. They lie dormant until you walk through them to your death. Here ... look for yourself." He motioned Sebastian to take his place beside the wall and moved out of the way. "You'll need my pattern to see it."

Sebastian gave him a look. "That goes without saying." Then he inspected the door with a narrowed gaze. "Is that ..." He scanned up and down and let out a low whistle. "Dore never taught me patterns like this. It's like a spider's web, only—"

"It would be the last thing you ever saw." Ean made a circle of his finger along a specific part of the pattern. "See ... it's designed to react to the fifth, to patterns like the variant one we're using."

Sebastian pushed away from the wall. "So if you can see it ..."

"It can kill you." Ean quickly found the pattern's point of separation where beginning and end connected and started its unraveling.

Sebastian watched him as he was doing this. "You're really kind of a miracle, aren't you?"

"Yes," Isabel said from behind them.

Ean cast her a sidelong look while asking his brother, "What do you mean?"

Sebastian was regarding him seriously. "I can see what you're doing because of the pattern you've given me, but seeing and unworking aren't the same thing. I wouldn't have had the slightest clue how to unwork that. This talent of yours—it's more than just *seeing* patterns." He leaned his shoulder against the wall and stared at Ean, making him rather uncomfortable with the force of his gaze. "In all the realm, how many people do you suppose can see *and* unwork patterns?"

"Two," Isabel said.

Ean turned her an expression of pained entreaty.

Sebastian looked to Isabel and met her hidden gaze. "My brother and yours."

She nodded. Then she nodded to the door. "Let's keep moving."

So they did.

Dore's message on the currents led them to a long hallway that appeared to run the entire length of the castle main. Ean led the way, scanning the wide corridor for patterns and passing room after room standing vacant and cold, host only to shadows and the rain beading against darkened windows. The passage seemed to go endlessly on—he'd covered barely a third of it when he came to an archway that opened upon a darkened gallery of tall windows. Something …

Pressing himself close to the wall, he scanned the archway and found another of Dore's patterns and unworked it. Beyond, deep inside the gallery, hidden from view save from that particular angle …

"It's Rhys—" Sebastian pushed past Ean into the room.

"Sebastian, *wait*—"

But it was too late.

Sebastian walked right through the nearly invisible pattern stretched from ceiling to floor, and the Labyrinth collapsed upon him.

Ean hissed an oath and dove into the room after his brother. Patterns like cobwebs covered the entire gallery, most of them making an attempt to conceal the Labyrinth.

He cast a broad sheet of the fourth through the room and seared away the illusion that had tricked Sebastian into his haste, as well as the one that concealed the armed men standing at the back of the room. Then he went to his brother, who'd fallen to one knee with his sword in his fist, head hung.

Wielder's lamps lit by patterns of *elae* flamed to life. Out of the shadows two dozen men emerged, led by a dark-haired Saldarian that Ean immediately recognized. Behind the well-armed host stood two guards holding a ragged prisoner between them—Rhys val Kincaide.

And behind these … three *eidola*. Something about them … Ean couldn't put his finger on why their presence made him suddenly uneasy. He slowly straightened and moved himself between the advancing host and Sebastian's bent form.

"It seems we meet again, Ean val Lorian." Raliax's voice had lost none of its smugness for Ean's having nearly cut him in twain in Tyr'kharta.

Ean rested a hand on his sword. "The better to best you twice, I suppose."

"Bold words." Raliax looked around at his men. "But I clearly have the upper hand. You'd be a fool to resist."

"I've been called worse things than a fool." Ean fixed a cool grey gaze on the man. "I'll bet you have too."

Raliax flashed a knife-sharp smile thick with animosity. "You val Lorians ... always thinking yourselves so superior."

"Only compared to some."

Raliax's eyes were twin coals of hatred. "Still ... we needn't be at odds." He seemed to bite the words as he said them. "You've brought what we want ... and we've got what you want." He waved for his men to bring Rhys forward.

Ean suspected the Saldarian's bold posturing had much to do with the patterns still cluttering the air—the ones seeking to entrap anyone working the fifth. But Raliax couldn't know that Ean had already set them to unraveling. He doubted Dore could make a pattern that he couldn't now easily unwork—the man was devious but predictable.

As the soldiers parted to make way, two Saldarians dragged the chained Rhys forward and dumped him roughly at Ean's feet. Ean kept his eyes on Raliax as he bent to Rhys, but then he swept his gaze across his captain. Rhys' condition brought a lump to Ean's throat. The weeks of captivity had made a wasted shell of the once-robust soldier; he'd been brutally beaten and looked ill with fever.

Ean pressed a hand to the captain's shoulder with gentle concern. This was not the reunion he'd hoped for. "*Rhys ...*"

The captain's voice came as a bare whisper across cracked lips. "Your Highness ... *kill* these bastards. They—"

One of the Saldarians jerked on the chain he held, and the captain flew backwards onto his side. He exhaled a forceful grunt of pain, which devolved into a coughing fit that sounded far worse.

Ean slowly straightened, his gaze arctic now. "And my other men?"

Raliax's smile could not have been more smug. "Just waiting for a word from me to be released."

"And what about the *eidola* hiding in the corner? What's their purpose? Impartial witnesses?"

Raliax spun a look over his shoulder to the supposedly empty corner where Ean knew the *eidola* were waiting. He hadn't bothered unworking that illusion, for the currents revealed the creatures readily enough.

Raliax's expression had measurably darkened when he looked back to Ean. "So ... you see how this will go." His black gaze flickered around the room as if trying to reassure himself that twenty men and a dozen *eidola* would be enough to contain Ean. Then he jerked his head towards Sebastian. "The wielder's useless to you now. That's the Labyrinth upon him—no getting free of it." He caught his bottom lip between his teeth in a smile that bespoke base desires. "Leave him. Take your captain and your men. That's the deal."

"My men." Ean felt sick as he shifted his gaze to the three *eidola* standing in the back. His heart went out to them; their blood would forever stain his hands. Likewise the guilt of their end. But he had no illusions that they were *his* men any longer.

Ean exhaled a slow breath. "Let's get this over with, then." He settled his gaze on Raliax, cold and hard as winter iron. "Where's your master?"

Raliax's eyes gleamed darkly. "You treat with me or not at all, little prince."

"Very well, if you insist." And he drew his sword.

Two dozen men drew theirs in reply.

Ean kept his gaze fixed on them but asked his brother, "Are you ready, Sebastian?"

Sebastian rose slowly from his crouch and stepped forward to Ean's side. He lifted his head and settled a penetrating gaze on Raliax. "Like there's no tomorrow, Ean."

The Saldarian took two reflexive steps backwards. His eyes darted between Sebastian and Ean. Then he rushed Sebastian.

The others rushed Ean.

Ean cast the fifth into the chains binding Rhys. Then he swept his sword overhead and spun into the *cortata*, noting mid-turn that Sebastian had done the same.

The room fell into chaos.

For many minutes, Ean knew only the clash of steel, the sounds of battle and the rush of *elae* in his ears. Men fell beneath his blade, others to bolts of the fourth which he cast like arrows. The latter sent men flying, often taking others down as their bodies plunged like boulders catapulted through the larger host.

But then the mortals grew wise and cleared away from Ean, and the prince found himself in the center of the long gallery with *eidola* coming at him from all sides.

Ean saw them as black forms against the currents, phantoms that absorbed *elae's* light—or perhaps repelled it completely—like the Merdanti blades they all carried. One of them started a rattling hiss that the others joined, so that a sibilating threat soon simmered in the gallery. It played counterpoint to the sounds made by the men still fighting Sebastian and to the rain washing the windowpanes.

Ean watched the creatures coming, their speed increasing with every step. Individually, he could take them, but all of them together … ?

He darted a glance down the gallery and its long row of rain-spattered windows. The *eidola* might be immune to the fifth, but the *room* wasn't.

Running, Ean flung the fourth at the windows. They exploded in a deadly spray of glass. The concussion sucked the rain inside, and the raging wind overturned and doused the lamps. Ean embraced the storm with his mind and cast it through the room, drenching all in stinging spray. Then with a thought, he turned everything to ice.

The marble floor became instantly slick—only Ean's feet found solid footing beneath his intent. The running *eidola* hit the ice and slid, fell, skidded—slammed into one another. Ean sent a bolt of the fourth towards three of them to augment their own momentum, and they flew out the shattered windows into the night. Three more he anchored in the ice with a thought. It would hold them for only moments, but he'd take whatever moments he could.

Spinning around, he ran to find the *eidola* who'd been his men. He owed them their freedom from the hell of Darshan's binding, and he would give them that if nothing else.

The closest one—who Ean recognized with a heartbreaking jolt as Fynn's man Brody—jumped for Ean, but he dropped into a slide beneath it. The creature soared over his head, hit the ice behind him, and went veering towards the far wall.

With a little help of the fifth, Ean slid back onto his feet and ran for the next one—*Dorin! Ah, Cephrael no.*

He'd been so loyal and such a fine scout!

The *eidola* who wore Dorin's stolen face hissed at him. Feeling a pain in his chest that was his heart rending, Ean dove for the creature and took him off his feet. They both sprawled onto the ice in a spinning skid. Wrestling the thing around beneath him, Ean reached into its mind and ripped apart the pattern that bound it to life. The body stilled while they were still sliding.

A third *eidola* fell upon him from behind, and Ean rolled to meet it head-on. Black eyes stared into his from the golem face of Cayal.

Cayal! Oh, Cayal! Not merely his man, but a friend in true—honorable, faithful, one whose counsel Ean had always respected. Ean swallowed the stone of guilt in his throat and grabbed Cayal's head between both hands. The *eidola* pinned powerful knees into Ean's shoulders and pulled a dagger from a sheath at its thigh. The blade was heading for Ean's heart before he saw it.

Ean shoved the fifth against his own body and sent both himself and Cayal skidding just as the dagger would've pierced his flesh. The blade sliced along his ribs in a line of heat and lodged in the floor, only to be ripped out of the *eidola's* hand as they flew away across the ice.

They spun in a tangle, and in that flicker of an instant Ean questioned himself. *Was* there a way to save Cayal? Could he sever the *eidola's* connection to the Prophet and somehow … ?

But even before he thought it through, he knew there was no saving this man who'd been so brave and traded his life in service of his king. When Ean chose to save Sebastian, he'd sacrificed these loyal men as surely as if he'd cast them himself into the flames.

And that was the truth Ean had to face. Cayal and the others were already dead.

Agonized, Ean twisted while they both slid across the ice, and grabbed for Cayal's arm. He knew exactly where to find the pattern of binding now—he barely had to look for it anymore, as his mind simply *found* it through any sort of contact—and with a surge of the fifth, he seared the pattern out of existence.

He who had once been Ean's friend fell back, no more animated than a broken statue.

As their motion across the ice slowed, the prince wanted only to stay there with Cayal's remains. He wanted to grieve for him and say the Rites for the Departed—for surely Cayal and the others deserved no less than this grace—but instead he gritted his teeth and rolled to his hands and knees—just as Brody raised his blade above him.

Sebastian spun into the *cortata* and raised his sword to block Raliax's downward stroke. Their enchanted blades clashed with the dull ring of stone on stone, but in Sebastian's mind, the sentient weapon sang. He felt it like an extension of his arm, a lengthened appendage jointed at the hand. Sebastian spun beneath their locked blades and swept his sword around in a forceful arc, slicing across the black scales of Raliax's armor. The Saldarian barely jumped back in time.

Sebastian pressed on the offensive. It thrilled him to fight cleanly, without the tricks Dore had made him use; the *cortata* fueling Sebastian's free mind gave him more power than he had ever hoped to wield. Downward he swung his blade, back and forth the weapon hissed, splitting the air with its razor edge, driving Raliax relentlessly back. The only thing Sebastian compelled was the Saldarian's desperation.

Another swing sliced for Raliax's chest, that time drawing blood. Even Merdanti armor couldn't protect against a sentient blade.

Raliax swore and scrambled back, scattering men behind him in his haste to escape. Elsewhere in the gallery, two dozen others were attacking Ean, but Sebastian suspected that his brother could hold his own. He only had eyes for Raliax—clear eyes, unimpeded by Dore's twisted illusions.

Sebastian stalked the Saldarian, who looked far less smug now than he had a minute ago. "I remember things." Sebastian swung his blade in its own deadly dance, keeping the form of the *cortata*. "Many things ... how you dumped me in N'ghorra, and even before. I remember *you*."

Raliax held his sword before himself warily, but he looked more keen to flee than fight. Resentment alone must've rooted him. "Oh, aye, I remember *you* ... *Prince* Sebastian, all pride and posturing, come to M'Nador to impress us with your rhetoric and velveteen smile." Raliax carved arrowheads out of his words, and he fired each of them at Sebastian laced with poison's bitter bite. "You were an arrogant prick then, and you're no better now."

"True, I am no better." Sebastian gave him a grim smile. "Now I am merely smarter." He took another step towards the man as he twirled his blade in the *cortata's* slow, twisting dance. "I have you to thank for that."

Confusion clouded Raliax's gaze. He lifted his sword as if to defend against an unaccepted truth. "What's this … wielder's trickery?"

"Gratitude." Sebastian took another step. "If I hadn't first endured N'ghorra's lessons, I never could've survived Dore Madden's." Abruptly he darted in with his attack.

Raliax matched his advance with a grunt of effort, and their battle paced a fast blur across the floor, blades flashing, until—

The windows exploded. Sebastian drew up short, letting the spray glance harmlessly off him—nothing so slight could penetrate the barrier of Dareios's shirt of mail—but Raliax threw an arm across his eyes and ducked for cover. Wind scoured the gallery then, extinguishing the lamps. Sebastian watched *eidola* go pouring across the floor after his brother.

He allowed himself a moment of wonder. Then he turned and ran after Raliax.

As he crossed the room in darkness, he thought he saw a figure wrestling with shadows. It might've been the captain.

Abruptly something struck beside his head and glanced off again, rebounded by Dareios's mail. Sebastian spun as a form rushed out at him, and he swung up his sword to counter the blade flying towards his eyes. Their hilts clashed with brutal force.

Raliax uttered a growl—fury mingled with malice. He tried to overpower Sebastian, but the latter slung his sword to free it and danced to the right. Their blades scraped along each others' edges as Sebastian slid safely out of reach.

They paced each other then, two predators casing the same hunting ground. "I remember you were different, too." Sebastian held his sword before him, grey eyes fixed on his enemy. "Raliax of Tambarré, Envoy and Adjutant. You had a promising career … that is, I suppose, until you failed to kill me properly. What happened after Viernan hal'Jaitar stole me away? What did your masters exact from *your* soul in punishment?"

The Saldarian's eyes were pools of black hate. "You know nothing of me." But the vitriol in his tone said otherwise. "Stop gabbing and *fight*, you gimp-legged jade!" he rushed at him.

Sebastian skipped aside, but at the same time he slid the fourth along his blade and flung it outwards like a rope. Raliax tripped across the thread of power and tumbled, skidded across a floor that had somehow become ice. He shouted curses under his breath as he scrambled to regain his feet, and then he called to his nearby men to attack in his stead.

Five Saldarians rushed Sebastian, albeit unsteadily on the icy floor.

Sebastian might've used any manner of patterns to subdue them, but honor kept such thoughts corralled. That he'd found honor again at all after so long still brought a choked feeling to his chest. He cast the fourth before his feet to crack Ean's ice and rushed forward to exact the cost of his vengeance on Raliax's men.

One, two, three fell to his blade. He thrust, he spun, he bounded over the fallen and ran his sword through a fourth.

Suddenly power flared in a halo around him, and he spun with an intake of breath to see Raliax flying backwards through the air. The blackguard had tried to attack him from behind.

Sebastian ducked beneath the swiping blade of a fifth man rushing in and spun. He surged upwards, sweeping his blade in a deadly, diagonal arc that cut deep. The soldier fell.

Instinct shouted and Sebastian threw himself sideways. Raliax's sword thrust missed him by a breath. The Saldarian snarled in outrage and barreled into Sebastian, and they crashed into the ice. Both of them lost their blades.

Raliax scrabbled for the advantage and managed to get his hands around Sebastian's throat. He smashed Sebastian's head backwards hard enough to shatter the ice skimming the floor. Sebastian felt his head hit the marble beneath, and pain exploded in his skull.

Ean rolled to avoid Brody's descending blade. The razor edge slammed into the ice mere inches from his head. He threw the fifth to push himself free and flew out from underneath Brody just as the latter was bringing down his blade a second time.

The group of *eidola* that Ean had pinned in the ice were helping free each other as Ean skidded past them on his back across the floor. Even as he watched, the last of them broke out of the ice block that had been encasing its feet.

Ean felt the beginning of a dull ache behind his eyes, the signal of impending exhaustion—he'd been working the lifeforce nearly nonstop since they arrived in Ivarnen—but resting meant dying, and dying wasn't an option. Ean saw the pack of *eidola* coming for him and felt a desperate sense of frustration. He needed time to figure out a way to handle all of them at once.

Breathing in determination, the prince caught up his sword as he pushed back to his feet. Then he summoned a third strand pattern and split time, fracturing each moment into multiples of itself, making seconds into minutes.

He stood then, chest heaving, head throbbing, while the world around him slowed. Rain seemed to hover in the air as it inched slowly towards the floor, the shifting mist took on a granular cast, and the *eidola* moved as if through stone. Sound ceased.

Ean listened to his rapid breath and the thudding pulse of his heart and tried to solve the problem of these *eidola*.

Think! What would Arion have done? How would he have solved it?

Out of the fog of exhaustion the Twentieth Esoteric blazed: '*The strands are divisions of energy ... thus the Laws of Patterning follow the laws of energy.*'

Mulling this over, Ean fixed his gaze on the slowly approaching *eidola*.

Patterns were energy. *Thought* was energy. He needed a way to destroy the patterns of thought-energy that bound the *eidola* to Darshan's mind ... to life.

Eidola were immune to direct attacks of the fifth, but the world around them wasn't. And while stone didn't conduct energy well ... water did.

Standing still within the continually expanding shards of time, Ean formed a plan—dangerous, insane. It would either work or be the end of him, but how was that different than any other day?

He drew in a deep breath and made his decision.

Ean reached for the storm and simultaneously released the third. Time slammed back again—all of those infinities of seconds collapsed into a single moment, but they brought into that moment the entire force of their expansion. The implosion jarred Ean so hard that he stumbled and nearly fell.

But he had hold of the storm. Embracing it to the fullness of his awareness, he pulled it upon himself and ripped the storm into the gallery.

Rain emptied into the room in a whirling deluge. Ean waved his sword, his talisman for this working, to collect the storm in a swarm around the approaching *eidola*. A whirlpool enveloped them. He ran towards the group, and as he did, he bound each molecule together so that it wasn't a whirlwind of water but a standing, swirling whirlpool. He collapsed the boundaries of this vortex to encase them tightly, until the *eidola* were spinning, twisting, tangling together, washed off their feet in a torrent of violently churning water. Then he dove into the pool.

Stone hands found him. Stone elbows and knees and toothless black gums bit into him. Ean let them pull his body within the tangle of their limbs. Water bound them all now into an airless cocoon. *Eidola* didn't need air, but Ean did. He had as long as he could hold his breath to make this work.

The *eidola* pulled and clawed at him while he sought the pattern of their existence. An elbow caught him in the temple, and painful stars knocked the pattern from his thoughts. But it also reminded him of something important.

'Patterns lie within the boundaries of Absolute Being.'

Keen to avoid the mistake he had made when sparring with Ramu—when he'd turned the entire Hall of Heroes to ice—Ean applied the Second Esoteric and expanded his being to include all of the *eidola* and his whirling pool of water.

His lungs burned. His head felt like it was ready to explode. His thoughts grew dim at the edges, and the creatures clung to him like chains dragging him deeper into the vortex of his own creation.

Ean finally got a handhold on one of them and found the pattern in its mind. He had one chance to do this right, one chance to sear not one pattern of binding but all of them from existence. He took it.

A flat sheet of energy flared outwards from the whirlpool and sheered across the room, incinerating everything in its path. Men dove to safety beneath it or were seared in two. A strip of fire raced along the wall with the expanding sheet of death.

The vortex fell apart.

Ean plummeted to the floor amid a painful tangle of inert stone bodies while his whirlpool splashed down around him. He choked and sputtered and tried to claw his way out from beneath the creatures crushing him. His head felt like *it* had exploded.

He finally rose unsteadily to his feet. He had a high-pitched ringing in his ears, and dullness veiled his eyes and thoughts. He stumbled forward, trying to regain his bearings, trying not to think about how for a split-second moment he'd been the source-point of elemental lightning.

Only then did his muddled mind realize that alarm bells were ringing, that Brody and two other *eidola* were attacking his brother, and that—

Something hard crashed across the back of his skull.

Light flared with blinding pain, and Ean flew forward onto the ice, lost his breath, lost control … and as his sliding body sped towards the shattered windows, lost consciousness.

FORTY-NINE

"The illusion called 'hope' is the most egregious
deception ever waged upon Man."

– The Prophet Bethamin

S EBASTIAN'S HEAD FELT like an anvil was crushing it as he lay pinned
beneath Raliax. He knew he needed to focus, to *do* something, but a wall
of incongruous thought separated idea from action. Raliax meanwhile
clung to him. His eyes fumed with a fulminating concoction of resentment,
envy and malice while his thumbs choked off all chance at breath.

"*Puppet ...*" The defamation frothed across the Saldarian's lips, unbridled
rage preventing all but choked-off words of hate. "*Madman's toy.*"

Sebastian felt blackness threatening. Warm blood soaked the back of his
head and took concentration with it as it seeped into the ice. The world spun
dizzily, dragging his stomach along on a twirling dance. Then—

A blur.

Raliax flew sideways, and a shadowed form stepped across Sebastian's body
in pursuit. Sebastian rolled to his side and pushed slowly to hands and knees.
With his breath returned some semblance of lucid thought. He turned to see
Rhys standing over a kneeling Raliax with a sword pushed against the hollow
of the Saldarian's throat. Sebastian retrieved his own sword and staggered to the
captain's side. Rhys looked as unsteady as Sebastian felt.

Raliax lifted his hands in resentful surrender and his lip in a sneer. "What a
touching reunion." He spat blood and glared acidly up at them.

"What do you want done with this filth, Your Highness?" Illness made
Rhys' voice faint, but nothing dampened the determination in his tone, and his
sword pinned at the man's throat remained amazingly steady.

The captain's formal address startled Sebastian, but he kept his expression
neutral and his gaze focused on the Saldarian. Eight years ago, this man had

befriended and betrayed him, given him to his enemies to be tortured, and then sold him to slavers. Vengeance was his due; yet as he stared at Raliax of Tambarré, all Sebastian truly felt for him was pity.

"Who is the puppet?" Sebastian pushed the sharp edge of his Merdanti blade beneath the Saldarian's chin and forced his head back. "The one bound to the strings of another man's will, or the one who jerks at his master's whims without any strings at all?"

Raliax's gaze burned with hate. He opened his mouth to retort, and Sebastian ran him through.

As the Saldarian slid off his blade, Rhys lowered his sword with a tremulous exhale. He looked ready to fall over. Then he crumpled.

Sebastian caught him around the waist and helped him to sit. Their eyes locked. Sebastian recalled too well their last interaction, when Rhys had been his prisoner. Sebastian had left that meeting feeling shattered. He'd never imagined the captain had recognized him.

"You *know* me." Sebastian searched the captain's eyes with his own.

Rhys held his gaze with deep lines creasing his brow. "Aye. I knew you even then. Would that I'd had the courage to admit it in that moment—" His eyes went round. "*Your Highness!*"

Sebastian spun to his feet just as three *eidola* descended upon him. To his horror, he recognized the tallest among them as having been one of Trell's men … the one they'd called Brody the Bull.

He brought up his sword to meet Brody's flashing weapon, and his sentient blade sang true in the clash, yet Sebastian felt the jarring force of their meeting blades reverberating all the way into his bones.

How in Cephrael's name does Ean fight these monsters?

Sebastian couldn't believe their strength. He tried to force Brody back to find the steps of the *cortata*, but he could barely counter the creature's power, much less maneuver it into the Adept dance of swords.

Suddenly one of the other *eidola* grabbed him around the waist. He struggled to keep Brody's blade locked with his, struggled to keep his feet beneath him.

And then—

He couldn't describe—couldn't comprehend …

The *eidola* that had been Brody was bearing down on him one moment, and in the next it and the third creature staggered back. The ratcheting hisses of the *eidola* trembled the air and then they …

Sebastian stared, open-mouthed. The creatures made it three paces before they dissolved—their last two steps sent them crumbling into black sand. Brody's sword clattered to the stones.

In his astonishment, Sebastian lost his footing and fell beneath the last *eidola*. His tortured head screamed as he landed on his back, and—

A flash of darkness blurred before his eyes. The *eidola* flew off him, backwards through the air, sprawling and hissing and spitting what could only have been curses, until—

It slammed into the floor and exploded into ash.

Veiled in illusion, Isabel van Gelderan stood in the hall outside the gallery where Ean and Sebastian fought. In her mind's eye, all three of their paths shifted around her tumultuously like a ship in hurricane seas. Sebastian and Ean's paths shimmered before her vision, their threads expanding and contracting, blurring and then solidifying anew, each time assuming a different shape. And of her own path, she saw a wavering gold thread extending into a wall of formless darkness. She felt unbalanced.

Windows shattered in the other room, and the castle inhaled a damp wind. Isabel sensed Ean fighting, felt his determination across the bond. She ached to help him, but she dared not take a single step in any direction for fear of over-tipping the dangerously lurching vessel that was his path.

Isabel gripped her staff in white knuckles and laid her forehead against its cool stone, willing herself to endure.

When she'd faced the knowledge that she would spend long centuries separated from Arion, she'd yet known they would meet again. Fortitude had kept her company. But since her recent dream, she could see nothing of her own path beyond the dark wall. She knew it must continue on, but what she would find beyond that blackness ... what she would *face* there? She had only vague visions to give shape to the future.

She'd never felt so afraid.

Suddenly instinct jarred her roughly from the far future paths she'd been traveling and thrust her indelicately back to the present.

A wall of darkness was coming towards her from the far end of the long corridor, but this darkness had shape and form. *Eidola.*

And behind them ...

Oh, no!

Naked eyes would not have seen him, for he was still too far away, but the lifeforce itself fueled Isabel's sight, and the painfully bright star following behind the *eidola* could be only one man.

It's too soon! She pressed a hand across her mouth. *They cannot meet yet!*

But Darshan was coming for Ean. She knew it in the fabric of her being, in the very threads that bound her consciousness to the tapestry. He'd seen Ean each time the prince severed his connection with one of his *eidola*, and he'd gained in those encounters a sense of Ean's mind. Now Darshan was following the star of Ean's awareness right to his location.

He's not ready!

Isabel felt ill with dread. If Ean and Darshan met now ...

We'll lose him from the tapestry forever!

For weeks she'd feared her presence was affecting Ean's path. Now she knew the truth to be much more painful: she wasn't influencing Ean's path, she was causing their two paths to *merge* into one path.

Her path.

Somehow she had to give Ean time to separate their paths again, to let him find his own way back to Darshan—a safer way, a longer way … the way he *should've* been upon. A route that would give Ean the opportunity to grow into his power, so when he and Darshan met in another future, in what seemed to her to be an inevitable contest of wills, Ean would have at least some small chance of surviving the encounter.

Suddenly the tumultuous sea around Isabel went still.

She saw all three paths converging.

On came the wall of *eidola* and the cold, fiery star that was their maker, while in the other room Ean was unmaking Darshan's evils one by one.

Along her path, frightening formless images shifted and became clearer, though no less frightening.

Isabel drew in a deep breath and let out a tremulous exhale. Then she closed her eyes and reassembled her resolve out of the shards of her fears.

She could forgive Ean anything—three hundred years of mistakes and separations, of failures and sacrifices and catastrophes for the sake of the noblest intentions—but she feared … she *truly* feared Ean would never be able to forgive her for this.

Isabel picked up her staff, exhaled determination, and accepted her path.

She slipped unnoticed into the gallery, gliding as a shadow into chaos. Even as she watched, three *eidola* descended on Sebastian. Further down, Ean was rising to his feet amid a sea of drowned *eidola*.

Behind her in the hall, the currents trembled. Darshan approached.

Isabel extended her staff, focused both her aim and her intent, and sent a piercing arrow of the fourth flying. It struck Ean across the back of his head and sent him skidding across the ice. Even as she set off towards Sebastian, Isabel flung a pattern of the fifth to halt Ean's momentum before he careened out the window, unconscious.

Let Darshan try to find him now.

Before her, Sebastian faltered. An *eidola* slipped beneath his guard while he was fighting one of its brethren and grabbed him around the waist. He struggled to keep his footing.

Running to his aid, Isabel spun her staff over her head and summoned a pattern she never imagined she would ever have to use—but sometimes only fire could fight fire.

Sa'shah'serrr …

The pattern hissed in her mind as she cast it forth—once, and again. Two bolts of violet-blackness caught first one *eidola* and then the second. They staggered backwards with rattling screams and collapsed into sand.

Isabel swept in and caught the third *eidola* in the back of its head with her staff as it was attempting to pin a fallen Sebastian beneath it. The creature flew backwards through the air, sprawling and hissing. Lightning quick, Isabel spun her staff again and cast a third *inverteré* pattern off its tip.

It hit the *eidola* in midair, and the creature landed in an explosion of ash.

Isabel rushed to Sebastian and helped him to his feet.

"*Isabel—*" His eyes were wide, his face bloodied. He looked stunned, shaken.

"Get Ean out of here, Sebastian—out of this castle. Out of Saldaria. Use Ivarnen's node. Ean should rouse by the time you reach it."

Looking aghast, Sebastian inhaled with obvious protest, but she stopped his argument with an upraised hand. "We have less than a minute, so listen well. Tell Ean he has to find a way to unmake entire companies of these creatures in one blow. Tell Dareios I said to use *inverteré* patterns if he must."

Sebastian stared at her.

Motion from behind drew Isabel's gaze, and she turned to find the captain struggling to his feet. She went and took him by the elbow and did what she could to ease his illness in their brief contact, but she could spare only seconds for Healing, and his sickness had rooted deep.

Even so, the captain must've felt her Healing, for he somewhat gaped at her. Then again, he might've been gawking at the blindfolded woman who'd just turned three *eidola* into ash.

"Come, both of you."

Isabel hastened towards an unconscious Ean. She knelt at his side and smoothed back his dark hair. Seeing him lying there, knowing she was leaving him … the moment stabbed her heart with a thousand knives. She could barely breathe.

Isabel looked up desperately at Sebastian. "Tell him Darshan was coming for him, and I …" Her voice caught in her throat. "I saw no other way."

"*Isabel,*" Sebastian murmured wretchedly.

"Take him." She swallowed her grief and stood. A wall of *eidola* approached in the hall. "Hurry."

Radiating uncertainty, Sebastian bent and gathered his brother into his arms.

Isabel held a hand to him and Rhys to stay where they were and rushed across the room. When she gauged herself far enough away, she turned to face them, spun her staff end over end, and slammed it into the floor. A thunderous, echoing clap preceded the jagged crack that speared as lightning through the floor. Tile and plaster disintegrated, and a chasm opened before her feet. She shaped the working to her desire as it spread, and a slab of the floor fell inward on an angle, sloping down to the level beneath.

In the corridor beyond, the currents raged. Darshan neared.

"The node." She pinned her gaze on Sebastian, demanding his full attention. "You know where it is?"

He nodded.

"Go, then." She pointed with her staff to the sloping floor.

He went, reluctantly carrying his brother. When he and the captain once again had their feet, Isabel threw them her staff.

Rhys lifted both hands and caught it, but he stumbled beneath its weight. Sebastian threw up a hand to catch the staff's descending end as the captain fell, and she saw him instinctively put *elae* into his touch.

As ever, your instinct guides you well, Sebastian.

Isabel called down to them, "The weapon knows both of you now. If anything stands in your path—magical or otherwise—use it."

Sebastian's eyes gazing up at her revealed his immense conflict.

"I'm on my path, Sebastian. Do not let him come for me. Remember all else I've told you."

A moment longer he stared at her, and then she felt the tension which bound him flattening with resolve. It was less a surrender than a concession to her understanding of things beyond his ken.

Sebastian bowed his head. "Your will, Isabel." Then he turned with his brother in his arms and led the captain away into the darkness.

"Who in the name of every god of this earth was that?"

Sebastian spared a look over his shoulder for Rhys. The captain was doing his best to keep up with Sebastian by using Isabel's staff for support. In his debilitated condition, Sebastian found it surprising Rhys kept apace at all. Without Isabel's staff, it would've been impossible. Still, Sebastian got the sense, even as Rhys likely did, that Isabel had given them her staff less to assist their escape than as a sacred charge.

Sebastian turned forward again feeling terrorized—more in view of what Ean was going to do to him when he woke up than because of what lay behind. He hiked his brother's inert form higher in his arms and blessed Ean for teaching him the pattern that was fueling his steps.

"That was … Isabel."

The Merdanti staff thudded dully on the floor as Rhys struggled to keep up. "Who is Isabel?"

"Isabel is Ean's … wife, I suppose. It's complicated." He shot him a somewhat desperate look over his shoulder. "Isabel van Gelderan."

Rhys missed a step. The staff's end struck unevenly against the floor, and the captain exhaled a pained grunt.

Sebastian supposed he understood how a statement like that must've sounded to a man like Rhys. No doubt the captain was pondering even now how Prince Ean had wed the sister of the world's greatest known traitor. How little he understood of what was truly going on.

How little any of them understood.

And by *Cephrael's Great Book*—what was Isabel *thinking*?

'Darshan is coming,' she'd said. So she'd knocked Ean out for gods knew *what* reason, given them her weapon and ... what? Walked out to meet the bloody man? It felt like insanity. It *had* to be insanity.

There was no way it was insanity. Isabel knew what she was doing.

But it certainly *looked* insane.

Sebastian forced his aching legs to keep moving. Whatever was happening in Ivarnen ... whatever greater battle had begun, his only job now was getting them to the node.

They reached a tower and Sebastian hurried down its tightly curving stair, nearly leaning into the wall to keep his balance while carrying his brother's heavy form.

"My prince ... my prince—*a moment*—" Rhys' breathless voice called to Sebastian from far back on the stair.

Sebastian paused and took a moment to reclaim his own breath ... but in that sudden stillness, futility pounced on him.

The node chamber seemed a world away, while his brother's form felt like a lead weight in his burning arms. Instinct told him an army of *eidola* waited between them and the node, the same army Isabel had perceived while down in the caverns. And how many more would soon be coming after them from above? With Ean unconscious, they didn't stand a chance.

Rhys caught up to him, pushed a hand against the wall and hung his head. He looked haggard. It took a lengthy span of wheezing for him to summon enough breath to speak. "Just a moment ... a moment to catch my wind."

Sebastian didn't think they had even a moment to spare, but he'd already abandoned Isabel—never mind that she'd forced him to—and he certainly had no intention of abandoning the captain when he was the whole reason they'd come to Ivarnen to begin with.

But the captain's 'moment' felt agonizingly long.

Sebastian set Ean's body down on the stairs and used the time to release his overtaxed muscles. He loosened his blade in its scabbard, adjusted his baldric and tried to think of any patterns that might possibly defend against *eidola*.

Just as Rhys was lifting his gaze and nodding wordlessly that they might continue on, they heard it—the pounding echo of stone on stone. *Eidola* running.

Sebastian cursed. He bent and shook his brother where he lay against the wall. "Ean!" He shook him harder. Then he slapped him.

Ean's eyes jerked open and he sucked in his breath.

Sebastian felt a wave of relief.

Ean pushed groggily up to sit taller. "What happened?" One hand felt along the back of his head as he looked around the stairwell.

Sebastian cast him a look of black chagrin. "Isabel happened."

"Isabel ..." Ean blinked. Only then did he seem to notice the captain standing several stairs above him, holding Isabel's staff. He swung back to Sebastian. "Where is she?" He surged to his feet and grabbed Sebastian. "Where's Isabel?"

"She's gone, Ean."

"They *took* her?" Ean gaped at him in horror. "You *let* them?"

"Of course I didn't *let* them! It was *Isabel,* she—" But Gods above, how did one explain such a thing? Sebastian shoved a hand through his hair and then flung it at his brother. "Darshan was coming for you. She—*thirteen hells,* Ean, I don't *know* what she did, but whatever it was, she did it so we could escape."

A cold and uncompromising fury settled across his brother's gaze. "I'm going back for her." He spun.

Sebastian grabbed his arm and exhaled a frustrated oath, but it was the captain who truly stopped Ean. He angled Isabel's staff diagonally in the narrow passage, blocking Ean's path, and fixed an equally belligerent and uncompromising stare on the prince. He seemed more than squarely matched against Ean's stubbornness.

"The lady said not to let you come back for her. She said to get out of Ivarnen, out of Saldaria, and to use the node to do it." Even wasted with illness, Rhys stood as a wall of conviction, steadfast and resolute. "Now I don't know what power Prince Sebastian can work, but I got the impression we needed Your Highness to travel the node."

Ean stared at Rhys, radiating a rage so formidable that Sebastian had to step back from him. The currents clouded around his brother, layer upon layer of formless power just waiting to be molded to his intent, and as furious as Ean was, he might've annihilated half the castle with one misthought.

"For gods' sake, Ean." Sebastian laid a tentative hand on his brother's arm, willing him to listen, to *see.* "We had no choice."

"You. *Left.* Her!" The words fulminated out of him, black explosions of condemnation. Sebastian felt each one in his gut.

He pushed palms to his temples, guilt-ridden and exasperated. "Ean ... she said she was upon her path—"

He heard his brother's sharp inhale, and his expression ... in an instant his face switched from enraged to utterly, completely ... *shattered.* The currents swarmed into a riotous tumult, a hurricane sea of devastation.

"She's upon her path ..." the words left Ean's tongue and whispered across his lips as though bled from them. He shifted tormented grey eyes away, red-rimmed and burning with too many emotions to name. "She's gone ... to him."

Sebastian reflected that this conversation might've been handled better, but they had no time. The *eidola* were nearly upon them.

"*Ean.*" He took his brother by the shoulders. "They're coming—can't you hear them? Can't you see them on the currents?" Sebastian was feeling the first real vestiges of panic. He searched his brother's gaze, trying to reach him through what seemed a veil of incurable despair. "*Ean*—don't make Isabel's sacrifice worth nothing!"

Ean stared at him, unseeing.

"*Ean!*" Sebastian cast it with a hint of compulsion, demanding Ean's attention to fix on him instead of on Isabel's loss.

His brother's gaze instantly focused. Instantly hardened. Then eased with understanding ... and split into a thousand shades of anguish. He dropped his head, pushed a hand roughly against Sebastian's shoulder and shoved past him on down the stairs.

Sebastian exchanged a look with Rhys. Then they set off after Ean.

Isabel watched Sebastian leading off into darkness. How strong he was! What honor he displayed as he embraced his new chance at life. Sebastian had reawakened beneath the dawn of her Healing, and all that had been pure in him had grown brighter and more vital.

The path she'd sown when Sebastian was newly waking had expanded into a wide trail. Sebastian would anchor Ean, while Isabel had unbalanced him. These brothers would find their path together.

Feeling hope for Ean, if none for herself, Isabel drew in a deep breath, let out a shuddering exhale, and turned and walked into the hall—

And directly into Dore's pattern lying in wait.

Eidola swarmed around her.

Black hands clutched at her.

Dark thoughts clung to her.

The currents ran as ink.

A cruel and familiar laugh rose above the sibilant *eidola* rattling, and Dore Madden pushed his way through the morass.

"*Oh ho*, I set a trap for a mouse and caught an eagle!" He thought he had her contained, which she let him believe. He spun a look back over his shoulder towards his master, the blinding star blocking all else from Isabel's view. "My lord—it is she, who I spoke to you about ..."

Dore continued his gloating words, but Isabel ... she saw only Darshan.

He towered over the *eidola*, over Dore—he would've towered over Arion had they ever met—and everywhere he walked, his will radiated forth like the sun's endless rays. Darshan worked compulsion as instinctively as Adepts worked their native strand. She saw this easily, though remaining unaffected by it took all of her skill.

Yet it fascinated her to see this being and study all that went into his innate construction ... to observe the way the currents simultaneously clung to him and flung outwards from him, the way his thoughts set them alternately trembling or glomming to him in great clouds of power. The currents were as helpless and malleable beneath his gaze as any living thing, all of whom he sought to dominate utterly.

Darshan would make all of creation submissive to him—bound beneath his steadfast, obdurate and inflexible will.

The sea of *eidola* parted to let him through.

Isabel urgently wrapped a shield around her thoughts—indeed, around her very *being*—closing off and concealing all but a thimble of the light that was uniquely her, like a lantern shielded but for a single slat that allowed some small glow to escape. Still, in the case of Isabel, this glow was not inconsiderable. She didn't yet know if this shielding would prove to her advantage or her ruin, but there was nothing more she could do to influence either eventuality.

"But where is your Arion?" Dore shoved his mouth against her ear. "Where? Where?"

She reminded herself that he thought he had her under his control and whispered, "Gone ... *escaped.*"

Dore stiffened beside her. "*No.*" The word emerged with his breath in a defiant gasp. Then he snarled. "*NO!*" He slung around and shouted at the *eidola.* "Find him! *Bring him back!*"

A slew of them streaked away down the hall.

Isabel cast forth the desperate thought, *Hurry, Sebastian. They're coming.* Then she dared think no more, for Darshan stood before her.

She felt his cold presence chilling her flesh, felt him exploring the pieces of her mind that she'd left glowing—a purposeful lure, that he might not delve more deeply. Even so, the touch of his mind scalded her, and his gaze ... he caressed her skin with darkness, with power, the lick of his eyes but a whisper. Any more than a whisper might've seared her from the ether.

He stood before her with skin as bronzed as the belt of metal that hung about his hips. Dark eyes watched beneath a wide forehead. His nose was long, straight, and like his brother's, slightly rounded at the end, but his chin was square, his cheekbones sharply contoured. A cascade of braids fell down his back. Darshan stood bare-chested, yet it was Isabel who felt naked beneath his gaze.

He lifted his hand and with long fingers traced the line of her jaw. Dore's pattern of binding she'd all but ignored. Darshan bound her with his gaze alone.

"You described her as formidable, Dore." He sounded amused.

At his resonant voice, the *eidola* quieted.

Darshan ran his finger beneath the curve of Isabel's chin. His touch sent chills racing down her spine, raised bumps upon her flesh, and made her heart quicken—in fear or aught else, she couldn't be certain. This man possessed a power that even she barely understood.

"But look at her …" He arched a brow as his fingers continued their gentle inspection of her face. "As fragile as a bird … and blind, it would seem."

"She wasn't blind in Tyr'kharta," Dore complained. His voice sounded like a whining child's next to Darshan's.

With his burning gaze holding her fast, Darshan cupped Isabel's head with both hands and ran his thumbs across the silk covering her eyes, lightly across her delicate lids. His power wrapped around her like a cloak, binding her to him, imparting to her *his* desire as if it were her own. Had he demanded anything of her in that moment, she wasn't certain she could've resisted him.

"No …" He released her face—allowing her at last to draw in a shuddering breath—but he left one hand resting on her shoulder, as if the continuing contact pleased him. "This woman poses no threat to me."

"But, my lord—"

"Do not trouble me with your petulance, Dore Madden." Darshan raised his voice but a fraction, yet his irritation thundered through the corridor.

"My lord, *my lord* …" Dore came nearly crawling back to him, head bowed and wringing his hands in a revolting display of obsequiousness. He licked his lips and turned a glare of hatred upon Isabel. "My lord, she deceives you—"

Darshan's eyes flashed, and his hand tightened on Isabel's shoulder. "*You forget your place.*" That time his voice boomed, Isabel's ears rang, and the currents seethed beneath his indignation.

Dore clasped hands and held them high above his bowed head, a placating gesture. "I mean only that she is … deceptive, my lord. She has power but … but she hides it. My lord—" he licked his lips and cast an urgent look towards the gallery. Then he dropped his voice and hissed, "She *murdered* your children."

Darshan frowned and looked back to Isabel. He took her chin and tilted her head back to better view her face, and his eyes examined her features while his mind explored her thoughts. She'd never felt so bare to anyone's inspection, nor so helpless to resist—

Nay … perhaps the will remained with her to resist—she was much stronger than she appeared—but she didn't dare try resisting just to prove to herself that she might. This was her path now. She had to walk it to know where it would lead.

"Hers is not the mind I felt," Darshan said after a moment of this intensely unsettling inspection. "But … defiance cannot go unpunished."

"*Yes* …" Dore sounded highly pleased. He rubbed his hands together, and his black eyes grew luminous.

Darshan's gaze narrowed. "Not by *you*, Dore Madden." The currents boiled with his displeasure. But when Darshan looked back to Isabel … oh, what menacing thought had brightened the depths of his gaze? It terrified her all the more for how deeply pleased he seemed by its ingenuity. "Yes." He smiled as he held her chin in his hand and her will in thrall. "I have a more fitting punishment in store …"

She felt his mind reach for hers, and she felt him ... felt him *closing* that tiny opening, the glow she'd allowed him to see, like shuttering the lamp ...

Ean ... forgive me!

The lantern closed.

Ean ... forgive me!

Ean stared, unseeing, as the thought impinged upon his consciousness—distant, faint, yet cast with such intention that he knew she'd meant for it to reach him across the world ... even across time itself.

In the next moment, he couldn't feel her at all.

Breath left him—nay, his heart simply stopped contracting, his lungs ceased expanding, thought ceased being.

A sharp pain daggered into his brain, demanding Ean's attention. He focused instantly on Sebastian, instantly furious, but then he understood why his brother had sought to impinge upon his thoughts. Still ... the crushing weight of loss was more than he could bear.

He pushed his brother out of his path and fled down the steps.

She couldn't be gone. She *couldn't* be—

No ... he could feel her still ...

Relief exploded with an intake of breath, shuddering and strained. But knowing she lived in no way lessened the abject fury that gripped him. Desperately he searched the bond to better sense her presence ... desperately he clung to its ephemeral glow, so fragile and wavering as to be nearly nonexistent. The flame that usually burned so brightly—even sometimes painfully—in his consciousness had been banked to its lowest ebb, mere coals darkened with ash.

But she lived. Until he understood more, it would have to be enough.

I am upon my path ...

Ean could almost hear Isabel saying those dreaded words. She'd been hinting at this moment for weeks. He'd known it was imminent. He'd just never imagined—he hadn't *let* himself imagine—it would actually happen.

Behind him, his brother cursed in pursuit of him—or else in flight from what pursued above, for they were all fleeing the torrential currents and the storm of *eidola* that drove them forth.

As they reached the tower's base, Ean flung open the door and bolted through, with Sebastian close and Rhys several paces behind.

"Ean—" Sebastian sounded desperate as he emerged into the corridor.

Ean silenced his brother with a look. He reached for Rhys and dragged the captain out of the tower. Then he narrowed his gaze and sent the fifth into the stones. Or ... perhaps it would've been truer to say he drew it *out* of the stones. Even as they watched, the walls began bleeding sand.

Ean grabbed Rhys' arm and hauled him away while spearing his brother with his gaze. "*Run!*"

They fled the crumbling tower and the avalanche that followed. Soon the corridor was filled with limestone dust and chalk, the fumes of dying walls. Ean summoned a pattern and let the currents guide him through dim light towards the node, but he hardly needed the currents to tell him what waited between themselves and freedom: A long corridor guarded by *eidola,* and a node chamber wall to wall with them.

"*Ean—*"

"I see them, Sebastian." Verily, the currents flowed like pitch with the blood of men made into monsters.

Ean kept a hand around Rhys' arm to help him along. The captain was huffing and wheezing, straining to keep apace. Isabel's staff clapped dully along the corridor stones with his uneven steps, an agonizing reminder of her absence.

Ean felt the *eidola* like a vein of cold water threading through a shallow pool, icy where warmth should've reigned; so did their presence flow along the currents of *elae*—not merely darkening them but depleting them of life, sucking warmth from the world as a Merdanti blade absorbed magic.

The wall of darkness at the end of the corridor broadened, and the currents roiled in response to the overwhelming numbers of the creatures that waited there. Their distant rattling hiss made the corridor seem an opening to a rattlesnake's den.

Reaching an intersecting corridor, Ean called a halt to let Rhys catch his breath if he could. Sebastian stopped and faced him, looking guilt-ridden. "Ean, I—"

"There's nothing to discuss, Sebastian." Verily, trying to *speak* of Isabel's absence would completely undo him.

Sebastian pressed, "I would've stopped her if I could—"

"Sebastian, I know." Ean looked to Rhys and then back to his brother. "We're getting out of here. I have an idea of how to do it."

Looking grim, Sebastian turned ahead and surveyed the wall of darkness lying across their path. "Your game, your rules, little brother," he muttered.

Ean clenched his jaw. Sebastian had it all wrong. This *wasn't* his game—he wanted no part in any game that took Isabel from him. And yet ... for all he wanted to shout this denial, he knew it would be a lie.

Though he'd thought of it as the First Lord's game, now Ean realized it had been *his* game, too—all along. *Their* game, the three of them. He could no more deny that than he could deny his love for Isabel.

Feeling as if the darkness at the end of the corridor was no match for what seethed in his soul, Ean set his gaze on the future. "Stay close." He set off at a run.

The hissing and rattling grew louder, the currents blacker, their pounding feet swifter. As they neared the *eidola,* Ean threw the fifth as a ribbon before them and forged a path over the monsters' heads.

Black hands reached for their feet as they ran on air thin of possibility and thick with an inhuman hunger. Stone bodies leapt and jumped and flung themselves to try to trip their running feet, to cling to them, stop them, drag them down into the black spume of that hell of Darshan's invention.

Ean held his sword like a shield before him and poured the fifth off of it, keeping the path clear ahead, while Sebastian flayed his blade left and right and the captain made a bludgeon of Isabel's staff. The dull clap of stone against stone became a constant assault on Ean's heart, shouting in an elemental tongue, *Isabel ... Isabel ... Isabel ...*

The corridor broadened, opened, and they reached the node chamber at last—a vast, columned hall with a rib-vaulted ceiling bathed in the cool light of wielder's lamps. And beneath, a floor seething with *eidola.*

Ean's head throbbed in a painful chorus to the pounding of Isabel's staff, while his body felt thin ... drained of life, drained by fear for Isabel, by the sensation of their separation ... yet he dared not stop. Momentum alone carried them forward now.

But the moment they emerged into the chamber, thunder without sound exploded. Ean caught the brunt of the force on his blade and simultaneously wrapped that ribbon of the fifth around himself and his companions, but he couldn't arrest their fall beneath the concussion. They tumbled, rolled, barreled through *eidola* to come to a halt near the center of the chamber.

Ean threw up a new shield and made it solid as he climbed over writhing *eidola* to reach his brother. The prince ripped the binding pattern out of every creature he touched along the way, so that by the time he gained Rhys' and Sebastian's sides, only the three of them remained alive inside his shell of air. The world felt eerily silent.

Utterly exhausted of heart and mind, Ean collapsed beside his brother and rested his head on Sebastian's chest, feeling threadbare. The shield which he held in place blocked all force, all sound, yet Ean *felt* the army of creatures battering wildly against it.

"Ean, are you ... ?" Sebastian placed a hand on Ean's head as he sat up.

Ean slowly pushed himself up as well. "I'm all right," but he felt far from all right. He felt shattered, abandoned. Desolate.

Sebastian exhaled an oath and looked around. *Eidola* amassed beyond Ean's dome, piling upon it like rats, but not even a whisper of their sibilant chorus reached their ears. "*How* are you doing this?"

Ean pushed palms to his throbbing forehead. "I don't know."

But he did know—after a fashion.

'*Arion was my brother's closest friend. Björn confided in him, taught him things no one else knows ... '*

Light flared against the shield and spread in a web of violet-silver. Ean felt it searing into his consciousness like Rinokh's thumb pressing again to his flesh. He staggered to his feet. Time was running out.

Sebastian jumped up after him and took his arm. "How long can you hold it?"

Ean clenched his jaw. Already he was having difficulty focusing his eyes. "Not much longer."

His brother squeezed his arm in reassurance. "We're close, Ean. We can make it."

Ean turned him a desperate look. "How?" He clutched his brother's shoulder in return, feeling like he could barely stand. "I don't ... when this shield falls, I can't ..."

Sebastian's gaze conveyed his understanding. "You still have to get us across the node."

Grimly, Ean bowed his head and pressed his forehead against his brother's shoulder. He feared if he worked any more of the lifeforce, he wouldn't be able to withstand the force of the Pattern of the World raging through him.

"If His Highness can't work his magic, then we do it the hard way."

Ean lifted his head with effort to look at Rhys. The captain was getting to his feet, leaning heavily on Isabel's staff. His face looked pale and drawn, and he was drenched in sweat. That he found his feet at all seemed a fair miracle to Ean. Isabel must've had something to do with his recovery.

Sebastian wrapped an arm around Ean's shoulder, sensing his equal waning of strength. "What's your idea, Captain?"

Rhys ran his eyes along the dark staff in his hands. "The lady said to use it against anything that stood in our path."

Ean cracked a threadbare smile. Ever Isabel was looking out for him. He forced back a welling sense of frustration ... forced his body straight, though he felt like the entire mountain was squatting on his shoulders. "Then that's what we'll do."

Deyjiin flared again, webbing across Ean's dome. He sucked in his breath with a hiss. Every time that power touched his mind he felt it dissolving his hold on *elae*.

They made haste to arrange themselves in a row with Ean in the center and Isabel's staff held horizontally before them, and they aligned their direction towards the center of the room and the node.

Ean gripped the staff with both hands and clenched his teeth. "I'll hold the shield as long as I dare."

Sebastian cast him an encouraging look. "I'll be right beside you, little brother. Ready, Captain?"

Rhys grunted.

And so they went.

Ean managed barely five steps into their dash before his shield gave way beneath another blast of *deyjiin,* but Sebastian threw up a shield of the fifth as Ean had taught him and they kept moving.

Ean had never known such gratitude for his brother as what he felt in that moment. *Right beside me, indeed.*

With Isabel's staff as battering ram clearing the way ahead, and their desperation pushing from behind, their mad rush to the node became less a flight to safety than the trampling force of a cavalry charge. *Eidola* fell, scattered by Sebastian's working and Isabel's staff, and then the node was before them—likewise the *eidola* who had been wielding *deyjiin.*

Three things happened at once:

Rhys cried out and staggered to his knees.

The *eidola* in front of them threw another bolt of *deyjiin.*

And Ean grabbed both of their arms and dove onto the node.

The Pattern of the World sucked him into its rushing embrace. Holding tightly to his precious cargo, Ean swam the current back the way they'd come, trusting—praying—that they both had hold of him in turn. For he sensed nothing but light, felt nothing but the raging, ripping *force,* saw nothing but the channels upon which he swam to bring them back to—

Kandori.

They landed in a heap in the tiled courtyard, which lay silent beneath the moon's luminous kiss.

Ean moaned.

Sebastian groaned.

Rhys made a choking sound that thrust Ean's heart into his throat.

He surged free of the tangle and reached for Rhys. The captain lay on his side with the hilt of a knife extending from his back.

Ean let out an anguished cry.

Dareios! He cast forth the thought with desperation, with every ounce of the fourth he could put behind it. *Help us!*

Then he moved to cradle Rhys' head in his lap. To have gone to such lengths to rescue him only to lose him now felt like being unmade all over again. He stroked Rhys' hair back from his face. "Hold on, Rhys … help is coming."

Sebastian set down Isabel's staff and looked over the captain's wound. His eyes, lifting to meet Ean's, revealed the truth.

Rhys gazed up beneath a labored brow to focus on Ean. "Your Highness …" The gruffly managed epithet held no rancor, no judgment, only sorrow. And perhaps a hint of Rhys' usual reverence that now weighed upon Ean's conscience like a ship dragging anchor.

"*Rhys* …" Ean took the captain's hand in his. "Help is—"

"Don't waste it … on me." The captain's gaze shifted to Sebastian … and a smile split across his wasted face. For a moment he gazed at the two princes, and then a look came into his eyes. Ean almost thought … it seemed amazingly like … *pride.*

"Knew you'd do it." Rhys shifted his gaze back to Ean, full of candid admiration. "… knew you'd find him … save him."

Ean turned Sebastian a swift look.

"... had to," Rhys gasped. Conviction alone must've fueled his breath. "He was ... your brother."

"*Captain* ..." Sebastian's face was tormented with apology.

Rhys shifted his eyes to him. "In Tyr'kharta ... lost my honor when I denied you. I couldn't believe it ... didn't want to. I failed you ... all three of you."

Though he didn't know what had transpired between Rhys and Sebastian in Tyr'kharta, Ean felt Sebastian's guilt resonating with his own.

"Later ... I knew ..." Rhys looked back to Ean. "When you didn't come for us ... the wielder's trap ..." His smile showed teeth stained with blood. "... knew you'd found your brother ... that you would save him."

Ean bit his lip, eyes welling. How could he have chosen any other way? Yet facing the very real and devastating consequences of that choice was agony.

Beside him, Sebastian opened his mouth to speak, but Rhys silenced him with a lift of trembling fingers. "It's right ... it's what ... His Majesty would've wanted." He gave his princes another pained smile that conveyed so readily his relief in seeing them together. "His *sons ... restored*—" He choked suddenly, and fell into a fit of coughing.

Ean gritted his teeth and dropped his chin to his chest. He'd abandoned Rhys and his men to a horrifying end; yet through it all, Rhys had lost not an ounce of respect for him. Ean didn't deserve the captain's esteem.

Then a sudden host of others were descending upon them in the night, a flurry of hands and low, urgent voices and whispering silks. Ehsan drew Sebastian off while Dareios and Bahman had to physically pull Ean from Rhys' side to let the Healers see to him.

With unshed tears burning his eyes, Ean looked to the sky in accusation, searching the night's stars for Cephrael's Hand—expecting, as it so often was, for the constellation to be shining down on his agony.

Yet the sky stood empty. As he hung his head and sucked in a shuddering breath, Ean knew then that these tragedies weren't Fate's doing—only his own.

FIFTY

"If the beard were all, the goat might preach."

–A popular Kandori saying

THE WIELDER VIERNAN hal'Jaitar stood on a balcony overlooking
the Shamshir'im torture chamber where the sailor Hafiz was being
readied for questioning. In that they were readying him with batons and
knuckles, and that this process had been going on for the better part of an hour,
Hafiz's answers were coming faster but far less coherently.

Viernan admitted the efficiency of truthreaders in these situations ... except
that truthreaders in *these* situations couldn't be trusted. Something happened
when you made fourth strand Adepts into inquisitors. They lost their moral
compass. The very quality you'd chosen them for—that inability to tell a lie—
somehow underwent a corruptive metamorphosis, which quite defeated the
purpose of using them at all. Then you were simply stuck with an Adept who
could read minds and had few compunctions about selling what they 'overheard'
to the highest bidder.

Thrace Weyland was such a one.

Thrace Weyland.

The Consul raised his lip in a sneer. He might've called Thrace by any one
of his many names—Mayanar Galandan, Joreth Wren, or the name by which
Viernan knew him best, Esfandiar Lahijani. *Oh,* if Viernan ever got his hands on
Esfandiar ... but the man was too smart to show his true face and far too adept
at hiding it.

A viperous rattle behind him alerted Viernan that the Prophet's creatures
had come to pry into his business. Bethamin had given them as 'gifts' to Radov,
but the Prophet's gifts were always poisoned sugar. Like the gift of absinthe from
Queen Indora of Veneisea, which had completely usurped his prince's will. Like

the 'gift' of the Prophet's blessing kiss that seemed to have claimed Radov's sanity in the giving so long ago.

Would that Viernan could give any of these gifts back—along with a few 'gifts' of his own.

Viernan cast the *eidola* a mordant eye. Ever the demonspawn followed him about, spying for their master and reporting to Bethamin on everything they saw and heard in the shadows of Tal'Shira. They lived inside Viernan's privacy like parasites under his skin. He couldn't step from his chambers without finding one of them watching his door—watching *him*. They never slept, never ate ... but my ... what he'd seen them *do*.

After observing a demonstration of one of the creatures against twenty of Radov's Talien Knights, hal'Jaitar no longer harbored questions as to what had become of his wielder, Kedar, and the company sent out with the King of Dannym. Kjieran van Stone *might* have eliminated them all by brute strength—but certainly his master's power would have accomplished the deed.

Luckily, few of the *eidola* worked this power. The creature called Tagn told him that the Prophet misliked too many of his offspring touching his power and that its investiture required a different pattern of binding. But Tagn worked it; likewise his silent partner.

The part of Viernan that desired retribution against the Akkad took this knowledge and basked with glee in its icy heat, but the better part of reason warned that a host of creatures with massive power and a miniscule sense of morality would only wreak havoc on their way to catastrophe.

The Prophet claimed to be Radov's ally—though Viernan had little doubt that as soon as their mutual usefulness had been expended, their alliance would evaporate like a drop of water on the desert sand. And after the Akkad and Dannym had fallen to his will, what if Bethamin decided to turn his aims against M'Nador? Who would stand up to an army of such *eidola* when mortal men could not?

"... Thrace ... Weyland ..."

The gasped words from the sailor Hafiz snared the Consul's ears and riveted his attention back to the chamber floor. He grabbed the railing and leaned forward. "*What* did he say?"

The black-robed interrogator lifted dark eyes to his master. His gaze spoke volumes. "He said he sold information about the prince to Thrace Weyland."

If a snake existed that could spit venom from its eyes, Viernan hal'Jaitar would've been it.

The *eidola* Tagn came up next to hal'Jaitar, forcing the Consul to swallow his natural revulsion, lest the urge to destroy such an abomination should overwhelm his reason.

"What does he mean?" Tagn's voice rattled like a pit viper's tail. "Who is this Thrace Weyland?"

Fury smoldered in Viernan's dark eyes. *A perpetual thorn in my side.* "Weyland is a purveyor of information—the worst sort."

"What is the worst sort?"

Viernan turned to him. "The kind who knows everyone."

"Why does this concern you?"

Hal'Jaitar looked the creature over vexedly. "The prince has powerful friends. We have reason to believe they may attempt a rescue."

The two *eidola* exchanged a look, and then Tagn fixed his inhuman black eyes on hal'Jaitar again. The Consul felt as if he stared into the dead eyes of a man-sized scorpion poised to sting.

"Our master was displeased to learn Trell val Lorian survived the attempt on his life five years ago. He would be even less pleased to find the prince walking free now."

How little you understand of it. Viernan looked back to the prisoner below. Taliah had sent word that she would like the sailor to be given to her once they'd finished their interrogation. Hal'Jaitar was of a mind to do it—better that all threads connecting to Trell val Lorian traced to Taliah.

"Where are you holding him?" Tagn clattered.

Viernan spun his head sharply. Why was this creature suddenly so interested in the val Lorian prince? He straightened and looked the *eidola* over, scouring it with his gaze. He'd seen these *eidola* kill and maim, but were such creatures capable of guile? For the first time it occurred to Viernan to wonder if they had some agenda beyond spying on him for the Prophet.

"What kind of a name is Tagn?"

"Our master renames each of us upon our rebirth. Tagn means claw."

The Consul grunted. *Fitting.* He looked back to the prisoner Hafiz below. "What's your interest in Trell val Lorian?"

"You've chosen not to kill the prince, despite my master's wishes. He would know then that Trell val Lorian is at least safely contained, Consul."

Viernan considered the creature suspiciously. "He's being held at Darroyhan."

"Perhaps more forces should be sent there."

Viernan's eyes narrowed. This creature was definitely trying to manipulate him. Well ... he would play along. Perhaps it would slay Trell and rid Viernan of the problem altogether.

"Yes ..." he drew out the word as though considering the possibilities. "Perhaps reinforcements should be sent. Perhaps you both should go with them."

Tagn exchanged another look with his silent twin. "We would not want to leave you unprotected."

Oh, how cunning it thought itself. Couldn't it see he could read it like a page in a child's picture book?

"When Cephrael's eye crosses these lands, Tagn, creature of Shadow, His gaze moves quickly on." He hoped it remained true. Fate's attention had never lingered long on Tal'Shira. More reasons to keep Trell val Lorian far away.

The Consul eyed Tagn speculatively. "If your master wishes to help us, let him lend his strongest resources to protect our most important prisoner."

Tagn bowed his agreement. "I submit to this wisdom."

Of course you do.

Tagn turned to go.

"Out of curiosity ..." hal'Jaitar's words halted the *eidola*, who looked over its shoulder. "How do you think you'd fare against a Sundragon?"

Tagn's black lips spread in a slow smile, and a violet-silver sheen crackled across the razor nubs of its stone teeth. Then both creatures blessedly departed.

FIFTY-ONE

"Grab luck by the balls when you can. Fortune has

a fickle heart and a short memory."

–The pirate Carian vran Lea

A MAN'S SCREAMS WOKE Trell in the night. He lay in bed listening, then not listening, *trying* not to listen, and finally hearing nothing else. When he could stand it no more, he threw off the sheet and stalked to his door, but the latch felt stiff beneath his fingers. So ... Taliah had locked him in. She wanted him to hear the stranger's suffering.

Very well.

Trell went to the windows and threw them open. Then he sat on the sill, laid his head back against the wood casing and closed his eyes.

He was still sitting there when his door opened shortly after dawn. The screaming had stopped perhaps ten minutes prior, so he knew it had to be Taliah come to see how well he'd endured the dark music of her night's performance. She came inside and closed the door behind her.

"Enjoying the fresh air, Prince of Dannym?"

He spared her a sideways glance, noting her approach. "Not as much as I would enjoy it elsewhere."

She came and stood beside him and ran her fingers along his bare chest. "Submit to me, and I'll bring you ecstasy like you've never known." Her hand slipped to his groin and her mouth to his ear. "Everything I know of pain, I know equally of pleasure. Both lie on the path of *mor'alir*."

His eyes went to her hand clutching him and flicked dismissively away. "All your talk of *mor'alir* stinks to me like specious justification."

She took a step back and stared at him in evident frustration. Then she turned and caught her thumb between her teeth. "I admit ... I expected to have gained your submission by now. This far into your brother's captivity, I had broken him."

Trell's heart went still, making his ears ring with silence. "What did you say?"

"Your brother Sebastian." She cast a little frown over her shoulder. "Before my father sent him to the salt mines of N'ghorra, he gave him to me to question. Like you, he'd proven remarkably resilient to conventional torture. Perhaps it's something in your val Lorian blood." She plucked at her teeth with her thumbnail. "I would need another of your brothers—or your father—to test the theory. Alas, your father vanished while in transit to the parley with the Emir. Dead, we fear."

Trell clenched his jaw and let out a slow exhale. Today she wielded words as weapons. "What do you want, Taliah?"

She spun to him, eyes hot. "You know what I want, Trell val Lorian. Your submission!"

"I told you in the beginning I would give you nothing freely."

"But that was before we began down the path of *mor'alir* together." She sounded almost petulant.

He grunted and shook his head and refused to look at her.

"I've given you many freedoms—too many, I think now." Taliah's tone boiled with malcontent. "Perhaps you would prefer I locked you in Darroyhan's dungeons, into darkness?"

"If memory serves, your father tried that already."

In the stormy silence that followed, he could nearly hear the convoluted cogs of her mind grinding and twisting. Then she spun and stormed from the room, slamming the door in her wake. Not much later, the nameless man started screaming again.

The day passed in this fashion.

The sun baked the stones and heated the air, and the man screamed. Trell drank all of the water in his pitcher, and the man screamed. The sea went from mercuric to azure to a gilded, ashen orange, and the man screamed. The worst part for Trell in all of the day was in recognizing how closely the man's screams mirrored his own, as if Taliah's techniques followed a sequence, enticing a dark melody that made cadence of a man's screams and built them into percussive crescendos.

Trell sat in the window and listened to the pitiful man and wondered if Taliah had really tortured his own body for so many unending hours.

After a certain point, the time and the pain had blended together. But hearing this man's hoarse screams all the night and day, and knowing she'd likely worked him personally the same way … it brought a renewed horror to those otherwise disjointed memories.

A lesser man might've heard the stranger's agonized howls and feared for himself, for his future … but Taliah's cruelty only hardened Trell's resolve. It proved to him that she didn't understand the most important elements of him, and that she'd spent too much time learning and practicing her black music to the screams of lesser men.

The sun fell and Cephrael's Hand rose in the west. Trell watched the Nadoriin manning Darroyhan's towers and walking its battlements and wondered why there seemed to be twice as many as before. His gaze followed one line of guards to the nearest tower, where two men stood in black silhouette. For some reason, their presence made the night seem darker.

Trell left the window and lay down on his bed. He clasped hands behind his head and watched Cephrael's constellation travel its slow, logic-defying arc. He was wondering how many of the stories about it were true when his door flew open and crashed into the wall.

The mute crossed the room, grabbed Trell out of his repose and dragged him off. He stumbled along willingly enough beside the giant man, who held his arm higher than was needed or comfortable, but when he saw where they were heading, his feet turned leaden.

The mute hauled him into the chamber and shoved him forward hard enough that he landed on hands and knees at Taliah's feet.

The room's high windows had been opened to admit the sea breeze, but it still stank of sweat and excrement and the peculiar tang of fear. Trell got slowly to his feet, brushed himself off and cast a wary gaze at the man lying naked, chained to the marble table. Just seeing the man made his own shoulders ache. He'd spent many tormented days in the same position, with those chains holding his joints just shy of popping out of socket. He pitied the man until he recognized him.

Then he knew only a churning anger.

Taliah went to stand behind the man's head and stroked his damp hair. He whimpered.

"Do you remember him, Trell?" She turned inquiringly. "Did I not tell you that you'd brought death upon two men with your carelessness? Hafiz seeks death now, I promise you." She kissed the sailor softly on his forehead. "Don't you, Hafiz?"

He whimpered again.

Taliah lifted her gaze to Trell. "There is a dagger," and a flick of her eyes indicated a slender knife lying at the table's edge. "Take it up. End his suffering."

Trell eyed the blade. He could end all of their suffering if he merely used the dagger on Taliah, but the mute stood beside her ready to protect her with his life.

Taliah stroked the sailor's head again, and he let out a low moan.

Trell frowned. Where was the trick in this?

"It was you who doomed Hafiz with your carelessness. Can you not find compassion for him? Have you not heard his screams?"

Trell looked from Taliah back to the sailor and frowned. He had to be missing something. This woman wouldn't know compassion if it stood nose to nose with her, shouting its own name.

Taliah stroked the sailor's forehead with her thumbs. "Such suffering. Will you not show him mercy? Wouldn't you want someone to do the same for you?"

And there it was.

He *had* wished for death many times when Taliah had been at him for countless hours—days … weeks. But he'd never wanted it truly. Not in the depths of his soul. Only in protest of enduring an agony beyond measuring.

A man might truly kill for mercy under certain circumstances, but if Trell took Hafiz's life now, he would be denying the sailor the right to make that choice himself.

Perhaps Hafiz sought death, as Taliah claimed, but Trell had been upon that same table, and even after all he'd endured, if a man had come at him with a dagger, he would've fought against him with every ounce of his will.

He took a step away from the table. "No."

Taliah's eyes flashed. "*Damn you*, Trell!" She threw out her hand in rage, and pain struck him everywhere at once.

He collapsed to the floor and curled reflexively into a ball, but the pain only intensified, so his body forced his legs compulsively away. He curled and extended then in rapid jerks, pulsing to the frenzied waves of her anger.

While Trell writhed in soundless agony, Taliah pushed her hand over Hafiz's forehead and concentrated. Then she ripped her hand away.

Hafiz roared. His back arched with the crescendo of his howl, legs and arms pulling against the chains until his joints distended, until his flesh became purple beneath the strain. Then he fell back against the table, dead.

"Put Trell on it," Taliah hissed.

Blinded with pain, Trell hardly noticed when the mute picked him up. Nor could he find the focus to struggle as the man forced him spread-eagle and chained his wrists and ankles. But he knew it when Taliah mounted him.

Laying hands against his bare chest, she spun her power to send heat into his groin and pump his heart and loins. Then she sheathed his erection inside herself. This always heralded the worst of her torments, for through this bond of body and mind she could bring him pain in impossible, inconceivable ways.

Which she proceeded to do with meticulous deliberation.

The sea of pain that crashed over Trell should have brought unconsciousness, but Taliah trapped his awareness so that oblivion couldn't claim him, so that he lay pinned against the floor of her will while waves of agony pummeled him.

How long this continued, he didn't know. Time excused itself to other diversions while Taliah assuaged her frustration via torment and misery. But when at last he surfaced from beneath that pounding, torturous surf, he found her face hovering close and her breath hot upon his parched lips.

"What do you live for, Trell?" She planted a kiss on his mouth, forced his teeth apart, and sent her tongue probing within. Her lips were cold, her mouth wet. It felt like Death kissing him.

She ran a finger along his cheek, and fire traced the line of it. "What do you live for?" Her thighs tightened, and her insides clenched around his shaft. Lightning speared through his veins. "What could you possibly have to live for?"

As the whips of Taliah's aggravation lashed him, welts appeared on his skin.

He sought oblivion, but she grabbed his chin and commanded him back. "Too quickly you seek to succumb to my pain." Her teeth were clenched as tightly as the muscles between her legs. "But not today. Today I will have an answer."

Where her fingers held his jaw, his gums began to bleed. He tasted the metallic tang ... welcomed it. Anything to mask the taste of her.

"Tell me!" She shook his head back and forth, making even his ears ache. "Why do you fight me so? What's the source of this contrary and dogged indomitability?"

Trell could barely find breath. The surface seemed so far and the water so murky. He managed, half expecting bubbles to appear before his burning eyes, "... honor."

"*Honor.*" She made the word sound a curse and drew back from him. "Always it's *honor* with you." She grabbed his jaw again in a painful grip. "You lie to me. How can such buoy you on the tides of *my* pain?"

Perhaps because she wanted an answer, the tide of pain ebbed enough that thought returned. He maneuvered his chin free of her and spat the blood from his mouth. "Taliah ..." He focused his gaze coldly upon her. "I cannot explain honor to someone who has none."

"Honor is a *word*," she hissed.

"Yet I'm whole because of it." He held her gaze with his own like hardened steel. "You're a fractured blade. You have no hope of splitting me."

Taliah gasped.

The fury that flooded into her expression couldn't be described, only experienced. And *oh*, how she made Trell experience it—long and arduously. She shattered a bone in his arm with a single thought, and another in his leg while he still screamed from the first. But her wrath knew no bounds that night, nor was there any boundary to the torment she wreaked upon him. Parts of him bled and others split, and she didn't stop until she was certain no man could look upon his body and call him whole.

When Trell at last escaped into unconsciousness, Taliah let out a scream of rage that quickly devolved into tortured, gasping sobs. "*Get out!*" she screamed at the mute, but then she turned wet eyes back to Trell and cared not what the giant saw or thought.

As the mute shut the door behind his exit, she pounded her fists against

Trell's chest and fell across him. She ripped her dress from her shoulders, pressed her small breasts against his form and clung to his neck and wept.

He was right.

He would never break beneath her. He would never look upon her with loyalty and adoration forged through pain. He would never seek her approval, desire her desperately, or give himself to pleasure her.

Taliah cried because she could no longer avoid the truth. She hadn't broken Trell; he had broken her. He'd won. She loved him desperately, and he despised her with every fiber of his being.

Wait …

Taliah sat up and wiped her eyes, smearing Trell's blood across her face.

There was a way.

It lay not upon the path of *mor'alir*—even *mor'alir* Adepts viewed compulsory bindings with disdain. But this wouldn't be a bond of compulsion. Rather … well, it *was* a bond, and unwillingly administered. The Sorceresy might curse her for it—*he* would certainly curse her for it—but as Trell found that he couldn't live without her, so he might come to accept her … in time. And in the end … perhaps he would even come to love her.

It was kinder than compulsion. The Sorceresy would forgive her once they understood, even if Trell never would. But his forgiveness didn't matter when he would be hers forever. Much could change during the slowly turning wheel of eternity.

Taliah placed her fingers on Trell's mouth and parted his lips gently. Then she held his face and kissed him. Her tongue captured his while her body clenched his shaft deep inside, and she sought his life pattern along the strands of the first.

Even after she had attacked it so angrily, still it glowed. She'd never seen a man with such vibrant life shining within. He seemed a god to her, so like perfection. It only followed that loving such a man would leave scalding wounds that never healed.

To his pattern she attached a first strand thread of bonding—a simple thing and easily cut if one knew to look for it, but no one would look for it. She attached the other end of this thread to her own life pattern, something all *mor'alir* Adepts were taught to find.

There.

It was done.

Yet … somehow even knowing Trell's life was now affixed to hers didn't allay the ache in her heart. Another sob escaped her, and Taliah climbed off his unconscious form. She laid a hand on his broken thigh and thought about Healing him. But then she decided a few days of suffering were in order—at least as long as she suffered for loving him. Yes, at least that long.

FIFTY-TWO

"There is no limit to what he can know."

— Náeb'nabdurin'náiir, Chaser of the Dawn,

on Björn van Gelderan

A WAVE OF RELIEF washed over the Alorin Seat Alshiba Torinin as she
entered her apartments in Illume Belliel. It had been a difficult day. Her
steward, Harryl, and two servants carrying armfuls of books followed
inside behind her. Harryl led them into her study to show them where to set
down their burdens. She didn't envy him the task of finding an open space.

Since Raine had spoken to her of Malorin'athgul many moons ago, Alshiba
had used every minute when the Council of Realms was out of session to learn
about those dark creatures. The cityworld's Archives—meticulously catalogued
and maintained—were supposed to hold copies of every important work from
the thousand realms, but even in this vast library, she'd found few mentions of
Malorin'athgul beyond legend and myth, even among the works of so many
varied worlds.

When Alshiba had first come to Illume Belliel long ago, she'd been surprised
to discover so many races with incredibly disparate histories and beliefs. The
diversity of belief had especially frightened her, for in her young naivety, she'd
thought that everyone knew the *angiel* Cephrael and Epiphany and that all
must surely follow the *Sobra I'ternin,* even as Alorin did.

Yet as the years had spun on and Alshiba had grown in understanding and
experience, she'd come to see that no matter how varied, nearly all beliefs shared
some common threads, as if somehow … somehow the same gods truly had
made all of the realms, leaving a trace of the story of their divinity passed on in
stone, parchment or oral tradition.

The other realms had different names for Cephrael and Epiphany, for
the one the people of Alorin called the Maker, and even for the strands of

elae—albeit every realm that joined the Council was required to agree to a codification of the strands for ease of communication among the Seats—but once she'd been willing to look past names, Alshiba had found the same core truths represented across the worlds.

Of Malorin'athgul, however ...

She was finding the task more daunting than she'd imagined. Alorin's own *Sobra I'ternin* spoke of these Unmakers, primarily in the *Qhorith'quitara*—an excerpted collection of writings considered too dangerous for mass public knowledge. These apocryphal volumes were not to be found in Illume Belliel's Archives—though they were certainly of immense importance—but were locked away in the vault of the Empress of Agasan.

This fact made her wonder what other valued works from other realms were also locked away in their own private vaults, perhaps considered too dangerous to share.

This idea troubled Alshiba immensely. She believed now that the Malorin'athgul were a true threat—though she had only the word of two men saying so. Yet Franco had been genuine in pledging his troth, and Raine would never lie to her.

Moreover, such a cataclysmic threat made sense of Björn's betrayal.

Well ... if it didn't truly make sense of it, at least it offered the faintest flicker of candlelight by which to inspect the Fifth Vestal's actions. Even this spark was preferable to the darkness she'd dwelled in for three centuries.

But where were the records that spoke of Malorin'athgul? It seemed unconscionable to her that someone would have knowledge of beings of such godlike power and not share this knowledge with other worlds.

Yet ... Alshiba was just as culpable as the rest. At any point she might've called for copies of Alorin's *Qhorith'quitara* to be brought to Illume Belliel, but she never had. Why? Because she feared they were safer where they were.

All of the realms must've been doing the same—keeping their most feared texts 'safe' in their own vaults.

And of the threat the Malorin'athgul posed?

Could the realms really fall to these ancient and volatile beings simply because everyone who knew of their existence was scared to say their names openly, too afraid to trust others with the knowledge for fear of the few who would find this information and try to use it to destroy? Yet not offering the knowledge broadly meant the creatures were free to do that very thing, and without a hint of awareness from those who might stop them—unmaking the world right beneath their noses.

That this indeed was Alorin's plight seemed tragically all too probable to her.

And that Björn had foreseen it from the beginning ... well, she didn't bother even questioning this truth.

None of this explained why he'd made T'khendar, slaughtered the Hundred

Mages—his own sister among them!—and ripped Tiern'aval from the world. It didn't explain why he'd allowed Malachai in his madness to nearly destroy their race, or why he now prevented three Vestals—himself included—from returning to the realm they were sworn to protect.

And it didn't explain why he hadn't trusted her with the truth all along.

But the candlelight which the explanation of Malorin'athgul shed did make it a little harder to hate him in the darkness of her thoughts.

"My lady, is there anything else?" Her steward exited the study and waved the servants out of her drawing room.

She realized she was still standing just inside the door. "No." She smiled. "Thank you, Harryl."

He nodded and left, closing the door behind him.

Alshiba took a deep breath and let it out slowly. Her eyes scanned her drawing room and the books and scrolls piled everywhere. Björn's once-immaculate apartments now resembled a scribe's back room.

Walking into her study and over to the sideboard, she poured a glass of wine and raised it—

"I like what you've done with the place."

Alshiba dropped her glass and spun with a gasp. The glass shattered against the marble floor, but nowhere near as badly as her composure. She stumbled into the sideboard while her other hand reached for the wall and she ended up somewhat crammed in the corner, wedged between shock and disbelief.

"This—*you!*—"

"This, me," he agreed with a smile.

Impossible! Impossible! cried her mind. *He's come! He's come!* shouted her heart. *Call the guard, you ridiculous woman!* screamed all logic.

And there he stood as though not a day had passed. His blue eyes were just as sparkling, his dark curls just as glorious, his smile every bit as devastating. What traitor had any right to be so handsome?

"*Björn*—" She couldn't tell if she'd said his name as a cry, a scream, a gasp or some embarrassing combination of all of them. "*How*—?" but she didn't bother asking how he'd found his way into her apartments. He might've walked right in through her front door, for she'd never changed the trace seal he originally put there. Not that a trace seal would've stopped him.

His cobalt blue eyes looked her over, but the smile never left them.

Oh, to truly look upon his face again! To know this moment wasn't just another spectral visit, a dream that would leave her heart shattered and agonizing anew.

In all their years apart ... through outrage and fury and the agony of his unconscionable and inconceivable betrayal ... for *eons* she'd tried to stop loving him, only to know in that moment that all of her efforts had been a foolish and fruitless waste. If only she could've *believed* the things she and Raine had made up.

Yet ... how *dare* he come to her like this! After she'd endured so much in his name. After so long? She wished she hadn't dropped her glass, that she might've thrown it at him.

Instead she reached a trembling hand and poured another. As she watched the sanguineous liquid filling the crystal, she tried to find breath enough to speak like a natural person. Her heart was a painful lump in her chest. It couldn't decide whether to beat again with joy or to quit altogether and free her from this excruciating moment. "I would that Cephrael had banished you through thirteen hells, Björn."

He leaned against the mullioned glass doors and crossed his arms. "That would be an interesting trick."

She glared at him over her shoulder. "It would be a kinder fate than you deserve."

"For hurting you? Unquestionably."

Alshiba slammed both hands on the sideboard. "Don't!" Couldn't he see her heart was breaking all over again? Damn him, of course he could. She clenched her teeth and stared at her glass and hissed, "You've *no* right—"

"To apologize for the pain I caused you?" He straightened and came across the room. "To explain why I abandoned you?" He reached her side, though she dared not look at him. His lips brushed her ear as he bent close. "To say how sorry I am that I saw no other way?"

Alshiba wanted to scream. Instead, she spun with a hand raised to strike.

He caught her wrist and pulled her into his arms.

"Stop!" She struggled, but he would've been stronger than her even without the fifth pouring into him. "Let me *go!*"

He held her gently but firmly.

"Three hundred years!" She slammed her fists against his chest. She might've fought stone for all the harm it did. "You can't just come to me after *three hundred years!*"

He pressed his cheek against her head, smelled her hair, trailed his lips down her neck. She felt his own ache in these actions, his own longing. She thought she would shatter into a thousand pieces.

"If I could give us back those years, Alshiba, I would." His voice came low in her ear, husky ... desirous.

"*Please.*" She stopped struggling and laid her forehead against his chest. Desperation held her far more tightly than his arms. "Please ... let me go."

His arms fell away, but he made no move to bring distance between them.

She closed her eyes and tried to breathe through the thousand emotions making a battleground of her heart. Surely her ribcage would at any moment burst from the pressure.

The cloth of his coat felt soft against her forehead. He'd always had the most exquisite taste ... so odd the thoughts that flashed to mind when your life seemed at its precipitous end. "Have you come to finish me?" she whispered.

He stroked her hair. "I've come to ask your forgiveness."

She wanted to pull away, but fear rooted her for that second's pause, the thought that this might be the last time she ever stood completely lost in his arms ... that she might never again know his love. Then she closed her heart and took a step away. "You can't have it."

She turned her back on him and retrieved her wine. It was truly appalling how badly her hands were shaking. She needed both of them to lift the goblet.

He came and laid hands on her shoulders. His lips found her neck again. "Do you think you suffered alone?"

She jerked free of him. "Don't talk to me of suffering." Her feet carried her across the room towards a chair, but her body balked at sitting. The idea of being still made her want to scream.

He poured himself some wine—damn him for having such steady hands!—and turned her one of his elusive smiles ... the kind that simultaneously melted and infuriated her—mostly infuriated because it melted.

She eyed him over the rim of her own goblet and conceived of a number of patterns she might've used to help his contrition along. But he stood shielded in the fifth—of course he did. He knew her well enough to know he wouldn't be safe in her company, not while she thought him a traitor ... and not even thereafter—assuming she ever changed her mind, which she saw no reason to do at the moment.

Unlike her, Björn seated himself comfortably with his typical grace. She wanted to strangle him. Instead, she said, "Return my Vestals unharmed and I'll seek clemency from the Speaker on your behalf."

Björn laughed. "I'm holding none of them against their will, Alshiba." His eyes danced as they watched her. Oh, yes, she must've looked quite the specimen of dignity, all wine-spattered and needing two hands to hold her goblet.

"I noticed you're attempting to replace one Vestal already. Do you intend to replace me too?" His eyes sparkled with mirth.

She glared in narrow accusation. "You think a traitor can't be replaced? No matter what power he claims?"

"I just marvel it took you so long to try."

She really considered hurling her goblet at his head but decided her wine would be better served calming her nerves than adorning his coat.

"So ... Niko?" He arched a brow above a humorous half-smile. "He was the best you could come up with to replace *Dagmar*?"

"I see I got your attention at least."

"Ah, there it is." He winked knowingly at her. "So you haven't lost your head."

She rolled her eyes. "Is that what you thought?"

"Isn't that what you wanted me to think?" The smile flickered again, irreverent, impertinent ... alluring. His finger drew an idle pattern on the chair arm. "What will you do with Niko now that your ruse has successfully lured me into the open?"

She cast her gaze around the room and took a sip of wine. "I don't see my Vestals returned as yet."

"They're safer in T'khendar."

Her pulse quickened at these words ... at the meaning behind his gaze. He wouldn't say it if it wasn't true. She knew this unequivocally.

"Surely you've noticed, Alshiba." He took a slow sip of wine while he let her think on what she was supposed to have noticed. "How many seats stand empty in the Hall of a Thousand Thrones? How many of those should belong to fifth-strand Vestals? The fifth strand is always the first to succumb to their influence, tied as it is to the Balance."

Alshiba sank down on the edge of the nearest chair. Sitting now seemed like an excellent idea, especially since her breath seemed to have found more hospitable places to be than inside her chest. "I've noticed growing absences of Seats over the years, but ..." She shook her head and pressed her lips together. She didn't see how Alorin's problems could be affecting all of the Realms of Light. "*Our* realm is out of Balance, Björn, not all of the Realms of Light."

His eyes upon her were sincere, intense. "Once you let the plague inside your house, closing a curtain won't keep it from spreading."

She barked an incredulous laugh. "You're saying their presence in Alorin can affect the entire cosmic Balance? That's bold."

One corner of his mouth lifted. "I see I need convince you of nothing." His gaze scanned the room and her piles of books—useless tomes. She'd get more value throwing them at his head. "You've seen already how Illume Belliel might be destroyed."

Her face fell at this remark. Damn him for always reading her so deeply, for seeing her fears when she herself was too afraid to face them head-on. "That day is not yet, and Alorin is worlds away." It was a vain protest, summoned out of spite. Never mind that she'd experienced the very premonition he intimated just minutes ago.

"They need only find their way here once, love, and the door will be eternally open to them."

Her gaze flashed back to him. "How? How would they travel here?"

"Shadow."

Now she really stared. "Shadow is a *dimension*—" but *oh* ... now she saw, or thought she saw. Shadow was the name the *Sobra* gave to the space between the realms, that connective tissue that bound the worlds together. If the realms were beads upon a chain, and the welds connecting the realms were the chain itself, Shadow was the air around them all. It permeated everything because it was a dimension, not a place. Theoretically it bound not only the realms but time itself, existing eternally from the beginning to the end of days.

She didn't know how the Malorin'athgul could use this dimension to travel, but she recognized the possibility. And if anyone would know and understand such a truth, Björn would. She didn't doubt him for a second.

Then it hit her like a punch to her stomach. By Epiphany's Blessed Light, *Björn* was sitting in her study—*his* study, once. She had to think the thought three times for it to sink in. Finally, she pushed a strand of hair impatiently from her eyes and settled him a heated look. "Why are you here, Björn?"

He chuckled. "Assuring myself of your mental welfare isn't enough?"

"As if you believed for a minute—" Yet ... if he *didn't* truly think her out of her mind for naming Niko to the Vestal Seat, why *had* he come?

She glared at him in frustration and pushed out of her chair. Emotion came in waves—one minute ebbing with heartbreak, the next rising with fury. The result was an embarrassing inability to find any semblance of graceful comportment. She walked behind her chair—she could at least ground herself by holding onto the back of it—and stood there watching him watching her.

In all the years, he hadn't changed. No matter what accusations, what names, what excrement of vindictive slander was slung at him, he stood remote, untouched and unsullied.

But the personal affront to her trust, to her heart ... this clung to him like bitumen. Indeed, it clung to both of them, binding them at two ends of betrayal.

Could such poisonous tar ever be dissolved?

He must've seen it in her eyes, seen the way her emotions in that moment tumbled over the edge, drawing her into a frothing cauldron of anger and indignation.

"Alshiba—"

"I've heard enough." She walked to the wall and a tasseled cord. She stared at him flatly as she pulled it.

Björn broke into a broad grin and pushed to his feet. "What a joy to see you haven't changed." He walked to the double doors and opened them.

"Two dozen Paladin Knights will be here in moments." Her tone held more gloat than warning.

He turned her a brilliant smile. "Then gaze upon the sunset with me until they arrive."

Oh, his hand held out to her, the soft entreaty in his gaze, his incomparable smile ... she could never resist him when he actually *tried* to charm her.

She walked over and accepted his hand. "I really despise you."

He wrapped her in the circle of his arm and kissed her hair as he drew her outside. "I know, love."

Her balcony overlooked a narrow strip of land far below, while beyond this stretch of manicured grounds, pink sand abutted an aqua sea that was turning to mercury as she watched. The orange sun hung low, caught between the chalcedony water and a flaming sky. These had been his apartments before they were hers ... still some of the best in the cityworld.

"We have oceans in T'khendar now," he murmured against her hair, his arm holding her body close to his strong form. She even smelled his familiar scent—*oh*, how this moment tormented her! "But they're wild seas," he went on, "treacherous, still pummeling the bedrock into sand. One day we'll have beaches like this."

"If the Council doesn't destroy T'khendar first," she groused.

He chuckled and laid his cheek against her head. Both arms moved to encircle her and draw her closer in front of him. He tucked her head beneath his chin. "You won't wish to destroy T'khendar once you've seen it."

"I've seen it." She tried to pull away, but crisscrossing arms bound her body like love bound her heart. "Or do you forget those days?" *She* certainly couldn't. She'd nearly died in that city of basalt.

He kissed her head and then shifted away slightly to aim a molten smile at her. "You saw Malachai's creation, not mine."

Yours would be different? she thought of retorting, but she only gritted her teeth and looked away instead, for she knew anything of Björn's devising would be … *damn him*, it would be as near to perfection as man could achieve. And a good deal more perfect even than that.

A distant commotion thundered suddenly, and the far doors burst open, disgorging Paladin Knights into her drawing room.

Björn stole a kiss from her lips. Then he swung himself up onto the railing.

Her eyes went wide. "What are you doing?"

He smiled down at her. "Stealing away into the night. Would you like to come?"

She spun a look over her shoulder at the Knights now flooding through her study. A sublime sense of vindication filled her. "They're taking you for Questioning, Björn. Three centuries overdue."

His eyes sparkled. Then he flipped backwards off the railing.

"No!" She threw her hands to try to catch him—

Then *she* was suddenly flying.

She didn't have time even to curse his name before her body slammed into his, and his arms were around her, and they were falling in a whirling rush—

The world jerked upside down. Alshiba spun head over heels and then hit up against something—not soft, no, though it didn't exactly crush *all* the breath out of her lungs.

A force spun her right side up, and then Björn set her down on her feet, but he kept her body encircled in his arms—in that moment of disorientation, she didn't entirely mind—and waved at the glowering Knights now staring down from the balcony two hundred feet above.

There among the tall trees, night had already claimed territory from the day. She could hear the waves lapping at the shore and cicadas beginning their evening song. The sky above shone with clouds painted in rose-gold and violet.

"*What …*" it took her a moment to regain her breath, moments more to dare meet his gaze for knowing how deeply it would pierce her heart. "Just what did this accomplish?" She joined him in watching the Knights lining her high balcony. "They'll only follow you down."

"Yes, but it will take them a few minutes to find the pattern." He turned his smile back on her, making her tremble inside.

Why couldn't she have fallen in love with someone less infuriating? The worst part was, Isabel had warned her—*oh yes*, but she hadn't listened.

'He is an easy man to admire, my brother, but a hard man to love.'

Alshiba had brushed aside Isabel's warning all those years ago—she and Björn were in love!—but in the crushing centuries since, Alshiba had come to realize that Björn's sister had already understood him in ways she never could.

Staring quietly down at her, Björn cupped her cheek and brushed his thumb across her lips. Knights began landing around them, but his eyes never strayed, and what those eyes said ...

His thumb traced her bottom lip again, and the love in his gaze stole every ounce of defiance from her heart. He leaned and kissed her lips and let his breath mingle with hers as he whispered, "So full of regret, love."

She closed her burning eyes. "What else was left to me?"

"Alshiba ..." His tone commanded her gaze to meet his. He held her chin, like her gaze, without even a flicker of contrition—damn the man his insufferable certainty. "I told you all would be made clear if you just had a little faith in me."

She looked defiantly away. "I'm afraid I'm fresh out." Who imagined so few words could harbor such immense bitterness?

He replied with a knowing smile. "Oh ... I think a little remains." His thumb lifted her chin and angled her lips up to meet his again.

Björn's kisses never tasted of anything but sunlight.

When he released her that time, he drew her close in the circle of his arms. His kiss, the feeling of being next to him again ... it was more than she could bear. *Why, oh why, were the Knights not taking him into custody?*

Her heart said, *stay with him—go with him!*

Her mind said, *make him tell you why he betrayed you!*

Logic said, *what in Cephrael's name is that flashing?*

Alshiba turned. Then she pushed him abruptly away. The Knights encircled them, but so, apparently, did a shield. The soldiers attacked an invisible dome with swords and magic and words of command, but their mouths and their steel moved soundlessly beyond Björn's barrier.

He was smiling when she looked back to him.

She ground her teeth. "Everything is just a game to you."

His fingers caught a lock of her hair, and he tugged her close again. She felt a magnet for him, always pulling him near, and he like the sun to her—scalding and immense, the unquestionable center of her universe anytime he was near. "It's the unspoken rule of life, dear-heart." Björn gave her another of those smiles that so easily enchained her to his gravity. "There must be a game; else, what are we all doing here?"

She drew breath to answer—she didn't know what, just something to deny him—but he fastened his mouth over hers, clutched her body against his and ruthlessly stole what breath she'd mustered.

She saw stars as he released her and drew away. "You know where to find me."

Alshiba made fists of her hands at her sides. "Easier said than done, I hear."

"I'm sure you'll manage with all the resources at your disposal."

He turned, but she grabbed his coat. Her eyes were hard. "If I come for you, Björn, I'll bring all the force of Illume Belliel with me."

Björn grinned. He took her hand from his coat and kissed her palm. "Love of my heart ... I'm counting on it." He gave her a sweeping bow and backed away.

Alshiba grabbed for him again, but her hand hit an invisible wall. In the same moment, the shouting of men suddenly accosted her ears. Now she and the Knights were somehow together *inside* the dome, while Björn stood without.

He placed a hand on the shield and mouthed three words. Then he turned and walked away.

Alshiba dropped her chin to her chest and forced back a sob.

"My lady?" One of the Knights placed a hand on her shoulder.

She shook her head, not trusting to words.

Three minutes later, the dome, like the man who'd conjured it, had vanished.

Björn stood in the shadows just beyond the pillars of the antechamber leading to the apartments of the Speaker of the Thousand Realms. Light from a massive crystal chandelier above the adjutant's desk chased the shadows from the room, so Björn had created some in which to stand unnoticed. He'd called off the guards with an illusion and was attempting to use a similar trick on the aide, but this man was proving both more logical and more cautious than his counterparts.

Björn sent another noise cascading down the passage. The aide looked up again with a frown. Anyone could read the questions in his eyes: where were the guards? What was the noise and why hadn't they taken care of it? Finally, he stood with a dramatic exhalation of annoyance and walked from the room to investigate.

Björn slipped around and into the Speaker's apartments.

The chambers of the supreme leader of the Council of Realms were appropriately gilded, pretentiously immense, and decorated with the spoils of eons of tributes from the thousand realms. It was rather like walking through a museum—the display was as exhausting as the distances between each set of doors.

After a long walk, Björn stopped before the towering double doors of the Speaker's office and watched the currents. They confirmed that the Speaker was out. He cast *elae* into the lock to depress the pins. The trace-seal upon the door he simply unworked.

Inside, he found the office as he remembered. Much like the rest of the Speaker's apartments, his office was elegantly appointed and lined in tall windows. An expansive balcony overlooked the sea. When Björn had held the Alorin Seat, the then Speaker had been an incompetent man incapable of seeing beyond a century or two. The new Speaker was better suited to his position.

Björn was sitting in a chair waiting for him when he entered.

Aldaeon H'rathigian, Seat of Markhengar and Speaker of the Council of Realms, moved with the characteristic poise of the Elven races, even while he balanced many ledgers in his arms. He wore the Speaker's robes, which glimmered with opalescent silk and Markhengar's own silver sapphires, but the elaborate adornment seemed almost crude against his graceful stature—the proverbial gilding of the lily.

He set down the ledgers on the corner of his desk and then happened to look up. Water-clear truthreader's eyes stared. Then they blinked and stared harder. Then he looked over his shoulder at the door, which he had just unlocked and worked a trace-seal to open—for Björn had of course relocked and rewoven the seal once inside—and turned back again wearing an expression of complete bewilderment. "I will never understand how you do that."

Björn's lips arced in a half-smile. "It was practically open."

"The door was bound with the fifth!"

"Perhaps a newer lock?"

Aldaeon grunted. "As if iron would stop you when a triform pattern cannot."

Björn's eyes danced. "One can't be too careful, Speaker. Word is there are dangerous men about."

Aldaeon arched a brow. "Yes ... my aide informed me of a commotion at the Alorin Seat's apartments. I confess, it never crossed my mind it could be you."

"I told you I would visit."

The Speaker grunted dubiously. "You know the Council would crucify me if they knew I was standing here like this with you. I can't think of anyone more sought after on our docket."

"And do you intend to tell them?"

Aldaeon observed him with a frown. "I haven't decided yet." Smoothing his silver-pale hair as the only indication of his discomfiture, he sat down in his chair, leaned back, and exhaled a slow breath. "Has it really been three centuries?"

"Give or take a few decades." Björn looked appreciatively around the room. "You've done well in my absence."

Aldaeon very nearly rolled his eyes. "You were the next sure candidate for the Speaker's seat. When you left, the votes fell to me ... but I suspect you knew that would happen."

Björn smiled. "It never hurts to have a friend in high places—especially when one expects to soon become a fugitive."

Aldaeon pressed at a miniscule speck on his desk. "I must've been your most vehement defamer." He glanced up at Björn beneath his brows. "I rallied the Seats against you."

"That you felt betrayal so deeply only proved the depth of our friendship."

Aldaeon gave him a considering look laced with skepticism ... a long look during which he was clearly deliberating. Finally he shook his head. "You didn't want the Speaker's seat. Politics bore you—even those as convoluted as Illume Belliel's." Casting Björn a frown, he rose from his chair and walked to a gilded credenza the size of a small village. As he was pouring wine into two crystal goblets, he looked over his shoulder. "You would've had us all wrapped around your fingers within a week, and then what?"

Björn grinned. "Indeed. Crisis averted."

Aldaeon came over and handed him a goblet. Then he sat in the chair across from Björn and considered him with a frown. After some time of this, he said, "I read your letter."

Björn arched brows and sipped his wine. "I wrote that letter many years ago."

"It took me many years to decide to read it."

"Fortuitous you kept it."

"You made it impossible to burn."

"One must take *some* precautions, even with friends."

Aldaeon grunted and shook his head. For a moment, he stared off absently into the night. "Until I read your letter, I thought you'd gone as mad as Malachai ... sure that something in that realm of yours spawned lunacy."

Björn traced the rim of his goblet with his thumb and gazed at his wine; in the dark liquid he saw a darker realm of brimstone and fire, and clouds laced with silver-violet lightning. "We spent half a century planning, Aldaeon, and a solid decade building it, and then, when the task was done and the realm created ..." he shook his head and looked back to the Speaker. "We had no idea what hit us."

"You spoke of *deyjiin* in your letter."

Björn gazed at the darkened windows and saw a reflection of that silver-violet power as it had first appeared, racing along the rim of the world. "We didn't understand it." He sighed resignedly. "We certainly didn't expect it. And before we knew what had happened, it had driven Malachai mad." He turned and met Aldaeon's colorless gaze. "He'd been our focal point, the group's talisman. We worked the entire thing through him."

"A grave tragedy."

Björn nodded in acceptance of Aldaeon's condolences. Even now, he felt Malachai's loss as his personal failure. There were all the reasons in the world to excuse himself from responsibility, but none which truly mattered. He should've foreseen it. The burden of Malachai's death would rest forever on his conscience.

"Suddenly we were in a scramble to save the realm we'd created—but it wasn't about T'khendar, Aldaeon, truly. It's what T'khendar was meant to do."

"In your letter, you described the realm as a fortress."

"The last bastion between the fringes of Chaos and the Realms of Light." He took a contemplative sip of wine and gazed out the windows, but instead of the blossoming stars, he saw the cosmic spiral of the thousand realms, with Alorin at its far tip and Illume Belliel at its center. "So long as T'khendar stands, the Malorin'athgul cannot unmake the realms from the plane of Chaos, where their power is greatest."

"But they're unmaking your realm even now."

He looked back to his friend. "Their existence in Alorin alone is enough to disrupt the Balance." He gave him a fleeting smile. "I was struggling to keep the entire game from collapsing. It was lose Malachai or lose T'khendar and everything we'd worked so hard to accomplish."

"You sacrificed him."

Björn held Aldaeon's gaze ... nodded. "Malachai's madness exacted a terrible toll." He grunted and looked away again. "But I had to keep the ultimate goal in mind—this wasn't about one man or one world but all the peoples in all the thousand realms." He ran his thumb along his goblet again. "I sacrificed him in a sense, yes ... and I sacrificed my own realm to a great degree. There are those who will never forgive me for it." He looked up to meet Aldaeon's gaze. "Perhaps they shouldn't."

The Speaker shrugged in acceptance of this truth. "Someone must atone for the genocide, or so demand your critics—Alshiba being foremost among them, I might add."

"Malachai more than atoned, Aldaeon." Björn turned a grim look out the windows again, lest Aldaeon see in his gaze how deeply the truth still speared him. "His soul ... *deyjiin unmade it.*" Fierce eyes swung back to meet his friend's. "That was Malachai's reward for bravery beyond mortal comprehension—to be removed from the circle of Returning. Eternal death."

Aldaeon paled. He set down his goblet as though it held this unwanted truth within its depths. "*Deyjiin* can do that?"

Björn leaned towards him. "*They* can do that. And with naught but a kiss of their power."

The Speaker looked appropriately horrified.

Björn leaned back in his chair and eyed him shrewdly. "It's only a matter of time before they find their way to Illume Belliel, my friend. And from here—the *center* of the thousand realms? What harm could be wrought?"

Aldaeon shifted uncomfortably in his chair. "What makes you think they're seeking the cityworld?"

Björn held his gaze. "It's what I would do."

At this response, the Speaker looked exponentially more disturbed.

Björn ran a finger along his lower lip. "*One* of them at least has made contact with the Shadow Realms."

Aldaeon stiffened. "You're certain of this?"

Björn gave him a telling look. "He twice used *inverteré* patterns to kill ..." the thought brought a sudden lump to his throat that gave him pause. Even with Ean Returned, Arion's loss remained a wound that would never fully heal. "... a dear friend."

The Speaker stared at Björn. "Couldn't he have gained these patterns elsewhere? Despite long efforts to confine them, *inverteré* patterns are still extant in the realms."

"These patterns were new, different. He pushed *deyjiin* through them, tried to unmake—" but he bit his tongue. Even now he couldn't say it—didn't dare think it. The idea of losing Arion from the tapestry forever, as he'd lost Malachai ...

Frowning with concern, Aldaeon picked up his wine and sipped it, holding Björn's gaze over the rim. Much passed between them during that enduring silence. Then the Speaker arched a brow as if with a new understanding. "By the Blessed Lady's Light ... you think they're making a pact—this Malorin'athgul and the Warlocks of Shadow."

"Made. It's nearly assured."

Aldaeon fell back in his chair, looking stunned. "But the treaty—"

"Malorin'athgul don't care about the treaties that bind the thousand realms, Aldaeon. When Alorin signed its pact with the Council, we shunned the Shadow Realms as was required of us, and the welds opening upon Shadow have been stricken from our weldmaps and charts. But Malorin'athgul aren't bound by the same cosmic laws." He leaned forward, draped his forearm across his knee, and pinned the shocked Speaker against the back of his chair solely with the force of his gaze. "Balance shifts beneath their feet like sand, my friend, and they have no compunction whatsoever about working *their* power, *our* power, or *inverteré* patterns corrupted by *deyjiin* to achieve their aims."

Mouth slightly ajar, Aldaeon lifted his goblet, held it to his lips without drinking, and then lowered it again. He wetted his lips. "And you think you have this grave threat in hand, do you?"

Björn shrugged and leaned back in his chair. "More or less."

As he sipped his wine then, he lifted his gaze to the cage of energy surrounding him. It stood invisible to the naked eye, but the currents revealed its shape to him, as well as the many patterns that comprised it. "This is really lovely work, by the way."

The Speaker gave him an agonized look and set down his goblet dejectedly. "How long have you known the *celantia* was in place?"

"Since you summoned it." Björn stood and examined the invisible shield that would prevent him from moving beyond a space of about four square feet. As his fingers touched this prison of light, sapphire-blue patterns spiraled outwards in a kaleidoscopic burst of color.

Aldaeon also stood, looking supremely apologetic. "One must take precautions sometimes ... even with friends." He bowed his head as he walked to the side of his desk, but there he paused with his hand on a gilded box. He spun Björn a regretful grimace. "They're not above Reading even me, you know—the Questioners of our illustrious Council."

Björn arched an amused brow. "Would you like to take a swing at me for good measure?"

Aldaeon looked faintly horrified at this suggestion.

Björn walked a few steps along the *celantia*, trailing his fingers across the walls as the currents revealed them, examining the spiraling sapphire patterns that burst forth at his touch. "I've really never seen anything like this."

Aldaeon opened the gilded box. "Are you keeping the other Vestals hostage in T'khendar, Björn?"

Björn placed a hand on the *celantia's* ceiling above his head. A burst of cerulean swirls spiraled away. "Yes, myself included. Can you not see the chains upon my wrists?"

"Alshiba claims you are," Aldaeon said tightly.

"She's claimed many things of me over the years."

"Are you—" But he bit off whatever he'd meant to say and settled Björn a tense look instead. "I said nothing to Alshiba because in your letter you asked me not to, but Björn ..." He pressed fingertips to the desktop and frowned. "All these long years ... she has grieved. I've never seen a woman more agonized by love."

The flicker of a sad smile graced Björn's lips, and he lifted his gaze again to the whorls above his head. He would make things right with Alshiba if it took an eternity to do it. "Ah, my friend ..." Björn looked back at him as he ran his hand slowly from high to low along the *celantia's* wall, "that tragedy, at least, I will one day put to rights."

Looking conflicted, Aldaeon turned back to the ornate box. He placed a hand inside, paused, frowned ponderously, seemed to finally make a decision, and pushed a button. Alarms rang. "You understand ... I have to—" but the Speaker's words halted on his tongue, for he'd just then lifted his gaze again and found Björn standing at the glass doors.

Aldaeon sat down abruptly on the corner of his desk as if his knees had simply collapsed, much like his attempt to reason out the impossibility before his eyes. He clapped a hand to his face wearing the candid color of astonishment. Nearby, the shouting of men could be heard over the continuing alarm, followed by heavy banging upon the Speaker's doors.

Well ... he hadn't rewoven the trace seal *exactly* like the original ...

The Speaker's colorless eyes looked from the space where the *celantia* had been and back to Björn, who remained by the doors. Apology flickered once more across his brow. He exhaled a resigned sigh and dropped his hand to his lap. "You won't fault me for trying, I suppose?"

Björn's gaze was warm. "I fault you for nothing, my friend."

Aldaeon clasped his hands and shook his head wondrously. "The *celantia* has been in use in my culture for over nine thousand years. In all of that time, no one has ever escaped it. Even I don't know how to escape it."

Björn opened the balcony doors and turned a smile over his shoulder. "Pity."

Aldaeon's face went slack. He stood in sudden alarm with a hand extended—

Spiraling patterns erupted around him.

Björn winked. "One must take *some* precautions ... even with friends."

Aldaeon shook his head, his eyes round. "Is there no physical law you cannot break?"

"Break, bend ..." Björn waggled a hand. Then he flashed a grin, winsome and insouciant. "One of the benefits of being a fugitive is that no one expects you to follow the rules."

"You never followed any of them to begin with."

"Well ... there is that." Björn's eyes danced. "As my sister might say, perhaps I was always destined for this path." He gave Aldaeon a bow, murmured, "Farewell my friend," and spirited himself away into the night.

FIFTY-THREE

"A truthreader cannot be corrupted save by the erosion of his moral compass."
— Valentina van Gelderan, Empress of Agasan

"I DON'T LIKE IT," Tanis said for about the fourteenth time. He shoved his hands in his pockets and leaned against the doors to Nadia's balcony, staring outside while she changed behind a screen.

"Tanis, you know there's no other way." Nadia's voice sounded muffled.

"There *is* another way." Tanis stared hard at the balcony railing to resist the temptation of looking at her. "I can go. I'll distract him while you and Felix search his rooms."

"You're the only one who really understands what he is, Tanis. Felix and I could walk right past some evidence and not see it. Besides," she added, coming around from behind the screen, "I'll be perfectly safe as Phoebe della Buonara."

Tanis turned to look at her and blinked. "But ... I've seen you before." He recalled the provincial girl he'd noticed standing beside Felix the night he met N'abranaacht. "You were at N'abranaacht's lecture."

Nadia smiled, and only then did Tanis see a glimmer of the princess beneath the disguise. She looked almost nothing like herself with her dark hair braided and hung in unattractive, dog-ear loops on either side of her head, while the wire-rimmed spectacles, tinted lavender in hue, somehow altered the shape of her eyes along with their color. Add an ill-fitting dress of olive drab, which drowned her slender curves in voluminous bulk, and no one would look at her twice, much less think to compare her to the ephemeral Princess Nadia van Gelderan.

Nadia spread her skirts and turned a circle. "How do I look?"

Tanis stood a little in awe. "I think you look ... awful."

She laughed and crossed the room to him. "You see? I'll be perfectly fine.

It would be far more dangerous for you to go. You said yourself he recognized you. There's no telling what he'll have planned."

Tanis exhaled and shifted his gaze away, trying to stay focused. Thinking of Nadia in the same room as Shailabanáchtran required him to use every bit of the training the zanthyr had impressed upon him just to keep from screaming. "You have to maintain a flawless mental shield, and under no circumstances can you let him touch you."

She nodded her understanding. They'd been over this already.

Tanis worked the muscles of his jaw. "He's dangerous, Nadia." He still wished they'd found some other way to do this. "It's safe to assume he took Malin. He could just as easily take you."

"I understand." She moved her head in front of his to capture his grim gaze. "As you said, he must have some end game for being at the Sormitáge, and I doubt he'll throw that away over an insignificant Healer like Phoebe."

Tanis frowned.

"Besides ..." Nadia looked at him somewhat perplexedly. "It doesn't make sense that he would've taken Malin simply because he knew this secret. I mean, who would have believed it?"

Tanis narrowed his gaze as he considered her point. "You think he took Malin for some other reason?"

She lifted one shoulder in a little shrug. "From everything you've told me of him—everything you said your friend Pelas told you of him—he seems the type to kill two birds with one stone."

Tanis let out a tense exhale. His entire body was rigid with apprehension. Just minutes from now, he'd be returning to the Sormitáge to send word to N'abranaacht that he would meet him for tea, thus giving the man time to bait his trap—which Tanis felt certain he would do. That Nadia would then walk into that trap ...

Tanis took up Nadia's hand and drew her close, and she moved into his embrace. He closed his eyes, rested his cheek against her soft hair, and focused in that moment only on the feel of her in his arms. How quickly she'd become important to him!

Yet ... when he allowed himself to think upon it, he feared a pairing could never be. Who was he, after all, to court the heir to an empire? They were young and foolish and 'quick in love'—as his Lady Alyneri would no doubt say—and this folly could only end in heartbreak.

The Empress chooses her Consort, Tanis. Nadia's thought impinged upon these gloomy fears. She tightened her arms around him, sensitive to his emotions even when he hid his thoughts from her. *My mother plucked Marius di L'Arlesé from among her Praetorian Guard—despite his protests, I might add.*

And smiling, she murmured at his ear, "One day we must ask the High Lord to tell you their story. My father recounts it much more amusingly than my mother."

"*Ahem* …" Felix's annoyed throat-clearing floated in from the other room. "Can I come in yet?"

Nadia disappointingly withdrew from Tanis's arms, but her smile when she looked at him offered the promise of future indiscretions. "Yes, come in, Felix."

Felix came striding in with a meat pie in each hand. He took a bite of one and asked through the mouthful, "You don't have to sit in on Twelfth-day proceedings today?"

She smoothed the folds of her woolen dress with a delicacy suited to finer cloth. "My mother is away, and my father has never had much patience for politics. He's already told me I need not attend."

"Handy," Felix mumbled. His mismatched eyes shifted between Tanis and Nadia. "So … are we ready?"

Tanis looked back to the princess. It was instinctive, this need to protect Nadia, and he found himself drawing from the zanthyr's example, acting as Phaedor did in moments of danger—leading without questioning his right to do so.

"Be careful." Fear for Nadia's safety lay sharp on his tongue and thick in his thoughts. The very air tasted of his apprehension. "N'abranaacht will probably be working the fourth from the moment he lets you inside. You won't be able to feel it." She opened her mouth to protest, but he held up a finger emphatically. "You *won't* be able to feel it. Assume he can tell immediately if you're trying to deceive him and do nothing to raise his suspicions."

Nadia arched an eyebrow imperiously. "I understand, Lord Adonnai."

He growled at her, "You're only meant to be a distraction, Nadia. Don't ask him pressing questions. Don't try to learn anything important from him. Just keep him occupied as long as possible."

Nadia squeezed his hand. "I'll contact you the moment I depart the literato's chambers."

Nadia kept her head low and her gaze downcast as she walked toward Literato N'abranaacht's office, though few, if any, would recognize her disguised as Phoebe della Buonara. It thrilled her to wander the Sormitáge halls unknown and unwatched—the oddest of sensations to someone who'd rarely walked a stretch of hallway without a froth of guards and an ocean of staring eyes.

Outside the literato's office, Nadia gathered herself, pressed out her skirts, adjusted her violet spectacles, and mentally checked her fourth strand shields. Then she took a deep breath and knocked.

The door opened to reveal a man dressed in a white, hooded cassock. He folded his hands in his sleeves and bowed his head so the hood's deep cowl hid his face.

When the man said nothing, Nadia cleared her throat. "Is ... Literato N'abranaacht within?"

The hooded man stepped aside that she might enter as he shut the door. Then he turned and led away. Nadia supposed she was meant to follow.

The literato's office was vast, dim and very cold. To her right, a floor to ceiling bookcase containing obviously rare volumes dominated the wall, while to her left, just beyond a long table, hung all manner of ancient weapons. She saw a particularly wicked saber among them with a dark, curving blade as black as iron and obviously Merdanti. She wondered somewhat nervously if that was the saber the literato had nearly used on Felix.

The servant led her down a hall, past several closed doors, and into a large drawing room where firelight flickered. N'abranaacht stood beside the mantel with his back to her. He was not wearing his hood.

This then, she surmised, was meant to be his moment of great revelation, when he unveiled his face to Tanis and watched him wilt with chagrin. It emboldened Nadia to deny the literato that victory.

N'abranaacht's black hair hung nearly to his waist, falling like water from the broad cliff of his shoulders. "Well, Tanis—" he began as he turned, but the words halted on his tongue. Dark eyes flashed to the man in white—questioning, castigating—and then went abruptly blank of emotion. A smile appeared, summoned in a blink, but the tightening of his eyes revealed his lingering displeasure.

"I fear you've caught me at a disadvantage, young lady. I was expecting another." His hands motioned to his bare head and face, the eyes now smiling too. "I would not otherwise present myself so."

The literato's almond-shaped eyes were so dark as to seem black. Nadia hadn't realized how tall he was until she found herself staring up at him. His features were striking but fearsome—the countenance of a predator. Thankfully he wasn't also wearing his sword, yet the very fact surprised her. Arcane Scholars were known to wear their blades even when in residence, for they lived such lives of danger beyond the university that they rarely walked unarmed.

Clasping her hands before herself, Nadia bowed her head slightly and drew in a breath to calm her suddenly racing heart. "Literato N'abranaacht, please forgive my imposition. I would have announced myself but your ..." she glanced uncertainly to the servant in white, "assistant ... somewhat confused me as to the protocol expected."

The literato gave her a gentle look, yet he radiated fury. She understood better now of Tanis's warnings, for N'abranaacht emanated emotions quite in disagreement with his courteous façade. Had he been openly enraged, she would've felt less frightened than in observing how adroitly he kept his true feelings hidden behind a mask of civility.

N'abranaacht motioned to his servant. "My ... assistant, as you named him, follows a vow of silence until accepted into our Order. I fear we must conduct the introductions ourselves. You are?"

"I beg your pardon, Literato N'abranaacht." Nadia had no trouble appearing flustered—just the force of his gaze unsettled her—never mind that she was about to tell a calculated and practiced lie. "Please allow me to present myself as Phoebe della Buonara." She gave an awkward curtsy.

That gaze looked her over speculatively. "And how may I assist you ... Phoebe della Buonara?"

His resonant voice reached out and enveloped her, wrapped and clenched around her. Nadia dropped her gaze and fought back the feeling of the air being slowly squeezed from her lungs. "I beg you to forgive my imposition, Literato. It's just ... I thought you might be ... I mean—I *know* who you were expecting."

He shifted his head slightly. "You do?"

She managed a fleeting smile, sheepish and apologetic. "I saw the new Postulant, Tanis, walking with another. They were discussing the Quai game tonight and talking about placing their bets, and then Tanis mentioned he had to hurry if they were going to get their bets down in time, because he had an appointment with you ..." It was all true of course—they'd purposefully staged the exchange to make it easy for Nadia to say ... though Felix was genuinely disappointed at the prospect of missing the game and had gone so far as to ask Tanis how long he thought they'd be snooping in N'abranaacht's apartments.

Nadia clasped her hands tightly in front of her. "I thought I might be able to speak with you for a few minutes ... since I knew your appointment would be late arriving."

"I see."

She looked up quickly. "I attended your lecture on the *inverteré* pattern you found. It was ... awe-inspiring."

"The *Sobra* Scholars are studying the Pattern of Awakening," he said in a low voice. Its timbre sounded so resonant in the high-ceilinged room that his words seemed to come from everywhere, like a god speaking from the heavens. "I'm afraid I cannot discuss it at this time."

"Oh, that's ... that's not why I've come." Nadia cast an uncertain glance at the eerily silent servant. "I just wanted ... I wondered if you'd be willing to speak with me about your faith."

He arched a brow. "You are interested in the Order of Holy Palmers?"

"Yes. I've studied the writings of Epiphany's Prophet and thought perhaps I could ask you a few questions."

He considered her for a moment and then nodded slightly. "I'm always keen to promote the tenets of our Order. While I'm awaiting my other guest," and something hidden in these words crackled with displeasure, "perhaps you would join me for tea."

She put on a smile to hide her nervousness. "That is most generous of you, Literato."

"It is my pleasure, Miss Buonara. Please ..." Long fingers motioned towards a near table already set for tea. It stood between two tall windows whose intrusive light had been blocked by curtains of heavy brocade. Nadia watched the literato as he flowed across the dim room, noting the way the silk of his white robes billowed with every motion. He seemed a flame floating among the shadows.

Nadia drew in a breath, carefully pushed up her lavender spectacles—the illusion crafted into the glass only worked if someone looked at her eyes through the lenses—and followed.

N'abranaacht settled into an armchair across the table while the servant came over to help Nadia into hers. She noted then that the ghostly apparition of a man even wore white gloves. He poured tea from an elaborate pewter pot, all the while keeping his head so bent and his face so hidden in the deep cowl that she marveled he could see at all.

Taking up his cup, N'abranaacht leaned all the way back in his chair so that his face fell into the shadow of its wings. Only his dark eyes were visible, luminous as moonlight on a midnight lake. "What questions do you have, Miss Buonara?"

Nadia dropped her gaze to her cup. She felt more comfortable watching the firelight dancing on the china than reflecting off N'abranaacht's eyes. "I wondered ... could you tell me if the Holy Palmers agree with the writings of Epiphany's Prophet?" She looked up again as she finished this question.

N'abranaacht considered her quietly while steam rose from his tea, forming a thin stream of haze across his darkly lambent gaze. "Epiphany's Prophet ..." Condescension permeated the currents. "Her writings are extensive. I cannot say that our Order agrees with all of the Prophetess's views."

"Could you perhaps tell me one area where your shared beliefs diverge?"

"The Prophetess and my Order embody different purposes, Miss Buonara. She professes to speak the Maker's will; we simply follow it." He gave her a humble smile at this, yet arrogance radiated through, searing away humility's gauzy strands with its prideful heat.

"Yes, I see." She was growing more unsettled the longer she stayed in the room with him. It was a strange sensation to sit so close to the literato—what with his broad shoulders and deep voice out of the void, just his eyes catching a spark here and there, or occasionally the glint of an earring peeking from beneath his long hair, rose-gold in the muted firelight ... startling to experience his gentle tone while something malevolent clearly hovered in the shadows of his darkly hypnotic eyes.

How did he do it? How had he fooled everyone so completely?

Nadia lowered her gaze and drew in a deep breath of the room's cold air. "I read that the Palmers believe that all men have paths but that fifth strand creatures do not. I haven't found anything mentioning this in the works of Epiphany's Prophet, Literato. Admittedly," she added with a shy smile and downcast eyes, "I haven't read all of the Prophetess's prolific writings, but I wondered if you might speak to me a little of this idea. Why does your Order feel these creatures have no path?"

Regarding her intently, he slowly set his teacup on the table before him. "You are well-versed in our collective teachings, Miss Buonara. Unusually so, for one so young." The comment fell with a leading edge, expecting explanation.

Nadia put down her tea untouched as well—she certainly wasn't drinking anything before he did. "I've long been interested in the Greater and Lesser Paths, Literato. While other children played at dolls and swords … I read." This, also, was quite true. She'd never been allowed to play with other children. Since she'd learned to read at the age of three, her days had been spent in study.

N'abranaacht reached a hand across the table, and she quickly removed hers from her cup into her lap, but his long fingers only took up the pot of honey. "I'm not an expert on what my Order calls the isolated threads." He dipped a tiny globule of honey into his tea and stirred slowly. "We believe that time is the great loom. The paths of men form the woof and warp of the tapestry of Life, the Great Pattern. The tapestry gains color through each man's actions along his path, while its integrity is governed by a man's intent. Ill deeds thin the tapestry. Honorable ones strengthen it."

She opened her mouth with a comment, but he preempted her with an upraised finger and a wry smile. "I am getting to your question, Miss Buonara." Still slowly stirring his tea, N'abranaacht continued, "This explanation outlines the paths of mortal men, but the fifth strand races are *immortal*. How, then, does one explain them?"

Nadia wetted her lips. "I'm afraid I'm missing some understanding, Literato." She was struggling to form a coherent sentence beneath the force of his interest, which was aimed upon her now like the unrelenting midday sun. "Why does their immortal nature change their path through the tapestry? Would they not merely weave a longer thread?"

"The paths we walk anchor us to the time continuum, Miss Buonara." His dark eyes gleamed as he regarded her with a frightening intensity. "One lifetime, one thread. The Prophetess, I believe, writes that a single being might walk the tapestry many times, but always upon the same thread."

His gaze fixed so strongly upon her set Nadia's heart to racing with disquiet. She fought the urge to squirm beneath the force of his attention. "I … fear I don't understand, Literato," she whispered, her voice losing both breath and volume to his consuming gaze.

"I think you understand quite keenly, Miss Buonara," he murmured in a deeply quiet voice. His eyes traveled, looking her over, smearing heat across her skin.

Nadia felt her face flushing, while a cold fear uncoiled inside her belly. "So, you're saying that because they're immortal, they … what?" She wished he would stop staring at her. She couldn't concentrate beneath his gaze anymore.

"An immortal creature cannot weave one path, one lifetime." His dark eyes held her in thrall, luminously hypnotic in the room's flickering firelight. "The tapestry is comprised of threads spanning single lifetimes. It is therefore apparent that an immortal creature has no path."

"Do … do you believe then that … that their …'" —by the Lady, it was so hard to think!— "that they still influence the tapestry?"

His lips parted in a slow smile, stirring fear. "Indelibly."

Nadia didn't think she could stand even one more minute beneath his gaze, less yet the vulturous emanations of his thoughts. She moved unsteadily to her feet. "Thank you for speaking with me, Literato. I … fear I should be going."

His dark gaze licked over her. "There is no rush, Miss Buonara. I believe my other appointment will not be coming after all, and you haven't taken any of your tea."

Her gaze darted to the cup and its amber liquid. "I apologize, Literato. I feel …" she pressed a hand to her throat. "I suddenly feel a slight malaise."

"A great shame," he murmured, but whatever thought lay behind these benign words sent the currents undulating out in waves that washed painfully through her consciousness. "Perhaps another time. I would be pleased to continue our conversation in greater depth."

Nadia did not trust herself to speak. She managed a fleeting smile and a curtsy and rushed from the room.

When Nadia was gone, Shailabanáchtran crossed one knee over the other and frowned. His gaze strayed towards the drawing room door, while a tightening around his eyes betrayed his malcontent. He wondered what game Pelas's little toy, Tanis, was upon. It nagged at him that the lad might have some inkling of his plans, or that the girl Phoebe might be part of a conspiracy to thwart them.

For a moment, Shail pondered what trouble Tanis could potentially cause. He couldn't see much opportunity on the boy's horizon, though with the High Lord di L'Arlesé as a sponsor, he had powerful allies in the mortal realm. Yet the only thing that truly concerned him was what Tanis might be reporting to Pelas.

He'd seen nothing of his older brother since the night he'd let Demetrio Consuevé have a chance at killing him, but he didn't for a moment believe the man had succeeded—if Shail knew anything of Pelas, he knew his penchant for escaping impossible odds.

It troubled him somewhat that Darshan, too, had been curiously silent for the past fortnight. If Pelas had gone to him in complaint of Shail's manipulations ... could the two of them have reconciled?

Shail immediately scoffed at this idea. Neither of his brothers would ever approach a median line; Pelas was too stubborn and Darshan too arrogant.

Shail shifted his gaze to his servant. *Have the girl followed. See who she speaks to, and when the time comes—*

Suddenly his skin prickled and he flowed to his feet. His silk robes seemed to dissolve and reform, and in this amorphous shifting they darkened from white to crimson, like blood soaking a cloth. "Someone has entered my chambers."

Shall I—

"Do as I've commanded you."

The servant bowed. *Yes, my lord.*

Shail summoned a portal and shaped Shadow to his will. As he stepped into the void, his gaze narrowed decisively.

Pelas could not be allowed to interfere.

FIFTY-FOUR

"A wise man learns from his failures. A brilliant man learns how not to fail."
— Ramuhárikhamáth, Lord of the Heavens

TANIS STEPPED OFF the *leis* into N'abranaacht's chambers feeling shaken and unnerved. He supposed that sliding haphazardly down the side of a dome three hundred feet above the earth would disturb any rationally-minded person—as compared to, say, Nodefinders.

He glared at Felix and hissed, "When you said you could get us in here, you failed to mention it would involve sliding down the side of the Physical Sciences *dome!*"

Felix tossed his calico hair from his eyes and grinned. "We've really got to work on your sense of adventure, Tanis."

Tanis turned away and shook his head. "You and Pelas would get along well."

Felix swiveled a look down a hallway leading out of the sitting room where the *leis* had deposited them and scrubbed at his arms. "Why in the name of my Sacred Aunt Bruna's goat is it so bloody cold in here?"

Tanis was wondering that, too.

N'abranaacht's apartments were located in a residential scholars' hall and as such should've shared a similar temperature. Instead, being in the room felt like standing in the endless void of space.

"I wonder what the other scholars make of this," Felix muttered, still briskly rubbing his arms. "'Come for tea, we serve winter year-round.'"

"I doubt he brings others here." Tanis looked around the apartment, which was richly appointed for all it might've been located inside an iceberg. "I can't see him deigning to entertain others. He would think it beneath him."

Felix turned him a curious look. "One conversation and you're suddenly an expert on N'abranaacht?"

"No." Tanis frowned as his eyes came to rest on an ornate lacquered cabinet that reminded him of a similar one in Pelas's seaside Hallovian mansion. "I just know how they think."

"Well ..." Felix screwed up his face. "Let's see what we can find. You go that way," and he waved nebulously towards the dim hallway.

Hugging his arms against the chill, Tanis headed down the passage. The place looked benign, yet an ill premonition seemed to mount with every step. By the time Tanis was halfway down the corridor, he felt washed in foreboding—deluged by it—his truthreader's senses accosted by a dark symphony of malignant wrongdoing that screamed through the corridor so loudly he marveled Felix didn't notice.

Tanis hunched his shoulders against the sensation and continued past a library to reach the end of the hall and the last two doors. One led to a bedroom, the other into a study.

This can't be right. He'd seen nothing untoward, nothing unusual, nothing to explain the intense chill—which reminded him all too nearly of Pelas' and Phaedor's nightcloaks formed of *deyjiin* ...

Even as the thought occurred to him, Tanis wondered if it was indeed *deyjiin* he could be sensing. His fair brow narrowed as he considered the idea.

Ignoring then the nagging voice in the back of his mind that roused too many questions about his own nature, Tanis envisioned the pattern his father had described in his journal to reveal the currents—indeed, had he not just practiced its construction in Chresten's dining room yesterday? *As mortifying as that experience was.* He filled the pattern with *elae*—with his *intention*, as his mother had taught him to do—and released it.

The currents illuminated the hall as if a painter had suddenly washed the passage in glowing paint.

Tanis stood for a moment in open-mouthed wonder watching the tides of *elae* swirling around him: rose-hued funnels of the first mingled with sparkling silver dust that was the omnipresent fourth, while the floor turned a burnished bronze overlaid with a translucent, knee-high river of rushing gold ...

To think that such marvelous power filled the empty spaces of the realm ... these spinning whirlwinds of kaleidoscopic light. All the airy world was actually a deep sea of variegated rose, silver and gold. He felt a sudden heady excitement ...

At least until he turned and noticed the golden, earthbound currents flowing through the wall at the end of the passage. The other currents too, in their way, seemed to be drawn there, as if a cyclone spun beyond the barrier, gravitating all forces in its direction.

Feeling that sense of foreboding burst to life anew, Tanis approached the wall and tentatively extended his hands to the plaster.

They passed right through—and the air on the other side of the illusion felt like ice against his flesh.

Tanis snatched his hands back with a sharp inhale. A host of thoughts accosted him—warning, scolding, encouraging caution and cowardice in the same instant—but ultimately, he had to find out what lay behind the illusion. Tanis drew in courage with his breath and stepped through the wall.

The icy air accosted his lungs and stabbed icicles into his unprotected skin. Tanis pushed his hands beneath his armpits and exhaled clouds with every breath as he walked between the long tables of a laboratory. Ancient looking books and scrolls littered the workbenches. Where any of them lay open, Tanis saw *inverteré* patterns that hurt his eyes.

But what really roused the hairs on his arms was the glowing, silver-violet patterns hovering in midair, twilit globes of *deyjiin* like snowflakes, every one unique—and all of them *inverteré*. They provided the room's only light while radiating their chill power. Tanis thought he walked carefully between them, but some of the patterns began to tremble slightly, soundlessly. The motion caused jagged ripples in the currents.

Indeed, *elae* swirled tumultuously around these patterns and moved on without touching them. Their aspect—that is, the negative force of the inverted patterns—repelled *elae's* currents on an existential level.

Tanis noticed that the earthbound currents were sweeping towards the back of the room, so he headed that way.

That's when he sensed another's presence.

Her thoughts floated to him suddenly: curious, frightened … and oddly ashamed. And beneath these, the echo of a being in anguish and pain. Her fear mingled with his own, rousing a sense of impending danger that sent the ghost of a shudder down the lad's spine.

Forcing a dry swallow, Tanis headed toward a grouping of couches and chairs arranged around a massive fireplace, its hearth dark. Just to the right of the mantel, he saw it—a black void in the wall.

Oh gods …

Tanis sucked in his breath and went still, staring at the glossy portal that could only be an entrance to Shadow.

That's why the air was so cold!

Suddenly he felt far more afraid than he'd been only moments ago. To think that Shail had erected a permanent portal—a permanent *hole* in Alorin's fabric—knowing that it would suck *elae* into the void of its existence … draining the very life slowly from the world …

Tanis shuddered and hugged his arms to his chest.

Phaedor had explained that *deyjiin* tore the fabric of the realm to gain the dimension of Shadow, which acted like filler between the realms while itself remaining formless. But he'd also explained that such rends in Alorin's fabric must be quickly sealed and tightly controlled, lest the rending spread and disrupt the entire tapestry of existence.

Seeing this ... this utter contempt for the realm's integrity ... Tanis realized just how deep the well of Shail's loathing really bored.

Instinct shouted to get out of there as fast as possible, yet duty rooted Tanis. He stood for a span of heartbeats staring at the space in the wall, wondering at its purpose ... worrying over it. Then the agonized thoughts filling the room became too loud in his mind, and he turned to seek their source.

As he moved further into the dark room, he saw her hidden in the corner between the wall and a long, glass-fronted cabinet: a gigantic bird sitting atop an ornate silver perch.

Bathed in the violet-silver light of the floating patterns, the hawk looked a bleached etching of herself. She was massive though—sitting easily three feet tall—and her wingspan must've been ...

But Tanis noticed then that her wings had been clipped, her claws ripped out, and her ankles tethered to the perch with a particular silver rope that made his skin crawl in recognition. He'd rather have not remembered his own experience with *goracrosta*.

The hawk shut her golden eyes and tucked her head away into the shoulder of her wing. In that moment, Tanis clearly heard her anguished thought, *Why must he stare?*

He caught his breath.

Then he caught his hand on the back of the nearest chair, for understanding rocked him. This was no mere bird. This was an *avieth*. And so vehemently abused—treated like a mindless animal, yet suffering a very human indignity.

Tanis felt sick. "I ... wish I could help you."

Her head flashed around, and a tawny eye pinned him.

If you would help me, kill me.

The despair in the thought wounded him deeply. Tanis even considered it for the space of an indrawn breath, but his compassion had already claimed the lives of two Adepts—and both times nearly his own as well. He still occasionally woke in the night awash in sweat stained with those Healers' memories, reeking of their broken hopes. He didn't think his soul could bear the weight of a third Adept life, even to give release to one so egregiously defiled.

"I'm sorry, I ... cannot." He dropped his eyes in shame. "I dare not."

The avieth flapped her wings and cawed a shrill protest, but her thoughts, cast even more loudly, put explanation to her reaction.

She hadn't realized he could hear her.

The eye pinned upon him again as she resettled, a fierce gaze. *Who are you? What are you doing here?*

Tanis looked around the laboratory at the glowing patterns, at the gateway to Shadow. "A grave fool."

You're not one of his ... not meant to become?

Tanis frowned. "I ..." He didn't understand her comment. "I know him for who he is, and I want to stop him, but …" he looked desperately around the room again. "I don't know what to do."

Run. T'was an anguished plea.

Yes, run is exactly what he *wanted* to do. Strangely, his legs had their own ideas. Tanis met the avieth's watchful gaze. "He's planning something, isn't he? Help me stop him."

He heard her mental scoff. *What could you do? You are a boy.*

"One with powerful friends."

She seemed to consider this. Then he felt her reticent thoughts pushing his mind away. *He will punish me for eternity.*

Tanis looked her in the eye. "What eternity will any of us have if he succeeds in his purpose?"

Silence followed, and Tanis's urgency grew, fed by that sense of impending doom that threaded like smoke through the room. Mingled with fear, it crystallized the air into shards, so that every breath Tanis took held a cutting edge, making his entire chest ache.

I know only shadows of their plan, the avieth finally answered. She spread her wings tetchily and resettled. Her thoughts resonated with the same suffocating fear that thrummed within Tanis. *They want Adepts for the Danes' war and they plan to take them from the Sormitáge.*

Tanis swallowed. He asked her, "How?" but he was thinking, *Who is 'they?'*

I do not know. A diversion of some kind, a way to collect many into one place.

"When?"

Soon.

Thirteen hells … Tanis pushed both hands through his hair and pressed his lips together tightly. He had to tell the High Lord about this, only—well, who would believe it?

He looked back to the avieth. "How can I help you? Perhaps …" the idea just came to him. "What if I take you with me?" He had no idea what he'd *do* with an avieth that couldn't fly, but maybe if she took her human form …

She seemed to understand his thoughts, or perhaps her avian eyes read the uncertainty on his face, for she confessed, to his horror: *He has bound me to this form, bound me to him. I'm beyond hope, for …* He heard the catch in her mental voice, the despair … … *elae has left me.*

Tanis stared wordlessly at her. This terrible truth stole the icy air from his lungs.

You must go. If he finds you here, he will make you eidola *like the others, a stone shadow of yourself.*

"*Eidola.*" Unease fluttered in Tanis's belly. "What's that?" Yet even as he asked, an image came to mind, bestowed by the High Lord when they'd arrived in port: the tortured and twisted travesty of a man with necrotic flesh.

Abruptly the avieth flapped her wings and cawed a raucous protest. *He comes! RUN! HE COMES!*

Tanis bolted.

He sprinted through the laboratory, dodging floating patterns like bees, and emerged through the illusion that concealed the room only to come to a sudden, jarring halt—whereupon that sense of impending doom collided with the present in a moment of screaming alarm.

Shail stood in the middle of the hallway holding Felix by his collar. The young Nodefinder looked both aggravated and chagrined; he didn't understand that the fingers clenching the scruff of his neck were actually the teeth of a tiger wearing silk clothing.

Seconds after his feet embarrassingly planted themselves, Tanis's heart skidded to a stop in his throat. He felt it lodged there now, making breath difficult.

Shail's lips spread in a slow smile.

Tanis's memory of the man's face had blurred since their meeting at Niko van Amstel's estate, but as he recognized the Malorin'athgul—with his deep-set eyes, angular features and imposing stance—that same instinctive fear of him returned tenfold, for now he lacked Pelas's protection.

"So, Tanis ... we meet again without the trappings of our mutual artifice— face to face, as it were, in the truth."

Trying his best to avoid the dry-mouthed panic beating down the doors of his composure, Tanis managed guardedly, "What truth is that, sir?"

Shail's dark eyes held a threatening gleam. "I shall be asking the questions." He squeezed the back of Felix's neck by way of emphasizing his point, making the boy cringe. "What have you told my brother? Tell me how you're contacting him."

Tanis fervently wished it might've been true—he would've given anything to reach Pelas. Instead, he strained his wits trying to guess the ramifications of admitting himself to be Pelas's spy versus denying it, weighing each of his options against the odds of survival in the few heartbeats Shail gave him to form an answer. Finally Tanis landed, as usual, at the truth.

"I'm ... waiting for him to contact me, sir."

"Then Pelas knows nothing?"

"I can't say what he knows, sir."

Shail grunted. He looked Tanis over critically, his eyes as blades knifing along the lad's flesh. "You're quite the accomplished truthreader already, aren't you? 'Drink intemperately of another's thoughts; speak only what is required in return.' That is the motto of the fourth's children, is it not?"

"I don't think those are the words exactly, sir."

Shail flashed a sharp smile. "My phrasing captures more accurately the essence of the truth." He squeezed Felix's neck again, eliciting another grimace. "Ah ... how ripe this moment. Once again, providence has shown its true colors. Ever does Fate shift the paths of others to fulfill my need."

Tanis regarded him grimly. "You speak as if our meeting was a foregone conclusion."

Shail's dark eyes bored into him. "My brothers and I are gods in this realm, little pawn. Fate bends to our will. Now ..." he shook Felix by the neck and received a black glare in return. "What of this Phoebe who came to see me today? Was she meant to be a diversion while you searched my apartments?" One corner of Shail's lip curled deprecatingly upwards. "Did you really think I would leave my home unprotected?"

Tanis kept a straight face and his mind empty, too afraid to think of Nadia in any capacity lest Shail somehow learn her true identity through his carelessness, but Felix growled, "Phoebe? My *cousin* Phoebe? If you've hurt her—"

"Be *silent.*" Shail's fingers clawed into Felix's flesh, and this time the boy's knees buckled and he sucked in a gasp. He grabbed awkwardly for Shail's wrist. The literato looked down upon him with barely veiled contempt. "The only reason you're standing, Felix di Sarcova, is because I have no desire to carry you."

Felix clung to Shail's wrist with his face twisted in a dreadful rictus of pain. The sight of him bled Tanis; sympathy welled as his composure waned, and fear swelled everywhere in between.

"Whatever her role in connection with you," Shail said then, shifting his gaze back to Tanis, "my servant will take care of her."

These words made Tanis physically ill. Anger rolled in to fill the hollow place in his belly that fear was carving out, and every curse he knew stormed through his mind, all of them aimed at himself.

Something hardened inside him then—determination? It felt more like righteous fury that he suddenly held clenched between his teeth.

Shail traced one forefinger along his lower lip, his eyes dark as they assessed Tanis. "I look forward to our getting intimately acquainted once my matters are concluded tonight. Until then ... a little time in Shadow's void will no doubt free your tongue for our discussion." His eyes licked over Tanis again, and a cruel smile lifted one corner of his mouth. "That is, if it doesn't drive you mad. Come—" Shail reached for him.

Instinct flamed like a wielder's lamp, fueled by the zanthyr's training.

The lad pivoted. His foot caught Felix forcefully in the side, sending the boy sprawling out of Shail's hold, and he caught Shail's arm in his hands as he spun beneath it. Tanis twisted violently then, pivoting his own body to become a fulcrum as the zanthyr had taught him, and flipped the larger man over his back. Shail grunted as he hit the floor.

Tanis grabbed Felix by the collar and hauled him up, and they sprinted down the corridor. If he'd had time to think about it, Tanis might've been amazed that the maneuver had worked just like the zanthyr claimed it would, but all the lad could think about just then was reaching the *leis.*

They were nearly there when thunder without sound lifted them off their feet and propelled them through the air. They landed in a jumble of arms and legs just shy of the *leis* and escape. Tanis heard Shail running after them and knew his fury would be immense.

"Felix!" Tanis shook the other boy. Felix must've hit his head on a chair as he fell, for his eyes looked dazed. Tanis struggled to get him up in his arms.

Shail rounded the corner in a billow of crimson silk, his expression murderous.

Tanis hugged Felix to his chest, looked Shail defiantly in the eye and skipped them into the future.

Time slowed. He saw the Malorin'athgul's hand inching higher, a word forming on his lips ...

Tanis threw himself backwards across the leis, pulling Felix with him—

The boys hit the dome beneath the blinding late-afternoon sun.

Then they were skidding, falling, the golden dome's smooth sides slipping past as they spun on their backs toward and over the gilded edge and—

Landed in a painful tangle on the walkway encircling the dome's base.

Felix groaned.

Tanis disentangled himself from Felix's limbs and pushed unsteadily up to rest his back against the dome's gilded tiles. His muscles felt like a piece of meat after one of Madaé Giselle's overly enthusiastic poundings, while his stomach churned in a sickly tumult.

Felix rolled onto his back and exhaled a long moan of protest. "*Bloody hells*, Tanis." He pushed the back of his hand across his forehead. "Even I had the sense not to fight him."

Tanis turned him a look. "That's only because you don't fear him enough."

Felix's fingers gingerly probed the bruised lump rising on his forehead. "I take back what I said about you needing a better sense of adventure." He winced and then pushed up on one elbow to aim a frazzled look at Tanis. "You're bloody insane."

Tanis pressed palms to massage his aching temples and gazed off through the wrought-iron railing. All around he saw peaked and gabled roofs and the sparkling domes, spires and towers of the city that called itself the Sormitáge University. Somewhere among that labyrinth of buildings, an unnamed menace was stalking Nadia.

Anticipation and dread ached in every inch of bone—but necessity stabbed even more forcefully than these. He opened his mind and sought Nadia.

A bond, unlike a binding, was limited by distance. He prayed she wasn't already too far out of reach. *Nadia* ...

A moment later, he heard her mental reply. *Tanis!*

Her tone held happiness and relief but also apprehension. Still, these were better portents than the alternative, which would imply Shail's 'servant' had already gotten a hold of her.

Tanis, I've been trying to reach you, but it was like—

Where are you? his concern for her safety overrode all else.

Heading towards the Quai game with a group of Maritus. I ... Uncertainty surged into fear. He could almost see her looking over her shoulder as she walked. *I think someone is following me.*

Stay with the group. We're coming for you.

Tanis grabbed the railing and surged to his feet. "Hurry, Felix." He spun the boy an urgent look. "Nadia's in trouble."

But as Felix was slowly getting up and muttering obviously uncomplimentary things in his native tongue, Nadia's words struck Tanis anew.

Oh, gods ...

His fingers tightened on the railing. Suddenly the avieth's confession returned with a clarity of understanding: '*... A diversion of some kind, a way to collect many into one place ...* '

Tanis clapped a hand to his forehead. "The Quai game!"

Felix observed Tanis's expression and his cat-eyes narrowed. He paused, halfway to standing. "What about it?"

Tanis let out a tremulous exhale. "Shail is planning to kidnap Adepts for the Danes' war. I think he means to do it tonight at the Quai game."

Felix glowered at him. "*Forthcoming* much?"

"I only just realized it myself, Felix. What's the fastest way to the amphitheater?"

The Nodefinder eyed him doubtfully. "This way." He turned and headed along the walkway towards the dome's east-facing horizon. "And how'd you learn of N'abranaacht's plans then?" he grumbled. "I don't suppose he just had them written in some secret journal like what you're always reading."

Tanis gave him a look. "No."

Whatever Felix saw in Tanis's gaze seemed to wither his indignation. "How'd you even get us out of there?" It wasn't really a question, and Tanis hadn't intended to answer it even if he'd had an answer to offer. Felix darted a look over his shoulder, uncertain now. "You're a wielder, Tanis?"

Tanis clenched his jaw. His urgent thoughts were split between finding Nadia and trying to imagine a way to stop Shail, but even had he thought upon it, the question had only one true response.

He cast his colorless gaze towards the forest and the distant amphitheater. "I am my mother's son."

FIFTY-FIVE

"Beware, beware the tunnel's light. Tis a dragon's hungering eye."

— Excerpted from *The Varahunaiya*,

a famous Kandori legend

"ISABEL VAN GELDERAN ..."

Isabel woke in darkness. She felt the whisper of his breath cold upon her neck, but the knife was colder still.

A circular room came into focus ... wide, with windows overlooking bleak mountains, broad strokes of charcoal and white. All the world seemed twilit and colorless, without even a hint of gold from the sun's radiant departure.

"Isabel ..." His voice in her ear made her jump, but she quickly stilled with a sharp inhale, for he drew the point of his knife lightly down the side of her neck and along her collarbone, scratching a whiter than white trail across her skin.

She realized she was bound. As awareness returned to her fully, she looked to find her arms and legs spread apart and a particular silver rope binding ankles and wrists to a pair of gold poles. She'd been stripped of her fighting clothes, of everything save her blindfold and a short linen shift ... but she hadn't gone into Ivarnen wearing that. It must've been a gift from him.

"Can you see me, Isabel? Even with that fold of silk across your eyes?"

She scanned the tower room, for she'd felt him moving away, and saw an ornate bed, a table, a hearth. He was leaning in what passed for a corner in the circular room, one shoulder braced against a window's frame.

"Pelas."

He had his arms crossed before his chest and a Merdanti dagger in one hand, and his eyes were very, very dark.

She'd known it would be him even before he spoke her name ... even before she walked unarmed to meet his brother. She'd known she and Pelas would meet again, but not the manner of it. She never imagined it would be like this.

Isabel swallowed and looked down at the shift protecting her modesty. Then she looked back to him.

He shrugged. "Out of respect for you."

"And the *goracrosta*?"

He smiled. "Out of respect for your ability."

An ache in her stomach and another in her head warned her she'd been unconscious for some time…hours, perhaps a day. She turned her attention to the window before her. These were no mountains she'd ever seen. "Where are we?"

He straightened and wandered along the curving wall. As he walked, he trailed his dagger behind him, scraping an uneven line. Reaching the window, he bent his head and peered out. "My best guess is Myacene. There's naught but what you see out there for hundreds of leagues. Such lifeless emptiness appeals to my brother."

She managed a dry swallow. "And this tower?"

He opened his arms. "This beautiful tower is a gift to me." He started walking the rim of the room again, tracing his dagger's uneven line. She saw thin ones and deep ones drawn across plaster and stone. Hundreds of lines encircling the room.

"A quiet place to 'ponder my disobedience'…somewhere away from distractions, where I might learn to reform my ways. He promised to check on me again in another century or so." Pelas shot her a bitter smile over his shoulder as he continued his slow tracing. "Being that I need neither food nor water to survive, Darshan considers this a suitable arrangement."

Isabel breathed in sorrow, for the air was thick with it. This was not the same being she'd met in Tal'Afaq—yet the darkness she now perceived in Pelas had been lying across his path even then. "What did he do to you?"

He shot her a look of fire and fury, of torment and agonized despair. "He took away my power."

She stared at him. "But…that's impossible."

He barked a caustic laugh and threw open his arms. "And yet here we are!" He plunged the dagger back into the wall and scraped a deep fissure as he dragged it behind him.

If she'd been talking to the same man that had faced her so calmly in Tal'Afaq, Isabel might've tried to reason with him, but she sensed that this version of Pelas had abandoned reason some time ago. And could she blame him, when no reasonable answer could possibly be found?

She watched him making his slow circle dragging his dagger, a predator chained in a cage. A god chained to mortal form.

"Why am I here?" She knew the obvious answer—that this is where her path had brought her, but why it had taken her there?

Pelas turned abruptly, tossed his dagger into his other hand and started dragging it back in the opposite direction.

"Why are you here?" He eyed her over his shoulder, and in that brief moment she saw something very dangerous in his gaze. An austere smile flickered and was gone again from his lips. "You're a present for my good behavior. Darshan's idea of sport."

Feeling a little lightheaded, Isabel tested the *goracrosta* at her wrists. The cuffs were tightly bound and had been artfully woven. Another piece of the enchanted rope connected each cuff to the metal poles. She couldn't free herself unless he gave her his dagger, which seemed...unlikely.

"But why you specifically, why here, like this...?" Pelas waved an airy circle with his dagger in a casual manner much in contrast to the acrimony in his tone. "*You're* here, Isabel, because you're a powerful Healer, and I..." Suddenly he dropped his chin and shot her a look so rapacious and hungry that her heart nearly stopped in her chest. "Thanks to my dear, sweet brother's *compulsion*, I've developed a particular taste for Healers."

She caught her breath.

Even in Tal'Afaq she'd perceived that Pelas hadn't been wholly himself. This compulsion then had been what she'd sensed, why he'd kept moving away from her...why she'd instinctively distanced herself.

She understood better the formless darkness that she'd seen shrouding her path, understood why she hadn't been able to see beyond it at the time...and why the world now remained a colorless twilight.

She and Pelas both had passed through Darshan's shadow, and now they were trapped together in a gloaming of his creation, trapped in some sense in Darshan's world—Darshan's *rules*—where all was a glamour.

Only the pain would be real.

Isabel forced a swallow. Though she could guess, she wanted to hear it from him. "What does...the compulsion require of you, Pelas?"

He stopped with his back to her. For a long time, all she saw was the rise and fall of his breath. Then he turned and crossed the room to a table with a linen drape across it. He tossed one corner of the cloth roughly aside to reveal a panoply of knives, and swapped his dagger for a thin silver stylus. Turning, he held it up for her viewing pleasure. "Let me show you, Isabel."

Her heart was racing when he halted before her and presented the stylus across his open palms. One end was needle-sharp, the other flattened to a razor edge—an artist's brush forged in steel.

His copper eyes looked her over, traced the lines and curves of her body. She thought she perceived a flicker of the man he had once been as he admired her form—a man he must still be somewhere, beneath the compulsion, confusion and loss.

He ran the back of his fingers across her collarbone, along her shoulder and down the inside of her upper arm, which lay open and bare to his inspection. "So lovely…too lovely to harm as I have harmed others."

The dark hunger in his gaze truly frightened her. She couldn't close her eyes to shut it out, for they were closed already—this was *elae* showing her what was, revealing only truth where human eyes had lied before. Pelas should've glowed standing before her, a sun too bright to look upon—even as his brother had appeared to her in Ivarnen's corridor…even with *goracrosta* diluting her *elae*-fueled Sight. Instead, Pelas was bound in twilight.

Somehow…somehow she had to free him from this shadow.

He dropped his arm to his side and his chin to his chest. "I tried, Isabel…" His voice came a bare whisper. "All day I've had you here…I've tried to disobey…out of fury and defiance…spite…but in the end…" He lifted his gaze. "In the end, we find ourselves inevitably back at our mutual beginning—subjects of Darshan's will." These last words sliced the air with animosity and hopelessness.

"You don't have to do this. You have a choice."

"No." He shifted his gaze away and clenched his jaw. "My only hope is to do what my brother tasks me with. If I…please him enough, he may give me back my own will."

It worried her to hear him say such words. "You cannot believe he will ever do that."

His brow twisted. She saw a spark of fury flare in his gaze and quickly die, replaced by smoldering despair. "I fear you're right." The smile he lifted to her then was as bleak as the mountains beyond their tower. "But that just leaves us…here."

Suddenly that dark persona appeared again—sardonic, caustic…coldly indifferent. "And where is here?" He narrowed his eyes and pursed his lips and spun the stylus through his fingers. "Oh, yes." The stylus flipped forward into an artist's practiced hold, and he set the needle point against the skin of her left shoulder.

His eyes flicked back to her, darkly inquiring, and he pierced the tip into her flesh. She inhaled sharply. "What shall we draw today, Isabel?" He drew the tiny razor end through her skin—not deep, no, but deep enough to trace a line of blood. Deep enough to leave a scar…that is, if she lived long enough to heal from this. If she *could* heal from this.

"A pattern—" she gasped. Then she caught her bottom lip between her teeth to keep from crying out.

He smiled into her hidden gaze. "A pattern. I hadn't thought of that." He drew a circle with the stylus and withdrew it from her flesh, leaving a streak that ended in a curlicue of blood. She inhaled a shuddering breath.

"You needn't be brave on my account." He looked her over while his fingers spun the stylus again. "A woman's screaming has never bothered me. Odd, I suppose. I doubt Darshan put *that* into his compulsion." His gaze narrowed. "But what pattern should we start with, you and I?"

Her heart was racing and she felt faint. She was finding it difficult to stay focused. "Something..."

He eyed her with dark curiosity. "Yes?"

"Something of the light."

This made him frown. But then he nodded. "Perhaps you should design it with me." Abruptly he spread his arms, backed away and barked a bitter laugh. "We're trapped in this hell together, after all, aren't we? At least..." his eyes looked her over again as his expression fell. "That is, for as long as you can last."

"Pelas..." She begged him with mind and tone and voice, but while the *goracrosta* couldn't keep *elae* from washing through her, it could and did prevent her from framing it to her intention. "Please—don't do this to yourself."

He drew back, blinking. "What?"

She tried desperately to find the right words to get through to him, to reach the being beneath the dark creature of Darshan's invention. "You're letting him win."

He stared at her for a long time, his face twisted with pain. The he laid his hands upon her bare shoulders and pressed his forehead against her own. "Isabel, can you not see?" He brushed his nose along hers, his breath cool across her mouth. "He already has."

Isabel roused from darkness into pain. She lifted her head and let the twilight seep back in. Her body felt cold except for her left shoulder and upper arm, where he'd—

She'd lost consciousness during the middle of his drawing. She looked now to the flesh of her shoulder. He'd blotted it, cleansed it of blood. The skin was red and slightly swollen around the swirling cuts, but the pattern ...

Even in that twilight world, it glowed.

She' didn't know if it was a real pattern with purpose or merely something of his artistic invention, but it collected *elae* to it like a star.

She knew why her path had brought her there now, but she didn't know how to move forward upon it.

Isabel looked around the room and found him standing at a distant window looking out. "Is there anything to drink?" She needed water if nothing else.

He turned from the window, and his brow furrowed. After a moment's thought, he grabbed a cup from the mantel, threw open a near window and scraped snow from the eaves into it. Icy air accosted her, rousing gooseflesh from neck to knees. Soon he had the window closed and set the cup by the fire to melt.

"I should've thought of that before. You'll last longer with water, and ..." he shrugged, "well, you're all the company I'm likely to have for a very long time."

He pushed his dark hair off his shoulders and came to look over his handiwork with a discerning gaze.

She watched him inspecting her arm. "What does it do, your pattern?"

He pursed his lips. "I'm not certain. It just came to me. It's beautiful, isn't it?" He lifted his gaze to her. Then he smiled sadly and stroked her cheek with a gentle hand. "Something must be left of me somewhere." The look in his eyes made a tortured confession of these words. "I couldn't bear to diminish the beauty in you."

"I suppose..." She had to work to keep her thoughts clear, for her head felt full of wool. "I suppose you've thought of trying to escape?"

He grunted derisively and flung one arm towards the window across from her. "Four hundred feet on that side." He opened his other arm to the opposite window. "A thousand feet over there." Then he gave her a pointed look. "So unless you can fly..."

She smiled. "Perhaps if you released me."

He cast his head in a chastising tilt. "But if I did that, sweet Isabel, what hope could I possibly have of pleasing my brother?"

She wetted her lips with a tongue too dry. "Perhaps *my* brother—"

He shook his head. "You and I both know it's too late for that. I should've listened to your warning." He threw himself into a low-slung chair by the fire and pushed out his legs. "I don't suppose it would make you feel better to tell me I told you so."

Isabel gazed sadly at him. "I would rather see you restored than humbled."

He grunted. "Would that Darshan shared your view."

"Pelas..." Her brow furrowed. "Would you really stay here a hundred years waiting for his forgiveness, even knowing as you must in your heart that it will never come?"

"And a hundred more, Isabel. What else is there for me to do?"

"You could..." Again she found herself searching for words to try to reach him, some spark to break through the melancholy, some hope to pierce the darkness. "You wouldn't consider living life...without your power?"

He lifted his eyes and held her blindfolded gaze. "Would you?" When she said nothing to this, for in truth she didn't know how to answer, he shrugged and murmured somewhat desperately, "It's all I know."

As Isabel gazed at him, she better understood his twilight horror. Pelas was an immortal being. What could he ever have known of loss? Perhaps he'd experienced it glibly on a small scale…observed it in the vain struggles of mortal men, but such trials had never applied to *him*—how could they? Pelas was a being who could never die. What was a hundred years in the grand scheme of his eternity? What was the loss of a single lover, or a building where he laid his head at night, or even a kingdom he'd once been fond of? Empires rose and fell while such beings deliberated on their next idle pursuit.

But now Darshan had given Pelas a taste of mortality. He couldn't throw himself from the tower, for he had no power to stop his fall. He couldn't call a portal of escape, for *deyjiin* was beyond his reach—and thus he felt that all of life was beyond his reach, now, without his power.

That was real loss—experienced perhaps for the first time in the countless millennia of his existence—and he had no idea how to emotionally or rationally come to terms with such a thing.

Pelas picked up her cup of snow, melted now, and brought it over to her. With the utmost care, he helped her drink. It cooled her parched throat but brought an empty ache to her stomach. He rested his cheek upon her shoulder while he held the cup to her mouth and watched her drink. "When this is gone, we should continue."

She pressed her lips against the cup for a moment and then turned to look at him where he rested his head on her shoulder. "What's the hurry?"

Abruptly he thrust himself away and turned his back on her. "I *hunger*, Isabel! It *burns!* Don't you understand?" He waved ambiguously at himself while he glared at her with abject anger pouring off of him in waves.

The currents pounded her, pinned her beneath the pummeling surf of his wrath. But it wasn't his ire that stunned her in that moment so much as the sudden shocking certainty that his power remained, only…somehow he couldn't access it—clearly, he couldn't even sense it.

Her mouth fell open with this realization.

"By Chaos born—" He stalked back to her, grabbed her around the waist, and dragged her body tight against his, straining at her bonds. She inhaled sharply. "I *can't* control it, Isabel." He buried his nose in her hair. "I'm sorry." Then he thrust her away and walked to retrieve his stylus.

Isabel tried to order her thoughts through the fear that clung to her. In the moment when he'd grabbed her, the spark of an idea had formed.

Pelas came towards her with darkness veiled across his gaze again and the steel brush of his stylus at the ready.

"What does it demand of you…the compulsion?" She turned her head to look at him as he came up behind her.

He swept her long hair aside and set the needle against her right shoulder.

His gaze narrowed with careful inspection as he pushed the needle tip slowly into her flesh and drew it downward.

Isabel sucked in her breath and clenched her teeth.

"It's difficult to say."

She turned away from him and tried to breathe through the pain.

"I thought for a long time it had something to do with a Healer's blood. Darshan bade me seek the Pattern of the World. We know it's mirrored within the first strand…" He finished off a curl, plucked the stylus out of her flesh and started another. Pain flared in fire and slicing heat.

Isabel gritted her teeth. She poured all of her intention into forming words. "It's true…a Healer carries elements of this pattern…but so does every Adept. Including yourself."

She glanced over her shoulder in time to catch a rueful arch of his brow. Isabel sucked in another shuddering breath. "But the pattern is too vast to be contained in a single Adept…or their blood."

He grunted.

"Even if you had it—" the words came out tightly, forced over pain, "the world cannot be unworked from within the realm itself."

Abruptly Pelas withdrew the stylus. He walked around and stood in front of her. "What do you mean?"

For a moment, she thought she'd reached him, but then she saw she'd merely intrigued that dark specter who had usurped Pelas's form.

"The realm cannot be unmade from within. It can only be unmade from the plane of Chaos."

Pelas frowned at her and spun his stylus absently through his fingers. "Darshan says that something stands between the realm and Chaos or Rinokh would already have reached us again…that is, since your Ean val Lorian unworked the shell my brother claimed on this plane." She couldn't tell if it was dark humor or wrath smoldering in his eyes.

"Yes." She sucked in a shuddering breath, for her shoulder burned badly enough now to bring tears to her eyes. "Another realm stands between Alorin and Chaos…made to be a buffer, a shield." She roused from the stupor of pain with effort. "My brother and his Council of Nine made it for this very purpose."

He regarded her strangely. "And invited us in—*why*…to level the playing field?"

"You were already here by that time, but yes, having you here requires you to play on the same terms as the rest of us—or as close as we can hope for."

He barked an incredulous laugh. It was almost his own. His gaze when he looked back to her was still shadowed, but it also held admiration. "I had no idea anyone knew so much about us."

Isabel doubted he would believe her if she tried to convince him that he still held his power, but perhaps she could give him *some* hope. "Pelas, we can help you."

His gaze darkened, but she couldn't tell what shadow overcame it. When he looked back to her, it was to level upon her a merciless stare. "Why would you?" He walked back around behind her and resumed his work.

Isabel bit back a cry as the stylus bit into her flesh. That time she couldn't stop the tears from falling.

FIFTY-SIX

"Thou art the avenger of the gods, judge and adjutant,

guardian of the gate. Thou art the Great Cat."

– Inscription on the Royal Tombs of the Kings of Cyrene,

circa 992aF

VAILE STOOD BEHIND Alyneri with her arms encircling her, her hands atop Alyneri's hands as she held Vaile's two Merdanti swords nearly touching, the blades extended straight. Alyneri and Vaile worked that day in a high meadow overlooking the *sa'reyth*, with a wide view of the green valley and the mountains beyond.

"When you separate the blades from this position," Vaile murmured at Alyneri's ear in her feminine purr-growl, "the right blade must turn flat as it lifts to the right, while the left blade stays vertical as it sweeps down to the left." She moved her arms to pull the blades as she spoke, drawing Alyneri's arms with her. "This motion twists the thread of the *cortata's* pattern properly. Without the twist, the pattern is incomplete. You will lose some of its strength."

Vaile released her and stepped back. Alyneri glanced inquiringly over her shoulder, and Vaile nodded and motioned her to work through the form again.

Alyneri did as instructed, bringing the blades back together in front of her and then separating her arms in a diagonal with one moving high while the other split low. She made sure to twist the right-hand blade flat as she lifted it.

"Very good. Now from the beginning."

Alyneri moved back to the center of the meadow, brought up her blades—Vaile's blades—crossed before her chest, and gave her teacher the formal bow of respect. Then she sliced her swords apart with a scrape of Merdanti steel and stepped into the *cortata*.

She knew this dance well now. Well enough to fall in and out of it without losing the overall thread.

"One sword," Vaile ordered.

Alyneri slung the left-handed blade into the scabbard on her back. Both hands met on the hilt of her remaining sword, and she turned, spun the blade over her head and slashed down; rose and spun, slashed again, and rose with the blade up in front of her.

"Two blades."

Alyneri reached for the left-hand blade behind her back. She brought both swords together and swept dual blades, united in their path, in an arc over her head. She split them apart as she turned and spun, arms extended, a spiraling top with daggered edges.

"One."

She sheathed the left-handed blade with a sweep of her arm and caught her remaining blade with both hands as she lunged with it, made a low sweep of her opposite leg to spin around. She launched back to standing with a circular twirl of the weapon.

So continued that day's practice.

As the sun fell into afternoon, they sparred. Vaile finally called for a break when all that was left of the sunlight was its golden kiss atop the trees. The zanthyr chose a spot on the hillside to sit, pulled out a bag of wine and offered it to Alyneri while she unwrapped a bundle containing nutcakes and hard cheese and apples so crisp and sweet that Alyneri suspected Balaji must've conjured them.

While Alyneri ate, Vaile leaned back against a rock and curled her legs beneath her. Far below, nestled in the bosom of undulating hills, the tents of the sa'reyth glowed copper in the lengthening sun, while the mountains across the grass-green valley—and indeed, the very air—reflected a golden sheen.

"What will you and Trell do when the game is won?"

Vaile always pushed Alyneri to envision her future and never allowed her to dwell on fears of the present. Sometimes imagining any possible future took greater effort than all the exhaustive sword forms she'd worked during the day.

In the dying light of that afternoon, after a hard day's lesson, she found it especially challenging. "Sometimes the fear hurts so much that I wish I could hate him," she confessed to Vaile after a moment, "or at least harden myself against him—against the loss of him. But I can't. I managed to let go of loving Ean by forgiving him, but I've nothing to forgive Trell for." Her eyes lifted to meet Vaile's, seeking understanding. "All I can think about is his bravery, his compassion, his sense of honor and his intelligence ..." she dropped her gaze, "... and of how incredibly special I felt beneath the warmth of his attention."

"Strong men rage through life burning as brightly as the sun." Vaile cast Alyneri a fleeting look while her fingers brushed idly across the grass ... reverently, as if each blade represented a treasured memory from her long life.

"Some great men burn for eons; others expire in an explosion of honor. But women …" Her gaze shifted to Alyneri with these words and then drifted away again, off towards the distant mountains. "Ever living in the shadows of their bold lives … women endure."

"*Endure.*" Alyneri swallowed. *Yes* … that was all she could say of herself at present. She was enduring … counting the hours and minutes of a life caught out of time while she waited for Fate to play his hand and decide her happiness or utter desolation.

Vaile reached over and cupped Alyneri's cheek. "In our hearts we carry the still-glowing embers of everyone we've ever loved. We can no more extinguish those embers than quench the desire to gather them newly. Men live for honor, women for love. Such is the way of life in this world."

Alyneri closed her eyes, nodded, and then turned away, trying to stave off threatening tears. She didn't like to cry in front of Vaile—not because the zanthyr was insensitive to her grief, but because she bore so much *more* of it personally. *Lifetimes* of grief. Learning of the things Vaile had endured … it made Alyneri feel small by comparison, her tiny fears petty and insignificant.

In the beginning she'd thought Vaile was helping her because the zanthyr also cared for Trell, but in their conversations since, Alyneri had come to understand that everything Vaile did, she did for the First Lord.

For love of him, she managed his *sa'reyth*; she slew his enemies, fought his battles, and waited timelessly for his infrequent and too-brief visits. For love of him, she helped those who were important to his game, suffered the indignation of close association with other than her own choosing, and even gave the gift of her wisdom when benevolence truly struck her. For love of Björn, Vaile endured … though Alyneri felt that if not for Björn, Vaile would not have lingered.

Because if ever a woman walked with grief shadowing her steps, Vaile did. Perhaps others saw this shadow and interpreted it as a zanthyr's typical remoteness, but Alyneri knew better now.

She'd asked Vaile once about the sorrow that lingered behind her every smile. The zanthyr had replied that some sorrows must never be forgotten.

Alyneri blinked dual tears and wiped them quickly from her cheeks. She looked back to the zanthyr and finally answered her, "I hope we'll live together."

The flicker of a smile danced across the zanthyr's lips. Her emerald gaze surveyed the valley while her raven hair made a velvet cloak over one shoulder. "Where would you live?"

"If I had a choice?" Alyneri tried to imagine a life without the looming shadow of the Eagle Throne. "Kandori perhaps. Or even the Akkad. Trell loves it there, and the Emir was good to him."

Vaile gave her an approving smile. "What will you do in your life together?"

Alyneri managed a fleeting expression of hope. "Make a home? Have children?" She shrugged and shook her head. "It seems so … improbable."

Vaile gave her an amused look—or possibly her amusement stemmed from Alyneri's suddenly blushing cheeks. "Children should be experienced," she agreed. "It is an adventure unlike any other."

Alyneri lifted her gaze back to her. "Do you ... ?" But the words froze on her tongue. She'd never heard of zanthyrs having children, and it seemed suddenly rude of her to ask if such was possible.

Vaile seemed to know her mind. "You're not wrong in your assumptions, Alyneri. A zanthyr mating with mankind will always produce an Adept child, but we cannot create our own kind together."

This truth startled her. "But ... *why?*"

"We are the Maker's children—like the *drachwyr*, like the *angiel* ... like Malorin'athgul. Only the Maker can decide when the cosmos needs more of us."

Alyneri frowned. "It seems cruel somehow, to have made you so."

"Sometimes the sun seems cruel, when the rains don't come and the crops die ... when nature is out of Balance."

Alyneri heard a significance in these words that ran far deeper than the statement alone conveyed, an undercurrent of meaning spoken as Phaedor often did—saying two things for every one thing spoken.

"Come now." Vaile pointed to the food she'd brought. "You've eaten but little, and we've more to do today."

Alyneri did as the zanthyr bade her, but food was the last thing she wanted just then. "It's so difficult, the not knowing ..." She frowned as she took another bite. "The mystery of where Trell is and what he's ... enduring. Not knowing if I'll ever see him again."

Vaile leaned on one hand. "The Mage says the best way to know the future is to make it."

Alyneri looked back to her. "Do you believe that's true? With everything that's happened to Trell ..." She shook her head while frustration and fear made an ache in her chest. "It seems like Cephrael stands against him."

"Not so, Alyneri d'Giverny. If the *angiel* stood against him, our Trell of the Tides would've died in the Fire Sea." Alyneri must've looked confused, for Vaile arched a humorous brow. "The gods of this world are naught but echoes of the *angiel*; incarnations of Epiphany and Cephrael in their various aspects." She placed a hand on Alyneri's knee and smiled. "Trell is a Player. His path stretches long before him yet—"

"Vaile!"

Both Alyneri and the zanthyr spun their heads at Náiir's call, which had resonated with unmistakable urgency. Alyneri spotted the *drachwyr* as he rushed over the rise of the hill just below them.

"*Vaile*," he said, planting his feet and sprouting a grin, which he shared with Alyneri when he spotted her, "they found Trell."

Vaile spun a look at Alyneri. Then she snatched her blades from the grass and sprinted down the hill. Even as Alyneri watched, Vaile seemed to pass through smoke—or else become of it—and when Alyneri's vision cleared, the zanthyr wore her fighting blacks. She sheathed both swords at her back as she ran.

Alyneri scrambled to follow.

Náiir waited on the rise for her. She'd never seen him offer such a smile as that which graced his features when she reached him. He took her hand in his own, kissed it, and then drew her rapidly down the hill. "This is good news, Alyneri."

Apprehension fluttered in her heart. "What *is* the news?"

"Trell is being held at the fortress of Darroyhan." He grimaced slightly at this statement. "Well, perhaps that, in itself, is not good news, but keep heart. Having knowledge of his whereabouts means action can finally be taken." He gripped her hand and drew her more urgently on.

When they reached the others inside the *sa'reyth*, an argument was raging. Náiir released Alyneri's hand to join in the fray between his sisters and Vaile, so she wandered along the edge of the tumult and sat down shakily on one of the couches. She couldn't decide if her stomach was twisting with knots of terror or if the currents, roiling from the immortals arguing before her, were simply battering it into a pulp. But in either case, apprehension had her hands twitching and her body trembling, and she couldn't sit still.

Nor could she understand a word of what they were arguing about until Mithaiya raised her voice to insist in the desert tongue, "We *must* wait for the Mage's command!"

To which Vaile snapped in reply, "Think you he'll say differently? They're brother-bound, Mithaiya. You *know* what Trell means to him."

In reply to which, Náiir said loudest of all, "I'm going."

"No, Náiir!" Mithaiya gasped. "If any of us, it should be Rhakar. He's already invested in the game."

Náiir's eyes were hard and uncompromising. "It's high time he had some company on the field, Mithaiya, don't you think?" The air around Náiir shifted as if with waves of heat and his form blurred. When the haze cleared, Náiir wore the *drachwyr's* fighting blacks and had a greatsword strapped to his back.

"At least take Rhakar with you," Mithaiya pressed. She sounded unhappily outranked.

Náiir began patting various places on his person, ostensibly inspecting for hidden blades. "I think I can handle a few Nadoriin, Mithaiya. Besides, Rhakar mans the lines at Raku."

"We should not wait for Rhakar," said an entering Balaji, "and the Mage has gone to Illume Belliel."

Vaile turned him a look. "Illume Belliel." Her green eyes narrowed. "To Alshiba?"

"The time to act is now," Náiir said.

Mithaiya's gaze begged his understanding. "Náiir, think about what you're saying—"

"I agree with Náiir." Vaile looked back to the others. "We must act now, before they can move Trell. Darroyhan is heavily fortified, but at least we know he's there."

"Exactly." Náiir gave Vaile a look of comradeship.

"Which is precisely why I'll be going also."

Náiir's eyes widened, and Mithaiya hissed, "Vaile—you can't mean it!"

"*Vaile* ..." Even Náiir sounded uncertain.

"But the Balance, Vaile—" Jaya began.

"Where will Balance fall if Trell is injured and cannot walk?" Vaile snapped, turning flashing emerald eyes on Jaya. Then she settled Náiir with a penetrating look. "We all know Taliah hal'Jaitar walks the path of *mor'alir* at Darroyhan."

"She will have tried to break him," Mithaiya murmured.

"Peace, Mithaiya!" Jaya glared at her, after which Mithaiya glanced apologetically at Alyneri.

Alyneri's chest in that moment constricted so painfully she thought her heart must've stopped. *A mor'alir Adept holds Trell?* Her nails dug into the velvet couch as if to somehow restrain her mind from exploring the horror of this news.

"Are you going to fight off an entire battalion of Nadoriin one-handed while carrying Trell of the Tides over your shoulder, Náiir?" Vaile hooked her fingers through the baldric strapped across Náiir's chest and pulled their noses closer. Her thumb traced the patterns inscribed in the leather while she held his gaze. "What power will you be forced to work to save him ... and what consequences will it draw?"

The room seemed to swirl around the two immortals while they stared at each other in silence. Finally, Vaile released Náiir with an arch look. "Exactly. I'm coming with you."

"Vaile ..." Mithaiya sounded desperate. "You cannot serve the Mage if you're dead."

Vaile spun her a glare. "Neither can Trell val Lorian," she hissed. Then she vanished.

Mithaiya threw up her hands and spun away in exasperation.

"Balaji, *do* something," Jaya protested.

Balaji in that moment became very interested in his wine.

"By the Lady's blessed star, have both of my brothers gone mad?" Jaya crossed her arms beneath her breasts and stared away. Alyneri imagined she could see nebulae exploding in her gaze.

"You *will* be careful, won't you?" Mithaiya asked Náiir. She glared accusingly from across the room. "Vaile is absurdly careless in her use of the fifth, and you're so unpredictable in these situations."

He looked affronted. "What's that supposed to mean?"

Mithaiya shook her head. "The Mage wouldn't appreciate another disturbance like Nab Kaleer right now."

"*Balaji* and *Ramu* caused the cataclysm that destroyed Nab Kaleer." Náiir flung a hand at an uncharacteristically quiet Balaji. "*I* had nothing to do with the city's destruction. *I* was minding my own business at the time."

Mithaiya snorted. "*Business* indeed."

"Balaji," Jaya turned back to him, "have you truly nothing to say?"

Balaji sipped his wine.

Náiir frowned at his sisters. "I have to go." He strode from the room.

"*Vincal*, Balaji!" Jaya swore.

Alyneri didn't understand the energy that was whirling around them, but at the same time she imagined that she probably didn't want to. Whatever had so upset the female *drachwyr*, it couldn't be pleasant. It probably wouldn't make her happier for understanding it better, and it most certainly wouldn't make her any less afraid. Besides, something else Vaile had said had her unsettled enough.

Alyneri captured her hands between her knees and shifted her gaze to the *drachwyr*. "What did Vaile mean when she said the Mage and Trell are brother-bound?"

Balaji looked to his sisters. "I will leave this to you." He left.

Jaya and Mithaiya exchanged a troubled look. Then Jaya came over and sat down on the couch facing Alyneri, so that their knees nearly touched. "Vaile said brother-bound," she began, looking hesitant, "because the Mage is bound, in a sense, to Ean val Lorian ... and therefore to Trell by extension."

For some reason, this answer made Alyneri feel shaky inside. "What do you mean, Ean and the Vestal are bound in a sense?" she could barely hear her own words, her voice sounded so faint.

Jaya placed a hand on Alyneri's knee. "Perhaps we should wait for a better time to speak of these things."

"Will there ever be a better time, Jaya?" Mithaiya came across the room. "It's time you knew, Alyneri." She spared a brief glance at Jaya. "As you know, Ean has Returned and Awakened, but what you don't know is that in a previous life, Ean was a man named Arion Tavestra."

"Arion Ta ..." It was a name out of history—a *famous* name. Alyneri's eyes grew wide as she looked up at Mithaiya.

"Arion Tavestra was one of the Mage's Generals," Mithaiya continued. "He sat on the Council of Nine and was integral in the creation of T'khendar. He was ..." Mithaiya glanced to Jaya, "he was the Mage's closest friend, but ..."

"But more than this," Jaya said, picking up the thread with a concerned furrow between her golden brows, "Arion Tavestra is the eternal soulmate of the Mage's sister, Isabel. Before the Adept Wars, Arion and Isabel bound themselves to each other with the Unbreakable Bond. They reunited in T'khendar, and ..." She cast a worried glance at Mithaiya.

Mithaiya came and sat on Alyneri's other side. "Sweetling ... Ean and Isabel bound themselves again in this life as they were bound in the beginning."

Jaya squeezed Alyneri's hand to regain her gaze. Hers conveyed the utmost compassion. "Ean is the Mage's brother now."

Alyneri pressed a shaking hand to her throat. She'd claimed to have expunged Ean from her heart, so why did this news make her feel so extraordinarily ill?

"Wait—Ean is Björn van Gelderan's *brother*?"

Everyone turned to find Fynn standing in the opening between tents. "As in my *cousin* Ean? Do you mean to say I'm cousin-brother-bound to—" Fynn paused to emit a long belch. "—Björn van Gelderan?"

Jaya cast him a look of stony disapproval. "It is by this grace that Vaile chose to save your life, Fynnlar val Lorian—much testing the Balance in the bargain, I might add."

Fynn came on into the room. "Oh, I'm most grateful, your worshipful sunful rivalness."

Jaya blinked at him.

Fynn threw himself on the low couch across from her. "Thirteen hells, who wouldn't want the most powerful wielder in the realm as a cousin by bondage? Besides, doesn't he—I don't know," Fynn waved airily, "own an entire realm or something?" He crossed a booted ankle over one knee and spread his arms along the back of the couch. "Do you think he'll be here any time soon? I have this investment opportunity he might be interested in."

"How can you joke at a time like this, Fynn?" Alyneri protested desperately. She sank back against the sofa and pressed hands to her cheeks. She felt like the entire world was slipping off its axis ...

"I never joke about needing money, Alyneri." Fynn waved with his empty goblet. "I find people who joke about needing money to be terribly rude. The indigent have no sense of humor, so jokes are entirely lost on them, which is a wanton waste when one is already down on his luck."

Carian just then poked his head around the curtains demarking the portal between tents. "Oh—there you are."

Fynn scowled at him. "Where've you been? You said you were going for wine an hour ago."

Carian shrugged a mass of his wavy hair off his shoulder and hitched up his britches. "I was occupied."

"Doing what?" Fynn and Mithaiya demanded in unison.

Then Mithaiya narrowed her gaze at him. "What are you doing here, Carian vran Lea? I told you to stay in your valley. You're already testing Vaile's patience being here at all."

"Yeah, but the cat just left didn't she?" Carian sauntered over to Mithaiya, loins in the lead. He grabbed her up by the waist, clutched her close, and proceeded to agitate her hips in a manner that looked extraordinarily unpleasant to Alyneri, although Mithaiya seemed to enjoy it, if told from the lustful smile she cast the pirate in return.

Balaji meanwhile came back in the room, walked over to Fynn and handed him a new goblet.

Fynn brightened considerably. "Why thank you, Lord of the Sky Who Walks the Sun."

"That doesn't even make sense," Jaya protested.

"Peace, Jaya, he's tasting." Balaji watched with a hopeful gaze as Fynn swished the wine around in his mouth, sucked in air with a great slurping noise, and then swallowed and smacked his lips. "Well?"

"It's still a little sweet."

Balaji looked crestfallen.

"Maybe you're not letting it age in the barrel long enough," Fynn proposed.

Balaji recoiled in horror. "My wine isn't *aged* in a *barrel.*" He couldn't have sounded more offended. "It is formed from the air in a complex blending of elements to produce the sublime flavors of cherries and blackberries with a hint of cassis, and a finish with undertones of vanilla." He waved a hand to emphasize the wide range of elements that combined into the conjuring of his wine.

Fynn seemed to not know how to advise him at that point. He put his nose back in the goblet and focused on draining it.

Carian came and plopped down between Alyneri and Jaya, forcing the latter aside. She cast him a glare like a displaced cat.

Carian looked Alyneri over as he made himself comfortable. "So, Your Grace, Fynn tells me you and our Trell of the Tides are betrothed. That makes a couple of princes on your dance card now, *eh?*"

Alyneri opened her mouth and clapped it shut again. She turned Fynn an affronted look instead.

"It's not like that, Carian." Fynn held up his goblet as he explained, "I don't think Her Grace was ever actually betrothed to Ean."

Alyneri's eyes widened. "That's hardly the point, Fynn!"

"Two princes is nothing to be ashamed of, Your Grace," Carian consoled. "Though, to be fair, it ain't much to write home about either. Now if that dance card of yours had a *pirate's* name on it …"

Mithaiya hissed at him.

Carian shrugged his eyebrows saucily at her.

She gave him a daggered glare and swept from the room.

Carian leaned back and draped his arms along the sofa, extended long legs and crossed his booted ankles with a flourish. "*Oh ho*, she's got it in for me now." He chuckled to himself. "I love it when she's spittin' mad. You won't believe the things she can do with her—"

"Do get on with whatever it is you came here for, Carian vran Lea," Jaya remarked with a pointed stare.

"I'm just waiting for Fynn, your lizardness."

Fynn exhaled a tormented sigh and stared into his now empty goblet. "I can't believe you talked me into this. I was happy here in my insobriety. Now I'll have to actually … you know … *do* something with my life."

"Only for a few hours. Look, Fynnlar, we need Cassius. He has contacts all around the realm and controls some ridiculous number of nodes—the man is critical to our rebellion. And you're about the only person in Alorin he'll talk to. Didn't you say you knew how to play to his indiscretions?"

"Insecurities," Fynn grumbled. "I said I can play to his *insecurities.*"

"Same difference." Carian sprang off the seat. "So come along then, mate. It's a fine night to travel the Pattern of the World."

Fynn pushed out of his seat with a sigh. He cast Balaji a pleading look.

Balaji said nothing, but a dark wine swirled up into Fynn's cup.

Fynn gave him a rapturous look. "You're a prince, my fine sir. I don't care what they say about you." He saluted the *drachwyr* with his goblet and followed Carian from the room.

Alyneri watched him go, feeling as if her world had been turned inside out. Her head was spinning, her heart felt cleaved, and apprehension and fear churned a toxic mixture in her stomach.

Balaji came over and offered her his hand. "Come ... walk with me, Alyneri. We will keep this vigil together."

Looking up into his eyes, Alyneri felt suddenly as if she looked not into a man's wheat-colored gaze but instead along the rim of the horizon, far beyond the curvature of the world ... even into the distant heavens themselves. In Balaji's gaze, the entire realm lay open to her inspection.

She got the impression that Balaji would know what was happening on the distant shores of Darroyhan long before Náiir and Vaile returned.

Swallowing, she took the *drachwyr's* offered hand and went with him into the night.

FIFTY-SEVEN

"Great minds are apt to work from hints and suggestions. A spark
of inspiration is often sufficient to inspire bold new thought."

– The Adept wielder Arion Tavestra

TANIS AND FELIX emerged onto the top level of the amphitheater just as one of the Quai teams scored a point and the left half of the oval stadium erupted into raucous cheering. Hundreds of rows below, on the 'field' of black and white marble tiles, the two teams broke formation to confer with their mates. All five Adepts of each team stood easily on a single massive tile.

The crowd maintained a fever-pitched hum that made just the thought of conversation daunting. Thousands of fans crammed the theater, eking out every available space from row, staircase, tunnel or platform. Tanis had never seen so many people gathered in one place—and simply to watch a ball game?

Admittedly, he had only a rudimentary understanding of Quai: each team of five Nodefinders hurled a melon-sized silver ball at the other team's players. If an opposing player was hit, the offensive team scored a point.

Where the game derived its challenge was in what happened when the ball missed its target. Depending on whether it landed on the opposing or defensive team's square, who caught it or touched it before it hit the tile, and what they then did with it, any manner of points could be lost or gained.

Actually falling off or knocking a player off their tile scored a weighted point and incurred a heavy penalty for the losing side. Likewise ending up with two players somehow occupying the same tile—which happened more regularly than one might think, considering that the players flashed randomly about the board like fireflies.

In these confluences and divergences governed by endless rules, Tanis quickly sank over his head into a Quai quagmire. He marveled the game needed so many rules when just hitting a player seemed challenging enough. Every player could appear and vanish at random—providing they stayed on their own colored tiles and off the tiles occupied by their teammates—but this often meant somehow catching the ball before it touched down if your team threw it and missed. Regularly a player would catch the ball thrown at him, immediately vanish, and reappear on another tile to pitch it at the other team.

Becoming skilled at Quai required insane talent as a Nodefinder, a head for strategy and tactics, and not inconsiderable athleticism.

"*Sancto Spirito*, what a crowd!" Felix made a face as he peered around. He took Tanis by the sleeve and tugged him along the broadly curving rim of the stadium. They wove among the standing observers until they found a clear view. Five tiers, each encompassing fifty rows, spanned the distance between themselves and the field.

"Must be so crowded because the Danes are playing. All the bloody Danes come out of their holes to watch their own team play." Felix shot Tanis a grin. "And everyone else comes hoping to see them beaten—by the Lady, half of Faroqhar must be here tonight. When the Danes played the Caladrian team, they slunk off at the end like shamed dogs. Now *that* was satisfying."

Barely listening, Tanis scanned the crowd for Nadia and Shail, already feeling overmatched. The fans standing closest to the field looked barely larger than ants.

Nadia ... Tanis let his mind travel the bond, trusting the path to take him to his intended end. *We're here. Where are you?*

A moment's pause, and then he felt her connection at the other end of the bond.

Tanis! Relief threaded through her mental tone, twining among a wider band of apprehension. He sensed her distantly. *I'm down in the first circle in the eastern quarter.*

Tanis snared Felix's sleeve and tugged him towards the closest staircase. *We're coming.*

Tanis ... He felt uncertainty and a budding fear tingeing her end of the bond. *I was so worried for you. N'abranaacht was exactly as you said. He—oh, by the Blessed Lady! He's here! He's—*

And then the feel of her mind vanished. Tanis came to a sudden halt and clutched Felix's arm.

Nadia? Nadia!

Nadia swallowed as the Literato N'abranaacht emerged from the crowd on an unerring course in her direction. Though he wore his white hood now, she couldn't mistake the set of his shoulders or the way his dark eyes speared the distance to fasten upon her. Even had she not recognized him from these attributes, she would've known him from the Merdanti blade strapped to his back.

Curving stone benches lined the row where Nadia stood, but the crowd was so thick that three people stood in every space intended for one. Somehow they all parted to let the literato pass, even when no room existed in which to move out of his way.

Nadia closed her mind immediately when she saw the literato approaching through the crowd, but this necessarily also shut Tanis from her thoughts. She'd never felt so trapped by uncertainty as she did in that moment, watching the terrifying man coming towards her. How had he found her at all?

"Why … Phoebe della Buonara." The literato's eyes were smiling as he reached her side. He clasped hands before his silk robes and gave a polite nod. "Providence shines upon us that we meet again so soon."

Nadia pushed up her glasses and turned an uncertain look towards the field. "I would that it might, Literato. Alas, my team is losing."

His eyes smiled at her, but his thoughts did not. "I think their luck is soon to change."

She sensed a deeper, darker truth beneath this statement, though the Rimaldi team *did* just then score a major point. The students near Nadia hooted and yelled and jumped up and down, and in the commotion, one of them knocked into Nadia, who in turn—and to her utter consternation—stumbled against the literato.

He caught her by the shoulders while she muttered a hasty apology.

"No harm done, my dear." His eyes smiled at her, but the mildness of his tone seemed quite at odds with the hostile emotions radiating from him. Worse, he kept one hand resting on her shoulder.

Nadia made to back away, and the hand became a claw firmly rooting her in place.

Dark eyes bored into hers then, yet his voice sounded soft and melodious as he inquired, "Now, *Phoebe*, where are your cousin Felix and his friend Tanis? Have you seen them since last we parted?"

She shook her head, not trusting herself to speak. The hand at her shoulder felt a vice anchoring her to the stone pavers.

"You planned to meet up with them?"

Her head nodded of its own accord.

"Here?"

Again, her head betrayed her by saying *yes* when she'd wanted to say *no*.

She couldn't understand how he was compelling answers from her when she felt no compulsion—exactly as Tanis had warned her!

"And are they here now?" His dark eyes scanned the crowd while her tongue treasonously answered, "Yes, Literato," quite against her will.

The chill seeping from his hand into her flesh was making her tremble, or perhaps it was just dread that had turned her bones to ice. Horrifying fears swarmed her—the danger of his learning her identity, how horribly she'd betrayed her mother's trust, how no one even knew she was gone from the palace—a litany of deadly, foolish mistakes ...

And on top of the consuming guilt of what now seemed enormously foolhardy decisions, she feared that Tanis would be walking right into the literato's hands!

Desperation gripped Nadia. While the literato's gaze searched the crowd, she opened her mind for a split-second to warn Tanis.

And the unthinkable happened.

Just as she felt his mind at the other end of their bond, *another* voice imposed into the silence, *Hello, Tanis.*

Relief flooded Tanis when he felt Nadia's mind open to him again, but then—

Hello, Tanis.

The lad's heart very nearly stopped. Pain in the form of Shail's anger flared through his head, so intense it felt the sun was exploding in his brain. Tanis stumbled and fell, hardly aware of the onlookers he dislodged in the process. Hands that must've belonged to Felix reached for him, but Tanis knew only blinding white light in a continuous explosion that seared away all capacity for thought.

Soon you will truly learn the consequence of defying me. Shail's voice lanced through the blinding pain, lightning bolts of agony further accentuating his displeasure. In the next moment, the man dove fully into Tanis's mind.

The feel of Shail inside his head was like a deluge of icy ocean pouring down upon his molten core—but the waters offered no relief, merely intensified his pain into a boiling torment. And the *horror* of it!

Shail scoured Tanis's mind like a river in flood, pouring into every chamber, filling it, absorbing its contents, and swirling on. Tanis had no command over his own thoughts, no way of even finding the door he'd once closed against the Endoge. The dark water swept his awareness on its tide that he might helplessly witness his own obliteration.

At last the water swirled into what Tanis felt must be the deepest parts of his mind, and there it banked against a solid wall, obsidian dark. This wasn't a wall of Tanis's devising, though he recognized someone had constructed it. As he felt the flood of Shail's mind rising against this wall, unable to penetrate it, Tanis made several important connections.

First, he realized that if Shail had been searching for the secrets of his identity instead of merely seeking to know his connection to Pelas, the Malorin'athgul would've found the truth, to deadly consequence. The same instinct warned Tanis that his parents were people whose very *names* held power, and that he must grant those names the same loyalty and protection he would grant to the people who owned them.

The second thing Tanis realized—a small but wondrous grace—was that Shail sought no further knowledge of Nadia. His dark waters merely washed disinterestedly by the truths of her identity, for his torrent had but one objective: to discern what his brother Pelas understood of his plans.

At last Shail's ocean drained away from Tanis's obsidian wall, but the man did not depart with his tide.

Phoebe belongs to me now, foolish boy. Shail's voice thundered so violently through his mind that Tanis's teeth chattered. He clenched them tightly and sucked quick, desperate breaths through them. *Go now and tell my brother that I will soon teach you both the price of interference.*

This last warning flared like sheet lightning through Tanis's mind. Then the overwhelming presence that was Shail vanished.

When the pain subsided and the spots cleared before Tanis's vision, he found himself on his hands and knees sucking in air in desperate, rasping gasps. A crowd had formed around him.

He blinked to focus on Felix's worried face. Seeing Tanis aware, Felix helped him sit back on his heels. Tanis pressed hands against his knees, feeling like he'd just been pulled from the icy sea. "I'm all right." He barely managed a hoarse whisper, still trying to scrape some breath out of the muck of his deluged composure. He looked to the many faces crowding around him and held up a trembling hand. "I'm okay."

"He's *fine*, he said." Felix glared at the onlookers. "Mind your business then!" Felix helped Tanis up and guided him away from those who'd seen him fall. Elbowing a space for the two of them to stand in, he took Tanis by the shoulders and searched his gaze for some explanation. "Tanis ... what by the Sanctos—?"

"He's got Nadia." Tanis felt sick just saying the words. "It's going to happen here, and it's going to happen soon. We don't have much time." Weak-hearted, Tanis turned away to find the stairs again.

"Wait—*what's* going to happen?" Felix sounded exasperated. He rushed to catch up.

They were pushing their way through the fans clogging the stairs when it began.

At first no one realized anything was happening. The game continued; players vanished and reappeared on their tiles while the silver ball danced around the field, pitched or caught or deflected by expert hands.

Until a player on the Dane's team vanished and didn't reappear. The game continued its fever-pitched pace for a few seconds more, and then one of the Rimaldi players vanished as well.

Seconds passed, and neither of the Adepts reappeared. The players slowly stilled on their tiles and looked around at one another.

Then they began disappearing, too.

The crowd inhaled a collective gasp. When the last Rimaldi player vanished with a cry of alarm, the rising dismay in the audience exploded into outrage. Accusations flung like Quai balls from one side of the amphitheater to the other. People began shoving and shouting as the fans on both sides blamed the opposing team.

Someone knocked Felix into Tanis, who in turn grabbed his friend's arm to keep them both on their feet. "He must've done something to the node!" Felix shouted into Tanis's ear.

"How?" Tanis shouted back.

"The whole Quai court is mapped into a node lying on the level just below it. It's how the court works, because the *leis* are all tied together on top of the node. N'abranaacht must've found a way to untwist that node—"

"Go see!" Tanis urged him off.

Just as Felix rushed away, a man appeared on the Quai court, casting a new ripple of astonishment through the audience. Tall and broad-chested, with blonde hair hanging to his shoulders, he wore leather over mail and brandished a broadsword as his only sigil.

Tanis heard loud thoughts rising on a tide of indignation. Some assumed it must be some kind of dramatic performance; many thought it a poorly conceived joke on the part of the Danes. Abruptly two dozen more armed men popped onto the field. They exchanged a look. Then they rushed into the crowd.

Only when the first onlooker fell back in a spray of blood did anyone realize these were real soldiers and the university was being invaded.

Chaos broke out.

A second wave of soldiers materialized on the Quai court and jumped into the audience after their brethren. They slashed through the hapless fans to form a spearing line. Then came a third wave.

Tanis leapt onto one of the stone benches and ran towards the center of the stadium where he'd have a clearer view, but he soon lost any hope of spotting Nadia among that chaos. The stadium appeared as a storm-washed sea, with people nearly climbing over each other to escape.

The university's Regiment Guard—bright spots of blue and silver—came rushing out of the tunnels and started fighting their way toward the mercenary force against an ocean of screaming people. A few brave souls attempted workings—Tanis felt energy flare and expand just before one explosion hit near the advancing line of mercenaries—but a black-robed wielder appeared on the court to deal with such resistance. A dozen bolts of the fourth cast randomly into the crowd nullified future attempts and stirred the masses into further frenzy.

Almost worst of all, Tanis saw maestros among the terrified students, but none of them lifted even a finger in aid.

Tanis pushed palms to his forehead. *Nadia, where are you?* He exhaled a frustrated breath and strained his eyes scanning the crowd. The cacophony rising from the frightened and injured made concentration difficult, but Tanis thought he saw a spot of white in the lowest circle of rows, near the field. If it was N'abranaacht, he was still over two-hundred rows distant—wide rows clogged with frightened people.

Tanis made for the spot he'd seen anyway, leaping from bench to bench, weaving among the crowd, dodging others also using the benches but heading away from the field.

Motion on the Quai court drew his eye as he ran, and he watched a company of Guardsmen rush onto the black and white tiles, led by two men in black robes. A sorcerous battle began then between the man Tanis assumed was Shail's wielder and the wielders for the Guard, with the latter trying to reach the former through concussive waves of power that flattened anyone unlucky enough to get caught in their cross-fire.

Tanis was beginning to hope they might succeed in stopping the enemy wielder when a man climbed the steps to the field … or … Tanis blinked to focus on the distant figure, for his eyes seemed to think the man's skin was entirely black.

He stalked onto the Quai court carrying an ebon-hued blade, and he walked with the manner of a fighter who knew he had the clear advantage. Two of the guardsmen broke formation to confront him, but he swept them aside with easy backhanded blows. They tumbled like twigs to lie still at the edge of the court. Six more soldiers moved to block the man's progress then, and a battle resulted. The black-skinned man easily held his own.

Tanis knew him then, for what else could he be than *eidola?* Had he been hiding in the audience all along, concealed perhaps, like Shail himself, in the passive robes of a Palmer?

Tanis observed all of this with one eye on the Quai court and the other guiding his way as he jumped from bench to bench, pushing through the masses still trying to escape. For all that his breath came fast from this effort, he felt cold inside.

A hand caught his arm roughly. Tanis grabbed his aggressor's wrist, jumped off the bench and spun, flipping the man over onto his stomach. He shoved the other's arm up behind him with the latter's hand turned in a torturous hold and exhaled a warning growl.

"*Yeow!*" Felix's cry sounded muffled, made as it was into the stone bench.

Tanis released him with an apologetic grimace. "Sorry." He extended a hand to help Felix up. The Nodefinder had a cut over one eye, a bleeding lip, and a nasty bruise blooming on his chin. "What in Tiern'aval happened to you?"

Felix glowered at him while dabbing at his lip with the back of his hand. "Nothing you didn't just make worse!" He exhaled forcefully. "Wouldn't you know? N'abranaacht's got a whole company guarding the entrance to the node chamber below the Quai court. If I hadn't been able to travel twisted *leis*, the bloody barbarians would've beheaded me."

Shade and darkness.

Tanis climbed back atop the bench and turned a desperate look around. The amphitheater remained in chaos, while the melee on the Quai court had devolved into a heated battle. Smoke and ash floated in a bluish haze, sparkling with lightning of the fourth. Tanis felt a constant tingling, like pins stabbing his skin.

He pushed a hand through his hair, feeling utterly inept and fighting off a crushing sense of futility. Any minute the mercenaries would have their Adepts surrounded and begin evacuating them across the node that Shail's wielder was protecting.

"Bloody Sanctos on a stake, Tanis." Felix had joined him on the bench and was casting his gaze around in horror. "What can we do?"

Tanis spared him an agonized look. "I—" But a sudden perception drew his attention to the lowest circle of rows, where he saw two figures moving against the exodus.

Nadia.

Tanis sprinted for her.

Nadia's shoulder ached beneath N'abranaacht's clawing fingers, which seemed to emanate icy cold so that her entire arm was numb beneath their hold. Yet the experience paled compared to the numbness she felt inside.

When N'abranaacht had taken over her mind and usurped her communication with Tanis, he'd somehow equally shut her out of the exchange. She had no idea what he'd said or done to Tanis through the bond, and the thought that Tanis might've come to harm because of her carelessness made her heartsick with fear. The worst of it was she couldn't even sense *elae* while the literato was touching her. She had no recourse to any of her gifts and no means of contacting Tanis again.

She'd tried pulling away many times, but escaping N'abranaacht's hold felt as much an impossibility as suddenly seeing dragons descending on Faroqhar in fire and flame. Yet ... that envisioning now seemed no more improbable than armed mercenaries invading the Sormitáge, or the black-faced ... *creature* that was fighting countless Regiment Guardsmen on the Quai court and winning.

In fact, the entire day's events had Nadia feeling faint with disbelief. Could the literato have somehow switched doors while they were taking tea, so that she'd emerged from his office into a world that looked the same yet existed on an entirely different plane?

She tried to keep her wits about her, but such dreadful thoughts kept presenting themselves for her regular inspection that it was all she could do to keep from screaming.

For the longest time, N'abranaacht had made her sit on a bench while chaos erupted around them, but now they were up and moving towards the Quai court. She didn't even remember being instructed to stand and walk.

That he could invade her mind, compel her cooperation, even usurp a bond—all through the touch of one hand ... this was a truth altogether unimaginable. Fear gripped Nadia as tightly as the literato's fingers.

She tried pulling away again, but her effort was half-hearted, and this time the literato squeezed so painfully that she gasped and her knees buckled. Even falling didn't free her from his grasp. He merely caught her other arm in a vice-like grip and kept her moving.

"Still thinking your young suitor will come to your rescue, Phoebe?" The malicious humor in his tone made the hair on the back of her neck stand on end.

Nadia didn't trust speech. She clenched her teeth tightly lest he somehow compel another truth from her wanton tongue. Fear made her feet unsteady, while guilt weighed heavily on her heart—*such* guilt! It would consume her should she dare think of the truths beneath it. But she didn't dare, for what if he could read her mind as easily as he compelled her tongue? What havoc could this man wreak if he *knew* he held captive the heir to the Agasi Empire?

They had to walk a fair distance, and Nadia was forced to step over those who'd fallen to an early blade. As they rounded one edge of the court, a man in a hooded cassock rose from a bench.

The literato thrust Nadia into the man's grasp. "Take her."

She looked beneath the shadowed hood, and fear lodged as a lump in her throat. The man's eyes were wholly black—likewise the flesh of his face and the hand that reached out to shackle her wrist in an iron hold.

"Get her across the node, but keep her isolated from the others until I return."

"Your will, my lord." The creature's voice sounded like pebbles rattling in a tin cup.

It pulled Nadia into the embrace of one iron arm. She turned a look over her shoulder, but N'abranaacht was quickly heading up a near flight of steps.

The man's arm around her shoulders felt as unyielding stone, yet relief flooded Nadia—for now that N'abranaacht had released her, she sensed the lifeforce again. She drew in *elae* like a man nearly drowned, a shuddering, grief-stricken inhale, and was just forming her intent to compel the creature to let her go when a resounding explosion rocked the air and sent her staggering into her captor's arms.

Ears ringing, Nadia clung to the creature's immovable form and looked for the source of the explosion. Midway up the stadium, a figure in silver mail and a red surcoat emblazoned with the imperial crest stood atop one of the tunnel arches.

The Imperial Adeptus—thank the Lady!

The wielder held a silver staff whose smoking tip remained aimed across the stadium at the mercenaries. Nadia swung her head to find their lines broken and the Adepts fleeing.

Another wielder of the Adeptus appeared on an adjacent tunnel roof. He raised his staff and aimed a murderous blast towards the battle on the Quai field. The wielder there deflected the pattern, which exploded against a section of the court and disintegrated the tiles into a massive geyser of ashen dust.

Red-cloaked soldiers came pouring in through several archways then, but they still had to battle their way through a terrified exodus to reach the mercenary forces, who were now reforming their lines. The two Adeptus wielders atop the tunnels began concentrating their fire against the black-skinned creature fighting the Regiment Guardsmen on the Quai court.

Then something—Nadia could only describe the force as thunder without sound—ripped through the stadium and flattened her painfully against the creature holding her; he himself stood as immobile as stone beneath the onslaught. She watched over his shoulder in growing horror as an invisible wave swept up the theater, taking down everyone in its path.

The Adeptus wielder standing atop the tunnel spun like a ragdoll in the surf. She didn't see where he landed and could only pray he'd maintained the wherewithal to protect himself.

Breathless, Nadia sought the source of the strange power and spotted another of the black-skinned creatures high on the other side of the stadium, standing upon its crowning colonnade.

Instantly the remaining Adeptus wielder retaliated against the creature, and the sky above the amphitheater lit up with the fourth. Soon all the wielders from both sides were attacking and defending. Deadly patterns flew like arrow volleys. No one paid any attention to how many innocents were harmed in the process.

Nadia stared. Was the world falling to pieces?

Everywhere she looked, Nadia saw chaos. Worst of all was the newest creature at the theater's rim, for he fired off constant lobs of thunder without sound that flattened or shattered everything they hit, while the wielders' aiming against him might've thrown feathers for all their patterns made any difference.

And then—*impossibly*—*No* ... it can't be ... ?

Nadia blinked at a white figure streaking along the colonnade at the stadium's rim, brandishing a black sword. A moment later the figure swung at the creature, and they met in a clash of blades.

"That's our cue." The monster holding Nadia dragged her off towards the nearest tunnel.

Wait—he's not taking me to the Quai court? But—

Suddenly every instinct screamed in alarm. She thrust her feet before her. She struggled. She tried compulsion. She even shouted. But the creature was an unstoppable force sweeping her inexorably on. *Elae* had no effect on it.

In a final act of desperation, she flung open her mind.

Taaaniiis!

Tanis got separated from Felix in the blast of *deyjiin* that ripped through their side of the stadium and cast the boys tumbling into a crowd of onlookers who'd stayed to gawk at the battles. The shaken lad was attempting to extract himself from the bodies that had graciously broken his fall when a streak of white at the stadium rim caught his attention. He blinked and pressed palms to his eyes. Then he stared.

N'abranaacht's silk robes clearly outlined his muscular form as he rushed to engage the *eidola—his own creature*—in combat. Thus began the pirouetting dance of a black marble statue against an angel in flowing white silk, with the stadium's majestic colonnade as a background.

It made no sense!

Tanis pulled his leg out from beneath an unconscious man and got shakily to his feet. Felix was still buried somewhere in the pile of people, but Tanis couldn't spare thought for him just then, for every sense screamed in warning.

The stadium had become a breeding ground for bedlam, yet what had truly shaken Tanis was the suspicion that he had it all wrong.

He scanned the scene: the mercenaries still trying to herd their captured Adepts towards the Quai court while staving off the soldiers trying to stop them; the wielders battling each other as well as creatures obviously impervious to *elae*; the same creatures easily battling a dozen men at a time; and N'abranaacht himself, by all accounts looking as though he was coming to the rescue ...

Oh, gods!

Tanis clutched his hair as the truth unfolded in front of him.

Diversion. It was all diversion.

No wonder everything remained in constant chaos. That was the point of the entire endeavor—creating chaos was *all* they were trying to do.

'*N'abranaacht's got a whole company guarding the entrance to the node chamber below the Quai court ...* ' Felix's words took on frightening new meaning. '*If I hadn't been able to travel twisted leis, the bloody barbarians would've beheaded me.*'

No. They hadn't been trying to behead him, they'd been trying to *capture* him.

Tanis pressed palms to his eyes and tried to breathe around the dread suddenly clenching his chest. He felt sick.

All those thousands of people—they'd all had to pass by the node chamber as they fled through the tunnels leading out of the stadium. The enemy could've picked Adepts off at their leisure with no one the wiser. They might have hundreds across the node by now.

Taaaniiis!

Tanis caught his breath at Nadia's sudden mental cry, which pounded in his head with the force of her alarm. He spun around in search of her and spotted two forms near the Quai court: Nadia struggling in the arms of a white-robed man—doubtless another of Shail's creatures—who was dragging her towards a tunnel.

In a moment of desperate clarity, Tanis knew if the creature reached that tunnel with Nadia, he would never see her again.

Concussions rocked the amphitheater as Tanis jumped from bench to bench in a desperate streak. A blast passing too near sent him sprawling, and as he pushed shakily to his feet again, scraped and bloodied, he realized he'd never make it in time.

In that moment, Tanis stopped thinking and just acted.

He needed time to reach Nadia, so he reshaped time around his intent.

Instantly the world shifted and slowed—smoke billowed lazily from the battle on the field; soldiers moved with sluggish limbs, taking seconds to match their swinging blades, even the sparkle of the fourth dulled—but Tanis flew.

He launched from bench to bench to stone staircase and took the steps three at a time. He blurred around and past fallen men and shattered stones, ducked flying bolts of the fourth and dodged through storms of patterns that swept across the stadium like rain. And all the while he kept his gaze pinned on the man dragging Nadia inexorably towards the tunnel, trusting instinct to deal with the rest.

The creature reached the tunnel just an instant before Tanis reached him. In the last, the lad leapt onto a bench and launched himself through the air. Hitting the man felt like diving into a marble column, but he did go down beneath Tanis's form.

The force of their collision knocked time out of Tanis's control, and they tumbled in a fierce and painful tangle.

Recovering quickly, the creature sprang to its feet, grabbed Tanis by the back of his shirt and flung him against the tunnel wall. Tanis slammed into the stone and fell painfully to his hands and knees. The *eidola* ripped off its robe and launched towards him.

Nadia screamed.

Tanis grabbed time again and wrapped it about himself like a cloak. The *eidola's* fist shot towards him, but Tanis easily ducked it. He spun into the *cortata* and pulled out Phaedor's dagger in the time it took the *eidola* to draw back its arm and swing at him again.

Tanis struck the creature across the chest with his dagger, and to his immense relief it staggered back. Such monsters couldn't bleed, yet Tanis knew he'd injured it from the way it pressed both hands to the contusion on its chest.

Tanis drew upon the *cortata's* power, and when the creature next grabbed for him, he ducked its thrusting arm and used the momentum to flip it over. He released time as the *eidola* slammed to the floor in a thundering clap of stone on stone, but then time yanked *him* back into its regular stream with a sudden jar.

"Nadia!" Tanis spared a glance for her over his shoulder. "Run!"

She had one hand on the wall and was struggling to rise, but he realized with a sinking heart that she was in no shape to flee. Blood streamed down the side of her face, pooling against her spectacles, and she looked dazed.

The *eidola* found its feet again and launched for Tanis. It caught him around the waist, and they flew violently backwards through the air. Tanis made time into a rope and climbed up it, slipping out of the creature's hold. He stood on its back while they soared past Nadia, and dove off the cliff of its shoulders just before it crashed violently into the tunnel wall. The floor shook in a rumble of falling stone as part of the wall collapsed atop the *eidola*.

Tanis rolled as he hit the ground. Then he scrambled for Nadia, who stood leaning against the wall. He exhaled a desperate breath, wrapped his arms around her and pulled her tightly against him, feeling such a raging conflict of emotions—she'd still be safe if not for him! "I'm sorry—I'm so-so-*so* sorry!" he murmured wretchedly.

Nadia's eyes beneath her bloodied spectacles remained unfocused, so Tanis slung her arm around his shoulders, spared a glance for the *eidola*, which remained buried under a small mountain of rubble, and then drew Nadia down the tunnel, moving as quickly as she could manage.

The thick stone walls soon drowned the explosions still raging in the stadium, but the sound of other dangers echoed among the maze of dim corridors: distant battle, snatches of men shouting, the chink of mail or boots on stone, the pounding of many feet or an errant scream.

"Tanis?" Nadia's voice sounded strained, a bare whisper. "I feel sick."

He hitched his arm more tightly around her waist and held hers more firmly around his shoulders. The corridor split just ahead, with a passage angling up and another angling down. He felt dubious about following either of them. "You hit your head pretty hard."

"There's something … important I needed to tell you." Nadia pushed a hand to wipe the blood from her eyes, but her fingers were shaking so badly that she only smeared it down her cheek instead. She flung her other arm around his neck and looked like she might pass out. "… I can't remember …"

Tanis clenched his teeth. All of this was his fault. He pressed his lips to her hair as she clung to him. "We've got to get you somewhere safe." He chose the passage angling up and started off again.

Tanis wasn't familiar with the tunnels on that side of the stadium. He didn't know which corridors led to safety versus leading to the node chamber beneath the Quai court, or which wound down to the hypogeum, a warren of rooms left over from the stadium's earlier, darker days.

If he'd thought to use his father's pattern to reveal the currents again, they might've shown him the way out, but the day's events were beginning to take their toll. He felt exhausted. He'd been blasted and blown about and flung into walls; his brain had been seared, and he'd done things with time that no wielder had accomplished in centuries. All of this had significantly drained the well of his energy. He wasn't as sharp-witted as he would've liked—as he *needed* to be.

As he struggled on, Nadia started weighing more heavily; his overtaxed muscles ached, and his body grew leaden while his head felt too light. It took him too long to realize the corridor had curved and was now leading in the wrong direction, or to notice the darker shadow ahead that was an intersecting tunnel. He didn't even hear the man until he stepped out in front of Tanis and raised his sword in warning.

The soldier called back down the adjoining tunnel in accented Agasi, "I think this is the pair you were looking for, Captain."

"Bring them!" came a distant reply.

The soldier motioned at Tanis with his sword.

Tanis wanted to fight—he wanted to grab time and strangle the man with it, but the lifeforce hovered just out of his reach, made recalcitrant by his exhausted mind. So with no other options open to him, Tanis gritted his teeth and turned down the tunnel, which was actually a staircase.

The steps were steep, and Tanis nearly fell twice. Nadia barely clung to him, for she was drifting in and out of consciousness. He was alone in keeping her on her feet.

Torchlight glowed at the end of the tunnel, and Tanis exited the stairwell into a wide cavern framed in ornate columns. The carved ceiling and tiled floor embellished with spiraling patterns of the second strand.

Four mercenaries stood at a far entrance—the main entrance—to the node chamber, blocking any escape. Well ... those, and the *eidola* standing beside a man who was obviously the mercenaries' captain.

Tanis's entire body clenched with frustration.

The *eidola* yanked a nearly unconscious Nadia out of Tanis's grasp and backhanded him. Tanis felt his jaw snap and then knew only a dazed blackness until hands grabbed him off the floor. His stomach heaved as they lifted him, but it had nothing to release back into the world, so it belligerently settled again.

Tanis blinked to focus. The *eidola* stood just inches in front of him. Its eyes were like orbs of obsidian with the slightest silver-violet gleam deep within—*deyjiin's* signature. Tanis felt the creature radiating hate.

"The master wants him alive, remember." One of the soldiers had spoken, but Tanis didn't know which one. He could barely focus beyond his own nose, beyond the fire throbbing in his jaw or his pounding skull.

The *eidola's* black eyes bored into Tanis. Then it turned away. "Bind him with the *goracrosta*," it said in a voice like tumbling stones, "and bring him with the girl." The soldiers holding him pushed him roughly into motion. Tanis stumbled in the darkness and nearly fell. One of their elbows found his jaw on the way down.

Blinding pain stole his breath. Then blackness claimed him.

FIFTY-EIGHT

"No rush is so consuming as the elemental fifth."
– Dhábu'balaji'ṣridanaí, He Who Walks the Edge of the World

AZIL, CAPTAIN OF the Guard, stood on Darroyhan's northernmost tower bathed in the gilt of a setting sun. The red-gold orb hung pinned between the darkening sea and the forward edge of a bank of charcoal clouds. Farther east, stripes of rain washed across the ocean, blanketing half of the horizon, while sunset painted the western clouds with angry light.

It was a potent finish to the day, but Fazil barely noticed, for his dark eyes were riveted on the two creatures standing atop a distant tower. They'd arrived along with reinforcements from Tal'Shira, the rumored 'bright stars' of Radov's new army, but Fazil thought they naught but drew darkness with them everywhere they went.

Supposedly 'secret weapons from the Prophet,' they'd been sent to help protect Darroyhan—from what, none would say—but the creatures in no way lessened the collective apprehension building among the troops. If anything, the presence of such things made it worse, for what kind of threat required demons to thwart it? Fazil just saw them as one more reason to stay on his guard.

If nothing else, the constellation proved his apprehension well-founded.

Every night that week Fazil had watched the seven stars of Cephrael's Hand rise in the west, cross directly over the tower where Trell val Lorian slept, and dive into the eastern ocean just before daybreak.

And Fazil wasn't the only one who'd noticed. It was whispered among his men that the constellation was watching over the prince. Others warned the stars were a beacon for Fate to come claim them all. Fazil had just decided to quell this talk—never mind that he quite agreed—when the reinforcements from Tal'Shira had arrived with those black-skinned demons, proving to his already superstitious men that deep trouble was afoot and heading their way.

Now Fazil watched the *eidola* standing together, seeming little more than dark shadows limned in dying sunlight, and he wondered why they'd really come to Darroyhan.

He didn't trust those things, no matter what lies Viernan hal'Jaitar spun into plausible truths. The so-called *eidola* were unnatural and nothing made by their gods. Just hearing them talk—with voices like dry seeds rattling in a hollow gourd—had unsettled him more than watching Taliah hal'Jaitar work her witchcraft.

That was two counts against Radov's Prime Consul, in Fazil's book. First the lie about Trell val Lorian being a turncoat and a spy. Second the letter telling Fazil to trust these *eidola* and to give them access to the fortress.

Well, Fazil had let them roam about—albeit unwillingly—but all the treasure in Kandori wouldn't entice him to trust them.

One of his men came up beside him and joined him in watching the creatures on the distant tower. After a moment, he made a deprecating grunt. "They're like death walking."

Fazil eyed him in silence, but he couldn't disagree.

From the northernmost tower where he stood, the captain had a view of all seven of Darroyhan's remaining towers. Even in the day's dying light, he clearly saw Taliah hal'Jaitar and her two mutes emerge from the south tower where she kept her prisoners and walk along the parapet to the tower beside it, where she kept her residence.

No sooner did she disappear into the latter than one of the *eidola* broke away from its twin. Fazil followed it with his gaze, watching it slide along the parapets like a shadow and enter the south tower Taliah had just departed.

Fazil's eyes narrowed. He looked back to the squall rapidly overtaking the entire horizon. Yes, a storm was definitely coming.

Trell woke in darkness. He lay with disorientation like a blanket over him, trying to remember where he was and what had happened. An attempt to move chained wrists and ankles answered the former, and the enduring ache in his joints and shoulders told the latter.

Taliah must've Healed him again, though he recalled lying in pain for a long stretch after her last tantrum—days perhaps, but it was hard to keep track.

He lay wondering what had woken him until he heard the door latch click. Moments later, the heavy door burst open and flew into the wall. Torchlight blinded him, and he squeezed shut his eyes until the spots behind them cleared. When he opened them again, the iron lamps were glowing and a demon stood at the end of the marble slab where Taliah had left him chained.

Trell blinked, but the macabre vision remained.

"You are the prince."

Its voice sounded like the clatter of pebbles down a stone stairwell. Trell couldn't quite believe the thing was talking.

It took a standing jump and landed in a squat at the foot of the table, jarring the room with a painfully loud clap of stone on stone.

Trell stared unbelievingly at the thing. Was this some new trick of Taliah's? Something conjured from her dark magic? *Shade and darkness*—could the thing have once been a *man*?

"What *are* you?" His voice sounded hoarse to his ears, dry from days without drink.

The creature grinned a bleak rictus, revealing a black, spiny ridge where its teeth should've been. "I am Death."

Trell laid his head back against the marble block and closed his eyes, resigned to whatever was to come—because, truly, what could he do about it? "It took you long enough to get here."

The creature made a sound that might've been a laugh. Did demons possess a sense of humor?

"It won't be long now, my prince, and it will please me to kill you, for my master wishes it too, but first—" Abruptly the thing sprang and caught itself low, with its hands to either side of Trell's head, its body poised lengthwise over his own. Now *that* was disturbing.

Its demonic face hovered inches from Trell's, close enough that he could see a spark of violet in the depths of its gaze. "My master wishes to know: why did Kjieran van Stone betray him? Why did he choose *you*?"

Trell blinked. Then, for a lengthy moment he just stared—the question was so non-sequitur. "*Kjieran* ... ?" He vaguely recalled the truthreader coming to him in his cell in Tal'Shira when he'd still been nailed to the wall—how long ago had it been? Trell had no idea. Weeks or months ... the days all blurred together. Kjieran had been trying to save him from Viernan hal'Jaitar, that much he recalled.

"I don't ..." he tried to focus his thoughts through the dull throbbing of his tortured head. "... Who is your master?"

The creature moved to its feet. Now it towered over him. "You will *answer*, and then you will die." It shoved a foot onto Trell's ribcage and pressed down. It felt like a bear was sitting on his chest.

Trell tried to draw breath. "I don't—"

"Kjieran van Stone betrayed our master!" Its voice came now in a rattling snarl, echoing in the stone chamber. "He tried to save you. Then he tried to save your father, both acts in defiance of our lord—*treason!* And after everything our master did for him. After such grace as our master's *love*, which none have known since—Kjieran *betrayed* him!"

Trell was seeing stars. The foot on his chest compressed so tightly he feared his ribs would shatter and pierce his lungs, and death really would come for him.

And then something dark blurred before his vision and slammed into the creature with a shattering of glass. The thing flew off of the table and smashed into the far wall in an explosion of stone.

Trell gasped in a breath that felt like needles stabbing his lungs. He saw one of Taliah's mutes standing over him, and then Taliah herself.

"Get that thing out of here," she hissed.

Chaos exploded around him. Trell closed his eyes and just focused on breathing. Glass from the shattered lamp had cut into his chest and arms. He felt the warmth of blood and the sharp fire of those cuts. Soon exploding stone peppered him everywhere else. It went on that way for some time, until—

A dull thud right beside his head bade him open his eyes. One of Taliah's mutes had just decorated the marble table with pieces of his skull. The other lay crumpled by the door. Taliah stood now between Trell and the demon with her hands spread against the table.

Her dark eyes speared it in accusation. "I know what you are." Her lips curled back so that her long teeth, like her father's, seemed to spit the word, "*Inverteré.*"

"*Witch*, my master cares not if you live or die." It stalked towards her.

Taliah threw her arms before her, and—Trell could only explain it as a dread darkness—rippled outwards from her core.

It caught the creature in the chest and spun it backwards into the wall. The stone shattered in another explosion. With all the craters marking the walls already, Trell worried the entire tower would soon come crashing down around them.

"*Inverteré.*" Taliah's lips curled back again as she snarled the word. She pushed up her sleeves and aimed her palms at the creature, who was just then pushing blocks of stone off itself. "I know such patterns as what crafted *you.*"

Reaching its hands and knees, the thing looked up at her under its bony brow. Its eyes were like black orbs of malice, and Trell saw something flash deep within them.

Thunder without sound ripped through the room.

The power shoved him painfully against the table, straining his chains, threatening to tear him *and* the chains from the stone; it sucked the air from his lungs, compressed his already stressed ribs, and finally sent him spiraling into darkness.

Vaile flew through the storm.

Tumultuous currents buffeted her velveteen wings, lifted and dropped her body, rocked her into uneven flight. All around, lightning burst into being, limning the charcoal clouds with great sheets of static brilliance. It couldn't harm her, only lacing her dark wings with rippling light.

She remembered when all of Alorin had slept beneath primordial tempests, waiting for the exploding land to be made ready for life. The *drachwyr* had been created in those fiery terrene forges, birthed of flame and smoke and sere sunlight; but Vaile and her brethren were the children of wind and clouds and starlight, born of the rippling energy of Alorin's first storms.

The fifth sang to her as she flew. It hummed into crescendos, charged forth in frenzied peaks, and fell into arpeggios of crackling static. Its song both bound Vaile and buoyed her, as if the lightning alone bore her through the damp and darkly crystalline clouds. She reveled in this elemental fugue, in the tension built in the humming downpour, the strings of the storm, and in the explosion of timpani in its thunder.

It had been a long time since she had felt so alive ... a long time feeling only a shell of herself.

Perhaps she'd adopted many identities in her long life. Not as mortals did, by changing shells, but in her own way ... selves reinvented or newly adopted for each millennia. But in the last many centuries, she'd spent too much time in her human form while the part of her that was uniquely *Vaile* drained away into transparency, bled of life like her dying realm.

Once great men had challenged her, enticed her ... even enchanted her ... but she held no love for humanity in this age, though she loved some humans individually.

She and her immortal counterparts, the *drachwyr*, varied in this view. The *drachwyr* were bound to humanity in ways Vaile had never understood. They possessed an infinite compassion and patience for mortal frailties, and seemed ever fascinated with those transient beings.

But zanthyrs had no such threads of sympathy binding them, no cause to love or care for the races populating the mortal tapestry. Increasingly Vaile longed to exist solely as her wilder self, her elemental self, the side of herself that was purely and essentially the fifth.

Was this storm your doing, Vaile?

Náiir swirled down out of the grey froth above her, his scales a glint of fire, wings trailing steam.

She angled a feline glance at him and then dove deeper, spiraling down into the denser storm. Powerful wings propelled her through darkness and flashing light. Let him follow if he dared. The *drachwyr* were not so fond of storms as she was.

I merely borrowed its usefulness, Náiir.

You're pulling it with us. He appeared nearby again, following close with outstretched wings, coppery-gold fire searing through smoke. He banked and sliced into the darkly swirling clouds, vanishing in a spear of serpentine tail.

Yes, but not off its course, she cast the thought back to him. *You give my intelligence too little credit.*

Nay, only your prudence.

Prudence has never troubled me. She flung her wings downward to lift herself over a mounding cloud and then dove through a hole just beyond it. Out of the clouds into the pelting rain she emerged, but only for the span of two thrusts of her raven-black wings, for she'd seen what she desired.

As she rose again into the clouds, she heard Náiir's mental sigh. *Exactly my point, Vaile.*

Vaile's emerald eyes narrowed in feline amusement.

But just as quickly they hardened again, for in that brief moment below the cloud line, what the currents had shown her of the activities at Darroyhan sickened her heart and roused her fury.

Vaile pulled the storm like a flowing cloak, so that as they came upon the fortress, rain pelted, lightning flashed, and thunder shook the world. She sent a pulse of the fifth to help the storm along, and a streak of lightning struck the spire on the northernmost tower. The men lining the parapets below scattered for cover.

Just within the gauzy lowest clouds, Vaile made a wide perch of the fifth and settled lithely upon it. Moments later, Náiir banked a close circle and then landed beside her. She dodged to avoid his taloned wings as he folded them behind his body. His spiked tail wrapped around the perch, and its razor tip came to rest near her paw.

Lightning flashed. Thunder resounded. The core of the storm shook the air.

This is a fitting overture for our entrance, don't you think, Náiir?

He angled a fiery orb in her direction.

Smoky clouds filtered across them, masking their forms from view of the men below, but even had mortal eyes noticed the immortal creatures hovering in the darkly shrouded heavens, they would've thought them figments of the storm.

Náiir turned his golden-eyed gaze down upon Darroyhan's towers. *How should we proceed? We don't know which tower they're holding him in.*

She gave him a look that might've been a smile if told from the number of sharp teeth it revealed. *I'll go provide a diversion while you find out.*

He sighed. *How did I know you were going to say something like that?*

Because I'm fonder of Trell of the Tides than you are.

Somehow that isn't the explanation I was thinking of. He aimed a look her way. *Perhaps it would be better if I created the diversion, Vaile.*

Nay. Viernan hal'Jaitar might be expecting one of you to come for Trell. Whereas me … ? The grin widened. *They cannot even imagine.*

They'll need imagine nothing in a moment, he groused. *Try not to kill them all—I need at least one to tell us where to find Trell.*

Vaile turned her head to him, and her gaze held that insolent cast all felines seemed to possess. *I should've brought Rhakar. He would've been more fun.*

Náiir cast her an annoyed look, which manifested in a sharp turn of his head and a hiss of steam from flared nostrils. *Rhakar would've bound you to the storm and rescued Trell himself.*

Ha! Vaile launched off her perch, which dissolved as she departed, forcing Náiir to pump his wings to recover. She laughed as she dove through mist. *He would've tried.*

She set her sights on the northernmost tower and its five guards. With the fifth singing in her blood, she tucked her head, drew in her paws as she flattened her body, and dove down from the heavens in a streak of velvet darkness.

Just inches from the tower parapet, she threw out her wings and thrust her hind legs forward, claws extended. The men saw her then—*my*, did they. Nadoriin scattered with shouts of alarm, but Vaile easily caught one man and then a second in her hind paws. She flung herself away from the rooftop with powerful thrusts of her wings.

Up over the pinnacle she rose, and then she dove into a spiral. The men spun, screamed ... spun ... screamed. Hundreds of feet above the sea, she released one and then the other. They tumbled through the air, still screaming, until they hit the charcoal water with tiny splashes that quickly vanished beneath the downpour.

Náiir had taken human form upon the tower when Vaile circled back around. Two soldiers lay unmoving in his wake, while a third stood pressed against a merlon with Náiir's Merdanti blade beneath his chin.

With the wind singing in her wings, Vaile hovered over the tower and released the form.

Darkness and light engulfed her as the fifth exploded through her form—dissolving, sculpting, reforming every inch of her. It felt like a plunge through the waters of sheer energy. A momentary disorientation cleared as she swam up through the swirl of transfiguration to assume her new shape. Surfacing, she took her next breath in her human form. Then she strode to Náiir's side.

The Nadoriin he held at sword-point stared with mouth agape.

"I asked you a question." Náiir prodded the man's memory with the tip of his blade.

Vaile looked the soldier up and down. "Their lives are not so valuable as you make them, Náiir. Kill this one. We'll find another to tell us what we want."

Náiir pressed the tip of his blade into the man's throat, barely piercing the skin. "Aid us and live; defy us and die. Choose wisely."

The man's dark eyes flew back to Náiir. "The prince ..." he gasped around the ebon steel threatening his flesh. "South tower."

Vaile directed her gaze through the storm. Two towers crowned Darroyhan's southern end.

Náiir motioned with his blade. "Show us."

The man pushed a hand to his throat and moved quickly into the tower. They descended the spiraling steps at a run. Several stories down, they emerged onto the ramparts as thunder rumbled another angry growl.

The soldier, their guide, drew up short. Likewise Vaile and Náiir behind him.

Soldiers were pouring out of Darroyhan's towers onto the walls.

Vaile arched a raven brow. "It appears they've noticed our arrival."

Náiir sighed. "Perhaps it was your making windmills of the guards that alerted them."

She tucked a strand of raven hair behind one ear. "Do you think they took offense?"

Náiir's dark brow furrowed faintly as he watched the crenellated walls filling with men like batter poured into a mold. "More than somewhat, Vaile."

She turned him a feral grin. "Good."

Náiir spun his blade horizontally in his hand, making the steel tip spiral like a drill. "This is quite a lot of soldiers for so remote a fortress."

"The Consul sent them." The Nadoriin's gaze flicked uncertainly between the two of them. "Reinforcements."

Vaile grinned. "How thoughtful of Viernan. He knows all of you so well, Náiir."

A mass of soldiers from the nearest two towers was streaming towards them in a raging wall of mail and steel and darkly bearded faces.

Náiir's frown deepened. "We'll need a better route."

"Very well. Let's make one." Vaile jumped up onto the nearest crenel. The wind whipped through her clothes and tugged at the dual swords strapped to her back. She turned Náiir a grin. "Coming?" Before he could answer, she flung herself off the wall.

She cast the fifth before her, and her feet struck down on a level even with the ramparts. She ran then, high above the lower bailey, high over the heads of the staring soldiers in the yard, spearing the fifth before her with every step. A glance over her shoulder showed Náiir and the Nadoriin not far behind on her bridge.

She and Náiir might've taken the form again and merely flown to the south tower, but seeing two immortals and a soldier running through midair would give the men below a better story to tell, and she wanted the tale of Trell val Lorian's escape from Darroyhan to be worthy of telling for a very long time.

The men lining the ramparts watched for a moment's astonishment, but soon they had regrouped and were chasing along the walls after them in a race towards the south towers.

Vaile reached those ramparts first, but the wall of armed humanity lagged only one tower behind. She stepped up onto the merlon while Náiir helped the soldier over the crenel, and watched the lines of men approaching from either side. They would try to pin her and Náiir between them, making a vise of the two forces.

Vaile's gaze narrowed. She turned and focused on a space of wall to her right and flung out her hand—but it was her intention that she truly flung across the distance.

Abruptly the stone beneath her gaze began crumbling, merlons tumbling, the ramparts dissolving as the entire section of wall melted into sand like a child's castle swept away by the sea. The approaching men drew up short and shoved backwards against their brethren to try and halt the momentum of the mass before they all tumbled over the edge.

Náiir grabbed her arm and with it her attention. "*Vaile.*" His eyes were hot upon hers, his tone sharp. "You take *too* many chances."

She jerked free of his hold and cast a daggered look in reply. "Ten chances would not be too many until Trell is safe."

Thunder sounded again, but further away. The storm was moving on, and so must they.

Vaile lifted her chin to indicate the horde still approaching on their left. "I'll stay to manage these. You find Trell." She jumped from the merlon and landed with a splash. She cast him another look over her shoulder, but his gaze, still fixed upon her, was dark with concern.

So he'd figured it out then, like Balaji before him. Well ... what of it?

She gave him a hard stare. "Find Trell, Náiir."

"My ... lord?" The Nadoriin seemed uncertain how to address Náiir and equally urgent to be off. How quickly he'd allied with their cause, yet she sensed no guile in the soldier. He motioned to the tower. "The prince is this way."

Náiir tore his gaze from Vaile's and followed him.

It felt suddenly as if Náiir tugged her resolve with him as he departed. Vaile closed her eyes and let the moment's indecision rake across her ... and move on.

She'd made her choice. It was time for this ... *long past time.*

Opening her eyes to a new moment, a firm decision, she reached back with crossed arms and drew her blades. In her hands, the sentient Merdanti weapons sang a new counterpoint to the song of the fifth ever humming in her blood. This ... this *connection* to the forces that bound the realm together, to the churning storm and the motion of the tides and the gravity propelling the swiftly spinning heavens ... this was what life was meant to feel like for one of her ilk. To live and never work the fifth was to exist without drawing breath.

Vaile turned to face the rush of soldiers.

As the first of them reached her, she spun with a swipe of flashing blades. He fell aside to find his death. Others quickly followed. Vaile spun her swords in the *ta'fieri* and carved a swath through the field of men.

On they came like the rushing tide and she the rock upon which they broke, wave after wave. None passed her. None escaped her. Bodies piled to left and right, jammed the crenels or toppled over the edge. How many would have to die before the others realized the futility of their intent? It mattered not to her.

Perhaps if they'd been Adepts, Vaile might've found compassion, but these men, mere blank threads in the tapestry and inconsequential to the Mage's game ... what care had she for their lives? *She*, a predatory being born of storms. If they meant to throw away their mortal lives, she would aid them in their goal.

Vaile spun. Her blades sliced. Now windmilling, now a figure-eight, from the *cortata* to the *ta'fieri*, back and forth. She knew every step, every spiral, every turn of wrist or elbow. She ducked and twirled, lunged, sidestepped. She launched high over the fallen and sliced as she flipped, and her black blades unerringly blocked every sword, dagger or fist aimed her way.

In Vaile's blood, the fifth sang, boundless and bright, raging, violent, beautiful ... and remorseless.

Finally, the mass of men before her fell back and the soldiers broke apart, a path opening down their center. The battle stilled beneath the pouring rain. Vaile sensed the stillness birthing a new kind of storm.

At the far end of the passage of men, darkness took shape.

The currents shied away from it—verily, the thing repelled *elae*. She knew then what it was, though she hadn't seen its like in two-thousand years, not since Warlocks from the Shadow Realms ran amok through the wastelands left by the last cataclysm. But no Warlock had made this thing. So she asked into the storm as the creature was coming towards her, "What manner of demon are you?"

Dark eyes fixed upon her, and in their depths she saw the violet glint of *deyjiin*. The demon spoke to her in a voice of crushing stone. "I am Fate come to claim you, bitch."

Vaile spun her blades. "Strange." She arched a raven brow. "I've met Fate, and you look nothing like him."

The thing made a rattling snarl and bolted at her in a streak of dark energy.

She caught its midsection in crossed blades and flung the demon up over her head. It hit the stones with a thunderous crack and somersaulted back onto its feet. Vaile turned to face it and simultaneously threw up a shield of the fourth at her back, lest any of the soldiers regain their courage and try to attack her from behind. The fourth strand was neither as invigorating nor as resonant as the fifth, but it had its uses.

Before her, the creature held its own Merdanti blade in both hands and considered her with dark eyes, oddly angling its head to view her out of first one orb and then the other, as if both were not centered on its face. "I know what I am," it posed in that ratcheting clatter, "but what are you?"

Vaile scraped her blades against one another and then flung her arms outward, swords extended, her entire body taut. Crashing thunder carried her reply.

"I am Alorin."

The fifth exploded out of her.

A razor bubble expanded around her, splitting rain, fragmenting air, shearing rock. The creature ducked its head against the onslaught and stood its ground while her working sliced away a curved section of the walls in its split-second passing. Then the rain returned.

Interesting.

The demon lifted its head with a triumphant grin. It launched at her then, but what did it really think—that being born of *inverteré* patterns and *deyjiin* made it invincible? That it had a hope of overwhelming a *zanthyr* in combat?

Vaile met its downward rushing blade with crossed swords, clamped hard. She twisted and turned her body and ripped the weapon from the demon's grasp. Then she spun, sheathed one blade, grabbed the demon's neck as she came out of the spin and rammed her other blade through its stomach.

It hissed that ratcheting snarl, black eyes burning in defiance.

Vaile snarled back. Then she ripped her blade upwards and sundered the creature.

It crumpled.

She spun and pointed her sword at the soldiers watching from beyond her barrier of the fourth. They all took a reflexive step backwards.

That's better.

Vaile gave them a feral grin and ran to join Náiir.

Trell started aware as something heavy landed across him and tumbled off again. From the brush of clothing against his bare chest, he assumed it must've been Taliah.

A storm raged beyond the tower. Trell knew this because wind and rain now whipped through the room, because his body was drenched and shaking, and because the howling wind seemed to have more of a hold on him than the chains—tearing at his hair and stinging his eyes. Trell strained his neck to look over his shoulder and found a gaping hole in the wall. Beyond lay only wind and rain, and a hundred feet below, a churning charcoal sea.

Only one of the tall iron lamps remained standing and alight, and Taliah used this to draw herself up. Her face was a bloodied mess. Likewise her torn and charred gown. Half her hair had been somehow singed away. Clearly she and the demon had continued battling while Trell lay unconscious.

A rattling drew his gaze across the room to the demon creature. It looked the same as it climbed out of another indentation in the stone wall, only ... perhaps a darker stripe marred its chest. *Yes* ... as it moved out of the shadows, Trell saw a gaping fissure there, as if skin and bone had been hewn away.

The moment she regained her feet, Taliah cast another dark enchantment at the demon. It ducked the blast as it launched towards her. She threw herself aside, but it caught her dress, spun her back into its arms and drove her into the wall.

Taliah screamed with defiance. She mashed her palms against its eyes, and a dark language frothed across her lips, a litany of hissing words that sounded like Agasi twisted inside out. The demon writhed beneath her hands and grappled for her throat while she swung her head and shoulders unnaturally to avoid its clawing fingers.

Trell swallowed and looked away.

Would this truly be how his life ended?

That he had endured so much, only to find himself pinned between evil and its darker twin ... it seemed so ...

Unbelievable? Unbearable?

Arrows of incomprehensibility lodged in a shield of disbelief. That Naiadithine had borne him, saved him, reunited him with friends and family, only to have him see *this* mangled end? Could his path really have been leading him *here*?

Or perhaps he'd been wrong—so *very* wrong—and his existence held no more purpose and was graced of no more divinity than any other man's. Perhaps he was not destined for anything and his life was simply purposeless ... one long race towards an inevitable death, as the Prophet Bethamin would have them all believe.

To meet such an end ... lying chained and helpless beneath this storm of evil, with neither outcome preferable to the other ... Trell could almost believe the Prophet had the right of it. It tore him apart to think so.

While his body shook from the blasting wind and rain—not to mention the host of other unimaginable wrongs it had recently endured—Trell pondered the unreality of the moment and nearly laughed. Surely all men experienced that same instant of rejection when they looked Death in the eye. A man might many times escape Death's near embrace, but he only met His consuming gaze once.

Then—

He almost missed the curse, for it was faint with incredulity, but he heard clearly the words, "Stand back," and the voice that had uttered it—*oh gods*, that voice! He had to be imagining it.

In the darkness of the shattered doorway, light blazed—no a *sun* blazed.

The world went silent and still. The storm, the wind, Taliah's macabre chanting ... everything simply ... ceased.

A moment later, a face appeared over his own. Dark hair fell across eyes of gold flamed with power. *Náiir.*

Trell shut his eyes lest emotion overwhelm all reason.

Náiir placed a hand on Trell's brow. "Oh, my friend ..." His voice was raw, fierce with fury, "this nightmare is almost behind you."

Abruptly Trell felt the shackles loosen. He opened his eyes to find the iron dissolving into sand and the world—around him, the world simply stood still.

Raindrops hung suspended, the brazier flames seemed sculpted from stone, and Taliah and the creature stood locked in their dark embrace.

"Can you walk, Trell?"

Trell struggled to believe this was really happening.

"… Trell?

He shifted his gaze abruptly back to Náiir, somewhat startled to see him still standing there. "I … don't know."

"I must release time to help you. Prepare yourself."

Trell thought at this point he'd be prepared for just about anything.

The world shocked back into motion.

The flash of sunlight vanished. The demon flung Taliah into a corner and her chanting broke off with a scream. The creature spun to face Náiir, arms splayed, with fingers as claws and a rattle in its throat.

Náiir drew his sword, leapt atop Trell's table and launched off it again. The demon hissed, and a streak of violet-silver shot towards Náiir. He caught it on his blade and slung it aside as he landed. It struck the tower wall and blasted a hole clear into the night.

The demon flung another violet-silver bolt, which Náiir cast aside with the same indifference. Then his sweeping blade came down on the creature and rent a crevasse from shoulder to chest. The demon fell back with a rattling snarl, scrambling onto all fours. Náiir advanced, spinning blade in the lead. The demon flung another ball of dark energy which Náiir again caught and cast into the walls. The demon hissed a raging snarl. Then it spun and dove out of the tower.

Náiir stared after it, frowning.

Taliah pushed to her feet with one hand supporting herself on the wall. "Whoever you are … you won't claim him." Her voice came as a gurgling rasp from pierced lungs. "Trell belongs to *me*."

Náiir turned her a look over his shoulder as if considering whether to bother with killing her. Then he moved to help Trell. He reached an arm around Trell's shoulders to help him sit up. "Can you stand?"

Trell slowly swung one leg and then the other over the edge of the table, but then he gripped Náiir's shoulder, fighting vertigo. "I think … with help."

"I think *not*," Taliah hissed.

Paralyzing pain shot through Trell. His body spasmed, and he fell back onto the marble slab.

Náiir spun to her, eyes aflame. "Release him."

She hung in the corner like a spider, arms splayed. "Trell is *mine*. We walk the path of *mor'alir* together!"

Trell wanted to tell her he walked nowhere with her, but he barely had breath enough to manage a guttural moan.

And in walked Vaile.

She took one look at Trell writhing on the table, and turned her gaze on Taliah. Then she was simply standing before Taliah with a hand around her throat and her body pinned up against the wall.

Taliah grabbed onto Vaile's wrist with both hands while her toes scrabbled for purchase and she struggled for breath—but she kept her agonizing hold on Trell's pattern.

"Release him," Vaile growled.

Blood frothed on Taliah's lips, and she wheezed a laugh. "I have *your* life pattern now." Her voice strained around Vaile's clenching fingers. "I can kill you … with a thought."

"And I have your throat. Which of us can squeeze faster, do you imagine?"

Taliah's eyes darkened, her gaze defiant. After a moment her face turned red, her eyes bulged, and muscles corded in her neck.

Vaile arched a deprecating brow. "Is that the best you can do, little witch?" She spun and flung Taliah contemptuously across the room. Taliah crashed into the wall and crumpled just shy of the hole the demon had vanished through.

The clenching pain vanished. Trell sucked in a gasping breath and curled his tortured body into an exhausted ball.

Vaile stalked towards where Taliah was struggling to rise. "I'm of the fifth, Taliah hal'Jaitar. You are *mor'alir*." The word could not have held more contempt. Vaile stooped and pulled Taliah to her feet. She held Taliah once more by the throat while her other hand held her Merdanti blade low. "You have no more hope of harming me than a shadow has of harming a stone."

Náiir helped Trell to sit up again. He braced himself and looked over at Taliah. She stood facing Vaile with tears streaming down her face. Their eyes met, hers beseeching, his unforgiving.

A gasp of desperate grief escaped her. She gave him one last look of longing, and he saw something in her gaze—

"*Taliah—*"

She grabbed the zanthyr's blade with her bare hands, and thrust herself upon it.

Trell drew in his breath sharply. Vaile jerked back her sword, but the deed was done. Taliah fell to her knees and then onto her side. She looked up at Trell as blood pooled beneath her, and a whisper fled across her lips: "I … will see you soon … my love."

Náiir turned Vaile a look of alarm. Then he moved to help Trell to his feet. Trell was beginning to feel like a china doll too many times broken and pieced back together. With an arm around Náiir's shoulders and Vaile close behind, they reached the stairwell.

Trell drew up short. Fazil stood in the passage with his sword in hand.

"Our sentry," Náiir explained with a smile. To Fazil, he added, "Let's get to the roof."

But before they could move, Vaile moved around and took Trell's face between her hands. She searched his gaze with her own.

Emotion beyond words flooded Trell. Knowing she and Náiir had come for him, knowing also that Alyneri must've reached the *sa'reyth*, that *she* was safe ... such relief and gratitude swelled in his heart that he almost couldn't breathe.

Then Vaile kissed him.

The zanthyr's kiss sent a cascade of electricity through Trell's flesh, bringing a feeling of rebirth where Taliah's kisses had only tasted of dying. While Trell felt rejuvenating energy flowing into him, invigorating him, so also he sensed Vaile was Reading of him, of his life pattern, doubtless ensuring he was hale enough to make the climb ... perhaps even testing the truth of Taliah's haunting last words.

She released him with a second sweet grace of her lips. Then she turned to Náiir. "*Now* we go."

And so they climbed.

Yet t'was not freedom but Death that awaited them on the tower roof.

Vaile emerged first, and *deyjiin* exploded around her.

She flung up a hand, but she was too late to catch and deflect the violet-silver energy, which rocked the air while sucking the life from it, stealing even the breath from Trell's lungs as he arrived just behind her.

Without the protection of her blades still sheathed behind her back, Vaile had to bear the force of this wrath. It sent her sliding backwards on her feet and bore her down until she was bent with one hand and knee on the ground. Náiir sprang around her and caught the last of the blast on his blade. Then he launched after the demon who had fled from him before.

The demon's sword flashed and Náiir countered with his own. They parried, and then Náiir twisted—Trell couldn't entirely follow the maneuver, he moved so fast—and ripped the weapon from the creature's hand. Náiir spun and slashed backhanded, right across the demon's throat. For a moment the creature stood as if frozen. Then its head toppled one way and its body the opposite.

Náiir spun and ran to Vaile. He wore a ravaged expression as he helped her regain her feet. She braced herself with one hand against the wall, but with her other hand she waved him off. "Get Trell out of here, Náiir."

"*Vaile ...*" Concern rang all too clearly in his tone, in his gaze as he looked her over.

She looked up under her brows. "I'll follow."

Trell had managed the tower climb, but now he felt weak-kneed and short of breath. He reached a hand for the wall, missed and would've fallen, but Fazil caught him around his chest.

Náiir still looked troubled. "Vaile, I think—"

"*I* think the Mage will never forgive either of us if you don't get Trell back to him *now*, Náiir." She gave him a hard look. "I *will* follow."

Trell heard the shouting of men echoing from inside the tower, a mass of voices rising above the waning storm. They were coming fast.

Náiir still looked conflicted, but he turned away and took the form.

The air shifted into waves of heat and a sun burst into being. Then followed a great shimmering, as if every single particle in the air exploded with light. It was painfully bright to look upon, yet nothing could make Trell turn away.

The shimmering deepened, took on color that shifted rapidly from gold to bronze to copper, every molecule collecting a different hue. Then the sparkling expanded into form, into shape ... into a powerful body and lengthy, spiked tail, into massive wings that hovered higher than the tower peak, and finally into the face of the dragon staring down at him from high above.

"And if I die now, I die fulfilled," Fazil murmured the words of a Nadori proverb. Trell had never thought the saying more apt.

Climb up, Trell. Náiir's voice resounded in his head.

Trell swallowed. He looked at the spiny back of the creature towering over him. He could see a place at Náiir's haunches where he might safely sit, but reaching it in his current condition, which seemed to be deteriorating with every breath ... ? "Náiir, I don't think I can."

"What can you not do?" Fazil made his arm tighter in support of Trell's weight.

Trell gave him a desperate look. "Climb."

"You will do it upon my shoulders, Trell val Lorian." And without waiting for Trell's agreement, Fazil marched him to the dragon's back and bent to one knee.

Trell stared wondrously at him. "Why?" He didn't elaborate on the question, but he didn't need to.

Fazil looked up and held his gaze. "You have showed me what honor is. I would serve you any day, and proudly." He held out his hand and motioned Trell up. Stunned, Trell took it and climbed from Fazil's knee to his shoulders, and, once the man had found his own powerful feet, to Náiir's spiny back.

Gaining the dragon's haunches, Trell looked down at Fazil and then over to Vaile once more in wordless gratitude.

In her emerald gaze as she locked eyes with him, Trell saw warmth and determination but also something else, something indecipherable ... something that almost seemed like ... accomplishment.

Then Náiir was surging into the sky with Trell gripping on tightly, and Trell knew only wind and charcoal clouds, and above these, the sun rising on a new day.

FIFTY-NINE

"Real trust, true faith ... these cannot be explained, only experienced."

– Excerpted from the collected writings of Epiphany's Prophet

ISABEL GRITTED HER teeth and took several fast breaths.

She was learning to manage the pain. It would spread and build until it was so intense that she thought she must surely faint, but often in that very moment, Pelas would remove the needle tip to start a new thread of the pattern and give her time to catch her breath.

Still, the world spun dizzily.

Darshan expected her to die beneath Pelas's knife, but Pelas seemed in no hurry to rush her along.

He sat in a chair at her feet, carving a pattern into her thigh. One hand pinned her hip, holding up the linen shift he'd provided her, while his other hand drew the stylus through her skin with an artist's steady precision. He attended his work with careful concentration, a faint furrow between his dark brows.

"What do you think about, Isabel?" He looked up at her. "While I'm working on you, what do you think about?"

She summoned her breath. "How to help you."

This made him smile. "Really?" He gave her a skeptical look that yet seemed pleased. "And have you made much progress?"

"Some."

He looked at her strangely for a moment and then sat back in his chair. "Some. What *some*?"

She'd been trying to get through to him, to reach *him*, not merely the shadowed entity that possessed his thoughts. But so far nothing she'd said had penetrated the membrane of hopelessness that had enveloped the real Pelas.

"You must..." she wetted her lips, feeling the dullness of exhaustion overtaking her, fighting to stay ahead of it. "You must know of the tapestry, of our paths."

"Some." He mimicked her with a shadowy smile. "What of it?"

"In Tal'Afaq, I got the sense that you…I perceived that you'd nearly chosen a path."

He set down his stylus and considered her. "I was told by someone I trust that I have no path."

She held his gaze. "Unless you choose one."

He frowned ponderously at this. After a time, he rose from his chair and wandered to the window to stare out over the bleak mountains. "There was a boy who followed me once." He turned her an unreadable look over his shoulder, his gaze intense. "A truthreader. I asked him why he knowingly followed me into danger, and he said he was simply following his path." Abruptly he looked to her. "I have no concept of that feeling, Isabel. I don't *feel* like I have any path. Nothing seems to stretch before me…" He leaned back against the wall. "No future and nothing behind."

"*Now*, perhaps," she conceded gently. "What about before?"

He growled in frustration and pushed off the wall. "Before, before—I hardly remember before." He flung a hand into the air as he wandered about the room. "All I know is now, and now feels like eternity, and eternity feels like *death*." Hit bit the word and cast her a glare bound by enmity, wrapped in fear. "In the void, ages passed in the blink of an eye. Without my power, a minute feels like a year, and a day a century."

"If you would let me help you—"

"How?" He moved swiftly to her, grabbed her and pressed their bodies close. "*How* can you help me? Can you remove Darshan's compulsion?"

Isabel's breath came fast, nearly as fast as her heart. "Not like this."

His face fell back beneath the shadow. He brushed a stray hair from her cheek. "Help me…" he barely breathed the words, a whisper of lost hope. After a moment, he shook his head and released her. Then he sat back down in his chair and retrieved his stylus. "There is no help for me."

Isabel summoned back the breath he'd stolen. "Let's say…let's say Darshan truly took your immortal power away."

He gave her a look that said clearly enough this wasn't open to debate.

"Even so, he cannot change your basic nature."

Pelas hung his head and stared at the stylus in his hands.

Isabel pressed on. "Your friend was right. You have no path—unless you *choose* one. But path or no path, by your very nature, Pelas, you summon to you whatever it is that you most need, whatever it is you desire…whatever you're most focused upon."

"Vortices." He glanced up at her under his brows.

She nodded. "It makes you powerful…even without power."

He sat back in his chair and considered her. Then he waved a little circle with his stylus. "By all of this, you insinuate that I drew you here to help me."

She held his gaze. "Facts are facts."

"Outcomes are all that matter." He returned his attention to her thigh.

Isabel roused from a fitful sleep with a sudden jerk against her bonds, against shoulders that throbbed and wrists that knew a numb ache deeper than the hunger in her core. Pain had become a jealous lover, keeping covetous watch over her form. Stabbing needles dug into her flesh, even in her sleep.

The latter came rarely enough, and when it did, it gave her no release, for that portentous dream of days past still haunted her. Over and over it played through her head, until she feared she must be missing something of vital importance.

Night lay over the mountains, but a luminous moon shone through the windows, limning the tower furniture in silver. She scanned the room—from fireplace to table, windows to bed. She couldn't see him, but she sensed him near. Then she happened to look down and found him lying at her feet staring out the window, his eyes half-lidded but awake.

"May I have some water?"

He pushed up on one hand to look at her. "You talk in your sleep." He got up and went to pour water for her.

Isabel watched him crossing the room, feeling a desperate need to help him. "I'm not sure that qualifies as sleep."

He turned her a look over his shoulder. "What then?"

She shook her head. "Nothing I can explain."

He came over and helped her drink. When she'd taken as much as she could, she nodded to him, and he moved away.

"Pelas?"

He looked over his shoulder as he set the cup on the mantel.

"How did you betray him?"

Firelight illuminated his twisted expression. "I chose...I chose..." He sat down on the hearthstone and draped elbows over bent knees.

"You chose...?"

He looked up at her desperately. "I suppose I chose to pursue a purpose counter to his own."

Hope made a sudden lump in her throat as she realized what he was saying. "You wanted to save this world?"

His gaze...she'd never seen him look so tormented. After a moment, he hung his head between his hands. "Yes."

He was *so close* to choosing a path! And what it would mean to the game when he did...it would be worth any cost.

"May I ask why?"

He looked up with a twisted smile. "Would you believe for love of a child?"

"Love is the best reason."

He considered her answer. "I don't know why it happened, our friendship. It shouldn't have, by all accounts. I told you once of this boy—he was a truthreader. I thought at first he was one of my brother's spies. But as I came to know him…" His brow furrowed. "I thought once that I perceived something of my Maker in him, just something impossibly….pure." He shrugged. "He's special to me now in a way I have no words to describe."

Isabel didn't need his words to understand; she knew what he perceived. "Where is he, your truthreader friend?"

Pelas shook his head. "I don't know." Then he grunted ruefully. "Waiting for me to find him again, I suppose."

"And will you?"

Suddenly his gaze darkened, and he shot her a rancorous glare. "Assuming he still lives when my two hundred years are up?"

Isabel's gaze held gentle understanding—no matter what he did to her in the throes of his compulsion, she wouldn't give him other than kindness in return. "Imagine he does. Would you seek him out?"

Pelas clenched his jaw. Then he pushed abruptly to his feet and walked to his table of knives.

"If you never choose a path, you will always be a danger to our world."

He grunted at this.

"Pathless, you'll continue to disrupt the paths of others as you pull them in to suit your whims. You're like the prow of a ship plowing through the waves, sending ripples in vastly different directions, disrupting the equanimity of the tapestry, tearing its pattern."

He pressed both hands wide against the table, bowed his head and growled, "How do I find a path when all the world is black, Isabel?"

She searched for words to help him. Threads spun before her vision, crossing and entwining, branching again. The threads looked oddly grey in the perpetual gloaming of their shared prison, but she knew somewhere the light was shining. The trouble was that Pelas didn't.

"I don't think the compulsion is the problem."

He cast a fierce look over his shoulder. He'd drawn that dark veil across his thoughts again.

"I know a little about compulsion, Pelas."

"High Mage of the Citadel, indeed." He looked back to his knives.

"What does Darshan's compulsion require you to do?"

"I tire of this line of questioning, Isabel."

"You haven't ever answered the question."

He turned with stylus in hand. "And yet, I don't have to answer it at all."

"If only you—" But the rest of the sentence came out in a hiss as he started in again on the pattern he'd been scoring into her back, and afterwards, she couldn't find the energy to ask him anymore.

Isabel hung her head. Exhaustion and pain flew in circles through her thoughts, spiraling ghosts, spinning … spinning …

Pain flared in her back—brilliant, intense, overpowering …

Images of Arion, then Ean, then the two of them somehow as the same person flashed back and forth before her eyes, tormenting her. They whispered that she'd chosen this path and abandoned them, and for what…? For what? To die in a tower halfway across the realm having accomplished nothing?

No, she couldn't let that happen.

Twice since waking in the tower, Isabel had caught a glimpse of the path before her and seen…well, if not exactly its end, then at least a door opening upon a new eventuality. But she didn't know how to get to that door from where she and Pelas now stood.

It was difficult not to give in to despair, yet she had to hold onto awareness—hold to *hope*, so that when Epiphany gave her an opening, she'd be able to claim it. For she understood that if Cephrael carried the staff of condemnation, Epiphany carried one of redemption. Even when Cephrael had set his sights against a man, Epiphany always gave him one last chance to prove his quality.

She didn't fear death; she feared failing all of those who believed in her, who were depending on her. She didn't want to leave her thread in the game unfinished.

For the first time she understood the torment Arion had endured in the weeks leading up to the Citadel, when he'd known he was going to die there.

Perhaps she shouldn't have told him, but he'd begged her to share what she'd seen among the shifting veils of the future, and she'd never been able to deny him anything. What courage he'd demonstrated in walking his path anyway, in going on alone and giving his life for her brother's game! They would've lost the Citadel that night if not for him.

Isabel thought of Arion in those days, and she thought of Ean now—so buoyant at times, and so overwhelmed in others, yet consistently brilliant if only he could see it in himself. How dreadful it must be for him to be constantly compared to and held up against his own genius, all the while knowing—*believing*—that even with all the knowledge and skill he'd possessed as Arion Tavestra, still he'd failed. Yet Ean chose to continue on.

In every moment, we bear the choice to embrace that moment or become the victim of it.

The temptation to feel that sorrow pounded constantly on the door of her mind, but she knew that once one opened the door of self-pity, it became nearly impossible to close it again. She might've seemed like a victim in this circumstance, chained and tortured by another man's knife, but she was the High Mage of the Citadel. She was Epiphany's Prophet. Outward appearances could be deceiving.

Pelas lifted the needle from her skin to her immeasurable relief. He wet a linen cloth with ice-water and spread it gently across the pattern he'd scored into her back.

Her body was almost covered in such patterns now.

The icy cloth on her back felt heaven's blessing. He must've heard her sigh, for he bent a kiss to her shoulder and then treated two of his other patterns—older carvings from earlier days—with their own chill dressing. Then he walked to a basin and washed his hands.

"What would Darshan say if he knew you were keeping me alive like this?"

Pelas shrugged without looking at her. "The point is moot. It will be decades before he returns."

"I would last longer as company with something to eat."

He paused in his washing. Then he turned and leaned back against the basin to stare at her. "You would choose to stay alive for this?" he waved a hand to encompass her bondage and all of the tools that brought her pain.

"Not for this, Pelas...for you."

Now he really stared at her. "You actually believe...you *believe* your path brought you here." He grunted with incredulity. "For *what*, Isabel?"

She held his gaze as best she could. "I think you know."

He slung the rag to the floor. "I *don't* know. I don't know *anything* anymore—not who I am, nor what I think, nor even why I bother trying to appease my brother when he has me *exactly where he wants me!*" These final words came out in a dreadful thunder.

Power darkened the room in shadowed clouds of static, responding to his rage. Even with *goracrosta* masking her from the full force of the currents, Isabel perceived this storm, but he sensed none of it as she did.

She hung her head and let the cauldron boil around her. Such power he possessed! She might've survived on his power alone had he channeled it towards giving her life instead of instinctively drawing upon it as fuel for his anger.

Isabel hung her head dizzily. "If you despise it so much, why do you not fight the compulsion?"

He barked an incredulous laugh. "You think this is me *not* fighting it?" He shoved off the basin and approached her. "Do you have any idea what this compulsion demands of me? What it *drives* me to want to do?" He caught her around the throat and forced her head back as he pressed himself close to her. His copper eyes flamed beneath a brow shadowed by fury and despair. She saw him grit his teeth, saw the muscles of his jaw tighten with anger. "Believe me, Isabel," he hissed, low and fervent, "I'm *fighting* it—Tooth. And. Claw."

He'd forced her head painfully back, so she had to whisper, "What does it demand of you?"

Oh, how he growled at her at this. "You really want to know?"

She nodded, the barest of motions against the constraint of his marble hand.

Pelas hooked an arm around her body and pulled her close, bringing his mouth to her ear while his other hand clutched her throat. "Need," he whispered, and he stroked his fingers down her neck. His breath fell cool across her, and his hand felt colder against her back than the icy cloth he'd dressed for her. "Hunger." His lips brushed her ear and along her neck. "Ache—yearning— heat and fury...*insatiable* want." He pressed his nose into her hair and smelled deeply of her.

"That's..." She tried to catch her breath with him still clinging to her. "Darshan cast a broad compulsion—formless. He would've given it direction as well."

Pelas laid his head on her shoulder and let his fingers trace down to pause in the hollow between her breasts. "He wants me to kill you—to kill all of you."

"Healers."

He nodded against her shoulder, and still he clutched her to him like a dying man. Her arms ached, strained against her bonds.

Then he simply pushed her away and stalked across the room. She feared for him as much as for herself. He posed the most danger when set upon by this mood, when Darshan's compulsive darkness wound about him like a viperous shroud, masking all that was innately him.

"I don't know why I fight it." He turned a brimstone glare over his shoulder. "Perhaps I shouldn't. Mayhap he knows even now that I defy him—how am I to know what patterns he's cast about this place? I have *no power* anymore!" He kicked at the table and sent the entire piece skidding, knives tumbling askew. Then he pushed both hands against the mantel and hung his head.

"Pelas..."

But there was no reaching him now. She saw that.

After a moment, he straightened and walked to his table. Her blood ran cold when she saw the blade he selected. "*No*—" She watched him desperately as he approached, eyes hooded and dark, his face twisted with despair. "Don't give in to it. Don't give up!"

He stopped before her and looked her over, jaw clenched. Then he ran the razor edge of the blade lightly down both sides of her neck and in an arc across her chest, as if mapping out the lines of his intended incisions.

More lines followed, tracing down across her shift, outlining her breasts, across her abdomen, another low arc from hip to hip. "Pelas, *please*..."

Oh, if only her mind were clear instead of plagued by this murky, sordid twilight, or if her thoughts weren't so fogged by exhaustion and pain. If only she could see the paths instead of these shifting threads, myriad filaments of possibility leading nowhere!

Abruptly he pressed the cold steel against her throat. Isabel caught her breath—at any moment he could lose his battle with the darkness and bring an end to both of them.

Holding his knife in place, he traced a hand down her face, watching her with hooded eyes blind to her pleas. Then his fiery gaze narrowed. "But I would see *you* when we do this, Isabel."

He ripped off her blindfold.

She gasped at the shock of it, at the sudden sensation of cool air upon her eyes, at a different sort of muted light...daylight, sensed more than seen. Her lids fluttered, and then Isabel blinked and looked upon the world with her naked eyes. Looked at him.

Pelas met her gaze hungrily, expectantly. Then she saw his brow tighten—

The knife fell from his fingers to clatter against the floor, and he staggered back—back—all the way across the room until he hit up against the far wall. She found no words to describe the horror on his face.

He gasped in a shuddering breath, pinned immobile. "*You're—*"

She nodded. She knew what he'd seen when he looked into her eyes.

"*By Chaos born!*" Still he was gaping at her. "If you knew...why didn't you *tell* me? Why did you let me—" but he choked over the words, suddenly sickened by what he'd done. He pushed off the wall and shoved both hands into his long hair and swore a litany of curses in a language of lightning and formless static.

Yet as she watched him, she knew she was seeing Pelas as himself again for the first time. The shock of seeing her eyes—of the recognition in their shape and color—had driven Darshan's shadows momentarily to bay. Pelas turned away, hands gripped behind his head, and—

Chills striped Isabel, for she experienced in that instant a Seer's duality, when life mimics the dream.

She saw the moment—his stance, the agonized expression on his face...

She understood it now, how to help him, but *oh*...the price was so high.

Isabel marshaled her courage. "A broad compulsion...can be rechanneled."

He threw her a tormented look.

"Compulsive hunger can be assuaged in more than one way." She strained to find her voice, her breath, to stay focused and aware. "Hunger and desire find harmonics up and down the scale. You can succumb to the craving in whatever form has been forced on you, or you can take charge of it, find a higher harmonic of the same driving impulse—direct it, own it...*sublimate* it."

He turned. Stared at her. His eyes searched her gaze for meaning. She knew he would find it there.

His eyes widened. "You don't know what you're saying."

But her gaze, holding his, said otherwise.

"Sublimate it?" Confusion and hopelessness twisted on his brow. "I...don't know how."

"Hunger is desire..." She dropped her gaze and summoned her resolve. Then she lifted her head and looked him in the eye. "Desire me."

In three quick strides he'd crossed the room and grabbed her into his arms. "I *do* desire you."

She turned her mouth to receive his, and he claimed of her a violent kiss...a powerful kiss that stole her breath and froze her deeply in the same terrible moment.

Suddenly he ripped away and staggered back. Misgiving and alarm made his copper eyes too bright, hot with accusation. He dabbed at his mouth with the back of one hand. "You would betray your love and give yourself to me just to secure your freedom."

"No." Her tone gentled the distrust in his rebuke while her gaze showed him the truth of her intent. "...but I would do it to secure yours."

For a moment, Pelas stared at her. Then he came for her. In a single motion, he swept his knife up from the floor and severed the ropes that bound her to the poles—though not the *goracrosta* cuffs that bound her wrists. Then he lifted her into his arms and carried her to his bed.

He nearly pitched her onto the mattress in his haste. She watched with naked eyes as he freed himself and threw his body down across her own. He sealed his mouth on hers and pressed her painfully into the mattress. His right hand pinned both of hers above her head, powerful legs forced hers apart, and Pelas channeled the full force of Darshan's compulsion into their copulation.

For a time, Isabel knew only the engagement of his lovemaking, intense with sensation and terrifying with guilt, but as Pelas found a sense of himself, his eyes sought hers again.

"Tell me..." he growled, low and feverish, "tell me how to do this."

Isabel held his gaze. This coupling had been her suggestion—it was the only way she saw to free him—but it was also a terrible betrayal. She felt the guilt of that betrayal far more deeply than any wounds Pelas had given her.

"You take the force of the compulsion...and you channel it to your *own* desire. This is how you overcome it."

He stilled for a heartbeat's pause, digesting that. Then he captured her mouth with his and spun her around beneath him.

Violent, fervent, desperate...the hours passed in this guise. Isabel became the vessel into which Pelas poured all of his fury and out of which he took everything he could to sate the compulsion's hunger.

At some point—she didn't know when, for the hours had become a blur—he pressed his forehead against hers and whispered, "This cannot be the way."

Isabel closed her eyes, but the tormenting truth still stared at her. "This is the only way."

He growled and thrust himself into her again, and the rhythm of their union paced the rapid beating of her heart. As he guided their joining, he unconsciously wrapped his power around her in a hundred arms, a thousand hands. His thoughts took flight and shaped themselves and claimed Isabel for their pleasure equally.

And so it went, this punishing, passionate, intemperate union. Pelas molded her body to his desires and carved his freedom out of her sacrifice, and though Isabel had chosen this path and now knew where it would lead, still each moment felt as terrifying as when he'd carved patterns in her flesh.

SIXTY

"When all else fails—panic."

— The royal cousin Fynnlar val Lorian

TANIS WOKE TO the pale light of wielder's lamps burning high on the
walls of a windowless chamber. The black marble floor radiated coldly
beneath his back, but it barely approached the frigid chill caused by the
goracrosta burning on his wrists. After being blasted and blown and battered
about, pain filled every space in his body not already occupied by guilt.

With hands bound in front of him, Tanis pushed up on one elbow and
looked around the octagonal chamber with its ornate marble walls of ancient
design. Then he got awkwardly to his feet. His jaw ached where fists and elbows
had met it. He shifted it slowly from side to side and found it functional at
least, thanks to the grace of his quick healing.

He walked to an arched opening and halted just shy of it. Beyond lay
a cavernous hall sheathed in obsidian. Shadows fell like curtains beyond the
nearest columns, but as far as Tanis could see, bodies covered the black floor.
Even in the muted light of wielder's lamps, silver cuffs and collars glinted—the
stolen Adepts. A rising sense of horror twinged in the lad's spine.

There must be over a hundred people in there.

Tanis turned his attention to the silver-violet sheen gleaming along the
edges of the archway that separated his octagonal chamber from the greater
hall. He could just see the curtain of *deyjiin* which stood in place of bars to
keep him enclosed—he more perceived it than saw it, with its cold breath and
tingling static.

Tanis frowned at the curtain of power. Instinct and experience both
whispered that he could pass through it unharmed—after all, he had a special
if utterly mystifying relationship with *deyjiin*. He suspected that at worst,

the curtain would shock him senseless, but at best ... Somewhere beyond his chamber, Nadia needed his help.

Tanis drew in a deep breath and walked through the archway.

It felt like passing beneath a waterfall formed of lightning. The hair rose all over his body and his breath fled in a forceful puff, but then he was emerging on the other side, unscathed save for his suddenly racing heart and electrified hair.

Tanis pushed his hair back down, drew in a tense breath and looked around the hall; his exhale came heavy with sorrow. So many Adepts stolen to be repurposed for an enemy king's war ... the tragedy of it tore at him—more so because he knew he could do nothing to help them.

Far worse was worrying for Nadia. How was he ever going to find her among all these bodies? And that was assuming they hadn't sequestered her the way they'd sequestered him ... which he somewhat feared would be the case. He tried reaching out to her along the bond, but either she was out of range of his thoughts or her mind had somehow been closed off to him.

With no other options in view, Tanis set off among the Adepts in search of Nadia, of escape, or of any sign that he still tread upon his path. The *goracrosta* binding his hands made his arms ache, and the gloom of the place quickly began to weigh on the lad. Everywhere Tanis looked he saw massive, sculpted columns carved with dark patterns that hurt his eyes. Who knew if the patterns themselves weren't designed to suck all the hope out of a person?

Memory accosted him—even as the patterns on the columns accosted his eyes. Too vividly he recalled the vision of Shail streaking along the stadium's rim, spinning into battle with the *eidola*. No one would ever believe N'abranaacht had planned the massacre now.

Tanis cursed himself for a fool. Shail had been ahead of him every step of the way—so far ahead he'd long since vanished over the distant rise while Tanis was still puffing up the first hill.

A plague of self-condemnation descended on the lad, black thoughts that quickly gained power in the shadowed room populated by uncannily still forms and corrupt patterns. Nadia wouldn't be in this situation at all if not for him. She could *die* because of him. And they were helpless now *because* of him, prey to Shail's malevolent whims. He had no idea what had become of Felix ...

Oh, the absurdity of thinking he could do anything against a force like Shail!

An *eidola* emerged out of the far shadows, and Tanis froze. His breath stilled while his heart raced.

Leveling him a castigating glare, the *eidola* stalked over, grabbed him with its stone hands and dragged him off.

Well, at least it hadn't punched him like the last one he'd met.

Tanis wondered where Shail had brought them. The entire place was sheathed in obsidian—from the shadowed ceilings of the great hall that the *eidola* had dragged Tanis out of, to the groin-vaulted hallways he then dragged him down. The place felt like a crypt—it was certainly as cold as one—and it had the same kind of ancient-looking ornamentation as the van Gelderan mausoleum at Calgaryn Palace.

At last the *eidola* dragged Tanis through a massive portal out into daylight. The lad turned over his shoulder to watch the façade of a temple growing into view behind him. The *eidola* led him down a wide set of black marble steps, pitted and broken, whereupon Tanis gained a wider perspective and realized the entire temple had been hewn right out of the mountainside.

Then the noise of men and metal drew his attention and he turned back—

To face an army camp of thousands.

Icy peaks surrounded the camp on all sides, and tents and men clustered in the valley between, stretching from edge to edge like an uneven carpet of drab moss.

'... *they want Adepts to fuel the Danes' war* ... '

There seemed little question whose army he was looking upon.

The *eidola* dragged Tanis along a steep trail skirting the forested hills that lined the protected valley. At the top of the rise they came upon a pavilion whose ancient construction looked as if it might've predated the forest that had grown up around it.

The *eidola* took Tanis through a series of salons to the back side of the building and a loggia with a commanding view of a mountain lake.

And Shail, sitting at a table draped in velvet.

Tanis felt everything inside him clench—fear, fury, apprehension all lodged in his chest.

The *eidola* jerked him roughly to a halt in front of the table. Tanis was just surprised the thing didn't force him to his knees.

Shail sat with his elbows resting on the arms of a wingback chair and his fingers steepled before his lips. His chilling gaze held Tanis captive far more adroitly than the *eidola's* clawing fingers.

"Well, Tanis ... here we are again."

"My thoughts exactly, sir."

Shail's razor gaze falling across the lad felt like blades slicing his skin. Tanis half expected to look down and see red lines bleeding through his shirt. After an uncomfortable moment of this, Shail motioned for him to sit, and the *eidola* forced him into a chair without giving him time to move of his own accord. Tanis glared up at it.

Shail dismissed the creature with a flick of his eyes. It retreated to stand in the shadows of a column, but Tanis could still feel its hateful gaze boring holes into the back of his head.

"So, Tanis ... it seems we shall have our tea after all."

"Yes, sir." Tanis couldn't miss the irony in the moment, nor the black humor in Shail's tone.

The man's lip curled in a smile that failed to touch his eyes. "Did I not explain to you that Fate bows to my will?"

Rather than acknowledge any possible truth in his statement, for it frightened him to think so, Tanis asked instead, "What have you done with Phoebe, sir?"

Shail's dark eyes licked over him, assessing, contemplating ... Tanis felt like a hunk of meat being inspected by a butcher's blade—*meticulously* inspected.

The lad tried a different question. "The other Adepts in the temple ... you drugged them?"

Shail stroked beneath his lip with the back of one finger while his eyes scrutinized every inch of the lad's corporeal form. "Yes."

Tanis had to work some moisture back into his mouth. "Why ... why didn't you drug me?"

Shail's dark eyes gleamed dangerously. "We did."

Tanis felt himself go a little pale.

A man in a white, hooded cassock came to the table carrying the tea service. He set down the tray and poured steaming tea into two cups. Tanis hadn't exactly seen where he'd come from or where he vanished to afterwards, for the lad couldn't remove his eyes from Shail's.

It seemed such a surreal moment, sitting there having tea with an immortal being whose purposes were utterly antipathetic to their world, with a tranquil lake on one side of the pavilion and thousands of men preparing for war on the other.

Tanis looked at the tea cup in front of him. He wasn't sure how he was supposed to manage the cup with his wrists bound together with magic rope. But then, Tanis hadn't really been brought there to drink tea.

For all he wanted to rage and howl and protest, for all he *wanted* to take the knife from Shail's side of the table and cut the *goracrosta* from his wrists and escape to find Nadia, Tanis understood—actually, he *sensed* more than he understood, but the sensation spoke quite loudly—that for whatever reason, Balance lay on Shail's side at the moment. The most Tanis could do was wait for it to lean in his direction again, and until that time ... well, he'd best cooperate.

He lifted his gaze back to Shail. "You must think me terribly fearsome to keep me bound in *goracrosta*, sir."

Shail stroked his finger beneath his lower lip again. "I don't know what I think of you yet."

Tanis dropped his eyes back to his tea. *That makes two of us.*

"For all his faults, my brother Pelas is no fool. He kept you close. I would know why."

"You would have to ask him that, sir."

"Yes, I intend to." Shail's gaze swept Tanis again, more accusatory than inquisitive. "How did you escape the chamber in the temple?"

Tanis attempted to pick up his cup, maneuvering awkwardly to do so. "You mean the curtain of *deyjiin*?" He managed to get the china rim to his lip and leaned slightly sideways to take a sip. He wasn't sure afterwards that the tea had been worth the effort. He looked back to Shail as he set it down.

The Malorin'athgul's gaze had gone very dark. "Yes, truthreader, I mean that exactly."

Tanis shrugged. "I just walked through it, sir."

Shail's eyes tightened. Oddly, the man no longer radiated such malevolent intentions as what Tanis had experienced from him in the Sormitáge, though the lad harbored no illusions that Shail's inherent disposition had changed. He was nothing if not calculating.

The Malorin'athgul regarded him quietly for a moment, much like a tiger's impassive observation of the prey struggling beneath its paw. Then he extended his palm. "Give me your hand."

Tanis exhaled a sigh and pushed his bound hands across the table. He knew what was coming next.

Shail took one of Tanis's hands and narrowed his gaze, and the lad felt *deyjiin's* chill come washing through him.

As he'd witnessed when Pelas had tested him in much the same way, Shail's determined expression soon changed to one of infuriated disbelief. He flung Tanis's hand away, sat back in his chair and stabbed Tanis with a Merdanti gaze. "Did Pelas work this craft upon you? Make you immune to our power?"

"No, sir. He was as shocked as you are."

"Shocked is not the word I would choose." Shail studied Tanis in silence. He looked thunderously displeased. "Truthreader, timeweaver, traveler of twisted nodes ... immune to drugged wine and *deyjiin*. What manner of wielder *are* you?"

Tanis exhaled a deep sigh. "I wish I knew, sir."

Shail considered this answer with an arched brow. Suddenly Tanis felt the fourth swirling around him like wind—just as obvious and just as insubstantial, for he could no more take it into himself than he could capture the wind in his palm.

"What other things can you do, Tanis?"

"I'm not sure, sir." The words came right out without a second's conscious thought.

This ... pattern—if it was a pattern Shail worked to compel such answers—must've been what Shail had used against him the night they walked back to Chresten together. Tanis wasn't sure why he could feel the working now but hadn't been able to feel it then. Could the *goracrosta's* intervention be making it easier to sense such things? Could it be acting as a filter of some kind? Or did it have something to do with the way Shail himself was wielding the pattern?

Shail moved his hand to the arm of his chair. "So you don't know your nature ... do you expect you can do other things with the lifeforce?"

"Yes, sir," answered his traitor tongue.

"Innately?"

Again the words flew out of his mouth. "I hadn't thought of it that way, but I suppose, yes."

"Did my brother Pelas send you to spy on me?"

The sudden change of questioning made the lad give a little start, but still he'd no choice but to answer truthfully, "No, sir."

Shail grunted. "The *real* truth this time."

Tanis felt compulsion land like a blow to his breastbone. He braced bound wrists against the table's edge to catch himself as he doubled over. The answer burst out of him with his breath. "He didn't send me!"

Shail skewered him with his gaze. He shifted in his chair, edgy with skepticism. "If you truly aren't my brother's spy, then he won't come for you."

Tanis's entire body was throbbing from that punch of compulsion, but the lad pushed himself straighter in alarm nonetheless. "What do you mean?"

"Last night I summoned Pelas."

Tanis heard this and went weak with trepidation. He knew that this conflict wasn't about him—it was beyond Shail to conceive of Tanis being a threat to him. No, this had always been about Pelas. And now, because of him, Pelas would be walking right into Shail's hands.

How many others would Tanis place in danger? Who else would come to harm due to his stupidity? Guilt pulled him rapidly down where shame and castigation boiled in a toxic pitch.

Shail leaned back in his chair and crossed one knee. "If you don't profess to be spying for my brother, then who? The High Lord?"

Tanis dropped his gaze to his lap. He had no idea what he was going to do ... where his path was taking him. He had to work to keep tears from burning his eyes—he'd be damned if he'd let Shail see him cry. "No, sir."

Shail grunted dubiously. "Just your own ill-fated interest?"

Tanis clenched his teeth. "I suppose."

Shail's razor gaze swept him, looking unconvinced.

The lad grabbed his courage and lifted his gaze. "What have you done with Phoebe, sir?" If he found out nothing else, he had to know this.

"Oh, yes ... *Phoebe*." Shail cast him a merciless sort of smile. "Miss della Buonara will be given the same choice as the others—to serve freely, or become *eidola* and serve eternally."

Tanis's chest became so bound with fury and protest that he could barely breathe. He wanted to scream. He wanted to fight. He wanted to summon every bit of *elae* he could muster and blow the entire pavilion from the firmament. Jaw tight, he ground out angrily, "Bound to *you*—"

Shail's laughter cut him off. "These hapless creatures aren't bound to *me*."

His laughter grew darker, bolder, loudly declaring Tanis's ignorance. "What need would *I* have for *eidola*?"

Something in the way he said this made the hair rise on the back of Tanis's neck. The lad deflated, struck by a painful volley of confusions.

Still chuckling, Shail took up his tea. He looked truly amused. "Admittedly, my brother builds an army of the creatures." He motioned airily with his cup. "But making weapons of *eidola* is not their true purpose. Any time you magically force a thing from its intended use, you run a risk of turning Balance from your favor—oh, yes, Tanis." Shail's dark eyes lanced into the lad. "Do you think me unaware of Balance and how it referees this world?"

Tanis's mouth had gone far too dry to mold any response out of the crumbs of his mortification.

"*Eidola* are creatures of Shadow, young fool." Shail's tone resonated a mirthful condescension. "Bound to a Warlock who cannot work your lifeforce, they harvest *elae* to fuel his power." His gaze shifted slightly, off over Tanis's shoulder. "Is that not right, Sinárr?"

Tanis felt him as he arrived, for he emitted a chill greater even than Shail's. The lad leaned around the wing of his chair to see a pillar of smoke and shadow coming across the room. With every step, smoke swirled into a shape that resembled a leg and then dissolved again. Sinárr trailed smoke like a man on fire, but only a deep darkness burned at his core. He stopped beside them, and only then did the shadows cling to form.

As the whirling smoke congealed, Tanis looked first upon a black-skinned face with golden eyes, reminiscent of a Whisper Lord, only more ... human wasn't the right word. Human-*like* perhaps, for his features were fey, if fierce. But those golden eyes—as purely golden as the *eidola's* were black—seemed less metallic than composed of light itself ... as if all of his stolen power glittered in his gaze.

The smoke continued its swirling descent into form, taking the shape of an elegant coat, velvet black, molded around a tall frame, and draping down into boots of shining leather. His shoulders seemed too broad for a natural man, his arms and legs just slightly too long. Human-*like*, but clearly not.

At last only the shadows swirling about his right arm remained. This darkness lifted to reveal a great bird's feet clinging to the Warlock's forearm. Then followed the rest of the avieth into view as the whirlpool of shadows unraveled upwards, revealing glinting feathers as captured light, and finally vanishing above her head in a violet spark.

Tanis stared at the avieth sitting on the Warlock's forearm and felt utterly ill.

'He has bound me to this form, bound me to him. I'm beyond hope, for ... elae has left me.'

He'd gotten it *all* wrong—horribly, inconceivably wrong!

'... *if he finds you here, he will make you eidola like the others, a stone shadow of yourself* ... '

The avieth hadn't been talking about Shail. She'd been talking about the Warlock. Tanis slumped in his chair while the world spun in a violent vortex of misgiving, and pins of dismay stabbed his entire body.

He'd made a *dreadful* mistake!

The portal in Shail's apartments, open to Shadow ... it had been open so the Warlock could come and go freely. Had the laboratory with its floating *inverteré* patterns belonged to Shail at all?

And the avieth's scream of '*He comes!*' She'd been warning him of Sinárr, *not* Shail. Tanis must've escaped just before the Warlock arrived.

The lad forced a dry swallow.

Shail's white-robed attendant approached Sinárr, and the Warlock handed off his avieth to him. Then he turned his attention to Tanis.

A black-fleshed hand reached for the lad's face. His nails held a curious golden transparency and were long and slightly pointed. Tanis stifled a shudder as those black fingers touched his chin.

"Who then is this?" Sinárr's voice sounded a whisper that echoed of deep darkness. The face came closer. All Tanis saw when he looked into Sinárr's inhuman eyes was *elae* trapped behind his sparkling gaze.

"This is Tanis." Shail's voice hinted of merciless humor. "He's one of my brother's spies, though he denies it."

Tanis couldn't look away from the Warlock. Sinárr's flesh touching his cheek felt as smooth and cold as ice. His hand moved to take a lock of Tanis's hair, and he rubbed it between dark fingers as if tasting of it. Tanis felt pinned immobile beneath this inspection. Only his heart remained free to race, which it did with frightening force, pounding painfully in his chest.

Sinárr cupped Tanis's jaw and brought his face even closer ... closer still, close enough that their noses nearly touched. He closed his eyes, inhaled deeply ... and smiled. His teeth were perfect and white.

Tanis shivered violently.

"He's not yours yet, Sinárr."

Abruptly the Warlock straightened—the flash of motion happened so quickly that the man seemed to magically shift from bending to standing without passing through the forms in between. Only a swirl of smoke denoted the change.

"This boy is strong. I would gain much power from an *eidola* with such a connection."

Shail's eyes licked over the Warlock, calculating. "You have much power already."

Sinárr turned away. Smoke and shadow swirled. Tanis suspected that the Warlock had no real form in their realm—only the appearance of form when he stood still, when he focused his power to assume a shape.

As he watched Sinárr moving away, the lad exhaled a measured breath and willed his heart to settle. He'd never imagined that running into Shail in his apartments had been a gift of providence, but he knew now that he wouldn't have survived that day if the Warlock had found him instead.

Sinárr walked towards a column. Velvet smoke swirled and solidified with his every step, trailing each motion like steam. A curtain of raven hair flowed down his back, shifting in and out of substance. "You called me. I have come." He turned a look over his shoulder.

Tanis couldn't take his eyes off Sinárr. There was something horribly compelling about this creature. It terrified the lad to realize it. He worried the man had somehow bound him already, claimed him with his mesmerizing gaze and his gilded nails, stolen his will with that deeply unsettling inhalation.

Shail shifted in his chair while his eyes followed the Warlock across the loggia. Tanis sensed a wariness in him—wary, but not uneasy. The two seemed comparable predators, lions momentarily united in a tenuous truce.

"You wanted to be here when the Adepts made their choices." Shail flicked an unreadable gaze at Tanis and then looked back to Sinárr. "We'll rouse them soon."

Sinárr looked to the lake and its tranquil view. "The prospect excites me."

"I have only to finish with Tanis and we can be about the task."

Abruptly Sinárr blurred and reformed at Tanis's side, a rearing shadow. The lad started and pressed himself sideways in his chair, angling away from the Warlock.

Sinárr reached out a hand and stroked Tanis's head. Black fingers threaded through his hair, brushing it away from his face. His unearthly gaze felt lustful.

Chills striped the lad.

"I don't understand why I can't have this one now." Sinárr's hand found the back of Tanis's head and encouraged him forth with gentle pressure. The lad felt himself flowing towards the Warlock, his body moving without thought or will, simply inclining in his direction.

"Sinárr, release him."

The Warlock spun with a look of frustration. Tanis fell back in his seat with a forceful grunt.

"Until I know what my brother knows of our plans, the boy stays with me."

Sinárr erupted into a swirl of smoke that quickly reformed again. "You are most aggravating, Shailabanáchtran." He looked back to Tanis. "Can you not see how the boy and I are drawn to each other?" Sinárr's eyes captured Tanis's gaze—his attention, his very *essence*. He traced a single gilded fingernail slowly down Tanis's cheek and whispered, echoic of the deep dark, soft as night's gentle kiss, "… our opposing natures call to one another."

Shail cracked a smile. "If you desire Tanis, Sinárr, you can help me with my brother. Then the boy will be free for you to claim in whatever way suits you."

Sinárr spun back to Shail. Smoke exploded, swirled, resettled. "I accept this proposal."

Tanis went utterly, completely cold. For a moment he wasn't certain his heart was still beating, so close the shock felt to death's grip around it. Then he felt the tiniest flutter and sucked in his breath with a shuddering gasp.

Shail grinned wickedly at him. "I see Tanis is equally excited by the prospect, Sinárr. Shall we be about it?" He stood and motioned to the *eidola* who'd been lurking in the shadows, and it came and hauled Tanis out of his chair.

Shail called a portal, and before Tanis knew what was happening, the *eidola* was dragging him through the temple again.

Reeling, Tanis tried desperately to think of some way out of this untenable situation, but his brain wouldn't focus. Instead of presenting him with solutions, all his mind kept throwing in front of his eyes was himself, saying to Felix, '*Shailabanáchtran is about the deadliest adversary you could imagine, Felix. He's probably worse than you can imagine … '*

Apparently he was worse than even Tanis could imagine.

The lad felt like all he'd done was offer himself and Nadia up to Shail like one of Madaé Giselle's turkeys, trimmed and tied and ready for roasting. He was supposed to be upon his path … yet he feared now that he'd made a terribly wrong turn somewhere.

Shail swept through the soaring obsidian halls with Sinárr at his side. Their continuing conversation suddenly yanked Tanis back to the present as Sinárr asked, "Why this fixation on Pelasommáyurek?"

Shail cast him a doleful eye. "Darshan has made an enemy of Pelas, and their enmity has bled onto my affairs."

The Warlock perpetually molted velvet-dark shadows, leaving icy wisps trailing behind him as he walked. "But you don't fear him?" It sounded more question than a statement of fact.

Shail's gaze tightened. "That Darshan fears him is enough. Pelas can cause us interminable trouble if not subdued."

"If he's as trusting as you claim, it should be no effort to bind him, but …" Darkness swirled, shifted, settled back into form with Sinárr's steps. "You would let me make a harvester of your brother?"

Shail swept through a vaulted antechamber. His crimson robes of silk flowed like blood in water as he cast a withering look at Sinárr. "A few millennia bound to you might moderate Pelas's infuriating intractability."

They entered a vast hall lit by iron chandeliers burning with the cold light of wielder's lamps. Shail motioned to the *eidola* escorting Tanis, and it marched the lad to the center of the chamber. Shail bound him there beneath a dome, with air and magic. The lad felt invisible threads wrapping around him, pinning him to immobility. Panic set in, and he shot a desperate look at Shail, rife with premonition. "He's *not* going to come for me, sir! He can't!" Verily, these words resonated in a way that broke Tanis's heart with their truth.

Shail's lip curled with a dubious smile. "We'll see."

"But I'm *not*—"

Shail pressed a finger across his own lips, and Tanis lost the rest of the words beneath a gag of air. Shail leaned close, bringing them eye to eye. "Your fate is set either way, young fool. If Pelas doesn't claim you, Sinárr will."

Then Shail and Sinárr departed to walk in a wide circle around Tanis. Thus, the lad only heard part of their conversation.

"… many to overcome him?" Sinárr surveyed the space with his golden gaze, but Tanis perpetually felt the Warlock's eyes straying back to him.

"I cannot say." Shail's voice resonated in the vast, empty hall. "It would be wiser to seal the entire area within a containment field." They stopped back in front of Tanis, seeming a tall flame of crimson and its night-dark shadow.

"If he's your brother, *deyjiin* won't contain him."

Shail crossed arms and then stroked his chin with one finger. His gaze narrowed as he assessed the dome above and its surrounding hall. "No …" he murmured, "not merely *deyjiin*—a web of it, woven to mimic *goracrosta*."

Sinárr sucked in his breath with an admiring hiss. "A dome of *invateré* patterns to steal his power. You're beginning to think like a Warlock, Shailabanáchtran." He walked in smoke a few paces past Tanis, surveying the scene. "I alone may draw power from my *eidola*. They and I will cross into the dome and take Pelas as easily as an ewe."

Shail grunted. "Don't underestimate my brother, Sinárr. This had better be enough to contain him."

"For Tanis, I shall bring the full force of my power to bear against him, Shailabanáchtran."

"Good." Shail's gaze shifted over Tanis's shoulder. "Ah … and here is our *coup de grâce*—my gift to you, Sinárr."

"Another gift? This is proving a bountiful day."

Shail's dark eyes glinted with cold humor as he looked back to Tanis and remarked, "It's always preferable to have a friend along when facing an eternity of bondage, don't you think, truthreader?"

Tanis jolted—for he knew immediately who Shail was bringing as a gift for the Warlock. Yet he could do *nothing!* To be pinned so helplessly in that moment was the worst feeling he'd ever experienced.

And of course it was Nadia who Shail paraded in front of him. Her dark hair had come unbound and trailed in waves down her back, but she seemed otherwise unharmed. She cast a desperate look at him as the *eidola* stopped her before Shail and Sinárr. Tanis saw that she, too, was bound with *goracrosta*.

Sinárr took up a strand of her hair and spun his finger around it. He pulled her head closer and leaned in. Then he smelled as deeply of Nadia as he'd partaken of Tanis. The lad wanted to scream. Everything in him swelled to do so, yet nothing emerged but a choking gasp.

"*Ah* ... this child is strong as well." Sinárr turned in a swirl of velvet smoke, so that his face vanished and reappeared around his glowing golden eyes. His teeth shone very white as he smiled. "What marvelous gifts you present me, Shailabanáchtran."

With a flick of his gaze, Shail instructed the *eidola* to move on, and the creature dragged Nadia across the hall. Tanis felt a volcano ready to erupt, but he managed only the barest puff of a furious exhale.

Shail chuckled, and his eyes glinted with dark amusement. "A prince and his princess. So quaint."

Tanis choked on his breath upon hearing these words. All fury fled from him, replaced by sure panic. His eyes flew to Shail's.

The Malorin'athgul arched a wry brow. "Did you really think a few braids and an illusion pinned to a bit of glass would keep *me* from recognizing the Empress's heir? Had you not just spent hours together the day before, no doubt plotting your doomed little coup?"

Tanis shook his head violently to indicate he wanted to speak.

Shail humored him.

Tanis blurted desperately, "But surely she'd be useful to you, sir—to your war!"

"*My* war." He grunted deprecatingly. "As if the politics of mortal kings could interest me." He spun in a billow of crimson silk and headed off with the Warlock.

They soon passed out of Tanis's hearing, but the lad hardly noticed anyway, for grief fought a battle with confusion while his soul bled with guilt. He watched the *eidola* tie Nadia to one of the twisting columns of a bronze baldaquin far across the hall. It was torment seeing her, knowing he'd brought her into this peril. She was too far away for the lad to see her clearly, denying them even the comfort of each other's gaze, and the *goracrosta* prevented any mental communication.

While Shail and Sinárr constructed their trap for Pelas, Tanis stood bound to misery, wondering with each inhale if this was really the path he was meant to walk and with every exhale fearing for Nadia and what he'd done. With nothing else to do but suffer his desperation, the lad made a clock of his fears and cycled through them with each passing hour.

Eventually Sinárr appeared again before Tanis—it was like the air split into a fissure and disgorged ebony smoke that poured itself into the Warlock's shape. Parts of Sinárr always remained amorphous; even his eyes shifted and sparkled, like golden glass beads tumbling in a goblet.

Those eyes fixed on Tanis again as the Warlock materialized in front of him ... studied him ... smiled.

Tanis's heart streaked into a panic.

Sinárr stroked his gilded nails upwards along Tanis's neck and drew them to a point at his chin. His unearthly eyes regarded him with a definite hunger. "No ... I think not *eidola* for you." He leaned close, bringing his lips to Tanis's ear, his breath icy as he whispered, "For you ... *concubine*." One nail caught beneath the lad's chin and pressed sharply.

Tanis got the frightening image of this unnatural being vampirishly feeding off of him for eternity, and suddenly nothing a Malorin'athgul could ever do seemed anywhere near as horrible.

"*Sinárr* ..."

The Warlock growled and exploded into smoke.

Tanis let out a shuddering exhale.

Then the two immortals departed, leaving Tanis to face his very uncertain future alone.

SIXTY-ONE

"The angiel are united in purpose but not always in action."
– *Sobra I'ternin*, Eleventh Translation, 1499aF,
On the Relationship of the Angiel to the Mortal Tapestry

ALYNERI HUGGED HER knees and gazed out across the valley of the *sa'reyth*, watching as the stars began to fade beneath dawn's early light. The night had been chill, but Balaji's arm around her shoulders had kept her warm. Though he usually unsettled her, that night she'd felt joined with him in their vigil, bonded through their shared purpose. She didn't exactly feel safe in his company, but she certainly felt protected.

She'd had plenty of time through the night to reflect on why Balaji made her so nervous. Outwardly it made no sense—Balaji was ever amiable, the *sa'reyth's* peace-keeper, equalizer and inimitable cook—but when she thought about it, she realized that she perceived in him an immense distance, as if only part of his mind wandered this earth while the greater part adventured eternally in the cosmic elsewhere.

His manner reminded her often of Phaedor, but whereas Phaedor presented himself with a zanthyr's aloof indifference, Balaji always offered an amiable and welcoming smile. She had the sense, however, that beneath Balaji's friendly façade lurked a wild being of untamed power. One could look at Balaji and see a youth of ten and eight, or gaze deeper and see a fiery dragon sharing kinship with the sun.

Despite her misgivings about his nature, all through the night Balaji had held her close, doubtless sensing the trepidation she must surely have been radiating. He in turn had watched the skies quietly, calm and unflustered, unfettered it would seem by bonds of love and thus by the emotions that accompanied those bindings. Yet Balaji clearly cared for Trell—she knew it was unfair of her to cast aspersions over his compassion.

As dawn's fire burned orange behind the eastern mountains and turned the near sky a deep, luminous blue, Alyneri hugged her knees closer and asked, "Does the passing of the endless years harden one's soul, Balaji? Does it make it easier to endure not knowing what's become of those we care about?"

Balaji turned his gaze from the sky and considered her as he held her within the circle of his arm. "A fair question, Alyneri, daughter of Jair. The Mage would say it is only our choices that harden us."

Alyneri pondered that, though her thoughts were sluggish after keeping their all-night vigil. She pushed a stray strand of hair from her eyes. "But what of tragedy and death, and things stolen and lost? What choice does one have in these?"

Balaji gave her a gentle smile. "One chooses how he will respond to them after all is said and done."

"That seems a callous way of looking at life," she protested wearily. "How can you not feel the loss of a loved one? Would the Mage have no one mourn their passing?"

"Ah, but it is *after* the mourning is done that one makes the choice to harden their heart against loving again, or not," Balaji pointed out with a smile.

Then his smile faded and his arm around her shoulders stiffened. "They near." He stood and abruptly froze again, like a predator smelling the air. "Something isn't right. Come, Alyneri." He offered her his hand, and she took it feeling suddenly ill with foreboding—a feeling that only intensified as Balaji drew her urgently down the hill towards the *sa'reyth*.

"The others—" she whispered.

"I have summoned them." He gripped her hand more tightly, and the world skipped beneath them ... blurred—once, twice, many times again. They crossed in heartbeats what had been half an hour's leisurely climb.

Alyneri felt a frightening duality as she rushed at Balaji's side. Part of her wanted to run as fiercely as she could into the imminent future, to be there when the moment arrived and do *whatever* she must to make her world whole again; another part desired to stay behind, to linger even in that past which had felt so agonizing only a moment before. For suddenly the not-knowing seemed a preferable state compared to what the future must surely hold.

The sun's rim cleared the mountain ridge just as Náiir's dark-haired head appeared over the rise of the opposite hill. Balaji must've known where his brother would return, for he'd been leading Alyneri in that direction all the while.

But as the rest of Náiir's form came into view, carrying Trell in his arms, Alyneri's feet turned as leaden as if all the blood in her body had fled there to cower. Balaji drew her relentlessly forth through a storm of fear that made all the world seem darker despite the sun rising brilliantly in the east.

"*Balaji*—" Náiir's tone crackled with urgency. "Summon the Mage."

"The Mage is in Illume Be—"

Náiir made a sound that was half-growl, half-roar and which echoed like a clap of thunder throughout the valley. "*Reach* him!"

Balaji drew up short, but now Alyneri couldn't stop. She picked up her skirts and ran to Náiir … to Trell draped unconscious against his body.

Oh, dear Epiphany, to see him again! She could hardly find her breath for sight of him, even cradled so in Náiir's arms. For weeks she'd dreamed of seeing him again, but always in her mind she feared she never would. Now here he was, and she'd never loved him more—truly, she knew she could never love *anyone* more than she loved Trell.

Náiir gave her a look as she gained his side. He didn't pause in his descent towards the *sa'reyth*, but he slowed to let her read of his charge. She spared but a moment to gaze upon Trell's face—*his beautiful face!* His closed lids seemed so fragile, his lips pale and barely parted—but then she placed her hands on his head and dove into rapport.

Tears of joy and tears of foreboding fell unnoticed from her eyes as she swam the current of Trell's lifeforce, seeking his pattern. When she found it … it made no sense! The light of his pattern was fading, yet the pattern itself appeared whole.

Her eyes flew open, and she found Náiir watching her as he continued his rapid descent. His gaze reflected what she had just learned. Something was *very* wrong.

Jaya emerged from the tent just as they arrived, and she held back the folds of heavy cloth to let them pass. "What is it? What happened?"

"The witch did something to him." Náiir rushed through the canvas corridors towards a bedchamber Alyneri had never noticed before. He laid Trell out on the wide four-poster bed.

Alyneri nearly threw herself to Trell's side and sank at once back into rapport. Again, she examined his life pattern, following its twists and curves, seeking explanation for the reason its light had already diminished. Finding nothing, she dove deeper—as Vaile had shown her how to do—deep into the heart of his pattern.

Now she swam among a maze of arches, looking up, down—all around within a vast complex of light. She threaded her mind among that rose-gold filigree of three dimensions, through the vaulted, spiraling arches and twisting columns that formed Trell's life-pattern, the very essence that was *him*. Yet despite this deepest of inspections, she found nothing to explain why his light was waning.

It frightened her beyond measure.

Opening her eyes, Alyneri pressed Trell's hand to her cheek and exhaled a shuddering breath. Her stomach felt sick, her throat clenched by fear. Whatever secret device this woman had worked, she'd hidden it alarmingly well.

Náiir meanwhile turned to Jaya and said in a low voice, "Trell walked from his cell in Darroyhan, but an hour after our escape, I sensed his consciousness fading. Now he won't rouse at all."

Eyes wide, Jaya moved to Trell's side, leaned on the bed and placed a hand on his brow. Alyneri watched Jaya close her eyes and concentrate. She remained still for a long time, no doubt following the same course of inspection that Alyneri had just completed. When she opened her eyes again, Jaya had measurably paled. "He fades with every breath!" She turned a gaze of fiery accusation upon her brother. "What could she have done?"

Náiir clenched his jaw. "She was a *mor'alir* Adept. What wouldn't she do?"

Balaji entered through a parting of drapes with Mithaiya close behind him. "I've called the Mage, Náiir, but I cannot say how quickly he will come."

Jaya spun to him. "By the Lady's blessed light, why didn't Vai—" Abruptly she bit off her words and leveled Náiir a dramatic look of unease. "Where's Vaile?"

Náiir's gaze narrowed to a smoldering, brimstone stare. He didn't seem to see Jaya anymore, only the memory of what he'd witnessed. "We met with some resistance at Darroyhan." His lips pressed to a tight line. "Vaile took the full force of a blast of *deyjiin* as we were departing with Trell."

Jaya pressed a hand over her mouth.

"And?" Mithaiya demanded.

Náiir gave her an unreadable look. "She said she would follow."

"So you just *left* her there?" Mithaiya grabbed Náiir's arm. "With *deyjiin* in her veins? What if she couldn't take the form?"

"Ah ..." Balaji's eyes were fixed on his brother. "You saw it too, then."

Náiir shifted his gaze to Balaji. Alyneri saw an odd acceptance in it.

Jaya dropped her hand to her side. "What are you saying?"

Náiir's expression was grim. "Vaile made her choice, Jaya."

Balaji looked over at Alyneri and gave her a soft smile. "She's been teaching Alyneri the dance of swords."

"That hardly proves—" Mithaiya began.

"*Amithaiya'geshwen*," Balaji's tone, though mild, yet silenced her. "Vaile gave Alyneri her own blades to use in her studies."

At this, both Jaya and Mithaiya stared hollowly at him.

Alyneri didn't understand the tumultuous energy that charged like lightning through the currents at this, and she really didn't care. Even the misgiving that something terrible had happened to Vaile sounded a faint whisper, drowned by the fear screaming in her head.

She shoved to her feet. "Trell is *dying* while you stand here bickering! Cannot any of you help him?" She cast her gaze urgently about the room, seeking any eyes to meet with hers. "*Won't* you help him?" Her voice broke, and she sank again at his bedside. His hand in hers felt cold.

Náiir touched her shoulder. "If it was within my power to help him, Alyneri, I would—Balance be damned."

"Náiir—"

"*Peace*, Mithaiya!" Náiir speared a condemning look at his sister. Then he turned back to Alyneri with deep concern furrowing his brow. "I searched his pattern all the while we flew, and still I could find no hint of Taliah's working."

"Nor I," Jaya said, sounding desolate.

Alyneri swallowed back a sob. Tears streamed down her cheeks as she pressed Trell's hand to her face. Still in rapport, she watched his life pattern fading before her eyes. All the while she'd been holding his hand, she pushed her own lifeforce into him, but it seemed hardly to make a dent in his degeneration. The life just kept trickling out of him. He grew paler by the breath.

Balaji came over and placed a hand on Trell's shoulder, and Alyneri saw a surge of *elae* flood into his pattern. He looked to her compassionately, nodded once, and withdrew. So followed Mithaiya, then Náiir, each one sending a pulse of *elae* into Trell's pattern, making it momentarily glow before it faded again, though it remained brighter after each surge.

After her siblings left, Jaya sat down on the bed beside Alyneri, placed one hand on Trell's leg and her arm around Alyneri. She cast a steady flow of the lifeforce into his pattern, even as Alyneri did.

Weak with desperation, Alyneri leaned into Jaya's embrace, and they rested their heads together.

"The Mage made Trell's body strong," Jaya murmured into Alyneri's ear, "and his will is even stronger. Trell's is the strength of a thousand men. Have faith he can endure even this."

Alyneri's face was wet with tears. Their salt collected on her lips and stained her cheeks, but she couldn't stop crying. The thought of losing him after all he must've endured, when freedom lay within his reach … it seemed so unbearably unfair.

"Jaya."

Alyneri looked over to find Balaji standing in the doorway.

"Any more and you risk shifting the Balance in *Trell's* life, never mind your own."

Jaya let out a slow breath. She stood and looked down on Trell quietly, her eyes dark with concern. "Once again, his life lies in the Mage's hands." She gave Alyneri an apologetic look and left with her brother.

Alyneri closed her eyes and laid her forehead on Trell's upper arm, her hands clutching his. She cast the lifeforce into him in a ceaseless flow. She knew the constant drain on her own ability would eventually make a sieve of herself, so that her pattern couldn't hold the lifeforce any more than his could. Yet what choice had she? *Trell* lay before her! He was dying! These were incontrovertible facts with an unequivocal response.

She would save him, or die trying.

Some time after daybreak, Fynn came in. He sat for a while in a chair at the foot of the bed and stared at his cousin, not speaking—not even drinking. Then, after an hour or so, he got up and left with red-rimmed eyes.

Carian came soon thereafter. He put a hand on Trell's leg and gazed at him for a time. Then he smiled and left.

It panicked Alyneri to think they were coming to pay their last respects.

Throughout the day people came and went. Alyneri rarely had the energy to spare a glance for them, but she often felt them there ... felt their grief or their worry ... their compassion. No one disturbed her. None tried to stop her, though everyone knew she was killing herself trying to save him. They also knew that nothing they could say would change that.

At one point in the early evening she heard a commotion that partly roused her from the symphony of rapport–Vaile's return. Alyneri listened long enough to ascertain that the zanthyr lived, and then she directed her attention back to Trell. His future was not so assured.

She drew upon the lifeforce, pushed it into Trell's pattern and considered the drain on her own energies as penance for her mistakes. They'd parted in the Kutsamak still riven by her duplicity. He had every right to be upset, but to think he might die believing she was ashamed of him—*this* nearly undid her. When she thought of her time together with Trell ... when she recalled his humor and his nobility and his incredible courage—*oh*, how *desperately* she loved him!

At some point, Balaji brought her a chair. Alyneri had lost track of the hours by then. Now she sat at Trell's bedside and rested her chin on her hands and gazed at him through eyes wet with tears.

For hours she stayed so, funneling *elae* into his pattern. For hours she watched as his face grew more pale, the delicate skin beneath his eyes grew shadowed, and the angular hollows beneath his cheekbones became ever more pronounced.

'If Cephrael stood against him, he would've died in the Fire Sea ... '

Vaile's words. Alyneri had to believe them now—they were all she clung to, in fact. She had to believe that Trell could survive even this; that somehow Balance would shift again in his favor. She thought of all the things she'd told Vaile that she and Trell would do together, and she promised herself it would come to be.

"I won't give up on you." Alyneri pressed a wet kiss to his palm and channeled *elae* into his life pattern despite the dangerous throbbing in her skull. "Don't you give up either."

She was resting with her head on his arm when again she felt a forceful presence enter the room. It took her half a minute to convince herself to lift her head to see who had come—the chains of her exhaustion bound her into that bent posture. When she did manage to lift her gaze, she looked upon another Sundragon.

Two of the *drachwyr* she hadn't yet met, but this man could only be Şrivas'rhakárakek, the Shadow of the Light. Jaya said he came and went always in the night.

Rhakar came across the room and stood opposite her across the bed. He placed a hand on Trell's shoulder, and because she maintained rapport, Alyneri saw a pulse of brilliant energy flowing into Trell's pattern, making it flare brightly before settling back again to the ashen hue it had become. Yet some of Rhakar's working must've lingered, for Trell's pattern seemed a little more solid than it had a moment ago.

Alyneri lifted her gaze to meet Rhakar's.

Yellow-gold eyes looked down at her. "I didn't pull him from a well so a witch could curse him unto death."

Alyneri pressed her lips together and blinked more tears from her eyes.

Rhakar held her with his gaze. His presence felt different from the other *drachwyr* ... uniquely powerful ... as though a thousand threads attached to him. She remembered Mithaiya saying that Rhakar was already invested in the game and got the impression that he walked the tapestry indifferent to the cobwebs of Balaji's analogy, that he never wove between them but merely passed on, letting them collect ... or searing from the aether any that sought to prevent his passing.

When Rhakar looked at her, as he was doing just then, Alyneri felt as if those electric threads, myriad filaments of Fate, reached out to bind her as well. "Trell is a Player, Alyneri d'Giverny. Isabel says his path extends long into the tapestry. You hold him here until the Mage comes. Don't let go."

A sob lodged in her throat at this—yet it was hope that caught it there. Desperately, she held his gaze and managed a nod.

He nodded once in return, pointedly sealing their pact, and left.

Alyneri lost track of time as she sat at Trell's side, pushing *elae* into his pattern. From the ache everywhere in her body and the interminable throbbing in her skull, she thought it must've been nearing midnight. She'd been awake for more than two days. Now it was less the fear of Trell's imminent expiration than of an overwhelming weariness that terrorized her, for she was the only force keeping him alive—her lifeforce anchoring his to this world—and if she failed ... if exhaustion claimed her into sleep or if the lifeforce suddenly denied her its touch, Trell would depart within the hour.

Indeed, the longer she held him to life, the more she felt that some force equally pulled him into the beyond, dragging him down to death's depths. She'd caught Trell while the anchor of death was still sinking, but now it wasn't enough for Alyneri to hold only Trell above those dark waves. She had to buoy him *and* the anchor. If she let it drop low enough to catch the bottom, it would yank Trell from her grasp.

Alyneri let out a shuddering exhale and rested her head on Trell's chest while she gripped his hand in hers. The world spun dizzily. She felt unimaginably drained … a mere husk of herself. Her fingers around his were cramped from clenching so tightly for hours unending, as if her hand alone held him to life; with every heartbeat, the light of the lifeforce seemed to move farther and farther away, like a candle being carried down a darkened hallway.

Each time she inhaled, she drew upon the lifeforce, but where once it had gushed as from a well too full, now *elae* came as barely a trickle.

She felt herself fading while the world spun around her, felt her own heartbeat slowing in time with Trell's. Darkness hovered on the edges of her vision … teasing, inviting.

Her muddled mind saw justice in their passing together into the beyond, as if in proving herself so willing to give up her life for him, she might make amends for having ever thought to live without him.

She tried to resist the pull of exhaustion's sleep, tried to resist the force tugging Trell into the depths, but suddenly she felt the anchor dropping. It slid from her grasp like *elae* had slipped, whisking away into the deep. The world spun with ghostly shadows, like sinking into a well of inky darkness. Alyneri felt herself being sucked down beneath the waves—for though she couldn't put life into Trell's pattern any longer, yet she wouldn't let go of it. Thus they both tumbled toward death's depths, struggling to draw breath through the swirling dark—

Light blazed in painful shards of color.

Alyneri's enervated mind thought at first it must've been Phaedor that sent his light into Trell's pattern, for whoever else could've shone so brightly?

A hand came to rest upon her head, and *elae* flooded into her even as it flooded Trell's pattern with a brilliance theretofore unmatched. It was as if the light was breaking away the char to forge the pattern anew. She roused and sat up with a start.

Looked up.

Blue eyes gazed into hers. "Sweet Alyneri …" His hand stroked her hair as he smiled upon her with wonder and awe. "How brave and selfless you are."

Alyneri caught her breath.

Björn sat down beside her. She didn't know where the chair had come from—didn't know where *he* had come from, this man who glowed on the currents like a star. No, a *core* of stars.

He laid one hand upon Trell's brow and extended his other palm open to her. "Give me your hand. See what parasite of vengeance tries to claim our Trell of the Tides."

Alyneri complied without thinking, such was the power of Björn's gaze. He interwove her fingers with his and then turned his attention to Trell.

Through Björn's eyes, Alyneri immediately saw a world bathed in the currents of *elae*, brilliant with color and gilded light. She saw what Björn saw as he dove with alacrity into Trell's mind and instantly arrived at his life pattern. He didn't seek it. It simply appeared to his view.

And she saw at once the dark pattern clinging there like a spider.

It stood out so prominently against Trell's life pattern! How could she not have seen it?

"You cannot see the pattern as I do." Björn squeezed her hand in gentle reassurance. "But I've shown you where it sits. Look now and see how it will present itself to your view."

Her vision shifted—Björn had closed off his mind—and she saw Trell's pattern again through her own rapport. She looked where Björn had shown her and saw a tiny thread of the lifeforce wiggling out of his now-glowing pattern. The thread was so small, so faint, that it nearly seemed a mirage.

It reminded her of stories she'd heard of a desert snake that waggled its tail like a worm with the rest of its body buried in the sand, just waiting for a hapless creature to follow its lure and be consumed.

"You'll know how to search for such parasites now."

"Yes," she whispered.

Björn squeezed her hand and opened his mind to her again. She watched as he seared the offensive pattern from existence.

Trell sucked in his breath with a gasp.

Alyneri's eyes flew open. She held Björn's hand tightly in her own, unable to breathe, just waiting ...

Trell's eyes fluttered open, and she saw his gaze slowly find focus ... shift ... settle on her. "*Alyneri* ..." he managed a smile. Then his lids fluttered closed again, and he slipped into sleep.

Alyneri burst into tears.

Björn moved to the edge of Trell's bed and drew her up into his arms. She sobbed into his shoulder as emotion and exhaustion and relief all flooded out of her.

When the deluge abated, he brushed the hair from her eyes and the tears from her cheeks. Then he kissed her forehead and encouraged her to her feet. "Go and find sleep. I'll stay, but we've nothing now to fear." Cobalt blue eyes looked her over. "You saved his life, Alyneri."

She pressed both hands to her mouth and stared at him.

He sat back down in his chair and smiled, his gaze holding a gentle insistence.

Alyneri complied, yet as she walked in a daze back to her own tent, rest suddenly seemed the last thing on her mind.

All Björn had done was show her a pattern, yet she felt as if he'd revealed to her an entirely new path branching with countless opportunities to make her life into anything she desired.

A day ago Alyneri had wondered at the many people who'd sworn themselves to Björn van Gelderan. Now she understood. She'd seen of him even as she'd seen of Phaedor. Björn's light seared all the shadows from the world to cast everything into stark illumination. There were no shades of grey while standing within that light, only truth.

She would follow him anywhere.

SIXTY-TWO

"The light always comes round again, if one can

stand the darkness long enough."

— A favorite Malchiarri saying

DAY AND NIGHT blended for Isabel while Pelas exorcised Darshan's compulsion, but finally a time came when they lay abed with moonlight as a blanket across their naked forms. Isabel lay on her back, Pelas with his head on her stomach. His long raven hair draped across the mattress, blending with hers, dark shadows amid a field of luminous white. Her fingertips traced the line of his temple and smoothed back his hair. His breath came evenly. He seemed at peace for the first time.

They'd been hours in this stillness, not speaking...perhaps not daring to speak. She sensed him waiting for the horror to return, for that repulsive, irresistible urge to do harm...for the dark desire that had always before overtaken and enslaved him.

"It's been three hours." She felt the roughness of his unshaven jaw scraping her belly as he spoke. The feeling reminded her heartbreakingly of Ean.

Though Pelas lay calm, serene, nearly whole again, Isabel felt shattered. Hunger was an ache she barely recognized anymore, so faint it felt compared to her guilt. Her raw and damaged skin touching or being touched threaded throughout this constant ache. But these hurts were part of her sacrifice—she would do whatever she must to ensure Pelas's freedom.

Her freedom...she wasn't sure she could ever feel free again with such a cilice of guilt around her soul.

"It just doesn't seem possible," he whispered.

She lifted her head to give him a smile, then slowly laid it back again. "Perhaps we should begin keeping count of the hours."

His brow furrowed faintly. But seeing him and only *him* as he looked at her...

"I cannot believe I'm free of it."

She stroked his hair. "Belief will come in time."

Abruptly he pushed to his hands and crawled up the bed to stretch out his body alongside hers. He rested his head on his arm and gazed at her, tracing his thumb idly across her collarbone. "But how will I remain free if I must have you to exorcise this demon?"

She gave him a look of soft acceptance. "You won't need me. Even so, I will stay with you if you wish it."

He lifted to his elbow. "You would stay with me—*here?*" He stared at her for a moment, but then a frown overcame his expression. "You cannot mean what you say. You have your own path."

"Pelas..." She drew in a deep breath and let it out slowly, the better to ease the tension binding her. She looked at him until he met her gaze again. "Your freedom *is* my path."

He heard this, but then he shifted his head slightly, and his eyes tightened. "No...I sense something in this—a truth you're not saying."

She gave a brief smile at his perception—proof again to her that no power had truly been taken from him—but she quickly turned her gaze away, that he wouldn't see the sorrow in it also.

"I am two. Even in a sense as you were two, yet mine is and has always been a battle between two selves. What I long for," she looked bravely back to him, "what the woman Isabel desires, must defer to the path I walk first as Epiphany's Prophet."

His gaze reflected his understanding, and his sympathy. "Then it's Epiphany's Prophet who gave herself to me, who I took to my bed, not the woman Isabel."

She nodded.

Pelas smoothed a strand of hair from her face and placed a chaste kiss on her cheek. "Dear, sweet Isabel...what you've sacrificed for me."

She turned him a fierce look softened with humor and darkened by grief. "I trust you will be worth it."

He chuckled. Then he laughed. "I can't believe it! How long I've lived with that...*demon* haunting my thoughts! Always fearing the inevitable moment when it would raise its head and consume me. If not for Tanis—" Suddenly he stopped himself, his eyes became round, and he gave her a wondrous look, for now he saw what she had already surmised. "If not for Tanis, Isabel," he said with deliberate slowness, "I would still be thinking I *was* that beast."

She lifted a hand and touched her fingers lightly to his lips. "Tanis truly saved you."

He held her gaze, nodded. Then he laid his head down beside hers again. "How did you know?"

"How did I know what?"

"How to help me?"

"It's just application of the Ninth Law. *'Do not counter force with force; channel it.'* Fighting the compulsion merely pits force against force—your will against Darshan's pattern."

He pushed up on his elbow to look at her better. "Explain this to me."

"As you learned," and she managed a smile on his behalf, "the way to escape compulsion is to rechannel its power to a harmonic of the pattern's original intent. Once you've learned to sublimate and channel a compulsion along one harmonic, you'll find you can channel it along any harmonic, any passion—be that a passion for sex, for exploration, for the creation of your art..." She held his quiet gaze and let her eyes convey more than words could ever express. "You'll find infinite harmonics to explore, Pelas."

She could tell from his serious expression that he truly understood now, whereas before, perhaps he had not.

"Darshan will never be able to compel me again—no one will." His eyes were very wide and impossibly bright. "Isabel..." He planted a sweet kiss upon her mouth. "You really have set me free."

She closed her eyes and smiled and tried to keep from crying, for while Epiphany's Prophet had set him free, she had surely imprisoned the woman Isabel. "Perhaps we should thank Cephrael," she offered quietly.

Pelas propped his head in his hand again and gave her an amused look. "Hmm...why?"

She opened one eye and closed it again. "You're laughing, but Cephrael wrote the Laws of Patterning to help Adepts solve the problems of Patterning. Had you known the Laws yourself, you might've found your own way free."

This made him quiet for a long time. After a while he murmured, "High Mage of the Citadel indeed," and fell back onto the mattress to stare at the ceiling. "There is much I still don't know about your Patterning."

"You have lifetimes in which to learn," she told him softly.

Her comment brought a sudden darkness to his gaze, which she immediately perceived. Before he could sink beneath those shadows, she forced herself to sit up and moved her body to straddle his hips. He smiled up at her curiously but with a hint of suspicion in his gaze.

She extended her wrists to him with their cuffs of silver rope. "Remove the *goracrosta*." When his expression hardened, she pressed, "Let me help you—I'm the High Mage of the Citadel, if you recall."

"I recall." Still, he watched her carefully, as if suspicious now of some hidden agenda.

Isabel took one of his hands and then the other and pinned them over his head. "Do you trust me, Pelas?"

He gazed seriously at her. "Trust was difficult even before Darshan took away my power."

She touched her fingers to his lips. "What does your heart tell you?"

He searched her eyes with his own and ran his fingers down her face. "I want to trust you, Isabel."

She closed her eyes and nodded. Exhaustion and pain were all intermingled now. It was so hard to stay alert to the shifting paths, but Pelas didn't know the way. She was his only guide. "Trust will be a new experience for you."

He chuckled. "*You* are a new experience for me. I like new experiences." He set her aside and moved off the bed. She lay quietly, eyes closed, trying to keep the path clear in her mind. But when cold steel touched her flesh, her eyes flew open.

He sliced the *goracrosta* cuff from one arm and then the next, and Isabel inhaled a shuddering breath of relief at the surge of life that *elae's* return restored to her. The currents swarmed around her in warm waves, like children greeting a parent too long away.

With *elae* so blessedly restored, her first action was to remove the concealment she'd worked to protect her mind from Darshan's inspection. She felt an immeasurable sense of restoration in doing this.

Cloaking herself in the lifeforce's blessed warmth, Isabel looked back to Pelas. He was regarding her with a deep furrow between his brows.

Isabel sat up and pushed him back on the bed. She straddled his hips and placed her hands to either side of his face in the truthreader's hold. "Do you trust me, Pelas?"

He looked nearly undone. "I trust you, Isabel."

She held his gaze, opened a truthreader's rapport with him, and flowed into his mind. Ah…treading upon the light of his mind was like swimming through the sun. Perhaps that boundless sky had once been shadowed by Darshan's storm, but as with all workings of *elae*, compulsion was merely a pattern; it collected *elae* and focused it around an intention.

Pelas had learned how to rechannel the power of that pattern into his own intention, and its darkness would never trouble him again.

His mind was powerful and free.

Except… *Ah, there it is.*

"What is it? What do you see?" His voice rang with concern, though seeming far away, for she was deep inside his mind now on her own wondrous exploration. That he felt barely a whisper of her presence was less a result of the vicious trick worked upon him than a product of her skill. "Isabel, please…I see it on your face."

"Be at peace, Pelasommáyurek," she whispered, using his full name in recognition of all that he was. "I'm merely sweeping up the brittle leaves of an illusion not long for this world." In that moment, she sent the smallest spark of the fourth to sear the offensive pattern from his mind.

He inhaled sharply.

Isabel opened her eyes, and her lips spread in a slow smile.

"I—" He gaped at her. Abruptly he sat up and took her hard by the shoulders. Fiery copper eyes searched hers. "*How?*"

She took his face in her hands and shook her head slowly from side to side. "You are immortal. No one can ever take away your power. It is only you who permitted it by allowing them to deceive you...and then by deceiving yourself into believing that your abilities could be lost."

He stared at her with a tormented expression, nearly as broken by this understanding as he had been in the belief that he really had lost his power. He looked as if he was about to speak, but instead he threw his arms around her and gripped her into a desperate embrace. That time she couldn't conceal the pain that flared, and she exhaled a whimper.

Pelas released her with immediate dismay. His eyes searched her face, scanned her body, and he seemed only then to remember what his demons had put her through, what she'd endured on the road to his salvation.

He leapt from the bed and grabbed his pants off the floor. Even as he was bent over putting them on, a silver line split down through the air.

"Pelas..."

He turned her a look that silenced her. Then he stepped into Shadow and the portal vanished.

Isabel inhaled a tremulous breath and buried her head in her hands.

There was no other way... There was no other way!

There had been no other way.

Oh, perhaps if she'd known that all of Darshan's efforts had been nothing more than smoke and mirrors, an attempt to deceive Pelas so that he would believe his powers to be gone—the ruse helped along by lengthy torture capped off by a tawdry illusion...Perhaps if she'd known how easily she could restore his power, she might've been able to convince him, to bargain her way free.

But if she had...

If all she'd done was restore his power, he would still be the prisoner of that compulsion which had so desolated him.

The *only* way to truly free him had been the path they'd walked together, and now he was *truly* free—more so even than if Darshan's compulsion had simply been removed, for now that he knew how to channel compulsion, he would never again become a victim of it.

As to herself...she was no victim in their interactions any more than a soldier could be considered a victim in battle. Epiphany's Prophet had walked knowingly into peril, and Isabel faced the consequences of her choices without diminishment.

But for the woman Isabel, those same choices would have grave consequences. She only prayed that Pelas's freedom would be worth the cost, for with a single act, she'd saved one good man but deeply betrayed another.

A silver line split the air, and Pelas returned through the portal carrying an armload of supplies. With a breath of the fifth and a dismissive glance, all the knives flew off the table. He laid his jars and baskets and other things in their place. Then he came across to her with water and linen and a salve for her wounds.

She looked up to meet his gaze.

A host of emotions flickered through his fiery copper eyes: gratitude, amazement, admiration…perhaps a hint of fury at how careless she'd been with her life, how she'd nearly let him kill her. Was he comparing her recklessness to that of another who had walked a similarly dangerous path with him? She thought he might've been, and the idea brought a soft smile to her lips.

He arched a brow at her, and she thought she heard his silent inquiry, wry and somewhat amused. *What memories are you looking at in my head, Isabel?*

To which she replied, *Loving ones.*

Then he was guiding her gently over onto her stomach and tending to the wounds he'd inflicted upon her back. "Would that I was better trained as a Healer." His gentle hands smoothed the salve onto her skin. "I have but small facility with such patterns, but I'll do what I can."

She felt him concentrating on using the first strand to ease her wounds and smiled in amusement. He would've had more success trying to work the first strand innately than by using patterns to do it, but some things he must learn on his own. Still, he managed to draw some of the pain from her skin, even if none from her heart.

After he'd treated her wounds, he fed her light fare—broth and bread and wine, what small amount she could take—and wrapped her in a soft velvet cloak he'd brought back with him. Then he held her in his arms on the bed, cradled like a child.

Isabel felt sleep coming and would embrace it when it arrived, for she saw that his path was set now and feared no more for his road. She let him enfold her with his arms and tried not to think about anything that would make her cry. What was done could not now be undone, and crying would not assuage her guilt.

Her voice sounded slow in her ears as she asked him, "How will you deal with Darshan?"

Pelas shifted his eyes to the metal poles she'd been tied to, and his gaze darkened. "Those were the poles he bound me to when he punished me. He brought them here for me to use in binding you. That's Darshan's idea of irony." He grunted and arched a rueful brow. "The real irony is that if my brothers hadn't elected me to be their enemy, I wouldn't have become one. Now…now there is no going back."

"You must be careful of them." She didn't think she needed to say it—she thought he'd learned what he needed to from this experience—but she said it anyway, because some truths couldn't be heard too many times.

"Isabel, I will be." He pressed his nose into her hair and breathed deeply. Then he laid his face against her head, and she felt him smile. "You smell like sunlight."

Isabel squeezed shut her eyes. *Why then do I feel so cold?* "Where will you go when you leave here?"

He let out a slow breath. "There's someone I need to find."

Sleep was coming for her. She felt it tugging on her consciousness, lowering its shade across her thoughts. She hardly realized the words left her tongue, for they were more thought than spoken word: "...and one day you will come to find my brother."

He chuckled. "To give him my oath, as Franco Rohre and others have done?"

Isabel let silence embrace her thoughts. "To shake his hand...and be welcomed to the game."

He must've said something in reply to this, but she'd already drifted off.

"My lady, your chariot awaits."

Isabel roused from sleep to find Pelas smiling over her. He looked striking in a long damask coat the color of wine, with his hair brushed and plaited, his jaw freshly shaved, and fine, starched linen at his cuffs.

She pushed up on one elbow and saw that he'd prepared food for her. She couldn't bear to tell him that she felt too heartsick to stomach anything but grief.

He was sensitive to her condition, however, and offered her but little things, fruit and the like. Then he made her drink of his wine to warm her, for he said her hands felt like ice. She knew it was merely an emanation of the regret coating her soul.

When he'd cared for her as best he could, Pelas stepped back from where she sat on the bed wrapped in his cloak, placed a hand to his heart, and swept an arm open in a bow. "Where would my lady travel?"

Isabel closed her eyes. She didn't know how to explain to him it was time for their paths to part.

Some might've looked upon him as a near tormentor, but Isabel only saw him as the man she'd walked a dangerous path to set free. And now that she had, now that he'd chosen a path, it would change the game.

Oh, Pelas would have his own consequences to face for the choices he'd made...for the lives he'd claimed under Darshan's compulsion, but she could already see threads shifting in the larger pattern.

Pelas sat down on the bed and brushed a tear from her cheek. "Whatever it is, Isabel, you can tell me."

She looked down at her hands, and two more tears fell from her lashes to mingle with others already glinting there, heralds of the pain yet to come. "I can't go with you."

He studied her face for a time. "You don't expect me to leave you here?"

She shook her head. "Not in the tower. Outside."

"Out—" he gave her a startled look. "*Outside.*" His gaze strayed to the windows and the bleak mountains beyond. "Out *there?*"

Isabel exhaled a slow breath that felt painful as it left her chest. "Someone will come for me."

"Someone…what someone? *Isabel…*" He took her chin and made her look at him. "What someone?"

Her eyes must've answered him enough, for recognition came into his gaze. Or perhaps it was just the light of realization dawning there. "I see." He drew back from her. "*He* will come." When she said nothing, Pelas leaned on one hand to study her. "Just like that?"

She nodded.

"Just…anywhere?"

She nodded again.

He arched a raven brow. "That's a nice trick."

"You should ask him about it," the flicker of a smile touched her lips, "when next you meet."

His gaze narrowed while one brow lifted upwards in a slant. "I'm not sure I want a path if it means becoming so predictable."

She gave him sharp little smile. "Too late, I think."

His gaze softened, and he leaned to take her into his arms. "Too late," he whispered into her hair.

At the bottom of the tower he set her on her feet, wrapped in his cloak. The day was cold but clear, breezeless. They seemed to be resting on the spine of the world—all around she saw only stark, granite mountains chalked with snow. But the springtime sun felt warm on her aching back, and the sky had never seemed so blue. Almost as blue as her brother's eyes.

"You're certain about this?" He looked her over.

She nodded, saying goodbye with her tears.

He pursed his lips, clearly considering the prudence in leaving her alone on top of the world. But eventually his brow relaxed with resignation and he reached into his coat and withdrew a strip of black silk from his pocket.

It was longer than her other had been and embroidered with patterns— *his* patterns, like those that still burned everywhere in her skin. She reached to receive the cloth from him and studied the patterns' construction, blacker than black thread against the midnight silk like the twisting spirals of endless space.

Pelas had been birthed of Chaos; these patterns were pure starlight.

"Allow me?" he offered.

She placed the silk into his hands and turned, and he replaced the blindfold across her eyes, tying it gently. Then he placed his hands on her shoulders. "You won't change your mind about this?" But he knew that she wouldn't.

She turned to face him again. "Be wary of your brothers. They'll use patterns to trick you again, if you let them."

Considering this, he drew in a deep breath and exhaled with a nod.

With *elae* now brightly showing her the world once more, she watched Pelas call a portal, watched its silver-violet streak splitting the gilded fabric of the realm, opening upon the dimension of Shadow, which was time itself—the stuff that bound all the realms together.

With one last glance over his shoulder—concerned...impossibly grateful— he stepped into Shadow, and his portal closed.

Isabel let out a sob that caught in her throat. Wrapping his cloak tighter about her form, she walked barefoot across the icy earth and sank down slowly on a rock. Then she called to him, reaching out along their bond.

She'd been an anchor for him once, when he'd navigated the formless stretches of Shadow across the centuries to regain her. Finding her on the other side of the world would hardly be a test of his skill.

Knowing him, he was probably already on his way.

I need you...

And oh, she needed him desperately.

The cold air embraced her with its chill. She hugged Pelas's velvet cloak about her and tried not to breathe too deeply, just letting her body tremble as it willed.

She might've made herself comfortable in the cold—it would've been easy to do. She might've even Healed herself to some degree, for she knew her own pattern and had done it before. But culpability weighed too heavily upon her. She felt wrong seeking comfort when the pain was only her due. Some discomforts were meant to be borne.

The sun had barely traveled in its arc when he appeared over a distant rise, a dark shadow crossing the frozen earth. Moments later he stood over her.

She saw his green eyes tighten—he would see what her cloak concealed. He would've seen all the moment he arrived.

"*Isabel...*"

Amazing how much horror and disapproval he could lace across her name.

She winced beneath the reprimand in his gaze. "Pray don't chastise me with 'I told you so's," she whispered. She'd never felt so broken. His censure would only pound the pieces into chalk.

The sky swirled as Phaedor swept her up into his arms.

She laid her cheek against his marble chest while her eyes burned with unshed tears. She knew those would fall later, in her brother's embrace. Phaedor held her tightly, and though he radiated fury over what she'd done to herself, still he pressed a kiss of absolution to her forehead. In Phaedor's embrace was a safety that would survive the shattering of the world.

With her ear pressed to his chest, Isabel heard his heart beating in resonance with hers. Their life patterns were bound in three—her brother and Phaedor and herself—as inseparable as the binding she and Arion had worked centuries ago. Then, Arion had sacrificed himself for her brother, for their mutual game... and sacrificed their love in the process.

And now she had done the same.

Phaedor had warned her it would be so...that her path and Arion's would ever be diverging and converging. She had wanted to prove him wrong just once.

The warmth of Phaedor's body eased her trembling. Or perhaps it was the Healing he worked upon her as he held her in his arms, frowning with unspoken rebuke.

"Please..." She pushed her face into his chest. "Just take me away from here."

"As you will, Isabel."

And he summoned a portal to take her home.

SIXTY-THREE

"A variant trait is like a twist in the game. Balance
doesn't know what to do with it."

– The Agasi wielder Markal Morrelaine

TANIS STARED AROUND the obsidian hall with foreboding and
guilt mingling in his soul. They were like oil and acid, fomenting an
unmixable concoction that churned endlessly. He felt as if Shail had
stabbed his heart and left the bitter steel there as a reminder of his foolish
mistakes, so that with every doomed contraction he might know again the pain
of failure. His every exhalation seemed to stain the air with fear.

Pelas wasn't going to come for him.

Tanis had never thought that he would … although he admitted a pale
hope had occasionally roused its head to be noticed. Pelas had his own choice to
make, and Tanis knew the importance of that choice. He couldn't bring himself
to truly hope the man would come rescue him. Pelas had to walk his path—as
much as Pelas *had* a path—and Tanis had to walk his, also.

It was hard to believe he walked it at all, but some faint part of him
recognized that he did. During the long hours, he'd many times tried to imagine
escaping with Nadia, but always those scenarios had met some opposing force
in his mind … as if the very fabric of existence was pushing back against the
idea.

Mostly his own incredulity stood in the way of any focused thought. He
just couldn't believe that his mother had gone to such trouble to train him—
and for what? So he could become a Warlock's concubine?

Tanis shuddered at the very thought—or would have, if Shail hadn't bound
him so tightly that even breath had to scrape its way in and out of his lungs.

But his disbelief over his circumstances made it difficult to think of solutions. What meager ideas he mustered just kept walking in circles in his head, leading nowhere.

The worst of it wasn't his own fate. That was too wholly unreal. No, the worst of it was worrying for Nadia.

Gods above, he'd been so stupid! Why hadn't he just told Vincenzé what they knew? Why hadn't he trusted the High Lord's calm rationality? How could he have imagined that three teenagers were any sort of match for Shailabanáchtran?

Verily, when he looked at it, Tanis could barely stomach his exorbitant stupidity.

And what of Felix? Tanis had just left him there, abandoned beneath a pile of bodies ...

Surely this must be what the zanthyr had meant when he spoke of Balance—or rather, of violating it. Somehow Tanis must've roused Cephrael's anger, for the *angiel's* scales of Balance certainly seemed to be weighing much more heavily on Shail's side than on his own. Either that, or the Malorin'athgul's claim that Fate kowtowed to his will was more than bold posturing. But if it was true, what hope did any of them have? If even Balance stood on Shail's side?

Tanis couldn't decide what was worse: contemplating an inevitable end, or the endless not-knowing. To just be pinned there hopelessly, impotently, with nothing to do but think on past mistakes, or else the grim envisioning of an unimaginable eternity ... and all the while just waiting ... waiting ... it felt an acute form of torture.

As the hours passed in this guise, what hope the lad had mustered faded away again. He tried to keep hold of his courage, but it felt a frail rope, many times frayed, and the tugging tide of fear so strong—

"Hello, little spy."

Tanis caught his breath. The familiar voice, coming low in his ear, seemed an impossible dream. Instantly he felt Shail's invisible bonds falling away. Tanis spun—

And there stood Pelas.

Tears of relief—and joy, and dire apprehension—brimmed in the lad's eyes. But then Pelas reached for Tanis's bound hands. "Sir, *wait*—"

Pelas sliced his dagger—Phaedor's dagger—through the *goracrosta.*

And a silver-violet dome sprang up all around them.

Tanis inwardly moaned. *Gods above,* now they were both trapped! And all of this was *his* fault!

Pelas lifted his handsome face to assess the dome. Then he turned back to Tanis, frowning as he noticed the lad's devastated expression. He drew him into a dear embrace. "Ah, Tanis ... how I've missed you."

Tanis hugged him tightly in return, jaw clenched, barely holding back tears. He felt pummeled by emotions too powerful to reconcile—fear and fury, apprehension, sorrow, shame, and a host of others, all of them swirling and pulling and tearing at him. This was no reunion. Tanis had just ensured Pelas's end along with his and Nadia's.

The lad drew back and pressed palms to his eyes. "Sir," he groaned wretchedly, "you shouldn't have come."

Pelas's copper eyes looked him over. Then he exhaled a regretful sigh. "I see Shail has been at you like Darshan has been at me." He shook his head and gave him a smile soft with compassion. "I never imagined our threads could've become so closely woven together, Tanis, yet I see so clearly of this truth now."

Tanis's eyes burned. He couldn't bring himself to look at Pelas and stared off instead, viewing the world through a black veil of fault. "Any minute all hell is going to open upon us, sir."

"Yes, my brother's trap." Pelas lifted a calculating gaze to the dome of *deyjiin*. "Like you in this moment, Tanis, I lost hope once." When he glanced back to the lad, his eyes were sparkling and bright. "Never again." He reached a hand and took Tanis's chin between his thumb and forefinger, making the lad look at him. "Promise me the same?"

Something indefinable cavorted in Pelas's gaze, mingling with deep affection and the irrepressible thirst for excitement that always danced there. Tanis couldn't decipher the meaning of this look, but the energy of it funneled into him.

That's when the truth finally claimed him: *Pelas* was standing *right in front of him!*

Finally—after so long, after so *many* months of desperately wishing to see him again! He stood right there looking as he always did—magnificent, dazzling, ready to take on anything the world dished out. Tanis had been so overcome by despondency that he'd failed to recognize the obvious truth.

This was *Pelas*.

Pelas had come for him!

Suddenly hope welled—no, it *surged* with tidal force, raging across the despairing landscape Tanis had been mired in to cleanse away the muck of disheartenment.

Tanis threw his arms fiercely around him. "You came!"

Pelas chuckled and held him close. The embrace of a brother couldn't have felt more true. "Of course I came," he murmured. "But leaving, I think, is our objective." He drew back and took the lad by the shoulders, and his smiling copper eyes looked him over once more. "Ah, yes, that's much better." His gaze shifted past Tanis then, and he straightened. "And here they come at last, the demons of our salvation."

Tanis's face fell slack and he spun. A host of *eidola* were coming their way, led by Sinárr. He braced himself against the onset of that incapacitating fear again, yet ... he couldn't find even a breath of it anymore.

Pelas had come for him!

It occurred to Tanis just how despairing he'd been—so deep into that well of hopelessness that he'd barely registered the lifeline being thrown to him. And he saw, too, that if he let Shail demoralize him so easily, then the man had won before the fight even began.

It was an important realization, but Tanis barely had time to process it before Sinárr burst into existence inside the glowing dome. Seconds later, his *eidola* walked through the shimmering walls—over a dozen in all.

Tanis instinctively moved closer to Pelas. He in turn placed a possessive hand on the lad's shoulder.

Swaths of darkness clung to Sinárr as he approached. "You would be Pelasommáyurek." Sinárr's quiet whisper scraped Tanis's ears, making the lad shudder reflexively.

Pelas's hand on his shoulder tightened with reassurance. "And you would be Sinárr."

"Shailabanáchtran would have me destroy you and claim the boy as my own."

The ghost of a smile flickered on Pelas's lips. "My brother never did learn to play well with others."

The Warlock vanished and reappeared in a flood of smoke in nearly the same instant, only now he stood but paces in front of them. His golden eyes fixed on Tanis, ardent with desire. "Come to me, child."

Tanis felt himself alarmingly moving forward.

Pelas held him firmly back. "Release him from your will, Sinárr."

"Nay, Pelas." His gilded eyes shifted to the Malorin'athgul. "You have no power here."

Pelas moved Tanis behind him with one hand while his other flashed out and closed around Sinárr's throat. Smoke exploded, swirled, congealed. Pelas's voice came as soft as Sinárr's. "Are you so certain of that, Witchlord?"

Darkness erupted, swirled, sucked violently back into form. Pelas had Sinárr pinned.

The Warlock struck in a flash of shadow—a Merdanti blade in a deadly swipe. Pelas caught his wrist and thrust him backwards, and they both vanished into a geyser of darkness. This angry vortex swept across the floor like a tornado as Sinárr and Pelas grappled within its mists. The *eidola* scattered before it, and then the swirling shadows crashed into the dome.

Violet-silver lightning streaked through the web. Tanis flinched away—and just in time, for the entire dome exploded in a charge of deadly static.

Thunder without sound rocked Tanis off his feet. He saw a pattern flash in his mind's eye, and then he was skidding across the polished marble floor. So disorienting was the moment that he barely registered the warmth of *elae's* sudden rushing return.

Lying on his back, momentarily stunned, Tanis first found his breath and then his vision. He rolled over and pushed up to his hands and knees, but the room spun dizzily. He felt unbalanced, like the floor beneath him—and even all the world—was teetering precariously upon a fulcrum that could easily tip along any of a compass-point of directions. It felt distinctly *dangerous*.

Then Pelas was at his side and had a hand beneath his arm and was helping him to stand. Tanis blinked and looked around. The *eidola* were scattered, the Warlock vanished. He watched a familiar silver line split down through the air.

No! Not yet! He gripped Pelas's arm with sudden desperation. "We can't leave without Nadia!"

Pelas searched his gaze. Then he arched a brow as if with recollection. "Ah, yes ... the princess." He turned a look over his shoulder towards Nadia. The silver line splitting the air vanished.

It occurred to Tanis that Pelas knew quite a bit more about Shail's activities than he'd anticipated.

Pelas read the question in his gaze. "We have much to discuss, you and I, but not here."

Abruptly, the air shifted.

Pelas hissed and spun his head even as Tanis saw a dozen silver lines splitting down through air. A heartbeat later, the portals opened and *eidola* came pouring out.

"By Chaos born, Shail." Pelas ground out the words as if they were a powder beneath the pestle of his ire.

Tanis watched the lines of *eidola* streaming out of Shadow and felt that unbalanced sense growing ever more vertiginous.

Pelas's gaze tightened. "These *eidola* are bound to the Warlock. That's why he fled me just now, to launch the next phase of my brother's ill-conceived plan." He clenched his jaw. "Shail doesn't know when to quit driving a wedge between us."

A wedge between you both, the lad thought, *and a hundred* eidola *between us and Nadia.*

"Tanis ..." Pelas turned him an intense look, searching the lad's gaze. "The use of Shadow is too dangerous now. If we seek your princess through this onslaught, you must be prepared for the possible consequences."

Tanis nodded grimly. He looked back to the creatures, who were spreading out like an army before them and blocking their path to Nadia. They moved oddly to his eyes, coordinated and yet ... not.

And then ...

Suddenly all of those crazy ideas that had been running in circles in Tanis's head speared outwards before him with inspired clarity, so that he could see how each would play out in a single instant.

He felt the unsteady floor tilting in a certain pliable direction.

"I have an idea." Tanis grabbed Pelas's wrist. Then he grabbed time and made a ribbon of it to wind through the masses of *eidola*. He darted forward along that thread, dragging Pelas after him.

"*Tanis,* what—" Pelas resisted him at first, but as the world around them shifted, he must've quickly understood, for he gave the lad an incredulous look, locked his hand around Tanis's wrist to bind their motion together, and kept pace at his side.

The *eidola* blurred as Tanis wove time—wove them *out of* time, carving the extended moments from the dark nothingness between seconds, between heartbeats and breaths. He and Pelas were a blur of light on the currents as they sped through the lines of *eidola* as mutably as the wind, slipping around and between the creatures even as Tanis slipped around the pylon seconds of time.

Elae sang in Tanis's veins, but so also did a sense of strength and power and purpose. Tanis didn't use patterns to carve time to his will; he merely knew what he wanted to cause and caused it—

Until a force like a flying stone wall slammed into him.

Tanis lost hold of time—lost his breath, even lost his vision—and flew sideways through the air. He felt something grab hold of him and spin him, and then he sort of hung suspended for a second before being released indelicately into a pile on the floor. With the strained return of his breath, the world blinked back into focus.

A dozen feet from where he'd landed, Pelas and Shail circled each other, both holding Merdanti blades. Tanis understood then that Pelas had somehow protected him from the brunt of Shail's attack. He marveled anyone could react so quickly.

He watched the two Malorin'athgul circling for a heartbeat more, whereupon he realized that Pelas was strategically keeping his body between Shail and Tanis, protecting him—

No—*stalling Shail.*

Tanis scrambled to his feet and sprinted for Nadia.

Pelas watched time being transformed as he ran beside Tanis, wrists interlocked. Yet more truly he ran arm in arm with amazement. Did the lad know he was working the third strand innately?

Seeing Tanis again after so long, after personally enduring and gaining so much, only to find that the lad had also come into his own ... the knowledge filled Pelas with feelings of pride and wonder.

This appreciation in itself amazed him. He'd never been attached to any of Alorin's children, but Tanis had bound him in ways he wasn't certain he would ever fully understand. It pleased him to wonder if he'd ever had a chance of escaping Tanis's determination to save him.

And he wondered now, upon leaving Isabel only to find Tanis with Shail, if the lad was somehow influencing his brother's path as well.

Suddenly Pelas felt the fabric shifting—a new and different tug upon the omnipresent fifth strand. He was coming to understand that all of the strands connected into the fifth—even the first strand, though more ephemerally—and that one needed only to monitor the fifth to sense shifts in *elae's* broader firmament.

Nearly in the same instant, a wall of force sideswiped Tanis and wrenched his wrist from Pelas's grasp. Pelas threw a bubble of the fifth around the boy to protect him from what could only have been his brother's working and spun out of Tanis's time-thread while the lad was still flying through the air.

Planting his feet, Pelas swept his arm over his head and drew his blade from the hilt at his back just as the sea of *eidola* parted to let Shail through.

His brother flowed in crimson silk, carrying his black-bladed weapon low. Shail boasted that he'd commissioned his blade from a master craftsman and used patterns of his fashioning to make it sentient. But Pelas had forged his own Merdanti weapon beneath a zanthyr's judicial eye, pounding patterns of sentience into each fold of steel.

The one thing he appreciated about Shail was how his brother constantly underestimated him.

"Pelas," Shail remarked as he neared.

"Shail."

"I warned you not to interfere in my affairs."

Pelas cast his gaze about the hall. "You invited me here, brother."

Shail's dark eyes flashed. "To claim your spy."

Pelas fingered the hilt of the blade in his hand. He remained aware of the lad, just rousing now behind him. "Tanis is no spy of mine. I thought he was yours in the beginning."

Shail's razor gaze held his, unconvinced. "If not your spy, whose?"

The ghost of a smile hinted on Pelas's lips as he thought of everything that had become of him since his first meeting with Tanis. "Perhaps Alorin's?" He shrugged.

His brother's expression hardened, and he looked Pelas over again with contempt notching his upper lip. "Darshan told me he had you contained."

Pelas motioned with his blade to the army of *eidola* funneling into the room. "This is a lavish reception for someone you didn't expect to come at all."

Shail's gaze tightened. "When speaking of you, Darshan has been known to exaggerate."

Pelas cracked a smile and moved to keep his body between his brother's gaze and Tanis. "I give you credit for doubting him. Would that you doubted him more."

"Darshan said you would betray us. In this he wasn't incorrect."

Pelas arched a brow. "Betrayal is a curious word. It assumes some agreement to begin with."

Fury simmered behind Shail's gaze. His ire churned the currents into whitewater. "Darshan has been far too lenient with you, Pelas. You won't find me such a patient nursemaid."

Disbelieving laughter burst out of Pelas before he could think to stop it. "The way you two go on about me—as if I were a wayward steed needing guidance and castigation equally—"

Shail growled a muted curse and advanced on him, raising his blade. "I know your weaknesses, Pelas."

Pelas moved sideways, forcing his brother to turn, keeping Shail's gaze averted from where Tanis now ran to free his princess. "Do you think me so unaware of *your* deficiencies, brother?" He flashed a sharp smile, his gaze alight with flames of goading. "My only endgame is stopping yours. Which of us faces the greater challenge, do you imagine?"

Shail's expression went as black as the obsidian hall. He growled another curse, swung his blade high and rushed Pelas in a billow of blood-red silk.

Pelas charged his blade with power and moved to meet his brother. Enchanted steel clashed in a flare of power that expanded in a ring of searing, violet-silver light. Even *eidola* fell beneath it.

The two Malorin'athgul scraped their blades free and immediately swung for each other again; again their weapons clashed with a thunder of intent that cast the currents into turmoil. Shail used his formidable stature to his advantage, but Pelas had grace and skill beyond his brother's brute strength. The tiger met the leopard on the plain and found an even match.

Pelas pushed Shail to keep his brother's enmity focused upon himself. Power pulsed with every blow of their flashing blades, sending shockwaves rippling across the hall. *Eidola* scattered or were crushed beneath the violent field of *deyjiin* that surrounded the fighting pair.

Shail threw patterns with every swing of his blade, but Pelas remained alert to them, thankful for Isabel's warnings—thankful to her in so *many* ways. He spun and swung his sword and kept himself shielded with his power. Until—

Shail's gaze strayed for the flick of an instant, but Pelas jolted.

Understanding roused every hair on his body in alarm, for he suddenly witnessed in himself the same failing he'd criticized in his brother. Yes, Shail had underestimated him ... but he'd also underestimated Shail.

Pelas tried to turn, and found Shail's sword blocking his path and his cold smile blocking his gaze. In the distance, the *eidola* started forming up ranks, which could only mean that their master had arrived to command them.

Tanis!

Pelas thought he'd been keeping Shail occupied. It seemed all the while his brother had been doing the same thing to him.

Shail chuckled. "You make it so easy, Pelas." He sidestepped again to block Pelas's advance, and again their swords clashed in a shuddering crash of power. Pelas flung his brother off him and spun away, but Shail moved swiftly to block any retreat.

They stalked each other like predators amid the dark field of demons. Spinning his blade, Shail speared Pelas with his gaze and salted the wound with the contempt in his smile. "Do I think of you as an intractable gelding?

Nay, brother—you're but a child manipulated with a bit of candy, or a glint of sunlight captured upon a mirror's edge."

He launched forward and with three heavy blows drove Pelas violently back, away from Tanis and the direction of his intent. Pelas worked the muscles of his jaw and parried his brother's attacks, trying to envision another outcome, a new plan. Fate bent a knee to their will—*his* will simply had to be stronger than his brother's.

Then he had an idea.

He ducked Shail's swinging blade, spun out of his reach, and slammed his palm into the chest of the nearest *eidola*. Power flared and focused as he channeled *deyjiin* in a massive pulse into the creature.

It flew backwards, limbs splayed, mowing a path through two dozen others; with every new creature touched, the pattern channeled newly, magnetically, so that silver-violet light careened like lightning through the assemblage, spreading in wildfire fashion the malady of Pelas's intent.

Shail exhaled a furious hiss and dove at his brother.

Tanis willed the *eidola* not to see him as he ran with his gaze set on Nadia. He pushed this intent as a wave before him, a shield of sorts, and the creatures all seemed to look away just as he was about to streak by them. Whether a product of his will, or luck, or the lack of their master to direct them, Tanis didn't know, but the *eidola* let him pass unmolested.

He watched them as he ran among them and finally realized what it was about their manner that seemed so unnatural. They moved *together* instead of individually—unlike a man with his own mind and thoughts, these *eidola* resembled a flock of birds, quite different in manner from the golem creature he'd confronted at the amphitheater. From this observation Tanis concluded that all *eidola* were not created equally. These had no individuality, no singularity of thought.

Is this what Sinárr would have Nadia and I become?

No, not eidola—the grim and quite unwelcome thought imposed upon his consciousness. It was as if he could still hear the Warlock whispering in his ear, *'Concubine ... '*

Tanis shuddered reflexively just as he reached the stairs leading up to the baldaquin. He took them two at a time.

Nadia roused as she saw him. Her tearing eyes widening, she tried to cry out around the silver rope gagging her mouth, but no sound emerged. Only her gaze shouted in warning.

Tanis skidded to a halt just as several *eidola* stepped out from behind the pillar to bar his path. The closest grabbed for him.

Tanis made a blade of time and let the *eidola* pull him into its embrace. Then he shoved his time-blade backwards into its chest. He had the forethought to snatch the *eidola's* weapon from its hand as his working thrust the demon several minutes into the future. It vanished.

Tanis spun into the *cortata* just as the next creature came at him. He parried its downward stroke, turned beneath their locked blades to free his own, and then sliced a deep arc across the *eidola's* chest. He threw a bubble of time at it as it fell back and jumped to meet the next one while the sundered one vanished.

The third *eidola* ducked Tanis's swinging blade, stepped into his guard and elbowed him in the chest. Tanis flew backwards beneath the baldaquin's stone canopy and lost his hold on the lifeforce. He somersaulted onto his feet again as the zanthyr had trained him, but his mind felt duller, stunned by the powerful blow, and his breath had deserted him.

The creature came at him, spinning its sword. This one clearly had known swordplay before becoming bound to a monster—*which* monster was the salient question. Tanis didn't for a heartbeat believe Shail's claim that Sinárr controlled all of these creatures. Their variable individuality indicated they had different masters.

The creature came at him, sweeping its blade in powerful downward strokes. Tanis dodged left, then right, but he had no choice but to parry its third swing. Without the *cortata's* power, the jarring blow reverberated through his bones all the way into his heels.

Tanis stumbled back and nearly fell. The *eidola* cast aside its sword and barreled into him, taking him down against the hard marble. The creature's hands found his throat while its stone body pinned the lad to the ground. Within seconds Tanis started seeing spots. He breathed in *elae* and called the currents into view, seeking any desperate way of getting free—

A line of violet-silver light sheared through the air. It caught the *eidola* across the back of its head and ripped the creature off him.

Tanis gasped a painful inhale and rolled to reclaim his sword. He scrambled on hands and knees then towards Nadia, keeping his head low to avoid the concussive waves of power that continued charging through the room. Blessedly, the baldaquin's twisting column protected Nadia from the brunt of this force. Even so, her eyes were wide and she was shaking when Tanis finally reached her.

He stood in the protection of the column and hastily cut the silver rope. Nadia fell forward into his arms and clutched him desperately. He took greater care with the gag of *goracrosta* around her mouth. Then she was inhaling a shuddering breath even as he'd done.

Oh, Tanis!

Tanis felt a tightness in his own throat as he held her close. How terribly he'd missed the reassuring presence of her mind connected to his own! Even more than her physical being, that constant mental connection had grounded him—*emboldened* him—in ways he couldn't entirely explain.

In the next moment, two things occurred: Tanis again felt that odd shifting, like the floor tilting beneath him. Then a sudden presence cast the currents into pelting turmoil.

Tanis instinctively threw up a shield of the fourth around himself and Nadia and thrust her behind him. He turned towards the source of the disturbance, but he knew already what he would find.

Sinárr was walking up the steps in a froth of smoke and shadow. A phalanx of *eidola* trailed at his heels, much resembling the flock of birds Tanis had envisioned. The lad put his blade between the Warlock and himself, pressed Nadia behind him, and backed away.

"*Oh*, Tanis ..." Sinárr's voice, for all it sounded a whisper, carried across the distance, drowning out the *eidola's* rattling, the clash of the immortals still fighting, and even *deyjiin's* concussive waves. His golden eyes pinned wondrously on the lad. "I'm so thrilled and amazed by the things you can do. When you and I are bound, you shall entertain me with your many talents."

Nadia caught her breath behind him. He pressed her farther back and took another step in retreat. He doubted his sword would be of any use against Sinárr, and he doubted his shield of the fourth would protect them from the man's power for long—if at all. Somehow his father's journals had failed to explain the correct way to battle a Warlock from the Shadow Realms.

Tanis summoned his courage and channeled it into a boldness he didn't feel. "You've no claim on either of us, Sinárr." He hoped his voice had sounded firm. His stomach felt like worms were writhing in it.

Sinárr's arms and legs molted smoke like blades new from the forge. "Where I come from, dear boy, one's *claim* and what one *can* claim are synonymous." The Warlock halted a few paces before Tanis's shield while his *eidola* fanned out, quickly and quietly encircling Tanis and Nadia.

There was something truly dreadful about the desire in the Warlock's gaze, as if he was already far along in his contemplations of a mutual bond with Tanis. Sinárr lifted his open palm to the lad and smiled meaningfully. "I think there's little question of my ability to claim the both of you. Come to me—"

But he bit the words into a curse and spun his head, doubtless distracted by the same cause that hit Tanis like a wave of disorientation.

The firmament shifted again, this time angling in what the lad sensed was a fortuitous direction.

Tanis grabbed Nadia's hand and bolted down the slope of Balance's capriciously tilting floor, while everything around him erupted into chaos.

Pelas lost his blade as he fell beneath Shail's weight, but before his brother could take hold of him, he made a rope of the fifth and yanked himself from beneath Shail's form. Shail's arms closed around empty air. He growled a curse and launched up after him.

Pelas rolled backwards onto his feet, called his sword through the air into his open palm, and turned and bolted for Tanis. All around him the *eidola* were falling into chaos.

Fast in chase, Shail shouted at him in a voice like a mountain's angry growl. "Pelas! What have you done?"

Pelas shot a grin at him as he dodged the milling *eidola*, some of whom had begun attacking one another. They were vicious creatures without a Warlock's bond to compel their thoughts. His working couldn't sever Sinárr's bond with them, but it went a long way towards momentarily disrupting it.

Pelas spun Shail a glance over his shoulder and called back to him as he ran, "Do you think you're the only one who forayed into Shadow?" Verily, what Shail thought he knew about *elae* hardly compared to what Pelas actually knew about *deyjiin*.

He ducked beneath an *eidola* as it made a mad swipe for his head and then dodged around another that was attacking its nearest companion; far across the hall, still the lightning of his working continued lancing from creature to creature, a violet incandescence dancing among the deeper shadows.

Shail cast a blade of *deyjiin* at Pelas's head. He felt it sizzling on the currents and dodged left; it exploded in the chest of an *eidola*. The force catapulted the demon off its feet and spun it, flipping head over heels, in an arc over its brethren.

Ahead, beneath the tall stone baldaquin, *deyjiin* flashed in rapid cadence. Despite Pelas's working to disrupt the creatures that fueled him, Sinárr still had enough power to threaten Tanis.

Hang in there, little spy!

Pelas dodged another bolt of *deyjiin* cast by his brother and increased his speed. He was going to have to ask Tanis to show him his pattern for timeweaving once they were safely away. It would've been a handy card to play right about then.

Pelas cleared the last of the mad sea of *eidola* and saw the lad fending off Sinárr beneath the baldaquin. As he rushed up the stairs, he saw the currents swelling towards Tanis. His eyes widened with understanding.

By Chaos born, Tanis!

Just behind, Shail snarled an explosive curse. "This isn't over, Pelas!"

Pelas threw the fifth behind him and launched himself forcefully through the air—

Tanis had hoped to make it to the steps, but the *eidola* were too thick surrounding the baldaquin, and now they were all in a fury. A violet static had seared from creature to creature, and they'd seemed to be dazed and then erratic. Some merely stood immobile now, but most clawed and rattled and climbed over one another wildly. Tanis found his escape blocked by a raging sea of madness that he dared not drag Nadia into.

With nowhere to run, he pulled Nadia into his arms and put every effort of his will into holding his shield of the fourth in place. Sinárr threw *deyjiin* at him in rapid bursts and moved in a circle around the shield, trying every angle for a weakness. It was truly awful watching the Warlock work this dark power so effortlessly and meticulously, with his golden gaze focused and intent and his brow narrowed in concentration.

Tanis gritted his teeth and pushed back against Sinárr's attacks of *deyjiin*, but every time that searing energy exploded against his shield, it felt like being hit in a helmet with an iron spike. The force reverberated all the way into Tanis's toes. He was sure his teeth would've broken if he hadn't had them clenched so tightly.

Again and again *deyjiin* burst against his shield. With every breath, Tanis felt it growing weaker—felt himself growing weaker. The fourth wasn't meant to withstand *deyjiin*.

Nadia clung to him. She seemed not herself, and Tanis worried Shail had done something to her.

Power flared again in a static sheet around them, sending an electric shock arcing along Tanis's bones. He clenched his jaw and held Nadia protectively close. He had to do something—and fast.

Think, damn you!

He scanned desperately through everything he'd learned from his parents—

Suddenly one of his father's journal entries seemed applicable. *'Give them one pattern and let them extrapolate the rest ... '*

Tanis realized he had a pattern he could use—or rather, one he could extrapolate to his own use. He'd seen Shail push *deyjiin* through a fifth-strand pattern to produce his thunder without sound. Tanis imagined he could compel the fourth and second strand together through that same fifth-strand pattern to cause a similar effect.

Or not use any patterns at all.

It was the First Law of Patterning—*KNOW the effect you intend to create.* Tanis knew what he wanted to cause—a charge so heady that the bronze baldaquin would shatter into a million shards and take out everything around them. He might just have enough time in the confusion to escape with Nadia. Then again, the temple itself might come crumbling down and they would all perish together. But taking their chances in the Returning was surely preferable to an eternity bound to a Warlock of Shadow.

A particularly nasty blast of *deyjiin* hitting against his shield nearly knocked Tanis off his feet and *elae* from his grasp. Recovering his footing, Tanis barely held off a pressing sense of panic. He'd have one chance to do this right.

He closed his eyes and opened every part of his awareness. Then he summoned *elae* forth—like opening the floodgates to the river. It was instinctive, this summoning; any Adept could summon his own strand. But as the lifeforce surged in massive waves towards him, Tanis realized with a shock that it wasn't just the fourth he was calling upon innately.

Even so, he grabbed every strand as it rushed to him, concentrated on the effect he needed to cause, and released the lifeforce along with his intention, impelling the strands—*propelling* them—forth together.

A tidal wave of the second strand merged with a similar wave of the fourth and exploded in a concussion that cast Tanis and Nadia both off their feet.

Everywhere stone exploded. The chamber exploded. *Light* exploded—Tanis felt like his head was exploding.

He lost his hold on his shield as he flew through the exploding air with Nadia screaming and his brain on fire, fighting desperately to regain his bearings before they crashed into something deadly and—

A force struck him from the side—

And they tumbled into darkness.

SIXTY-FOUR

"Cowards dream of failure. The brave, only of victory."
– The Agasi wielder Markal Morrelaine

TRELL WOKE IN a massive ebony bed draped in diaphanous silk. He blinked, inhaled deeply and looked around, instantly recognizing the ornate furnishings of the Mage's bedchamber—and across the room, sitting at an elegant desk littered with books, the man himself.

Trell pressed a palm to his forehead and then drew it down across one sand-filled eye. "This seems … familiar."

Björn looked up from the book in his lap. "You do seem to be making a habit of nearly dying at my *sa'reyth*."

Trell managed a rueful grin. "And they call *me* the conscientious so—" But the phrase lodged in his throat, impeded by a sudden staggering realization.

Trell sat up forcefully. The world spun—not from the vertigo of injury but of shock. He turned a vivid look upon the Mage. "I *remember*."

Björn was smiling softly at him. "I imagine that you do."

Trell pushed palms to his temples as if his hands alone might prevent the memories from escaping his head again. His incredulous eyes saw not the Mage but the river of his life leading all the way back to his youngest years. He could pluck a memory from the waters and examine it, recall every moment of it, even reach other related experiences associated with it …

His memory had been restored.

Trell's heart thudded in his chest like a device that fueled his smile. Both heart and smile revealed an overpowering elation.

Björn rose and set down his book on the desk. "A truthbinding from Raine D'Lacourte is not easily broken … they tried, those men who invaded your ship in the Fire Sea." He came across the room towards Trell. "The Questioning you endured would've driven a weaker mind to madness. Considering the stipulations of Raine's truthbinding, coupled with the trauma of a near-drowning, it's no wonder your memory fled."

Trell had to summon his breath back to form words. "… And now?"

Björn shrugged. "I removed the truthbinding. I don't believe I've betrayed my oath-brother's confidence in freeing you from its hold. Doubtless he would've done the same, were he here."

Trell didn't know whether the emotions threatening to explode out of his chest urged laughter or tears. "*Thank* you." The words seemed such a dreadful understatement. Twice this man had saved his life—more than twice, if he took all events into account—yet they'd never even formally met. But introductions seemed unnecessary now, even insulting, for the Mage had known him from the beginning, and Trell had come to understand so much more of him in turn during the intervening months. He'd told Phaedor in Rethynnea that he would've given the Mage his oath, and he'd meant it.

Björn seemed to hear every sentiment Trell couldn't find words to express. His eyes sparkled as they held his gaze. "You're welcome."

Trell exhaled forcefully and dropped his eyes, shaking his head in wonder. How looping his path seemed—circles upon circles—each one taking him far and away and back again to some point of beginning. What seemed but hours ago, he'd thought he was staring death in the face while rounding the apex of a circle that began in the Fire Sea, looped through the Akkad and slung him right back into the clutches of Viernan and Taliah hal'Jaitar. And now … well, now he found himself at the ending of an entirely different circle, yet somehow right back at what felt like its beginning as well.

"Is everyone's path so convoluted?"

Björn chuckled. "Our paths are rarely straight, but I admit some astonishment at how many coils yours has made. But the three of you are like that. Even when your paths circle wide, you somehow turn them back to cross again."

"The *three* of us." Trell had the distinct impression the Mage was speaking of him and his brothers, but Sebastian—

It came to him on a flood of memory—a face and voice in the Kutsamak that he couldn't recognize then, but could and did recognize now that Björn van Gelderan, Mage and First Lord, Fifth Vestal of Alorin, had returned his memory to him. Remarkable how many graces the man had bestowed upon him … how much he owed him in return.

Trell's eyes flew back to Björn. "Sebastian—"

"He lives. Freed now of the compulsion that dominated his will. His is a story as convoluted as yours, even tracing a similar trail as yours."

A laugh burst out of Trell. He pushed hands through his hair for lack of any other way to show his desperate joy and stared, seeing only the binding threads of wonder. "My brother *lives*."

"More importantly, he lives free. In no small part, thanks to you."

Trell blinked. "Me?"

Björn cast him a knowing gaze. "I'll let you dress. Then perhaps you'll join me in breaking your fast?"

"Of course, but—"

"I imagine you've some questions, also, which I'll do my best to answer." He placed a hand before his heart, bowed his head in a grace of parting, and left Trell to ready himself.

Trell nearly jumped from the bed.

But then he just stood there, locked suddenly in the gorgeous miracle of it all, feeling choked by gratitude and relief, his throat tight for the first time with freedom instead of fury.

For a moment, he let himself experience these feelings, intense and wonderful and overwhelming—

He was standing there as a free man.

He *knew* himself.

His life and the world were an open canvas before him.

It seemed too incredible to be believed. What had he ever done to deserve such grace? For a moment, he merely stood there. Then he dropped his chin to his chest and acknowledged the many people to whom he owed a grave debt. The Emir, Graham, Istalar, the Mage, Vaile, Loghain, Balaji, Carian vran Lea, Yara, Náiir ...

Trell pressed a hand to his heart. *I promise you—all of you—somehow I will repay you for your kindnesses.*

It was a singularly odd experience getting dressed in front of the Mage's massive mirror again, this time with full recollection of who he was—indeed, it was as if his memory had never been taken from him at all!

Every time he had a thought, it still surprised him to be able to connect it to something old, something understood, some deeper belief that he'd always held true. It was so odd standing there looking at his face for the first time and *truly* knowing who he was. Odd also to once again find clothes set out for him, and his sword—

His sword.

Alyneri.

Oh gods, Alyneri!

Trell pushed a hand through his hair and sat down abruptly on the near chair. Alyneri, who had made it to the *sa'reyth* against all odds, who'd bought his freedom with her courage, who'd doubtless had a hand in saving him from whatever ill-conceived craft had been worked upon him in Darroyhan.

Alyneri ... who he'd barely thought about since being taken hostage.

Trell dropped his hand and slumped back in the chair, heart racing with sudden recognition and guilt.

He knew his initial circumstances had made it hard to think of anyone or anything but the pain they were inflicting on him; and later he'd eschewed thoughts of Alyneri for fear of tainting her memory with the pain or disgust he was experiencing.

He supposed many men would've turned to thoughts of those they loved to give them the strength to endure. But he'd shuddered at the idea of bringing Alyneri into those tortured moments. He'd purposefully avoided thinking of her to keep her disassociated from Taliah, so as not to confuse his mind later with unwanted correlations or connections.

Still … he felt a sudden extreme guilt in having done this, for he knew without a doubt, without even asking her, that *she* had not stopped thinking of him.

And *oh*, the tortures he'd undergone during their months apart. Trell thought of the many indignities he'd suffered at Taliah's whim, of the rapes and depravities she'd inflicted on him and what she'd made him give in return for ameliorating the pain.

He'd refused to feel the shame Taliah had tried unceasingly to engender, but the thought of speaking about her to Alyneri … of confessing what he'd done and endured … of the compromises he'd made to survive … that *would* shame him.

Letting out a slow exhale, Trell pushed from his chair and finished dressing. At the last, he belted on his sword feeling a renewed sense of ownership that resonated quite poignantly with him. So many times he wished he'd had the weapon at his side during his torturous adventure. How relieved he was to find it safely returned to him now. And how grateful to Alyneri for ensuring it would be so.

Yet in conceiving of the coming conversation with Alyneri, he felt suddenly as if he was staring out across a wide swamp full of hidden pitfalls. Somehow he was going to have to find his way through that morass, and in that adventure, he knew his sword wouldn't help him at all.

When he walked from the Mage's bedchamber, Trell almost expected to see Balaji, Vaile and Loghain in conversation again. That the sitting room stood empty felt a slight disappointment. But the thought fled as soon as it had come, for the world held a brightness that Trell hadn't experienced in a long time—too bright for any shadows to linger.

So he'd quite recovered his smile by the time he pushed through the next set of drapes and ran into Balaji.

He Who Walks the Edge of the World had just entered from the other side of the room, but he drew up short upon seeing Trell. Then he threw open his arms and grabbed him into an embrace.

"Ah, my friend, it is magnificent indeed to see you again!"

"It's magnificent to be here," Trell murmured. Anew, that sense of marvel beset him, bringing a sudden joyful dampness to his eyes.

Balaji released him only far enough to take him by the shoulders. He looked him over, full of admiration. "How far you've come since last we parted. How much you've gained in experience and understanding."

Trell lifted brows resignedly. "Not all experiences I would choose to endure again."

Balaji nodded in acknowledgment of this. "Yet, if it cannot be avoided, at least let us find a way to make experience useful to us, for all experience is worth having to those who can become its master instead of its slave." He cast Trell one of his sharp smiles upon this idea, the kind of smile that always gave Trell the impression of a dragon's needle-toothed maw superimposed over Balaji's white teeth. "I know *you* are such a one, my friend. But, oh—the others will be so pleased to see you up and about when they return! So also your cousin, Fynnlar—though he's strayed further from our pleasant field with your friend, the pirate Carian vran Lea.

"But look at me, delaying you so when the Mage awaits." He wrapped an arm about Trell's shoulders and guided him off. As they walked the *sa'reyth's* labyrinthine corridors, Balaji aimed a knowing gaze Trell's way. "Now you will get all of those questions answered, eh?"

Trell gave him a quiet smile. For all he still had questions, so few of them remained from those he'd harbored the last time he'd come to the Mage's *sa'reyth*. It surprised him in that moment to realize how much he really had grown in understanding, like Balaji had claimed of him.

They parted ways outside, with Balaji directing him towards a red-violet pavilion crowning a hill east of the *sa'reyth*. As Trell neared the top, a glorious world spread out around him. He realized he still had no idea on what continent or in what kingdom the *sa'reyth* was actually located and had a sudden intuition that it wasn't in Alorin at all.

The First Lord sat at a table beneath the peaked and tasseled tent with his boots extended to the mountain view. He looked up as Trell arrived and waved him take a seat across from him. The table, Trell noticed, was set for four.

"For the lovely Alyneri and her tutor," the First Lord advised, reading the question in Trell's gaze.

Trell slowly sat. "Her tutor?"

"Vaile has been teaching your Alyneri the dance of swords, among other skills."

Trell fell back in his seat. "Alyneri is learning swords from *Vaile*?"

Björn cast him an amused look. "So I have been informed."

Trell spent a moment trying to envision that. Then he spent another minute wondering why. When he lifted his gaze back to the First Lord, Björn was regarding him quietly with his chin on his hand.

Trell felt suddenly at a loss for words.

"Where should we begin, Trell?" He leaned forward and poured tea for both of them, eyeing Trell as he did so. "With the Emir, perhaps? Or have you other questions more pressing?"

Trell shook his head. There were so many things he might've asked, but only a few held any real importance to him. "Vaile. That demon hit her with something—"

"*Deyjiin.*" Bjorn took up his tea and sat back in his chair. "A dark power, antipathetic to *elae*. She ... survived it."

What was it in his gaze? Trell couldn't decipher the look. But Vaile lived. That was a relief and a weight from his conscience.

The spicy aromas wafting up from the tea in his cup called to Trell, and he absently retrieved it from the table with his mind caught up in a whirlwind of thoughts. How heady to once again have access to knowledge long lost, to be able to connect ideas to their rightful source and form suspicions and conclusions based on knowledge he'd always believed he should've had but couldn't remember.

He sipped his tea and then lifted his gaze back to Björn. "What of the war?"

"Stalemated, as it was when you left, but I think not for much longer."

"And the Emir?"

"He's well, and admittedly anxious to see you."

Trell furrowed his brow in a frown and exhaled a measured breath. "He thinks I'll be angry, but he owes me no explanation. I owe him my life. I wouldn't offer suspicion where gratitude is better suited."

Björn settled his chin on his hand again, and his eyes conveyed his admiration. "You three are such wonders."

Trell looked back to him. "We three ... your Kingdom Blades?"

An enigmatic light danced in his gaze. "So you read that, did you?"

"Your journal was open to the very page. Was I not meant to find it?"

"Indeed, Trell. I hoped very much that you would." Björn shifted in his chair and gave him another smile. "But as my sister would say, one never knows exactly where the seeds of possibility will find purchase when cast across a man's path. The best one can do is wait and see where each blooms."

Trell went to drink more of his tea and realized he'd finished it. He set the cup down on the table with a frown. "When I left here all those months ago with Gendaia and a fortune in Agasi silver—*your* silver, your horse—I told Balaji that I thought you were making me into one of your pieces."

Björn leaned to refill their cups from the ornate silver pot. "And now?"

"Now ..." Trell exhaled an explosive breath. "Now I would willingly take any part in whatever it is that you do."

Björn smiled as he sat back. "I hoped you would feel that way."

Something in his gaze as he said this made Trell feel especially proud. The idea that *this* man—who'd earned the loyalty of immortals and men far greater than him—would desire Trell's help …

"Phaedor said—" Trell shifted his gaze away and back again. "He said you would accept my oath if I offered it."

Björn held his gaze evenly. "Are you offering it?"

The question sounded so benign, yet Trell sensed such gravity in its meaning. "Yes."

"Then I accept it."

Trell waited for more. Then he blinked at Björn. "That's … it?"

Björn smiled crookedly. "You were expecting a crash of lightning? Blood in a chalice … ?"

"Words of an oath …" He cast him a somewhat pointed look.

Björn leaned towards him in return and fixed Trell with his gaze. "*You* are not a man who needs words to shape his intention, nor one that requires the bonds of magic to hold his honor true." He sat back again. "I would never insult you by considering otherwise."

Trell regarded him wordlessly. He received this admiration less with pride than with a sense of ominous duty.

Björn smiled at him, and something in his gaze seemed to acknowledge the subtle challenge in his declaration; but his expression also offered encouragement and the sure certainty of his faith in Trell's ability to live up to his esteem.

Then his gaze shifted slightly and his eyes became softer. "But see who comes to greet you."

Trell turned around the side of his chair to see two figures approaching across the meadow. It was like the two women had traded identities, for Alyneri wore slim britches and a long tunic many times bound with leather bands crisscrossing around hips and waist, chest and arms, accentuating her slim form; while Vaile wore a desert gown of emerald green much like she'd been wearing the day he first set eyes upon her miraculous form. The zanthyr walked with a shawl of soft wool around her shoulders and wore her long hair as an added cloak, flowing and free.

But for all of Vaile's voluptuous beauty, Trell really only saw Alyneri.

He'd forgotten how her features conveyed such vulnerability, yet her gaze held an amazing strength of spirit. He'd forgotten how lovely she appeared in the daylight and how innocent beneath night's desirous kiss.

And this graceful creature, so frail-seeming and fey, had somehow kept Fynn alive while finding her way through miles of desolate desert?

My yes, he loved her.

But he had confessions to make—what seemed a lifetime of confessions from but a few months—and he had no idea how to put words to many of those truths.

Trell stood and turned to receive the women, whereupon Alyneri saw him and broke into a run. Heartbeats later she flew into his arms.

Trell clutched her close, feeling her beating heart and her tears wet against his neck, himself choked with wonder and admiration and gratitude. He marveled sometimes that Naiadithine had delivered him a woman so constant and brave. However could he have questioned her love for him?

Alyneri pulled away to look at him with tears of joy making her brown eyes lambent. He searched her gaze for a moment in wondrous silence. Then he planted a fervent kiss on her mouth. Afterwards she laughed and threw her arms about his neck so tightly that she seemed unlikely ever to let go.

"Perhaps we should lower the drapes for them and break our fast elsewhere." Vaile's voice hinted of amusement.

Trell repositioned Alyneri to cast the zanthyr a look of gratitude. He couldn't quite forget her last kiss. "My lady, I cannot thank you enough."

Vaile sighed and looked to the Mage. "Trell insists on calling me a lady," she complained as she took a seat beside him, though her eyes were smiling. "I've been unable to disabuse him of the idea."

"There are worse crimes." Björn settled his chin on his hand. "How went your training this morning?"

"Alyneri has the *cortata*. I've tasked her now to teach it to our Trell of the Tides."

Trell finally extracted himself from Alyneri's arms, but he gave her a kiss on the cheek that the separation of a chair's width might not feel too torturous a distance. He kept her hand in his as they sat down. Then he asked, "What's the *cortata*?"

"The Adept dance of swords," Alyneri said.

She blushed a little at this, and Trell wondered why. Did she imagine he wouldn't want her learning to defend herself? On the contrary, it made her that much more appealing to him. Ever Alyneri surprised him with her courage.

Björn served them all tea and looked up under his brows as he poured. "The *cortata* is a pattern. It is most closely aligned to *elae*'s fifth strand, but it's truest to say the pattern draws upon the lifeforce in its fullness, for hints of each strand can be detected in the power it provides the skilled practitioner."

Trell turned to Alyneri. "And *you're* going to teach this to me?"

She smiled into her tea.

Vaile pulled her woolen wrap closer about her shoulders, earning a look from the First Lord that Trell couldn't quite interpret. "I know where I found you at the end of your path," the zanthyr said to Trell, "but not how they overcame you at its beginning. You could've held your own against even a host of men, Trell of the Tides. How is it they claimed you?"

Alyneri's hand tightened around his own.

Trell leaned against the side of his chair, the better to be nearer to her. He sighed. "They had a wielder with them. A man called Işak'getirmek." He shifted his gaze to the First Lord, who was watching him with quiet compassion. "He was my brother Sebastian."

Alyneri gasped.

"Neither of us recognized the other, and yet ..." Trell frowned, holding the First Lord's gaze.

Björn nodded. "Yet you both knew each other."

"On some level, I think we must have. Even though he tried to hide his face from me ... perhaps *because* he hid his face from me, I felt that I knew him—that I should've known better of him—and I felt in my heart that our paths would cross again."

Alyneri was staring at him. "Sebastian is *alive*? But I thought—"

"Lies." He shook his head and pressed his lips together, tight with a fury yet unavenged. "All lies, crafted by Radov and his wielder, Viernan hal'Jaitar. A web of lies intended to draw Dannym into their war."

"Effective, if predictable." Vaile arched a deprecating brow as she sipped her tea.

"But then—" Alyneri shifted in agitation. "Where is Sebastian now? Is he—"

"He's with Ean."

All eyes shifted to Björn.

He regarded each of them in turn. Then he motioned to the many silver domes upon the table. "Let us eat, my friends, and I'll speak of what I know."

When all plates were filled, Björn told the tale as he had pieced it together. First he told Rhakar's story from his interaction with Sebastian while still in the Kutsamak, and how the *drachwyr* had followed Sebastian's group to the mountain castle of Tyr'kharta. He explained how his contacts in the Cairs had received a demand for ransom for Trell's men—Ean's men—and how Ean and Isabel had gone to save them while Rhakar had continued searching for Trell.

Finally he told Isabel's tale as she'd relayed it to him, describing how Ean had come upon Sebastian in Tyr'kharta, how he'd seen the terrible compulsion binding his brother, and how he'd sworn to free him from that torment.

Björn crossed one knee and leaned back again with a sigh. "Ean's entire path shifted in that moment."

"But he succeeded?" Alyneri sat nearly on the edge of her chair. "Ean freed him?"

Björn blessed her with a dazzling smile. "Yes."

Alyneri pressed both hands to her mouth. She darted a look to Vaile, and her fingers slipped but an inch to free the words, "He's grown so powerful."

"He was always powerful," Björn murmured.

These estimations of his brother puzzled Trell. "Are we speaking of the same person? My little brother, Ean?"

"Who is Arion Tavestra, Returned," Vaile remarked with a zanthyr's characteristic bluntness.

Trell frowned. He remembered Alyneri explaining to him that Ean was a Returned Adept, but he couldn't reconcile Ean the Adept with the images he had of his twelve-year-old brother. Though he admitted a sudden welling gratitude again that he could reach those memories at all.

Trell looked around the table at the others. "Who is Arion Tavestra?"

Three answers came at once:

"A gifted wielder," said Vaile.

"Isabel's eternal soulmate," breathed Alyneri.

"My closest friend," answered Björn.

"They bound themselves to each other, Trell," Alyneri went on before Trell could process any of that information. "Ean and the Mage's sister—in Ean's last life and in this one." Her eyes darted to Björn and back again. "Ean is the Vestal's brother now."

Trell felt a little unbalanced beneath so much information. He rubbed his forehead, trying to process it all, and turned his gaze to Björn. "My brother ... your sister?"

Björn nodded.

Trell dropped his hand and sort of stared at him. "We're ... family?"

Björn opened palms and smiled in acceptance of this truth.

Trell felt a little unbalanced. "I think I see what you meant." He poured some wine and quickly drained his glass. Then he gasped, "About our three paths turning back to cross again."

The Mage just smiled.

When the meal was complete, Björn stood and bade Alyneri and Trell enjoy their afternoon. Then he offered Vaile his arm, and they walked into the hills together.

Watching them depart, Trell suddenly felt uncomfortably alone—alone in his indecision of how to move the conversation forward, of how to set things right with Alyneri so they could proceed in building their lives together ... assuming she wanted that. He hoped she wanted that.

He turned his chair to face her and took her hands in his, but then words wouldn't form. As he searched her gaze, so open and naked to his inspection, he saw only the things he couldn't tell her—things he *wouldn't* tell her—so many truths he dared not burden her with. Yet *he* was the one who'd admonished her that only truth and trust could lie between them.

Abruptly Alyneri pushed to her feet and tugged on his hands. "Can we walk? I need to walk."

Trell stood and let her lead him into the daylight, feeling oddly lost. He tugged on her hand to stop her before they'd gone too far. "Alyneri ..." He cupped her face with one hand and gazed intently at her. She felt such a treasure to him, and he so blessed to be alive. "*Thank* you."

Her eyes grew bright beneath his inspection, her cheeks flushed. "I think what it means to love someone is that you never need them to say thank you."

He stroked her face with his thumb. "I wouldn't be here if not for you." *Oh, never had he said anything more true!* The weight of his sword at his hip was testimony to this. It would forever stand as a reminder of her troth and courage.

But at his gratitude, a deep furrow creased Alyneri's brow. She turned and drew him off again. "There's something you need to know, Trell, and I can't wait another moment to say it—I dare not." She glanced at him over her shoulder, and he took heart from the endearment in her gaze.

She looked forward again, and he saw her shoulders lift and fall with a sigh, perhaps summoning the courage he still hadn't found. "In those hours when I thought I was losing you ..." She shook her head and glanced at him again. "I felt tremendously ashamed."

He pulled on her hand to stop her and immediately brought their bodies close. His hand went to her neck and his fingers twined within her hair. The longer he spent in her company, the more he felt drawn to her. Taliah had only repelled him, but seeing Alyneri again engendered such amazing feelings of desire. He felt almost as if those terrible weeks might be expunged by her kiss alone.

"Whatever could make you feel that way, Alyneri?" he whispered.

"You."

He blinked in surprise. "Me?"

She brought up her hands to make a V around his face. "You are perfect and—and *immaculate*, and I betrayed your trust and made you feel as though I was ashamed of you when really I was just such a fool!" She pushed a hand to her forehead and dropped her gaze. "I was so afraid of being chained to someone else's path instead of being free to follow my own that I didn't stop to think about what it would be like to walk that path alone." She dropped her hands to her sides and looked up to meet his gaze again. "But now ..." Tears filled her eyes. "Now I can't imagine a worse hell than living one more day without you."

A joyous warmth bloomed upon hearing this. Trell took her hand and searched her gaze with his own. "Do you imagine I don't feel the same?"

"I don't know how you feel. I sense a great distance in you ... and we parted under such dreadful circumstances."

Trell drew her into his embrace. "The distance you perceive is my desire to protect you from my own nightmares." He kissed her forehead and then drew back slightly to look at her. "I want to restore truth between us, but, Alyneri ..."

She stopped him with fingers across his lips. "You need tell me nothing of what happened, Trell—or all of it, as you desire. I care only that you're here and safe and *whole*." Her gaze shifted away beneath a furrowed brow and then darted back to find his, resolved suddenly. "We're not the same people who said goodbye in the Kutsamak. We can't be. We shouldn't be—I don't want to be that girl."

He gazed quietly at her. "That girl saved my life."

She gazed defiantly back. "This girl did, too."

He broke into a smile. "*This* girl ... who learned blades from a zanthyr and is going to teach me the *cortata*."

"That girl, yes." She flipped a strand of pale hair from her shoulder and cast him a determined look. "That is, if you will have her, Prince of Dannym."

He felt desire filling him. Doubtless it filled his gaze as well. "I will, Alyneri d'Giverny."

"Well then." She took his hand and spun on her heel and pulled him off again. "As Vaile would say, the sun grows long and the day short."

But the night ahead of us remains longer still.

He didn't think she'd heard the thought—she was a Healer, not a truthreader—but from the smile she shot him suddenly over her shoulder, he wondered if she'd heard it after all.

SIXTY-FIVE

"Don't seek to live within a world framed by others' dreams.
Dream new realities and dare to explore their vast reaches of wonder."
— Attributed to the *angiel* Epiphany

TANIS ROUSED FROM a kaleidoscopic disorientation feeling a strong arm bracing him against a marble-hard chest.

Pelas.

As his vision returned and he recognized a hall in Pelas's home in Hallovia, Tanis exhaled a tremulous sigh fraught with relief, incredulity and no small measure of *did-I-really-just-bloody-do-that?*

Pelas chuckled. "Here all this time I thought my brother feared me, when really he should've been fearing you, little spy."

Tanis managed to get his feet solidly beneath him and straightened away from Pelas's support. He pushed a palm to his pounding forehead. "Please, sir … don't remind me."

Pelas chuckled again.

"Tanis?" Nadia was leaning in the curve of Pelas's other side. Her voice sounded unexpectedly weak. Then her knees buckled.

Pelas caught her up in his arms.

"*Nadia!*" An alarm went off in Tanis's head. He took her face between his hands and tried to hold her attention with voice and mind together. "Did Shail or Sinárr put their power into you?"

Nadia's head lolled. Her eyes were barely open. "He … put his thumb …"

Pelas hissed an oath and took off down the hall. Tanis followed close on his heels, his heart keeping a rapid pace with apprehension.

Pelas laid Nadia down on a bed in the first room they reached, and Tanis nearly threw himself onto the mattress beside her. She looked frighteningly pale, as if death had already claimed her with a final kiss. Tanis spun a desperate look at Pelas.

The Malorin'athgul placed his hand on Nadia's forehead and narrowed his gaze in concentration. The furrow between his brows deepened. "Tanis ..." his gaze shifted to the lad. "I can pull *deyjiin* from her veins, but much damage is already done."

"Just—" Tanis couldn't hear him speak such words. "Just do it—*please!*" He took Nadia's face between his hands and dove into rapport with her—the connection was the same whether worked by a Healer or a truthreader. In the same moment, he sought Pelas's mind, casting forth the invitation, knowing Pelas would perceive his entreaty.

At once the Malorin'athgul opened himself in return. Pelas's powerful mental presence felt painful to Tanis's ravaged brain, like sunlight on already burned skin. *Help her, sir—oh, please help her!*

He watched with his mind and the currents both as Pelas began drawing *deyjiin* out of Nadia's form, not unlike extracting a poison from her blood. *Deyjiin's* negatively-charged power churned the currents into tiny rippling waves, like a pelting rain on an otherwise still pond, but in the currents, too, Tanis saw that her life had reached a dangerous ebb.

Instinct drove Tanis from the shores of desperation into uncharted waters.

As he'd seen the zanthyr once do, he let the currents guide him to Nadia's life pattern. He instinctively recognized it when he found it, but—

Not merely frayed, her pattern had started coming *unbound*.

Tanis couldn't lose her like this. He *wouldn't* lose her at all!

'Take each fraying edge and make it smooth ... '

His mother's words from a lesson on Healing found him, calmed him, though she hadn't told him *how* to make the frayed edges smooth.

Tanis took a deep breath and imagined his mind as a beam of light, which was an easier way of conceiving of what he was really doing—that is, creating a focal point for *elae* and casting his intention through it. He swept the beam across one of the frayed edges of Nadia's pattern and watched the tendrils seal back into themselves. It surprised him to realize it had actually worked.

That was ... interesting.

When her pattern didn't immediately come apart again, Tanis felt hope thrill through him. Okay, he could do this.

He set to work.

Tanis was new to a Healer's technique—though he understood much of their craft from his mother's teachings and from his observation of Alyneri's work—so he continued his Healing with methodic and careful attention.

When he'd resealed every escaping tendril of Nadia's life pattern, he inspected it again from every angle to assure himself there were no more frayed edges anywhere. Even as he watched, her pattern began to glow vibrantly again. Then Nadia drew in a deep breath, and her eyes fluttered open. "Tanis ... ?"

Tanis nearly cried with the relief that flooded him. He pulled out of rapport and gave Pelas a look of desperate gratitude.

Pelas shook his head in wonder. "My little spy." His eyes were warm, his smile impossibly bright.

Tanis returned his smile with a nearly overwhelming sense of joy.

Nadia blinked up at him. "I thought I was ..." Her eyes strayed off with confusion. Then they moved to meet his gaze again. "Did you *Heal* me?"

The barest smile hinted upon his lips. "Yes, Nadia."

Her eyes regarded him with uncertain wonder. "How do you know Healing patterns, Tanis?"

Tanis felt a smile of pride twitching in the corner of his mouth, because for the first time, he owned the truth. "I didn't use patterns, Nadia."

Her eyes went round. "A variant trait?"

He nodded.

Possibly because he didn't hide his next thought, Nadia came more fully awake, though her voice grew fainter with surprise. "Do you ... are there other things you can do innately?"

"A few."

She searched his gaze in wonder. "Like?"

The smile twitched more impatiently on his lips. "I've had some success traveling nodes and with other workings of the second." Albeit he admitted his last working—where he'd nearly incinerated the temple and himself and Nadia along with it—might've been a tad over-ambitious. "And timeweaving."

"A truthreader with *three* variant traits?" Her colorless gaze strayed to Pelas, who was watching this exchange quietly, and then shifted back to Tanis again. "No one has *three* variant traits, Tanis."

"How else would you explain it?"

Nadia frowned as she tried to think of another answer. Then something, whatever she'd thought of, made her come fully alert. "Not three variant traits," she whispered with understanding coloring her tone. Her gaze flew back to meet his and she squeezed his hand. "*One* trait. One variant trait that makes you a native of *four* strands."

Pelas grunted as if this proved a theory he'd long suspected.

Tanis gave him an odd look. "I've ..." He turned back to Nadia. "*Is* there such a variant trait?"

Nadia sort of stared at him. "Only one person has ever been known to possess it."

Tanis felt a sudden welling apprehension. His mouth went suddenly dry. "Who?"

Nadia's eyes darted between Tanis and Pelas again. "Epiphany's Prophet, Isabel van Gelderan."

Isabel van Gelderan.

Though he'd heard her name a hundred times—a thousand times—*this* time Tanis knew its truth. The obsidian wall that protected the memories of his parents—the same wall that had banked the deluge of Shail's invading mind—suddenly began dissolving away as if washed by the surf, and upon that rising tide came a flood of memories.

Tanis heard his mother's voice, saw her face—saw his father's face for the first time. *At last,* his father! In whose features Tanis found so many echoes of his own.

And his father said, *'You are the son of Arion Tavestra, my son.'*

And his mother bent and kissed him and said as she withdrew, *'You are the child of Isabel van Gelderan, my child.'*

Then together, they said into his mind, using a bond Tanis only then realized still existed, *'And you are dearly loved.'*

Tanis gripped Nadia's hand tightly, for such emotion threatened to burst out of him that he wasn't sure he could contain it.

The son of Arion Tavestra. The child of Isabel van Gelderan.

And behind their names ... hundreds of memories, scenes from his earliest years. He could perceive them hovering in the space behind the obsidian wall ... a wall he realized he could now raise and lower at will.

Why had hearing his mother's name this time released those memories? But of course, he knew.

Because this time I was ready.

Tanis pushed a hand through his hair and left it lodged there, all but forgotten in a moment of new understanding. His parents had built the wall to protect him until he was old enough to protect himself, until he'd gained enough understanding of his gifts to raise and lower it with a simple thought. Which he did just then, raising it up again to protect those cherished truths.

Tanis let out a forceful exhale and dropped his hand. He closed his eyes feeling a sense of reverence, of awe, and of immense gratitude to his parents. When he opened his eyes again, he felt as if he gazed upon a brand new world.

Nadia was staring speechlessly at him.

Pelas was smiling.

Only then did Tanis realize that he'd shared the entire experience with both of them—for he still shared Pelas's mind from the moment of their Healing, and with Nadia through their bond.

"Tanis ..." Nadia breathed wondrously.

Tanis pushed a palm to his eyes and found both a little damp. He felt—well, he could hardly express how he felt. Elated? Joyful? Overwhelmed? Even a little bit frightened.

Nadia watched him dabbing at his eyes and laughed suddenly. "Tanis—you're Arion Tavestra's *son!*"

I'm Isabel and Arion's son.

Never mind how impossible it seemed, how improbable that he'd been born three centuries ago yet had seen only fifteen name days—no matter all the reasons why it shouldn't be true, Tanis knew unequivocally that it was.

Equally incredible was the fact that the two people in the room with him, who were undeniably the most special people in his life, had been there also to witness what was quite possibly the most significant moment of his existence.

Tanis reflected on the many dangers and desperate moments that had defined the last twenty-four hours, and on how despite uncountable odds, they'd somehow escaped death's swiping claws only to land here in *this* moment of impossible wonder.

He looked to Pelas with eyes round with wonder. "Your brother claimed Fate bent to his will ... but ... perhaps Cephrael turns a benevolent eye my way sometimes, too."

"Perhaps he does, little spy." Pelas's gaze sparkled with equal parts admiration and affection, and both of them in that moment felt limitless to Tanis. "Perhaps he does, indeed."

Tanis followed Pelas from the room where Nadia was now sleeping, but he could barely sense his feet beneath him. How impossible it all seemed, and yet so profoundly magnificent at the same time. He felt as if that rapid and dangerous descent into Shail's enmity had been worth every second, since it had ultimately resulted in this moment.

He watched Pelas on the currents as he followed him down the dark hallway of his home, and a sense of marvel beset him anew—this time at the change he observed in the man. This wasn't the same Pelas he'd said goodbye to in Rimaldi. A darkness had hovered about that man, clouding his spirit. This man blazed on the currents like a star.

Yet for all the excitement of the night thus far, a cord of tension still threaded through the lad, for he didn't know if they would be able to stay together now that they'd reunited. If Shail's summons had called Pelas from his path before he could make his choice ... ?

Tanis didn't know what he would do if he and Pelas had to separate again. Every time the lad thought of walking his path without him, he felt that same odd resistance he'd experienced back in the temple.

And what *had* he experienced in the temple? In retrospect it seemed like he'd been perceiving the very shifting of Balance itself. He'd said only moments ago that perhaps Cephrael turned a benevolent eye his way. In some ways, it seemed the only explanation. How else could he account for their miraculous escape, save for having followed that tilting sensation when he sensed it leaning in a fortuitous direction?

But could one really sense the tides of Balance? Surely if such awareness existed, his father would've written about it.

His father. Arion Tavestra. Tanis felt a bit unbalanced just thinking about it—but in the best possible way.

Pelas paused at the landing to wait for him, and they headed down the wide staircase side by side. Tanis felt like the question of Pelas's choice both bound and separated them as they descended the stairs together, like opposite sides of a coin. He couldn't find it in his heart to ask him for the truth ... not if the answer meant having to leave him so soon.

"I never thought you'd come," Tanis said in tense confession. His hands felt twitchy at his sides, so he made them into fists and shoved them in his pockets. Colorless eyes stared forward, seeing both the solid marble of the stairs and the gilded, ephemeral currents superimposed across them. "I *wanted* you to come—but I didn't at the same time, because I knew it was a trap, and I knew you needed to walk your own path ..."

"I came as soon as I received his summons, Tanis." Pelas cast him a sidelong look, his gaze considering. "How could I not when he had *you*, and I ..." He arched a brow and exhaled a slow breath, turning ahead once more. "I'd been trying to find you again nearly since the moment you left."

Tanis dropped his gaze back to the stairs. A warm flush came to his face, for he felt the same way.

"It wasn't my intention to make you wait so long for rescue," Pelas continued with a slight grimace, "but I had to devise a way to tap into Sinárr's *eidola* to fuel my own power while beneath their *goracrosta* dome."

Tanis turned back to him with sudden understanding. "The 'demons of our salvation,'" he quoted Pelas's words.

"Just so." The Malorin'athgul arched a sardonic brow. "Unfortunately it took longer than I would've liked to learn of their plans and then derive the necessary patterns to turn them to my advantage. I had to experiment on quite a few *eidola*, and all the while maintaining my cloak of *deyjiin*, lest my brother take notice of me." They reached the main floor, and Pelas placed a hand on Tanis's shoulder, stopping him. "It pained me to see you suffering. I would've ended it sooner if I could've."

"It's not important now, sir." Tanis only cared that their paths had reconnected. He prayed they could remain so.

Again the question rushed to the edge of his tongue and hovered there, unspoken.

Pelas held his gaze quietly, as if waiting to receive the question they both knew hung between them like a shielded lantern, requiring one of them to open its flaps. When the moment hung even as the lantern of question hung, Pelas motioned them off again, that time towards the kitchens.

"I have much to tell you, little spy, things we should discuss, but I would know first of you." He cast him an endearing smile. "You've learned much, it would seem, since we parted."

Tanis exhaled a measured breath. "Yes, sir." He'd actually lost count of all the things he'd learned. He feared it would take a decade now to recount them all. "Where should I start?"

"You gave me your magical dagger and left with your zanthyr ... and then?"

Tanis rubbed at one eye. The idea of referring to Phaedor as *his* zanthyr threw him somewhat. "We traveled through the Navárrel ..."

Over the course of the next hour, while Pelas found food and drink for them, Tanis told him everything that had happened since they parted in Rimaldi—at least, everything that seemed relevant.

They were sitting at a table on Pelas's patio, beneath the night's stars overlooking the sea, when the lad began speaking of his time at the Sormitáge. When he reached the part of his story where he met Shail, he slumped back in his chair and exhaled dramatically. "*Gods above*, I was so stupid."

Pelas sat with one hand draped over his chair arm, a wine glass suspended between his dangling fingers. "I suspect neither of us is well matched against my younger brother." He lifted his goblet and drank from it. "I confess a certain naivety myself in predicting Shail. Don't let these missteps dishearten you though, Tanis. We've gained much in understanding."

Tanis frowned towards the horizon. A thunderstorm was moving off to the west, trailing the tattered wisps of its expended fury, and its departure revealed a moon nearly full. "I'm not so sure all's well that ends well, sir." Verily, Tanis expected to have nightmares for many moons to come. Just thinking of Sinárr made him shudder.

"How not?" Pelas cast him a look. "We live to fight another day, and we've learned from the experience." He lifted his goblet in salute. "All experience is worth having."

"Yes, I seem to recall your mentioning that before."

Pelas chuckled.

Tanis turned his gaze back to the star-filled heavens and thought on everything that had happened to him. Pelas was right. He *had* learned much— of Shail, of his own abilities, of his parents ... this last joy had barely settled into place in his understanding. Yet he knew nothing of the road Pelas had traveled, and the tension of this uncertainty had become a constant ache in his chest.

Pelas's soft chuckling roused Tanis from his thoughts. He looked over at him.

Pelas just kept chuckling.

Tanis frowned. "What?"

The Malorin'athgul waved his goblet with airy amusement, his eyes bright. "It's only that you seem to have a thousand questions in your gaze, little spy—or perhaps only one question that yet seems to weigh upon you as if a thousand—while your tongue speaks not a word."

Tanis had forgotten how acutely Pelas could read him, even when their minds weren't consciously connected. He shoved his hands beneath his legs to keep his twitching apprehension from plaguing them and stared off to sea. "I haven't asked because ... well, because ..."

"You're afraid of what I might say."

Tanis gave him a swift look, redolent of confession.

Pelas held his gaze. "You want to know if I've chosen a path."

Tanis nodded.

"And what if the path I've chosen isn't the one you're hoping for?"

The lad turned away with apprehension welling against a wall of protest. He drew in a deep breath and let it out slowly. "Every time I think of leaving, I ... it's like there's an anchor dragging me back again." Pelas himself had said that he believed their paths had become entwined; Tanis had felt connected to him in some indefinable way ever since the drums of duty had called him to follow the man in Rethynnea.

Pelas flowed from sitting to standing. He pushed back the long folds of his coat, slipped hands into his pockets, and gazed out to sea. The night quieted beneath his inspection.

"I think I made my choice the moment you left, Tanis." He regarded the lad gently over his shoulder. "It just took me some time to realize it." He exhaled a long breath, and a host of unreadable truths passed over his features, momentarily darkening them. "I've come to understand that my brothers and I have no path, unless we choose one ... but I wonder if you truly know what that means." He settled his gaze upon Tanis inquiringly.

Tanis felt suddenly pinned to his chair with his breath caught far beyond his reach. "I'm ... not sure, sir." It took immense courage to ask the obvious next question. "What path did you choose?"

The hint of a smile flickered across Pelas's lips. "Yours."

A wave of elation propelled Tanis from his chair. He threw his arms around Pelas.

Smiling, even laughing a little, Pelas returned his embrace. "Ah, my little spy ... you have no idea what you've done for me."

Tanis drew back and pressed palms to his eyes. His heart felt too full, like he'd called too much *elae* and now couldn't contain the forces surging through him. "What happened to you, sir?"

Pelas laughed. "What happened to me?" He flung up a hand and turned the lad a brilliant smile. "*You* happened!" Then his gaze strayed past Tanis towards the sea, and he dropped his hand and added almost reverently, "Isabel happened."

Tanis blinked at him. "Isabel? My ... my mother?" He searched Pelas's eyes with his own. "You knew?"

"I only recently learned this truth." He regarded the lad for a time with a considering gaze. Then he nodded towards the cliffs. "Will you walk with me a bit, Tanis?"

The lad dutifully followed Pelas off the patio onto a path that wove along the sheering cliffs. The recent storm had cleansed the world, and now the crisp air seemed to magnify the starlight, amplifying its intensity. Tanis saw every blade of grass on the high precipice, every luminous wave marbling the sea far below. Even the silver threads in Pelas's damask coat glowed as if their patterned whorls were formed of starlight captured and bound.

Or perhaps it was just the joy Tanis felt that made the world appear so bright.

He wanted to know everything—*everything*—that had happened while they were apart, and not the least of these how Pelas had learned of his mother. Suddenly all the things he couldn't ask before demanded voicing all at once. "Was it Darshan, sir? Did he remove his compulsion?"

Pelas grunted dubiously. Then he cast the boy an enigmatic look that found its resolution in a smile. "I've confessions I need to make to you, little spy, but atrocities committed beneath my brother's compulsion will never again plague my conscience."

Tanis hadn't thought his heart could grow any larger, yet the relief and happiness he felt upon learning this seemed tenfold what he'd experienced even a moment ago. "Then ... you're free of him?"

Pelas smiled quietly, but his gaze held a fierce intensity. "I'm free in a way you cannot imagine." He stopped and turned to Tanis. "Free to *choose*, Tanis—thanks to you."

He reached beneath his coat and withdrew Tanis's dagger. Eyeing it meaningfully, he flipped it and caught it by the point, even as Phaedor had so often done. He put the hilt into the lad's hand.

"I've forsaken the brothers my Maker gave me." Pelas kept hold of the blade as he captured Tanis's gaze. "I would choose my own this time."

Tanis stared at him. Pelas's gaze holding his seemed to say, *You spoke it first. Do you recall?*

And Tanis did remember—*so vividly*—how he'd stood in the courtyard in Rimaldi and told the zanthyr that Pelas was the brother he'd never had. But Pelas had already left by then ... hadn't he?

Feeling suddenly unbalanced in the most heady of ways, Tanis looked down at the dagger mutually held between their hands. It took on an ominous new meaning. Even so ... the lad thought surely he must've misunderstood. His gaze conveyed this when he lifted colorless eyes back to meet Pelas's again.

"I believe your immunity to *deyjiin* is inherited through the bond you share with your zanthyr, Tanis." Pelas held the lad's widening gaze, pinning him between earth and endless sky. "I would offer you the same protection."

Now the lad really stared at him. "Sir ..." he barely croaked out the word around his startled awe.

"You have no idea what you've done for me."

"But, sir ..." Tanis stared vainly down at Phaedor's dagger in his hand.

He couldn't have released it if he'd tried—he couldn't have moved from that moment if he'd tried, for a force far greater than himself suddenly bound him to it. It seemed as if all the world hung upon his words, waiting for him to make a choice and set it spinning again. "Whatever I did ..." his voice sounded so faint against the vast listening void, "you owe me nothing in return."

"Tanis ..." Pelas pressed the dagger's hilt more firmly into his palm and held the lad fixedly beneath his attention, which felt not unlike the baking summer sun beating down on him. "The moment you followed me from the café in Rethynnea, you bound me to your path. I don't know *how*," and the hint of a smile flickered across his lips, "but I know this truth." His copper eyes dazzled with meaning and challenge both. "Tell me aught else if you can."

Tanis slowly, wordlessly, shook his head. He couldn't deny it, even if it made no sense whatsoever.

Pelas's eyes were immensely warm as they gazed upon him. "I'm bound to you already, little spy."

Tanis could barely find words to respond. "Sir ..." He gripped the dagger in his palm. It suddenly felt a lifeline mooring him, lest the whirlwind of impossibility carry him away. "I was so young, I don't even remember when Phaedor bound himself to me. He said he did it because he promised my mother he would protect me—"

"I would make her the same promise."

Tanis felt that whirlwind pulling violently at him. He looked off into the night, seeking something to ground him. "But I don't know the working—"

"In all your many lessons, your mother—*High Mage of the Citadel*—never taught you a pattern of binding?"

Tanis's eyes flew back to Pelas's. He swallowed. "She taught me ... one."

Pelas's eyes danced as if his point had been proven. He looked to their hands, implying clearly his intent.

Tanis exhaled a tremulous breath and looked at the dagger they held together. Pelas closed his fist tightly around the enchanted blade. Then their eyes met again above the dark weapon.

Tanis swallowed. He pulled the blade free.

Pelas gripped his fist harder, and blood pooled between his fingers. He nodded to Tanis to continue.

Swallowing nervously, Tanis reversed the dagger and closed his fist around the blade's icy edge, slick now with Pelas's blood. He lifted his eyes to meet the Malorin'athgul's gaze again, and Pelas took the hilt and pulled the dagger across Tanis's palm. Heat flared.

Pelas dropped the dagger to the grass and gripped Tanis's hand. His fingers felt icy in the lad's grasp, cold as the blade that had just sliced his flesh, as deeply cold as the vast reaches of space. But Pelas's gaze was sunlight itself.

Tanis summoned his courage. There was no room for error with a binding.

Pelas opened his mind to the lad. Ever he seemed to predict Tanis's next thought—or perhaps some natural bond truly did exist between them already, some thread in the tapestry that acted like a chain and made an anchor of each of them for the other.

For this binding, blood is the catalyst, the first strand foundation ... the warp through which the threads of two are newly woven into one. Tanis remembered his mother's words as she'd first described the working to him. *Blood, representative of the first strand, forms a bond of connection, allowing the one forging the binding to find the life-essence of both who will be bound.*

This essence appears as threads extending from each person's life pattern— ephemeral, intangible—yet perceived through the blood-bond. These are the threads to be woven together.

Gripping Pelas's hand tightly—more for reassurance than any further need to seal the connection—Tanis closed his eyes and sought the bond as his mother had taught him. He expected it to be difficult to find the threads of which she'd spoken, but the moment he called the fourth to fuel his awareness, he saw them as clearly as silk scarves blowing on a clothesline—or rather, two clotheslines, where the scarves of each were blowing towards the other.

Tanis took one rose-hued, silken thread from each line and joined them with his intent. They twined into one another as they sealed. He moved on to the next pair.

As he bound more threads, a pattern began to form; the newly bound threads inclined towards each other, like a snowflake's crystallization, or the rivulet channels of rain running down a windowpane, each newly formed connection branching and rejoining. He bound the threads, yet the *pattern* of their binding grew organically.

Throughout the process, he felt Pelas working the fifth, but because the Malorin'athgul compelled this strand innately, Tanis couldn't see any patterns to determine what he was doing. As the binding neared completion and the lad's awareness of Pelas's mind grew and deepened, Tanis realized with a start that with every thread he was binding, Pelas was likewise weaving in *his* intention of permanence.

He was binding them with the fifth.

When Tanis sealed the last thread, that budding awareness wakened into full bloom. Light blossomed, flowering out from the binding's core, from a stem woven of threads from them both, cool starlight and warm sunlight intermingled. The kaleidoscopic light only grew in intensity as the pattern of binding continued drawing *elae* unto itself, until it filled with power and hovered there, secure in its own gravity like a newborn sun.

As this awareness reached full strength and the connection between their minds solidified into permanence, Tanis felt like the very fabric of his soul was expanding towards infinity, being pulled towards the light that was now an integral part of himself, a circle of perception that extended through Pelas's own far-reaching awareness and came back to him.

Floating in this expanse, Tanis imagined he could see infinity at one end of the universe and the core of cosmic creation at the other. If not for Pelas's hand grounding him, he thought surely he would've dissolved away, every particle of his own self stretched and dispersed to be reabsorbed by the greater existence ...

Tanis's knees went a little weak. Then Pelas's strong arm was around him and helping him sit down. The moment he felt the earth beneath him, Tanis lay back in the grass. The world spun dizzily.

Pelas lowered himself slowly beside him. He seemed a star on the currents, so bright it hurt to look at him. Tanis closed his eyes, but the searing light remained.

"That was miraculously done, little spy."

Tanis exhaled a tremulous breath. There was something immensely reassuring about the hard earth pressing against his back. "Somehow I don't think that was the same working Phaedor used, sir."

Pelas chuckled. "And yet, it feels very right to me."

Tanis wasn't sure *right* was the word he would've chosen. *Sensory overload* seemed more appropriate. *Overwhelming*, certainly. *Incomprehensibly and mind-alteringly description-defying*? Closer.

Then the enormity of what he'd done suddenly doused Tanis back to a chill reality. He let out a low moan of disbelief, pushed both palms to his eyes and tried to keep his head from spinning away.

What had come over him that he went from one desperately bold act to the next without any thought or consideration as to the consequences of his actions? He had no business being bound to one immortal, much less *two*. What by Cephrael's name did he think he was *doing*?

Humoring me. Pelas's thought hinted of deep amusement.

Tanis turned him a look of pained protest.

Pelas chuckled and fell back in the grass beside him. He pushed hands behind his head, stretched out long legs and gazed up at the stars. "Through me, you're bound to the heavens, and through you, I'm bound to the earth. Each of us becomes a child of two worlds, little spy."

Tanis tried closing his eyes again, but it only made the world spin more. *You were always a child of two worlds, sir.*

Yes ... Pelas cast him a look of affection mingled with wry humor, *so I've come to see.*

Tanis drew in a deep breath and let it out slowly, willing his pounding heart to settle. On the one hand, this connection he sensed so deeply filled him with excitement. On the other—

By all the gods in the known, he'd *bound* himself to a *Malorin'athgul!*

The realization just kept deluging him, the ramifications branching into more and more frightening directions. And yet ...

For all that the enormity of what he'd so impulsively done was still sinking in—would likely continue sinking in for some time—Tanis felt *right* in having done it.

In the space of his awareness where he'd once felt that odd resistance, there now resonated only a sense of correctness, of satisfaction, like a purring cat curled on a sun-warmed cushion; he got the distinct impression that the cat wasn't really a cat at all but some far greater force, which now abided, momentarily content.

Indeed, when he looked back on the entire night—from the moment he'd first felt the world's tablature shifting beneath him—he realized he'd felt guided. Or, if not guided exactly ... well, *something* at least had been shouting at him from the sidelines and pointing in the direction he ought to run.

Tanis turned to look at Pelas, who was lying beside him with hands braced behind his head and a smile curving his lips. Their minds were connected now in a marvelous and breathtaking and entirely mind-boggling way. He felt immense amazement at it all.

When he looked back to the sky, the low bank of clouds had moved mostly out of view, revealing Cephrael's Hand rising out of the west.

It almost looked like the constellation was winking at him.

EPILOGUE

H E WOKE TO see a woman swathed in robes of emerald green bending over him. Her face swam before his vision, but the world beyond her remained too bright for his eyes, which felt dry and rough from sleep. As he lay amid disorientation, she settled dark, almond-shaped eyes on his to ground him and placed her hands to either side of his head.

"How long … ?" His first words emerged in a rough whisper.

"Over a fortnight since they brought you to me." Her accent gave a unique sharpness to the common tongue. "For many days you lay unconscious. Many more I kept you this way, to aid my Healing and see it complete."

She might've smiled as she straightened—it was hard to tell what shape her lips took beneath the strip of silk that concealed her face—but her next words remained with him like seeds sown in his head. "But now the Healing is finished." Odd to hear words so clearly without seeing the mouth that spoke them. "Do you recall your name?"

He held her dark-eyed gaze. "My name … is Gydryn val Lorian."

That time her eyes crinkled with what could only be a smile. "Jai'Gar has given you another chance at life, Your Majesty. Use it well." Then she pressed her hands together, bowed and departed.

He lay in bed letting his eyes adjust to the bright day and thought deeply and long upon those words. Having stared into many faces of death on that long night—the last night he remembered—and having been certain as he lay bleeding out on the searing sands that he wouldn't see another sunrise … to then wake and find himself whole, healed, *cared* for, treated with gentleness and honor … he did indeed feel as if he'd been gifted of a divine grace.

He didn't know what it meant, but he hoped it might herald another chance to right the mistakes of his rule; another chance to spare his army from war and his kingdom from the Duke of Morwyk's greed; an opportunity to earn back the respect of his men.

Another chance at life in all its vagaries, complexities, sorrows and joys.

Once his eyes were working properly, Gydryn lifted the sheet and looked down at his naked body. He knew how close to death's lands he'd traveled. It must've required powerful Healing to carry him back. The scars of his ordeal looked weeks old but still told a macabre tale. Likewise the lingering invalid's weakness that made his arms tremble just holding up the sheet.

He looked out the open balcony doors. A pale city of glittering domes winked back at him.

That he'd been taken somewhere into the deep desert was evident, but who had claimed him from the sands, Healed him, cared for him? And why they'd offered such generosity to an enemy king—these answers evaded his understanding.

A knock came, rooms away. He heard the distant door open and close and footsteps passing from tiled floor to carpet. Then he felt a presence arrive.

Gydryn turned his head. The man who stood in the portal was of medium build and height and wore a grey and black-striped turban. Dark eyes, deeply lined, regarded him shrewdly above a prominent nose and a heavy beard flashed with grey. He wore reserve like a cloak.

"Your Majesty." He pressed a hand to his heart and bowed his head respectfully. "I am Rajiid bin Yemen al Basreh, Prime Minister of the Akkad, and we have much to discuss."

When dawn broke upon the day, Pelas left Tanis to see a meal prepared for them. Tanis lay still atop the cliff, bathed in the light of a gilded sky. There was one last thing he had to do.

The knowledge hadn't been in his lessons from his mother, yet he knew instinctively how to find the bond he shared with her, how to use it to travel the distance in a single thought.

And now ... now he knew it was time to do so.

Letting his mind explore those wide vistas which joining minds with Pelas had opened to him, Tanis reached out across the bond—tentative, hopeful, jittery with anticipation. He'd bound himself to a Malorin'athgul just hours ago. Contacting his mother ought not to cause such unbridled nervousness.

Just when he thought he'd gotten it wrong, he felt her presence open to him, like a flower of light blooming in his mind. Her mental touch was so similar to the idea he'd formed of her during her lessons, and yet so much *more*.

Then he heard her voice, perceived her smile, and felt the warm sensation of an ethereal caress. Suddenly he was a babe in her arms again. He didn't ever want to be anywhere else.

Tanis, love of my heart ...

Mama!

KEEP IN TOUCH

"We are as close as a thought away."
— The High Mage Isabel van Gelderan, to her son

Melissa loves hearing from her readers with feedback or comments or just discussion of Alorin and its peoples. For updates on the fourth installment in A Pattern of Shadow & Light and other topics of conversation, follow Melissa's blog at http://melissamcphail.com/blog

To see Melissa's picks for her cast of characters and the realm of Alorin, visit her Pinterest boards: http://pinterest.com/melissagmcphail

For daily news, follow Melissa on twitter:
http://twitter.com/melissagmcphail

Melissa can also be reached via these social media sites:

Facebook: http://facebook.com/melissagmcphail

Goodreads: http://goodreads.com/melissagmcphail

Google+: http://google.com/+melissamcphailauthor

APPENDIX

THE LAWS OF PATTERNING

(Laws 1-12)

1. KNOW the effect you intend to create.
2. What applies to one applies to all.
3. Create newly each effect.
4. Positive determinism is necessary to the intended effect.
5. A wielder is limited by what he can envision.
6. Energy responds to positive thought.
7. A wielder succeeds in the alteration of energy, space and time in inverse proportion to his agreement with the material universe.
8. All patterns are the result of effort channeled along a specific vector; thus, patterns are the product of force.
9. Do not counter force with force, channel it.
10. Energy cannot be unmade, merely transformed.
11. All things are formed of patterns.
12. A pattern need not be perfect, but the wielder's concept of it must be.

THE ESOTERICS

(A sampling)

1. Absolute Being is the entire concept of actuality. Corollary: Absolutely Being is the exact form, material composition and position in space as modified by time.
2. Patterns lay within the boundaries of Absolute Being.
3. The wielding of Form must encapsulate Absolute Being.
4. Time results from the application of an intention that matter and space will persist. Thus, time and space are monitored by Absolute Being.
5. Absolute Being must equal the scope of a wielder's concept of effect.
11. A wielder is limited by what he can envision himself envisioning.

12. Space, energy, time and form are the result of thought applied to intention.

15. Doubt of intention results in diminished effect on a gradient scale.

20. The strands are divisions of energy as applied towards creation of life, form, time, thought, elements. Thus, all laws of patterning follow also the laws of energy.

21. Actuality is monitored by the wielder's point of view. Reality is monitored by collective thought agreement.

22. Illusion becomes reality when a) collective agreement is achieved on the existence of the illusion and b) when enough agree that the illusion should persist.

DRAMATIS PERSONAE

THE FIVE VESTALS

Alshiba Torinin—the First Vestal and Alorin Seat, an Adept Healer

Dagmar Ranneskjöld—the Second Vestal, a Nodefinder

Seth Silverbow nach Davvies—the Third Vestal, an avieth of the Wildling races

Raine D'Lacourte—the Fourth Vestal, a truthreader and raedan

Björn van Gelderan—the Fifth Vestal, also called the First Lord

THE MALORIN'ATHGUL

Darshanvenkhátraman (Dar´shan – vin ka´tra mahn) called Darshan whose name means Destroyer of Hope; also known as the Prophet Bethamin

Pelasommáyurek (Pe´las – oh my´yur eck) called Pelas whose name means Ender of Paths; also known as the artist Immanuel di Nostri

Rinokhálpeşumar (Rin´och – cal pesh´oo mar) called Rinokh whose name means The Mountain That Flames

Shailabhanáchtran (Shale´ – ah bah nock´trun) called Shail whose name means Maker of Storms

THE SUNDRAGONS (DRACHWYR)

Dhábu'balaji'şridanaí (Da´boo – ba lah´gee – shree´da-nye) called Balaji whose name means He Who Walks The Edge Of The World

Şrivas'rhakárakek (Shree´vas – rah kar´akeck) called Rhakar whose name means The Shadow Of The Light

Jayachándranáptra (Jai´ah – shan´dra – nap´tra) called Jaya whose name means Rival Of The Sun

Ramuhárikhamáth (Rah´moo – hareek´amath) called Ramu whose name means Lord of the Heavens

Amithaiya'geshwen (Ami-thi´ya – gesh´win) called Mithaiya whose name means The Bosom of God's Nectar

Náeb'nabdurin'náiir (Ni eb'– nab dur'en – ny'ear) called Náiir whose name means Chaser Of The Dawn

On Tanis's travels in Agasan

Phaedor—a zanthyr

Madaé Lisbeth—Seneschal of the Villa Serafina

Madaé Giselle—Head cook of the Villa Serafina

Nathalia—a cook at the Villa Serafina

Loghain—a Tyriolicci (called Whisper Lord by the races of men)

Dional—Huntmaster of the Villa Serafina

Kendir—A huntsman at the Villa Serafina

Birger—Tanis's valet at the Villa Serafina

Liam van Gheller—Endoge of the Sormitáge

Felix di Sarcova della Buonara—a Devoveré Nodefinder studying at the Sormitáge

Malin van Drexel—a Nodefinder working on his Maritus thesis at the Sormitáge

Isahl N'abranaacht—a literato at the Sormitáge University

Monseraut Greaves—Imperial Historian and maestro at the Sormitáge University

Giancarlo—A truthreader in the service of the High Lord of Agasan

Vincenzé—An Adept Nodefinder and wielder in service of the High Lord of Agasan

Sinárr —a Warlock from the Shadow Realms

Agasan's Imperial Household

Valentina van Gelderan—Empress of Agasan

Marius di L'Arlesé—High Lord of Agasan, Consort to the Empress

Nadia van Gelderan—Princess-Heir of Agasan

On Ean's Travels

Isabel van Gelderan—Epiphany's Prophet, High Mage of the Citadel, sister to Björn

Immanuel di Nostri—An artist and painter from the Fourth Age; Pelas's alias

Dareios Haxamanis—Prince of Kandori

Ehsan Haxamanis—Princess of Kandori

Yasmin Haxamanis—Princess of Kandori

Nîga Haxamanis—Mother to Dareios

Bahman—Cousin to Dareios

Naveed—Brother by marriage to Dareios

Dorn, Baz, Lem and Poul—men in service to Isabel

In T'khendar

Carian vran Lea—a pirate of Jamaii, an Adept Nodefinder

Gwynnleth—an avieth from Elvior

Julian d'Artenis—a fifth-strand Adept from Jeune, Veneisea

Markal Morrelaine—a wielder, one of the First Lord's three generals

Balaeric de Parma—a pirate from Alorin, now a gypsy Iluminari

Björn's Council of Nine

Björn van Gelderan—the First Lord and Alorin's Fifth Vestal

Cristien Tagliaferro—an Adept truthreader

Anglar Tempest (deceased, revived as a Shade)

Dunglei ap'Turic (deceased)

Parsifal D'Marre (deceased)

Arion Tavestra (deceased)

Markal Morrelaine—a wielder, one of Björn's three Generals

Ramuhárikhamáth—a drachwyr, one of Björn's three Generals

Malachai ap'Kalien (deceased)

THE FIFTY COMPANIONS

(those known to be living)

Pavran Ahlamby—a truthreader

Usil al'Haba—a Nodefinder

Elien ap'Gentrys—an Adept wielder

Gannon Bair—a truthreader

Karienna D'Artenis—an Adept Healer

Laira di Giancora—an Adept Healer

Mian Gartelt—an Adept Healer

Viernan hal'Jaitar—an Adept wielder

Socotra Isio—a Nodefinder

Ledio Jerouen—an Adept Wildling

Dore Madden—an Adept wielder

Mazur of Elvior—an Avieth of Elvior

Franco Rohre—a Nodefinder

Delanthine Tanner—an Adept wielder

Thessaly Vahn—An Adept Healer

Devangshu Vita—a Nodefinder

Niko van Amstel—a Nodefinder

MEMBERS OF THE ROYAL FAMILY OF DANNYM

Gydryn val Lorian—King of Dannym

Errodan Renwyr n'Owain val Lorian—Queen of Dannym

Ysolde Remalkhen—the Queen's Companion; a Fire Princess from Avatar

Ean val Lorian—Prince of Dannym, the youngest son

Trell val Lorian—Prince of Dannym, the Queen's treasured middle son

Sebastian val Lorian—Prince of Dannym, oldest son and heir to the Eagle Throne

Creighton Khelspath—ward of Gydryn, blood-brother to Ean (now a Shade)

Ryan val Lorian—brother to Gydryn, posted as Dannym's Ambassador to Agasan

Fynnlar val Lorian—son of Ryan, the royal cousin

THE WARRING PRINCES & THEIR ALLIES

Emir Zafir bin Safwan al Abdul-Basir—Akkadian Emir, Unifier of the Seventeen Tribes

Rajiid bin Yemen al Basreh—Prime Minister of the Akkad

Radov abin Hadorin—Ruling Prince of M'Nador

Viernan hal'Jaitar—Radov's wielder (see The Fifty Companions)

Taliah hal'Jaitar—daughter of Viernan; an mor'alir Adept

The Prophet Bethamin (also known as the Malorin'athgul Darshan)

Dore Madden—an Adept wielder serving the Prophet (see The Fifty Companions)

Raliax—a Saldarian mercenary serving Dore Madden

The Karakurt—a female truthreader, leader of an infamous ring of assassins

Fazil—Captain of the Guard at Darroyhan

Hafiz—a sailor at Darroyhan

Thrace Weyland—an Adept truthreader and purveyor of information

THE KING OF DANNYM'S CABINET & GUARD

Morin d'Hain—Spymaster

Donnal val Amrein—Minister of the Interior

Mandor val Kess—Minister of Culture

Vitriam o'Reith—truthreader to King Gydryn

Kjieran van Stone—(deceased) Agasi truthreader; killed on assignment in Tambarré

Rhys val Kincaide—Lord Captain of the King's Own Guard

Jasper val Renly—a captain in the Dannish army in M'Nador, elder brother to Bastian

Bastian val Renly—a lieutenant in the King's Own Guard, younger brother of Jasper

Cayal—a soldier in the King's Own Guard, taken hostage in the Kutsamak

Dorin—a soldier in the King's Own Guard, taken hostage in the Kutsamak

Brody the Bull—bodyguard to Fynnlar val Lorian, taken hostage in the Kutsamak.

Of the Peerage of Dannym & Their Households

Gareth val Mallonwey—Duke of Towermount and General of the West

Tad val Mallonwey—Heir to Towermount

Katerine val Mallonwey—daughter of Gareth, engaged to Creighton Khelspath

Lisandre val Mallonwey—daughter of Gareth

Loran val Whitney—Duke of Marion and General of the East

Killian val Whitney—Heir to Marion

Melisande d'Giverny—(deceased) mother to Alyneri

Prince Jair—(deceased) Prince of Kandori, father of Alyneri

Alyneri d'Giverny—Duchess of Aracine, an Adept Healer

Tanis—an Adept truthreader, Melisande's ward

Farshideh—(deceased) a Kandori midwife, Seneschal of Fersthaven

Stefan val Tryst—Duke of Morwyk

Wilamina—Dowager Countess of Astor

Ianthe d'Jesune val Rothschen—Marchioness of Wynne

Wilem val Rothschen—Marquess of Wynne

The Contessa di Remy—wife of the Agasi Ambassador's Aide

The Seventeen Gods of the Akkad

Jai'Gar—the Prime God

Azerjaiman—the Wind God

Sons of the wind god—North son, Shamal; South son, Asfal; East son, Sherq

Daughter of the wind god—West daughter, Qharp

Shamash—God of Travelers and the Poor

Inanna—Goddess of War

Naiadithine—Goddess of Water

Enlil—God of Earth and Agriculture

Inithiya—Goddess of Restoration (Spirit)

Angharad—Goddess of Fortune (Fate)

Thalma—Goddess of Luck (Virtue)

Huhktu—God of Bones

Baharan/Baharani—The two-headed God of Blood/Goddess of Birth

Ha'viv—the Trickster God, patron of thieves

GLOSSARY OF TERMS

UNDERLINING WITHIN DEFINITIONS denotes words that may be found in this glossary.

Adendigaeth (aden′– di gay′uth) [Old Alæic] 1 Rebirth, regeneration 2 A festival in celebration of the Winter Solstice lasting varying lengths but traditionally ending on the Longest Night.

Adept (a′-dept) n. [Old Alæic] 1 One born with the instinctive ability to sense and compel one of the five strands of elae 2 A race of such persons, each with attributes intrinsic to the strand of elae that modified them [an adept of the third strand] 3 A Healer, Nodefinder, Truthreader, or Wildling.

Alir (ah -leer′) n [Agasi] 1 lit: heart-light 2 The path followed by an Adept during the course of his life; also referred to as the path of destiny, especially in the vernacular of the Palmers 3 Indicating either of the two valid paths of elae able to be followed by an Adept inducted into the Vestian Sorceresy. See also hal'alir and mor'alir.

Angiel (ahn gēl′) n. [Old Alæic] The Maker's two blessed children, Cephrael and Epiphany, who were made in the Genesis to watch over His worlds.

Ascendant n. [Cyrenaic ascendere, to climb] A priest or cleric serving the Prophet Bethamin. Ascedants are marked by tatooes denoting their rank and function.

Avieth (ay′ vee uth) n. [Old Alæic, bird] A third-strand Wildling race of shapeshifters with the ability to asssume two distinctly separate forms: human and hawk.

Awaken (ah wā′ ken) v. [Old Alæic] Adepts who have Returned awaken to their inherent abilities usually during the transition of puberty but sometimes as early as two years of age.

Balance (bal′ans) n. [<Veneisean <Cyrenaic, bilanx two+scale] The term used to describe the highest force of cause and effect in the realm of Alorin; the natural laws of the realm which define how far the currents may be twisted out of their natural paths by wielders of elae before

manifest retribution is incurred by the wielder. These laws are of much consideration among the various Adept Guilds and a topic of intense speculation and theorization.

Catenaré (ca-ten ah´-ray) n. [Old Alæic, catēna, a chain] The second ranking of Adept enrolled at the Sormitáge University. Adepts wear the Catenaré cuff until they pass their invocation trials to advance to Maritus status, usually a span of five to ten years of study.

Cephrael (sef´ray-el) n. [Sobra I'ternin] The Maker's blessed son. Ascribed as the Hand of Fate, Cephrael is responsible for administering the Maker's ultimate justice. See also Angiel.

Companions – See Fifty Companions

Devoveré (de-voh ver´-ay) n. [Old Alæic, to vow] The fourth ranking of Adept enrolled at the Sormitáge University. Adepts are awarded their Devoveré ring (often called a Sormitáge ring) upon successful completion of the Devoveré Trials. Gaining a Devoveré ring automatically entitles an Adept to membership in the Guild respective to their strand.

Docian (dos´ see-an) n. [Old Alæic docilis, readily taught, equivalent to doc (ēre) to teach + -ian] The first ranking of Adept enrolled at the Sormitáge University. Adepts wear the Docian collar from their earliest years until they pass the invocation trials to advance to Catenaré status, usually a span of five to eight years.

Drogue wolf (droag) n. [Origin unknown] A sentient animal, larger and more intelligent than a common wolf, which roams the mountains of Agasan. It is most often found in the Navárrel, the Geborahs and the wild ranges of the Hallovian plateau.

Drachwyr (drak´wēr) n. [Old Alæic] An Adept of the fifth strand of elae: the drachwyr were banished to the icy edges of the realm in the year 597aV. Also called a Sundragon.

Elae (e-lā´) n. [Old Alæic, elanion, life, force; the power of life] 1 The itinerant (roaming) energy that, in its accumulation and formation, creates the pattern that becomes the foundation of a world 2 Pertaining to any of the five codified strands of this energy, each with distinctly separate attributes.

Epiphany (ē pif´fany) n. [Sobra I'ternin] The Maker's blessed daughter.

Epiphany is the speaker of the Maker's will and is often turned to in prayer by those seeking divine blessing. See also Angiel.

Espial (espy′-al) n. [Cyrenaic espyen <es- + spähen, to spy] See also Nodefinder. The term used to describe a Nodefinder of the highest degree who has gained license from the Espial's Guild to travel between the realms.

Fhorg (forg) n. [origin unknown] One of the Wildling races most notably known for their use of blood magic.

Fifty Companions n. [Colloquial] The name given in reference to the Adept survivors of the Battle of the Citadel on Tiern'aval.

Hal'alir n. [Agasi, light of the heart] The light path of elae. Adepts following hal'alir wield the lifeforce primarily towards constructive or creative aims.

Healer (hēl′er) n. [Old Alæic haelan > hal whole] An Adept of the first strand of elae who has the ability to see the life patterns of living things and compel the creative forces of the first strand to alter them.

Khoda Panaheh (lay) n. [Kandori, "God protects"] 1 A tattooed mark upon the forehead which is gained when an Adept of the royal lines of Kandori takes the oath of immortality and works the Pattern of Life.

Leis (lay) n. [Old Alæic leis] The shortest pathway available to a Nodefinder when using the pattern of the world to travel, often connecting spaces within a small geographic area.

Literato n. [Old Alæic literati, learned, scholarly] A scholar at the Sormitáge University whose focus is on research of the strands of elae or into the history of the realm or the Adept race.

Maestro n. [Old Alæic, master] A teaching scholar at the Sormitáge University.

Maritus (Mer′i-tus) n. [Old Alæic maritum, act worthy of praise] The third ranking of Adept enrolled at the Sormitáge University. Adepts wear a Maritus bracelet until they've completed their thesis and passed the invocation trials to advance to Devoveré status, often a span of five to ten years.

Marquiin (mar kwen′) n. [Myacenic, chosen] A truthreader who has been chosen by the Prophet Bethamin to be cleansed in a "purifying" ritual involving, in part, the insertion of Bethamin's Fire into the Adept's mind.

Merdanti (mer dan´tē) n. [Agasi] 1 An impossibly hard black stone named for the region of Agasan in which it is found 2 A weapon forged using the fifth strand of elae and made from this stone.

Malorin'athgul (muh lor´en – ath´gool) n. [Old Alæic, they who make the darkness] A race of beings from beyond the known realms of Light who were birthed by the Maker to balance Creation by unmaking the universe at its far unraveling fringes while it is constantly expanding at its core.

Mor'alir n. [Agasi, dark of the heart] Adepts following mor'alir wield the lifeforce towards primarily destructive aims.

Na'turna (nah toor´nah) n. [Old Alæic < nare turre, of the earth] A non-Adept; mortal.

Node (nod) n. [Old Alæic nodus, knot] The points where the pattern of the world conjoins. Nodes connect places in vastly different geographic regions and allow a Nodefinder to travel great distances within a few steps. In the realm of Alorin, nodes also connect to the neighboring realm of T'khendar due to the nature of the latter's formation.

Nodefinder (nod-fin´der) n. [Old Alæic nodus, knot + findan, find] Adept of the second strand of elae who sees the points where the pattern of the world conjoins (called nodes) and can use these points to travel vast distances; see also Espial.

Qhorith'quitara (Cor´ith kee-tar-ah) n. [Old Alæic] The collection of apocryphal books derived from the Sobra I'ternin.

Order of the Glass Sword n. [Origin unknown] The name of Agasan's spy network.

Palmer n. [Caladrian, pilgrim] A religious order devoted to the study of Alir and the influence or interference of destiny or fate upon an individual's path.

Patterning (pat´ərn·ŋ) v. [Veneisean patrun, patron, hence something to be imitated, pattern] The codified methodology encompassing the use of patterns to compel the strands of elae to move against their natural course, an action (also called wielding) which is often erroneously referred to as magic.

Raedan (ray´ dan]) n. [Old Alæic raedan, to guess, read, counsel] 1 One trained to read the currents of elae and thereby able to discern the workings of patterns and their effects throughout the realm.

Realm (relm´) n. [Veneisean, realme (altered by assoc. with reiel, royal) < Cyrenaic, regere, to rule] 1 A kingdom 2 One of the thousand linked worlds, each represented by an elected Seat and four Vestals in the governing cityworld of Illume Belliel 3 The realm of Alorin.

Return (Returned, Returning) (rē turn´) n. [Veneisean, retorner] An Adept who has died and been reborn. See also Awakening.

Sanctos n. [Caladrian sanctus, hallowed] In the Caladrian belief, sanctified ancestral spirits who watch over their descendents.

Sobra I'ternin (so´ brah - e turn´en) n. [origin unknown] The ancient text, most often attributed to the angiel Cephrael, which details the natural laws of patterns in thaumaturgic application. The book is itself written in patterns and has yet to be fully translated. Many Orders are dedicated to its study, translation and adaptation for use in the Adept Arts.

Soglia-varcarés / soglia're (So´-lee AHR´-ay) [Caladrian, bridge across the earth] Nodes or leis magically constructed into permanent portals that anyone can travel with or without a Nodefinder present and with or without any Adept talent. Soglia'res bridge two specific points, only those two points, and cannot be used to travel anywhere else but between those two points.

Sorceresy (also Vestian Sorceresy) The predominant school of Adept learning in the far-eastern land of Vest. The Vestian Sorceresy believes both paths of Alir have equal merit, but they're known for their Blackshard Council and its exploration of the mor'alir path.

Stanza segreta (Caladrian, secret room) 1 The term given to a leis which a Nodefinder has pinned to his personal life-pattern or to an object in his possession, the use of which allows the Nodefinder to secret away or store items for later use. Colloquially called a "coach."

Strand (strand´) n. [Agasi, strônd] 1 Any of the parts that are bound together to form a whole [the strands of one's life] 2 Referring to any of the five composite aspects of elae and its five attributive fields of energy (respectively: strand 1:creative energy, 2:kinetic energy, 3:variant energy, 4:energy of thought, 5:elemental energy).

Thread (thred) n. [Old Alæic thræd, to bind] A colloquial term used when speaking of a group of four men of a specific race, as opposed to a String, which is a grouping of six.

Tiern'aval (teer′- navol′) n. [origin unknown] An island city, one of the Free Cities of Xanthe, which vanished at the end of the Adept wars circa 597aV. The city's fate remains a mystery.

T'khendar (tuh – ken′dar) n. [origin unknown] The realm created by the Adept wielder Malachi ap'Kalien out of Alorin's own aether, which sacrilegious act resulted in fierce denouncement from the Council of Realms and indirectly, his later madness.

Truthreader (trooth′ rēd er) n. [Old Alæic treowe, true + raedan] An Adept of the fourth strand of elae who is able to hear (and sometimes see) the thoughts of others and is thereby able to discern the time, place and form of any occurrence in their memory, i.e. its truth.

Tyriolicci (teer′e-oh – lee′chee) One of the Wildling Races of the Forgotten Lands. See Whisper Lord.

Vestal (vest′-al) n. [Cyrenaic, vestir, to endow] 1 An Adept elevated and empowered with the responsibility of enforcing the laws, regulations, activities and codes of his respective strand of elae, and of overseeing all Adepts subject to it 2 one of five highly-trained and advanced Adepts elected as voting members of the Council of Realms, ranking just below the Seat of the realm in authority.

Weld (weld) n. [Cyrenaic, welden, to be strong] The most major joints in the pattern of the world. All leis and nodes connect through a weld, thus a weld allows travel to any location. Welds also form the joints between the realms and thus allow travel from realm to realm.

Whisper Lord n. [Collq.] One of the Wildling races (also called Tyriolicci) known for their frenzied fighting style and ability to make small skips through time.

Wielder (wēld′ər) n. [Cyrenaic, welden, to be strong < Old Alæic, valere, a show of strength] A person of any race who uses patterns to compel one or more strands of elae, thereby influencing the strand's properties to create the effect he has postulated; a sorcerer in the realm of Alorin. Adepts and men alike become wielders through intensive training and study.

Wildling (wahyld´-ling]) n. [Old Alæic wilde] 1 (Collq) An Adept of the third strand of elae 2 Any of the twenty-seven non-human races whose native abilities are attributed to the third strand of elae but who may or may not be possessed of paranormal abilities.

Zanthyr (zan´thur) n. [Old Alæic] An elusive Adept of the fifth strand of elae; zanthyrs can shapeshift between two forms: one human, one animal. Many have been seen to work elae. The extent of their abilities is unknown.